2233

REAP THE WHIRLWIND

KENNETH TAM

2233
REAP THE WHIRLWIND

Martian War - Omnibus 3

KENNETH TAM

ICEBERG

Published in Canada by Iceberg Publishing, Waterloo

Library and Archives Canada Cataloguing in Publication
Tam, Kenneth, 1984-
    2233 : reap the whirlwind / Kenneth Tam.
(Martian War ; omnibus 3)
Contents: The Canary wars -- The Forge fires -- The Mercury
    asssault -- The fleet crash.
ISBN 978-1-926817-00-2
    I. Title. II. Series: Tam, Kenneth, 1984- . Martian War ; omnibus ; 3.
PS8589.A7676T845 2010   C813'.6   C2010-900093-5

Iceberg Publishing
55 Northfield Drive East, Suite 171
Waterloo ON N2K 3T6
contact@icebergpublishing.com
www.icebergpublishing.com

Cover Image: Wesley Prewer
Cover Design: Kenneth Tam

Inscriptions

The Canary Wars

"It was involuntary. They sank my boat."

– Jack Kennedy, *Former-skipper of PT-109*

The Forge Fires

"There seems to be something wrong with our ships today..."

– Admiral David Beatty, *Jutland, 1915*

The Mercury Assault

"The Nazis entered this war under the rather childish delusion that they were
going to bomb everyone else, and nobody was going to bomb them.
At Rotterdam, London, Warsaw, and half a hundred other places,
they put their rather naive theory into operation.

They sowed the wind, and now they are going to reap the whirlwind."

– Arthur 'Bomber' Harris, *Air Marshal, Royal Air Force Bomber Command*

The Fleet Clash

"Never do anything that can denote an angry mind; for, although everybody is born with
a certain degree of passion, and, from untoward circumstances, will sometimes
feel its operation, and be what they call 'out of humor'... a sensible
man or woman will never allow it to be discovered.

Check and restrain it; never make any determination until you find it has entirely
subsided; and always avoid saying anything that you may wish unsaid."

– Cuthbert Collingwood, 1st Barron of Collingwood
Admiral, second in command at Trafalgar; friend of Horatio Nelson

THE CANARY WARS

THE AUTOBIOGRAPHICAL REMINISCENCES OF
ADMIRAL THE LORD KEN BARRON FOR 2233

THE MARTIAN WAR - 9

KENNETH TAM

From The Author

Look close enough at any war and you'll find sideshows from the main action — stories of shipwrecked sailors, marooned soldiers, or downed airmen. These stories often make for good movies because they're self-contained adventures, and they don't rely too much on the larger conflict to make sense. *The Canary Wars* is one of those sorts of stories.

Taking us away from the Martian War, this book gives us a chance to see one of the few so-called 'non-civilized' peoples left in the solar system. Every Empire has its 'barbarians', be they the indigenous people of the American West, the various societies absorbed by the British Empire, the rest of the world as seen by the Confucianist Chinese Empires, or the original Germanic barbarians that menaced Rome. In my opinion, this isn't just a matter of coincidence: I think every Empire and large society looks for a supposedly cruder one with which to favorably compare itself. You know: "Look how savage they are... we're much more civilized... but they are very interesting..."

I don't think this is done maliciously... I think it's more a matter of seeing those supposedly 'uncivilized' people as being an exciting and adventurous alternative to the relative stability of life within a large and efficient society.

But the Earth Empire doesn't have access to many 'inferior' peoples. Remember that under the Articles of Empire, all humans are seen as equal, regardless of race, gender or faith. Does this mean humans of the 2200s are beyond looking down their noses at each other?

Nope, I don't think it does.

So enter the Canaries and Pions, a couple of isolated 'tribes' of humanity through whom we can explore some of those issues of Imperial-'barbarian' relations. It's always a complex relationship —and make no mistake, it's often a two-way street. It's too easy for either side to accuse the other of being completely responsible for the woes of the other. The reality, to quote a scholar who has looked extensively at European relations with North American First Nations, is that there is often a 'middle ground'. It doesn't always last — one side can gain an advantage in the end — but when it works, it makes for a fascinating relationship.

Of course, the Pions and the Canaries have a society that is the stuff of nightmares, so that complicates things... but I won't spoil anything. You'll see soon enough!

As usual, it's time to give thanks. Many of the characters you'll read about in this book are based on real-world friends of mine. Thanks to all of those fine people —I hope your characters do you proud!

My good friend Peter Caron must be thanked for always being a great sounding board for ideas —and for identifying the bad ones! Wes Prewer's cover images and ideas for character development earn him special thanks too. As ever, I'm much obliged to these gentlemen. Of course most importantly, I must thank my parents and Iceberg partners, Jacqui and Peter. By now you know how awesome they are. Don't you forget it!

And Atlas. As always, thanks.

– Kenneth Tam

PREFACE

We're about to enter 2233, the last year of official hostilities during the Martian War... and it's going to be a rough one. As you'll see shortly, this book is actually going to start in the last days of 2232, when some of the strife was set up... but I'll get into that momentarily. This year saw a lot of big fleet battles, as we went through the final rounds of fighting against the Martians. Lots of big, epic fleet actions...

Oddly, though, the year doesn't start with any of that. Instead, it starts with a sideshow that really had very little to do with the fate of the Empire... but which had a lot to do with those of us in the Jupiter Force.

In studying history, I've found that wars are full of sideshows... full of strange stories that have nothing to do with what scholars are prone to calling the 'metanarrative' (yeah, I don't know where they get it either), and so get overlooked in the big history accounts. In that vein, then, the story that follows doesn't really further our understanding of the war. It's just what happened to us.

One of my editors wondered why I wrote this book. If we could just skip it without missing anything essential to the battle against the Martians, why bother to write it? Well, there are a number of reasons, but the most important is simple: this mission didn't change the war, but it definitely changed us. If I didn't tell the story, some of the things that happen later might make less sense.

I personally would liken it to the story of an American PT boat in the Second World War, number 109. It was sunk, and its crew, led by one Lieutenant Jack Kennedy, struggled to survive in the islands of the Pacific ocean. The fate of one boat really meant nothing to the war... but the story gets told, largely because Jack Kennedy became a bit famous later on (when he was known by his full first name, John Fitzgerald).

So this is a sideshow story, that won't add much perspective on our climactic battle against the Martian fleet... but, well, I was there.

And yes, there's another reason I feel obliged to write about these events: they involve the Pions and the Canaries. These two tribes are the bogeymen of choice for many movies, and they are much misunderstood. When you get to know them, they're even worse than the movies make out... largely because for all their butchery, they're both smart and capable. I hate them. I think they're disgusting. And you better believe they think the same about us. But we had to deal with them.

For those of you unfamiliar with Canaries and Pions, let me provide some context. Brace for a grizzly history lesson.

Mining colony XV-001 was the baby of the Wainwright Celestial Mining Firm. Founded in 2066, with grav-plated facilities being constructed in 2079, it was one of the first large attempts made by an Earth-based company to exploit the minerals of an asteroid.

And, of course, when I say 'attempt', I mean it failed quite miserably. And tragically.

The colony was tunnel-based — this was a century before the Earthgreen dome was made economical enough for mining colonies to use — and huge. Powered by a nuclear fission — yes, *fission* — reactor, it was the pinnacle of Earth's engineering at the time. Nearly 2,000 people were shuttled out to it, on ships that took over three months to get from Earth to the asteroid.

Then Mars rebelled in 2088... and guess where the head office (and all the records) of Wainwright Celestial Mining were? The company personnel were able to mostly escape under the escort of DCSF and the Imperial Army, but they lost all their files, and most of their backups.

That was bad enough, but then the universe decided to toss a rock into the mix... literally. A comet passed through the asteroid belt... well, we assume that's what happened... and it shifted the orbit of the XV-001 very slightly. By the time the Wainwright people set up a new office on Earth, and tried to get in touch with the colony, it was gone.

Since that was a time when ships took months to get to the asteroids, a search mission was more or less doomed to failure, though Defense Command tried. The cruiser *Adventure* spent a whole year looking, but in that year the ship could only cover a very tiny portion of the Belt. It took them six months to cover what would have taken one of our corvettes a couple of weeks to look over... and it was alone.

XV-001, it seemed, was gone.

But, of course, it wasn't. It was lost out there, and the 2,000 people in the colony (only 587 of them women) lived on. It didn't take long for their social order to fragment, and in a way so reminiscent of that 'lord of the flies' paradigm, things got uncivilized rather quickly.

The colonists eventually divided themselves into two camps: the Pions — *Pioneers* — who had worked in the administrative, support and logistics parts of the colony, and the Canaries, who were the miners themselves. 'Canary' is apparently a reference to a very old mining practice, dating from before the time of noxious gas sensors. A canary would go down the tunnel with miners, and if it died, that meant there was something poisonous in the air — everyone had to get out.

Evidently, the miners had a sense of humor when they picked their name.

Now, we have no idea how all that played out — the Pions and the Canaries didn't exactly keep written histories. This is just how we found them, and since then caricatures of them have turned up in bad action movies across the Empire. After all, they're the closest things to real 'savages' we have these days.

That's right, they dress in rags, they capture and rape women (sooo many things to clarify there, but I'll save that for later), they live in dark tunnels like troglodytes, occasionally eat each other, and they fight with savage-seeming bladed weapons and cudgels, all built from remnant tools of the old colony.

Naturally, they're great subjects for movies.

Unfortunately, as much as I love to pan movie versions of things, I can't deny that many of the portrayals of both the Pions and the Canaries don't get *everything* wrong. Certainly, the movies that have them somehow attacking passenger liners and freighters are ridiculous — there's no way for the Pions and the Canaries to get off their rock — but the way we often see them terrorize and fight in the movies... well, that's based in truth.

All members of both tribes have lived their lives in the darkness of relatively narrow tunnels, still with gravity from those unfailingly reliable Type 2A Felix Wolfe grav plates, without ranged weapons, and fighting for the bare essentials of life. The things they know how to do with an improvised axe make me shudder.

Anyway, we're pretty sure that during the years that they were 'lost', the Pions and the Canaries occasionally had unwelcome guests — civilian ships found their asteroid, and landed looking for salvage (assuming, logically, that no one could have survived centuries in a lost asteroid colony). When one of our ships happened across them in 2188, the first landing party was butchered, and the SF sent in to get retribution didn't come back. The ship left, and reported to Admiralty House, though the next response was delayed.

In 2195, Lord Hawke sent a company of Special Branchers to clean out the rock. One hundred of our best special forces went in, thirty-one came out, and they had no interest in going back. The tunnels, you see, are a nightmare of a battleground that completely favor the defender... I'll get into that later.

By the time all that happened, the media had gotten hold of the story, and with the scattered after-action reports from Ian Hawke's Admiralty, they pieced together the Pion/Canary story, and thus gave us the Pions and Canaries: the movie bad guys every producer loves. The tribes entered our popular consciousness.

From then on, stupid civilians occasionally tried to go down to the rock to see the Pions and the Canaries up close, but missionaries, aid workers, hunters and adventure-seekers alike all failed to return.

So, when Charlie and I got orders to go to the Pion rock in *Friendly*, we were understandably unenthusiastic. But that adventure I'll hopefully recount in another book... it was years before the war, and basically, we were there because the Canaries wanted to make a deal with the Empire: we fix their fission reactor (which was finally going on the blink) and in return, they let us know when they see pirate ships cruising by.

That was a nightmare of a mission, but we managed to get through it...

This next return to the Pion rock, though, would be a real mess.

Alright, I think that's more than enough exposition. I apologize for all that background... particularly if you knew it already.

So this book is called *The Canary Wars*. Technically, we're dealing with one Canary 'War', but my editors have said (and I agree) that 'Wars' sounds better for the title. And let's be honest, the Canaries and the Pions have had plenty of wars, so it's not as though we're being outlandish.

Let's get started.

CHAPTER ONE

THE 2232 BIT

This chapter will cover 2232's contribution to this book. For reference, I should point out that the following takes place about six weeks after our return from the dark cruise. The Jupiter Force was holding station at Belt Two, repairing damage, doing maintenance and replacing the people we'd lost. More on all that later.

What matters for now is that two of the ships that had come back with us, *Kansas* and *North Carolina*, had joined Marshal Samuels' Belt Squadron. Just to remind you, the 'Belt Squadron' was a force dedicated to escorting convoys of trade ships through the Empire — Marshal's force was over twenty hulls strong by the end of 2232, though many of his ships were old. Either way, they were escorting convoys, protecting Imperial trade and making sure pirates and Martians alike were disappointed when they came looking for easy prey.

When we'd come back from our Jupiter patrol, Captains Kishko and Akuma, both formerly of the Jupiter Squadron, volunteered their ships to join Marshal's force. This, I have to say, took a lot of character: those two ships had been alone at Jupiter for seven months, surviving on minimal rations for all that time… and now, as soon as they returned to the Empire, they volunteered to take on new duties.

Those ships, skippers and crews had my respect in *The Dark Cruise* for surviving what they had, and that respect just kept growing.

Anyway, it is with one of those ships, the frigate *North Carolina* under Captain Simon Kishko, that we have to start *The Canary Wars*.

Kishko's ship was one of three escorts on a large convoy that was heading for Earth, but due to the orbits at that time of year, the trip was destined to be tricky — the convoy had to pass very near to the Martian asteroid colonies. The other two escorts were aged *Canada*-class corvettes, *Canmore* and *Summerside*, so Kishko's was the biggest and most powerful vessel, and he was the escort's commanding officer.

Now, recall that Simon Kishko was himself an older man, who'd been with the service longer than I'd been alive. He had a sense of honor and pride in the Navy that more 'modern' cynics like myself didn't express so well. He also hadn't seen action much at all over the past decades.

When he was woken from his sleep period by battle stations alarms late one night, neither that advanced age, nor the lack of recent combat experience slowed him down. He was on the bridge in moments, and with a patriarchal calm he addressed his executive officer, Commander Lam Meili, "Report, please, Commander Lam."

"Sir, *Canmore* is detecting the approach of a raiding force of two pirates, a Martian destroyer escort and a destroyer. They will converge with our course in two hours."

Standard operating practice under conditions like these was to scatter the convoy. If the attackers overwhelmed the escort while the convoy remained in formation, then the attackers would be able to go up and down the line, destroying the merchants. Scattering the convoy would mean the attackers would have to chase individual merchants (who they'd almost certainly catch)... but they wouldn't be able to chase everyone, so many could escape.

That would be standard procedure, but Captain Kishko wasn't ready to abandon the convoy just yet.

"Very well," he said slowly, then approached the front of *North Carolina's* aged bridge. "Send to *Canmore* to take command of the escort. We will attempt to dissuade the attack force."

This was old-school thinking at its finest — tactics from a time when Defense Command went straight at the enemy, under every circumstance. Some can argue that it doesn't make the most sense under these circumstances... but I don't care. Call it nostalgia, or a misplaced sense of old Naval honor, but there's something about a frigate standing its ground to protect civilians that feels right to me.

North Carolina accelerated away from the convoy on an intercept course, and an hour later the ship's crew was at battle stations, a few minutes away from a fight. Captain Kishko stood solidly at the front of his bridge, watching the range tick down.

"We will make the destroyer our first target, Commander Lam. Laser one, do as much damage as you can. Prepare the torpedo as well. Its target will be the destroyer."

Kishko was going to do his best to dissuade the Martians and pirates from attempting to raid the convoy, and if he could disable the destroyer, they'd be fools to try — the escort's remaining two corvettes were easily a match for a destroyer escort and two pirates.

But four-to-one were not the best odds for *North Carolina* to start with.

One of my editors has (quite logically, I suppose) inquired as to why Kishko didn't take his whole force out to meet the Martians, if our three ships would have had a good chance against their four. I think Kishko's concern was that this might be a feint — an attempt to draw our escort away from the convoy entirely, so another force could attack them while our ships were locked in a fight. He wanted to keep most of his force close to the ships they were protecting.

Yes, it's a debatable decision, particularly since there turned out to be no further attack waiting in the wings, but I can certainly understand the caution.

"We must dictate the range of the engagement," Kishko continued his instructions to his bridge crew. He was saying things that, on the bridge of *Wolf*, everyone would have already known, but to many of the less combat-experienced people on his crew, it was necessary information.

"Range in two minutes, sir," Commander Lam reported from her station at the back of the bridge.

Kishko nodded, "Very good."

North Carolina closed with the Martians, and the Martians adjusted their courses to come straight at the frigate — they figured that, four-to-one, it'd be easy pickings.

I won't play coy, or try to overdo the buildup here: when the range came down, Kishko gave his order, "Shoot."

North Carolina was a Belt Squadron ship, but not one of the old, *elite* Belt Squadron ships. Commander Lam was a solid officer, but she didn't quite have the targeting finesse of Matt Baxter or Jim Hannigan. When the frigate's number one laser fired at maximum range, it completely missed the destroyer.

"Launch torpedo," Kishko was unfazed by the failure of the first shot, and his order sent the warhead from *North Carolina's* tube racing towards the enemy formation.

"Open fire with magnetic disrupters. Continue to plot laser solutions, and report when you are ready for your next shot," Kishko persisted with his commands, and *North Carolina* closed with the enemy.

The Martian destroyer began to return fire seconds later, lasers sweeping out from the red ship's turrets and crisscrossing over *North Carolina's* flight path. What beams hit, however, slid off the fast-moving frigate, and then Defense Command mags began raining back in reply.

North Carolina's mags hadn't been upgraded since the ship had been constructed, so the weapons didn't repeat as quickly as a *Predator's* rapid-fire models, but a torrent of golden energy nonetheless hurtled through space at the Martian destroyer.

"Launch Starbursts for missile defense," Kishko now loosed his nineteen F-184 Starbursts from *North Carolina's* flight bays. Had *North Carolina* been newer and faster, it might have been dangerous to launch those planes — a *Predator* moving at full speed can often outrun (and thus ram into) its launching fighters — but the Starbursts were able to jump out of the bays at 197 kps, to *North Carolina's* 189 kps.

The planes, all of which had seen better days, peeled away from the bow of their ship, then formed up into their respective NorCar and NorCarStar Squadrons, sweeping back and forth on the forward quarters of the frigate to shoot down any missiles that were launched by the Martians.

By this time the Martian destroyer was starting to feel the stab of mag bolts, but its laser fire didn't slacken. Instead, the destroyer escort added its own, smaller lasers to the onslaught, but again, *North Carolina* was riding in too quickly, and presenting too slim a silhouette, to be seriously hit by the fire.

"We are ready with a new laser solution, sir," Commander Lam reported, determined this time to make the shot tell.

Kishko nodded, "Shoot."

North Carolina's mag fire stopped and seconds later an angry red laser shot stabbed out from its bow emitter. The powerful beam crossed space at light speed and found the destroyer amidships. The Martian turned to spin off the beam, but Lam adjusted the solution just enough to keep contact for an extra handful of seconds.

The laser cracked the Martian's armor, and sliced into the ship's primary hull before it could get out of the way. Its acceleration dropped by thirty percent and it turned away, its EM cannons firing wildly to try to screen the retreat.

"Well done, Commander Lam!" Kishko's approval was warm, and he smiled as he turned back to look at the operations consoles.

North Carolina then bucked out from under his feet.

The destroyer escort's lasers found *North Carolina's* bow pod, and one of the pirates — a mid-sized hauler hull originally — had a laser on it. A powerful laser. That beam blew straight through *North Carolina's* high drive pod, sending a surge into the power grid that tripped the overload breakers for half the ship. Fifty percent of the ship's internal systems went dark for seconds.

While *North Carolina's* Helm and Navigation Officer threw the frigate into a spin to get away from the fire, Commander Lam cut loose again with her mags, and the pirate took the brunt of that onslaught. Being a civilian ship by design, the vessel lacked adequate protection against mag fire. As Lam found the range, that pirate's laser went silent and its own power grid burned out.

The other pirate didn't run, though: with guts uncharacteristic of a pirate, it opened up on *North Carolina* with Martian-manufactured EM cannons, closing up next to the destroyer escort as it did.

"Prepare a laser shot for the destroyer escort!" Kishko ordered sharply, managing to brace himself on the railing in front of the main screens. "Turn us back toward the convoy!"

This is where the bridge log from *North Carolina* abruptly cuts out — we have no visual record of the rest of the engagement.

I can tell you what happened, though: the Martian destroyer, seeing that its frigate adversary was wounded, opened up with its rear lasers, and put a shot right through *North Carolina's* bow pod. The shot cut all power to that section of the ship, meaning the bridge went dark, and sensors went down.

Communications were still working, so over the intercom Kishko passed commands down to the auxiliary steering position, and pilots from the Starbursts he'd launched called in realtime alerts about vectors and locations — they'd say 'hard to port, incoming!' and he'd pass the orders on.

North Carolina's mag gunners switched to independent fire — mags that had power were targeted and fired individually by spacers at their controls, though without sensors they could see precious little. They were down to aiming by enhanced visual feeds from their hyper-zoom targeting cams.

After several minutes of scrambling around blindly, Kishko gave an order, "Withdraw from action… any direction that appears clear."

Continuing to fly blind, *North Carolina* withdrew from the fight, being chased by a slightly wounded destroyer, a determined destroyer escort and a gutsy pirate.

The convoy was saved…

Chapter Two

Reunion

Several days after *North Carolina* tangled with the Martians, Karen and I were standing in one of Belt Two base's receiving lounges, waiting as a frigate finished docking.

It had, as I say, been a couple of months since we'd gotten back from the dark cruise, and Karen was doing just fine after her Phosgene exposure. But that damned stuff had killed many of our crew, and we'd just finished another personnel shuffle to fill the gaps it had left.

Only one development that you'll likely recognize: replacing Kyle Stranks, our fallen commander of SF, was *Lion*'s former SF commander, Lieutenant Omar Cunningham. Omar had been Karen's chief of SF when she'd left *Lion*, and had stayed in that position when Kris had taken command of the ship. Now that *Lion* was laid up for repairs, and Kris was in hospital on Earth recovering from the epic radiation poisoning she'd suffered in *The Sinope Affair*, Omar was available, so we grabbed him.

In fact, all the people we lost to the Phosgene on the dark cruise were replaced by survivors from *Lion* — those women and men who'd gotten off our sister ship were able to stay in the Jupiter Force family, so to speak.

Anyway, back to Karen and me. Like I say, we'd handled all the personnel stuff already by the time 2233 rolled around, and now we were waiting to welcome some guests to Belt Two.

"So the publicly released story is that she has the flu?" Karen's arms were folded and she was leaning back against one of the columns in the waiting lounge. "What about all the people who're going to see her here?"

"They leaked a second story, that she was actually coming here for secret meetings on the creation of a new combined assault force," I replied, yawning. As seems to be a common theme with these recent books, I was tired again.

Karen frowned slightly, "Isn't that why she's actually coming?"

I shrugged, "I thought so. But you never know with her."

We continued to wait until the light over the entrance to the chute went from red to green: *Nova Scotia* had docked securely with Belt Two base's airlock. Soon enough, people would be coming down from the ship.

"Did they just dock?"

Charlie Peters appeared next to Karen, seemingly out of thin air. Our intrepid Special Branch Major has that ability — you know, you're looking at an empty room, then you blink and he's standing there. Damned Special Branch skills...

Well, I actually shouldn't *damn* them, owing to how many times they've kept me from dying. And since Charlie's my friend, probably shouldn't damn him. Sorry Charlie!

Karen, of course, didn't seem at all surprised to have Charlie suddenly appear beside her, and she simply nodded, "Yup, just went green."

"Why's she coming out here, anyway?" I looked back at Charlie, and he gave a genuine shrug.

"I really don't know. I don't think it's the assault force thing."

We all fell silent. There was no telling what was going on here, so we waited two minutes, and then people started coming down the chute.

First to arrive was Commodore Christian 'Mik' Mikaelsen, a passenger we were expecting. I smiled and approached him with an outstretched hand, "Mik, good to see you!"

He took my hand and nodded back, "Good to see you too. Glad you got back in one piece... good to see you too, Karen, Charlie..."

Mik shook everyone's hand in turn, and then before any conversation could start, Wes Pellew exited the chute, "Morning all."

Turning back to Wes, I frowned, "It's the middle of the afternoon, Wes."

He smiled, "Is it?"

Then we all shook hands again. One of my editors commented a while back that the amount of hand-shaking we officers seem to do is irritating. I'm not sure what else we could do, though. I'm not one for hugging, and I don't think greeting each other with some sort of traditional dance would be appropriate to the decorum of the Navy. So yes, we shake hands a lot.

It seems I've really mistimed that rant, though, because when Charlie stepped past Wes and me and got to the entrance to the chute to greet the next person off *Nova Scotia*, it wasn't with a handshake.

Sorry for trying to be somewhat coy about who the third person was, because you obviously have already figured out it was Lia Hawke.

Karen, Wes, Mik and I all talked quietly amongst ourselves while Charlie greeted Lia for the first time in a little over a year, but I have to confess, I stole some glances in their direction. My sixth sense was picking up a weird vibe from Lia. She didn't seem like herself, at least not to me.

Remember back in *The Hawke Mission*, when she greeted Charlie in Hawke One's receiving lounge with one of those kisses that would fell any man but a Special Brancher? Remember how playful she was?

Well, there was no kiss this time. Charlie's probably going to kill me for being this descriptive (Lia never minds, of course), but she had her eyes screwed shut, her chin on his shoulder, and by the look of it, her hug was a vice grip.

In other words, Lia wasn't just happy to see Charlie, she desperately *needed* to see him. After a few minutes of that vice-grip hugging, she pulled her chin off his shoulder to give him a modest kiss, but suffice it to say that her greeting seemed much more serious than usual.

As soon as she pulled away from Charlie and they both turned and approached Karen and me, she flipped a mental switch, and raised a wall of mischievousness to mask any vulnerability.

"So what'd you bring me back from Jupiter?" she asked Charlie with a coy smile.

Charlie shook his head, "Nothing, really..."

"What does 'nothing *really*' mean? It means something?" she was back to her crazy self.

"He brought you lingerie," Karen said with a small smile of her own, and all the men froze in place (though, as one editor has pointed out, that fact would be obvious to no one since we were already standing still). But lingerie wasn't the sort of thing they were supposed to talk about in front of us, and Karen knew it — Lia's mischievousness was rubbing off on her.

Charlie — poor Charlie — almost turned red, but since he's a Special Brancher, he didn't, "It was Carly's idea. We'd just shot a Commando in a lingerie store... I waited outside and she handed me a bag..."

Lia's smile broadened, "That's sweet... but didn't you tell her all my lingerie is tailored?"

She is so bad.

"Wes, how's... the squadron?" I asked loudly. I'm very subtle when it comes to trying to change the subject.

"It's the only way to go," Lia continued unabated. "Karen, I can send you my tailor's name if you like."

"It's good," Wes replied, even louder than I'd been.

I think Lia's the only person who could get away with making that sort of suggestion (even as a joke) to Karen, and Karen smiled back, "I'll have to think about that."

"Mik, how's your battleship?" my volume increased to match Wes', and Mik just laughed and shook his head.

"You're not going to get them to stop by shouting," was his reply.

He was right — they kept at it. We all fled, looking for Greg's office. The crazy Lady and her new accomplice followed.

CHAPTER THREE
RAISON D'ETRE

The title to this chapter seems to be in French, and as anyone who frequently writes or speaks French can tell you, there should be an accent over the first 'E' in D'Etre. Unfortunately, my system (which does put accents on words like cliché) won't put one here... and I don't know how to force it to do one. I tried turning on my transcription system, so I could say 'Raison D'Etre' and have the computer automatically put in the accent, but it spelled it 'Raisin Debtor'. I could get my publishers to fix it, but they won't even spring for maps, so what are the chances?

Yeah, not holding my breath. Apologies, then, to anyone offended by the lack of an accent on the top of D'Etre.

There is a good reason for the title, though. It indicates that the meeting I'm about to recount was Lia's raison d'etre for coming to Belt Two — it was her plausible excuse for being out here, just as it was Wes' excuse. I think Mik was actually here for only the meeting (without any other secret intent) but I don't know for sure. I'll have to ask him.

Anyway, the meeting.

Admiral Greg Noyce and Commodore Marshal Samuels were waiting for us in one of Belt Two base's conference rooms — from the receiving lounge where Karen had encouraged Lia to start talking about her unmentionables, it was about a five-minute walk. And we weren't wasting any time getting there.

When we entered the conference room, we... wait for it... shook hands. Greg and Marshal hadn't seen Mik and Wes since around the time of *The Gallant Few*, a year prior, so they exchanged greetings and congratulations on jobs well done. Rightly so.

Lia, of course, was something of a different story. She was still working under her crazy-Lia guise, so when Greg smiled and extended his hand to her, she rushed forward and gave him a big hug.

"Uncle Greg!" she exclaimed, and Greg chuckled, hugging her back before she stepped away.

"I see you haven't lost your sense of humor, Lia," he said approvingly, and Lia shrugged girlishly.

"Keeps me insane," she replied with mock-sheepishness, then she turned to Marshal. "You're Marshal Samuels, aren't you?"

Marshal braced himself, then nodded, "It's a pleasure to meet you, Lady Hawke."

Lia sauntered up to him and shook his hand, "Your Belt Squadron is doing very fine work, getting shipments to us safely."

That compliment — actually serious and on-topic — caught all of us off guard. It wasn't quite in character, despite being a very appropriate thing to say.

Marshal nodded, "Thank you, m'lady. I'll be sure to pass your compliments along to all the Captains and Commanders who are doing the work."

"It's Lia," she smiled in reply, then turned to Greg. "Now, no offense to anyone wanting to chat, but can we get down to business? After we're done here, I have to haul Charlie away for reasons he wouldn't like me to talk about in distinguished company, and I'm impatient."

Ah there, she was back.

Charlie didn't look impressed, but he didn't look horrified either. None of us did, really — we all either had plenty of experience with or more than enough fair warning about Lia's personality.

Taking our chairs all around the table, we settled in.

And yes, I'm going to make you sit through this. Or at least part of it. Because this meeting is full of important exposition that will set up the rest of 2233. Can't just gloss over it with my usual intricate verbosity… you know: 'And then we had our meeting.'

"I'm sorry to have to get you three down here as soon as you docked, but I've been in frequent contact with John at Admiralty House, and it's necessary that we get your perspectives as soon as possible. We are planning to begin our counteroffensives in the coming months, and we want your forces to spearhead our operations."

Well that made sense. Sorry, I know that probably sounds conceited, but you had in this room some of the best officers in the fleet (myself excepted, obviously). Mik had proved himself a hell of a leader, coordinating a mixed bag of warships with Hawke Command and turning them into an effective force. Wes had taken the disgraced Independent Squadron and turned it into the elite fighting formation it always should have been. Marshal was effectively defending the trade of the Empire against all comers. Lia, for all her insanity, was the commander-in-chief of Hawke Command. Karen had commanded the Jupiter Force, and I suppose to be fair, so had I.

Taking that all together, the people in this room were the best ones to involve if we were going on the offensive.

"Our thoughts are that the Jupiter Force and the Independent Squadron should remain as they are, but we will add new ships to the Hawke Force and the Belt Squadron. The increased numbers will allow you to divide your formations into defensive and offensive units, and the offensive units can join our assault force."

Alright, I'll slow down here to explain that, top to bottom. Greg and John Fiora were planning to build an assault fleet — a combat formation with the power to defeat the Martians anywhere we cared to go. Great idea… one problem: where do you get the ships? If you pulled the entire Hawke Force or Belt Squadron off its station, you'd leave important colonies unprotected, and that wasn't acceptable.

So John and Greg had a plan: they'd increase the size of the Hawke Force and the Belt Squadron by sending them newly-commissioned ships. Then, when their strength was suitably increased, they could be divided, with some of the ships staying on the defensive, and others being assigned to the assault fleet.

Meanwhile, the Jupiter Force and the Independent Squadron (with no particular defensive responsibilities) could simply go on the attack as-is. As-was. Whatever.

"What are your thoughts on this? It's still a preliminary plan," Greg finished. "We do need a decision as soon as possible, though."

Marshal leaned forward immediately, "Greg, will you be commanding the assault force?"

Greg nodded, "I'll be one of the commanders. Marlene will be commanding a section of Venus Squadron ships, and John will be taking the *Bonnies* out. He'll have overall command."

"Then I can't leave," Marshal shook his head. "I'm sorry, I really wish I could join you, but the convoy system right now is too fragile. And I don't like the thought of pulling all our experienced people out of the Belt colonies when the offensive begins."

"Agreed," I nodded quickly in support. "I'd prefer to have Marshal watching the back door... if we all left, I'd constantly be worried about the Martians raiding in our absence."

"Very well, Marshal can take overall command of the Belt Station, and we'll keep the Belt Squadron here," Greg concurred.

Yes, a major decision was made just that quickly. I can almost hear my editors saying, "What, wouldn't he have to clear that with John and the Admiralty?" Nope. The reason we were having this meeting was to tell Greg, and by extension John, what seemed realistic to us. Neither Admiral had the complete picture of the situation we were each facing in our operational zones — we had first-hand knowledge and they were quite willing to defer to that knowledge.

"I can turn operations for the Hawke Force over to Latisha Genda," Mik spoke up next. "I can also afford to pull *Cyclops* out, give you another battlewagon."

Mik, remember, commanded (jointly) the Hawke Force, a mixed Defense Command-Hawke Command formation of ships. His Hawke Command opposite was Rear Admiral Latisha Genda, a capable officer who he knew could operate that mixed squadron effectively in his absence.

"And we can definitely release some of our ships to join your operations," Lia added in a somber tone. "We can put together an elite squadron out of the Hawke Force for you, Uncle Greg."

"We're ready to fight as we are," Wes added after that.

Karen and I looked at each other, then she provided the first part of our own status report, "We're ready for operations now, too, but we're under strength. We adopted *Trusty* from the old Jupiter Squadron, but even with Nancy on board, we're down to three corvettes and two frigates."

Greg frowned at those words — as he later said to me, "It was a little bit of a shock to hear out loud how weak the Jupiter Force was after the mission to Io."

He's right about that. Of course we'd all known how much the Jupiter Force had lost in 2232, but to bluntly hear that we were down to five effective ships — *Wolf, Cheetah, Friendly, Lady Grace* and *Trusty* — was still shocking every time. Remember, *Lion* was laid up for repairs, and *Lady Grace* was only just back out of the yards after having a replacement drive pod installed.

Compare that to the eight or ten ships Mik and Lia could probably provide, or the seven Wes had. We were the smallest squadron in the proposed assault force, and while five ships wasn't all that weak by pre-war standards, 2232 had reminded us how quickly numbers could dwindle.

"I could send you some of my best from the Belt Squadron," Marshal, as always, had a solution in mind. "Actually, my best are *Alberta, Generous* and *Sackville*. How about a reunion?"

Remember, *Alberta*, *Generous* and *Sackville* had all been with us in the old Belt Squadron. We'd be beyond happy to welcome them back into the fold now.

Despite that, though, I frowned — Marshal was offering quite a sacrifice, "You want to gut the Belt Squadron of its veterans?"

With a shrug, Marshal leaned back in his chair, "You need them more than I do. I gave *Alberta* to Kasia Hu, and she's doing very well. I think they'd be an asset to the Jupiter Force."

I smiled, "Well, we appreciate that very much."

We certainly did.

Greg was nodding approvingly, "That's excellent, Marshal. So we will have three squadrons from the Belt: the Hawke Force, the Independent Squadron, and the Jupiter Force. I will also have a separate battleship unit built around *Warspite* and *Goliath*. The home fleet might detach additional battleships on the way, and we'll add two newly-commissioned frigates and three corvettes... so that makes four formations in our assault force."

"The Martians are in for a fun time," Wes nodded with some satisfaction as he sat back in his chair, and we all chuckled.

The meeting continued, but now I can just say that it did. I've managed to get a good deal of the necessary exposition out of the way... onwards with the narrative.

CHAPTER FOUR

THE REAL REASON (PART ONE)

About an hour later, we all filed out of the conference room, and as we were leaving, a number of different things happened. First, I found I was walking out next to Marshal, so I asked about *North Carolina*.

"Anything on Captain Kishko?" was my exact question, and Marshal shook his head.

"Nothing. The convoy pulled into Earth safely about twelve hours ago, but no one's heard from him. I'm starting to fear the worst."

I nodded, "It doesn't seem good."

Shortly after Kishko had led the Martians away from the convoy, *Canmore* had sent a comm burst informing Marshal what had happened. We'd all been wondering after *North Carolina's* fate, but we couldn't obsess over it too much. There were too many other things happening for one missing frigate to absorb all our attention. We were all still hoping *North Carolina* would appear at one of the outer Belt colonies, wounded but still flying.

As the days… just over a week now, actually… wore on, though, chances of that were seeming slimmer and slimmer.

Anyway, that was the first thing, because just as Marshal was opening his mouth to add something to the conversation, Lia tugged on my sleeve from the other side, "Need to talk to you."

The tone of her voice was no-nonsense, which in itself got my attention. I must have frowned or something, because Marshal quickly picked up on my surprise, "I'll catch up with you later, Ken."

He went on, and as he did, he passed Wes, who caught my eye and then nodded to me before turning away and leaving. With them on their way, I turned to face Lia, and found that she'd rounded up Karen and Charlie too. Her face was serious, and she waved us down the corridor, "Is there somewhere here to talk?"

"Best place for that is back on *Wolf*," Karen said softly.

Lia frowned, nodded, and then looked over her shoulder, "Is it this way?"

"This way," I bobbed my head in the opposite direction. I could have joked about her poor sense of direction, but for some reason I didn't think that would be right.

About ten minutes later we'd made it to *Wolf*, and we set ourselves up in the Captain's dining room (Andrea was busy, and later I'll get into why and how she was doing). For those of you who haven't been aboard a *Predator*-class ship, the dining room is *not* connected to the Captain's cabin. In some older versions of the *North America*-class, they were linked or close together. Not in *Predators*.

Anyway, we snuck into the dining room, and Lia closed the door behind us, then locked it. As I sat down at the table next to Karen and across from Charlie, I wondered for a moment if Lia was just orchestrating some sort of joke — a pretend secret to play with us.

"My dad's going to die. Soon."

Well, no, that wasn't any sort of joke.

Lia's words were soft, simple, and gut-wrenching in their own way. She dropped her façade completely and started pacing back and forth at the head of the table, her hands working nervously in front of her as she tried to explain.

"He... the stroke killed his brain... doctors said if there was no improvement by now there never would be... He's on a machine... it's breathing for him... no one knows... only Doctor Sykes... me and Sykes and four people on the palace staff. He has no brain function... I mean, he's... dead. They say we should pull the plug soon..."

She stopped pacing and looked at us, and I immediately understood why she'd come all this way. Lia looked totally and genuinely lost, and that's not a look Lia often gets.

I can't adequately describe the pain she was so obviously radiating, but my editors have asked me to try. It's difficult, I know, to understand why Lia would be in pain about the death of her father — a man she really did *not* get along with. Well, in my experience, there are two kinds of bad relationships with parents: the ones that are genuinely horrific, that truly leave the child with no connection to home... and the ones where the division and dislike coexist with a real, deeply-felt love.

That probably sounds very antiseptic — as usual, I describe things with the emotional weight of a robot writing a formula. But I hope you know what I mean. The one time we've seen Ian Hawke in this Martian War series, he was at his very worst, and Lia genuinely hated aspects of the life he'd pushed her into.

But except for him and Charlie, and to a lesser extent, me, she was also alone in the world. She was so many things to so many people, always had a façade up. Her father was her only surviving parent, and while she didn't like him much of the time, the connection was vitally important to her.

"I couldn't tell anyone... it'd be a mess... I don't know what to do... as soon as we pull the plug it's all on me. All of it..."

By now, with his blinding Special Brancher speed, Charlie had taken up position next to Lia, and had his arms wrapped around her.

Karen and I were genuinely dumbfounded. We obviously hadn't known that Ian Hawke was ill, and I had no idea how to respond.

"I..." was all I could mumble for a moment.

"So sorry, Lia..." Karen, for once, was equally unable to find the right things to say.

Charlie was whispering something to Lia that neither of us could hear. Tears were starting to slide down her cheeks — tears that she'd been suppressing, she told me later, for six months.

Imagine that, for a moment. Your father is dying, and then has a stroke that renders him brain dead. You're obliged to tell the world that he's fine, just on bed rest, and to keep the fact that you're losing him a secret.

Every day you go and visit him, and stand next to his bed and squeeze his hand, vainly hoping he might come out of it, and be okay.

But as soon as you leave that room, you have to be chipper and playful — you have to pretend that everything's normal, because you don't want anyone to know that it isn't. Even for someone like Lia, who has a chameleon-like ability to fit herself into any situation, that had to be emotionally crushing.

Well, no 'had to be' about it. It was taking everything she had to keep the façade intact. When the opportunity came to visit Belt Two for this meeting, she knew she had to take it. She had to share the situation with people she could trust, and I am eternally honored that she trusted Karen and me with this knowledge.

Now, before I get back to Lia, my editor has asked a very good question: why was Ian Hawke's medical situation being kept secret? I probably did a bad job of explaining the intricacies of the Hawke governmental system in *The Hawke Mission*, so I'll try to give a simple answer.

First of all, if the information was made public, it could cause a PR nightmare. Yes, I feel somehow sick to have to say this, but public relations — the media spin — was one of the reasons Lia had to hide her anguish. Remember, she'd grown up in the Hawke Court: some of her first memories were of her father explaining to her the importance of appearances.

If the leader of the Protectorate was dying, it could cause a massive wave of concern, or a lack of confidence in the government. People could fear that the administration at the head of the colony was going to collapse, because Ian Hawke had, for years, *been* that administration. Those in the know would realize that the government had been well-developed over the Lord's latter years, so that in the event of his death the bureaucracy could continue without him... but the apparent loss of leadership could be damaging, particularly during war.

Well, you say (rightly) wouldn't Lia take over as leader? Certainly, she'd have to — she'd be in demand immediately, in fact. She'd have to go before every camera she could find, attend every rally her publicists could set up. She'd have to do everything conceivable to convince people that the Protectorate was going to live on, strong and proud even in the absence of its aged patriarch.

Then she'd have to run court to reassure the nobles of the very same, and host the heads of all the Protectorate's largest guilds and industries, to let them know that things were stable.

After that, she might be able to get back to organizing the war effort. If her father died right now, Hawke's ships would still be in the fight, but there'd be no way for her to help organize an assault squadron. She'd essentially have to turn overall control of Hawke Command to an officer like Rear Admiral Genda, who wasn't ready for that much responsibility.

Let me just reinforce that point here: for all her antics, Lia was running Hawke Command as surely as John and Daragh Ryan were running Defense Command. And if she was required to replace her father now, Hawke Command would lose its most experienced commander-in-chief just when circumstances required the surest possible hand.

These were the political and military reasons why Lia was keeping her father's condition a secret — there would simply be too much to deal with as soon as the people found out he was dying.

There would also be no chance for Lia to say goodbye to her father, to grieve and to heal. The minute he flatlined, she'd have to be on her game. She'd have to take over the leadership of the Protectorate.

And she didn't want to. She really, truly didn't want to. She'd be forced into the mold her father had made, and while over time she could stretch that mold, she'd still be confined by it. What freedoms she'd enjoyed — and they were few to begin with — would be crushed by the weight of a responsibility she couldn't shirk.

If you want to criticize her for wanting to hide from those responsibilities for as long as possible, while also being unable to pull the plug on him because, for all his faults, she loved him, go right ahead. Send your criticism in writing to me or Charlie for a start, and he and I will have a race to see who can be first to kill you in a duel. And I bet he'll win.

Lia's life — and she'd never say this herself — had an air of tragedy. I suppose it's cliché to say someone can be trapped by responsibilities they never asked for, but it's true. She was losing her father, who she loved despite everything, and she was losing her freedom.

She knew she couldn't prevent either from happening, and she needed to tell someone.

Charlie was whispering many comforting things to her, and she was past the point of speaking. She buckled at the waist, sobbing in the hoarse, excruciating way that the movies avoid showing (I presume because in its authenticity, it isn't attractive enough). At that point, Karen and I quietly got up and left.

There was nothing either of us could do. She needed to be alone with Charlie, and I'll be honest, it wasn't easy for us to see.

It was like watching paradise burning.

We left.

CHAPTER FIVE
THE REAL REASON (PART TWO)

Andrea Kiley was on an off-duty shift, doing paperwork at her desk. This, I must say, was progress. She was focusing on her job, and for the moment it was keeping her from reflecting on the terrors of the past. Though, as Andrea tells me, the losses and the horror were never particularly far from her mind. She was getting better at ignoring them while she got her job done, but they definitely hadn't disappeared.

Not at all.

A lot had happened to Andrea in the time since we've last seen her...

Actually, no. Not much had.

Sorry, that blatant contradiction actually makes sense to me, so I'll see if I can explain. Andrea had made a lot of progress in terms of refocusing on her job over these past couple of months. And she'd done that by establishing her routine, and sticking to it.

How was this different than the situation on the run out to Jupiter? Well, on that trip, she had been inserting new things into her routine, like nights spent with correspondents, in an attempt to distract herself from the horrors she saw in the dark.

Now she didn't need the overt distractions.

Not, I should add, that there's anything wrong with distractions. I got slammed by some readers because they thought I was saying casual sex was evil, and that it made innocent Andrea a horrible person. I was just saying it wasn't in character for her — a sign that she wasn't quite her old self anymore.

So in a superficial way, Andrea was getting back to being who she'd been, and this seemed like progress. The prisoners of war had gotten off *Wolf* in good health, she'd proven herself a very able Captain, restoring the morale of our ship after the tragic events with *Idaho*, and all in all, Karen and I were more comfortable with her mental state than we had been for quite some time.

But our comfort wasn't stopping us from getting another opinion. Neither Karen nor I had experienced anything approaching the kind of psychological trauma that Andrea had suffered. Was this just a lull — was she repressing pain (albeit successfully) and setting herself up for a proper breakdown, or was she healing?

And even if she was healing, was there a way we (or any of our old Belt Squadron family) could help?

These were our questions, and the man with the best chance of getting answers was Commodore Wesley Pellew.

It was therefore Wes who knocked on Andrea's hatch while Lia was telling us about her father.

Andrea frowned at the interruption, got up and answered the door. Wes was looking away when the hatch opened, but he turned her way quickly, "Andrea, good morning."

"It's afternoon, Wes," she answered with a slight frown. "Is there something I can do for you?"

With a nod, he pointed at her couch through the hatch, "You could let me in. We're supposed to have a talk."

It took a few seconds for Andrea to realize what he meant — she was truly focused on her paperwork just then, and the suggestions Karen and I had made that she talk with Wes weren't in the front of her mind. As she remembered, she nodded and waved him in, closing the hatch behind him.

"Can I get you something to drink?" she asked smoothly.

Sitting down on her couch, Wes shook his head, "I think I'm fine for now."

Andrea raised an eyebrow, "I see. Well, I suppose you'll be checking to see if I'm fine?"

"That's the general idea."

Returning to her office chair, Andrea sat and shuffled the pads she'd been working on into stacks. Then she laced her fingers together and rested her hands on the desk in front of her, "So ask, then."

Wes detected an edge in Andrea's voice, but he couldn't figure out just what sort of edge. There was only one way to find out, so he leaned forward, "Are you fine, Andrea?"

She paused for a few seconds, then smiled sadly, "Not even close, Wes."

Wes liked that answer. He'd never done this before, so all he could expect was the movie-cliché answer — the 'I'm fine' protests from Andrea, until at last he made her admit that she wasn't. Then there'd be tears and hugging, and an unusual attraction that'd lead to a violin-backed kiss… ah the movies. This was much easier (and less awkward).

"Well," he said slowly, "I think I might be able to help. A bit."

Andrea grinned, "Oh come on now, Wes, don't get my hopes up with all those promises."

"Just managing your expectations is all," Wes smiled back. "I think I know some of what you're feeling."

Andrea's grin faded and her eyes narrowed slightly, "Ken and Karen have been hinting at that, but they've been damned cryptic. You have a dark spot in your past?"

Wes nodded, "I do. I doubt that it compares to that week you spent on Egesta, but it was bad for me. And it changed me a lot."

He let those words hang for a few seconds, and Andrea studied him as he paused. She wasn't sure what to expect, though as she tells me now, she was all set to be politely dismissive. She was quite certain that nothing Wes had seen in his past would compare to Egesta. He wasn't dark enough for him to have seen the sorts of things she'd seen.

"I was married, once. A long time ago now, it seems," Wes began the story, and Andrea leaned back in her chair and folded her arms, just avoiding a frown. "Sara… she was incredible. I loved her… well, the way you're supposed to love your wife. I was a Lieutenant in *Alberta's* fighter group, and Ken was my wing commander. This was before he moved over to the command side… before *Friendly* and before you would have known us."

Andrea nodded once to acknowledge that; she could already tell where this was going.

"We had a little house down in Belt Two Dome Four. She was a nurse, she did the night shifts in the dome hospital. We didn't get to spend much time together, but I was looking at a transfer to SF so I could be with her more. You know, did the small arms courses and so on..."

Another nod from Andrea.

"Well, I came home one night, and found my front door off its hinges. And I found Sara inside, dead."

Wes had rehearsed that line to himself many times, trying to make it easier to say. I should mention that this is not a story he tells... ever, really. The very fact that I'm recording it here is the result of a long discussion where he, Andrea and I decided it was necessary to include it. If we didn't, none of the advice Wes gave Andrea would have any real teeth at all — his attempts to counsel her would make no sense.

So he agreed to let this story be included, and my eternal thanks to him for that. Because it's not a happy story.

"The local Belt Widows had noticed her at the hospital when one of them was getting treated for a stabbing. They followed her home. They spent almost a day raping her. Then they killed her."

Andrea's face tightened slightly, and she nodded again.

"None of the neighbors paid any attention to the screaming. I don't know why. When I got home, the door was open... I don't know why someone walking by didn't check. But it doesn't matter. It didn't matter then. She was dead... and... I went to a dark place."

Wes tells me that he wasn't satisfied with the way he was telling this story. It seems to me to be a fine, honest account of what happened, but understandably, Wes doesn't think his words quite relayed the pain they needed to.

But let's be honest, what words can do justice to that pain?

"It didn't take long for SF to find the bastards. And because Sara was the wife of one of ours, they worked extra hard. We got the whole gang — seven men and four women. We got them within a day. They were tried and convicted within the month. The ringleader was hung, the rest got long prison terms."

"But you weren't satisfied with that," Andrea knew where this was going.

Wes nodded, "Right. So I challenged all of them to duels. Real duels. We signed DNRs. One of them nearly killed me, but I got them all. Dead *dead*."

As you probably know, most duels to the death these days do *not* end with final death. As soon as someone is killed, they're resuscitated. It's basically as fatal as fighting to first blood. Unless, of course, you and your opponent agree to sign DNRs — Do Not Resuscitate agreements. Then it's a real fight to the death — you don't use mags on 'lethal' (which kill you by overloading your nervous system, so you can be resuscitated). Instead, you fight with them set on full, so they punch a hole in the human body. Remember Kate Levec on Io? That's the setting you use in a DNR duel.

I remember Wes fighting those duels. I remember trying fruitlessly to convince him that he shouldn't go through with them... and I remember thinking my words would be pretty useless. These people had done unspeakable things, and it was his right to seek final revenge. All those Widows agreed to the duels, took their chances, and lost.

I was incredibly relieved when he didn't die — he was one of my best pilots, and of course, my friend.

"The problem was that I wasn't the same after that, Andrea," Wes pushed on, trying to sound calm. "I started finding other gangs of Widows, and challenging them. I was flying like a madman when I was on missions with *Alberta*, and then as soon as we got into port — any port in the Belt — I looked for a duel. And I nearly lost a couple."

Wes isn't exaggerating here: he fought over twenty-five duels in the course of about six months (a lot considering we were in space for most of this time, fighting pirates). All of them DNRs. And he was flying like a madman — the nothing-to-lose sort of flying you'd expect from a man who'd lost everything that mattered to him.

"Finally Ken pulled my flight status, and at the next port, he came down after me. He'd tried to tell me I had to stop what I was doing... I was going to destroy myself, and I'd probably kill some of my squadron, but I wouldn't listen. So after I killed the local chief Widow in a duel, he challenged me to a DNR duel."

Andrea hadn't seen that one coming, and she sat up slightly, leaning forward again.

"I didn't want to do it, obviously. But he started in on me. He called me a coward. He said I'd failed as a husband. Said I'd let her die. He said all the things I'd been saying to myself for months. He *said* them to me, and he made me so angry I agreed. So we did it right there in the Widow side of Dome Two on Belt Five. I was so mad... he made himself the focus of all the things I was hating about myself."

By now, Wes was so lost in retelling this story he was only half-aware of Andrea. Ever had that happen? You get engrossed in reliving something so painful that you basically start telling the story to yourself, as much as anyone else.

"He outshot me. I don't know if I missed him on purpose... if I subconsciously didn't want to shoot him because he was my friend, or because I wanted him to kill me because I thought he was right... but he shot me down, and I didn't get him."

His voice trailed off, remembering the day.

"And despite the DNR, he'd only set for lethal?" Andrea asked quietly.

Wes blinked, again almost surprised that he had a listener. He shook his head, "He didn't even set it to full. We were in the middle of the Widow side of town. If I'd actually died, there'd be no ambulance to resuscitate. I was shooting full power, though. He faced me down... he... um. He could have died, but he stood his ground, and he stunned me."

Andrea was silent, and Wes took a couple of blinks to bring himself back to the present.

"All that self-hatred nearly killed me, and more importantly, one of my best friends. I realized then that I had to come to terms with what I was thinking, and that I had to get past it."

"Yes, I know the feeling."

Wes' eyes settled on Andrea's, "I'm not offering a duel, because I'm pretty sure you'd win. But can you confront some of the things you're torturing yourself with? Can you, will you, get past them?"

Andrea understood now why Wes was the right person to have this talk with her — he'd been to a pretty dark place, and knew more of what she was feeling than just about anyone else in our close-knit family.

She nodded once, "I've recently come to the realization that I can't take my pain out on others."

Wes began to nod, but stopped with a frown, "What about the second part? Will you get past it?"

A small smile crossed Andrea's face, "Thanks for the advice, Wes."

"No, don't deflect the question. Will you get past it? You need to try..."

Andrea held up a hand, her smile fading, "After you found Sara, when you closed your eyes, what did you see?"

It was Wes' turn to recognize where the conversation was going, "For a while, I saw her lying there. After a while... nothing."

Taking a deep breath, Andrea nodded, "I really, truly appreciate you coming here, Wes. Please don't think I don't appreciate it. And I'm so sorry for your loss... I never knew... and I don't think I have the words... but as you said, it is different."

Wes took a deep breath, "I understand. Hopefully... hopefully some of it will help a bit. And if you ever want to talk, you call me. I don't know exactly what it's like for you... but I probably know better than some."

He came to his feet with that, a grim, sickly feeling settling over him. He wasn't angry at Andrea, nor was he offended — he could understand that his experience and hers were different. But he'd hoped sharing Sara's story would do more good... that what Sara had suffered, and what he'd done afterward, could help Andrea more than it had.

Heading for the door, he was about to leave when a question came to his mind. This is a question he, Andrea and I very much considered leaving out, because... well, you'll see.

"Andrea... when you close your eyes, what is it you see?"

Andrea wasn't looking at him when he spoke, and she didn't turn towards him to answer. But she answered, because, in her words, 'somehow I knew I had to say it out loud'.

"I... third day I was on Egesta, after Mark had taken *Honesty* and the refugee ships out for help. Gwen Jameson and I responded to a call that the Guild was emptying a shelter at one of the elementary schools. When we got to the school, it was empty, but someone said they were heading to the locks."

I didn't put this into *The Independent Squadron*, because... well, I couldn't. But I have to include it now.

"We got to the locks, just Gwen and me. And they had the kids... all of them, no more than ten years old... they had them lined up. They were sending them into the airlock in groups of five, and they were just blowing them out the lock. Must have been hundreds of kids."

Wes swallowed hard. Andrea was no longer in the room with him — she was back on Egesta, and there were tears streaming down her face.

"I don't know why they did it. I still... I still can't understand who would do such a thing. They were children. Just children, y'see. And I screamed at them. Gwen and I screamed at them. And we were ready to attack, just the two of us. We were going to kill as many of the bastards as we could, and save as many kids as we could."

She stopped talking for a moment, and then she turned and looked at Wes. To use Wes' words, hell was in her eyes. I don't know if that sounds melodramatic, but I rather think it's accurate.

"Then the Guilder who was leading the operation... never got her name... she said if we tried it, they'd kill all my people in the dome, and no one would be saved."

Somehow, Andrea's voice didn't crack.

"And… and I ordered Gwen to stand down. And I didn't do anything. It was a few hundred children, and we had thousands under protection at the stadium. It was the greater good, you understand? But…"

Wes started to hold up his hand to interrupt her, but she held up her hand in reply, "It was the decision that had to be made. But this one little boy, he stared at me. And stared. He didn't say anything, just kept his eyes on mine the whole time. Right until he went into the lock. He was too short to see through the window, so that was it. And then he was blown out into space."

Her voice trailed off. She took a deep breath.

"I see him. When I close my eyes, I see him. And many more. But always him. The ones I couldn't save, you understand? They're who I see. And Wes, I very much doubt I'll ever get past that."

Wes couldn't react to those words. How could he? He'd lost someone he loved so much… but Andrea had sentenced hundreds of children to their deaths. Their deaths were on her shoulders. And there was no one she could blame but herself. It had been her decision not to save those children.

No, sorry. It had been her decision not to die, and not to condemn all the people under her protection to death, by making a vain attempt at saving those children. I don't know if you can agree with the choice she made. I don't know if the 'greater good' argument works for you. The thousands of people who were ultimately saved survived because of decisions like that one… but it's the most horrifying choice imaginable.

And Andrea had to make it. Does the fact that she was still torturing herself for it surprise you? Maybe it makes a lot more sense now. Maybe I should have been up front with this in *The Independent Squadron*.

Andrea's hell was of her own making.

Finally, Wes managed to move, and he took a step towards Andrea, "I'm so…"

Andrea's eyes, which had fallen, flashed up to lock on his, "Don't say sorry, Wes. I'm the one who'll be forever sorry. I don't deserve pity."

She said that firmly, and Wes stopped in mid step, then nodded, "Alright."

"Now… if you could leave…" Andrea turned away again.

Wes opened his mouth to suggest that he should stay, to continue this excruciating talk, but Andrea pulled a pad off a stack, "I'm not going to shoot myself, Wes. But I need to get lost in my work again. That's enough for today. I'll call when I need to talk."

Reluctantly, Wes nodded, then he turned and left.

Sorry, let me take a deep breath here. I wasn't in that room, but hearing about it from Wes and Andrea, and writing it for you… it's a bit intense.

That was the reason Wes had come up from the Protectorate. His story in itself may not have helped Andrea, but perhaps, he suggested later, it had shown that he had the credentials — the personal experience with agony — to at least hear about her pain.

And as Wes knew well, talking about one's pain really is helpful. The movies make that into a bit of a cliché, but it's true. And that's a good thing, too. Otherwise we might have completely lost Andrea.

CHAPTER SIX

ELSEWHERE IT WAS LESS GRIM

In an effort to get the mental image from the last chapter out of my head, I'm going to hop us back to Earth right now, where John Fiora and Daragh Ryan were meeting about the state of affairs at the start of 2233. What's talked about here will be important to keep in mind throughout this book and the rest of the year…

"So Thea really doesn't know where she is?"

"The unexplored belt. All Thea knows is there's some sort of new government cropping up out that way, and dear Haley got a tip saying the new boys were a threat or something such," the Irish Second Lord explained.

He was referring there to Haley Briand who, if you'll recall from the start of 2232, had departed from Earth and then Belt Two on a mission that was so secret her boss didn't even fully understand it. After ten months of silence from Haley, Thea Fostopolos of Defense Command Intelligence was considering sending more agents to find out what had happened to her star operator, and had mentioned that to Daragh in their briefing earlier in the day. Now Daragh was passing the news along to John.

"Well, I hope she's alright," the First Lord nodded. "She deserves better than to die out on some godforsaken rock."

"That's true enough," Daragh agreed quietly.

Sorry, as usual, I've failed to set up the location of their meeting (no, I never do learn, thank you very much). They were sitting in John's office, with Daragh facing the First Lord across the desk. John drummed his fingers on the tabletop, thinking for a few seconds about the implications of a new government in the unexplored belt, then shook himself back to the present.

"Alright, the carriers on their way to the Forge yet?"

Here we go, more exposition. Sorry, but as seems to be inevitable with the first books of each year, there's a lot of setup to do!

Now, I think I explained pretty clearly in past books what the Forge is — the vulcanoid asteroid that circles the sun between the orbits of Venus and Mercury. In the old days, Daragh had operated his force from the hot little rock, and now John had promoted Shauna Cass — one of Marlene's Venus Squadron officers — to Rear Admiral. Her mandate was to build up the Forge so it could serve as a staging point and a flanking threat for our assault on Mercury.

Shauna had been fortifying the Forge quite effectively for most of 2232. She had gotten off to a slow start, but with the promise of new battleships coming online to join the Venus Squadron, Marlene had been able to send her *Warlock*, one of her two veteran battlewagons. Ophelia Zhukov's *Medusa* had also been detached from the Heavy Squadron of the Home Fleet and added to the Forge Squadron, along with three new *Asia*-class frigates and five new *Australia*-class corvettes.

In other words, the Forge was pretty well armed at this stage — as formidable a military post as Venus. This was important, because from a strategic perspective it would massively complicate the Martian defense. Think about it: if we were building up an invasion force at Venus alone, they would have been able to come out and meet us. Because we now had two possible bases from which to attack, they couldn't risk trying to meet us halfway. If they sent forces to block one avenue or the other (we were pretty sure they didn't have the resources to protect both) they'd leave the back door open.

That meant they had to sit and wait at Mercury — it seemed to John and Daragh that it'd be too risky for them to come out to meet us.

Anyway, Shauna was set up and her base was growing more formidable every month. Now John was sending ships that, frankly, you wouldn't expect *him* to send: two carriers.

Yes, carriers.

The last time I mentioned carriers in these books was in *The Almost Coup*, when *Yorktown*, *Essex* and *Hornet* were destroyed in the Battle Over Earth. If you'll recall, the lightly-constructed ships had gotten much too close to the Martian battle line, and despite the self-sacrifice of the battlecruisers *Invincible* and *Indefatigable*, they'd been destroyed. Only *Ark Royal*, the assault carrier, had survived that mess — we were hoping to have that ship back later in 2234, after extensive yard time.

The two carriers John was referring to here were *Akagi* and *Kaga*, two ships that were a decade older than the carriers lost in the Battle Over Earth, and which were smaller and frankly very bad as warships. There's a long and sad history of how those ships came to be, but I won't bore you with it here. Bottom line: they were not exactly the sort of combatants you'd expect a member of the Fiora Ring (let alone John himself) to send into a fight.

"*Akagi* and *Kaga* left yesterday. Still can't believe you're sending those buckets of shit out though, Johnny boy."

Ah yes, remember how Daragh doesn't share my disdain for swearing?

John shrugged and smiled, "You don't believe most things."

Now, as I always say, a movie would have John re-explain to Daragh things Daragh already knew about the deployment, for the benefit of the viewers. I'll do that here — and quickly: the carriers and their squadrons of old F-174 Sunbursts and F-184 Starbursts were going to be used for recon *only*.

In other words, the plan was to send them towards Mercury, and have them launch their fighters for long patrols, covering as much space as possible. That sort of non-combat recon, the carriers could do… albeit badly.

The unstated reason carriers were being deployed in that role (as opposed to frigates or battleships) was simple: if the carriers got caught in some sort of trap and were destroyed, it would be no great loss. That's an incredibly cold thing to say — there were brave crews on those ships — but it's true. The carriers served no critical purpose in this war; losing them would not hurt us. It might even help us, if they prematurely sprung a Martian trap.

"That's good. I'll want them doing sweeps as soon as they get out there," John continued, returning us to the narrative.

"I suppose it is good, so it is. But damned if I'd want to be flying off one of those thin-skinned bastards in the middle of a proper war," Daragh put in one more shot before he finished on the subject. The *Akagi*-class ships were roughly of his own vintage — an age when starfighters were still effective as fleet combatants — but even in those days, pilots like our mad Irishman preferred flying off maneuverable, fast frigates, not the carriers.

Sorry, I'm getting so close to a rant here I need to side-step.

"Talked to Greg this morning. He says Lia Hawke and Commodore Mikaelsen have confirmed that they can put together a Hawke Force for the assault fleet. Wes Pellew's obviously on board with the Independent Squadron, and Ken's got the Jupiter Force ready to go. Greg himself will have his Belt Assault Unit with the battleships and escorts," John moved the discussion along.

Daragh frowned, "Samuels can't pull the Belt Squadron out?"

"Not if we still want our convoys to keep coming through safely," John shook his head. "I've ordered Xi Xelin to use her Coalition Force to reinforce Marshal on the convoy routes. I think we'll have enough firepower on the attack, when you add in the Bonnies and the Venus Squadron."

That last comment was made with a small smile — John had ordered the combined Defense Command and Coalition (of Unaligned Asteroids) warships, a force of ships not unlike the Hawke Force, to stay in the Belt to serve as backup for Marshal's Belt Squadron and the convoy escorting jobs. He'd done this, frankly, because we already had more than enough ships to win the war on the assault, and he could thus afford to keep a cushion of ships on the defensive side.

Hence the smile: we were in good shape.

This meeting obviously went on, but I don't know how much more exposition you (or, honestly, I) can handle just now. You're caught up on the important stuff, so let's skip a few hours ahead, and back to Belt Two.

Chapter Seven

Bouncing Back

Lia Hawke is a hell of a Lady. I suppose that's a really obvious first line for a chapter — you're sitting there thinking 'well of course she is!' — but I think it deserves repeating.

About four or five hours after Karen and I had slipped out of the briefing room to give Charlie and Lia some privacy, there was a knock on my cabin hatch. Karen and I had just settled in for our nightly dinner, and were somewhat surprised by the interruption, but after I dislodged my tray from my lap and got to the door, it made sense.

Lia stepped in quietly, wearing the smile that Karen and I had both seen before — the never-fails, mischievous smile that Lia can use to such great effect when she needs to.

"Just wanted to say hi. I think Wes is boosting us back to the Protectorate in the morning, and I've got somewhere to be tonight, so I wanted to stop and say goodbye."

Karen pushed her tray to the side of my bed and hopped up to her feet, "So... what's the plan? You and Charlie figure something out?"

Lia bit her bottom lip and nodded, "My dad's staying on life support until we're finished with the Martians... and then... well... then I'll..."

She stopped herself because her voice began to quiver. Her smile didn't flinch, but her eyes did, so she stopped. She didn't *need* to keep a brave front up with us, but if she could keep her composure here, she knew she could keep it anywhere.

"Anything we can do to help in any way at all, let us know," I said that in the somber but hollow way you make that sort of offer. I'm sure you know what I mean — someone you care about is in pain, and you know there's not much you can do to help... but you offer anyway.

Lia nodded with a couple of quick jerks of her head, "Yeah. Thank you..."

She bit her bottom lip for another second, and we could see she was focused on remaining composed, "Listen, I'll see you both when we rally the big battle force of doom for the assault. I'm going to take the Hawke Force out with Mik."

That was a surprise.

Lia was a great commander-in-chief, but she had never really been an operations commander. We hadn't really expected her to join the assault.

I think my expression immediately betrayed that surprise, and even Karen's question seemed to slip through to her face, so Lia countered, "Come on, you two don't get to have all the fun."

That wasn't a bad answer. I prepared to backpedal and accede the point, but Lia didn't stop.

"And I need the experience. It'll give my people more confidence if they know I have combat experience like dad does. It'll make things easier in the long run."

I actually didn't know how to respond to that. Lia was leaving the side of her father's deathbed because she had to serve the Protectorate in a war, and from a political standpoint, reassure the citizens of Hawke that she had some fighting qualities.

Politics.

Again, I don't know if you think Lia was doing the right or wrong thing, but really, I don't think you can accuse her of running from responsibility with this call. Running from responsibility would be going home and pretending that everything was alright, not joining an assault fleet.

That's my opinion, anyway. Believe what you like, but as I said earlier, don't be too vocal if you have nasty things to say.

Anyway, as I was rather incompetently failing to say something reassuring, Karen intervened in the conversation with the right response: she gave Lia a big hug. Hard to believe these two had only known each other since the start of the war... they were like sisters already.

"We'll see you out there. Take care of yourself and stay insane," Karen almost whispered.

Lia squeezed back, closing her eyes. She was clearly close to losing her composure again, but she held fast. Karen pulled away, then I swept in to reinforce the hug.

I didn't say anything — I was afraid if I said something that (by fluke) managed to be appropriate for the situation, she might really have lost it, and I didn't want to see that. You know how awkward I get in emotional situations, and selfish as it was, I didn't want to have to see Lia in such pain again.

Lia pulled away and left Karen and I to finish dinner. She spent the night with Charlie, and then headed out in the morning.

Speaking of the morning, I'm going to skip there now, in the same chapter, to finish off this little story line. We have Pions and Canaries to deal with shortly, but for now Wes was taking *Nova Scotia* back to Hawke One, and Karen and I were rather curious about how things had gone with Andrea.

After an early breakfast, Karen and I had hurried down the chute from *Wolf* to Belt Two base, then up the chute into *Nova Scotia* — the first visit for both of us to that ship. As one would expect of a Pellew command, the frigate was in fine condition, everything gleaming and the crew happy and efficient. We got some surprised looks as we passed through the corridors, a few of the crew Wes had pulled from *Cheetah* in *The Gallant Few* acknowledging us with waves, some of the newer spacers actually saluting us.

Eventually, we got to Wes' cabin, where we knocked. Wes opened the door almost instantly — he'd been on his way to the bridge to do pre-departure preparations — and then immediately stepped back and waved us in. Obviously we didn't have to ask about the meeting... as Wes told me later, it was the only thing on his mind that morning. Hell, it was one of the reasons he was going to the bridge so early — he needed to take his mind off it.

As the hatch closed behind Karen and me, he shook his head, "She's in bad, bad shape. She's handling it as well as any human could, but what she's been through is so evil."

Karen and I traded glances. We'd both been down on Egesta during the second week, but as any good history text on the first crisis will tell you, the first week was the worst.

Well, the worst of the two weeks for which Defense Command was present. According to witnesses, it had been even more horrific before Andrea and Mark arrived there... but I won't get into talk of comparative evilness.

"I think she's on the right road to come back from it," Wes continued quietly, grimly. "It's a very long road, though, and I don't think she'll ever come all the way back."

I frowned, "But part of the way?"

Wes sighed, "It's like she's tied to a chair and forced to watch it over and over... I don't know if that'll ever stop."

Andrea says she couldn't have put it any better herself.

"But she's learning how to deal with it. She knows to comm me if she needs to talk more, which I hope she does. She's an incredible woman; she's fighting this, but she needs to keep talking."

Karen and I both started nodding slowly, and then we both stopped, neither of us actually wanting to ask the question we both had in mind.

Wes, thank God, was one of us. He knew what we were wondering, and he answered that, "She's fine to stay on her bridge. I don't think she's going to let her control slip again."

That drew relieved sighs from Karen and me... obviously, we knew Andrea had had a handle on her problems since she'd returned to duty after the *Idaho* situation, but we'd never been sure that, if the going got tough again, she'd be able to keep it together.

And while Wes was by no means a mental-health professional, and he wasn't clairvoyant, we trusted his read of people.

Andrea would be able to continue in her role as Captain of *Wolf* without endangering her crew or herself.

We chatted with Wes for a couple of more minutes, said our goodbyes and our 'See you at Venus!' sendoffs. We did *not* tell him about Ian Hawke. That was for Lia to do, whenever she was ready. One of my editors thinks it's strange we didn't let him in on the story immediately... but then, this book is probably the first Lia's ever heard of what happened to Sara. I'd call that even.

Nova Scotia pulled out of dock later that morning, about six hours before Marshal Samuels received an unexpected and grim message.

Yeah, you know what the message was.

CHAPTER EIGHT

ENTER THE HORROR MOVIE

When Marshal called me to Belt Two C&C later that day, I had no idea why. I suspected it might have something to do with the fate of *North Carolina*, but I wasn't expecting what I got.

Even if you haven't seen any of the seven movies about this situation, though, I expect you know what I'm on about.

As I arrived in the C&C, Marshal turned from one of the big screens and waved, "Ken... you probably aren't going to like this."

"Well, that's a great way to start any meeting," I smiled wryly, figuring I might as well start things with a sense of humor.

Marshal nodded, "Sorry. Mister Pinh, run the message please."

I was about to make some smart remark when the screen lit up, and I stopped talking. I don't know how to describe the feeling I got right then... maybe I could compare it to the feeling you get when, as a student, you wake up one morning and realize you forgot there was a big exam that day. Yeah, that's close, at least.

Holly was on the screen.

Holly is a fixture of every Pion/Canary movie, usually played by very beautiful actresses, and more often portrayed as a bare-breasted Amazon who's lusty, fierce, and yet submissive to the hero of the movie once he proves his manhood.

Well, fierce is sort of right. And she certainly has been bare-breasted (though despite what the movies suggest, Pion and Canary women don't just go around like that all the time). But lusty or submissive... or beautiful? No no no.

"Message here for Bear. We got people of yours here, ship called *Nortcarol*. Shot down over our rock, all the survivors here. But we only got the half of them. Pions got the rest. Of course pleasure be ours to give you ones we got. Even women. But Pions want to trade for theirs. Say they got twenty, they want even trade women for the six men, they want keep the fourteen women, or trade for other women, even trade. They respects the uniform for now til response, though. You need come down, Bear. Bring Charl too, kay? See soonest."

I could rant here about the Pion and Canary dialect of English — how it's not nearly as ridiculous or unsophisticated as many movies suggest — but I won't bother. Suffice it to say, the Pions and Canaries can speak English well enough. Yes, their grammar and syntax is odd, but I think it's basically understandable.

To summarize what dear Holly was saying, though: *North Carolina* had been destroyed over the Pion rock, and lifeboats had gone down on both sides of the asteroid. Crew who went through the top locks would be in the hands of the Pions; those who (luckily?) went through the bottom locks were in the hands of the Canaries, the closest thing to friendly people on that rock.

I'll explain the overtones about women-trading and the rest of it in a while. It's something that's very often twisted and misunderstood by neo-suffragists and macro-chauvinists alike... people who apply our society's standards to a culture — yes, *culture* — that developed with a set of challenges we can't even imagine.

For now, Marshal looked at me, "I think you need to get to Pion rock, fast."

I nodded without saying anything.

The Bear was going back to Pion rock.

We wasted no time boosting. We didn't even take time to call the two dozen people who were on leave back to the ship. Why the rush? Well take a guess. We had people, Defense Command officers and spacers who we'd brought back from Jupiter with us, down in one of the most hellish places in the solar system.

We'd plan on the fly — it was a five-day run from Belt Two to Pion rock, and there was no time to waste.

My editors are suggesting that I be more explicit. I have to admit, in describing the situation so far, I'm assuming you've already heard the story of *North Carolina's* crew on the Pion rock, but if you're reading this decades from 2233, the story might have (finally) passed out of circulation. I won't try to fill it in all at once, but I will explain more of it as we go.

Anyway, when *Wolf* shipped out, *Cheetah* and *Friendly* came with us. Nancy Whitehorse kept *Trusty* at Belt Two, because over half her crew was off-ship, and because we felt uncomfortable taking the whole Jupiter Force (such as it was) out with us.

Why did we need escort at all? Aside from *Wolf* being a flagship traveling in wartime, Pion rock was in fact very close to the Martian asteroid colonies. That was one of the reasons it was a great place for collecting intel on pirate movement — it was a part of space where DC ships didn't venture too often.

In the middle of a war, it would have been unwise for us to head that way without enough firepower to guarantee our safety.

It was quite a surprise for all of our crews, though, to be going cruising on such short notice. Rumors started spreading that we had to head off a Martian attack force, or an attack on a Belt colony, so we decided to be open about what was going on: we sent the recording of the comm signal from Holly to every department.

I know, we probably shouldn't have been so casual about spreading the word... but then, at the same time, we knew our crews weren't going to get scared off by the Pions and the Canaries. Everyone on the ship knew *North Carolina* had been a survivor of the Jupiter Squadron. Many had been aboard that frigate at Io, helping repair it, and meeting the brave crew. The thought of those people being at the mercy of the Pions (and to a lesser extent, of the Canaries) was enough to get them fired up.

We had a lot of people approaching Charlie and Omar Cunningham (new Lieutenant of SF) asking to be part of any landing forces. Those were gallant sentiments, but the answers were universally *no*.

Only the best-trained people would be going down into that mess of tunnels.

Well, the best-trained people and *me*. Because I was the Bear.

And to get us away from exposition for a minute, let me address that.

Shelby McLaws had the watch that first evening of the cruise, and Karen, Jim Hannigan and I were watching the message from Holly on screen three. Jim had been Sensors and Communications Officer on *Friendly* when we'd been to the Pion rock before. Karen had never been, but she'd heard my detailed stories, and thus knew as much as most of the people who'd stayed aboard *Friendly* on the last mission.

Shelby, though, knew only what she'd seen in the movies.

Let me be clear: there is no shame in knowing 'only' what comes from the movies. The problems start when you assume that the movies are perfectly accurate, and Shelby wasn't doing this.

"Sir, if you don't mind my asking, the lady there is requesting a 'Bear'. That's you, sir?"

The question caught me off-guard, largely because I was spending far too much mental energy simply dreading the job we were going to have to do. After taking a few seconds to process Shelby's question, I nodded.

"Yes… they like to take our names and make them into something a little… edgier, I guess. Bear is what they got from Barron."

Shelby gave an 'aha' and went back to her watch duties.

"Do they even know what a bear is?" Karen asked quietly as Shelby left.

I shrugged, "Big, loud, dangerous, perhaps cuddly…"

Karen managed a small smile, "They think *you're* a bear? A humanoid bear who speaks English and happens to be an Admiral?"

I chuckled. She was right, it had an air of the ridiculous — imagine a bear commanding a warship, or a fleet. Or a lion commanding the same. Or a wolf! How silly.

Ahem.

Anyway, we were on our way to the Pion rock, with virtually no preparation, and with a very urgent mission to help our comrades who'd been a hell of a lot less fortunate than we had.

CHAPTER NINE
PIONS AND CANARIES

I have a lot of myth-correcting to do in this book, and I fear that it's going to turn into quite the social science lesson... but it's necessary. You'd be surprised (or maybe you wouldn't be) by the number of myths and half-truths about the Pions and the Canaries that were held as fact, even by our excellent crews. It's a symptom of the media madness over those two tribes... very rarely does anybody peer deeply into the reasoning behind what they do. When all you ever see is movies about the Pions and the Canaries in which they're the two-dimensional villains, it's easy to stop peering deeper.

It's quite possible that you, dear reader, are in the same boat. There's no shame in this at all — before I went to Pion rock the first time, I was the very same way. The reality is that it's not a fun subject of study... one of my editors finds it downright disturbing, and understandably so.

That all being said, we still have to go through it now, or the rest of this book isn't going to make a great deal of sense.

So we needed to inform *Wolf's* crew about the realities of dealing with the Pions and the Canaries. We had to make these horror-movie villains into a real society, so that our people would be ready to deal with any contingency that occurred.

Well, as ready as they could ever be.

As such, we did one day of intense briefings, with three sessions (all the same information, but offered at different times of day so we could reach the entire crew). Running these sessions were Charlie, Jim Hannigan, Andrew Jenson, Alicia Morgan, and me — officers who'd been with *Friendly* back in the day.

On *Friendly*, Matt Baxter was telling his crew about that old mission, and on *Cheetah*, Erica Martin (our former Helm and Navigation Officer, and now Mark Gunney's XO) was doing the same.

Basically, for this chapter, my plan is to splice together parts of the briefings on *Wolf*... if this was a vid, it'd probably come out as a montage sequence, with audio. But it's critical information, and it'll ensure you never again watch one of these Pion/Canary horror movies the same way.

"Everyone knows Pions and Canaries are coming for your women," I said blithely at one of the sessions, and the crew listened with rapt attention. "Well, that's true. They want women, as many as they can get, and you better believe they're going to rape them."

That, when I re-state it here, sounds far too casual. Sorry. At the time it was taken in the correct, grim, mood.

"What the movies never bother to explain is *why*," I went on. "It's not Egesta. They're not doing it for pleasure, or for torture. This is a societal imperative."

I got a lot of frowns with that introduction, and I expect you're also wondering what the hell I mean. How can a society promote rape? Egesta's Guild aside, not easily.

Recall that, when XV-001 was first isolated, perhaps a third of the population of the colony was female. That being the case, we think the women were quickly relegated to a secondary, breeding role, to keep the population numbers up.

Alright, cue the macro-chauvinists high-fiving each other and barking 'hell yeah, women in their place!'

However — and here it gets complicated — women were so important in the resulting society that it became a matriarchal one. Women who bore children were of a higher social status than any men.

Now, cue the neo-suffragists high-fiving each other and yelling, 'men are pigs!'

So the very strange result was a matriarchal society that promoted the capture and rape of as many women as possible.

Cue the macro-chauvinists and the neo-suffragists starting to puff up and cheer, then stopping in confusion and looking at each other without any idea of what to do.

Yes, I know, it's confusing as all hell. Let me see if I can make it even more confusing.

The specifics of how society developed on the Pion rock are, of course, a mystery to us. As we knew it then, the Canaries and the Pions both held women as a prized commodity, and child-bearing became their first objective.

Over time, this importance led women to take overall command of the society — ultimately, they would become the leaders and decision makers, but only if they were deemed 'strong'.

What you get, then, is a social order determined by number of children birthed. Women who are 'barren' (can't have children) are at the bottom of this order. If they fail within five years of the start of puberty to become pregnant, they're declared barren, and they are shunned. All they are allowed to do is 'train' the young men of the society in the mechanics of impregnation.

That's me trying to politely say that they're treated as objects, and die miserable deaths after being sexually abused for most of their lives.

Men who have not fathered children within five years of puberty are the next step up. They can at least fight, so they're used for the riskier missions. The barren men, as they're called, always have something to prove, and usually die young while proving it.

The men who do father children are the next rung up. They're the proper warriors, and the only ones who can ever come to lead the warrior class (in other words, be generals).

Women who become pregnant, but miscarry or have the baby die, are roughly on par with these men. They have the same rights as fathers, and yes, they can be warriors. Women with one surviving child are of the same class, but are more revered — like the most accomplished warriors.

Women with two children are a special class of notables. They form a council that runs the domestic side of the society… they're sort of like Mayors.

The women — the very few women — with three surviving children become the leaders for the entire society. They form a council of sorts that deals with the opposing tribe, leads wars, and all that sort of stuff.

The eldest of these three-child women (the 'triples', as they are known) becomes the overall leader of the society.

For the Canaries, that meant Holly, who was the ripe old age of twenty-nine.

There are usually many questions about this social order. First of all, is it really that hard to have three kids? People do that all the time!

Well, it's not so easy living in the tunnels of Pion rock. It'd be incorrect to suggest the Pions and the Canaries didn't have some means of looking after children, but they certainly didn't have modern medical science. Nothing even close, actually. The infant mortality rate was over thirty-five percent.

Worse than that, though, the mothers had something like a one in five chance of dying while pregnant. Without proper nutrition and the sorts of relaxed lifestyles we lead, the wear and tear on their bodies made bearing children a very dangerous job for them.

That brings me to a quick sidelight: the Canaries and Pions are often portrayed as sexy savages. They're not. Sorry, this is a shallow thing to say, but they're uniformly ugly. We like at least one bath or shower a day, we brush our teeth regularly, we care about our looks…

They live in dark tunnels, eating food out of hydroponic gardens (that, to the credit of their original designers, are still regrowing every cycle on schedule) and have none of the health habits we do. To them, healthy means able to bear children, able to fight, or both. They do not look like super models in rags. They are, frankly, disgusting.

Anyway. The second question that often gets asked is about the capture and rape of women from the outside. The stories about the Pions and the Canaries taking civilian women and raping them are true. As far as we know, though, no Defense Command women had been adopted — any who'd been captured had resisted too strongly, and were ultimately killed for their trouble.

The thing is — and don't mistake this for me trying to defend rape, no way — the story doesn't stop at the rape. What these two 'tribes' are doing is called (to them)'adoption'. Basically, the Pions and the Canaries need every woman they can get their hands on, because more women means more babies, and more babies means a larger population. A larger population puts you in a better position to defeat your enemy — the other tribe — so… well… it's like an arms race, but of mothers and babies instead of ships or troops.

So any woman they can find, they take, and they do their damndest to make her a mother.

And all the class status points I just talked about apply to her. If she becomes a mother, she becomes equal to all the men, and so on.

Women from outside the Pion rock are actually much prized by both Pions and Canaries, not because (as one commentator suggested) they're prettier. No, the women coming in with missionary or anthropology teams are coveted because they were raised in the Empire, and are *healthy*. It makes them more likely to bear more children.

So that's what's behind the women trading and it makes my skin crawl to explain it. I simply refuse to imagine what it must be like for those women who are subject to 'adoption'… well, as soon as I say that, I start to imagine.

I mean, just think about it. You're part of a team of anthropologists, determined to prove that the Pions and the Canaries are just another culture of humanity, and you end up watching every man in your party horribly killed as they scream and plead for mercy. You tell the tribes that you want to help them, want to study them, to tell their story…

instead, the men are killed horribly, and the women are assigned 'studs' and are raped repeatedly until they become pregnant.

Then, if the child comes to term, those women are expected to *join* the society.

Not really as sexy as the movies let on, eh?

Of course, Holly herself is a perfect example of this. She was ten or eleven and on her father's freighter when it had a reactor failure. She and the rest of the crew spent two weeks in a lifeboat and ended up at the Pion rock, where all the men on the crew were murdered, and Holly was adopted.

Now, almost two decades later, she was one of their longest-lived Canary leaders in memory.

At twenty-nine.

Oh, I should clarify that too: the Pions and the Canaries didn't live long.

I don't expect you need me to explain why. Between their hard lives and their constant wars for food and women, you can probably guess.

There's one more thing to explain before I can leave this topic. Look back at the message: Holly says the Pions were 'respecting the uniform'. What does that mean?

Well, Defense Command personnel were, after our last visit at least, not considered to be like the other visitors who came occasionally to Pion rock. Even though it failed, the Special Branch assault of 2195 had earned Defense Command respect — we died just like the civilians, but we took plenty of tribe fighters with us.

In a society where births are few and so obviously coveted, the power to kill gets respect.

Last visit, despite having no children of our own, Charlie and I thus were given respect. They actually thought it funny that my last name was 'Barron', which sounds, obviously, like 'barren', and is their most reviled word. We earned their respect because when we landed, and some of their barren men (trying to prove their manhood) jumped us, Charlie and his half-squad of Branchers killed them. All of them.

I didn't actually do much, but as I was the designated leader, I also got respect.

After that, part of the deal we struck with both Pions and Canaries (in return for the reactor repair) was that 'the uniform' would always be respected. Women taken in a Defense Command uniform would not be raped, men would not be killed. It was a promise we extracted from the tribes, though we'd never been certain it would be honored.

Now it seemed that it was being honored… though the Pions weren't going to be patient indefinitely. If they didn't get their trade, they were going to break their word. They respected our killing ability, but they weren't terrified of us. Hence the situation we were in: we had time to get *North Carolina's* people out of there… but there was only so much time before the needs of the tribes started to outweigh any threat we could deliver.

So, that was the situation, more or less….

And I just realized I've been prattling on in straight exposition this whole time. I was supposed to deliver all this as dialogue from the briefing sessions we had on the third day of our cruise.

Uh. Sorry.

Let's… uh… pretend those pages and pages of block paragraphs were in quotation marks, with lame descriptors of me walking and talking mixed in.

CHAPTER TEN

BOOM TALK

The day before we got to Pion rock, Charlie was in the Special Branch weapons room with Rufus Chang, going through some boxes of special toys. When I say 'special toys', of course I'm talking about weapons, and in this particular case, explosives. The room Charlie was standing in now was full of them.

Rufus likes explosives. I think that much might have become quite apparent when he used them on *Idaho* to deal with the booby traps in the engine room and with the 'alien'.

Now don't get me wrong, Charlie likes explosives too. He could, I promise you, put a hole in a tank with a wine bottle and some C6. Hell, he could do it with a wine bottle and C4, he's that good.

But Rufus' relationship with explosives is a little more... personal. Charlie knows how to use them very, very well. Rufus, well, might be a little obsessive. I don't consider that a bad thing. In fact, at this moment, it was very useful.

Before I continue with the scene, I'll just explain that Rufus was still aboard *Wolf* because his previous ship, *Lion*, was in dock for a year's worth of repairs, and we were definitely seeing some utility to having two Special Branch teams aboard, particularly with the Mercury assault ahead of us.

And this Pion mission too. We were very lucky to have Rufus along for this.

"Sweet merciful crap, Rufus, you have a lot of explosives with you," Charlie had gone slightly wide-eyed and shook his head at the copious quantity of boom devices in the room. Most of them had been stored separately from the rest of the Special Branch gear in this prep room (which the two squads were sharing). Rufus had kept it stashed in his cabin, in a special blast-proof locker that he'd built himself, when he'd been stuck on Luna Six.

"The shortest distance between two points usually involves blowing a hole in something," Rufus said with the cool matter-of-factness you usually see from the slightly crazy arms specialists in the movies.

Charlie tried to come up with a non-cliché response, and I approve of the result: "You must be great to have on a road trip."

Rufus chuckled, then started picking up different devices and checking that they weren't about to explode... or maybe he was just admiring them. Charlie started to do the same, looking at various detonators and pre-packed charges, figuring out just how he'd use them.

"It's close quarters down there... all tight corridors, relatively dark, a lot of rooms where they could hide and ambush us... a real mess. Last time I was there I was strongly in favor of *not* getting into a fight, because it'd hurt."

Charlie was obviously trying to reinforce for Rufus the sort of carnage that could ensue if things got violent. Remember back to *The Sinope Affair*, how Charlie faked overloading the Io dome reactors in order to get the Commandos out of the underground complex, because he didn't want to take his people down there?

The scenario on Pion rock would be like that, except worse, because here we weren't facing Commandos, we were up against Pions and Canaries. I don't know if Charlie would actually agree when I say this, but to me Pions are scarier than Commandos. Commandos are special ops infantry — they are, when it comes down to it, soldiers. Pions and Canaries aren't. They live in dark corridors, they move more like apes than people, and they fight with savage implements of death.

And they're entirely unpredictable in combat.

Remember how Charlie was able to guess (quite accurately, in fact) where the Commandos would set their traps, and how they'd fight? We didn't have that sort of read on the Pions — their social and cultural makeup was so different than our own...

Have you ever read about the clash between the European troops and the North American first nations in the years before 1815? The clash of completely different fighting systems? In hindsight we can sit and point and laugh at those who took a long time to adapt to the enemy's fighting system.

But it's damned scary being in that fight without hindsight to tell you what not to do.

And to answer the questions of those who just think Pions are savages with clubs, who should fall before our civilized mags, you're so wrong. Mags are great. They let you shoot at long range.

However, within about twenty feet, the ranged weapon is no more likely to be lethal than is a club. Studies have proven this. Basically, the idea is that it takes a gun-wielder as long to turn and engage an attacker as it would for the attacker to cover twenty feet and to stab/beat/bash/slash the gunner. Special Branchers are better than that average... but if they're outnumbered in a corridor that's dimly lit and only six feet wide, a guy with an improvised axe could jump out of an air shaft and behead Charlie before someone could turn to shoot him.

Remember, the Pions train with their weapons as much as... probably *more* than Charlie trains with his. And that's a *lot*.

So when you see in the movies that the Pions can get the drop on SF and even Special Branch, it's not all just the magic of movie horror. It's quite possible, and Charlie was determined to make sure it didn't happen.

That in mind, he stopped rifling through the cases of explosives with an "Oooh!"

"What you got there?" Rufus frowned and leaned over the table slightly as Charlie pulled his hand out of one of the boxes.

"Concussion grenade. Have many?"

Rufus frowned thoughtfully, then sidestepped and shifted a couple of boxes out of the way to reach the crate underneath, "Here we go. Liberated these from the armory on Luna Six... have about fifty."

Charlie grinned, "You, sir, are very prepared."

"Better than magbangs?" Rufus asked, handing Charlie the crate, and our intrepid Major Peters nodded.

"I don't think a magbang flash is going to spread far enough to incapacitate attackers hidden in ducts and things."

Rufus grinned, understanding immediately.

I, of course, had no sweet clue how old concussion grenades were going to be any different than nice, modern, civilized magbangs, so Charlie enlightened me. Concussion grenades are old technology — we stopped really using them in the mid 2220s because the magbang came along, and was more civilized.

But in a situation like this, a concussion grenade was perfect. When a grenade detonates, the force of the explosion sends out a shockwave of atmosphere. That shockwave penetrates any crack or crevice that's around — in other words, any hiding place you could think of — and it's enough to kill or stun.

Seriously, the invisible pressure wave caused by a grenade will at the very least make your ears pop and your nose run. If you're too close, I believe Charlie said it'll make your brain melt.

Compare that effect to a magbang, which can stun or kill, but only uses an energy pulse to do the job. The concussion wave moves particles in the atmosphere, and thus is more pervasive. The magbang's like a light source — if you can find shelter from the flash (like a good hiding spot with only a couple of cracks to peep through) you'll probably only be tingly after it hits.

So that's why Charlie was so happy to see concussion grenades.

Alright then.

Sorry, after a chapter with a lesson on society, I just switched to a lesson on weaponry. I promise, the setup is pretty much finished — we can get back to the story soon.

Anyway, Rufus and Charlie continued to talk about blowing things up, and how they'd handle the tight spaces on the Pion rock. I'll leave out the rest of that in the interests of getting to some dialogue. New chapter time...

CHAPTER ELEVEN

ALMOST THERE

I stopped by the Special Branch briefing room (they have one on *Wolf*, and I don't think I've ever mentioned it) later that evening, and caught the end of Charlie's talk to his squad. Rufus had done his own squad briefing the hour before, because the room wasn't big enough to comfortably accommodate two complete teams.

You know most of these officers by now: you have people like Captains Carly Henderson and Raza Weiss, and Lieutenants like Ben Belete and Terry Schroeder... obviously there were seven more.

I slipped into the back for the last few words of Charlie's briefing to these elite Branchers, and I'm sure they all noticed I was there (even though I was very quiet). I mean, they're Special Branchers.

Anyway, the point of this chapter isn't the briefing — you've already soldiered through enough of those so far — it was to get a word in with Charlie. We really hadn't had time over the past several days to talk about anything on the personal side... namely, to talk about Lia. It's amazing how things like that can get away from you when you're preparing to literally enter a horror movie. Again.

Just occurred to me that this was a pretty miserable follow-up to *The Dark Cruise*. For the second straight mission (albeit months later) we were sending Charlie's team into a very messy place, right out of a summer blockbuster of carnage.

Charming.

As the briefing wrapped up and the room cleared, Charlie hung back and shrugged at me, "Ready as we can be. Carly's been telling the uninitiated about the last time we were here, and the fight with the barren men."

Carly and another of the team members had been with us back on *Friendly* when we'd been to Pion rock, so there was more experience to be shared. That was good — the more the Branchers knew, the better they could prepare.

"I figure we'll make do. I just realized we haven't talked about... well, the Lia thing."

Charlie's 'we'll get it done' expression creased into a slight frown, "Lia *thing?*"

I shrugged, "Sorry, pedestrian way to put it. But how's she doing..."

Something had been percolating in the back of my mind since Lia had headed back to Hawke, but I wasn't just going to come out and say it.

Charlie, of course, is much more adept at reading people than I am, so he figured out what I was getting at, "Am I leaving?"

I snapped my fingers and pointed at him, "That's exactly what I'm asking!"

Frown deepening, Charlie looked at my finger, "You just snapped your fingers and pointed at me."

"What, too much?"

He shrugged, "Just strange."

"Oh, sorry," I lowered my hand.

Charlie didn't waste any more time, "I told her... I told her she didn't have to deal with this on her own. If she needs me, I'll be there."

Of course he did, because Charlie is a first-class fellow. Top of the line, don't find people of better character anywhere.

"What do you really think?" I asked flatly, and he looked away and winced slightly.

"I don't want to leave in the middle of a war. You and the team... I don't want to bail out before this is done. But I will if I have to. I hope you'd understand."

"Of course I'd understand," I probably should have smiled when I said that, but I didn't feel like smiling at the prospect of Charlie leaving, or at Lia's situation. I tried to follow up my statement with a qualification — that I knew where he was coming from, or that Lia obviously deserved his help... something like that. I didn't manage to figure out what to say, though, so I remained silent.

It was strange to think of Charlie leaving. He and I had known each other for years, going back to the days when I was flying planes off *Alberta*, and he was one of the junior officers in ship's Special Branch squad. He'd come over to *Friendly* with me, and then we'd been partners in crime for years and years and years.

This was an unusual conversation (or non-conversation, based on the amount of awkward silence) to be having with him, especially when we were heading for Pion rock.

"But she doesn't want you now?"

That reads differently than it sounded when I asked it, and Charlie (understanding what I was trying to say) shook his head, "Not the right time. She doesn't want to pull me away from my people in the middle of this fight, and she says she can handle things on her own."

I did smile (selfishly, I think) at those words. Lia understood Charlie, and while she knew he'd do anything for her, she didn't demand that he did. I call that a functional relationship.

And, of course, Lia could handle things on her own — she always did. Remember, she and Charlie tended to go years without seeing each other, and though I still have no idea how they survived that, they did. It's no surprise, at least to me then, that she didn't need Charlie to immediately ride his white charger right up to her side.

But the writing, it seemed, was on the wall. They'd be together at some point — some point *soon* — and when that happened... well. No more Major Peters on DCNS *Wolf*.

That was a change I didn't want to think about, so true to form, I changed the subject, right back to the cheerful question of the Pions.

"So, we ready for a scrap? Because I think there'll be a scrap."

Charlie accepted the change of subject and shrugged, "As ready as we can be. Like I said last time, anyone who has to fight those guys in that place is asking to die. I'm just planning to ask very quietly."

"You're planning to use explosives quietly?" I frowned at the metaphor, and Charlie paused.

"Well then, I'm just going to blow up as many of them as I can so I don't die. That work better?"

I shrugged, "Yes. Makes much more sense."

We paused for a minute, for no particular reason, and then I continued, "I'm figuring that Holly will return her *North Carolinas* without any trouble, but we may have to go in and rescue the twenty the Pions have."

It's funny, in a strange way, that Charlie and I hadn't talked explicitly about this yet. Goes to show how hung up I'd gotten on the dangers of Pion and Canary society and culture… as opposed to the more practical concerns of how to accomplish our objectives. We could have taken five minutes any time during the cruise out here to do it… but we were too caught up in the particulars of the environment. Ah well, we were doing it now anyway.

Charlie agreed with the assessment, "Seems likely. It'll be a mess if we do… there's no way we can even be sure where the prisoners will be. I'm hoping we can get some of Holly's people to help."

"Yeah great. Join in a Canary war, just what we need…"

Oh ha, there's the title of the book.

Charlie and I kept talking for a while. We'd deal more with the Lia issue (first a 'thing', now an 'issue') later.

Chapter Twelve

Innocent Looking Rocks

When you arrive at Pion rock, you almost expect to find a graveyard or something… perhaps a giant, creepy monument that says 'go no further' or 'beware, death awaits you'. You know, something needlessly melodramatic but at the same time unmistakably eerie.

But there are no such monuments. Even the warning buoys we try to put in orbit of the asteroid never seem to last more than a few months — the gravity in orbit around the rock is not very good, and they get lost in space along the way.

No, what you find when you arrive at Pion rock is just another rock. There are a couple of crude, meteor-impacted structures left standing on the surface, out-buildings and docking structures that date all the way back to the 2070s, but aside from that, you have only a collection of airlock columns sticking out of various craters.

"It's not as menacing as I expected," Karen observed with a frown as she stood next to me on the bridge.

"A letdown, isn't it?" I asked, trying to keep the mood as light as possible.

She smiled smoothly and glanced at me, "I'll just keep deluding myself that this won't be too bad."

With a grin, I nodded back, "You do that. I'll douse you with the cold water when the carnage starts."

It was, I have to say, particularly grim humor — a sort of humor we were exceedingly good at, especially at times like these.

"We're now in orbit over the rock," Shelby McLaws made that announcement a few minutes later, and as Andrea stood next to the Helm and Navigation consoles, she nodded directly at our southern belle Lieutenant.

"Thank you, Shelby. Felicia, let's see what we can see."

Felicia Khalid had stayed on as *Wolf's* Sensors and Communications Officer. Her appointment during the mission to Jupiter had been temporary (remember, she got the job when Kate Levec was shot) but after her solid service throughout that entire mission, we'd elected to make it permanent. She'd definitely earned the job, and now she was really settling in.

As Andrea requested the scans, Felicia patted the back of the appropriate technician, and the main screen ahead was abruptly filled with data.

"We really should paint a big red pentagram on the surface, or something," Jim Hannigan observed dryly from behind his ops consoles. "Looks so harmless."

I glanced back at Jim, a grin maintaining a tenuous grip on my mouth, "A *pentagram*, Jim? Do you think that might be a tad overdramatic?"

He locked eyes with me for a second, then looked thoughtfully towards the ceiling, "Hmm. *No.*"

I chuckled and looked back at the screen. Right he was… there was nothing to warn travelers that this rock was dangerous… and that fact had contributed to the predicament the crew of *North Carolina* now faced. If their sensors and navigation had been down, as they almost certainly were, then this rock might have looked as innocent as any other.

But to the Martians, with their sensors active, it was anything but. I didn't know it as I stood on the bridge then, but I did find out much later: the Martians knew exactly where they'd chased *North Carolina*, and they'd done it for kicks.

Bastards.

Anyway, enough judging by appearances. Time to get on with the job.

"So, we going to sit around and rate this rock by looks, or are we going in?" Mark Gunney, I should have mentioned, was up on Battlelink, along with Matt Baxter.

The Briton scowled at the suggestion, "Much as I'd like to sit back, I fear we don't have any time to waste."

I nodded reluctantly, and my grin disappeared, "Yeah. Alright, Felicia, look for the antennae we planted. That'll be the side we need to go in on."

Last time *Friendly* had been here to fix the nuclear reactor, we'd planted a transmitter next to the main Canary lock — the transmitter through which Holly could call us with intel about pirates moving overhead.

"They'll probably have seen us out here by now," Jim observed from the back of the bridge.

I nodded again at those words. Some of the barren-men from both the Pions and Canaries were employed with orbit-watching. If a ship was in orbit of their asteroid, there was a good chance it would send people down, and people — particularly women — were important prizes. Whoever saw them coming down first could have an advantage in capturing new tribe members… unless, like us, the people knew which locks to go to, and had 'allies' in the rock.

Yes, *allies*. That's a good word for the Canaries.

"I have located the transmission tower," Felicia reported after another moment, and I nodded to her.

"Record me."

There was virtually no delay between that order and Felicia's nod — as I say, she was definitely finding her footing in the job, predicting our needs and taking initiative.

"Holly, it's Ken Barron. Thanks for your call, we're here to retrieve our people. I'm coming down to your main locks… the ones next to your transmitter… with a heavily-armed party. Don't try to kill us, alright Holly? See you shortly."

That was the extent of my message, and Felicia sent it.

Karen was looking at me as I turned away from the screen, "So… you want me to come down with you?"

I laughed, "Given the choice, I'd take blockheads down with me. I'll take anyone stupid enough to come, which means you should stay."

Karen flashed a warm smile, using it to draw attention away from what looked to be nervous (yes, *nervous*) eyes, "I have my stupid moments."

"Hanging out with me too much…" I started past her towards the door. "Andrea, look after things up here. If you don't hear from us in an hour, blow this rock to small, small pieces."

"I bloody won't," she called as Karen fell into step next to me.

I didn't argue.

"We call these the 'main locks'. Don't know what the Canaries actually call them, and I don't think it matters. We used them to get in last time because they're close together, better for mutual support," Charlie had both his own Special Branch squad and Rufus' standing before him in the waiting room next to flight bay two, and behind him on the screen was a picture of the locks we were going to dock with.

"Close together, easy for mutual support," Rufus repeated Charlie's thought, and every officer in the room nodded. These people didn't generally need the reasoning behind their deployment explicitly explained to them, but because of circumstances, the two Majors were making sure the basics were well covered.

There was a slight undercurrent of anxiousness in the waiting room. These Branchers were essentially being tasked with a rescue op in *hell*, so they deserved to be a little unsettled.

"We're operating in a horror movie. Again. Let's hope they don't make a habit of asking us to do this sort of work," Charlie closed off his comments, alluding there to the horror movie they'd all been in aboard *Idaho*. That horror movie (with the 'alien') had been a hoax. This one was going to be all too real.

"Come on, boss," Carly pitched in with a jaunty grin. "We do this, they'll send us out to kill Satan. And that'd be a story for the grandkids."

"Or for the pub," one of Rufus' officers countered with a grin, and a current of chuckles battled some of the tension.

With surprisingly good timing, Karen and I chose this moment to slip into the lounge. We weren't going to be taking our fighters down to the rock, as having them docked with the Special Branch assault shuttles would have slowed down a rapid evac if one was needed.

"Here come the amateurs," I called from the back of the room. I'm pretty sure I was overcompensating at this stage — forcing just a little too much humor, trying to keep things light.

Karen let that one go, though, and together we arrived at the front of the room to stand opposite Charlie and Rufus.

"We set?" I asked the dumb question (of course they were set).

Charlie didn't seem to take offense, "All set. You riding with me?"

I nodded, and Karen looked to our other Major, "I'll ride with you, Rufus, if you don't mind."

The Chinese man with mismatched eyes offered a curt nod, "We're pleased to have you ma'am… you think it's safe for both of you to go down?"

Karen looked at me, and I looked at Karen. Then, in stereo, we both blurted, "No."

That earned us a couple of laughs, and then I followed on with the actual rationale, "I don't have a choice, Holly wants to see me."

"And I have to go along to make sure he doesn't take up with any of the local women," Karen said with a totally deadpan expression.

That got us more laughs, and our enforced 'light atmosphere' stayed intact.

A few minutes later we boarded the assault shuttles.

CHAPTER THIRTEEN

WELCOME BACK TO HELL

I was actually wearing a tac vest.

You know I *never* wear a tac vest, but I was wearing one now (as I had last time we were here). I'm fine storming a pirate house in shirtsleeves. I'm good shooting it out with Martians while wearing a tunic. Pions and Canaries? If I had a full suit of medieval armor, I might well try it.

I'm actually not being sarcastic there… which is sort of scary.

But yes, I was wearing a tac vest as Chet Srisai edged Charlie's shuttle up to the airlock on the left. Rufus' shuttle was, obviously, docking on the right.

I tugged at the vest uncomfortably as I listened to the lock cycle. The snug-fitting protective gear wouldn't save me from having my face impaled/crushed/torn off, but it would absorb solid body blows if I was jumped. It was better than nothing.

Pulling my sidearm out of its holster on my hip, I got myself ready. Charlie, obviously, wasn't letting me go first — that honor was going to Captain Raza Weiss — but I wanted to be prepared to go into the dimly-lit tunnels when my turn came.

Charlie was standing just ahead of me in line, and he was clearing his MAG-90 for action. As soon as that was done, he let the weapon hang from its harness on his vest and drew his ill-used fighting knife from its sheath.

Special Branchers, as you know, can fight with just about any tool. Charlie, for instance, could kill you with a bag of sedated cats. And yet, despite all the hype, Charlie tried to avoid knife work — he didn't like showing off, and he preferred the flexibility a mag offered in terms of how much damage to do to a target.

But for Pion rock, he was bringing out the steel… and apparently, the bombs.

"Are those concussion grenades?" I frowned as I noticed them on his vest.

He nodded, "Rufus brought toys."

My eyebrows went up, "Guy comes prepared."

"That's what I said," Charlie agreed, and then just as we were getting our cadence up for a quick repartee on being prepared, the lock clunked, and there was an audible hiss as atmosphere flooded the chute.

Chet Srisai got out of his pilot's chair with his MAG-90 in hand, then stood in the doorway of his compartment — an extra gun at the ready in case we were rushed. Raza Weiss stepped up to the lock and nodded to his half of the squad, "Let's go."

He popped the hatch with no ceremony, and then with blinding speed the Branchers were out of their shuttle and into Pion rock. I followed with rather less eliteness.

Yes, I'm betting eliteness isn't a word. My editors have given me permission to create one new word a book. Sporting of them.

Entering the dim, stuffy tunnels — with their indescribably strange smells — was not fun. Behind me, Chet shut the inner hatch of the shuttle, and that was it: I was back in Pion rock.

For those of you wondering, yes, it basically looks just like the higher budget movies you've seen: the walls to the right and left are bare, brown rock, worn relatively smooth after a couple of centuries of use. The floor is made up of Type 2A Felix Wolfe plates that, true to their centuries-old promise of never failing, still work — though they have been scuffed and dirtied from their original silver color to that of a grimy black. The ceiling was originally silver as well, and because there's been no foot traffic on it over the years, parts of it are still a dull silvery-gray.

The smell, however, is almost indescribable. The recycling systems for the air were still going, using the *original* supply of air. It's beyond stale.

This is a point I should actually stop to explain: the entire colony was still running on the same kit that had been installed in the 2070s. There are simply fewer things that can go wrong with old-school technology. The grav plating, for instance, was the same physics-defying roto-atom Felix Wolfe design from the 2050s, and it was soldiering on in most parts of the rock. The water, air and food growing systems were still running, and as I mentioned earlier, the reactor had only started failing in the 2220s… that's 170 years of straight use before it died.

They don't build them like that any more.

But let's not over-romanticize — not everything was working just like new. Parts of it weren't working at all, and some systems had been patched and bastardized with equipment off ships that had since docked here. Things were operating just well enough to allow the Pions and the Canaries to continue their wonderful lives for a little while longer.

Whoops, that was sarcasm.

By the time I got into the tunnel, Charlie's team had fanned out into the junction of corridors connected to the two main locks. Six separate hallways converged in an open space similar to a docking arrivals lounge, so Charlie's Branchers covered the three tunnels on the left, and Rufus' team had the three on the right.

And, predictably, everything was just too damned quiet.

Karen came up beside me after a moment, shaking her head, "Am I allowed to be cliché, since we're actually inside the biggest cliché in Imperial culture right now?"

I shrugged, "Sure, I guess."

She nodded, "Alright. It's quiet. Too quiet."

Charlie was walking past us towards Rufus and volunteered a groan. Karen and I looked sheepish and shut up.

"Terrible lighting for us… it's like twilight… too bright for night vision," Rufus observed as Charlie stopped next to him.

"Yeah, it's not the best lighting," Charlie agreed. "I have no idea which way Holly would be coming from…"

There was no need to brainstorm: Rufus' three officers watching the right-most tunnel tensed and tightened their grips on their weapons, "Here's company!"

The Branchers didn't need to be told to hold their fire — they were at the ready, but no one would squeeze a trigger until ordered. In the meantime, Charlie, Rufus, Karen and I moved quickly to stand behind them, our weapons up, as a half dozen Canaries came towards us with their distinctive gait.

Up front, and *not* bare-breasted, thanks, was Holly.

"So it's Bear and Charl bring friends, yeah?" she called, her grin revealing her abysmal dental state.

I waved my hand and attempted a transparent smile, "Hi Holly."

Charlie had his MAG-90 trained on Holly and her compatriots, but he managed to wave too, "Excuse the weapons, we're just not very trusting."

"Know you we can do the wallop," she shuffled to a stop about three meters short of our defensive position, and her minions halted behind her. "Well, good faith is giving, no concerns there you should. Look and come us…"

As she was saying that, she seemed to take first notice of Karen, and Karen raised an elegant eyebrow as their gazes met. If Karen qualifies as goddess-like (as she does) then Holly qualifies as goddess-of-the-dead like. She doesn't have snakes for hair, but there's nothing refined about her.

Sure, some of the spiritualists might say that natural is the way we should all live, but they don't mean *this* natural. Trust me, it's not healthy or idyllic. It's certainly not sexy. It's not the movies.

So when Karen and Holly locked eyes, it was like watching the opposite extremes of humanity.

"Holly, pleased to meet you. I'm Karen McMaster," Karen said politely, though she didn't lower her guard.

"Karen," Holly chewed on the word. "Master. I think Master. Guess I should you barren like Bear?"

"No children, no," Karen shook her head very slowly.

"Leader in except of it," Holly observed, sidling forward again. "Spose that makes you like Bear. Strange lot you, but word's given respect the uniform. Healthy is what you some look, yeah?"

Narrowing her eyes slightly at the strange phrasing, Karen went to work deciphering Holly's dialogue, and after a moment she nodded slowly, "I'm healthy, I'd hope."

Holly laughed, "Slow she. You well and will learn speaking. Fight too, I spose? Bear she belonging you to, fight better me than she."

Karen stepped out past our line of Branchers, which I have to point out was a very bold move. Holly's grin stretched as she approached, and her escort of Canaries bridled. These guys were all mostly naked and carrying a variety of nasty clubs and cleavers fashioned out of bits of mining equipment. As they perked up, the Branchers behind Karen did too.

If it had been anyone but Karen I would have said something — reminded her that calm was needed.

But it was Karen, so obviously I was less concerned.

She stopped close to Holly, and leaned down to go nose-to-nose with the leader of the Canaries, "I think I *well* and *will* learn your dialect. And I do know how to fight. And who said he doesn't belong to *me?*"

Holly's head pulled back slightly at the smooth words, "Boss woman in charge?"

Karen straightened up, "We tend to share. I'd say you need to learn to do the same, but somehow I doubt you'd care to."

She was goading Holly… and Holly was digging it. Holly snorted a laugh, "Empire types and fairness. You know good not to force us."

"You really should learn how to speak properly," Karen smiled, "but again, I know you probably take pleasure in irritating me with your savage brogue, don't you?"

"Master stands tall for a barren woman," Holly stabbed a finger at Karen. "Only you wrong is no a baby. Has you a baby, you be like us."

Karen's eyebrow slid up, "I certainly hope not."

Holly cackled, then kindly made an effort to clean up her language for our benefit, "You come to see your people. We got them up put neatly."

With that, the Canary matriarch turned and waved her escort back down the tunnel.

Turning around to face us, Karen gave an exaggerated lady-like shrug, "Guess she likes me."

Charlie and I must have had some pretty astounded expressions on our faces. I mean, you don't just walk up to the leader of the band of savages from the horror movies and tell her to learn syntax.

Well, *you* shouldn't try, dear reader. And I won't be in any rush to.

"Come on, I think they're taking us to their share of the survivors," Karen pointed her thumb back down the corridor, then wheeled and followed Holly.

Charlie and I chased quickly, with the rest of his squad bringing up the rear (which was a very bad deployment scheme, generally).

Rufus and his squad stayed at the intersection, protecting our route of escape.

We were going deeper into Pion rock…

CHAPTER FOURTEEN
RELATIVE GOODNESS

On Pion rock, you take what goodness you can get. We were about to get some... but let's be clear, what passes for 'goodness' on Pion rock would probably be considered horrific anywhere else.

The Canaries and Pions live in the corridors of the old XV-001 colony, and there are a lot of tunnels. Each tribe has control over about thirty percent of the network. The Pions control mainly the upper levels, the Canaries have the lower ones, the mining sections. In between is a buffer of tunnels (about forty percent of the installation) which are just impossible to defend because of the plethora of access points.

I bring this up now just to give you an idea of the lay of the rock. We were in the Canary section of the tunnels, which is probably why I thought of that glowing bit of exposition. This was the bottom half of the asteroid, and it was the part Charlie and I had spent most of our time in during the last visit, because the reactor was down here.

We recognized some of the intersections we went through — including one in the vicinity of the place we'd been ambushed last time — and then we started getting into the more communal areas.

This was not pleasant. The Canaries live in conditions that still defy my ability to understand. They don't bathe, and because of the closed, microbe-free environment they've lived in for centuries, there isn't too much in the way of disease — there just aren't enough microorganisms around. They don't care much about clothing, or about body shape... they defy all the 'standards' we in the Empire set for ourselves.

Case in point: when Holly looked at Karen and called her healthy, she was making note of things like her *teeth*, not her elegant neck and jaw line.

I don't know if I'm adequately describing the difference with the Canaries, sorry. Just trust me when I say that none of the movies correctly portray their look and their smell. They aren't the hot Amazon babes of space, and they're not the butch bodybuilders either. They're distended, stringy, long in all hair, have uncut fingernails, generally saggy everywhere there's anything to sag, and they never wash.

Sound gross?

Good, because it is. I apologize to the anthropologists who'll tell you that they're people too... I mean, those anthropologists are right. It's just that they're disgusting. Yes, I said it. They call us weak, I call them disgusting. We trade insults equally. I'm not trying to exterminate them because they're gross, I'm just observing that, by my standards, they're gross. Get over it.

My editor says you probably are over it, so I'll shut up.

For Charlie and me, walking through these narrow corridors being eyed by these people was not a pleasant return. Of course, as a Special Brancher and a generally decent person, Charlie wasn't as judgmental as I was... but even he didn't enjoy the company.

For the Branchers following us who hadn't been here before, this was a rude greeting. Occasionally one of the warriors we passed would bare his teeth... er... his toothless gums... and pretend to start lunging. Whenever that happened, the warrior would come nose-to-nose with a MAG-90, but he'd only cackle and leap away.

It was surreal, horror movie-ish. And, to reference the chapter title, it was relatively a good thing. At least they weren't actually attacking us.

We finally arrived at a communal chamber — a room we're pretty sure used to be a lunch cafeteria for miners, centuries prior — and Holly led the way in.

"Come now in to looked at your uniformered," she said with as much flourish as can be managed by someone who doesn't conjugate verbs but does conjugate nouns.

Sorry, went all literary snob right there. Which, as you know, is rather ironic.

Karen was first through the door after Holly, and I followed next, inside were twenty-two men and women from *North Carolina*, looking filthy and hungry, but decidedly alive and unmolested.

They were all pretty tired, and they didn't recognize us immediately. One of the women sitting towards the back of the group eventually caught sight of us, then looked up and narrowed her eyes, not quite believing what she was seeing.

I rather casually held up a hand to wave at her, and her eyes popped wide, "Admiral!"

She grabbed the shoulder of the woman sitting next to her and climbed shakily to her feet, "Rescue! Rescue!"

Then everyone else started sitting up, recognizing us, and expressing their relief. It wasn't awkward... at first. There were cheers and smiles from the first people up — the ones, I suppose, who'd born their condemnation to this hell with the least immediate emotional or mental trauma. The ones slower to their feet were in rougher shape.

I should be clear here, this place wasn't as bad as Egesta — or at least, I wouldn't say it was — but it was pretty nightmarish in its own, grizzly way. And these people had been through hell... together they'd survived nine months of hide-and-seek on minimal rations out at Jupiter, and now shortly after getting back onto active duty in the Empire, they'd lost their ship and ended up in a horror movie. I wasn't about to condemn any of them for being emotional just then — they'd earned the right.

Maybe these people weren't as elite as the officers and crews of the Jupiter Force, but they were solid and very close-knit.

Holly stood aside as the filthy (but not nearly as filthy as the Canaries) survivors stumbled over to shake our hands and thank us. As the awkwardness rose, I started interrupting them.

"Glad to see you're all safe. Now let's get you the hell out of here..."

No, wasn't too subtle about that.

As I was speaking, Karen was on her comm to *Wolf*, "Andrea, we have the first party of twenty-two... should be able to get them all into one shuttle. Send it to the lock closest to the right main lock... know the one?"

Andrea confirmed, and *Wolf* dispatched a shuttle.

Charlie started moving his squad into position to escort the survivors out of the room, and as he did Holly approached me, "So Bear better be pleased. Healthy women there with uniform respected."

"I do appreciate that, thank you," I nodded, actually sincere in my sentiment.

"And guess lemme. You didn't women for the trade along. Twenty is what the Pions call about and you don't have for the Pions. They don't have respect in the uniform quite my way, you know."

Holly was condemning the Pions, and pointing out that they weren't nearly as cooperative overall as the Canaries were. This seemed likely enough — they weren't going to be sympathetic to our survivors if they knew we were on the rock and that we hadn't brought women along for trade. We didn't have a lot of time to get the *North Carolinas* out of their hands.

"You and Charl and Master is tough, but not so tough. Pions shit beat and kill all if you do the run in for the uniformered. Better trade is you do."

Holly's voice was lower now, but despite her impossible grammar, I was getting a sense from her inflection that she was getting ready to set me up. The movies generally assume that Canaries and Pions are simple or stupid, but my experience with Holly demonstrates quite the opposite.

She was playing me. She knew it, and I knew it, and she knew I knew it.

She also knew that if I wanted to recover the people the Pions had taken, I needed to cooperate with her, at least for the short term.

The question was what she wanted out of this playtime... I couldn't yet be sure, and there was only one way to find out.

Just imagine how maddening the dialogue is going to be in *this* meeting...

CHAPTER FIFTEEN
DEBRIEF AND DISCRETION

Karen, Charlie and I went next into a meeting with Holly, but I'm not going to take us there right now. Instead I want to follow the survivors back to *Wolf*, so we can find out what happened to *North Carolina*.

The shuttle that Andrea sent down to Pion rock was empty but for the pilot and two SF. Carly and the rest of Charlie's squad escorted the survivors to the lock and sent them on their way in this shuttle, and after a short flight it landed in *Wolf's* bay one.

Alicia Morgan and most of her medical staff were waiting there as the *North Carolinas* disembarked, as was Andrea Kiley herself.

As the filth-covered crew emerged, Andrea was actually the first person they were seeing, and she repeated the same words softly to each person she greeted: "I need to speak to whoever's in charge."

After a moment, Lieutenant Commander Lamia Makanga stepped up with a stiff salute — not unlike the one Captain Kishko had once given us, "Ma'am, Lieutenant Commander Makanga, Helm and Navigation Officer."

Andrea returned the man's salute, "Commander, as soon as you're cleared by Doctor Morgan, please join me in my day cabin on the bridge."

Makanga nodded and then returned to his crew under Alicia's supervision.

Half an hour later, Andrea lowered herself into her seat in her day cabin, and Lieutenant Commander Makanga sat opposite her.

"Ma'am, on behalf of my crew I am obliged to thank you for coming to our rescue. Hope was, I must be honest with you, beginning to fade."

Captain Kishko had certainly influenced his crew, or at the very least, his senior officers. If you'll recall from *The Dark Cruise*, Kishko himself was a very formal gentleman, an officer of the old guard. His young Congolese Helm and Navigation Officer was keeping with that tradition, despite his lack of years.

Andrea's reply came with a sad smile, "I'm sorry the situation required us to come. Mister Makanga, what precisely happened to your ship? All we know is that you detached from the convoy."

Makanga nodded slowly, "Yes ma'am. Captain Kishko led the attacking Martian force away from the convoy, but in the process we received damage. We damaged the destroyer leading the Martian formation, but a powerfully-armed pirate and a destroyer escort remained intact. The destroyer was also functional. They chased us, but our sensors had been destroyed."

We'd guessed something to that effect based on the information provided by the escorting corvettes that had remained with the convoy, so as Andrea nodded, she wasn't hearing anything surprising.

"Captain Kishko turned us away from the sun on dead reckoning. Our hope was to enter the asteroid belt and find local support, while leading the enemy away. We were also hopeful that they would give up their chase, perhaps. They did not."

"I suppose they wouldn't, no," Andrea shook her head. "And how'd you come to be here, on the Pion rock?"

Remember, we still didn't know at that point.

Makanga shook his head grimly, "I can only assume by bad luck, Captain Kiley. Every time we were attacked by the Martians and the pirate, we made a course correction to attempt to avoid them. We thought for a time that they were attempting to herd us in a certain direction, but I do not believe that to be the case. I do not know why they would intentionally bring us here."

Andrea avoided saying what popped into her mind at that moment — that she wouldn't put such heinous 'herding' past any bastards who would use *Idaho* as a trap the way the Martians apparently had.

"Some of my people have suggested that after *Idaho*, the Martians would do anything. I do not believe, though, that they could have so effectively herded us to make us come here."

Well, Andrea didn't need to be silent about her biases then... but she still didn't mention them. Instead her eyes narrowed slightly as she studied Lieutenant Commander Makanga; as the Helm and Navigation Officer on *North Carolina*, he would of course be the most aware of the difficulties of herding an enemy ship to a particular point, like Pion rock.

But she wouldn't put it past the Martians. And she was right not to.

"Well, whether the Martians meant to or not is irrelevant. There were twenty-two of you in the Canaries' custody. Do you happen to know how many were taken by the Pions?"

Makanga shook his head, "I am sorry, ma'am, I do not know. When the final attack came and Captain Kishko ordered us to abandon ship, I was in the auxiliary steering position, because our bridge controls had been disabled by mag fire. I do not believe Captain Kishko abandoned, ma'am. In fact, I believe he attempted to ram the Martian destroyer, though I do not know if he was successful."

Brave man, old Captain Kishko had been. Andrea nodded solemnly, "Very well, Lieutenant Commander. I'll let you get back to your crewmates. Rest assured we'll be getting the rest of the survivors back from those Pion bastards quick as we can."

"Thank you, ma'am," Makanga came to his feet and snapped to attention, again offering a militarily-perfect salute.

Standing in response to the formal gesture, Andrea issued a salute of her own, and then Makanga left.

The moment the hatch shut, Andrea keyed her intercom, "Jim, could you come in here? And Felicia, I need realtime with Mark and Matt please."

Jim Hannigan came through the door just seconds after the request was made, and Andrea's wall screen flashed up two *WolfNet* loading windows at the same time.

"As we suspected?" Jim asked as Andrea waved him to the seat Makanga had just occupied.

Nodding, Andrea waited another second for Matt and Mark to appear on her screen before elaborating, "So as we thought, we have a wounded destroyer, a healthy DE and a well-armed and gutsy pirate out here somewhere. If they're smart, they'll have moved on... but they could have brought *North Carolina* here as bait. They could be lined up to hit the rescue party."

"Another trap?" Matt Baxter asked coolly. He was still rather angry — to use a British understatement — about the last one.

Mark grunted, "If the fuckers who set this one up want to come looking for trouble, I'm all for it."

Go figure, Mark wasn't mincing words. He also had a good point — if the Martians had brought *North Carolina* here and destroyed it so the survivors would be bait for a Defense Command rescue force, they were going to get a rude surprise when they found two frigates and a corvette waiting for them. If the same destroyer and destroyer escort were the ones behind the trap, they'd find themselves thoroughly outgunned.

"I want to cut these bastards' throats, but I've lately been made aware of the fact that I'm slightly more... *aggressive* than I ought to be," Andrea said quietly.

Mark grinned, "Well at least you have an excuse for your aggression. I'm just a horrible person."

"Makes three of us," Matt nodded in agreement. "But I assume you're concerned about taking that too far?"

Andrea nodded, then glanced at Jim before looking back to her fellow skippers, "We could hide the two of you, so if the Martians come back they see only *Wolf*... make us bait for the bastards, and when they come in you two pounce. But that's a risk, and it's not the mission."

Matt and Mark both nodded slowly — their job out here was to make sure we got the survivors out safely, and there was nothing safer in war than compelling the enemy to run before any shots were fired. If this was a trap, and the three-ship Martian force came in to attack us, they'd see that they were outgunned as soon as they got into sensor range. Being clever, then, they'd doubtless turn tail and run, denying us the chance to destroy them.

If *Friendly* and *Cheetah* went to silent running and hid on the opposite side of Pion rock, then the Martians would probably see only one Defense Command ship if they returned. With numbers apparently in their favor, they might come in to attack, and then Mark and Matt could pounce on them.

But that wasn't the mission — we weren't out here to find the bastards who'd done this, as much as we'd have liked to. Avoiding a fight wasn't something we Belt Squadron/Jupiter Force types often did, but in this case, discretion wasn't necessarily a bad thing.

"I think we just sit and wait, don't get too cute with it," Andrea said quietly after a moment. "I'd love to bait those bastards in... but it's too risky separating us. Particularly if they come here with reinforcements. Could have us over a barrel then."

Slow nods came from Mark and Matt, and from Jim Hannigan as well. If the Martians came, they'd see the entire squadron waiting for them. If they wanted a fight at that stage, that was up to them, but we weren't going to try anything overly fancy to bring them in.

Andrea wasn't about to risk her ship and her mission to feed her anger. And that, as I probably don't need to point out, was a very good step for her.

+++

My editors asked a good question after this chapter: why weren't Karen or I in on that conversation, since the Jupiter Force technically belonged to us? Well, for one thing, we were in a delightful meeting with Holly. For another, when I'd left the bridge and told Andrea to 'look after things up here', what I was doing was putting her in squadron command.

Karen and I had our hands full with the survivor situation — it was up to the skippers we'd left above to make whatever arrangements they needed in order to keep orbital space secure. Strictly speaking, I hadn't ordered that they do this, but again, these were our elite people — Andrea, Mark and Matt knew to take initiative, and to get the job done.

And we knew they knew.

When I left the bridge, then, I hadn't done so thinking 'Andrea will make the deployment arrangements to protect our orbiting ships in case of an ambush, and she will do so with appropriate discretion'. Instead I'd thought: 'Andrea will look after things up here.'

Actually, no, I'd thought 'Andrea, Mark and Matt will look after things'.

That's one of the biggest advantages of an elite formation like ours: you could trust that, without itemized instructions, the important things would always be taken care of.

CHAPTER SIXTEEN

WHEELING AND DEALING

I am not, in fact, going to try to repeat the meeting Karen, Charlie and I had with Holly. You think normal briefings are bad because they have too much dialogue and exposition? This one would kill me if I tried to write it, and it'd axe-murder you if you tried to read it. Yes, words on a page would actually axe-murder you — the dialogue would be that jagged. I mean, pages of discussion in which words are randomly excluded or put in the wrong places, or conjugation is completely messed up?

I realize you're probably used to bad writing from me by now, but this is on a whole different level than, say, having publishers who spell *Jupiter* with an extra 'e'.

So I'm going to skip past the excruciating dialogue and give you the summary I gave our officers when we returned to *Wolf* a couple of hours later.

To set the scene, I'll tell you that when our meeting with Holly was over, we all left Pion rock — both assault shuttles came back to *Wolf* with their full complements of Branchers. We weren't leaving anyone down there to maintain a presence. Arguably, it might have been a good idea to keep people in the tunnels, observing and showing the flag, but I just couldn't ask any of our people to do that.

Pion rock is not a place where you leave people. Even temporarily. Period.

When we got back to *Wolf*, I'm pretty sure most people from the landing party went immediately to the showers — just being around the Canaries makes your skin crawl. Tough characters like Charlie probably didn't, as they're not fazed by such feelings, but Karen and I surely did.

After that, we called Andrea, Jim, Andrew Jensen and Alicia Morgan to the conference room, and piped in Mark and Matt via realtime. Andrea filled us in on the last chapter's discussions of how to handle orbital defense, and after that we addressed the problem of the survivors who were still in Pion hands.

"So... basically, no one knows exactly where they're being held," that was the start of the subject, and as I spoke I leaned back in my chair and steepled my fingers. "The Pions have undoubtedly seen us in orbit, so we're on the clock, too. If we're here for more than a few spins without getting in touch and offering trade, they're going to lose their respect for our uniforms."

That was interpretation passed on directly from Holly, though obviously she'd said it in her own half-intelligible brogue. A 'spin', I should clarify, is the time it takes Pion rock to rotate 360 degrees. It's tracked by observing the position of the sun from airlock windows, and measures about five or six hours on our clock (depending on the angle the rock holds towards the sun at any given moment).

As you might imagine, the Pions and the Canaries had little use for precise measurements of time... if one spin was longer than the next, no one was going to lose sleep over it.

Er. Maybe they would, actually, if it was a shorter sleep spin than the one prior…

Anyway. The point here was that Holly had no intel on exactly where the Pions were holding the remaining survivors. We didn't have any women to trade for those survivors, either, which put us in an odd spot.

"I know this isn't as easy as it sounds, but we're going to have to smash and grab, right?" Mark Gunney asked the inevitable question, and I had to nod slowly, as did Charlie.

"It's the only way we're going to get them out of there," our intrepid Major replied.

"But there are too many compartments and tunnels," Matt Baxter's tone was properly grim. "We'd need a battalion to sweep them all, and the casualties would probably be enormous."

There was no disputing that. If we decided to go all jingoistic on the Pions, we'd end up getting a lot of people — ours and theirs — killed. As much as big-Empire types like to assume that the might and technology of the black sun can shatter any adversary, there are situations where we simply aren't superior. In those tunnels, we're at best on a level playing field, and frankly, I think we're at a major disadvantage.

"Holly offering any help?" Jim asked that question, his eyes narrowing thoughtfully.

His implication was pretty clear — would the Canaries send their warriors to help offset our own disadvantage in the corridors if we mounted an incursion into Pion territory?

I scratched my temple, "Um. Sort of. That's why Andy and Alicia are here… they'll help, but only if we can offer them something to make it worth their while. I mean, they'd be starting a war for us, so they'd want to get something out of it."

"I love how savages with no teeth and no personal hygiene can understand capitalism," Mark commented gruffly, while Alicia and Andrew both looked at each other in surprise.

What did we have to offer the Canaries?

Well, there were the trusty old tried-and-true staples…

"Weapons?" Andrea asked, almost chewing out the word (remember, the last time she'd seen weapons traded to a population it hadn't gone so well).

I shook my head, "They don't want them. There's maybe five places down there where a ranged weapon is going to have a clear advantage over a club, and about a hundred places where it's a liability."

"And they don't have the ability to maintain them," Andy Jensen added helpfully. "They know how to patch up some of their systems with parts they pull off ships that come down, but they always… uh… *outsource* the complex work."

By 'outsource' he meant 'keep the engineers from unwise expeditions to Pion rock alive long enough to fix the problems before killing them'. Or, as we'd seen last time, make agreements with Defense Command for engineering support.

Anyway, offering mags wasn't going to get us anywhere.

"Supplies…" Alicia let the word trail off as she started to say it. What supplies could the Canaries really want from us?

That might seem a stupid question, but it's quite serious: the Pions and the Canaries had an entire society built around the equipment they could find in their own rock. They knew how to make everything function with what they had available to them, and anything we offered in small quantities would be rejected. Why? Because if we were the sole source of a new tool that changed their way of life, they'd suddenly become dependent on us.

And dependency is not something the Canaries or the Pions much believe in.

"Is there anything you could do to augment the reactor, make it run better somehow?" I looked at Andy with that question, but he shook his head.

"When I fixed it last time, I fixed it right. It'll be running when my grandkids are going gray. I could probably fix up some new grav plates for them, though. Last time we were here I remember there being entire sections where the plating had failed or been pulled out."

I mentioned earlier that the Type 2A grav plating was still functioning, and obviously it was — we'd walked around down there. Andy was correct, though: many sections of the rock's tunnel system had failed, or had been completely ripped out to replace those that had failed in other, more important areas.

And *yes*, they did know how to relocate grav plating without the help of outside engineers. Part of that is because the clunky old 2A Felix Wolfe panels are idiot proof — they even have color-coded connectors — but part of it is because the Pions and Canaries aren't stupid.

And the reason why new grav plates wouldn't work is equally not stupid.

"They use the zero-gee zones as ways to cover their flank down there. I don't think reopening areas will do them any good… it'd just give them more entrances to defend."

I was starting to feel poorly about how this meeting was going — I felt like all I was doing was gunning down ideas, but the Canaries were a tough people to bargain with. We all settled into an unproductive silence for a moment.

Then a thought started formulating.

"All they seem to want is women," Karen observed quietly. "Why *women?*"

Charlie leaned back in his seat and glanced at her, "More women means more possible mothers… bigger population. It's the core of their society."

The tone of Charlie's voice made it clear he wasn't sure where this was heading. Karen's eyes narrowed thoughtfully at the reply, "So what they really want is more *babies*."

Well dammit, Karen had their number.

Not sure that really required a 'dammit'…

The Canaries and the Pions were both small societies, each numbering perhaps a thousand people. For them, as I've already explained, having children was both the primary aim and the primary status-giver in society. Having children was of maximum importance. What if we offered them the chance to have more babies *with the same number of women?*

Everyone caught on to what Karen was suggesting pretty much instantly, but it was Alicia's job as the doctor to weigh in on whether it was practical.

"Fertility drugs?" our fine doctor asked with some deserved surprise, and Karen nodded.

Pausing in thought (thought that I am in no way qualified to attempt to understand — you know, including medical words with many syllables and such) she started to nod slowly.

"Well, the most powerful drugs would be too much for them. They can't have the right medical facilities to monitor pregnancies the way those drugs would demand. There could be too many complications with any multiple pregnancies…"

She paused, again pondering her medical options.

"*But*, some of the over-the-counter stuff, the lighter grade fertility enhancers… those could work. They're low in terms of complications, and you're looking at a success rate of about seventy percent in healthy women."

Jim held up his hand, asking the question that popped into many of our heads right then, "Success rate?"

This is one of the few times when we didn't all immediately understand what one of our peers was saying in a briefing, and thus had to ask a question.

"A pregnancy from a woman who couldn't previously conceive, or twins instead of a single baby," Alicia explained quickly. "In Canary women… well I don't expect their health is very good, and there'll be complications because of that… but I'd say you'd still get a decent number of successes."

I started to nod, "That could be a bargaining chip, definitely."

Technology, perhaps, could help these people.

Charlie then added his usual dose of reality to the discussion.

"Their social rankings are based on number of surviving children… three being the most any woman has ever had. If we artificially enhance the chances of pregnancy and child birth, we could turn their social ranking system on its head," he said those words with a certain reluctance.

Charlie Peters. Again, let me tell you, this guy is the antidote to Jingoism everywhere. He sees the good that a powerful force like the Empire can do, but he is ever-conscious of how we throw around our weight, and the possible effects of our actions.

We're all much better off for his attention to these details.

And what he was saying here, obviously, was quite right: if we gave a supply of fertility drugs to the Canaries, then their barren women might become child-bearers, and some of their child-bearers might exceed three pregnancies. The increased number of pregnancies *might* be accommodated in the social order that had been established, or it could cause great difficulties as the number of leadership-class women ballooned.

Simply stated, we'd be potentially destabilizing a society.

"No offense to the Canaries, but I don't care," Mark Gunney was the first to voice his opinion on that one.

I winced at the abruptness of the words — I had been going for more delicate wording than 'I don't care', but now I shrugged.

"It could completely destroy their society. I hope it doesn't, but that's not my problem. We need to get our people back, and this is probably the only thing we have to barter with," I looked down the table to meet Charlie's gaze.

He thought about it for a moment, and then with a single, slow nod, he agreed, "The survivors are our top priority."

That, again, is another great Charlie quality. Same as on Egesta and everywhere else: he makes sure we know the ramifications of what we're doing, be it lying about free elections or doling out fertility drugs, but even when we're wandering through a gray area, he keeps a simple question in mind: how do I save lives, and is it worth the price?

In this case, potentially destabilizing a crude society was worth the return of the twenty *North Carolinas.*

Yes, that sounds cold, but it's what we thought then, and it's what I think now. This may make me a cruel, arrogant Imperialist, but there were twenty men and women down in that asteroid, who needed to get out of there. Those people had been through hell once out at Jupiter, and now they were going through it again in the Pion rock, and I'd be damned if I was going to abandon them.

Under other circumstances, would I have condoned any attempt to destabilize Canary society by the introduction of fertility drugs? Probably not. But in this case, I'd do what I had to in order to get our people out of there.

"We'll warn Holly about the possibilities when we make the offer," I said quietly, my eyes drifting down to the table. That was my concession — I wasn't just going to tell Holly that these drugs would be wonderful, I'd point out some of the potential problems.

Charlie nodded, "That seems fair. And bottom line, it'll be up to her to accept them or not."

He was right about that, and made me realize I'd been making a very foolish mistake. I'll come back to that in a moment, because there is a practical narrative point that has to be dealt with first.

"There's another problem, though," Alicia sounded slightly sheepish, and all eyes turned towards her. "We don't keep fertility drugs aboard. We've never had any use for them."

Oh.

Whoops.

"Belt Eleven's about thirty hours behind us... I can go and raid a pharmacy or ten," Mark offered from his place on the screen.

I thought for just a second about that — despite Andrea's sound decision to keep us all together, it seemed we might need to split up.

"We'll see what Holly says... if she wants them, then you're on," I agreed after that pause. "So... I suppose I'll ask her."

The meeting ended.

CHAPTER SEVENTEEN

ARROGANCE

I met Holly at the entrance to the main lock, with two of Rufus' Special Branchers flanking me. Charlie's team was stood down, so I'd come over in Rufus' shuttle with four of his officers — we didn't need a full complement, since I was only planning to chat at the lock.

I explained to Holly what we were offering — fertility drugs, that could make barren women fertile and already fertile women even more fertile — and she smiled in a way that I could only describe as 'thoughtful'.

"So women not what pay you'd bring, but you make more babies of the women of we got," she repeated the ideas I'd conveyed in a low, pondering tone. "How total much you going hereto?"

God, sometimes what she was saying was not easy to decipher. But on the plus side, I suppose, at least it was essentially English.

"We can bring in as much as you want. We'll have to send one of our ships to go pick it up… we didn't plan ahead enough to bring some along. But you tell us how much and we'll bring it."

She nodded with an exaggerated jerk of her head, "Bring here you enough to ten thousands, it make us last generations."

I tilted my head, wondering if fertility drugs could expire. Ten thousand doses would last a long time for a population of women as small as the Canaries'.

"I don't know if it expires over time."

"Fruit rotting like," Holly nodded. "Wants the 500 in a year doses. They go bad, you bring more for 500 yearly. Deal that okay?"

Well, it was a steep price I suppose, but then all things considered, having to possibly run doses of the fertility drugs to this rock over the next twenty years wasn't so bad. Presuming we didn't default on the payments at some point…

And defaulting was not something I'd recommend. While the Canaries couldn't come looking for you if you didn't pay up, they were certainly not the sort of people you'd want annoyed with you in future, in case something like this happened again.

I nodded my agreement, "Deal."

Then my guilt kicked in. Yes, occasionally, I feel some guilt, and this was one of those occasions.

"Holly… before you agree… you do realize, making pregnancy easier could really change the way your society structures itself. I mean, if there are more successful pregnancies, there could be many three-child women. It could turn your social order on its head."

Charlie's caution was important. We had to warn these people of exactly what we might be getting them into.

Holly looked at me, "Uh. Yeah obviously. Thing that I first thought is that."

Oh.

"We just control who to gets the fertie drugies. If wants someone particular in power, her will get lots. Ones don't I want get none. Usefully."

What she was saying there, in case it didn't make sense to you (and by no means should you worry if it didn't) was that the instant I explained the purpose and effects of the drugs to her, she'd figured out what their uses could be, and what the potential political and social implications of their effects could be.

And she had decided how she'd use them to her personal advantage as a leader.

In other words: we didn't need to worry.

More to the point, though, we were being patronizing.

Yes, we were. Not Charlie so much, he'd warned *us* about the problems we could create, but had pointed out that it'd be Holly's decision (thus respecting Holly's right and capacity to make an important decision for her people).

I, on the other hand, assumed that the Canaries, being a gross, crude and violent society, wouldn't be sophisticated enough to foresee the problems fertility drugs could create. I assumed they'd just start using them, destroying their own way of life and not realizing what they'd done until it was too late. In retrospect, that assumption was so incredibly stupid. That's the nature of Imperial arrogance right there — the patronizing belief that we're the only ones who understand how a society works, that we know it even better than the people who *built* the society in question. Hence my guilt — I thought we were giving them trouble that they had no way to predict.

This arrogance of ours is insidious, and it really does infuse just about everything we do.

I'm a citizen of the Empire — the civilized, shiny Empire. More than that, I live an Earth-style life, as do all the people living in Earthgreen domes in the independent colonies out there. As much as they don't like to admit it, the Martians do too.

We all look at tunnel-dwellers like the Pions and Canaries and assume they're stupid, and that we need to think for them. We're not the first great 'civilized' society to have this patronizing outlook, and I doubt we'll be the last. Look through history and you'll see it over and over — the incredible hubris of Rome, the dangerous and destructive arrogance of the Confucian Chinese Empires, the catastrophically misguided perspectives of the European Empires and later 'superpowers'. Empires *always* assume that the 'other guys' aren't as smart as they are, and thus need to be taught. Otherwise, they couldn't be 'beneficiaries' (or 'victims', to those opposing interaction with them) of our massive, enlightened intelligence! Oh no!

The worst part is that we Empires don't generally realize we're doing it. We're patronizing, thinking we're being helpful, when really all we're doing is telling them to be like us. Act as we do, disregard thousands of years of your own tradition. Abide by our economic practices, because they're better. Abandon your own definition of human rights, because ours are obviously the only correct ones. Stop cooking that food, because ours is better. But better by what universal standard, exactly? This is the problem — one, thankfully, that the Articles of Empire forced an end to on Earth. All races of humanity being equal under the law helps a lot, but when it comes to the Pions and Canaries, we're right back where our ancestors were. Arrogant. Embarrassingly so, at times.

Sorry, I'll now step down off my soap box. Er. That's an old expression. Means I was ranting.

Anyway, in the case of me and Holly, my arrogance was leading me to believe that if I didn't warn her, she'd never figure out the negative ramifications of the drugs we were offering. Which, obviously, is ridiculous — as gross as I think she is, she's able to figure out the particulars of her own society.

"So got you none for the sampling now," Holly observed while I realized my foolishness. "So trusting you is what's want."

I nodded slowly, "Well, even if we had a sample here, it'd take a bit too long to hand out the doses and see if babies survived their first year, don't you think?"

Cackling, Holly bobbed her head again, "True and that. Trust giving alright. Bear know bettern't mess us, right?"

"Indeed. I'd never dream of cheating you, Holly," I managed a slim, somewhat genuine smile with that assertion, and Holly cackled again.

"Yeah deal its. We helping, but plan be needed, yeah?"

"We'll worry about that shortly. I need to head back up there to send a ship to get your drugs. I'll bring down a full planning team in a couple of hours."

Holly nodded her head again, and I left.

The deal was done.

CHAPTER EIGHTEEN

SETTING UP

"I'll be back before you can say 'too many babies for the savages,'" Mark Gunney grinned on the Battlelink monitor, and I shrugged.

"Be careful walking into pharmacies on Belt Eleven asking for fertility drugs. If the media starts broadcasting that Mark Gunney's starting a brood, daughters across the Belt will be locked in their rooms," I met humor with humor.

Mark didn't skip a beat, "Heh, like a locked door would stop me. Be back in sixty-five hours."

"Fly safe," I nodded as his signal disconnected, and *Cheetah* turned away and accelerated back towards the Belt colonies.

Karen was, go figure, standing next to me, and she elected to take a deep sigh, "So, do we wait until he gets back with the payment, or is Holly going to trust us so we can start now?"

I mirrored the sigh, "Well, I think she trusts us enough to give us the help we need right now."

Managing a slightly sly smile, Karen leaned towards me, "I suppose you look somewhat trustworthy. Good teeth."

I shook my head, "Nah, it's because you made such an impression."

Our fumbling attempts at banter were reflections, I'm sure, of our general reluctance to get down to the business of helping the Canaries start a war. Don't mistake me: we had to do it, and we weren't going to waste any time when the lives of those twenty *North Carolina* survivors were on the line. But we really, *really* weren't looking forward to this.

Gee, can you guess why?

"Alright, let's call in all the brains we can for a meeting," I mumbled as our weak humor melted. "We'll talk ideas before we go back to Holly."

Karen nodded, and the orders were issued.

Matt Baxter came over from *Friendly* personally for this meeting. He had been my Lieutenant of SF in *Friendly* when we'd been here last, and between him and Charlie, we had the two most experienced shooting specialists in Pion/Canary affairs in the Empire.

Whoa, apologies for that sentence. Sort of slipped out of control. But you probably get my meaning.

Along with them were me, Rufus Chang, Andrea, Karen and Omar Cunningham, our new Lieutenant of SF (remember, off *Lion*?).

"Holly doesn't know where they are, but some of her warriors will know the Pion tunnels pretty well. That'll be a help," I was restating things we all knew, as though we needed the refreshing.

Well, we did.

We all knew what Holly had to offer us in terms of tactical personnel (if you can call warriors 'tactical personnel'), but I was hoping that by repeating what we knew, I could subtly get us talking about what we didn't know — about how to get to the survivors.

Charlie took my dumb hint and was charitable enough to get the real ball rolling, "I don't like the idea of roaming from tunnel to tunnel down there, calling their names. We need to find out where they're being held before we go in..."

"Or we need to control where they'll be," Rufus casually inserted himself into the middle of Charlie's remarks, and Charlie halted.

"That's what I was about to say."

Rufus blinked and glanced at Charlie, "Uh. Sorry."

I think I probably smiled at that, but we didn't dwell on the exchange — Charlie went on, "Getting them to move the survivors is my preference. We get them to neutral ground and set up an ambush."

"And not an ambush at the exchange site... they'll be expecting that. We ambush them as they're bringing the women back to their tunnels. Pick some neutral ground with only one way back to their tunnels. We hit them after they think they've done the trade," Rufus followed on immediately, and Charlie gave him another slightly surprised 'I was about to say that too' look.

But wait a second... insert the sound of the needle being abruptly dragged off a vinyl record (look it up, mid-twentieth century): *done what trade?*

Andrea cleared her throat politely, then leaned forward, "Rufus, you know exactly what I'm going to ask, so if you wouldn't mind convincing me..."

Rufus and Charlie both opened their mouths to explain, but Matt Baxter managed to beat them to it, "Andrea, there simply isn't a better way to get the survivors out. We find twenty volunteers from Special Branch and SF and we offer them as trade. When they bring the survivors for the swap, we take them."

Oh boy. I doubt I even need to explain to you what a dangerous game this would be — if we tried it, we'd basically be asking twenty women from *Wolf* and *Friendly* to offer themselves up as 'trades' for the survivors. When we met to exchange these women with the Pions, we'd even turn them over to Pion escort. We'd just have to intercept them on their way back to the Pion tunnels.

The advantage to all this would be simple: we'd force the Pions to bring the people we were trying to rescue out into an agreed-upon space, allowing us to control the circumstances.

It wasn't a great plan, and Matt, Rufus and Charlie knew that. But there weren't too many other options — if we didn't offer the trade, the survivors would stay in some dark back-tunnel deep in Pion territory, where we couldn't get at them.

"Our two squads have nine women total," Rufus observed, narrowing his mismatched eyes as he glanced at Charlie.

"We'd want to keep two or three in kit, and visible up front during the trade. Otherwise they might start wondering where our woman officers were," Charlie nodded slowly. "Good core of highly-trained ladies there, though."

"Gwen has three on her half squad as well. We can fill in the rest from SF. I'm sure we'll have enough volunteers," Matt pitched in.

Karen, Andrea and I didn't really need to be there for this — the three shooters were figuring out everything.

"We keep one of our squads at the site of the trade, use the other for the ambush on the way back?" Rufus asked after that, and Charlie nodded.

"Make it look good at the swap — like we've got all our people there. The Pions might have a rough idea of how many Branchers come with a ship... if they do, then *Wolf* having an extra team will work to our advantage," Charlie was virtually thinking out loud.

They went on for a couple more minutes, pointing out different criteria that would need to be met — the kind of location we'd want for the swap, and more importantly, the sort of tunnels we'd want the Pions moving the women back through.

Karen and I were feeling so redundant that, no word of a lie, we started playing tick-tack-toe on a pad while we waited. That probably sounds horribly irresponsible — this was a meeting about the safety of not just the twenty *North Carolinas*, but also of everyone engaged in their rescue...

But really, would you get in the way of Charlie, Rufus and Matt when they were in the planning groove? Didn't think so. Us ship-shooting types sometimes need to stand (or sit) aside and wait for the bullet-point summary.

"Are you two playing tick-tack-toe?" Charlie's question had an edge of friendly incredulousness.

Karen's eyebrow arched and she shook her head, "Of course not. That would be thoughtless."

"Callous and unbecoming," I added as I dropped an 'x' in to block Karen's line.

She countered with an 'o' that got her another line anyway. Just can't win with her... don't know why you'd want to.

I looked up fleetingly as she reset the board, "So, have it figured out?"

Charlie nodded, "Yes. Would you like to hear it now or later?"

Karen beat me again, just like that, and I pulled my hand away from the pad, "Now is good."

Shaking his head and hiding a smile (I *think*), Charlie filled me in.

Chapter Nineteen

Combined Planning

Holly grinned toothily and her head swung downward, then moved from left to right, "Sooo, bad is what that. Good bad see my meaning?"

That one caused me to blink a couple of times as my brain tried to follow the syntax. Then I nodded, "Yeah, we're playing dirty."

We'd just filled Holly in on what Charlie, Rufus and Matt had decided, adding a few more qualifications about the sort of place we'd need to do the exchange, and the amount of help we expected to need (or not to need) from the Canary warriors.

Charlie, Rufus and Matt were reluctant about having too much involvement from the Canaries, because there was no way to be sure of their discipline. Yes, I suppose you can argue this is another case of us underestimating them — assuming they were incapable of understanding our advanced tactical thinking or whatever — but I look at it differently.

An ambush to retrieve the twenty women we'd turn over to the Pions absolutely had to be precise. Many lives would be on the line. Now, the Canaries were no doubt smart enough to understand the importance of our planning, but culturally, their values were quite different.

What if they decided to attack at a different time than we'd planned for, because in their experience — with their weapons — it made more sense? Maybe it would work better than our way, or maybe it'd put our people at risk. It didn't make sense to take that chance: Charlie and Rufus knew exactly how to orchestrate this operation, and it was better to avoid the complications of integrating their warriors (and their rather unrefined combat style) into our op teams. Pardon the cliché again, but lives were literally depending on them.

"Stupid not the Pions and they know," Holly had sobered slightly, and now she looked at me squarely. "Smelling traps."

"We'll take our chances. We're hoping to catch them off guard by waiting until they're taking the women back. That's why we need a good place to ambush them on the way," I hope I didn't sound patronizing there.

Holly gave a single, slow, somewhat exaggerated nod, "Best is then."

God this is annoying to write. Also, I should mention that I could be getting some of it wrong. You know how sometimes you can look at a jumbled word or sentence and read it as if it were correct, missing the mistake because your brain automatically reorganizes it? Well it's quite possible that I'm remembering Holly's exact dialogue incorrectly for that reason. I've looked back through our recordings and notes in the archives, and transcribed as much as I can, but there's stuff (like this meeting) that weren't on any cameras, and we weren't recording on our comm logs. Usually I can muddle my way through on the dialogue for such meetings by talking to the other participants, but I wasn't really in the mood to go back to Pion rock as prep for this book.

So apologies if the poorly-syntaxed dialogue doesn't sound authentically Canary. I think it's ironic that I just made up the word 'syntaxed'...

Anyway, Holly was agreeing that this was our best chance.

"Warriors out of ambushy, attack Pion tunnels timely same?"

I frowned, "Depends. How quickly do you think they'll respond to an ambush?"

"Fast how is. Way in we get, block em up for the war start."

Holly had raised yet another good point — the Pions would doubtless send reinforcements to assist their team escorting the women when we launched our ambush. How would they find out? The Pions and the Canaries had been fighting in these tunnels for centuries. I don't know *how* they communicated so effectively from one end of their complex to the other, but they did have a way.

If we jumped the escort bringing the women in, even if we shot them all down in the first volley, there was an even chance the Pions would get wind of it and come for us.

So having Holly's warriors in position to intercept reinforcements, or to attack the Pion tunnels as a diversion, could buy time for our recovery operation.

I thus nodded again to Holly, "Alright, so now we just need a good spot for the swap."

"Have," she replied, meaning she had one in mind.

Moving deeper into Pion rock is almost counter-intuitive. Your instincts generally tell you to get out of that place — to get as close to the outside as you can, and to stay there. Only grim things can happen in the central levels of the colony.

Holly had a spot in mind for our exchange, though, so we had to check it out. We weren't traveling too heavily either — it was just me, Charlie, Rufus, and a half dozen Canary warriors. We were hoping not to call too much attention to ourselves, and since we hadn't started the war with the Pions yet, we had to hope there'd be no trouble that would have required the assistance of the rest of Charlie's and Rufus' squads.

Imagine how comforting such hopes were in the dark center of Pion rock.

Yeah, not very.

"Here places," Holly turned a corner in the dark corridor and led us into an open area. "Gymansium."

That's not a typo, she actually pronounced it 'guy-man-sium'. The room was, of course, a fitness centre — one of the relatively austere fitness facilities that the corporation behind XV-001 had installed for its personnel. The room likely had once been full of exercise machines, but after a couple of centuries they were all gone... I'd guess treadmills and weight machines and such had all been broken down and their parts turned into weapons or other tools.

No one can say the Pions and the Canaries aren't resourceful.

"Large, empty, reasonably central," Rufus took a couple of steps past Holly and looked around the open room down the barrel of his MAG-90.

"How many approaches?" it was Charlie's turn to finish Rufus' thought, and Holly grinned gummily.

"Just is two. To Canaries is the one and to Pions elsewise," was her answer, and Charlie started to frown.

Taking a couple of steps past Holly in a different direction than Rufus, he looked down the barrel of his own weapon and started counting the very obvious doors.

There were four — one in each wall.

"Holly, you savages do know how to count, don't you?" I asked that with a little bit of humor, and she cackled.

"Gravie plates now is gone other in-two," she explained.

That's to say, the gravity plating was down in the other two corridors leading into the gym, which didn't make them impassable, just incredibly easy to secure. Fighting in zero-gee is not something any proficient fighter wants to do — if you get hung up floating in the middle of a corridor with no handholds in reach, you're as good as dead. Combat in such situations is thus reliant on bouncing (in a controlled manner) from surface to surface, and having to deal with potential adversaries in every direction — up and down included.

But fighting from a gee position against a zero-gee opponent is different. Think of it this way... Pions' greatest asset in combat is their closing speed — as soon as you see them, they're clubbing in your skull or tearing off your face. You don't get any warning time. But what if they try to charge at you through zero-gee?

Well, they float.

Now, don't get me wrong, they can move fast, pulling themselves along the walls, but they're still just floating, unable to really take advantage of explosive bursts of speed that come with the human body in gravity.

One good Special Brancher with a MAG-90 could thus stand in the doorways to these two grav-free corridors and stop onslaughts of dozens of Pion warriors, simply because those warriors would be 'bogged down' by the zero-gee.

In effect, then, there were only two usable ways into this room... which meant we could control the way the Pions would come in with their survivors, and the way they'd leave with their prize women.

"I think it could work," Charlie nodded slowly, thinking all those things as he continued to sweep the room.

"We'll just need to find a good ambush site in the corridor," Rufus added, and Charlie spared him another glance, though didn't say what he was thinking (that Rufus was finishing his sentences again).

Those two were very in line with their tactical thinking, that's sure enough. They headed out the Pion-side entrance and started scouting, leaving me alone with Holly and her warriors.

I said nothing, and they kindly obliged me by doing the same.

CHAPTER TWENTY

VOLUNTEERS

"You're not going to be one of the women, so don't even think it. Let alone say it."

Not my most friendly greeting, but when Karen came through the hatch into my cabin wearing an expression that blared 'troubled thoughts', I knew exactly what was going on in her mind.

Of course she wanted to be with the twenty volunteers who were going to be essential to this piece of theatre — they were her people as much as they were mine, and her natural instinct was to be there with them. Rightly so.

Karen had stopped and shut the hatch behind her, a quizzical look on her face, "I was wondering if one of my shoes was in here. I'm missing a left shoe."

Yes, I am brilliant. Way to jump the gun, eh?

I must have started turning red, and I definitely started to stammer as I laid the pad I'd been reading on the floor next to my chair, "Uh... left shoe... uh... how do you lose one shoe..."

I got to my feet and avoided eye contact, and then turned around and checked behind the chair. No shoe there.

"Nothing here... I don't seem to ever remember you kicking shoes off in a violent manner. And wouldn't you notice leaving here with only one shoe?" Watch me back-pedal like a cyclist, it's great.

I stopped stammering when Karen's hand slid up my right arm, and nudged me to turn around. She was smiling in that way you smile when a small joke has distracted you from much darker thoughts...

"I was kidding, I always make sure I have both my shoes before I go anywhere," she said softly. "The first thing you said was the thing."

I let out a sigh and shook my head, "You're learning way too much from Lia."

I unceremoniously pushed her back to the bed so she'd sit, and then lowered myself back into my chair with a groan, "So no. No you can't be one of the twenty unluckiest members of this crew."

Karen's smile faded and with a sigh, she looked down at her hands, "Yeah..."

She really hadn't thought she could join the volunteers... in fact, she'd *known* she couldn't. But she wanted to hear me say that — to back up her own conclusion — and understandably so.

This is another of the reasons why Karen's the best skipper... Flag Officer now I guess... around. She cares so much about her crews, and it kills her to put them in danger. But she does it anyway. That probably sounds cold, but it is as it should be.

You can't command if you can't put people you care about in dangerous situations when necessary. That's what we all signed on for. Don't get me wrong, I think you know by now that we don't casually look for opportunities to put people in tough situations, but when they come, we can't always lead the way into the danger.

One of my great flaws as a CO, I think, is that too often I'm still that idiot who wants to jump out of the airlock before Charlie's team can clear the area. Hell, that I'm even with Charlie's assault teams at all is quite bad.

My editor just pointed out that Karen does that too, but... well, don't try to rationalize my opinions of Karen, mister editor!

Also, don't mistake me: plenty of other Defense Command skippers, in the Belt Squadron and out of it, cared as much as Karen did, and were nonetheless similarly able to detach themselves. That quality alone wasn't what made Karen the best, but in my opinion, it was part of the tapestry...

Sorry, I think I'm sliding off into Karen-worship here. One of my favorite subjects of all time, certainly, but not exactly helpful to the narrative.

Karen = Goddess. Moving on.

"Hey... you with me here?" ironically, my thoughts had drifted off as I'd been staring at Karen, and now she verbally prodded me.

I blinked a couple of times, "Yep. Yep, Charlie has already started putting together the volunteer force. It'll be six Branchers and fourteen SF."

"I heard. Carly's commanding, with Gwen Jameson as 2IC," Karen confirmed with a nod.

That in itself meant the twenty-woman party was going to have a hell of a lot of umph behind it. Six Branchers were inevitably going to be dangerous, but when Carly Henderson was leading, and Egesta veterans Gwen Jameson and Mikka Hong were along for the fight, it'd be a match for anything the Pions could throw at them.

That was what I was telling myself anyway. Sound like wishful thinking to you?

Karen took a deep breath and leaned back on the bed, planting her arms behind her to prop herself up at an angle, "I hate this, I have to be honest."

That sentiment actually surprised me a bit — no one ever has fun at Pion rock, but Karen had seemed to be doing relatively well. But then, that was Karen. Always appearing unflappable, no matter what she actually felt inside.

I shifted back in my chair with a groan, rubbing my eyes with the palms of my hand and yawning, "You know, I'm right there with you."

We sat in silence for a while, both contemplating what was to come, and enjoying the reassurance of each other's company.

Dealing with Pion rock — even with an impending war and prisoners to rescue — was much easier for me this time than it had been last, because she was there.

Sorry if that seems sappy to some of you, but it's just plain true.

Charlie, Rufus and Matt stood at the front of the gym on *Wolf's* rec deck, having just spent two hours selecting fourteen women from the fifty-one — yes, that's *fifty-one* — from *Wolf* and *Friendly* who'd volunteered to join the six Special Branchers. What I'm trying to emphasize is the point that we had announced we needed fourteen women to join the six Special Branchers, and fifty-one people turned up at the selection meeting.

Now, I know some of you think I'm laying it on with a trowel, but I have to say again how incredible the spacers of Defense Command, and particularly, *Wolf* and *Friendly* were. I've commanded both of those ships, so obviously I'm biased about them, but, *come on*. I'm not making up the numbers, they're on file in the fleet archives.

We said we needed fourteen people to be traded as veritable *chattel* (unarmed and in civvies) to the Pions, and fifty-one showed up. Obviously they knew it was going to be a ruse — that we weren't going to actually trade them — but as anyone who's seen a horror movie featuring the Pions knows, this could get messy. They weren't deluding themselves, they weren't underestimating their adversary... they were willing to offer themselves as bait in Pion rock so that we could get survivors back from *North Carolina*.

I can think of few more terrifying situations to ask people to go in to, yet here they were.

So if I'm using a trowel and laying this 'we have the greatest crews imaginable' stuff on thick, sorry. As far as I'm concerned, these men and women earn every scrap of praise I can give, and somehow I expect you understand that, so thank you.

Anyway, because of the number of volunteers, Charlie, Rufus and Matt had been forced to do quite a lot of sorting, and they did so by running some hand-to-hand drills. The most proficient in unarmed combat were selected, for reasons that I think must be obvious.

The fourteen who had been chosen were now drawn up in front of our three planners, and were looking somewhat tense.

Matt explained the plan to them, and as he did, Charlie and Rufus called in Carly and the rest of the Special Branch team that was going to be working with these volunteers — the Brancher ladies had been training at the far side of the gym, practicing their own (much more formidable) hand-to-hand skills.

Now Carly came up alongside Charlie with a thin smile, "So these are the volunteers?"

He nodded, "Brave people. Look after them."

She grinned, "What, not going to tell me to look after myself?"

"You always do," he chuckled.

Shelby McLaws had the watch on *Wolf's* bridge, and was pacing the deck none too comfortably. She, of course, was not destined to join this mission, but even just thinking about it unsettled her. Shelby doesn't mind admitting this now (she wouldn't have dreamed of saying it then) but she'd always, *always* been terrified of Pions. Shelby's not a scary-movie sort of person, largely because of an exceptionally bad dating experience had while watching one of the most spectacularly terrifying Pion movies around (even to we who've been down to the Pion rock).

I won't elaborate any more than that, but if you can ever get the story out of her, it is hilarious... in hindsight.

In any case, Shelby had the watch, so when the signal came in from Holly, she was the one to see it first.

"On screen two, please," she said with a charming southern-belle smile and the technician who held the watch for Sensors and Communications piped the signal to the appropriate display.

The message had been addressed to 'ship up there', not to me, so it wasn't like Shelby was opening my mail. After a *WolfNet* loading screen cycled up, Holly appeared with a gummy, pre-recorded grin, and Shelby contained a shudder.

These Canaries might be our allies, but they were also just plain disturbing to our Lieutenant McLaws... and to me... and to every other human from a civilized world, pardoning my 'civilization' hubris again.

"Got we day... be the three spins. Come the two spins and ladies too. We'll get readying."

Shelby winced at the syntax but thought she deciphered the message: the exchange would take place in three spins... roughly fifteen to eighteen hours from now... so we needed to be down there in about twelve hours to prep for it. By our clock, that put the operation just after lunch of the following day.

Shelby contained her uneasiness with the signal and turned back to the technician at Sensors and Communications, "Send that along to Rear Admiral Barron, Commodore McMaster, Major Peters and Major Chang, please. And to *Friendly*, if it wouldn't be too much trouble."

Of course it wasn't too much trouble — even if the man at Sensors and Communications hadn't been Shelby's subordinate, her polite and charming way of asking would have obliged him to cooperate.

We were going to be in Pion rock trading prisoners in half a day...

CHAPTER TWENTY-ONE
ASIDES

John Fiora and Daragh Ryan were meeting again, in what was mid-morning Earth time. We on *Wolf* were all sleeping (or making a futile attempt to sleep) because it was our night cycle, but you know how time zones can be.

"I think the bastards want control over the Mercury assault," Daragh leaned back in his chair opposite John's desk and grumbled out the comment.

Placing the pad he'd been reading on his ever-cluttered desk, John nodded, "Probably. So another whole *brigade*? There's no way the Guild is causing them that much trouble."

As asides go, this is going to be a dark one. Where's the one place in this solar system I think is worse than Pion rock?

"That's four brigades on Egesta," Daragh replied with a nod. "They're staging their bloody blockheads there. The bastard Emperor is going to demand we let them command the assault. I can just smell it."

They were obviously talking about Egesta, and specifically, the fact that the Imperial Army was moving large numbers of troops out to that rock. Now you know what this is all about, but at the time there was no way for John or Daragh or any of us to do more than guess.

Daragh's guess, though, was quite a good one. The Emperor knew his popularity had been seriously hurt by his support of the Caldecott Inquiries at the start of the war, and the relative calm of 2232 had been credited completely to John, Daragh, and their circle in Defense Command — those who had opposed Caldecott's plan.

If His Highness wanted to regain some of his popularity, he needed to be seen as contributing to the war effort, and that meant he needed to get his Imperial Army blockheads off Earth, and out to the Belt.

Now, thinking back to Egesta, remember how one armored brigade had shown up with enough tanks and heavy weapons to quell any resistance? Exactly, there was no reason to have two more brigades out there, and another on its way.

That was just about 10,000 blockheads on the rock... more than a match for the Guild, who if you'll recall, fielded maybe 1,000 hard core fighters when we were there. Unless the hundreds of thousands of other Guild members had taken up arms, there was no reason for the extra troops.

So this smelled like a staging exercise. The Emperor knew the assault on Mercury was one of our objectives, and he wanted to make sure his blockheads got as much of the glory as possible when the landings on the Mercury domes were made.

Seemed obvious enough, and there were no reports coming out of Egesta to suggest it was a bad assessment.

"Bastards are going to want the reins on our operation," Daragh muttered again. He didn't like the Emperor or the Army much.

John answered with a nod and a sigh, "Well, we'll deal with them as best we can. I've got a meeting with Craig MacDonald this afternoon, I'll give him a warning about it too."

Daragh nodded — the Foreign Secretary needed to be aware that the Emperor was starting to jockey for position. Neither of these men had forgotten Haley Briand's warning that the imperious Luther Gregory III was going to come after them as soon as the war was done, and if he was going after the heads of Defense Command, that meant he was going to come after the Parliament as well.

Once we beat the Martians, we'd have a constitutional crisis to deal with. Fun.

The meeting continued, of course, but I've pulled the ominous snippet from it already, so I'll just leave the rest to your imagination.

Several hours later, the receptionist sitting behind the desk at the Rock-Hard Drugs Pharmacy corporate headquarters on Belt Eleven looked up from her work to be greeted by Mark Gunney's smile.

Now, as you know, Mark was then (and still is now) as much a celebrity as any of the Belt Squadron veterans, so the pretty young receptionist recognized him instantly, and immediately gasped. This was *Mark Gunney*, wait until she told her girlfriends! They'd never believe her luck! But how much luck...?

Mark's reputation was, by that time, legendary.

"Good morning... Eve..." he smiled as he read the name plate on her desk, and she blushed.

"Good morning Captain Gunney... it's a real... honor to meet you..." she said breathily, and Mark kept the charm going.

"It's a pleasure to meet you. I'm hoping you can help me this morning."

"*Anything*," she blurted instantly, her hand fleetingly reaching back and scratching the side of her neck.

Mark's smile widened, "I need fertility drugs. *All* of your fertility drugs."

We don't have any vid recordings of Eve's reaction to those unexpected words, but Mark tells me it was priceless. Because, of course, Mark has a reputation, and reputations like his usually hinge on the opposite thing to what he was asking for.

"I... uh..."

Mark couldn't resist, and I can't blame him: "This Empire has been without a brood of Gunneys for far, far too long. I figure on 100 sons, and 100 daughters."

Eve really wasn't ready for that. Mark has a way of tossing people off their comfortable balance, and this was just too good an opportunity for him to pass up.

"That's... that's a lot," Eve stammered... then she surprised Mark. "I've always wanted kids."

Mark laughed, then shook his head, "We'll talk. Right now, can you call your boss?"

Eve had to shake herself mentally before she could do her job, and as she hit the intercom and called for the director of Belt Eleven's branch of Rock-Hard Drugs, she avoided eye contact with his still-smiling face.

Mark kept the charm going, and using a bit of his star power combined with the promise of Imperial compensation, he convinced the director to release all the doses of fertility drugs we needed. As it turned out, the brand Rock-Hard Drugs carried was never supposed to 'rot' (expire), so we wouldn't need to do follow-up shipments.

That suited me fine.

Mark made quick arrangements with the director to gain access to the Rock-Hard Drugs warehouse, so that his SF could go down with a couple of heavy landers and do the pickup.

When he finished with the director, he turned and headed for the door, but Eve stopped him with a smile and a piece of paper with her comm address on it.

She beamed at Mark, and Mark gave her a grin and a nod before leaving.

We got our drugs, and he got her number. Mark was on his game.

CHAPTER TWENTY-TWO
LEADING UP

"Everyone have their tracker?" Rufus returned to the front of the Special Branch briefing room and turned to survey the cluster of twenty volunteers he'd just moved through.

Nods were the only reply, and satisfied, Rufus laid the box of tracker bugs back down on the desk next to him, then put the lid back on. The women going into Pion custody wouldn't be carrying any comms, so it was necessary to put trackers on them, just in case.

We didn't use tracker bugs much these days — they'd been very useful tools in the pirate hunting days, but not during the war. The little guys were tiny — only the size of fleas — and they were smart. Usually they stayed in someone's scalp, but their tiny little AIs had the ability to recognize when they were being hunted, and to evade.

Unless you put someone in a scanner, a tracker bug was hard to locate. It could be *anywhere* on the body, creepy though some people (myself included) find that.

Rufus had planted a bug on each woman's neck, tapping them on the shoulder as he'd done it. As such, the ladies hadn't seen the bugs go on (they wouldn't know if one of the little guys accidentally slipped onto the floor, which would be bad) but his asking made certain that he hadn't forgotten anyone.

Pulling out his comm, Rufus activated our standard tracking program, then waited as the unit made contact with each of the bugs. After just a few seconds, twenty signals registered, each one colored green. If the bug had fallen off, and was no longer detecting a warm body under its itsy-bitsy feet, the icon would go blue.

That's one thing we learned back in the old days of Syndicate fighting: your bug needed to be able to tell you when someone found and removed it.

Right now it told Rufus that the women were good to go, so with another, final nod, he slid his comm back into its belt holster, "Alright everyone, I want to wish you the very best of luck. We'll be covering you, but stay on your toes."

He was really speaking for the benefit of the regular SF in the room — it went without saying that Carly and the Special Branchers would be ready for whatever occurred.

With that, they all filed out of the room.

Charlie was standing with Karen and I in the dark reception lobby in Pion rock. We'd come over in regular and assault shuttles with over sixty Special Branchers and SF, and that number didn't include Rufus' team or the twenty volunteers.

We were prepared for a scrap.

As prepared as we could be, anyway. I suppose this point is getting whipped to death, but Pion wasn't a place where any of us 'civilized' types could be fully prepared for a fight.

It really, truly, honestly is as bad as a nightmare. And fighting nightmares is not something we have a lot of experience with.

"The shuttle with the volunteers is on its way down from *Wolf*," Matt Baxter was sliding his comm back into its belt pouch as he came over to us with that news. "Jim also received a comm from Belt Eleven, Mark's on his way back."

I nodded, "Good... tell Holly, would you, Matt?"

The Briton nodded, "I will."

Matt moved on to find Holly, and Karen, Charlie and I continued to stand in silence. We probably should have been trying to keep loose — to tell bad jokes and to banter — but we didn't have that in us. There are times, as you know, when even *we* can't be as inane as we'd like.

Charlie glanced at his watch, "We're going in... three hours."

I nodded without reply, and Karen took a deep breath, "Yes we are."

Rufus' shuttle actually docked before the one carrying the twenty volunteers; as his squad cleared the lock and started to coordinate with Charlie's Branchers, and the four left from *Friendly's* detail, Rufus joined us.

"They're all bugged and as ready as they'll ever be," the Chinese man announced as he settled into a squared-off stance beside Charlie.

"Good way to put it," I replied with a sharp nod.

I don't think I'm going to try to drag this out any longer. We'd needed to land early with all our people, just to make sure any last minute complications (meaning Holly and the Canaries getting pissy) could be dealt with. But Holly was good to her word, and the arrangements stood — her warriors were dressed for battle, and she was ready to go all in.

I still don't like the woman, or her society, but they were sticking with the agreement. I suppose I should respect that.

The shuttle with the volunteers docked moments later, and after that we all started to make our way down to the exchange room.

Rufus parted company with our column of SF and Special Branchers long before we got to the gym, taking his team (a full twelve bodies because two of *Friendly's* Branchers had joined them for this op, replacing the women who'd volunteered to join the hostage party) to the ambush site. He'd have to be in position and covered up before the Pions came through that area for the trade, so we wished him luck and sent him on his way.

If all went to plan, we wouldn't actually see him until we were back on *Wolf*, or at the very least, until we were all back at the locks, ready to depart.

Charlie and his Special Branch squad (similarly augmented by the last two of *Friendly's* Branchers) led the way for our column, with only a handful of Holly's warriors out ahead of them. Behind Charlie's team were thirty SF guards under Matt Baxter's orders. The twenty women came next, and then the last fifteen SF, led by Omar Cunningham, brought up the rear... along with Karen and me. We weren't leading the way — neither Charlie nor Matt would allow it, in case the Pions had staged an ambush for *us*.

Does that sound paranoid? Well, maybe it is, but Pion rock is the last place in the solar system where you want to discover you've made incorrect assumptions about security.

We weren't arguing with Charlie and Matt on this one.

It was bad enough that we had to be there in the first place. I should clarify that Karen didn't *have* to be there — the Pions didn't know her the same way they knew Charlie and me — but she wasn't letting me go into nightmare-land alone, which I hugely appreciated and wasn't going to turn down. Anyway, that was the makeup of our column.

Holly was right behind Karen and me, protected by a half dozen of her own warriors. She'd be there to act as a diplomatic intermediary, and to allay any suspicion that her tribe was going to be causing mischief. If she was in the exchange chamber, her warriors presumably wouldn't be willing to start any wars — she'd be in harm's way.

Yeah, like she didn't have the guts to start a war herself if necessary...

After a long walk, we reached the chamber, and found it quite empty. That was good, as one of our slight concerns had been that the Pions would arrive first. In itself, that wouldn't have been the end of the plan, but it would have meant they were being a little more cautious and attentive than we'd have liked.

But no, we were clear for the moment.

"I'll secure the rear," Matt announced as our large party pooled in the chamber, and then he began barking orders to a couple of the junior SF officers with him. Twenty of our green-clad shooters exited back the way we'd come, setting up secure positions with good fields of supporting fire.

If the Pions smelled a trap and tried to flank us, they'd meet resistance. No telling if that resistance would be equal to the task of stopping an onslaught, though — even *Matt's* SF had to be very wary when dealing with Pions.

Omar Cunningham deployed the rest of the SF around the chamber, putting three each at the side entrances (remember, to the corridors with no gravity) and then spreading the rest of the guards around the twenty women. Charlie's Special Branchers formed a loose, open line in front of the volunteers and their guards, with Charlie in the middle.

Karen and I edged our way forward to stand next to him. Now that we were in an open and reasonably secured area, he was fine with us presenting ourselves at the front end of the Defense Command formation.

Holly followed us up, swaggering with her hands resting jauntily on her hips, "Fancy look to the oprat, is."

She was saying she was impressed by our show of force, but the way she said it was a message all its own. What she was thinking, I'm sure, was that we could bring out all these well-armed, uniformed, healthy-seeming shooters... and she figured we'd only last ten minutes if we really got into it.

Well, I hoped we wouldn't find out, one way or another.

Time would tell... we were half an hour from the 'exchange'.

CHAPTER TWENTY-THREE

BAD TIMING

Some days the timing just works against you, and this was one of those days.

Sort of.

Andrea Kiley was in command in orbit while we were waiting for the exchange to happen, and both *Wolf* and *Friendly* were at full standby readiness. If things came to their very worst, one of those ships might have been asked to try to drill a laser into Pion rock, potentially to crack a tunnel, but more likely just to cause a massive seismic disruption.

One of the things about Pion rock that was so insidious was that it was hard to chew with energy weapons — XV-001 was set up to mine its minerals for use in high-heat applications like reactors, after all. Cutting through to decompress a tunnel would not be easy... or terribly smart, since the anti-decompression compartmentalization likely wouldn't work.

But if you hit a hard rock with a barrage of laser fire, you could potentially shake things up — create a distraction that could help buy us time to run if things got messy.

That was why Andrea and *Wolf* were at standby... circumstances demonstrated that there were other good reasons to be ready for action.

"Sensor contact... it's out there ma'am, but I have one... two... three now ma'am, closing our location at 185 kps," Andrea eavesdropped on the report as one of the Sensors and Communications technicians delivered it to Felicia Khalid.

Felicia didn't even need to be asked by Andrea, she immediately ordered the contacts to go up on screen one, and to get the technician to clarify bearings.

"That's a vector from the Asteroid colonies," Jim Hannigan observed in a dry tone from his position behind the operations consoles.

Andrea nodded, having already made that determination herself, but happy enough to hear it again from her XO. This looked like a return of the bastards who'd driven *North Carolina* here, possibly intent on shooting up the rescue ships.

"Three of them," Andrea said softly, though she tells me her mind was in the process of taking flight.

A lot of feelings were battling within Andrea, and the first one to appear was anger. She hadn't known *North Carolina* nearly as well as *Lion*, or obviously *Wolf*, but for the third time in the last year of fighting, she was finding herself witness to a crew being gutted or victimized in some way, and that absolutely infuriated her.

To avoid too much melodrama, this part of her psyche was very keen on revenge.

But — and she credits this to the realization she'd made back in *The Dark Cruise*, as well as to Wes' words to her back at Belt Two — that voice in her mind was no longer the loudest.

To use Andrea's words, she was starting to get her wits back in order.

Three ships were a potential problem, but not an insurmountable one. If there was indeed a Martian destroyer and destroyer escort, backed by one pirate, *Wolf* and *Friendly* would have a solid chance in a fight against them. If Mark was here with *Cheetah*, there'd be no contest at all... the Martians would undoubtedly turn and run immediately, not willing to risk their own destruction.

But with only two Defense Command ships on their screens, the Martians had to feel... ambitious. The odds were more or less even, so the temptation to get into a shootout was inevitably there.

And six months earlier, Andrea would have undoubtedly been very glad of that fact. She'd have wanted a fight — she'd have been desperate to get her hands (or lasers and mags) on the underhanded bastards who'd done this to *North Carolina*, even if it meant putting herself and her ships at risk.

Not anymore. Certainly, she wanted them dead, and she wanted them to hurt... but her perspective was balanced again, and she knew it wasn't a good idea to get into this fight if it could be avoided.

Battlelink had been up since we'd landed for the exchange — it would make any orders to fire on the rock that much easier to carry out. Now, Lieutenant Commander Fahd Haas, Matt's XO, frowned on screen two, "What do you think, skipper?"

Fahd had been appointed XO by Andrea just before she'd moved over to *Wolf*, so they worked together quite well.

Andrea advanced towards the screens at the front of *Wolf's* bridge, folding her arms as she did. Her eyes narrowed in thought, and soon options were running through her mind at a solid clip.

"Bring our reactor levels up to full," she said after a moment, then her eyes moved to the local space map on screen one. "Felicia, show me the local rocks please."

What Andrea was referring to — and what Felicia instinctively knew — was that Andrea needed to see what small bits of rock were floating out there, in the general area around Pion rock. These chunks weren't particularly large, but in a tactical sense they could be very helpful.

Screen one flashed briefly, and then the rocks appeared, a few of them being good candidates for what Andrea had in mind. She took a second, looked each one over, and then pointed to her choice.

"That one. Fahd, Felicia, start sending burst transmissions to that rock. Shelby, mark whatever course you'd think was best if we were going to try to draw those bastards past that rock. Keep us close to Pion, though — close as you can."

Shelby didn't need to have that elaborated on — remember, she'd been Andrea's Helm and Navigation Officer for years aboard *Friendly*, before following her skipper over to *Wolf*. Felicia was slightly less certain, never having seen this trick used.

"Stick close, Fahd," Andrea said that quietly, and then she watched *Wolf's* icon on the screen as Shelby McLaws fired the engines and gently nudged our frigate out from Pion rock on a clever angle.

For a minute, this theatre continued, and *Wolf* and *Friendly* cruised away from us and the rock with increasing speed, all the while following a course that seemed a little too innocent.

To explain what's happening (if you've never seen this trick in action before) let me switch perspective to that of the Martian commander. I'm not going to elaborate on who that bastard was, but I did have the decided *pleasure* of meeting him later, after the war. I'll save the stories about him for books about those years... presuming I write them. Presuming my editors *let* me write them. Maybe I should stop abusing them so they let me... nah I'll take my chances.

Anyway, what he saw was something that looked a little *too* good to be true: two Defense Command ships, seemingly without escort, moving away from the rock on a course that he could easily intercept *if* he rushed for them, passing a large piece of rock on the way.

Meanwhile, they were sending low-power signals to that rock — signals, he assumed, they thought he couldn't see.

Now, you can hide plenty of things in the lee of a rock in space. Remember all the way back to *The Rogue Commodore*, when Mark Gunney tucked *Honesty* behind a rock over Asteroid Theta? Exactly.

There wasn't actually anything behind this rock, but any Martian commander who was a crafty enough piece of... boy I nearly swore right there... who was enough of a bastard to do what had been done to *North Carolina*, would see the potential trap. And he'd have a strong enough sense of self-preservation not to spring it.

Sure, he could ride in to see if it was a bluff, but what if it wasn't? The potential risk wasn't worth the reward, especially considering that even if it was a bluff, the odds of him winning the ensuing gunfight would at least be relatively even.

Basically, victory wasn't certain enough to make this move worth the risk.

So, to return to *Wolf's* bridge...

"They're reversing drives... backing out the way they came!" Felicia had a little excitement in her voice as she passed on that report, and Andrea nodded and smiled thinly.

"Love it when that works," she said quietly again, silencing the part of her mind — and it was still a sizable part — that was grumbling about giving chase.

Wolf and *Friendly* were required to stay over the rock, in case we needed them.

"Get Adrienne's squadron in their cockpits. I want rotating sweeps around Pion rock and local space, in case they try to creep in from another angle," Andrea's voice was a bit louder with that order. She was staying on the defensive, she wouldn't go looking for blood.

"Let's hope," she said sharply, "that they're not fool enough to come back."

Much of her really hoped the Martians were gone. Part of her still wanted to get into a vicious, care-free murder fight, no matter the cost or consequences.

But let's not pretend this wasn't *huge* progress. Andrea was getting back to the same sort of decision making she'd always been known for...

In the meantime, we were about to start our delightful little exchange. Changing chapters... *now*.

Chapter Twenty-Four
Best Laid

I don't know why people try *laying* plans. We all know that best laid plans can turn out badly, so my suggestion is simple: don't lay down plans... carry them, or sit them in a chair, or float them in zero-gee... just don't lay them down. It's when they're laying down that they always seem to fall apart.

Hm. That really was a horrible piece of attempted humor. I apologize. But I'm still leaving it in.

Watching the Pions file into the far side of the gym was a genuinely skin-crawling experience. I wish I could say the Pions looked somehow more sinister or evil than the Canaries, but to be entirely honest, they were just equally filthy and heinous looking.

What the Pions had on the Canaries in this situation was... well, I don't think 'connotation' is the right word, but it's close. We had these bastards built up in our minds as devils — as being worse than the Canaries because they were our enemies. So that made us, or at least me, see them as more sinister, even if a neutral observer mightn't notice any difference.

Perspective and such.

Anyway, a dozen Pion warriors led the way, and following them was their leader, Josie. If I say that Josie was in no way as sophisticated and charming as Holly, will that be saying enough?

I shifted my weight from one foot to the other as they came in — I was getting a little too anxious, and I wasn't proving particularly adept at hiding it. I spared a glance to Karen, and her confidence seemed painted on her face, but her eyes were darting from Pion to Pion as they entered.

That meant that even the unflappable Karen was a bit anxious. This is what these people do to you. Doesn't matter if you're a combat professional, they make you anxious.

I looked the other way at Charlie, but his eyes were locked firmly ahead. I started to frown at his composure, and through a locked jaw (to hide any visible indications that he was talking) he waved me off, "Yes, I'm anxious. Not showing it."

I actually smiled at that, despite myself. I didn't even bother wondering how Charlie knew what I was thinking anymore — years of rolling together did have that effect.

But now probably wasn't the best time to marvel at it.

Holly stepped forward two paces and held up her hands towards Josie, "Uniforms bringing for trade?"

Josie stepped forward two paces from the line of warriors who'd accompanied her, eyes darting over our uniformed SF and Special Branchers. She wore the same sort of arrogant smirk Holly had when looking at our people — we didn't intimidate her in the least.

Then she made a strange movement that rocked her shoulders and twisted her head from side to side, "Terms tradeon is ours, Holly."

I should paint a slightly better picture of Josie for you, since any movie that includes her presents her as a purring savage sex kitten who most red-blooded humans who are attracted to women would want to be devoured by. Well, Josie had no teeth, she was filthy, was slightly shorter than Holly, and had much worse fashion sense — her ragged clothing was barely adequate to cover her. She was, if I recalled correctly, almost Holly's age, and she was a conniving, cut-throat woman.

So no purring was involved.

Anyway, as Josie issued that statement — that this trade would be on Pion terms — I decided it was my time to do some solid posturing, "Josie, good to see you. Give me back my crew or I'll cut your throat."

Hmm, no, there's no real way I can make that statement sound any less savage than it was — I was posturing, I needed to go big.

Josie cackled (all Pions and Canaries cackle when they laugh), "Bear balls big and sec men bolden up him."

What she was saying was that having a room full of SF was making me braver than I deserved to be, which was clearly wrong. I was anything but brave at this moment.

"Try me," I taunted her, taking a step forward. Now, being taller and clearly healthier than the meagerly-nourished Josie didn't really have the intimidating effect one might hope for, but the fact that I was stepping up to challenge her would hopefully demonstrate how serious I was about this.

Before Josie could react to me, though, Karen had stepped further forward than either Holly or myself, and with that classy smile she could wear in any situation, she tilted her head slightly and met Josie's eyes, "Are Pions good for their word?"

"Be who?" Josie sidled sideways to line up a glare at Karen, and was met with a shrug.

"Holly's dubbed me 'Master'... with good reason, if I do say so myself. And don't listen to Ken... to *bear*. He won't cut your throat."

I blinked and frowned — for a fleeting second, I wondered what Karen was at, because polite diplomacy tended not to work well on the Pions. I'd learned that last time... you had to posture, you had to try to go toe-to-toe with them, and make it worth their while to obey.

"Right damned," Josie grinned, showing us her lovely toothless gums.

Karen crouched slightly now and took a couple of steps towards Josie, stopping just a meter from the Pion leader.

"I, however, will cut out your heart, and show it to you, if you don't oblige us. Do you need me to translate that into your ridiculous syntax, or is it clear enough?"

Karen's back was to me, but she told me after that she was still smiling her painted-on smile as she delivered that icy threat. The tone was one I've heard Karen use only on a few occasions — one being when she was dealing with the Governor of Egesta, if you remember that scene back in *The Independent Squadron*.

When Karen goes cold... when she decides to release all the anger that she so often keeps restrained... you don't want to be the person (Pion or otherwise) she's staring at.

She definitely hadn't misread the diplomatic style here.

Josie's grin faded, and she leaned in closer to hiss at Karen, "Master teeth I could use for me."

Karen nodded a couple of times, "You do need dental work."

Not being familiar with the term dental, Josie swung her head from side to side, rather in the style of an animal (yes, I know, being arrogant, civilized guy again), then decided it was better not to try to trade threats with the 'Master' before her.

It takes a lot to intimidate a Pion leader. It takes the threat of righteous fury that only a goddess can provide.

Josie waved a hand back to her warriors, then straightened up slightly from her crouch, causing Karen to do the same.

"My part and does it my way," Josie's voice was sharper — she wasn't playing with us anymore, which was both good and bad, I think.

Karen nodded very smoothly, "Thank you. I'll wait over there… don't make me wait too long."

With that, she did something no one ever does: she presented her back to a Pion. I probably don't have to tell you why turning your back on a Pion is usually a bad idea, but Karen was making a point. She wasn't afraid of this leader.

When she arrived at my side again, she turned sharply on her heel and locked her jaw before speaking very, very quietly, "How was that?"

"Great… the heart thing, nice touch."

"Yeah…" somehow, even when her words were barely audible, Karen sounded slightly nervous (I know, *nervous*), "…I should probably read some biology books. I don't know if that's even possible."

I almost shrugged, but restrained the gesture to try to keep our chat hidden, "I'm sure you'd find a way."

Gruesome banter, I'm sure you'll agree. And you might think Karen's threat was an empty one for show. Well…

The first five *North Carolinas* were pushed out of the Pion entrance into the gym, their eyes widening and then relaxing slightly with relief as they saw the room was full of DC SF and Special Branch.

I nearly let go a sigh of relief as I saw them, then I realized there were *only* five.

Holly frowned and studied this move with a sweeping gaze, then went forward to Josie, "Twenty was."

Josie grinned again, and looked past Holly at us, "Twenty is. Traps isn't. Five by time, so traps isn't."

The exact words that went through my head at that moment, and you have to forgive my language, were these: *That clever little savage bitch.*

What she was saying was simple: she didn't trust us, and as such, she was only going to trade our people back *five at a time.* That meant at least fifteen of our volunteers would be in Pion custody and presumably back in the Pion tunnels before we got all of the *North Carolinas* out.

Our ambush would be worthless. If we ambushed the Pions taking the first five back to the Pion tunnels, they'd kill the fifteen *North Carolinas* they still had in custody. If we waited until the last trade and ambushed the final five volunteers, the Pions could kill the first fifteen volunteers.

That clever, savage little bitch. She was bartering with the lives of Defense Command personnel, and she was grinning about it.

Karen took two steps forward and narrowed her eyes, "That *wasn't* the deal."

"Dealed fuck. Way be… or dead."

Amazing how sentences that make no sense can make perfect sense.

Karen straightened and nodded, pulling out her comm, "We do it five at a time. Make the arrangements to convoy the survivors back in groups of five."

That message was meant for two people: it would tell Matt Baxter that he'd need to move the *North Carolinas* safely back to Canary territory in four separate groups, which would be a tactical challenge all its own, and she was warning Rufus Chang that the ambush plan was gone to hell.

We wouldn't need to say any more than what Karen had said to Rufus — he'd immediately recognize the implications of doing the trade in batches of five and he'd have to figure out a way to deal with it.

Grinning little Josie had buggered us.

And Karen didn't like it any more than the rest of us, so she took two more steps forward as she slid her comm back into its holster, "We'll be seeing your heart later, Josie."

I think you can tell Karen was angry. Josie's grin faded again, and she stepped in closer to Karen, "Master talk-big."

Karen smiled and tilted her head sideways, "A right I've earned over the years. Those crew better be untouched."

Josie tossed her head, a little frustration at Karen's refusal to be intimidated starting to gain purchase, "Respect the uniform was. Now five women, them give."

As the Pion leader tossed a nod in the direction of Carly's volunteers, Karen straightened, "Of course. Charlie, bring up the first five."

Charlie turned around and waved for two of his officers to lead five forward. If they were going to do this in four batches, he was going to want at least one of the six Special Branchers in each party. And Carly was up first.

Trying their best (and frankly failing) to look meek and afraid, the first five volunteers were sent across the gap between the Pion line and our own. Five *North Carolinas* were sent across at the same time. Trade one of four complete.

I stood silently and watched as Carly and her four fellow volunteers were pressed roughly into the Pion entrance, and I have to say, I started to let slip some of my already tenuous self-discipline.

We shouldn't have given any indication that we cared about the twenty women we were trading — that was as good as tipping our hand to the clever Josie that we hadn't thought we were actually going to *lose* them.

But I ground my teeth together and then shifted a grim stare down to Josie all the same. There is something fundamentally horrid-feeling about participating in a trade of humans. My mood was rapidly getting to Egesta levels, but here, in Pion rock, I didn't feel the same obligation to be restrained.

We weren't protecting thousands of innocents here.

First chance I got, I could well kill Josie. If Karen didn't get her first.

Hopefully — yes, that's not a mistake, *hopefully* — we'd get that chance.

CHAPTER TWENTY-FIVE
ON THE FLY

Rufus watched silently as the first party of five volunteers was pushed down the corridor in which he was located. He and the rest of his team were still in hiding, ready to launch their ambush, but now he knew he couldn't...

Waiting until the Pions and the women they were escorting were safely out of earshot, he drew his comm and activated its connection to the trackers the volunteers were wearing. He had to see where the ladies ended up. If he knew where in the Pion tunnels they went, then he could hopefully launch his team on a recovery mission while Holly's warriors started the war.

The chances of that going well were not good, though, and he knew it.

Silence dominated as Rufus watched the green icons move — everyone in the squad had heard Karen's message, but every man and woman in the ambush party knew they had to wait for their Major to make the call about how to respond.

These were Special Branchers. They were extraordinarily aware of the need not to go off half-cocked.

The green icons halted well short of known Pion tunnels, and only several minutes away from the very place where he was lying in wait.

Rufus' eyes narrowed at the stoppage, and then he waited patiently... one second... two seconds... three...

After they hadn't moved for a whole minute, Major Chang started to reorient his thinking. Perhaps the Pions were being efficient — they knew they couldn't bring all the *North Carolinas* to the gym for trade at once, in case it was a trap, but running four trips of five people from the gymnasium all the way to their own tunnels would take hours.

So perhaps they'd moved all the *North Carolinas* to a staging point far enough away from the gym to be presumed safe from an ambush, but close enough to facilitate a speedy exchange. Crafty, logical... and an opening.

Checking to make sure the way was clear, Rufus tapped his headset comm and selected a frequency that only Special Branchers would receive — his team and everyone in Charlie's as well.

"They have a staging area about five minutes from our ambush site. We'll move there and prepare to take it by force, as soon as the last batch of *North Carolinas* are safely in our hands."

Needless to say, he whispered that so quietly that the Branchers only barely heard it. He then did hand gestures (visible in the shadowy corridor thanks to night vision kit) and his people moved out.

Charlie didn't so much as blink to acknowledge that he'd heard something. He was front and center with Karen and me, so any sign that he'd been in communication with someone watching the trades from behind Pion lines would have been bad.

After a few minutes, another five *North Carolinas* arrived in the bay, and Charlie turned around to wave the next five volunteers to be brought forward by his team. As he made that turn, he nudged me with his elbow, making it look like he'd just accidentally bumped into me.

I turned after the bump, as if to look at the women we were sending over next, and as our faces pointed casually away from Josie, he filled me in through a locked jaw: "Staging point five minutes out. He takes it when we have all the survivors."

I didn't nod, I didn't react, I just turned back with my same dark glare and shot daggers at Josie with my eyes. If she thought I was still hopelessly hating her, maybe she wouldn't realize we were in a better position than she thought we were in.

Her eyes darted from me back to Karen, who was still up close, still staring at her with cool disdain, and steely eyes. It's a look that no one ever wants to get from Karen, but some unfortunate people do. Often one of the last things those people see.

I kept my façade up, and tried to make sure the minor relief I felt at knowing where our volunteers were being held didn't show through. I don't think it was difficult to hide, though — there was still rather more anger than anything else.

As the next batch of *North Carolina* survivors passed me with thankful expressions, I did nod to them in turn. While I was standing there stewing about the lives we were putting on the line, these twenty spacers and officers from Captain Kishko's valiant old frigate were again being redeemed from grim fates.

These men and women had survived months hiding over Jupiter, and now they'd survived Pion rock. Realizing that, I decided that any who asked to be honorably discharged from the service would have my full support. People generally couldn't be discharged without medical grounds during the war, but these survivors had done more than their share.

Rufus Chang is a Special Brancher of the best quality. Like Charlie, he has an instinct for ground war that transcends anything you can get out of a book, and he uses that instinct judiciously. I can't remember if I've said this yet, but we were incredibly lucky to have him aboard *Wolf* with us after the Jupiter patrol. If we'd only had Charlie, we wouldn't have been able to carry off this rescue attempt because both the Pions and the Canaries remembered Charlie from our last visit, and if he wasn't there for the trade, it would have raised suspicions.

So having Rufus out there, using his instincts to move twelve Special Branch officers into position to assault the former-cafeteria holding the women and the *North Carolinas* who hadn't yet been traded, was pure gold.

There had been no proper reconnaissance of this area, so Rufus didn't know all the approaches, the angles, or the places where a Pion ambush might be waiting for his team. He had to think on his feet, and doing so, he found a couple of darkened, dead-end tunnels and split his Branchers between them.

He then tapped his headset and whispered very, very quietly, "In position. Ping for go."

Ping for go meant that all Charlie had to do to tell Rufus that we had all the *North*

Carolinas was send a comm ping — something that could be done at the touch of a button. We rarely used pings, to be honest, because we were rarely in situations like this where silence and covert movement were so genuinely critical.

We'd need it today though.

A question one of my editors asked was why Rufus didn't go right then, when he got in position. Why did he sit and wait in darkened corridors, taking the risk of being discovered? What was the point of waiting for all the *North Carolinas* to be behind our lines before launching?

Well, this was a judgment call, made on the fly by Rufus, and supported completely by Charlie, Karen and me after the fact. The basic reasoning here is simple: if Rufus had gone the moment he got into position there would have been twenty people in the cafeteria, half of them our volunteers, the other half malnourished *North Carolinas*.

After having been through what they'd been through, we couldn't expect the *North Carolinas* to be in any condition for a close-quarters fight against their Pion guards, while our SF and Special Branchers were fresh and ready for one. It thus made more sense to Rufus to wait, so that he could know for certain that his attack would be supported by volunteers who, while unarmed, could still assist his squad.

That's why he held off… that and because the longer we waited, the more arrogant and careless the Pions got. They thought they'd flummoxed us, and to be fair, they damned near had.

But we weren't going to surrender ourselves to the horror movie quietly…

CHAPTER TWENTY-SIX

COLLISION

The next ten minutes were predictably slow. You know how it is — waiting for the fight to start is the worst time, even (or especially) when you're standing in the room, looking at the person you're going to be fighting with.

I had time to think about all the problems with our new plan — the fact that only Charlie, his squad and I actually knew what was happening being chief among them.

Karen didn't have the information — she couldn't break off her staring contest with Josie to check in with me without implying to the Pion leader that we were up to something.

Omar Cunningham and his SF couldn't know either — they were all carrying comms, not wearing headsets, so they had to wait, covering our flanks with their MAG-90s, but only assuming that we had a plan to retrieve the women we were sending out.

Holly couldn't know. She might have thought Josie had snagged us, or she might have been putting together her own plan to get our volunteers back. I never asked her.

Many of our people would have to react with virtually no information on what the plan was… though Charlie would no doubt find a way to explain quickly and efficiently once the shooting started and there was no further reason to make it seem like we were actually doing this deal.

And yes, the shooting would have to be here, in this room. As soon as the last *North Carolinas* came past Charlie and me, his Special Branchers would have to gun down the half dozen Pion warriors who'd escorted Josie in, and who were now standing smugly behind their leader, laughing to each other about Defense Command's useless over-preparations, our stupid clothes, or whatever else they thought was idiotic about our approach to things…

After that, we'd all have to watch the doors — particularly the door the Pions were using, but the others as well — because after being this cautious about setting up the exchange, we could be fairly certain Josie would have at least another dozen warriors waiting in the hall beyond.

That might not sound too complicated, but I knew better than to think it would be easy. The Pions would have a trap in place, those clever bastards. They'd probably cut the lights to lessen the meager advantages of our ranged weapons, and then they'd rush across the gap and try to get in amongst us, so that our SF couldn't really do anything with their MAG-90s.

We'd have to be diligent on gunning them down short of our line, then. And if the lights went down, our Branchers would have to get their night vision optics working fast enough to shoot the incoming Pions.

There was a lot that would happen, and in the ten minutes we waited, I thought through every variant I could imagine. I tried not to sweat, or to appear outwardly as though I was anything but furious about losing the volunteers.

And then the last five *North Carolinas* stumbled into the gym.

Josie grinned at Karen, "Good worded, see. Thanking trade."

Karen's icy steel eyes found the Pion's, "You're very welcome."

The *North Carolinas* stumbled past her, then past me, and then into the protective ring of SF that Omar Cunningham had set up to get them out of the room. Charlie took a deep breath and shook his head, still acting as though now he had to send the last five women to their fates. He turned around to face his team, then tapped his headset to ping Rufus, and raised his arm.

"Optics now — they'll cut the lights!"

He didn't actually order his team to gun down the Pion warriors — he didn't have to. The fire was fast and precise, everything you'd expect of these veterans. The smirking warriors all went down — dead, because the Branchers were taking no chances with lower power settings here in Pion rock.

And just as expected, the lights went down almost instantly.

The SF behind us scrambled, none of them having night optics. Omar barked orders, getting them to collapse around the *North Carolinas* and the five remaining unarmed volunteers, and to back out of the gym. The SF would only be targets in this room — if the Pions got in close, they weren't trained for the kind of hand-to-hand fighting they'd have to do, and they weren't wearing tac vests. Better that they backed off as much as they could.

This, in my opinion at least, was a brilliant set of rapid decision making from *Lion's* former SF commander (Omar).

I didn't have night optics either, so I dropped to one knee and drew my sidearm, letting Charlie and his team move up past me. The room started to flash as though a strobe light was going in a club — when a MAG-90 fires in darkness, the light from its EM pulse is pretty striking.

And there was plenty of firing.

The Pions were trying to rush through the door now, but because Charlie and his team knew exactly how bad things would get if any made it through that choke point, they were letting fly.

In one of the bursts of rapid flashes, someone landed next to me with a thud, and I turned and trained my mag on the woman, only to find it was Karen, with blood on her face. She wasn't out, though, not by a long shot. Another figure came on through the strobing of the mag fire (this really was like something you'd see in a dramatic shoot-out movie... one of those scenes lit with just mag shots). It had to be Josie.

I swung my mag around but, of course, she moved too fast, and rapidly had Special Branchers behind her in my line of fire. If I shot at her, I might hit one of Charlie's team. Moving as fast as I could manage, then, I dropped my mag back into its holster and leapt up and forward at the Pion leader, aiming to tackle her hard.

I missed. I'm not the fastest hand-to-hand guy around, though I do like to think I can handle myself reasonably well. But a Pion — *any* Pion — can handle him or herself extraordinarily well. It is a skill they rely on for survival, and they practice it all the time. Small wonder that they can be so devastating.

As I realized I'd missed my tackle, I slid to a halt and turned, expecting Josie to be right on me. In that second, too, someone at our end of the gym managed to override whatever the Pions had done to the lights, and got some of them back on. It wasn't full lighting, but it was enough to see without the mag flashes — thank God Omar was thinking clearly.

Charlie's team yanked their optics away from their eyes as the light started to come up, and they kept shooting, as still *more* Pions came. In the minute since the shooting had started, they must have downed over twenty... how many were out there?

Well, more than twenty, and the MAG-90 power cells were starting to run dry. That was fine — the Branchers obviously had more cells — but reloading would give the Pions a chance to start pushing in through that door.

"Fighting pairs!" Charlie barked, meaning that the twelve Branchers would pair off for reloading, one still shooting while the other swapped cells.

The fire didn't stop, but it slackened, and a half dozen Pions surged into the room, their crude, brutal weapons raised.

That was happening to my right. To my left, at the very same time, Karen was leaping to her feet with all the effortless power she possessed, and then as Josie leapt at her, she dove at Josie. They collided with a crunching sound, and healthy Karen, with her superior body mass, knocked Josie off angle and dropped hard on her.

In a fight against a pirate, Karen landing on the offender would have ended it, but Josie was used to worse impacts. The Pion leader writhed under Karen, her filthy body like a whipcord of stringy muscle, bucking with such power that it was almost impossible to contain.

And even as she was doing that, the Pion leader was driving a spike of some sort towards Karen's already bloody face.

I moved, pulling my mag back out in a blur and lining up to blow Josie's head clean off. But that damned woman was so fast, and I was at a bad angle...

As I leapt desperately to get in position, Karen saw the spike, and stopped its massive blow with her hand... the hard way. She didn't let out a sound as the spike went through her left palm. Instead, with a savageness that even seemed to earn Josie's respect, she wrenched her impaled hand to the side, ripping the spike out of the Pion leader's grip.

Wasting no time, she pulled the spike out of her hand, and just as I raised my mag and lined up a shot on Josie's still-writhing head, Karen inserted the spike into Josie's left ear with such force that the tip of the crude weapon emerged from Josie's right ear.

Yes, it was exactly as gruesome as it sounds, and as if we needed any more proof of that, Holly bounced over with a grin and slapped Karen on the back, "Master good killing!"

With the amount of adrenaline running through her veins, Karen wasn't sluggish when she got to her feet and drew her mag from her hip with her right (intact) hand. I spared a second to look at her, in all her grizzly state, and then spun my mag back toward the door.

While Karen had been dealing with their leader, seven Pions had forced their way in — and *only* seven, thank God.

Charlie's team was ready for the bastards.

Charlie himself gave a perfect demonstration of what one should do when going hand-to-hand with Pions. In his fighting pair with young Ben Belete, he dropped his MAG-90, letting the weapon dangle from his vest, then tugged his combat knife out from its sheath. He did this, I should add, only because the Pion coming for him was just too close... I don't think words can adequately demonstrate how fast the attacker was moving.

Actually.

There, read the word 'actually' out loud. When you start with the first 'A', that's when Charlie noticed the warrior coming. When you hit the 'ly' that's when the Pion was swinging his weapon for Charlie's head. In between is when Charlie dropped his MAG-90, pulled his fighting knife, ducked and dodged.

Not kidding. That fast. This is why, Karen excepted, only Special Branchers had a chance in this mess.

The giant war hammer missed our intrepid Major by a few inches, but it was already up and coming around at Charlie again with impossible speed. See, for one of us untrained types, a heavy weapon like a 'war hammer' is a one-use thing... swing it big and miss, and it takes time to reset. But for someone who uses it as his primary weapon in fights of the worst kind, it seems light as a feather.

Charlie dodged the next blow, but down the line from him, a Pion caught Captain Raza Weiss by surprise with a sharpened club. Raza managed to get his arm up to protect his head, but the impact shattered his forearm, and cut deep into his flesh — even despite the protective webbing in the sleeve of his tunic.

Pions don't pull punches.

Still Charlie dodged, and then as the Pion he faced started to weave and reposition, our elite Major slipped forward and took a few swings with his fighting knife. He didn't land a single blow, which again will tell you something about how damned good these Pions are.

What Charlie did, though, was avoid getting hit, and much more importantly, he turned the Pion around just enough.

Ben Belete, like every Brancher, was a crack shot: the Pion's head exploded as soon as the angle was even close to right... then Charlie had his knife sheathed and his MAG-90 up to sweep the room again.

All in such a blinding flash it was difficult to follow.

With that method, Charlie's team put down the Pions, and then they secured the corridor outside the Pion-side entrance with a simple and effective method: concussion grenades and follow-up headshots.

After that, we took the better part of a minute to catch our breaths, before getting the hell out of that room.

CHAPTER TWENTY-SEVEN
RESCUE

Things in the gym had gone well. Raza Weiss was in bad shape, and medic Terry Schroeder had taken some punishment too (he had a foot long gash across his stomach, but if not for his tac vest, that cut likely would have gone through his ribs and wedged into his spinal column). Karen was probably worse than Terry, but she was better off than Raza, and between them, those three represented the worst of our injuries.

Things had gone well for us, and there was one clear reason for that: we'd been able to control the flow of Pions.

When we'd attacked, we had surprise on our side, and most of Josie's reinforcements had been out in the corridor. Why had she positioned them there? Well, probably because out there they'd be safe from fire — she probably thought that if she'd brought everyone in and it had been a trap, we could have gunned them all down before they closed to fighting distance.

Gunning down close to thirty Pions wouldn't have been easy, but between Charlie's team and the SF under Omar, we probably could have managed it.

But with the reinforcements outside, the lion's share of her force would have been spared from our initial, surprise attack. Cut the lights, and as far as she knew, we'd be unable to see to shoot them as they came in.

I should mention that the Pions had good natural night sight — a 'benefit' of living your entire life in a tunnel system with only dim lights at the best of times. Attacking under the cover of darkness is something they're prone to do, and if you've seen the movies, you know that. Bottom line is Josie probably didn't expect Charlie and his team to have matching night sight. Even if she knew about Special Branch night optics, she likely didn't think we'd expect the lights to go down...

Basically, she thought she had set her forces up smartly, and she had. Raza Weiss and Terry Schroeder would completely agree.

But we'd still done well.

Rufus, unfortunately, didn't have such a favorable situation to contend with. He'd located only one entrance to the cafeteria in his brief sweep, and when Charlie's ping came, he wasted no time in surging to his feet and moving through it. The second Brancher in line swept in right at his shoulder, covering the opposite direction as Rufus moved, and then the rest of the squad followed, all having to use the same single entrance... as the Pions had been forced to at the gym.

There were eleven Pion guards in this room, which may not sound like a lot when you factor in Rufus' twelve plus the fifteen volunteers (remember, the last five hadn't been sent down). But then, I suppose by now you know better than to think that in close quarters one of us is generally going to be a match for one of them.

The third Brancher in Rufus' line was abruptly decapitated before any of the team had managed to get a shot off. Seeing this, the fourth person in line dropped to one knee and proceeded to separate the offending Pion from his legs at the kneecaps, and then to finish him off with a shot through the head. MAG-90s started singing their deadly song.

But it was very, very close quarters.

"Pairs!" was the only order Rufus managed to bark in the flash of time before seeing a huge warrior coming, and charging to meet the Pion.

As he tackled the big bastard, Rufus drew his own blade — not a regulation fighting knife like Charlie's, but a Japanese-style tanto with a mean edge — and used it to remove part of the warrior's face.

While Rufus did that, the volunteers were leaping into action, trying to tie up the warriors long enough to let the Special Branchers gun them down. It didn't work so well.

Three of the women, all SFers, pounced on a single warrior, but with his slippery Pion skill, he got loose of them, and then using his massive, jagged club, he shattered each one of their heads. Now, watch how you read that: 'shattered' is a word we writers (in my case, 'hacks') use for dramatic effect many times, but rarely mean quite as literally as I mean it now.

The force of the blow that these women each absorbed in the shocking space of just seconds was incredible, and pieces of skull and scalp did flake off, and scatter.

The time it took for that bastard to do his work did give one of Rufus' Lieutenants a chance to gun him down, but... well.

I don't need to explain the 'but'.

A second Brancher from Rufus' squad was torn from his fighting partner and slammed up against a wall, at which point a long spike was driven through his forehead. That warrior then managed to get his hand on his first victim's partner, and he inserted a second spike into her lower abdomen before she was able to insert her fighting knife into his eye, and then to follow it up with a full-power mag blast.

This wounded Brancher was Lieutenant Harriet Chow, and she stumbled out of line as the man who'd stabbed her dropped in her direction like a ton of bricks. She wasn't yet feeling the seriousness of the wound that she'd received, but logically she knew the injured area was potentially serious, so she called for the squad medic.

I go into this much detail with Harriet because, even as she called for the squad medic, another warrior came at her from behind, too fast for her to turn and engage.

That's when Carly intervened. Carly Henderson, you know by now, moved damned fast, and though she had no weapon, she was able to catch the arm of the man trying to swing his club at the back of Chow's head, stopping the blow.

The warrior grunted and started to turn on Carly, but with a sharp jump forward, she butted the bastard's head with her own. Unfortunately, his skull was much bigger and emptier than hers was, and the butt had no effect. She swung a fist at his face, connected, and broke his nose instead.

But as she did that, his free hand pushed her away, and he started to spin. Sensing that there was trouble to the rear, Harriet Chow turned and opened fire with all the speed a Special Brancher can muster — a lot, we know.

The man's chest started to explode, but momentum carried his weapon on its perfectly-aligned swing. Carly tried to stop it with her arms, but the blade on the leading edge of the weapon cut mercilessly through her forearm block. The weapon went in through the right side of her slim, unprotected body, and by the time momentum wore off, it was cracking her spine.

Carly Henderson.

That's right, Carly Henderson.

If somehow we haven't already established that this was deathly serious, that this place from the horror movies really was a horror movie from the very depths of hell, that oughta bring it home to you. Carly Henderson dropped from her feet and mercifully died immediately. I can't imagine the look on her face. I don't want to imagine it.

Carly had been with Charlie's team for years. Back on *Friendly*, it had started as the Charlie and Carly show, and then that joke had gotten old, so it'd just been, well, Charlie and Carly. She was always there, she was always reliable and deadly. She made sure he brought gifts home for Lia. She'd been one of the first people to *know* about Charlie and Lia.

And now she was dead, in Pion rock, during a rescue of the survivors of *North Carolina*.

The rest of this fight in the cafeteria was equally brutal. Eight of Rufus' squad came out of it on their feet, and two more were dragged out alive. Of the fifteen volunteers who'd been in the fight, eight lived.

I'll talk about them more in a short while. For now, just know that the Pions guarding the volunteers all eventually died. Rufus, his bloodied squad, and the volunteers got the hell out of there, dragging the wounded and dead with them.

CHAPTER TWENTY-EIGHT
ESCAPE

Realizing that Rufus' quickest way to safety was likely the same route the Pions had been using to transfer people back and forth to the staging area, Charlie had moved back through the gym and set up a defensive position in the corridor beyond the Pion entrance.

Karen and I waited at the opposite entrance to the gym — the entrance we'd controlled through this whole mess — with Omar, eight of his SF guards, Holly and her six warriors.

Yes, Karen and I should have been high-tailing it back to the relative safety of Canary territory, but we couldn't. Our discipline and our command instincts should have required us to get out of harm's way, but it's *us*. As stupid stuff goes, this was pretty much top of the list, but we were doing it anyway.

I'd managed to pluck a first aid kit off one of the SF guards, and with it had sealed Karen's copiously-bleeding scalp wound — one she'd gotten, I found out, when she'd very narrowly missed Josie's first strike with the spike. Karen didn't even know where that weapon had been hidden on the Pion leader's rag-clad body... it really didn't matter.

The wound on her hand was, obviously, much worse. I couldn't close it with some quickseal out of a tube. Instead, I'd bandaged it clumsily, tying the dressing as tight as I could to try to keep the bleeding down. Still on the adrenalin when I'd done that, Karen didn't so much as wince.

We stood and waited.

Holly was giddy, though, which was in itself very difficult to handle.

"Victoried big Bear. Master spiked Josie good ear!"

I can't remember all Holly's natterings, but there were two particular themes: first, Karen knew how to kill really well, and second, Josie was dead and the Pions would be easy pickings in this war because of it.

It was tasteless cheering — what kind of person is thoroughly giddy about such carnage? A Canary, right. And before anyone criticizes me for perpetuating a negative stereotype, let's get a couple of things straight: Holly *was* happy about the carnage, so if it's a stereotype, it's an accurate one.

More important, be it a stereotype or an observation, the statement that Holly was enjoying the carnage is not a 'negative' one. It's negative to us — from our point of view, it seems savage. But remember, this is the world in which Holly grew up. It was entirely valid for her to enjoy it... we just don't have to like hearing about her enjoying it.

As it was, we didn't react in any way to Holly's cheers. We remained silent as we watched the gym and waited for Charlie to lead Rufus' team through.

I spared intermittent glances at Karen, and after about five minutes of waiting, her expression changed. She began blinking frequently, and she starting biting down on her bottom lip, her breathing growing heavier as she did.

I switched sides of the door frame to stand closer to her, then whispered, "Starting to feel the pain?"

The adrenaline was wearing off, and as it did her mind was starting to process the agony being caused by the hole in her left palm.

She closed her eyes and nodded a couple of times in answer, "Yes."

Her soft word was tenuous, indicative of her determination not to give in to the acute throbbing. She ground her teeth together, her nostrils flared with each breath, but she opened her eyes and kept her gaze locked on the gym. Her grip on her mag (in her right hand) never slackened.

We waited another few painful minutes before Charlie's team started leading Rufus and his people through. Karen and I both stilled as we watched the number of lifeless bodies being dragged, and then I recognized Carly.

I tried to murmur some word to express my shock at seeing her body being hauled through the gym, and then out into the corridor and back towards Canary territory, but there was nothing I could say under my breath that felt adequate.

Charlie was the last man out, and as he stepped clear and we locked eyes, neither of us had words. It was one of the few times in life when I could clearly see that Charlie was hurting. Obviously he was keeping that contained — it wasn't obvious to everyone. But after all our years together, I knew what the burdened look in his eyes meant, even if his all-business demeanor masked the message.

He then shook his head, "Should have told her to look after herself."

That remark didn't make any sense to me at the time, because I didn't know about his last proper conversation with Carly — the one where he'd told her to look after the SF volunteers, and she'd asked him why he hadn't told her to look after herself.

Charlie knew, as did Karen and I, that innocent comments like that meant nothing in the universal calculus that dictated who lived and who died. He wasn't going to blame himself foolishly for the death of one of his officers because he hadn't told her to look after herself. He just had to say that to quell the superstitious part of his mind, and because he didn't know what else to say.

And then the 'mourning' time ended abruptly, because a party of Pions leapt into the gym from the entrance on the far side.

Omar's SFers saw the bastards first, and cut loose with MAG-90 fire. The SF are generally very good shots, but it really does take a Special Brancher to hit a bounding Pion. Charlie was the only one we had with us, but he wasn't in the mood.

Plucking two concussion grenades off his vest, he thumbed them active and tossed them into the room, then slammed the hatch behind them. The thuds of the grenades were muffled by the heavy door, as were the surprised wails of the Pions as their heads were badly shaken by the bursts.

Charlie then re-opened the door, and with the help of Omar's SFers, finished off the stunned party before it could find its feet.

After that, we ran for Canary territory.

+++

It was surprising how much relief we felt when we reached the Canary tunnels. That anywhere at all in Pion rock could feel somewhat *safe* was frankly shocking, but it did. Canary warriors rushed past us several times as we made our way out of the neutral tunnels — the war was clearly going into full swing.

Holly stuck with us, making sure we got back safe. I'm so conflicted in my opinion of that woman... I can't abide by her values, her society... it makes my skin crawl. But she was also true to her word. That should, theoretically, be grounds for her earning my respect. And yet the thought of respecting her just doesn't sit right. That probably means I'm an elitist Imperialist bastard.

But I've been called worse, and with better justification, so I'll let it ride.

As we reached the Canary tunnels, Holly grabbed my sleeve and stopped me. Turning, I found her looking right up at my eyes with a more serious expression then was her norm, "Head the for war now... trust your bargain. Cheating not, yes?"

I suppose my expression must have been fairly stark, but I nodded, "We're not going to cheat you. We'll stay in orbit and look after our wounded until Mark gets back with the drugs."

Holly nodded in an exaggerated fashion, then turned and nodded to her escort. They were going to war.

"Good luck," Karen called, rather surprising me.

Looking back with a gummy grin, Holly waved at us.

I looked across at Karen and she shook her head slowly, tiredly, "They earned the luck, at least."

Sure, they'd earned that much.

CHAPTER TWENTY-NINE

RECOVERIES

Alicia Morgan was already working briskly by the time Karen and I arrived at the med lab. She'd been forced to send the *North Carolina* survivors to a conference room near the infirmary to be checked out by some of her medics, because the number of grievously wounded people coming in from the Special Branchers and the SF was more than sufficient to fill the med bay.

Triage is never a pretty thing, but triage after fighting on Pion rock is positively horrific. Explosions during ship-to-ship actions can mangle bodies in gruesome ways, but the amount of destruction that can be wrought by a determined Pion with a twisted piece of metal is something different... it's personal.

Shattered bones, flesh hanging from the bone as if a person had been carved like a turkey... it's heinous. Most of the casualties were, of course, from Rufus' squad and from the volunteers. Many of those people had walked out of Pion rock only because adrenalin and first aid drugs kept them functioning — when they got under Alicia's scope, internal injuries, fractures and even some sizable gashes appeared that had been unnoticed.

She had her hands full, then, when Karen and I slipped through the hatch.

Walking into this room still prompted a bad reaction — it had only been a couple of months since we'd seen Jocko, Summer and Destiny die here, along with Kyle Stranks and his security detail. And since Karen had feared for her very life here.

Obviously, we couldn't let the bad feelings stop us from coming, and we certainly couldn't reveal how we felt to anyone, but we silently shared the reaction.

At least this time, the injury to Karen was one she'd had complete control over... more or less. What I mean is that Karen had been cut and beaten up in a fight — her actions, as much as Josie's, had dictated her current physical state. It wasn't underhanded poisoning, like that goddamned Phosgene had been.

Standing quietly, we observed the goings-on in the med bay for several minutes before Alicia even noticed us. She was hurrying from bed to bed, prioritizing patients and designating the people who would go for surgery first... actually, she was just heading to the scrubbing station to get ready to go into the operating theatre when she noticed us.

She frowned for a minute (I'd helped Karen wipe the blood off her face, so her injuries weren't immediately evident), but then Karen raised her left hand and waved, "Puncture. Not too bad."

Frowning, Alicia stepped over, then quickly but delicately unwrapped the bandage I'd applied. She looked at the wound from a couple of angles, held a scanner over it, then called for one of her medics before looking back at us, "Nerve is damaged but not badly. Juan will have you patched up in no time. Take it easy on the hand for a couple of weeks; you'll probably feel like you're missing your fingertips for a while."

Karen frowned slightly but then nodded. She liked feeling her fingertips... hopefully the sensation wouldn't take long to come back.

With a parting nod, Alicia turned away and headed to the scrubbing station. There were people in dire need of fixing, and, of course, some who couldn't be fixed at all.

The temperature in the small cargo bay was just below freezing, to make certain the bodies didn't start to decompose. Charlie personally undertook the grizzly task of moving the two uniformed Special Branchers from Rufus' squad, and the five dead volunteers, into this place.

It was the very least he could do.

Carly's remains were in a terrible state — the massive cleaving damage had left her body nearly in two pieces, which made moving her with any respect quite difficult. But Special Branchers had a way of making 'difficult' look easy, especially when it mattered.

Those who'd passed the triage medical scans, and those like Charlie who'd known they were fine, had moved the bodies of the brave and fallen to this small bay — a bay I've not actually mentioned in these books, but which, because of its size, often became the last resting place for our dead.

It was on the lowest level of *Wolf's* 'neck', so when you turned down the compartment heating, space did the job of cooling it for you... preserving the dead until they could be examined by the physician and a cause of death officially recorded.

Yes, we all knew how these seven people had died, but protocol required a doctor's signature on the form that said 'killed in action'. If someone else signed off on it, the Navy would not accept the certification, and the benefits paid out to the families of the dead would be affected.

Defense Command personnel killed in the line of duty left behind them the best damned benefits package one could find in the Empire — three years of full salary at the usual pay intervals, followed by half-pay for an additional ten years. Private companies often wonder how we could afford to set that up. Well, Defense Command is a huge part of your tax dollars, for one.

For two, all things being equal, we don't face that many killed-in-action casualties... at least, we hadn't before the war. The war did massively increase the costs to the pension system, but we were able to set up a fund from the Imperial treasury to handle that... I'll probably explain the hows of that in a later book. It's actually an under-appreciated but instrumental part of the political wrangling that happened right after hostilities ended.

Anyway, Alicia had to sign off on the causes of death for the seven men and women whose bodies now lay in the cargo bay.

Charlie stood in silence with his arms folded as he looked down at Carly. He'd dropped his vest and his MAG-90 at the door, and now he just stood and stared. It was a thousand-yard stare, as he calls it — one that sees more than just eyes can see. There was so much history between him and Carly. She'd been his trusted friend. For so long.

He just stared and stared. No dramatic dialogue. No monologues or soliloquies. Just silence. He couldn't bring himself to leave her side quickly or easily.

Eventually, he knelt next to Carly's cold, cleaved form, and his hand came to rest on her shoulder. His eyes fell on her lifeless face, and he let out a sharp breath, then tightened his grip briefly. That was his goodbye. It was all he could do... all he needed to do.

Carly Henderson was gone.

Standing slowly, Charlie turned for the door. He walked purposefully, in a way that would look no different than usual to most observers. But Lia would have seen, and even I would have seen, that there was something different in the way he was moving.

He collected his vest and MAG-90, and left Carly and the other volunteers to their peace.

Andrea Kiley appeared in the med bay just as Juan Marcos, the medic Alicia had assigned to Karen, was finishing his work. Karen didn't notice our Flag Captain's arrival, but I did, and for a moment I held my breath.

Yes, Andrea had been making great progress, but how would she handle the carnage the Pions had wrought on some of her people? Was she going to draw a MAG-90 from the armory and try to go down there, hunting for blood?

No, of course she wasn't. We were getting Andrea back, thank God.

Moving from wounded person to wounded person with a calming, almost motherly expression, she made the rounds. She smiled warmly to greet each one, and laying a hand gently on them, she asked how it had been down there and told them how well they'd done. She told them that the ship was incredibly proud of them, and that she was grateful for their efforts.

She said the things that a good Captain thinks to say after the kind of grinding fight these men and women had just been in.

This, I should say, is what the crew probably had needed after the incident with *Idaho* — the reassurance Andrea knew well she hadn't given them. She was determined never to let that oversight happen again, and today those who'd gone into the nightmare of the Pion rock and come back with wounds and trauma were the first real beneficiaries.

By the time Andrea had made her way around the room to us — the last stop based on the direction she was traveling — Juan was just stepping away, having handed Karen an injector with a couple of vials of a good painkiller.

Andrea's warm, reassuring smile stayed in place as she stepped over to us, but as soon as she was out of the peripheral vision of the other occupants of the bay, it faded, "Talk in a cabin?"

Karen and I glanced at each other, and then nodded. We wanted to say nothing here that would darken the spirits of those who needed to heal. They deserved to enjoy the fact that they'd done their jobs well, and successfully.

We went to Karen's cabin, because she was the one who'd most need the rest... and because her cabin was directly between mine and Andrea's. Nice and central.

"Three Martians tried to come for a visit while you were down there," Andrea announced as she closed the hatch.

Karen was lowering herself gingerly onto her bed — she was realizing now that in her wrestling match she'd managed to pull or micro-tear something in her torso, which made the move painful. Those words brought her gaze abruptly back up to Andrea.

"I take it you scared them off?" I asked the question Karen was thinking, and then seeing that Karen had seated herself, I dropped into the chair next to her bed.

Andrea replied with a nod, "The old rock signaling bluff. I have Adrienne running constant sweeps to make sure they don't creep up on us, but we may well see the bastards again."

I glanced at Karen, and she raised her eyebrows and rubbed her head with her right hand, "Good. Well if they come back, we'll have more options. I don't know if it'd be a good idea to fight without Mark."

"We'll play it by ear," I assured, not really wanting to get into such a tactical discussion now. Andrea had made the right call before, in scaring them off without confrontation. The situation could be different if they came back and we weren't bound to the Pion rock orbit… we'd see.

For now, it wasn't something I thought Karen really needed to worry about. She needed rest. Come to think of it, this was the second mission in a row when she'd been put into rough shape, but at least this time she could say 'you should see the other guy'. Well, other woman. But in the first draft I tried it as 'you should see the other woman' and it sounded weird. So I changed it back to the standard cliché.

As if that boast is consolation. Hell, as if that's not in bad taste. Josie had a spike sticking out her ears.

"We lost seven?" Andrea asked quietly after we'd assimilated her news, and with a very deep sigh, I nodded again.

"We lost seven. Carly Henderson with them."

"Christ," Andrea shook her head, and I noticed that her jaw was clenching.

Andrea's gaze slid away from mine and for a moment got lost in the void between Karen and me. Later she explained to me what was happening in her head: she was feeling anger, but she was also feeling relief. She wanted revenge for her people, but she was determined not to let that get out of hand.

You know what I mean. Andrea was fighting with herself — she was in a knock-down, drag-out battle with the demons she'd earned on Egesta and since. And she was winning.

Perhaps that sounds corny or melodramatic, but it's what was happening. She was accepting loss again, and detaching yourself when people die in action is something you need to be able to do. Remember, *not* detaching myself when Kate Levec got shot was what I'd been beating myself up about in *The Jupiter Patrol*.

It was necessary, and it wasn't easy to do.

Andrea was getting used to it again… she was a little bit more like herself.

We talked for a short while longer, then Andrea left Karen and I, and we elected to clean up — a difficult experience for Karen, with her hand still in agony.

Still, for her, pain was a small price to pay — we wanted to wash away the gore of Pion rock.

That'd take two or three showers.

CHAPTER THIRTY

CANARY WARS

What many people don't understand about Canary and Pion wars is the length: a Canary war is short... very short. To the Canaries, a war lasts between five and fifteen spins. The longest Holly ever told me about went twenty-five. Assuming a spin of five hours, that means wars for these tribes run between twenty-five and 125 hours, roughly one to five days by our time scale.

Short wars.

Why is this the case? Well, when you have a small population that is so obsessive about reproduction that it bases its scale of social worth on number of children produced by a person, it's almost inevitable that you don't like to see large numbers of dead warriors. Replacing losses is not easy, so one side tends to sue for peace when it loses more warriors than it feels it can replace... or if it's smart, just before that point.

One thing we did do when we started this particular war was kill almost fifty Pions. That's a big number for their society, and they were lost for nothing. When Holly's onslaught followed, it involved over 200 Canary warriors rushing the outer Pion tunnels, capturing one of the hydroponics bays that was close to Pion territory, and killing another six warriors.

Yes, only six. At the cost of nine of their own. Those numbers are indeed very small, which is why the fifty-odd fatalities we inflicted were so striking. When the Pions attack the Canaries, it's not quite the same fight-for-life that it is when they attack us. We don't have the skill base to survive hand-to-hand with the Pions, but the Canaries do.

I've never personally seen it, but I believed Holly's explanation: a fight between two warriors can indeed go on for hours. The first move is to disarm the opponent, and then as much as anything else it can become a wrestling match. Because the tunnels are narrow, and the numbers of warriors can be small, singles combat can in fact hold up entire campaigns. This is something they're good at — something they train for all their lives.

But the same way the Pions and the Canaries would be useless in a special ops fight like the one Charlie had been in on Sinope, we were next to useless in the battles in the corridors. It was alien to us, so we either died quickly (as Carly had) or we killed them with our impressive energy weapons.

Fights weren't overly drawn out.

It's actually rather strange when I review everything I've just explained: Canary wars tend to be short because they don't like high numbers of casualties, and at the same time, individual battles can be quite long during those wars. The formula ultimately means that, in this case, the Pions sued for peace before Mark Gunney returned.

Without Josie to lead them, and having lost a considerable number of warriors in our trap at the exchange, the Pions had lost their stomach for it... and rightly so, I should say. We earned their respect that day, in the most horrific and yet indisputable way.

We killed a lot of them. And we were the first force of humans from outside their rock to successfully do that... well... ever. Even the Special Branchers Ian Hawke had sent in decades prior had lost more than they'd killed.

For our seven dead, we'd killed almost fifty.

I don't think that's something we can 'take pride in' — I try to make a point of not taking pride in killing. But we'd done our job in getting the *North Carolinas* out, and had accomplished that with surprisingly few of our own dead.

All this brings me to a meeting with Holly, the morning after the exchange and the war. Mark Gunney had pulled into orbit the night before, and his shuttles were loaded up and ready to fly with the fertility drugs — I just had to meet with Holly first, to arrange the drop.

I went down to the rock with Charlie and two of his squad. Karen stayed behind, ready to command our three ships in action if the Martians who'd arranged this gruesome piece of theatre came calling, and because she had no interest in going back down to the tunnels, to be congratulated on how well she killed Josie.

Karen already knew how good a killer she was... she didn't need gleeful reminding from the Canaries.

When we got to the entrance lounge, the area was abandoned. Holly had sent one message up to us the night before, saying that they'd won and that it was over, but finding the tunnels abandoned made us wonder if a counterattack hadn't been launched. We were thus very cautious as we headed down the shaft towards the core of Canary territory.

I had my mag out, and Charlie was looking at everything down the barrel of his MAG-90... we were on our toes.

But the Canaries had won. The tunnels were empty, we discovered, because most of the population had gone into celebratory orgy mode after the triumph.

Yes, orgy. No, Charlie and I didn't walk in on anyone at inopportune times, we just saw many rooms full of post-orgy clumped-up couples, fast asleep.

I'm past the point of trying to explain or rationalize Canary behavior. If they wanted to celebrate their victory by trying to produce more warriors and child-bearers, that was entirely their business. The less said about it the better, actually, because if we asked Holly what the point was, she'd inevitably offer to find women ready to have children so we could find out for ourselves.

Hopefully, by now, you know that such an offer would not be the raunchy, sultry sort of one that the movies suggest it would be — instead, it'd be a genuine request for new blood in the breeding lines.

Anyway, we didn't ask, so they didn't ask. We just pressed on through the masses until we found Holly's headquarters, or whatever she called it. Holly herself was far too old to mess around with having kids again, and since sex to these people is not about pleasure, just breeding, she'd found another way to enjoy her night: with fresh fruit.

The hydroponics bay they'd captured was full of fruit — strawberries, cantaloupes, grapes... all the things it had been programmed to grow back when it was installed in the twenty-first century, and that it continued to grow without fail.

Holly knew that she wouldn't be able to hold that bay for long — it was close to Pion tunnels and far from her own — so she'd ordered its harvest stripped, and now she was enjoying a disproportionate share of the tastiest fruit it had to offer.

That, to her, was ecstasy, and I suppose that's one place where she and I actually don't completely disagree… I do enjoy fresh fruit. The rest of it, though, we don't see eye to eye on.

Ahem.

"Victorious ours!" she raised her hands to the air and squealed as we stepped in. "Killem you good and did!"

She was under no illusions that she'd won this war on her own — she knew we'd done a huge amount of the essential killing, and she was kind enough to give us the credit.

"Won't again though. Trick knowed… any down to Pions won't respect uniform."

It was true. If the Pions got a hold of ours again, they'd have no reason to respect the uniform.

"I don't know about that," Charlie said in a cool tone. "We did finally prove that we can do a lot of damage. Maybe they'll think twice before assuming they can push us around."

Holly waved her hands around in the air, "Maybe. Whats the ferties?"

I have to laugh writing that. I didn't laugh then, hearing it, but for some reason now it strikes me as funny — not because what Holly said was unreasonable, but because she damned well wasn't going to let us off the hook.

"Mark Gunney pulled in last night. We can bring them down whenever you like, probably when your people wake up and can help move it. There'll be a lot."

Holly stopped waving her arms around and nodded, "Fairlike. Bring where come you… next spin on."

"We'll be there," I wasn't going to draw this conversation out for too long, so I replied with speed that would have undoubtedly been seen as rude in any other company.

With another nod, Holly let us take our leave. Her fight was over, and she was victorious. Now we just had to pay the bill, and go home to our own war.

CHAPTER THIRTY-ONE

DEAL DONE

I'd vastly overestimated the number of boxes of fertility drugs we had to move. Ten thousand doses sound like a positive ton, but when you get down to it, the bulk-packaged drugs were in fact reasonably compact.

It came down to something like fifty 'cases', each one carrying 200 disposable injectors... not terrible at all. Mark was able to get them down to the locks in two shuttles and a single trip, and when they got there, Holly personally opened a few just to make sure she counted 200 in each one.

Yes, she could count to 200. I don't mean that as a joke, or to be unkind: most Pions and Canaries couldn't count that high. Those who became leaders — part of the three-child caste — would be educated by their predecessors, to make certain they could understand some things that the rest could not.

Charlie and I returned to the rock with Alicia Morgan and one of her medics after the drop was complete, so that Holly could learn how to use the injectors. A few women had been selected as candidates for the first doses, so Alicia did the first two, and Holly did the third.

These were home-injection kits — more or less idiot-proof. Holly and the three-child women she'd assembled to learn the workings of the injectors were more than able to understand the technology... and, of course, to identify how useful the needles on the injectors could be as points for darts or something similar once the doses had been expended.

Have to hand it to those Canaries, they're always innovating and recycling...

Once the instructions were given, we sent Alicia back to the shuttle and Charlie and I remained behind for a while to properly say our goodbyes.

As much as we didn't like this place, and as often as I'd gladly tell Holly that she was a savage and needed to learn to structure her sentences better (rich criticism, coming from me), she had kept her word, looked after twenty-two *North Carolinas*, and helped us get the rest back.

We'd helped each other, it was only proper that we said polite goodbyes.

"Tellin Master she welcome be here evertime," Holly grinned at us. "Can't make her your babies, our warriors will!"

She was trying to goad me, and I knew it. My answer was thus a slim smile, "Doubt they could handle her... but I'm sure she'd rather never come back here. I sure as hell don't want to."

Holly cackled, "Civilized and so... too mean we are cause we kill hard... you kill millions said time last here."

I had told Holly about that, when she'd asked us how human 'civilizations' made war. That was back in the *Friendly* days, before I'd been in a war, but I'd been speaking of things like the pirates and the conflicts of Earth's past. Holly had thought it ridiculous to fight wars when you couldn't look into the eye of your adversary, and when machines made the difference for victory.

Now I could try to go off on a tangent here about how awful technological war is — how our machines make it so deadly, and how easy it is to forget there are people on the other end of that laser. But that argument has been made cliché by all the self-righteous people out there who have some romantic notion about what war should be.

Yes, there's something to it — wars are quite different now than they were back on Earth in the old days, when people waited to see the whites of the enemy's eyes before attacking. Ultimately, though, war is war. The intent hasn't changed: it's about people trying to kill other people, hopefully for a reason they believe is a good one.

Whether you fight with a Pion warhammer or a shipboard laser, that intent doesn't change, and I think that's the important thing to remember.

Anyway, I wasn't going to be baited by Holly's jeer, so I shook my head, "We're different, you and us. You're savages, we're civilized. That just means we do things differently."

That was unusually philosophical for me, so Charlie stepped in and bailed me out, "And it's been nice to see you again, Holly. Good luck with the drugs."

Holly cackled again, then nodded, "Equal is us and you, thanks."

To her, my philosophical statement — that we were different, but that neither of us were inherently superior to the other — was a joke. Obviously, she knew the Canaries were superior.

"So good warring be outer way. Back here needing us when you do!" she waved us away with a grin.

She'd said that we should come back when we needed her. That was... nice... of her.

Charlie and I turned away and walked through the Canary corridors away from Holly, raising a hand to wave goodbye.

After a few minutes, we were clear of most of the Canary people, and I spared a sigh, "I really, *really* don't *ever* want to come back here."

"That's what you said last time," Charlie made an effort to say it playfully, but it came out flat.

I concurred, "It's exactly what I said last time."

Charlie was silent for a moment, then he nodded, "I agree even more now than I did last time."

"Yeah. Yeah I know."

We headed back to our shuttle.

CHAPTER THIRTY-TWO

RETURN TRIP

By the time we left Pion rock (without any further visits from those Martian ships, by the way), the matters that had loomed so large before we left were distant memories. Lia facing the takeover of her Protectorate, Andrea's situation… it all took some time to get back on the radar after Pion rock.

But we did have to get back into it. For all its gruesomeness, and despite the lives it saved, this mission really had just been a sideshow to the rest of the war. A sideshow that had cost lives… that had seen the first fatality of the entire war on Charlie's Special Branch team. Just pause and think about that for a moment: all that his officers went through at Sinope… all the battles we'd fought that were important to the fate of the Empire… they'd even beaten the Phosgene trap. But not the Pions. Not this sideshow.

That's something that's quite maddening about war, I think. When someone dies in the pursuit of the enemy, at least you can try to console yourself with the fact that they were doing an important service to the Empire. Sometimes that consolation works, other times it doesn't.

But what about losing people in a bitter horror trap like Pion rock? Well, obviously those we lost had given their lives to save others… but it wasn't part of the war. It wasn't part of the grand 'metanarrative'. That was next: we were heading back to the full swing of the bloodiest year of the Martian War.

And that had to take precedence. Pion rock had to be left behind, in all senses of the expression… a difficult task, it must be said.

Does it surprise you that putting Pion rock behind us was a little easier said than done?

We weren't spending our time during the days mired in thoughts about it — Andrea immediately started running ship action drills, and as the members of Charlie's and Rufus' squads started getting healthy, they began running fire-and-maneuver drills, refreshing the skills that would be useful in an assault on the Mercury domes.

In other words, we spent the days plunging ourselves back into the reality that was the Martian War.

But when it got later in the days, and particularly during the night periods, it was a little bit more difficult to stay focused on the Martians. There was actually a considerable increase in the downloading and playing of Pion and Canary-related horror movies from *Wolf*Net's entertainment database, I'm guessing by the people who weren't down in the rock with us, and were trying to get a sense of what they missed. I can't imagine anyone who had been there downloading those movies — at least not so soon after. Though I suppose it's possible.

For me, though, sleep wasn't coming easy, and no movie about Pion rock would help. I don't know if it's cliché not to be able to sleep after participating in a real-life horror movie, but if you think it is, why don't you go to Pion rock and see how you fare. If you survive, and then you don't have nightmares, I'll gladly admit that I'm more mentally fragile than you are.

Sorry, that was adversarial — needlessly so. Guess I felt my dignity was in jeopardy when I admitted I couldn't sleep for the first few nights.

It didn't help, I suppose, that Karen was in rough shape. She was healing on schedule, of course, but there was something slightly unsettling about seeing her wince every time she sat down in a chair, or had to pick something up with both hands. Just little things, but disturbing nonetheless.

We weren't back to normal, whatever normal was for us by that point.

So while I couldn't sleep, I did the predictable thing: I walked the decks of *Wolf*. I could have done paperwork (that very boring and tedious task that Rear Admirals have to do even more than Commodores, and which I've been making effort to keep out of these books). But I didn't want to... so I walked.

Night watch on *Wolf* is generally quite quiet, with two thirds of the crew bunked down or taking some R&R time. The particular night I want to refer to right now was our second out of Pion rock, when we were already back within the perimeter of the Belt colonies, but were still a ways out from Belt Two. I was walking aimlessly along the rec deck, contemplating getting something to eat at the Officers Club when I passed the crew theatre.

Predator-class frigates have all sorts of amenities, and one of them is a theatre that can seat up to seventy people... more if they don't mind piling on top of each other. It wasn't anything fancy, really — there was no sloping floor, just lines of seats in two isles — but it was a nice touch, and a big improvement on watching movies in crew messes as we'd done in the old *North Americas*.

One of the Pion movies that had been released in 2229 was playing in the theatre — I obviously won't give you a title, because movie studios hire some mean duelers. Suffice it to say it was one of the more graphic, gritty, realistic movies about the Special Branch incursion into the rock back in 2195.

The star was, as I walked by, trying to encourage his officers to keep their heads together — even though they'd lost a quarter of their number and killed no Pions or Canaries in return, they could still make it.

The audience inside the theatre — again, I'm guessing people who weren't down there with us, but were trying to see what it was like — watched with rapt attention. What was more interesting, though, was that Charlie was leaning against the door frame, hands thrust into his pockets.

I frowned and closed the distance to the theatre entrance, wincing as one of the Branchers started screaming about how it was 'over, man — game over'... a rip-off of a classic movie that few people these days have seen.

"Think most people know where they stole that line from?" I asked, trying much too hard to be casual as I leaned against the opposite side of the door, and Charlie shook his head.

He wasn't surprised to see me appear suddenly — as a Special Brancher, he automatically knew I was there.

"Pretty sure no one does," he reinforced his head shake with the words.

We stood and silently watched the action unfold for a little while. This was one of those 'hyper-real' action movies — the sort that looked so real you could almost taste the Pion rock stench. Well, you couldn't actually *taste* it — they banned those ridiculous attempts to include taste and scent markers in movies in 2211, after three people had strokes during a viewing of *Ragnarok Now* (another ripped-off movie, by the way).

But yeah, we just stood in the doorway and watched, seemingly unnoticed by the crew inside.

After a while, I glanced at Charlie, "How long's it been?"

"Vance Rock," he replied without skipping a beat, or looking away from the screen.

Vance Rock had been a mess of an operation in its own right, due in no small part to Grant Merger and his Syndicate henchmen. I won't go into the detail now, but as you can probably guess (or as you may know) that was the last operation on which Charlie had actually lost one of his team.

Between then and now, there'd obviously been casualties — people wounded, some of them seriously — but he hadn't seen one of his people killed in many years. That's a great track record for a Special Branch squad, considering the number of dangerous spots they're put into, but it somehow made a loss like this one even harder to bear.

Well, 'harder' being a relative term. Charlie tended to handle this sort of thing pretty well, at least outwardly.

"Doesn't get easier," I said quietly, stating the obvious in a bland way to indicate that I knew he knew what I was talking about.

He shook his head, "No, it doesn't. Might get harder. I can't tell yet."

I thought briefly of my state of mind since Egesta, then nodded in reply, "You may be right."

Again we fell silent, and continued to watch the screen. Some actors who were altogether too attractive and had too many of their teeth were swinging around now, in the dramatic strobe lighting of mag fire (like the gym when Karen and Josie fought, remember) clobbering, cutting and gouging the Special Branch squad in the movie.

Charlie didn't even blink, though I could tell he was remembering the gym fight when that came on. He'd seen it in real life... as had I, come to think of it. In a movie, it looks impressive. In person, it's damned terrifying.

"Mercury will be very bad," Charlie said quietly as the fighting went on. "Pions do it scary. The Martians will do it efficiently."

I didn't respond for a moment, then I sighed, "That's true."

More silence. This, I suppose, was unusual for us — our dialogue is so often rapid-fire and desperately attempts to be clever, but right now we were thinking about things that would be insulted by attempts to make them seem clever.

"So when are you going?"

That was my question, and it earned me a look from Charlie... I expected it to.

He knew exactly what I meant: I was asking when he was going to leave us to go to Lia's side. Interpreted another way, I was asking when he was going to abandon his squad. Interpreted yet another way, I was asking how much hellish horror he could take before it killed him.

I was asking when we were going to lose him.

He stared at me for a few seconds, frowning very slightly at his own thoughts, then looked back at the screen.

"I... don't know."

That answer spoke volumes, at least to me. Charlie's not the sort of man to run out on his squad — the people he's been committed to for years and years. He's also not a fool who thinks he can stay ahead of the demons he's been collecting for the rest of his life. He's also a good person, who wants to do the right thing.

The sum total of all these truths was a difficult one: he wanted to be with Lia, but he couldn't tolerate the thought of leaving his officers while he could still be of use to them. It was a very, very fine line to walk, and he knew it.

But as far as I was concerned, there was no one better to walk that line than Charlie. You know by now how much I trust him — that I vet my craziest schemes with him. During the war, I'd been reasonably balanced in those schemes... I'd yet to suggest a course of action that made him give me a solid look, and tell me I was taking it too far. I think Karen's presence aboard *Wolf* had helped with that because she too had a way of moderating my occasional madness... as I moderated hers, now and then.

Charlie, though, was an unwaveringly moral person. If anyone could figure a way to make his situation work, it was him.

So I left the question with him.

"Let me know when you know. I think Rufus will be sticking around, so if you go you won't be leaving me completely defenseless," I said that wryly, figuring Charlie had already thought of the unique and somehow poetic reality that he was sort of passing the torch of *Wolf's* Special Branch commander to a new guy who was already finishing his sentences.

But Charlie wasn't done yet.

"Whatever you want, I'll see to it," I finished up my solemn words, and Charlie was silent for a moment.

Then the mood turned, instantly.

"Ooh listen to mister big-shot, your wish is my command..." a smile spread on Charlie's face, and he glanced at me.

I chuckled, "I'm just saying is all. A Rear Admiral now, you know."

"Yes, Godfather..." Charlie looked back to the movie.

We kept watching, right until the surviving Special Branchers got away, and their CO declared that any Defense Command personnel who ever went back to Pion rock would be either supremely arrogant or completely insane.

I don't need to tell you that between us, we were probably both.

CHAPTER THIRTY-THREE
MOVING ALONG

I was sitting quietly in my cabin, the lights down and a stack of pads sitting in its usual spot next to my chair. I didn't want to be doing paperwork, but I'd decided I'd spent enough time *not* doing it for the time being. Of course, a decision like that doesn't actually make paperwork any easier... just the opposite, really. I've always found that when I try to force my unwilling brain to do tedious jobs, I'm about as productive as... oh... Martian industry.

Zing.

Yeah that was bad, sorry.

I rubbed my eyes with the palms of my hands and sighed. This was the day before we'd return to Belt Two, so I was starting to get everything in order to reconstitute the Jupiter Force, and to prepare for our cruise to Venus. That was going to be an important mission — arguably, one of the most important missions Defense Command had ever undertaken... I thus had a healthy respect for the paperwork involved.

Yep, I was respecting it the whole time I wasn't getting it done.

Then my door opened, and Karen half-stepped, half-stumbled in, still wearing her sleep clothes and with her eyes barely open. She rubbed her forehead with the back of her bandaged left hand and shut the hatch with her right.

"It's late..." she paused to yawn, "...why didn't you wake me up?"

I lowered my palms from my eyes and frowned, "You said you needed to get some sleep. I thought that made sense, given your condition."

I winced as I said the last part, and Karen lowered her hand from her forehead and blinked a couple of times, failing to clear enough sleep from her eyes to open them wide, "Condition? I'm pregnant?"

Shrugging, I winced and held up my hands, "Surprise?"

Too tired (or perhaps too unsympathetic to my bad humor) she shook her head and shuffled forward to my bed, then dropped face-first onto it in a rather unceremonious way, "Oww... Your bed is comfortable."

I leaned back in my chair and raised my eyebrows, "So I've been told..."

She didn't say anything, and I wondered then if she'd suddenly fallen asleep.

Then she lifted her head and turned it around to look at me... before letting her cheek drop to the comforter.

"Hi," she said.

I frowned again, "Are you on drugs?"

She tried to nod, but since she'd gone face first onto a bed, that gesture had to be done sideways, which apparently confused her, "The painkillers. But that's no excuse."

That was true. Painkillers have virtually no side effects, not unless Alicia had gone retro and prescribed morphine without telling me.

"I see," was the answer I managed, and she smiled, her winningest half-asleep smile. A pretty damned winning smile, I must say.

"Just here to visit. Not at all because I keep waking up from troubled subconscious voyages or anything like that. Not at all."

"Right. Not at all."

"Not at all," she nodded again. "Not. At. All."

We were silent for a couple of minutes, just taking in the complete lack of structure in this conversation.

"Well, if it helps, I've been having trouble sleeping too," I eventually said.

Karen lifted her head off the bed and scrunched up her brow, "How does *that* help? That means you don't have any valuable advice."

"I… uh. Oh."

"Yeah, see," she shook her head and then let it plummet to the bed again. "I'm getting tired of seeing things I don't want to see when I go to sleep, you know?"

I nodded, "I do know. First Egesta, now this?"

"*Lion's* crew too. It's horrible to say… but I'm glad Kris' face stopped melting. I'd never be able to sleep if she hadn't started to get better."

The way she said that was intriguing… her tone was playful, like one of our fun conversations, and somehow appropriate for the scene she set by flopping face first onto my bed in her powder blue sleepshirt and gray sweats and with her hair unbound.

Notice how I subtly included a description of what she was wearing and how her hair was arranged in there. Nice, eh? My editors asked me to pay more attention to those details. Also, I'm shallow and this look really worked for Karen. Most looks do.

Anyway, I've fessed up to my shallowness…

The thing about the way Karen said those words, though, was that I could see through… *hear* through, I guess, the playfulness. She didn't want to be haunted by the things she'd seen, but more importantly, she really didn't want to be seen as complaining about them. She knew, as I did, that whatever Andrea had seen must have been much worse. We both knew that what we had seen could in no way compare to what those people who'd been killed and injured by it all actually went through.

As I've said before, it was much, much easier to watch than to die.

Now, you can rightly point out that Karen had been a victim of the Phosgene in *The Dark Cruise*, but again, she'd come through pretty well. You could say that she'd been the victim of Pion violence in the fight with Josie, and she had been.

But if you asked her, nothing worth mentioning had happened to her. She didn't see herself as having any right to be as affected as she was by the things that had happened.

Clearly, this is not fair to her: anyone who'd seen these things had a right to be affected by them. But I couldn't say that, because I absolutely agreed, albeit for myself. I wasn't sleeping well — and no, I won't tell you about my dreams — but I had no good reason not to be sleeping, so I sure as hell wasn't going to complain about it.

While I thought Karen had a right to be distraught, I thus couldn't tell her that she had a right to that feeling, because then I'd be a hypocrite.

See how dysfunctional martyrdom can get into a stupid, self-perpetuating cycle?

"This is stupid, self-perpetuating martyrdom, isn't it?" Karen asked that question to break the silence I'd fallen into as I pondered her tone.

I looked at her in surprise, "Well, I was going to say 'this is dumb', but your answer sounds more smarter."

She laughed into the comforter, and then rolled onto her side with a winced, "Oww."

I winced when she winced — it wasn't easy for me to see Karen in discomfort like that. Sorry, call me corny or old-fashioned or something, but I get awfully sympathetic (and don't tell the neo-suffragists, but I also get a little bit manfully protective, even though Karen needs no protection).

"So we need to stop being all dumb and pretending like we're not allowed to be messed up after everything we've seen," I kept my eyes on her, and she opened her lids halfway.

"Yeah. And you still need to stop blaming yourself about allegedly losing your impartiality when Kate got shot, but I'm wounded so I don't want that argument now. But yes, we need to be okay with the fact that we're having bad dreams," her voice was a bit strained, as her pulled torso muscles were getting irritated from lying on her side.

"Roll onto your back, you sound like you're being stabbed," I actually sort of demanded that, and Karen's eyes opened all the way.

"This is not the way I sound when I'm being stabbed, thank you very much."

That one stopped me. I blinked once, and then I laughed. Karen started to laugh then too, but that immediately caused her side to hurt, "Owwww…"

Being mister idiot protective, I hopped out of my chair and bounced onto the bed to sit beside her, then quickly pushed her over onto her back.

"There."

She 'hmphed', "Well that might be more comfortable."

"I'll bet," I nodded. Then I proved my stupidity, "How do you know what you sound like when you're actually being stabbed?"

See, when I said stabbed back there (and I still don't remember how I earned enough genius to think this one up), I'd somehow not thought about Josie's spike — I'd been thinking of corny movie stabbings with little knives.

That's just bad humor under the best of circumstances. Given our recent history, I should have aimed for a more tasteful joke.

Top marks, Barron. Once again.

Karen opened her eyes and — bless her — smiled, "Well, it's not the sound I made when Josie spiked me."

As she raised her left hand towards me, I paled and winced, "Yes. That… is true."

She laughed softly for a second, trying to deflect the open wound of the subject, but that didn't really last. Her eyes darted to her hand, and then she bit her bottom lip, clearly remembering what she'd done.

"That's what I see in my dreams, honestly. Not just Pions, but what I do to them. I don't… I don't like when I get like that."

"It's been a while," my tone had grown more somber quite quickly.

Her eyes bounced back to me, "It's never been quite like that, though. I mean… I've never put a spike through someone's head before."

Yeah, she'd never actually had a spike handy before. But deep down, when she let slip the leash, there was a lot of cold fury in Karen, and it could come out. I suppose she'd say the same of me. Maybe that explains us… I don't know. But she had questions to ask herself.

"You protected yourself. You beat down a Pion leader," I felt the words weren't adequate as soon as I said them. "After Egesta… and *Lion's* crew… you've had enough anger backed up, I think. You're entitled. Even Charlie's starting to feel a little of that."

Lowering her hand back to lie on her stomach, Karen frowned up at me, "Maybe. You haven't really let it slip, though."

That got her one of my 'what the hell are you talking about' expressions, but she kept a serious gaze on me, "Don't try to call that Kate thing a letting go. You were in control the whole time, even if you didn't know it. But you haven't driven any spikes through heads."

"Charlie doesn't let me play with sharp toys," I immediately tried to side-step with humor.

Karen's right hand grabbed my left, and she shook her head, "Look, it's good. It's a good example for the rest of us. God knows you know how to go off. You're setting an example for all of us… for me especially."

Now, you know how I take praise. You especially know how I take praise that I believe to be completely inaccurate. Simply summarized: I don't take it.

"I… *no*…"

Karen struggled upward, and seeing that she was coming up I got a hand against the small of her back and helped her get into a sitting position.

"No, listen. It's one of the reasons you're the Admiral and I'm not…"

"Don't start that. That's luck, that's all that is."

"Fine, but listen, it's good. It's good for everyone to see… for Andrea to see and all the crews to see. It's really good for me to see. You're doing it well."

Come on, how am I supposed to take lies like that? Well, I'm supposed to stop calling them lies, I think. This was the first time since I'd begun attacking myself in *The Jupiter Patrol* that Karen's words on this subject were starting to have any resonance with me. Maybe, I started to concede to myself, I wasn't *showing* how difficult (or impossible) it was for me to completely isolate my emotions anymore.

Maybe my façade was helping.

And, of course, I've been saying in this book, and I think others, that a façade of confidence was the most important thing. Karen was telling me to just admit that to myself, and to give myself a little credit.

Now, I know all this self-help stuff might irritate some of you readers… some of you will probably be screaming at me saying 'yes finally listen and stop criticizing yourself!' Well… hmph. Stop screaming. Use your inside voice.

Karen leaned closer to me, drawing my mind away from the questions of my own recent performance as an officer, and let out a sigh as she studied one side of my head, "So how do you do it?"

I jerked away from her slightly, and shook my head a couple of times before coming up with an answer, "Well… having you around, and Charlie around… that makes it easy. Good people, see…"

Karen frowned instantly and jabbed a finger into my ribs.

I jolted sideways and yelped, "Hey! I'm not deflecting, it's true!"

Spreading a bright, blinding smile across her face, Karen held up the finger she'd used — on her left hand, "Sorry, just checking if I can feel the tips yet."

"There are more fun ways to figure that out," I rubbed my side, embellishing my pain.

Karen chuckled, "Only a few..."

We laughed... and about damned time, our laugh was entirely unforced.

Wolf blazed on for Belt Two.

AFTERWORD

So ends *The Canary Wars*, and when I think about it, I have to say the last four books — from *The Jupiter Patrol* up to now — really are the ones that to me make up 2232. Yes, I know *The Gallant Few* is officially in 2232, and this book is officially in 2233, but I've always associated the year 2232 with the hangover from Egesta, and all these grizzly, non-war-related experiences… so I think of *The Jupiter Patrol*, *The Sinope Affair*, *The Dark Cruise* and this book as all being part of that shadowy time, even though they don't conveniently fall into the same twelve-month bracket on the calendar.

With the next book, *The Forge Fires*, we're back to the war proper. It's a testament to how bleak my 2232 was when I say I'm looking forward to getting back to shooting at Martians… not being in the far reaches of the solar system, months away from anything that matters, and not dealing with their schemes and traps.

It goes without saying that the psychological hangovers from what we'd experienced would remain, but Karen and I had a decided advantage in coping with them (cue the violins, sorry to be soppy): we were in it together. That made all the difference, as I found out later.

Charlie had decisions to make, Andrea had more steps to take on her trip back, and everyone had other stuff to deal with. No, I won't be more specific.

That all said, *The Forge Fires* will ironically deal less with us and more with Shauna Cass and her situation at the Forge. We'll be in it, obviously, but most of the action in that book happens without us present. Sort of like *The Gallant Few*, but different again. If you don't already know the story of the Forge, then you'll just have to see what I mean.

In the meantime, we're done here. We're done with Pions and Canaries, and good damned riddance. Time to beat the Martians, even if they get a few swings in on the way.

Thanks for hanging in — see you next book!

THE
FORGE
FIRES

THE AUTOBIOGRAPHICAL REMINISCENCES OF
ADMIRAL THE LORD KEN BARRON FOR 2233

THE MARTIAN WAR - 10

KENNETH TAM

FROM THE AUTHOR

As we come to the mid-point of the Martian War series, I have to say we've been pretty spoiled. Aside from glimpses at some of the less-than-effective officers who were cruising the independent belt (back in *The Hawke Mission*) and Sean Cook's travesty of a command (*The Independent Squadron*) we've spent most of our time looking at the war from the perspective of elite, professional fighting women and men.

The Belt Squadron veterans are damned good at what they do, and it's bad luck for any unfortunate Martian who comes up against them.

But no Navy in history has been made up only of the elite.

This book gives us a chance to look at professional officers of a different caliber — officers who, by association, were assumed to be elite. It also gives us a chance to explore the differences between professional officers and reservists. Basically, reservists are people who don't crew Defense Command ships for a career: they have jobs and families at home, but take extra training so that in case of war, they can join the Navy to defend the Empire. When I was researching my MA thesis, I came across a lot of discussion of such reservists, largely because the Royal Canadian Navy in the Second World War was overwhelmingly dependent on them.

There is always concern that the weekend warriors, or whatever you want to call them, will not be equal to serious operations, and sometimes this is undoubtedly true. But there are cases, too, where reservists with natural talent and drive can exceed their professional colleagues. They often do this with a different style of command, but they get the job done.

So getting back on point, this book takes a look at what happens when unremarkable professional officers and remarkable reservists are faced by the very best the enemy has to offer.

Oh yes, that's right, the Martians come to play this time. I think the old adage that a wounded beast can be the most dangerous often plays out in history: a state that is losing a war can pull out all the stops, and really threaten to change the course of a conflict. Sometimes that doesn't work, sometimes it does, but either way it's a damned scary occasion for the side that thought victory was assured...

Anyway, cryptic messages from the author aside, I have thanks to give! Many of the characters you'll read about in this book are based on real-world friends of mine. Thanks to all of those fine people — I hope your characters do you proud!

Once again, thanks go to my good friends Peter Caron and Wes Prewer. Perpetual sounding boards, sources for great ideas... I'm very lucky to have such friends.

As usual, and most importantly, I must thank my parents and Iceberg partners, Jacqui and Peter. After ten books of Defense Command, I literally have no better way to say this: they are awesome. The awesomest, actually.

Atlas... thanks old friend.

– Kenneth Tam

PREFACE

So we come at last to the matter of the Forge. I've been craftily (well, I think it was crafty) inserting references to the Forge since John and Daragh came up with the idea of using the base to help stage our assault on Mercury. Now, at last, we get to deal with the well-known matter of that base, and Operation Sunbeam.

Ah yes, Operation Sunbeam. You have to really appreciate the Martians' naming conventions. I'm glad the war didn't last too long... next it would have been Operation Rainbow, or Operation Lollipop, or Operation Cute Puppy Dogs And Kittens And Yay! My editors think I'm taking the last one too far, but I'm standing by it, probably (inevitably) to my detriment. Ahem.

But I'm sorry, Operation *Sunbeam?* Sounds like the title of a movie about trying to harness the energy of the sun to melt a planet or something. Just doesn't sound very military.

Unfortunately for us, though, whatever the name made it sound like, it was *very* military.

And by 'us' I mean Rear Admiral Shauna Cass, one of my counterparts, and her people at the Forge.

For those of you who don't know, the Forge was once a major base of operations for Defense Command. It was set on a Vulcanoid asteroid... a rogue asteroid that got caught in our sun's gravity and is now in orbit... probably will be for another century or so before it manages to swing far enough out to escape.

The asteroid's orbital circuit is entirely contained within Venus', but Mercury's orbit is entirely contained within the Forge's. In other words, if you were to draw three rings, one inside the next, Venus would be the outside one, Mercury the inside one, and the Forge would be in the middle. Hey, maybe the publishers will put in a map... stop laughing. They might.

Lord Hawke had set up a base on this asteroid in the old days, and quite a base it was. It had a dome, of course, but lacking any sort of atmosphere, the place was severely pounded by the sun's radiation. By 2233, our radiation shields were more than capable of dealing with the huge doses you get at the Forge, but back in the early days, it was so 'hot' it was called 'Hell Base'.

I believe it was Daragh Ryan himself who dubbed the place 'The Forge' instead of Hell — Daragh had no intention of allowing anyone to think he'd listened to them and actually gone to hell, and he also saw that operating at this difficult post could really *forge* some tough crews. See, it was clever.

Back in those days — long before Marlene turned it into a crack unit — the Venus Squadron was more or less a joke. It was a patronage unit, where young men and women from the rich families on Venus could make their way up the rank ladder without having to fight or command or perform any of the other pesky duties we tend to do in the service.

That being the case, Lord Boscawen sent Daragh to the Forge to try to get a handle on the piracy that was really getting out of control around Venus. The Venusian pirates, either not caring about exposing themselves to radiation, or having better shielding against it than we thought they had, were working out of stations in orbit around the sun. The Martians weren't doing anything about them (in part because Mercury was comparatively poor, so the pirates never hit it), and it was up to Daragh to deal with the problem.

The Irishman thus earned his reputation, and eventually his peerage, while running his operations out of the Forge.

But the base fell into disuse when Marlene took command of the Venus Squadron and cleaned house, turning it into the sorceress-led pirate and Martian-basher we knew by the start of the war. But 'disused' didn't mean 'gone entirely' — there was a large dome on the asteroid, and plenty of base infrastructure, so John and Daragh decided to ramp up DC presence there during the second year of the war.

As I think I've mentioned, Shauna Cass was put in charge. Shauna is remembered in various ways, depending on the movie version of this you watch, or the book you read. Many people have attacked her on a variety of fronts, blaming her for all sorts of things. Some of these criticisms have merit, but many have gone much too far.

My perspective on Shauna has always been that she was my counterpart... she was supposed to be to Marlene what I'd been to Greg: one of the solid officers who could be trusted, fully capable and competent, and fit for command. Questions of whether she was as 'elite' as advertised have been raised, but I won't repeat them just now. Either way, what transpired at the Forge falls on her shoulders.

I've never liked the idea of second-guessing a commander from the comfort of an armchair after the fact, so I'm going to try not to do too much of that here. My aim is to give you an inside perspective on the tough decisions Shauna faced, and how she came to her conclusions — even when those conclusions are at variance with what we Belt Squadron types might have done. And I have to admit, I always feel an element of 'there but for the grace of God go I' when I talk about Shauna at the Forge, so I will sympathize with her (to my editors' frustration).

Ultimately, I aim to be fair. Whether I succeed or not... well. We'll see.

I suppose by now it must be clear that this book is going to be one of the few in this series that doesn't focus on us. As with *The Gallant Few*, we'll certainly have a presence, but I believe we'll be what the fiction people call the 'B' plot. The story begins about six weeks after we'd returned from Pion rock, and by this time all the strike forces that were destined to join the Mercury assault had left the Belt and were on their way to either Venus or the Forge by way of Earth. This was a largely inactive time for us... we were in transit.

For the Forge, though, this was anything but an inactive period.

Sorry, one more aside. My editors are somewhat nervous about my approach to this book... they had some concern that telling this story mostly from the perspective of those on the Forge (or telling it at all) would disconnect readers from the series.

Evidently, I have more faith in you than they do, and I won the argument.

Of course, you've probably seen some of the movies about this whole situation, and there's a reason that so many are made about it: it's a compelling story. If I can keep my act together as a storyteller, I should be able to get it across without too much loss of interest... hopefully.

Let's find out.

CHAPTER ONE

THE NEW CAST

Shauna Cass swung her legs out of her bed and rubbed her eyes. She'd been worrying greatly about her situation at the Forge, for the reasons I've already described. Having her based on that rock was a move designed to divide the Martians' attention — they probably knew that we were coming for Mercury next, but if we'd been coming only from Venus, they could have launched their Mercury Squadron against that planet in a preemptive strike.

Because we had two bases of operation in the Mercury area, we could attack from either… they couldn't risk striking out with the Mercury Squadron against one and not the other, because to do so would leave Mercury vulnerable to a counterattack.

That said, Shauna knew her situation at the Forge was in some ways quite precarious, and it was costing her sleep.

What if the Martians were foolish and did decide to sortie — to try to hit Defense Command first, even if it meant the end of their attack force and left Mercury defenseless?

Worrying, you see, was not something unique to me… not by a long shot.

"Can't sleep?"

Shauna lowered her hands from her eyes and shook her head, "No, I don't suppose I can."

The question had come from the man in her bed, a certain Colonel of Special Branch named Hwangbo Yang. Hwangbo (his surname) was a Venus native and a hell of a Brancher — he'd made his bones as one of Marlene's best Special Branch Majors when she'd crushed the Venusian Pirates, so when the Forge had needed an overall commanding officer for its many Special Branch teams, he'd been a natural fit.

Over the past year, Yang and Shauna had discovered a certain amount of chemistry existed between them, and around the time Karen was recovering from her Phosgene poisoning, they'd finally gotten up close and personal.

Yang sat up and shuffled sideways and let his legs drop over the edge of the bed, sliding an arm around Shauna's waist, "Well then I won't sleep either."

Shauna chuckled, "Aye, well for you sleep's more of a luxury than it is for me, isn't it? You Special Branchers, I dunno…"

I should mention that Shauna's English is neatly accented by her native Scottish brogue. No, I don't know why so many people in the fleet seem to be Irish, English, Scottish or from Capital Island… maybe it's part of the tradition of the North Atlantic or something — being in a fleet, I mean.

"Sleep is never a luxury. But you shouldn't have to do without… things are under control here," Yang offered evenly.

That was true — business at the Forge seemed to be going quite smoothly. The base had two battleships — *Warlock* and *Medusa* — on station, along with the carriers *Akagi* and *Kaga* (believe it or not, they were actually proving useful), four frigates and seven corvettes. Of the latter two classes, three of the frigates were new *Asia*-class ships, right out of the yards, and five of the corvettes were equally new members of the *Australia*-class.

In other words, they had plenty of firepower, and combined with the shore-based batteries, the Forge had to be considered fairly secure.

But that didn't stop Shauna's worrying, which was fair enough if you ask me.

The couple sat on the edge of Shauna's bed for a few minutes, not saying anything, before Yang took Shauna's hand and squeezed it, "How long until Noyce gets here?"

"Eleven days, fourteen hours, twenty minutes... give or take..." Shauna replied without missing a beat. "Suppose I'm looking forward to spreading the weight around."

Yang laughed, "A little eager, I'd say. We'll be fine. Seriously, you know the Martians wouldn't be fool enough to come out here and make trouble... if they did, Fiora would be all over Mercury."

Shauna stopped the attempts to reassure her with a slight scowl, "Come on now, you know better."

Know better than to try to talk her anxieties down, she meant. Shauna knew better than anyone else exactly what situation her base was in — it was (to insert more convenient exposition) orbiting ahead of Venus at the moment, so while Mercury and Venus were almost on opposite sides of the sun at this point, the Forge was actually somewhat exposed.

Or so it felt.

If — *if* — the Martians decided to make a play against the base, now would be the best time, before Venus caught up to the Forge and before Mercury flew around the sun and started to pass them both again.

No matter how strong a force Shauna had in place, and no matter what Greg was bringing with him, she had to be concerned.

Hwangbo Yang decided to concede the point, and they continued to sit in awkward silence as time ticked by, while Shauna tried to control her heart rate. I know what she was going through. Sometimes, when there's a lot on the line, just thinking about trying to stay calm can in fact make you more anxious. It's a delightfully vicious circle that can utterly destroy sleep.

That said, I was never as vulnerable to such sleepless nights after Karen boarded *Wolf*. Where Yang couldn't really convince Shauna that the situation wasn't as potentially bad as it appeared, Karen could always convince (or coerce) me to worry about it the next day, not in the wee hours of the morning. I like to think I could offer the same support to her.

This isn't a criticism of Yang or Shauna... really, it's a testament to Karen's remarkable calming skills.

"I dunno, I think I might take a walk and burn off some nervous energy," Shauna said after a while, and started to shift off the bed.

Yang's grip on her waist tightened and Shauna glanced back at him quizzically.

"Think about what you just said, and where you're sitting," the Colonel said with a smile.

Shauna frowned, then shook her head, "What… a walk?"

"Nervous energy to work off," he wasn't terribly subtle about that, and after a second to process what he meant, Shauna indulged him.

Captain Kelly Monahan skippered the battleship *Warlock*, and was the senior CO in the Forge Squadron. While Shauna was sleepless and reducing her nervous energy, Monahan was sitting in her cabin, entertaining a visit from an old classmate.

Captain Ophelia Zhukov was the skipper of the battleship *Medusa*, formerly of the Heavy Squadron, and if you'll recall, one of the ships that fought in Glorious February.

The two battleships had been on station together at the Forge for months now, but Ophelia and Kelly still liked to get together some nights to share drinks and remember the old days. They'd been relatively casual acquaintances at the Academy, but at the Forge — where shoreside entertainments were few — casual acquaintances could rapidly become intimates.

"I hate this place," Ophelia's accent was thoroughly Russian (I don't know, by the way, if she was descended from the famous General Zhukov), and she was properly forthright about her opinion. "The sooner we get on to attacking Mercury, I say, the better."

Kelly Monahan was from Boston, and she just laughed, "Now tell me what you really think."

"I just did," Ophelia replied shortly, and took a shot of the vodka she'd rather predictably brought with her.

Monahan was of Irish descent, so she wasn't cowed by the Russian's appetite for the drink, "We'll get our chance soon enough."

"It's already not soon enough," Ophelia smiled and poured another shot. "Promise me we'll drink together when we're finished destroying the Mercury Squadron, yes?"

Kelly Monahan laughed, "You ask me to promise that every time we drink together."

"Don't want you to forget," was the stern reply.

Finishing off another shot of vodka and screwing up her face, Kelly shook her head, "Good point, enough of this shit and I will forget."

"Precisely," Ophelia poured another shot.

The Captains got drunk together.

While veteran officers were either trying to sleep (or were otherwise occupied in bed), drinking or doing something else entirely, Commander Puruhi Arama of the new *Australia*-class corvette *Adelaide* was pulling an all-nighter.

"I wish to hell they'd installed this correctly the first time," his XO, Lieutenant Commander Francine Fuentes, grunted rather bluntly, but Puruhi couldn't gather the breath to reply.

He was using all his strength to help keep the console he was holding from dropping onto his XO — any break in his concentration would likely have ended badly for her.

"Got it… no wait… got it!" Fuentes slid out from under the console, and with a proper grunt the Commander lowered the console unit back onto the deck.

"Thanks, Bruce," Fuentes got to her feet and wiped her hands off on her pants.

'Bruce' was the pronunciation most non-New Zealanders used when they couldn't do justice to Puruhi's Maori name — he was, of course, a Kiwi of Maori descent. And being from Capital Island, I'm going to go with 'Bruce'.

Bruce and Fuentes weren't the only two working on consoles on the bridge — most of the bridge crew were here, as well as a handful of engineers. This rewiring had become something of a ship project. Essentially, it had been discovered that the civilian yard that had built *Adelaide* had skimped on the finishing touches: the conduits and cables that connected most of the consoles on the ship to the power taps in the floors and walls were only *civilian* grade. This meant that, if the corvette took a heavy hit and the power grid surged, those cables and conduits would either melt or explode.

Either way, the ship would be deprived of its control surfaces, unless all the cables were replaced. Needless to say that Commander Arama had decided the replacements were necessary.

Of course, Bruce was going about this in an unusual fashion. He'd filed a request with Forge Repair Section, but the small team of engineers based on the rock were tied up doing serious overhauls to the reactor buffers on *Warlock*. Remember the problem that caused reactor radiation spills when secondary systems were hit with beams? They were fixing that in a battleship, which trumped the power-line problems in a corvette.

Bruce had said that was fair enough, then had requisitioned all the military-grade conduits and cables so *Adelaide's* crew could do the install work themselves.

They'd been working all day, and now all night, and pretty soon it would be another day...

"Bruce, Helm and Navigation is all done," *Adelaide's* Helm and Navigation Officer, Walter Borjigin, stepped up behind his skipper, wiping his hands on a rag. "I'm going to head down to aux helm control to give them a hand, if that's alright."

Turning with a nod, Bruce grinned at the Lieutenant, "I'm not going to stop you."

Matching the grin, Borjigin saluted loosely and barked at a couple of his people to depart the bridge with him. Bruce watched them go as he sucked in a deep breath. He was pretty sure he was going to feel the burning in his muscles tomorrow... he'd been lifting consoles for his XO all day, and even though they'd dropped *Adelaide's* shipboard gravity by thirty percent to make the job easier, he was getting tired.

Bruce was a big man — sturdily built and strong. Up until 2231, he'd spent his days as a general contractor in Auckland.

So now the logical question is why and how he found himself commanding a corvette.

Well, Bruce had been a Commander in the Defense Command Naval Reserve. I believe I've mentioned the reservists before, in relation to the mobilization of personnel to crew all the new ships John was building. Here we are, on one of those new ships, and every single member of Bruce's crew was from the Reserve. This is relatively unusual — policy tends to hold that you should mix regular force personnel in with Reserve crews to make sure there's enough experience aboard ship... there simply hadn't been anyone available to put aboard *Adelaide* when the corvette had been ordered out to the Forge.

Theoretically, Shauna was supposed to assign some of her regular personnel to augment *Adelaide's* crew, but after seeing how Bruce and his ship were performing, she'd decided there was no reason to.

Sometimes you get lucky, and *Adelaide* certainly had: the crew of reservists had gelled very well, and the majority of them proved to be excellent spacers, even though many of them had been on Earth full-time for their day jobs. Believe me when I tell you that this sort of success was not common — most Reserve crews needed plenty of time and coaching from full-time personnel to achieve the standard that *Adelaide's* crew had easily reached. Part of the credit for that obviously goes to Bruce, the rest to his fine crew.

As you might be able to see so far, though, the culture aboard a reservist-crewed ship was a bit different. Bruce, for instance, wasn't 'Commander Arama' to anyone. This is something else we found aboard reservist ships... there was a much, much less formal atmosphere. Skippers and spacers could drink together, play cards together... they were almost expected to. Classically-trained officers like Dave Caldecott would have blown blood vessels if they saw such behavior in practice... I just would have been aloof and useless at it. But it was necessary for these crews, for whom the discipline of full-time military life was new.

This wasn't a phenomenon unique to our service, of course. Right back to the Canadian Navy of the Second World War, reservist ratings and officers had been interacting much more informally than the rule books said they should.

Whatever works, I say.

All in all, Bruce was doing a fine job, and the spirit of teamwork aboard *Adelaide* was making this thirty-six hour maintenance entirely pleasant.

Mildly painful, but pleasant.

"Need the Adlenol again?" Fuentes slapped Bruce in his meaty upper arm and he laughed.

"That and a soak in a hot tub, maybe. We have one of those on this baby?"

Fuentes shrugged, "Your ship, you find out!"

They stood back and took a break for a few more minutes, then started on the next console. Though small, *Adelaide* had a lot of consoles. They had many hours ahead of them.

CHAPTER TWO
ON OUR WAY

While Bruce Arama was lifting things, and Captains Monahan and Zhukov were drinking, and Shauna was… er… while all that was happening at the Forge, I was sitting in my chair, with a tall stack of pads on one side, and a much shorter stack on the other. Karen was lying in her usual spot on my bed, with two similarly-configured piles in front of her.

She wasn't looking at the pads, though — she'd stopped working on her Commodorial paperwork and was studying the palm of her left hand.

I looked up over the pad I was reading at one point, then lowered it with a frown, "Stop picking at it."

"I'm not picking at it," she protested in a decidedly child-like fashion.

"Well, stop staring at it. Staring's not going to make it go away."

Karen frowned and glared at me out of the corners of her eyes, "I've come all this way without a scar, I don't want one now."

I released a sigh and let my head fall back against the back of my chair, "It'll give you stories to tell after the war."

"I'd still have stories without the scar," she looked grumpily back at her hand. Sorry, I can't think of a better descriptor than grumpily. You have to understand, she wasn't being foul or unpleasant… she was more like a puppy who'd been confounded by having her favorite toy stuck inside a clear plastic tube, and was trying to figure out a way to release it.

Yes, I just compared Karen to a puppy. She really did look incredibly cute with that frown. Yes, I just called Karen cute, after having compared her to a puppy. You already want me to get out of this scene and go back to the Forge, don't you? Sorry, not yet.

"Well," I pushed on, baiting her a little, "they say scars are sexy."

"I'd still be sexy without the scar," she mumbled before she thought about what she was saying, and then she turned red and really glared at me. "Hey! You tricked me!"

I grinned, "You said it, must be true."

"Bastard. Talk to me about deployments."

You could tell I had her on her heels — a rare thing, but then, it was rare for Karen to be scarred by her infrequent hand-to-hand altercations. A testament to the physical combat prowess of the Pions, I suppose.

"Pfft," I shook my head, "you're not going to change the subject now. I'm going to make you preen some more."

I was discovering a certain evil joy in tricking Karen into saying things that she would never normally say. I can't remember precisely when it had started… perhaps during our layover at Earth, when we'd dropped in to visit her sister Kathy (who is rather Karen's opposite) and she'd come away unimpressed by how much Kathy thought of herself.

"Talk to me about deployments," she insisted, so I held my hands up and shrugged.

"What do you want to hear again?"

"Hmm. Um..." she paused. "Never mind. I have reading to do."

"Yes, you do. Don't stare at your sexy reflection too much in the pad screens."

I ducked just in time to avoid the pad that flew at my head, and then I picked it up and tossed it back onto the bed with a grin. We were enjoying our long, quiet transit out to Venus.

Aboard *Nova Scotia*, just down the line from us (the Jupiter Force and the Independent Squadron were heading to Venus in a combined formation), Wes Pellew was sitting in his chair trying to do the same thing I was doing.

Well that's not true, he was actually trying to work, and wasn't interested in harassing anyone. See, Wes is a responsible grown-up, who likes soup and doesn't like heights.

He was interrupted, though, by a comm call. His screen flashed once and he looked up, then grabbed his remote and scrolled to the message. It was from *Wolf*, so he figured it was just me calling over to give him grief (I was really getting up to no good on this trip, and I have no good excuse for that poor behavior). He accepted the realtime signal without a second thought, then went back to his reading.

"What this time, Ken?"

There was silence for a moment, so Wes' eyes darted up over his pad, and then locked on the screen. Whoops.

"Andrea, hi, sorry," he dropped his pad into his lap and frowned. "What can I do for you?"

Andrea Kiley was in her sleep kit, which wasn't the usual attire one wore when comming a Flag Officer like Commodore Pellew. As Wes noticed almost immediately, though, the Irish skipper was soaked in sweat, and her expression seemed tight.

"I..." Andrea started with that word... and then stopped.

She was silent for another moment, and Wes was already figuring out what was going on: she'd had a particularly bad nightmare about Egesta. That was normal enough.

The weird part was that she was calling him about it. She hadn't done that before. Ever. She hadn't said a word to him about Egesta since before the mission to Pion rock. Granted, they'd not been in realtime range much since then... but even so...

"Just... checking in, Wes. Is... everything alright?" Andrea was suddenly feeling quite embarrassed about making this call at all, and while she knew her attempted back-pedaling was quite flimsy, she had to try.

Wes narrowed his eyes slightly, considering what he should say. Sure, he was the only member of the old Belt Squadron family to have any scant experience with the sort of pain Andrea was experiencing, but he was decidedly aware of the fact that his pain couldn't compare to the enormity of hers.

He thus had to think like a counselor, not just as a compatriot who was mildly familiar with agony. I hope that makes sense.

Would it be better to press her for the real reason for her call... or just to let her back away?

He decided fast, "Everything is fine, Andrea."

Biting her bottom lip, she nodded, "Good."

"Thanks for checking in," he continued. "Please do, whenever you want to."

Andrea swallowed and nodded, "I'll keep that in mind. Good night, Wes."

"Good luck, Andrea," Wes gave her a last nod before she cut the link, and then stared at his blank screen for a moment.

It took him a while to shake the conversation and get back to work.

Charlie Peters had just finished sparring with his new 2IC, Captain Ben Belete. You might remember Ben… I think he was first mentioned in *The Sinope Affair*, when he was a Lieutenant driving Charlie around in Io dome. With Raza Weiss laid up on Earth getting his arm reconstructed, and with Carly Henderson lost on Pion Rock, Ben was Charlie's choice to fill the second-in-command role.

Even Charlie was willing to admit that it took some getting used to.

Finished with the session, Charlie bade Ben a good night and headed for his quarters to shower. His squad had been working hard on their assault tactics, and on integrating the new members who were replacing the dead and wounded. Some were familiar faces — Gina Bertram was Charlie's other new Captain, and she'd been with him on Io… remember in *The Sinope Affair*, when she'd led her provisional team of nine in defense of the dome HQ building?

Others were fresh out of selection, and needed time to get oriented with their new unit. All of that was keeping our intrepid Major busy, which he took as a good thing. He was finding that his focus had been slipping a little lately — not when he was working, obviously, but when he had time off.

The question was looming over him: when was he going to pack it in, and hang up the MAG-90?

I know — the thought was almost inconceivable to us, too. But for all his superhuman abilities, Charlie was still human, and the wear and tear from the past years was taking a slight toll on him. Combine that with the fact that Lia Hawke really was going to need him soon, and he was facing some huge choices.

He'd decided so far that he wasn't going to leave before the assault on Mercury. He couldn't conceive of leaving his squad before that operation. They needed him. Indeed, he'd probably wait until the end of the war… but what if the war went on and on…?

Those were the sorts of questions that were preoccupying Charlie, despite his stalwart attempts to simply tell himself to decide later. It was almost beginning to irritate him, which was why he was enjoying the simplicity of training. At least working got his mind off it.

Being preoccupied all the time was no fun.

"You going to walk into me?"

Charlie stopped instantly, looked up and discovered Rufus Chang was standing right in front of him. Rufus was heading in the direction Charlie was coming from, obviously on his way to the gym for a Special Branch training session of his own.

"I was going to see if I could find someone to do some move-and-shooting with. You interested?" the Major with the mismatched eyes asked the Major with mismatched thoughts, and Charlie frowned thoughtfully.

Well… why not?

"I'm in."

The two Majors went off to practice shooting things… as if they weren't already deadly enough.

Wolf, the Jupiter Force, and the Independent Squadron hurtled on towards Venus.

CHAPTER THREE
THE OVERVIEW

John Fiora had brought the *Bonaventure* Squadron to Venus, and when he'd arrived it had been quite a show. The Venus stations and domes are packed with some of the richest and most arrogant people in the Empire… and I don't mean to say that the rich ones are the arrogant ones. Sometimes the two overlap, but just as often the most arrogant people are those who pretend to be rich — people trying to fit in with the supposedly arrogant culture of wealth, not realizing that the so-called 'old money' of the Empire is actually pretty personable.

Anyway, all the money and the arrogance in Venus local space meant plenty of yachts and other small craft had flocked around *Bonnie* and her sisters as they entered Venus orbit, getting pictures and saturating the ships' comm grids with welcome signals.

It took twenty minutes for Marlene Stoll's first message to get through to John, and he didn't even manage to meet with her on that first day. Instead, the Venusian Council of Lords had invited him to visit them down in one of their illustrious surface domes, and with specific orders from the Prime Minister to be 'cordial', John had to comply.

I won't bore you with the details of that meeting. The Lords are not bad people, but… well, they're not regular people either. Living in those domes on the surface of Venus keeps them isolated — and isolated by choice. I still have a hard time believing that wealthy people enjoy living in domes on the surface of a planet with an atmosphere over ninety times thicker than Earth's, but then, I don't mind rubbing elbows with regular people.

If you want to live in a private community with only other wealthy people and carefully screen service staff, then a Venus dome is for you.

John went down almost as soon as *Bonnie* tied up at *Venus One*, the chief military station in orbit of the planet. He spent the rest of that day (into the night, in fact) being thanked by all the Lords for bringing the most prided battleships in the fleet to their aid, and being promised that they'd see his title perpetuated so that he could come live on Venus with them.

He didn't agree to anything, obviously.

It was the next morning when he finally got a chance to shake hands with Marlene, and now the two of them were sitting in John's office on *Bonaventure*, discussing the plans for the Mercury assault.

Alright everyone, this is it… MARLENE IS BACK! YAAAAY! MARLENE MARLENE MARLENE MARLENE MARLENE!

Too enthusiastic a greeting? Well in the first draft of this book, there was a whole page of MARLENE copied and pasted for effect. The editors cut it down — to the bare minimum, if you ask me. If you've been reading all the way up to this point, you know why I'm using the all-caps. Since *The Almost Coup*, book two, Marlene's been on the other side of the Empire. Finally — FINALLY — we get to see the sorceress in action again.

YAY!

Sorry. Quieting down now.

"So you survived the Lords?" Marlene smiled as she settled into the chair opposite John's desk, and he chuckled and tugged at his collar.

"They're promising to perpetuate the title. Never have I wanted so much *not* to be Lord Fiora."

Marlene laughed, "Price of being good at your job."

"You watch it, I'm very much considering recommending you for peerage, for the job you've done out here!" he shot back.

Marlene frowned, "But I've been doing a good job, why the punishment?"

They shared a laugh at the Venusian Lords' expense, but I'm sure the Lords will understand. As I say, not bad people... just very insulated.

"Ken and Wes are on their way out here," John slid a pad across his desk towards Marlene. "This is the update to the package I sent ahead before I left. You saw that I didn't bring any escorts with me?"

Marlene nodded as she picked up the pad — *Bonnie* and her sisters had flown from Earth to Venus alone, with no frigates or corvettes screening them. That was potentially a risk... but then, they were the *Bonnies*. Their battle record was so far beyond impressive, it was superpressive.

Yes, I made that word up. And though they protest, I know my editors secretly love it. They let me make up one new word per book.

"Wes has five frigates and two corvettes. Ken's got three frigates and five corvettes, which I don't think has changed either. They're coming here to reinforce us."

Just to add the necessary exposition (sorry, you know how the start of books are big on exposition), Wes' Independent Squadron hadn't changed its makeup at all since he'd brought them back from the Barbary Cluster — he had the frigates *Nova Scotia, British Columbia, Nunavut, Yukon,* and *Prince Edward Island,* along with the corvettes *Corner Brook* and *Port Aux Basques.* His ships were all specially tuned for pirate-hunting, meaning they had acceleration rates higher than ships like *Wolf,* and other assorted tricks that were prohibitively expensive to install, but were damned useful too.

The Jupiter Force was stronger than it had been since leaving for Io, though — and the best part of that was the fact that the ships we'd gotten back were all veterans of the old Belt Squadron, albeit with some new faces commanding.

We had the frigates *Wolf, Cheetah, Alberta* (commanded by Kasia Hu instead of Marshal Samuels, who was now running operations at the Belt), along with the corvettes *Friendly, Trusty, Generous,* and *Sackville.* That meant Commanders Togo and Romanov were back with us, after their sabbatical escorting convoys and doing something else... now what was that... oh *right,* joining Greg and Mik for the raid on Mars during Glorious February.

Sorry, that was a little juvenile of me — I just want to make sure Isoruku and Katya are remembered for their part in that fine operation. It was great to have them back...

"Greg and Christian Mikaelsen are taking their forces to the Forge to reinforce Shauna. Lia Hawke is with them too, personally commanding a contingent of Hawke ships," John waited as Marlene scrolled down to that section of the pad, and then the sorceress frowned.

"I didn't know Lia was coming out herself."

John nodded, "I was surprised when she turned up in my office at Admiralty House. You know how she is about surprising people."

"Good at it. Did she meet Daragh?"

John shook his head with a smile, "He was out shooting up some contractors' offices, I think. If those two ever meet… it'll rip the fabric of the space time continuum thing."

"There'll probably be gunfire," Marlene agreed with a laugh. "Well, if she wants to command her own ships, that's her right. Greg will take over at the Forge when he arrives?"

John nodded. Greg was taking his force to the Forge, as was Mik. I'm going to go ahead and list all of these forces right now, and who knows, maybe we can get a chart to organize them all. Maybe… if there's a typo on the cover of *The Canary Wars* or something…

Anyway, Greg's squadron consisted of four battleships, *Warspite*, *Goliath*, *Empire* and *Rodney*, the latter two having been detached from the Heavy Squadron of the Home Fleet. He also had the new *Asia*-class frigates *Guangxi* and *Jilin*, and the corvettes *Perth*, *Canberra* and *Nanton* (now skippered by Commander Lisa Sims, not Mik's old troublemaker Guy Vivar, thank God).

Mik himself had overall command of the Hawke Squadron, which was what we were calling the combined Defense Command-Hawke Command force. Lia was his deputy. His Defense Command ships were his battleship *Cyclops*, the frigates *New York*, *Maine*, *New Hampshire* and *Utah*, plus the corvette *Amherst* (still commanded by the formidable Nikhil Jones). Lia's Hawke component included the frigate *Whirlwind* and the corvettes *June*, *Daisy*, and *Helen*.

So, pulling out the calculator, that meant Greg was bringing four battleships, two frigates and three corvettes, while Mik and Lia were providing one battleship, five frigates and four corvettes. Total number of ships heading to the Forge were five battleships, seven frigates and seven corvettes.

Oof, that took a lot of effort. You might want to flag this page for future reference as to what ships are where… well, only if you care about that sort of thing. If you don't care as much about the minutiae of what ships are where, then don't worry about it. I certainly wouldn't blame you! That said, I still have one more list…

Marlene's Venus Squadron, less the ships she'd sent with Shauna to the Forge, included the battleship *Sorceress*, the frigates *Kodiak*, *Newfoundland*, *Ontario*, *Hunan* and *Guangdong*, and the corvettes *Gallant*, *Noble*, *Melbourne* and *Sydney*. Total forces under Marlene's command right then were thus one battleship, five frigates and four corvettes.

Running the tallies, that meant we were going to have twenty-nine ships at Venus, and thirty-four ships at the Forge. We'd be ready for a joint attack as soon as our relative orbits to Mercury suited our designs. I should point out that this was the largest force Defense Command had ever assembled, and we were pointing it at the Martians.

So getting back to the narrative, Marlene looked up from all these numbers on the pad and frowned, "We all going to hit Mercury at once?"

John gave a slow nod, "I'd like to, though it may not be possible. When Mercury gets around the sun again, we'll send *Akagi* and *Kaga* up to check it out. If the Martian squadron there hasn't moved, we'll all go. If they're missing, Greg will lead with the Forge force, and you'll take Ken or Wes and move out as well. We can't leave Venus defenseless if we don't know where the enemy is."

That was very prudent thinking — much more prudent than the thinking Grand Admiral Garvey had employed during Glorious February. The *Bonnies* by themselves would be able to protect Venus from any sort of attack by the Martians, leaving the rest of the assault fleet to hit Mercury...

But hopefully it wouldn't come to splitting our forces like that. Ideally, every ship, including the *Bonnies*, would go after Mercury, all together. Hopefully.

Marlene nodded slowly and laid the pad back on John's desk, "Well, I've never seen this many ships deployed anywhere. This is over sixty percent of our pre-war strength... all hitting one target. That's really incredible."

"It is."

There was nothing to do but agree.

Anyway, this meeting obviously went on, but as is my habit, I'm going to leave it there. I'm quite conscious of the fact that more exposition will likely cause a brain hemorrhage or some frustration.

On we go, back to the narrative!

Or... well, blame the editors for this one. Seriously, if you're close to having your brain melt, skip it. A good question was asked: what defenses were left at Earth? Don't worry, I can sum this up quickly. Earth had the supercarrier *Ark Royal* (not fully repaired after the beating it took in *The Almost Coup*, but now well-enough restored to be able to fight in a pinch) along with *Revenge* and *Royal Sovereign* (in different states of repair). The new battleships *Hokkaido* and *Honshu* were there too, along with a strong guard force of escorts under the command of Shannon Hunter.

Two more battleships, *Shikoku* and *Kyushu* were out at Belt Two, reinforcing Marshal Samuels' Belt Squadron.

So we had heavy cover in most of the key places, despite the huge commitment we'd made to capturing Mercury.

Alright, that covers it all!

CHAPTER FOUR

UNEXPECTED

Shauna Cass was in her quarters in the Forge dome, working through a pile of pads. Paperwork (yes, we know it's an anachronistic term since we all use pads) is something no Flag Officer can escape, and Shauna was trying to reconcile herself to that fact. It wasn't working so well for her... the pile of pads was frustrating.

Yet another sentiment I quite understand.

As she was trying to work her way through a requisition for more power conduits (*Adelaide* had used up half the base's supply), a message flashed up on her screen. Her remote was sitting in her lap, so she grabbed it and accepted the incoming message, and as she did Captain Monahan appeared.

"Shauna, just got a signal from *Kaga*. One of their planes is missing."

A frown crossed Shauna's brow, and she laid down the pad she was working on and came to her feet, "Out on its patrol run?"

Monahan nodded, "Was checking in fine on regular intervals until it got out to the extreme end of its flight... about fifteen hours from *Kaga's* position."

Shauna looked down from the screen for a moment, then nodded, "Alright, it could just be comm failure. Has *Kaga* sent a plane out after it?"

Monahan shook her head, "Not yet. They wanted to report back before they did anything."

"Of course..." Shauna bit off the end of that sharp reply. The carriers were proving useful so far, but both their skippers were relatively conservative, and tended not to work well under their own initiative. I suppose I can understand that to some degree... the Battle Over Earth had proved how vulnerable the carriers could be, so conservatism might have been sensible.

But 'sensible' wasn't always helpful.

"Tell them to send out another plane to investigate, and put Commander Ivanov and Commander Arama on alert. We might need to send them out to have a look around," Shauna narrowed her eyes in thought as she gave those orders.

"Yes ma'am," Monahan acknowledged and then faded from the screen.

A missing fighter — particularly if it was one of the aged Sunbursts the carriers were flying — wasn't in itself terribly unusual, but it was better to be safe than sorry. Better by far.

For now, though, it was back to paperwork.

"You definitely have some micro tears. Were you doing a lot of deadweight lifts during the rewiring?"

Bruce Arama winced at the question as he lowered his arms back down to his sides, "You know how it is, doc. Need to make sure the crew sees me pulling my weight."

Doctor Krista Lapolo shook her head and turned away from her Commander, "You can put your shirt back on. And no, you don't actually need to show off your strength, skipper. Don't see Ken Barron out there servicing mags with his crews, now do you?"

This is creepy. They were referring to me and I wasn't there... and now I'm writing about them talking about me.

"Yeah, but you don't see me in the press all the time either," Bruce grimaced as he pulled his shirt back on. "Belt Squadron officers can lead any way they like. This isn't a Belt Squadron crew."

Bruce wasn't criticizing his crew when he said that, nor was he criticizing us. He was just pointing out the very real differences between an elite, professionally-filled Belt Squadron crew and his reservists.

One thing was for sure: Bruce knew how to lead the sort of spacers and officers he had. I certainly wouldn't doubt his methods... and Doctor Lapolo wasn't doubting him either. In civilian life she was a family doctor, and a mother of three — aboard *Adelaide* she was rapidly becoming the 'ship mom'.

Turning back to Bruce with an injector gun and a little cup with some pills, she shook her head, "Well, if you're going to do the heavy lifting, at least recruit an extra set of hands. This shot will accelerate the knitting, you're going to be chewing the Adlenol for a while, though."

Bruce gulped down the painkillers as Doctor Lapolo injected him, then nodded, "Well, the rewiring's done, so I should be able to have a break from lifting."

"Good," Lapolo finished up and patted him on the shoulder. "All done."

"Thanks doc," Bruce hopped off the medical bed he'd been sitting on, and with a parting nod he left *Adelaide's* med bay, heading for the bridge.

He took the long way, making sure to admire the shining decks of his new ship. *Adelaide* hadn't been out of dock for long, so everything felt new, and added to that, his crew was proudly keeping every deck and corridor spotless.

Anyone he passed greeted him with a smile and a nod, and he gladly returned the gesture. He quite liked the ship's company, and he wasn't afraid to show it.

Eventually, though, he had to get to the bridge, and get back to business. In fact, he was turning the corner into the last corridor on the way to the bridge when his comm beeped. Slowing slightly, he drew the unit from his belt and fumbled with the key, "Bruce, go."

"Orders from flag, Bruce. Need you on the bridge," Lieutenant Commander Fuentes reported, and Bruce nodded to himself.

"On my way."

He entered the bridge a moment later, and Fuentes turned to greet him with some surprise, "That was fast."

"I was just down the hall when you commed," he smiled in reply. "What does Admiral Cass need?"

Fuentes turned towards the main screen at the front of *Adelaide's* bridge and pointed, "Looks like *Kaga* had a plane go missing. Could be a mechanical issue, but in case it's something nefarious, she wants us and *Earnest* ready to go have a look."

Bruce frowned thoughtfully as he stepped forward to join Fuentes, and examined the information on the screen. *Kaga* and *Akagi*, the two carriers assigned to the Forge, were both constantly out on deep-range patrol missions, increasing the chances that Martian or pirate mischief would be detected. In order to cast the biggest net possible, the two carriers were operating separately, both about twenty hours out from the Forge.

With additional long range tanks, their Sunbursts and Starbursts had the ability to patrol out an additional twenty hours — meaning a round trip patrol for each plane of forty hours. Bruce certainly wouldn't want to be one of those pilots, crammed into a cockpit for that length of time.

I'm personally very glad I was never put on a patrol that long. A day in a Starlight (which is a much more spacious plane than a Starburst) was too much for me...

But the pilots from *Akagi* and *Kaga* were willing to do the job, and that meant that there was a line of scouts out there, constantly watching to make certain nothing unexpected reached the Forge.

Hopefully, then, this was just a mechanical failure. If that was the case, the fate of the lost pilot could certainly be in question, but at least it wouldn't mean the Martians were coming.

"Think the Martians are playing at something?" Fuentes asked, sparing Bruce a glance.

Frowning and folding his arms... then wincing at the microtears in his muscles as they changed position... he shook his head, "I don't know. I guess it'll be up to us to find out, if nothing more is heard."

Fuentes nodded but said nothing, and Bruce took a breath to pause and think through what would need to be done to prepare *Adelaide* for a patrol.

"Alright, inform all department heads that we are going to patrol standby. Let's make sure we're ship-shape before we get sent out," he said smoothly. "Ready for some adventure, Francine?"

She grinned back, "Always ready, Bruce. You know me."

He laughed. Back home Francine was a preschool teacher — she had adventures all the time, they just usually involved things other than weapons, explosions and death.

As you can hopefully see, the brave men and women from the DCNR came from all walks of life, and were fine people.

Adelaide made preparations to cruise.

CHAPTER FIVE

GROUNDWORK

While Shauna was preparing various scouting options to investigate the missing plane from *Akagi*, John was involved in one of his many coordination meetings for the Mercury assault. Sitting with him in his office on *Bonaventure* was a woman who, according to Charlie, is 'tougher than something that is very, very, tough — and probably even tougher than that'.

She's so tough, he can't think of any real-world similes that make her sound as tough as she is. That, I think you'll agree, means she's tough.

The woman, of course, was Brigadier General Peri Oktar, the most senior General in Defense Command, and the commanding officer of Defense Command Special Branch. There was no one higher ranking in the Special Branch command structure — she reported directly to Vice Admiral Hirobumi Tesso, the Admiral in charge of SF.

That made her the top Special Brancher in the Empire.

While I often like to point out how people in reality tend to defy the stereotypes we expect of them, Peri Oktar did not. She was powerfully built and she carried an air of invulnerability. She'd started in Special Branch back in Daragh's day, and all these years later she was still in, and still able to kill a room full of enemy Commandos with, oh, a pigeon. And the pigeon wouldn't even be hurt in the process.

These days she'd moved up to top command-level work, which meant she was John's chief planner when it came to the assault on the Mercury domes. That was what they were meeting about, indirectly.

"We have a total of 2,120 Special Branch officers available for this landing," Oktar was explaining. "That includes the officers from every ship in the force. It is obviously not enough to do the job."

John nodded, "How many SF has Tesso added to the mix?"

Oktar seemed unimpressed as she recited the answer, "He has provided 7,144 total. But many of these are police volunteers who are not properly trained for the mission. They are not as well trained as I think they must be."

Oktar didn't mince words, and it would probably be awkward if someone like her tried to.

The answer, though, was not a good one from John's perspective — roughly 10,000 'troops' (twenty percent of them massively over-qualified for the landing, eighty percent of them not trained for it all) was not a great force to be moving in with. The Mercury domes held a total of three-and-a-half-million Martians, with probably 10,000 or 15,000 security personnel mixed in there.

Which meant Defense Command really couldn't come up with an argument to stop the plan that was in motion...

"So there's no way I can keep the Imps out of this?" John asked with a sigh, and Oktar shook her head.

"We need Imperial Army troops, or this assault will fail."

John leaned back in his chair and rubbed his forehead — of course it would. The damned blockheads, for all their brutality and general stupidity, were a fully-trained, armed and equipped Army. That's why we'd called them to Egesta (so help us), and that's why we'd need them at Mercury.

John hadn't *really* thought there'd be a way to exclude the blockheads from the invasion, but just in case he was wrong, he'd wanted to ask his Turkish Brigadier one more time. Was there any way the formidable Brigadier Oktar could do it with Defense Command forces alone?

But there wasn't.

"Well, that's going to be music to the Emperor's ears," John said after a long break.

"In the absence of a Marine Corps, we are forced to cooperate," Oktar observed coolly, and John nodded in reply.

Alright, hold onto your chair: time for a historical aside. A Marine Corps, if you're not familiar with the distinction, is a force trained for ground combat, but which is an integral part of the Navy. No Emperor had ever let Defense Command start a Marine Corps out of fear that it would give Defense Command too much independent power. All ground combat missions of any considerable size had to be handed to the Imperial Army, which reported directly to him.

Obviously, there were developments on this front after the war, but for the moment John had no option — Defense Command had no marines, just Security Forces that were somewhat experienced in combat (but weren't trained infantry) and Special Branchers who were over-qualified. He needed the Imperial Army.

Great.

Picking up one of the pads on his desk, John tossed it gently to Oktar, "Came in this morning. The Emperor has done us the *favor* of sending reinforcements. Major General Ronald Frederick Hubert III is bringing 30,000 of his best and brightest out to Venus in several different convoys over the next week. Most are coming off Egesta, as Daragh and I had figured."

Oktar took one look at the pad and her face soured, "I know Hubert. If he commands this mission we will lose."

John's head fell back against his chair and he let out another sigh, "That's what I figured. I'm going to make sure you have overall command, but I'm sure Hubert will be *displeased*. We'll deal with him... but he's going to be a pain in the ass this whole way, isn't he?"

Oktar nodded, "Count on it, sir."

As if assaulting Mercury wasn't, in itself, going to be tough enough, now we had to play nice with the blockheads in red. And many of them, I should add, were later proved willing participants in the Egesta Crisis.

Charming.

Anyway, back to the Forge...

Chapter Six

Recon

The carrier *Akagi* was twenty hours out from the Forge, and its skipper, Captain Jens Holbrook, was feeling somewhat exposed. Jens had been a Wing Commander in *Yorktown*, and had survived the Battle Over Earth in the cockpit of his Starlight, watching all the capital ships of his squadron getting mauled around him.

That had definitely informed his perspective as a carrier CO. He now had no interest in letting *Akagi* get caught within laser range of… well… anything.

Akagi and *Kaga*, I should say, were very old ships, and were both slow and thin-skinned. That being the case, Holbrook's caution wasn't unfathomable, it just removed any chance of derring-do from his ship's repertoire.

"*Akagi*Star AA23 to base, I have reached the patrol area," a voice came over *Akagi's* bridge speakers, and as he heard the words, Holbrook began to pace. AA23 was the plane they'd sent out to investigate the missing recon Sunburst from the last sweep. Would trouble be found?

Holbrook stopped at the front of his bridge and watched the data stream that the Starburst had sent from its burst comm, then started tapping his foot. He wasn't yet accustomed to the sensation of standing on the carrier bridge and waiting for answers — he'd been trained up in the Light Squadron to be a pilot, to be the man who led the way into danger.

Standing back and waiting for it was a different beast entirely, as I think we've covered so far in these books.

But waiting is exactly what he'd have to do — there was nothing in the scout's report that would shed light on the situation.

"Their plane just got onto the patrol grid, about forty-one hours out," the Sensors and Communications Officer in Forge Command and Control reported after decoding the burst message from *Akagi*. "Nothing suspicious yet."

Shauna was pacing back and forth across the C&C deck in the Forge's HQ building, and now she nodded, "Thank you, SCO."

Waiting for news was as brutal, if not more brutal, for her… the gravity of the situation was potentially enormous. Where had the plane gone? Was there an attack force on its way?

But Shauna rightly didn't allow those questions that were bubbling under her skin to surface — pacing aside, she did her very best to project a façade of confidence to her people, and she succeeded. She was Marlene's protégé, remember, and there is no question that she had learned some things from the sorceress. Like how to wait.

+++

Allow me now to do some reconstruction.

*Akagi*Star AA23 was piloted by Ensign Will Flynn, a young flier who'd only gotten his wings during 2231. He had spent twenty hours flying from *Akagi* out on the same course that one of his squadron mates had taken a couple of days prior, on the previous patrol cycle, and let me tell you, twenty hours in the cockpit of a shiny new Starlight is not easy.

In the cockpit of an old Starburst, it's verging on cruel and unusual.

But he was only twenty, and he was excited to be doing his part for the war effort. He was undoubtedly terrified too, though, and rightly so — he was flying out beyond any help, looking to see if one of his buddies had suffered a mechanical failure that would almost certainly have killed him... or if the Martians were out there.

Getting out past the point of his predecessor's last comm check, he was now in potentially hostile territory.

For the first few minutes, he saw nothing on his sensors panel. He had his Starburst's hurriedly-upgraded recon sensors blaring away on full active scan, and they were coming up blank. While he might have been holding his breath as his plane flew out into the danger zone, he started to feel some relief.

No sign of Martians.

No sign of the debris from his buddy's plane, either, but if there had been an explosion, debris could have scattered all over in the hours since *Akagi* had lost contact with the missing craft.

For about half an hour, Ensign Flynn cruised ahead, his scanning computer sending *Akagi* reports on what it was seeing — or not seeing — every ninety seconds. This was much more frequent reporting than most recon flights provided, but because Flynn was in an area of suspicion, increased contact was necessary.

Then, as Flynn started to relax, a blip appeared on his panel. He undoubtedly panicked for a split second, then figured out what to do: he brought his combat systems online and primed his burners — he'd be ready to squeeze every little bit of thrust he could out of his aged Starburst if this blip proved to be a Martian.

Correction, if *these blips*.

His sensor computer sent back one more scan of its display to *Akagi*, and then a pack of Interceptors dropped like falcons on Ensign Flynn. He undoubtedly jinked and tried to escape, but he was dealing with the combat patrol of a battleship squadron. He didn't have a chance. No single pilot would have.

As I say, this is all imagined by me, based on what we got from Flynn's regular burst check-ins. I don't know for a fact that that's what happened to him... but we do know what he saw in that last terrifying instant of his life.

"Send this through to Forge C&C immediately!" Captain Holbrook's voice was quite urgent as he stood at the front of *Akagi's* cramped bridge.

*Akagi*Star AA23 hadn't been able to send in a clear threat assessment of the force out there, just a basic picture of blips. Blips didn't give actual classes (though we could estimate based on size), but it certainly gave an idea of numbers.

There were seventeen blips on this scan.

"Sending signal now," *Akagi's* Sensors and Communications Officer reported quickly, and Holbrook nodded.

"Good, request orders from flag about what we're supposed to do."

"Seventeen…" Shauna's façade very nearly collapsed when the sensor feed from Flynn's plane appeared on the C&C's main screen. "SCO, do what you can to guess classes based on the sizes of those blips. I'll be in my office, when you have a report let me know."

Waiting to receive a nod of confirmation from her commander at Sensors and Communications, Shauna took a deep breath and left the C&C. Every step she took towards her office pushed her heart a little higher into her throat. Including *Akagi* and *Kaga*, two ships that were largely useless in combat, she had only fifteen vessels at the Forge.

This could be trouble. There were Martians less than two days from her rock, and Greg's reinforcements were still a week away.

She stayed calm as she walked, but already Shauna had a very bad feeling about what was coming next. John had to be informed.

Chapter Seven
Damnation

John's jaw was set as he stood in front of the screen in his office and looked over the sensor scan from the ill-fated Ensign Flynn. Seventeen blips, three of them probably battleships. Based on the estimates from the Forge's sensors operators, the squadron makeup was three battlewagons, six destroyers and eight destroyer escorts — a force largely comparable to Shauna's... except for that extra big gun...

Well, that's how it looked according to the estimates.

Marlene was standing back from the screen, arms folded and eyes narrowed, "Why are they just sitting out there? If they shot down the first plane, they would have known that we were going to send another... they can't be foolish enough to think we didn't see them."

With a nod, John turned away from the screen, "Best guess is they're waiting to rendezvous with more ships... maybe... that'd be the only reason I can think of that would keep them in place."

Making rendezvous in space is never easy, so if you say you're going to meet someone at a certain set of coordinates, it's best to stay there unless you positively cannot. Otherwise there's a good chance the rendezvous won't happen at all.

"And DCI had no idea they were out here?" Marlene asked the question quietly.

"None. Their [best guesswork] put the Mercury Squadron in Mercury local space, and the Mars and Asteroid fleets in their home orbits..."

Uh-oh, it's the return of the hated [square brackets], denoting a source of information that I still can't reveal. Remember *The Gallant Few?* Well, here we go again. Why is it these brackets only appear in books in which Karen and I take a back seat?

"Well the [guesswork] is wrong, so we better get DCI to start looking over its [guesses] again. Meantime... what do you think about this? Greg's still a week away... I get the feeling these blips are going to head to the Forge long before he can intervene."

When Greg, Mik and Lia arrived at the Forge, they'd have with them more than enough ships to tip the balance back in favor of Defense Command. Remember, he was bringing five battleships with him. But these Martians were forty hours from the base, and Greg was a week away. Venus was five days away from the Forge, given their orbits just then, so if John took the *Bonnies* over they'd still be days late... and that wasn't an option in the first place: the Venusian Lords would never have stood for their battleship protection leaving them.

Let me pause quickly to expand on that point: some have suggested that, had John immediately broken dock from Venus and taken the *Bonnies* at full burn to the Forge, everything that we're about to discuss would have gone differently. That's undoubtedly true, but remember that John couldn't know whether this was a feint, or if there was in fact another force getting ready to attack Venus. And Venus, with its millions of people and very politically-connected Lords, was much more important to defend than a radiation-saturated Naval base with few civilians.

In fact, to be quite blunt, one of the reasons the Forge had been built up was to make it the lightning rod for any counterattack the Martians could hope to mount. If the Martians got wind of our plans to hit Mercury (which we assumed they would) then we'd provided them two targets to hit with a preemptive strike. Venus, with its huge population, many stations, and large defense force would be the tougher of the two targets. The Forge would be more attractive.

Of course, if you go to Defense Command staff college, every officer there will point out that Venus was still the better target — it was what Clausewitz called a 'center of gravity', meaning that, in military terms, it was a very valuable target. It would have meant more to the Martians to capture Venus than it would have to capture the Forge…

But that didn't matter. The Martians chose to attack one of our two bases to slow down our assault on Mercury, and they'd picked the more vulnerable option. To answer one editor's question, we did predict this — John and Daragh had guessed that, if the Martians decided to counter, they would pick the Forge. What was surprising, though, was that the Martians were doing anything at all: we hadn't expected them to have enough ships, or enough will, to go on the offensive without severely weakening Mercury's defenses.

But here they were, managing to both menace the Forge *and* protect their outer capital.

"We're going to have to let Shauna deal with them," John said quietly after several moments of thought. "With those numbers, she should have a pretty level chance. If they can deal with the extra battleship, they'll be alright."

Marlene agreed with a slow nod, "The shore defenses can make up for their deficit in mobile units."

Her voice trailed off, and she took a couple of steps towards the screen, "But do you think she should go out to meet them, or wait for them to come in?"

John stared at the blips thoughtfully and let out another long sigh, "If it were me, I'd go meet them. Worked last year."

"Yes, I'd tend to agree," Marlene concurred softly. "How about we leave it up to her judgment, but recommend she goes out."

"Sounds like a plan," John agreed. They recorded a message to Shauna.

Shauna was sitting in her office when John and Marlene's signal came in. While those two venerable Admirals had been mulling over the options, she'd been on the line with Captains Monahan and Zhukov, having a very similar discussion.

"Their battleships can't be anything new… Noyce's raid on Mars destroyed their hulls under construction," Monahan was remarking. "That means they have to be old wagons. Either damaged and repaired, or ancient and put back into service. We can handle them."

"Ophelia?" Shauna wanted Captain Zhukov's perspective on that claim, as *Medusa* had been with Rachel Butler's force during Glorious February. The Russian skipper knew very well what the Martian battleships could do.

"I believe that Kelly is correct. If they had any new battleships, intelligence would have informed us so. I believe these must be old ships detached from their home fleet, and that we can likely defeat them if we seize the initiative."

Ophelia was making some assumptions there — assumptions based on her gut feelings. This is something we do all the time, as I think we've established over the books so far. Sometimes, in the absence of information, you have to trust your gut and make the call. Our best leaders — people like John, Greg and Marlene — got to their top spots because, through luck or through skill, their gut reactions always seemed to prove right, or pretty close to right.

Shauna had to go with her gut now too...

Then John and Marlene's message came in. She paused the meeting for a moment while she watched it in a small window on her main screen, and then nodded to her two battleship skippers, "Well, First Lord Fiora and Marlene recommend that we go out there and try to make a mess of the Martians' plans. Better to try to fight them in open space than here, where we'd be limited by the Forge."

What Shauna was saying was that, given the choice, she'd prefer to fight the Martians where there were no objectives to protect. If her squadron waited at the Forge for the Martians to show up, then she'd constantly have to worry about staying between the Martians and the base when battle was joined. If she went out to meet them, then at least in an immediate tactical sense she could maneuver as she liked. It improved the situation for the Forge Squadron if they fought in open space.

"Alright, so we go," Kelly Monahan sounded slightly eager. She hadn't had much opportunity to face the Martians yet in the war, so she was looking forward to the chance to do her part.

Shauna nodded, "Let's assume the Martians started coming this way at full burn as soon as that plane found them... I'll order *Akagi* and *Kaga* to rendezvous at a point seventeen hours out, and we'll meet them there, then start looking for the Martians. Does that make sense?"

Monahan and Zhukov nodded in agreement, and Shauna thoughtfully tapped her fingers against her desk, "We'll have to keep the fighter recon up as much as we can... we cannot afford to let the Martians slip past us in space."

"Good thing we have two carriers full of planes out there to track them, then," Monahan added. "You going to fly your flag from *Texas*?"

Shauna looked up, "Yes, of course."

"Good. When are we departing?"

I think you can tell that Monahan was really the most eager of the three involved in this meeting, and Shauna needed a second to catch up to the enthusiastic question, "Let's... well, we need to move immediately. One hour. I'll be in touch from *Texas*."

With additional nods from the two skippers, Shauna's screen blanked. She sat still for a moment, then got on her comm again, issuing orders to get her squadron ready to cruise.

They were going to go looking for the enemy.

CHAPTER EIGHT

LOOKING FOR A FIGHT

The air aboard *Adelaide* seemed to be full of nervous excitement as the corvette prepared to boost from orbit around the Forge. This was the first time the crew of the new ship had ever been sent towards possible action, and they weren't even getting a chance to start small.

"Seventeen ships? Wow..." Francine Fuentes sounded like someone trying *not* to sound nervous, and Bruce nodded.

"It's one of the biggest forces they've put together," he agreed, "but only three of them are battleships."

That wasn't a huge comfort, but it was something. The Forge Squadron was made up of two battleships, two carriers, four frigates and six corvettes. That meant they were outnumbered in every class but for the carriers, but only outgunned by one or two ships in each case. Now, thinking back for a moment to *The Gallant Few*... remember how I explained about the advantage of one ship allowing for double-teaming? That was the concern that the Forge Squadron faced.

Just to review more explicitly, the Martians would have an extra battleship when battle was joined, which meant one of Shauna's battleships would be double-teamed by two Martian heavies, and would theoretically die twice as fast. That was bad news, though as had been seen in Glorious February, being outnumbered didn't always prove as devastating to the smaller force as the rulebook suggested.

All this theory was something that Bruce Arama knew, but it wasn't something he could afford to worry about. His responsibility in the coming days was his ship, and making sure his untested crew was ready to participate in one of the larger Naval actions of the war.

"Once we're squared away for cruising, I'm going to go section to section and talk to the crew. We need to make sure everyone stays calm and remembers their training," Bruce said in quieter tones.

He and Fuentes were in his day cabin, so there was no particular reason to speak quietly about something like ship morale, but Bruce somehow felt he couldn't say it too loudly.

His concern was apt, of course — as far as I'm concerned, the way he was thinking about the state of mind of his crew is proof that he was fit to command *Adelaide*. Many regular-force officers are wary of reservists getting commands without a history of space duty... and usually I *am* one of those officers. But occasionally you get natural leaders who have excellent minds for their new jobs... those women and men are worth their weight in gold.

Fuentes nodded slowly at Bruce's words, "Yes, right... of course. We'll make sure everyone is feeling steady when we get out there."

Bruce studied his XO for a moment, "And that includes you, Francine. How're you doing?"

She smiled nervously, "How do you think?"

With a soft, gentle laugh, Bruce half shrugged, "I'm the same, I think."

"Really?" Fuentes eyed him curiously. "You really don't seem it."

The Maori Commander laughed a little more heartily, "Then I'm a good faker."

"I suppose you are. How long do we have until we boost?"

Bruce's eyes darted up to the chronometer on his wall, "Forty minutes. Let's get out there, make sure that we're ready to go."

Shauna Cass stepped onto the bridge of her longtime frigate, the *North America*-class ship *Texas*, and allowed herself a deep breath. She'd been skippering *Texas* since I'd been skippering *Wolf*, so she had a long history with the ship, and was comfortable aboard it. As commander of the Forge station, she'd been obliged to do a lot of work from the base's C&C, which had left her homesick for her ship on more than one occasion.

Captain Calleigh Tong had taken over as CO of *Texas* in Shauna's absence, and now the skipper approached her Admiral with a smile, "Good to have you back, boss."

Despite her anxieties, Shauna replied with a broad smile of her own, "It's very good to be back, thank you Calleigh. Are we ready to boost?"

"All set," Tong nodded.

"Good. Establish Battlelink and let's get ready to move out."

Shauna headed to the front of her trusty old bridge and stopped at the railing, running her hands back and forth over the cold metal rods in a move that had always given her comfort during stressful moments.

The faces of her squadron's commanders began to appear on the screens before her, and she nodded to each of them as they turned up. There were so many, in fact, that *Texas'* bridge didn't have enough screens, so windows in the main screen were used to show those who signed on last.

"All ships ready to boost?" Shauna straightened up and asked with a practiced calm. If you watch the logs, she looks and sounds every inch the professional — unfazed and ready for whatever was to come.

Of course, you know by now that anxiety is the enemy of every commanding officer in this fleet. How we deal with it is one of the things that can make a real difference in action.

For the moment, a chorus of 'yes ma'am' and 'aye aye' was the answer to Shauna's order, and she smiled smoothly and nodded, "Excellent. Alright everyone, we're going out there to look for a fight — potentially a rather large fight. I know we've been sitting here for quite a while, but we need to shake off any rust, and do our very best. I trust that you all will."

One thing I'd never done much was give little speeches like that... I always felt too awkward to do them, because I knew that in the Belt Squadron and the Jupiter Force, they were largely unnecessary. But Shauna was under different circumstances — without the benefit of an elite and professional force — so she decided to offer the rousing words. Her comments brought some anxious smiles to the faces of skippers who'd never seen action, or to those who hadn't seen action in command. These men and women — and their crews — were nervous, and as far as I'm concerned, they had every right to be.

I don't think going into battle is ever *easy*, but it's probably tougher to do the first time than any other. Actually... no, it may not be. It's undoubtedly different for everyone, so I shouldn't attempt to generalize.

Anyway, Shauna was still giving orders: "We'll boost in formation established by the squadron orders. Speed is to be 190 kps, and we will rendezvous with *Akagi* and *Kaga* in seventeen hours, long before the Martians could reach them. Clear?"

Answered by a similar chorus to the one that had come before, Shauna linked her hands in front of her and nodded, "Squadron, let's get under weigh."

"Helm, mark our preset course and make our speed 190 kps. Get us into line," Captain Tong gave the orders for *Texas* behind Shauna, and on the Battlelink, every skipper gave essentially the same orders in their own unique way.

The Forge Squadron was heading out from its base on short notice, looking for trouble with some Martians who'd decided to preempt our assault on Mercury.

CHAPTER NINE
SPREADING THE WORD

"We're slowing down for our scheduled comm stop, Jim."

Jim Hannigan had the watch on *Wolf's* bridge that afternoon, and he was rather tired. While we'd gotten rid of our reporters after 2232, John had decided that we should keep a camera aboard *Wolf* during 2233, to record footage that could prove useful for our recruiting adverts, and so on. Defense Command Public Relations had offered a team, but after a request from Jim, Karen and I pulled some strings and got a civilian into the job.

Yes, you guessed it, we got Bunny Fox a full-time job on *Wolf*.

This wasn't just a matter of us helping Jim out with his love life: everyone on *Wolf* knew Bunny after the Jupiter mission, and since she'd lost the rest of her camera crew and Jocko in *The Dark Cruise*, she'd been an orphan at her news agency. If we were going to have a camera aboard ship, then, it seemed like a solution to many different people's problems to give it to Bunny. We knew we could trust her, it gave her a place to be with familiar, friendly faces, and it kept Jim happy.

And tired.

As I was saying, Jim was a bit tired on this watch. Now, now, let's not be juvenile, this isn't the Geraldine Coilier Show!

Anyway, Shelby McLaws made that report about our designated comm stop, and Jim nodded somewhat sluggishly, "Felicia, send to *Venus One* with our standard report."

What we were doing here was actually stopping our cruise towards Venus at a pre-designated hour and checking in, so that Venus could know exactly where we were to send back an update. Arguably, this was an unwise thing to do — if the Martians somehow tracked Venus' comm laser, they could find out where we were, and potentially ambush us.

But remember, 'us' included the entire Jupiter Force (now massively reinforced) and the entire Independent Squadron… we weren't terribly worried about being ambushed. On the contrary, we were much more concerned about turning up in Venus local space uninformed about any moves the Martians were making.

It seemed quite possible to us that the Martians would try something preemptive — that they'd mount an attack against Venus or the Forge to try to hold up our assault on Mercury. If they did that, we might have to cruise somewhere other than Venus, to intercept, reinforce or whatever else. Hence the daily comm stops. They didn't slow our progress appreciably, and they kept us informed. Win win.

Greg's force heading for the Forge was doing the same thing, I should add.

Anyway, Jim was only half paying attention as Felicia Khalid, our now-veteran Sensors and Communications Officer, oversaw the receipt of John's latest update package from Venus, and routed it up to the main screen.

He woke up with a jolt when he saw its lead message, though.

"All senior officers to the bridge," he ordered immediately.

+++

"This is going to be bad," I was pretty forthright about my expectations as I stood in the lift with Karen and Andrea. They both looked at me with slightly tight expressions, not needing to say anything to communicate their agreement.

We all had a feeling... that's about the only way I can describe it. Karen and I had been going over personnel files on some of the new faces we were seeing in the ships that had rejoined our force, when the hasty call from the bridge had reached us. And we both knew that such an urgent call from Jim would only come if there was a negative development.

"Well... I suppose the Martians could have surrendered," Andrea offered with a shrug.

Andrea was starting to sound more naturally relaxed than she had for over a year, which was very nice to hear. Her half joke was taken with a smile, and Karen let out a deep breath.

"We can hope," she said softly.

Hope indeed. There's no question, after what we'd been through out at Jupiter — the hard battle we'd faced against the Martians there — we were very conscious of how tough an assault on Mercury would inevitably be. Obviously we were going to participate, and we weren't going to complain that we had to... we were just well aware of how much Mercury was going to cost us.

If we won there, the victory could very likely end the war — having control of Mercury meant we would have a bargaining chip that could force the Martians to sue for peace. That was why John had long ago decided Mercury had to be the target, instead of the Martian asteroid colonies. The Martians could lose a dozen asteroids... hell, they could lose *all* of their asteroids... and it probably wouldn't bother them terribly.

Comparatively poor though it was, Mercury was their outer capital — their version of our Venus. If we took it, they'd be virtually out of options.

How did I get onto this tangent? Oh right, we weren't looking forward to the assault, but knew it was important. Right.

Anyway, Karen, Andrea and I arrived on the bridge several minutes after our summons, and as we appeared, Jim pointed to the main screen, "The Forge seems to have guests."

We studied the seventeen blips uncomfortably for a moment, and then Wes Pellew called over from *Nova Scotia*, having just seen the same thing, "Looks like the Martians figured out what we were up to."

I nodded in reply to Wes' words, "Looks like... and Shauna's going out to get them."

"Gutsy," Andrea remarked quietly from behind me. "She must be certain this isn't a decoy."

I swallowed and nodded. John and Marlene must have looked over this data and recommended Shauna go out to tackle the Martians, but there had to be a fear that the seventeen ships were just a decoy force — that they would draw the Forge Squadron out while more Martians swept in behind to take the base.

Such was the risk that had to be taken, though. And chances were that no second force existed.

"If they're sitting out there, letting two different planes see them in the same spot, then they're waiting for reinforcements," Karen said quietly. "Or... like you say, Andrea, they could be bait. But hopefully the Martians wouldn't use seventeen ships as bait."

What Karen was suggesting was that, if the Martians were just out there to draw Shauna away from her base so a second force could attack it when it was defenseless, they probably wouldn't have committed seventeen ships.

But what if they'd faked the seventeen ships... creating false warship signatures on sensors was possible...

Jim Hannigan somehow knew what I was thinking, and he interjected, "I checked. Before they shipped out to the Forge, they upgraded the recon sensors on *Akagi's* planes. I don't think these are decoys."

We all nodded at that, quite confident in Jim's opinion.

Even so, though, this was a scary thing to see. The Martians knew what we intended, and were trying to do something about it. While it seemed likely that they couldn't actually stop us from hitting Mercury, we couldn't afford to underestimate them.

And, as you'll recall from *The Gallant Few*, we hated watching things like this build up while not being in any sort of position to do anything about them. We just had to wait and see what Shauna and her squadron were able to accomplish, and hope they'd be able to win...

Wolf began to accelerate from the comm stop a few minutes later. We'd have to wait for tomorrow to find out what happened next. We were still four days away from Venus.

Chapter Ten

Carrier Anxiety

Captain Holbrook had been a flier for too long to stay out of the briefing that his pilots on *Akagi* received about an hour after Shauna cruised away from the Forge. His carrier was dropping back to the designated rendezvous coordinates as per Shauna's instructions, but even as it pulled back, it was necessary to keep all the planes aboard cycling through constant patrols, trying to see if and where the Martians were moving.

"We're going to focus recon in the direction of Flynn's contact. With all squadrons, we're going to fly a pattern that covers 130 degrees on the *x* axis and fifteen degrees on the *z*. When *Kaga* joins up with us, they'll overlap the course…" *Akagi's* Wing Commander already had the planning well in hand.

Holbrook simply stood to the side with arms folded and a grim look on his face. He remembered what had happened to *Yorktown* when the Martians had come to grips with the Light Squadron. I don't think anyone can blame him for being anxious about the prospect of having his carrier and *Kaga* sitting alone in the path of a new assault force.

"Each one of you is going to have a spoke that covers five degrees on the *x* and on the *z*. You will not be on each others' screens, but if someone tries to slip between you you'll see them. Comm bursts every three minutes for the first five hours, then down to one-minute reports after that. Expect to run into the Martians out there, and if you do, see if you can get a closer look at their force. Bottom line, though, come back. Don't take unnecessary risks."

Holbrook started nodding at those last words, and he stepped forward out of the corner, "Todd, if I can cut in."

The Wing Commander looked back over his shoulder, "Of course, sir."

Holbrook cast his gaze over the pilots sitting in the large ready room, "I wish I could be out there with you. This is going to be one of the riskiest recon missions ever flown by Defense Command. It's not going to be easy. But look after yourselves and come back. We'll be waiting for you, and we'll need you to help beat these Martians when the squadron arrives. So be careful out there, no risks."

That was *interesting* advice to give. It was these pilots' job to risk their lives to find the enemy. Period. It's a cold reality, but it's *necessary*. And Holbrook didn't seem to accept that.

"Carry on, Todd," the Captain glanced at his Wing Commander, and the man nodded and went back to his briefing.

Holbrook didn't wait around — instead he turned and left the ready room.

About twenty minutes later, six squadrons of Sunbursts and Starbursts being tasked with the recon mission — every plane *Akagi* had ready to fly — went out.

The next hours passed with a dreary slowness. Shauna spent several of them in her cabin, trying to catch a nap, but by the time the Forge Squadron passed Waypoint George, one of the outer beacons in the Forge's sensor grid (lying about ten hours out from the rock) she was back on *Texas'* bridge, sitting in her chair.

Her mind was racing, trying to sort through every option available to her. The Martians had three battleships, she had only two... how could she compensate for the difference? Was it simply a matter of sending *Medusa* and *Warlock*, both of them older battleships, straight at the Martians, and trusting that Monahan and Zhukov could get the job done?

That was the easiest answer, but as you'd expect, Shauna was mulling over her options again and again, hoping that a new idea would change everything...

"We're now seven hours from the designated rendezvous point," Captain Tong lowered herself into her own chair next to Shauna's at the back of the bridge, offering that report quietly.

Shauna's reply was a nod, but she said nothing.

If the Martians had started coming towards the Forge as soon as the second recon flight had detected them, they'd have to run into *Akagi's* fighter recon grid within the next hour or so... she actually would have expected to see them already.

So were the Martians coming, or were they sitting out there and waiting for her, baiting her away from the Forge?

"SCO, contact Forge C&C and check in. Make sure the sensor grid is clear of intruders," Shauna gave that order with a frown. She had no intention of being flanked.

Because the Forge Squadron was within a day's cruise of their home base, its ships didn't need to halt in space to communicate (the way we had to with Venus). It's a lot easier for a comm laser to find a moving ship when it's within a day's travel than when it's a week out, as you probably know. That's why our communications ships always stay on pre-planned cruising routes, and cruise slowly... otherwise it'd be next to impossible to contact them.

Anyway, Shauna wanted the reassurance that the Forge wasn't about to come under attack, and that was fair enough. There'd be news soon anyway.

"Hold it... we got dead air that time... from DD08... skipper!"

Holbrook overheard the slightly breathless exclamation of his Flight Operations Officer and hurried over to the Flight Operations consoles (a bridge section unique to carriers) before he was actually called.

"Which spoke was he running?" was the Captain's question, and the Flight Ops Officer moved over to one of the large, transparent screens that was suspended from the ceiling of *Akagi's* bridge.

After a quick check, the Lieutenant Commander keyed up the markers of *Akagi's* planes, and the colored lines showing the spokes of the patrol flight (they're called 'spokes', by the way, because they look like the spokes on a wheel, radiating out from the centre to points all along the semi-circle that represents the maximum range of the recon flight).

"She was dead center on course for the Martians... they must not be coming in on an angle," the Flight Ops Officer said, again sounding slightly panicked.

Holbrook put a hand on his junior officer's shoulder, "It's alright, Don. Let's see if we get another signal from her... could just be a signaling glitch."

Tense seconds — just seconds, but I'm sure they felt much longer — passed as the Flight Ops crew of *Akagi* waited for DD08 to report in. The next minute marker passed with no message from that plane, and then for good measure they waited one more minute.

No signal. The Starburst's comms had either crashed... or the Martians had blown right through the recon plane without it having a chance to send off an alert signal.

"Send word back to the Forge, have them forward it to Admiral Cass. The Martians are coming right down our throat," Holbrook turned to his Sensors and Communications Officer.

He then stepped away from the Flight Operations consoles for a moment, and took a deep breath as he eyed the main sensor display on the main screen. *Akagi* was sitting at the rendezvous point now, waiting for the rest of the Forge Squadron to join it. Shauna was just under seven hours out, and *Kaga* was just over an hour away.

If the Martians continued on course and at the speed they were evidently making, they wouldn't get to this place in space for another thirteen hours, meaning Shauna would arrive and have six hours to play with when it came to figuring out deployments.

That was fine, but all of *Akagi's* planes were also close to thirteen hours away, which meant Holbrook's ship would be without any strike ability when battle was joined.

"Call back all planes, right now. Tell them all to burn their drives hard, I want them on my flight deck in twelve hours, so we can rearm them for combat," Holbrook's tone was insistent, and he turned to his Flight Ops Officer as he said the words. "Clear?"

The Lieutenant Commander frowned, "Sir... I don't know..."

The Flight Ops Officer didn't know if the Sunbursts and Starbursts could actually accelerate to a high enough speed, and hold it for long enough, to get back before the Martians. Keep in mind, one of the big problems starfighters face these days is that they can't actually fly any faster than big ships. The scouts were all at least as far out as the Martians were, but with their aged engines there was no telling if they could out-run the Martians to the rendezvous point.

But Holbrook wanted them back, and as a flier himself, he was confident that they could make it, and be in position to help with the coming battle.

The Flight Ops Officer sent the orders ahead, and the fighters were recalled.

Now, you might be thinking a couple of things here, so if you are, let me answer in advance. First of all, Holbrook did seem awfully confident that his planes — sixty-one aged F-174 Sunbursts and F-184 Starbursts — could do some good in a battle, didn't he? After what he'd seen at the Battle Over Earth, shouldn't he have known better?

Well, all I can say to that is Holbrook was in a very awkward spot, much as George Parks-Dawes had been in during the aforementioned battle. Neither *Akagi* nor *Kaga* could contribute anything to a fight if they didn't have planes, so however slim the chances might have been that the Starbursts and Sunbursts would do any good, they were better than nothing.

The second question, I think, is whether it was wise to call all the planes straight back in, instead of leaving some out there to try to keep track of the Martians' location. Those planes that were on spokes close to DD08's could potentially have angled their way in and located the Martians. It would have been risky, but it would have kept eyes on the enemy ships as they closed.

But Holbrook decided not to keep eyes on the enemy, for reasons that I do not know. I can guess, having been a flier myself, that his concern (conscious or subconscious) was for his pilots, and that he didn't want to send them into the midst of the Martians in ones and twos to be destroyed. But that's only a guess.

Either way, he had called all his planes back. I won't give you my opinion of that decision, yet.

"Confirmed from Holbrook through Forge C&C, the Martians are coming right down our throats," *Texas'* Sensors and Communications Officer delivered the news, and Shauna allowed herself a slight sigh of relief.

Perhaps that was an odd thing to be relieved about, but at least she knew where the Martians were coming from. There wasn't going to be an attack from the rear or anything such. They'd come straight down, and the Forge Squadron would meet them gun to gun.

"Well, with *Akagi's* planes out there, we should have eyes on them the whole way," Captain Tong came to a stop next to Shauna and said that with some relief. "Now we just need to figure out how to beat them."

"Oh, that little detail, right," Shauna managed a smile at her Flag Captain.

They stood silently and continued to think the problem through.

My editors wanted me to be explicit about what was said in that last little scene — when Tong mentioned that *Akagi's* planes would definitely keep an eye on the Martians as they came in. Well, I just explained that Holbrook had called in his planes, so they *weren't* going to have eyes on the Martians... why did Tong think they would when they wouldn't?

This is a classic misinterpretation on the part of two different skippers. Shauna had ordered Holbrook to locate the enemy, and had assumed that when he located the enemy, he'd do everything in his power to track the Martian ships. Holbrook had interpreted the orders differently: once he'd located the Martians, he didn't believe he needed to track them.

It was a simple misunderstanding, really — the sort of gaff that could have been corrected by a single comm call. And yet neither Holbrook nor Tong nor Shauna realized the gaff was taking place.

After all the time we've spent in these books with the Belt Squadron and Jupiter Force, this seemed to my editors to be the sort of mistake Defense Command simply doesn't make. Well, unfortunately, Defense Command *does* make mistakes... you just don't see them as often in professional units that have been together for years.

One of the great strengths of a unit like the Jupiter Force is the fact that, because we'd all worked together for so long, we could fill in the blanks for each other. This was one reason John had sent us to Jupiter in the first place — to keep us together so we didn't lose our team, and thus that dynamic. If I said to Mark Gunney that we needed to find the enemy, he'd know that I didn't just mean to locate them once. He'd understand that I wanted as much information as possible, for as long as possible, about where they were going and how they were getting there

In a new unit, like the Forge Squadron, where officers had a variety of backgrounds and levels of experience, that ability to leave things unsaid didn't exist. Shauna could tell Holbrook she wanted the Martians located, he could emphatically agree, and neither of them would realize they were talking about slightly different things until it was too late.

And that's precisely what was happening.

Many critics have said that Shauna should have been careful, and sent ahead clear orders. In hindsight, of course she should have. That's easy for us to say, looking back and knowing what transpired...

Though, when one of my editors asked me what I'd have said if someone like 'Mik' Mikaelsen or Wes Pellew made the same sort of error, my answer was straightforward: they wouldn't have.

Shauna and Holbrook had put themselves into a difficult position. There was more still to come.

CHAPTER ELEVEN
MISINTERPRETATIONS AND BLINDNESS

Texas led the Forge Squadron as it decelerated at the rendezvous point, and joined *Akagi* and *Kaga* there. Shauna had taken a break for food in the last seven hours of the run, though her appetite had not been particularly impressive. She'd managed to force herself to eat a high-protein MRE, knowing that she needed some fuel in her stomach… but that was a chore.

Shauna had a very bad feeling, and while she wasn't going to share that with her crew, she was certainly letting it creep into the back of her thoughts.

Something about all this felt wrong.

"Captain Holbrook on Battlelink," *Texas'* Sensors and Communications Officer reported, and Shauna shifted her position slightly to stand before the screen that popped up with a *TexasNet* buffering graphic.

Jens Holbrook then appeared, his face dark, "Good to see you, ma'am. Looks like we have trouble on the way."

"It seems so," Shauna agreed. "I take it the Martians haven't changed course or speed?"

Holbrook stared straight at her for a moment, and I really think you can see the confusion behind his eyes when you watch the recordings of this exchange. How the hell was he supposed to know if they'd changed course?

"I… wouldn't expect them to have, ma'am," he said, and his tone reflected confusion as well.

Shauna didn't understand his uncertainty for a moment, "Have your scouts reported any changes in their approach vector?"

"Ma'am, my scouts are all burning their way back here," Holbrook's answer was forthright, and Shauna's heart threatened to leap out her mouth.

Which is a really gross metaphor. Ick.

"Your planes aren't watching the Martians?" Shauna's tone hardened instantly. "Why aren't they tracking the enemy?"

Holbrook started to pale, not fully realizing the gravity of his mistake, but recognizing he was about to get a heap of Scottish fury over Battlelink, "Ma'am… I didn't know you needed us to keep them under watch… I recalled my planes so they could be rearmed for the battle."

Rearmed for the battle? What Shauna wanted to say, but didn't, was that the damned old Sunbursts and Starbursts *Akagi* carried would be about as useful in the upcoming battle as a bloody sandwich. The job of those planes was to make sure the Martians didn't slip away, and they weren't doing that job?

You can see the fury that started to consume Shauna on the recordings. She very barely held it in check, with a measure of self-control that does her credit, "Call all your scouts, they are to change vectors and converge on the Martians' previous base course. Where are *Kaga's* planes?"

Holbrook's eyes were wide at the edge in Shauna's tone, and his answer came in a stammer, "Four squadrons are landed and arming, one squadron is on combat patrol here, the other is an hour forward on the Martians' base course."

"Order all *Kaga's* planes into space," Shauna directed that order to *Texas'* Sensors and Communications Officer. "I want a halo of fighters all around this RV, in case the Martians have changed course and we can't find them. Get them up *now*."

She wasn't yelling, but no one could mistake her anger. The orders were sent immediately.

"Captain Holbrook, find the Martians. Find them *quickly*. All ships go to general quarters while we wait. If they're not where we expect them to be, they could turn up anywhere, any time now."

Shauna turned away from the screen and stepped out of range of the viewfinder, taking a moment and a few deep breaths to try to calm herself. She wasn't terribly successful, though she did have one minor consolation: she knew why she'd had that bad feeling.

Or at least she thought she knew.

Had the Martians held their course and speed, they would have needed six hours to reach the Forge Squadron's RV (rendezvous, can't remember if I've used that acronym before) point. The next five hours made it seem quite doubtful that the Martians had held their course.

First, Shauna watched on one of the screens on *Texas'* bridge as the planes from *Akagi* started sweeping back and forth over the Martians' expected vector, finding nothing. The planes, many of them low on fuel after opening the taps on their rush to return to their carrier, then began to branch out. Some went high, some went low, others left and right.

But space is big, and when you lose something — even something as big as a squadron of seventeen warships — it's quite possible that you won't find it again... that it'll find you instead.

While the planes from *Akagi* failed to locate the Martians, the planes from *Kaga* circled the RV point, staying about half an hour out to provide early warning of any approaching enemies on the flanks of the Forge Squadron.

The twelve planes waiting an hour ahead of the Forge ships saw nothing, though — the Martians had definitely changed their course.

After-five-and-a-half hours had elapsed, Shauna recalled *Akagi's* planes, as many of them were about to hit bingo fuel (meaning they'd soon not have enough to get back to the RV if they stayed out there). A cold, dark feeling gripped her as she realized that, because of Holbrook, she had no idea where the Martians were.

They could be slipping right past the Forge Squadron, heading for the base... they could be anywhere.

At six hours, when the Martians should have appeared, Shauna shook her head and glared at Holbrook, "As soon as your planes finish refueling, send them out on lateral sweeps. We need to see if we can catch them trying to pass us. We'll be withdrawing towards the Forge."

Holbrook nodded, looking so pale one could mistake him for being quite ill. His planes had mostly landed now, and their exhausted pilots were being jacked up with quick food intake and some stims while their Sunbursts and Starbursts were refueled and prepared for another long recon mission.

Shauna stepped away from the screen occupied by the carrier skipper and looked to her other Captains and Commanders, "Let's go to double column cruising order and head for the Forge. Stay at general quarters… they could come at us any time now. *Kaga's* planes should give us some forewarning."

The other skippers nodded in turn and gave their verbal sounds of agreement. Shauna was making a good decision here: there was no point staying put in space when there was a very good chance that the Martians were in the process of slipping by.

The Forge Squadron reversed its direction and headed back toward its base. Somewhere not too far from them, a larger Martian battle group was preparing itself for action.

CHAPTER TWELVE

CLOSING

About half of *Akagi's* planes had launched when one of *Kaga's* patrolling Starbursts sounded the alarm. The Martians were closing in from above, getting set to drop on the Forge Squadron.

Shauna was relieved to hear this — after the uncertainty about where the Martians were, it was a great reprieve to discover that she would, indeed, have the chance to lock horns with them.

Now all she had to do was figure out a way to win.

"Coming down from on high... they're closing with us at about 194 kps, ma'am," *Texas'* Sensors and Communications Officer reported, and Shauna nodded.

She at last was able to square herself off at the front of her bridge, and with the skippers of her fifteen ships on the screens before her, she began to give confident orders, "Let's reorient the squadron ninety degrees up..."

That first command was logical enough. Space being a weightless, three-dimensional battlefield, you could point ships in any direction, and Shauna was thus going to meet the Martians on the angle from which they were approaching.

"Corvettes will form up and screen the battleships. Remember to stay clear of their laser arcs — *Medusa* and *Warlock* must have clean shots," Shauna continued, reminding some of her less experienced Reserve skippers that the plucky little corvettes truly had no business getting between titanic battleships. The corvettes would be tasked with shooting down missiles more than anything else, at least to begin with.

"Frigates form on *Texas*, we're going to try to torpedo the third battleship," Shauna said finally, explaining her plan to try to level the odds in favor of *Medusa* and *Warlock*. Shannon Hunter had had success torpedoing Martian battlewagons during Glorious February... hopefully Shauna could manage the same.

Bruce Arama came out of his chair and walked to the front of his bridge, doing his best to keep his heart rate under control. Through the entire flight out to the RV, and through all the waiting, Bruce had managed to stay relatively cool. He was a laid-back person by nature, and that had helped him keep his crew reasonably relaxed as the enemy remained unseen.

But now that the Martians had been located, and were just twenty minutes away, Bruce's calm was beginning to slip. He knew he had to hold onto it, though — he needed to remain in control, if he wanted to lead his people effectively.

That's a very easy principle to state, but Bruce knew it wouldn't be easy to pull off. *Adelaide* was heading into its first ever fight... and it was a big one.

"Put me on internal comms," Bruce nodded to his Sensors and Communications Officer, and a chirp over the loudspeakers announced to the entire ship that he was about to speak.

"The Martians have been sighted, and we're in the process of turning up to engage them. *Adelaide* will be part of the line of corvettes that will provide screening protection for the battleships. Everyone get ready... we'll be engaging in about twenty minutes. Bruce out."

One thing that Bruce was determined to do was keep his crew — his entire crew — completely informed. During an engagement, word of what's happening in the bigger picture often doesn't get down to the crew — that's just the way it is. Commanding officers are busy giving orders, and while bridge officers (the Helm and Navigation Officer, for instance) pass on quick updates to their departments whenever possible, there usually isn't a direct line of communications from the skipper down to the lower decks.

In the Jupiter Force, we do everything possible to let the crew know what's happening, but that usually means we just give access to the bridge plot information to all sections below... sorry, I think that sentence might have been too laden with jargon. On *Wolf*, for instance, the main sensor display that Karen, Andrea and I work from is made available to every screen below decks, so spacers can follow the action as it happens. Other ships have their own methods.

Such communication is enough for our professional crews, who have often been in the Navy long enough to be able to put things together on their own.

Adelaide's reservist crew didn't have the benefit of that long experience in space, and they probably needed some reassurances as they cruised into a battleship fight. Bruce was therefore doing everything he could to bolster their confidence.

After closing his address, Bruce looked up at his bridge screens. Commander Ivanov from *Earnest* was the senior corvette skipper in the Forge Squadron, so she was naturally in charge of the corvette line.

"Commander Arama, you'll take the extreme left, please, off *Medusa's* beam..." she gave him his assignment, then went on to order the rest of the corvettes into line. Bruce turned away to order Lieutenant Borjigin to position *Adelaide* accordingly.

The corvette sidestepped quite smoothly, and along with the rest of the ships under Ivanov's charge, it fell into position ahead of and slightly below the two battleships, which were now drawing up alongside each other.

"Our job today is to try to keep as much fire away from the battleships as possible," Ivanov explained in cool tones, conscious of the fact that four of her six corvettes were new, and crewed in part or in whole by reservists. Only her own *Earnest* and its companion *Loyal* were veterans of Marlene's Venus Squadron. "The Martians have missiles on all of their ships, and we should expect those missiles to be used. Stay out of the battleships' lines of fire, but if you see a missile coming, shoot it down."

Bruce took a deep breath and nodded at Ivanov's words, as did the other less experienced skippers from the corvette group.

"If you start taking fire from the Martians directly, respond, but only if it doesn't jeopardize your ability to cover the battleships," she continued. "Hold your fighters until we get the order from Admiral Cass. If we have to withdraw quickly, we don't want to have to leave them behind."

Ivanov's reminders continued, and as the Forge Squadron closed with the Martians, Bruce forced himself to calmly memorize them again. He had to be ready.

+++

Captain Kelly Monahan grinned jauntily at Captain Ophelia Zhukov on the Battlelink screen, though because it was Battlelink, it probably looked like she was grinning at everyone. Either way, her mood was quite obvious.

"So this is your third big battleship fight, Ophelia?" Monahan asked, and Zhukov nodded.

"It is, and I believe it may be the most difficult yet."

"And the most glorious," Monahan said. "We'll get the bastards."

Shauna Cass interrupted their open-channel exchange, "Kelly, I think they're stacking up on your side. Looks like you'll be the one receiving double the attention."

Monahan nodded, "We'll be ready."

The sensor sweeps run by *Kaga's* planes hadn't given a clear picture of exactly which ships the Forge Squadron was about to face, but as the two formations got closer to each other, shipboard sensors were starting to provide a clearer picture. *Warlock* was a larger ship than *Medusa*, so that was probably why the Martians were lining their battlewagons up on Monahan's command.

"Anything on the battlewagons we're facing?" the skipper from Boston asked.

Shaking her head, Shauna frowned, "They've scattered their escorts ahead of them, I can't get enough detail on the scans to see which ones they are. They do look big, though."

Monahan's grin widened, "It's too bad bigger things can't actually fall in space. Because they'd fall harder."

Shauna spared a tight smile at the confident words, "Just make sure you're ready, Kelly."

"Always," Monahan nodded.

The forces continued to close.

"Our battleships will be in weapons range in one minute, Martians in an estimated eighty seconds," *Texas'* Sensors and Communications Officer reported, and Shauna nodded.

Her hands slid back and forth over the rails at the front of *Texas'* bridge, and she took a deep breath. She still had a bad feeling, but at least now it was buried by the relief and urgency she felt at the promise of action...

"Good luck everyone," she said to the skippers on Battlelink, and they offered it back to her.

She watched the clock... thirty seconds until *Warlock* and *Medusa* could engage... twenty...

All hell broke loose.

CHAPTER THIRTEEN

THARSIS – THE MONS

Medusa exploded.

Commander Bruce Arama had never fought a major fleet action before, but he was pretty damned positive that battleships weren't supposed to explode when they were twenty seconds outside their own engagement range.

"Incoming lasers from the Martian battleships!" his Sensors and Communications Officer barked instantly. "Incoming debris!"

The next second lasted an eternity as Bruce figured out what had happened, and what he had to do. *Medusa*, the ship he'd been screening, was in pieces — and some of those pieces were flying right at *Adelaide*.

"Walter, spin and climb, get us out of the way of the debris, then close us up with *Warlock!*" he didn't sound calm as he issued those sharp orders, and Walter Borjigin didn't sound calm as he barked the necessary commands to his Helm and Navigation crew.

But *Adelaide* moved in time. The next corvette over, *Ararat*, didn't, and one of *Medusa's* drive pods slammed into it with ferocious speed, snapping the small ship's neck and instantly decompressing many of its sections.

What the hell was going on?

Kelly Monahan's grin had died instantly, and Shauna Cass' heart seemed to stop as she stood still on *Texas'* bridge.

"Return fire," she rasped out of instinct, but Monahan shook her head.

"We're not in *range!*"

Then *Warlock* bucked under her, and she was jolted out of the frame of her bridge viewfinder.

"What the *hell* is going on?" Shauna demanded in a half-yell, and the fact that she dared to ask such a question on her bridge was a clear sign of how acute her shock was.

No one had an answer, but *Warlock* had taken two lasers in the starboard drive pod. Having seen what happened to *Medusa*, *Warlock's* Helm and Navigation Officer had been ready to dodge fire, and thus had saved the ship from being crippled... but *thirty-two* Martian lasers were crossing the battlewagon's bows.

Then the third battleship fired, making it forty-eight beams.

Shauna didn't know how, but the Martians had built bigger battleships, with longer-range lasers.

Three of them.

And they were charging down at her force the way John and the *Bonnies* had hit Grand Admiral Garvey's battleship squadron during Glorious February.

In that second there were a thousand questions filling Shauna's mind — how... what... when... why... who...?

And of course, there was no time to even attempt to answer them. The fact that the Martians shouldn't have had the ability to do what they'd just done — to blow a Defense Command battleship (albeit an aged one) to pieces in one volley, beyond our maximum range — didn't matter. Shauna had to deal with what the Martians were doing, not what they *should* have been able to do.

"Frigates advance quickly, torpedo solution on the nearest battlewagon!" she barked, and Captain Tong ordered *Texas* to increase speed to 198 kps for the torpedo run.

"I'm in range... shoot!" Kelly Monahan made the report and gave the order to return fire in the same breath, and the Forge Squadron gave its first answer to the Martians.

Warlock's crew was impeccably trained — the ship was Marlene's second battlewagon from the Venus Squadron, after all. Both of its lasers rammed home on the center battleship in the Martian line, and the behemoth wasn't able to sidestep the hits as smoothly as *Warlock* had just seconds prior.

Shauna felt a very brief few seconds of relief as the lasers connected — she was in engagement range, thank God. She could fight back.

But now it was one battleship against three, and they were clearly bigger and tougher than anything Defense Command had ever seen from the Martians...

"Destroyers and destroyer escorts closing to engagement range!" *Texas'* SCO denied Shauna any time for relief or questions.

Her eyes darted up to the main screen, and she saw the icons of the Martian escorts surging ahead, no doubt instructed to intercept her frigates and keep them from launching against the new battleships.

"Corvettes forward, we need to break their screen!" Shauna gave up trying to protect *Warlock* in that instant. When the odds had been two against three, trying to protect the battleships had been most important. Now that she was down to one, it was more critical to get her frigates into torpedo range. It was the only chance they had left to even the odds.

The six... no, five corvettes started to push forward behind the frigates, and as laser range was reached, a chorus of 'shoot!' came across Battlelink. At least the frigates still had a range advantage over the destroyers...

Two of the Martians sustained moderate damage, but then the frigates and the corvettes ran smack into a wall of energy fire, most of it being generated by the third Martian battleship, which had turned its interest away from *Warlock*.

Texas was forced to sidestep and drop at full speed, a move which severely tested the ship's artificial gravity and Shauna's grip on the bridge rail.

Sichuan was destroyed by a direct hit from two of the battleship's lasers, and *Hubei* was caught by two destroyers and crippled. *Texas* and *Gansu* were suddenly the only two frigates left in the Forge Squadron, and they weren't the only ones suffering.

The lack of coordination that came with a new squadron was evident in this fight, and *Earnest* became a victim of it. While the ship was professionally-crewed and one of Marlene's best, it was still at the center of a formation that was closing in too tight. The nervous skippers of the Reserve-crewed corvettes had clumped together in a frankly amateurish manner, so when three of the Martian destroyers and four of their DEs locked on, there was no room for maneuver.

Earnest went first, being completely destroyed as lasers converged on it. *Darwin* was knocked into a tumble when one of its drive pods was burned through, and then a DE chased it down and finished it off with a missile. *Loyal* and *Hobart* succeeded in keeping good spacing between them, and fighting as a pair, they managed to burn through a Martian DE with their lasers. Then one of the Martian battleships swatted *Loyal* like a fly.

At the very same time, *Albury* charged in against one of the destroyers that was attempting to track *Texas* and unleashed a small torrent of mag fire… just enough mag fire to get noticed, without doing any damage to the larger ship.

The rookie mistake cost *Albury* a drive pod, and then a reactor overloaded and ended the lives of everyone on the brave little ship.

Captain Tong managed to get *Texas* back around and burned right through the destroyer that had killed little *Albury*, but then two DEs closed on the frigate and again kept it well away from the battleship it wanted to attack.

Only *Adelaide* remained near *Warlock*.

"Two destroyers closing with missiles, Bruce!" Fuentes was at her operations station, directing the fire from *Adelaide's* lasers, and now she had two Martian targets to pick from.

"Focus fire on the one to starboard," Bruce replied with no pretense of calm, then looked up to Captain Monahan on his screen. "Ma'am, missiles incoming, we'll try to stop them."

Monahan wasn't paying any attention, as her ship was again being pounded and dodging madly to avoid *Medusa's* fate.

It was around this time that fifty F-174 Sunbursts and F-184 Starbursts rushed into the space around *Warlock* and *Adelaide* — the planes from *Akagi* were joining the fight. Captain Holbrook had launched them on his own initiative, and as they arrived Bruce allowed himself a moment's hope — with fifty planes offering strafing support, they could keep missiles off *Warlock's* back.

While *Adelaide* and now several squadrons of fighters tried to keep her ship from being stabbed by the destroyers, Kelly Monahan roared orders to shoot at the Martian battleships again.

She wasn't allowing herself to think that all hope was lost. Things didn't look good, but there was still a chance… there had to be a chance. It was unlikely, but *Warlock* was a hell of a ship. If any battlewagon could take on these three Martian behemoths on its own, it was…

It was *Bonaventure*, but *Bonnie* wasn't here.

Warlock exploded as the lasers from two of these seemingly-unscathed Martians converged on its lower bow pod, and pierced their way into the ship's fighter ordnance bays. The amount of armor those beams burned through to cause that secondary explosion was considerable… but they did it.

Thirty-two laser beams, the strongest lasers we'd ever seen from Martian ships. Ever.

♦♦♦

"Debris incoming again!"

Bruce didn't even think as he heard the report — he didn't have time to think, "Walter, climb and break. Warn the planes and get them to follow to cover us."

With their primary targets gone, the Martian battleships turned on the smaller survivors of the Forge Squadron, and there weren't many to choose from. Mags... or whatever the Martians were calling them... started raining in lethal numbers, and the fighters ended up absorbing altogether too many of them.

Of the fifty-odd planes that *Akagi* had launched, thirty-three were caught in the downpour and died.

Adelaide took some hits, but the determined little ship climbed out of the targeting bracket the Martians had set for themselves too quickly to be disabled.

Then the battleships opened up with lasers again — but this time they'd noticed the two carriers that had been hanging to the rear.

Akagi and *Kaga* evaporated in vicious fireballs, the same way *Yorktown*, *Hornet* and *Essex* had a couple of years prior. The age of the carrier was well and truly over.

As those bright explosions distracted some of the Martians, Shauna did the only thing she could do: she ordered the retreat.

Texas and *Gansu* managed to close together, and then the two frigates poured all the thrust they could out through their drive pods. Accelerating to a desperate 202 kps, they climbed and turned towards the Forge.

Hobart followed them, burning its new engines for all they were worth, and making a shaky 203 kps on a matching course.

Adelaide was the last to turn away from the Martians, and Bruce found himself breathless as he realized the Martians would have a solid ten seconds to shoot at him as he crossed their front on his run towards the Forge. There were no other options of course — he had to head for the Forge...

Those ten seconds passed like ten hours... but they all passed.

The Martians had had their fill for the moment, and in an act of magnanimity on the part of their commander — who was himself quite shocked at his success — they let *Adelaide* fly away, dozens of demoralized Sunbursts and Starbursts clouding around the corvette.

One of the most astounding defeats in the history of the Defense Command Navy was complete.

The Martians' prized *Tharsis*-class battleships — *Olympus Mons*, *Pavonis Mons*, and *Arsia Mons* — had joined the war.

They now began launching search and rescue craft.

Chapter Fourteen

What?

Shauna found that she couldn't breath. She didn't know how it had happened, or why. Her knuckles were white and her hands hurt from the death grip they were keeping on the railing at the front of *Texas'* bridge. She couldn't let go of that railing because her knees were shaking so badly she knew she'd fall if she did.

Many things were going through her mind. Many horrible things.

Each of those battleships had taken more than 700 crew with them. The two destroyed frigates meant another 1,000 men and women lost. And the four corvettes would have taken another 600...

How had that happened? How had... how had that happened? She couldn't understand it. Stunned silence settled over the bridge as the ship redlined its drives, running from the Martians.

After a few minutes they discovered that the Martians weren't chasing, so they slowed very slightly.

Weren't chasing *yet*, that was.

It took twenty minutes for Shauna to force her mind to work, and then another ten to compile all the data from the brief and devastating engagement into a message to send on to Venus. As such, it was about forty minutes later when John and Marlene, standing in *Venus One's* C&C, saw the results of the battle.

The entire bustling C&C fell to a deathly silence as the battle played out through sensor logs and enhanced vid recordings. A great cold darkness seemed to grip everyone in the room — John and Marlene included.

Not since the loss of the Light Squadron had our fleet seen so epic a tragedy. And the Light Squadron had been one of Dave Caldecott's formations, without any proper battleships. That a squadron led by one of the Fiora Ring could be so defeated... it was almost inconceivable.

Almost inconceivable.

The shock settled in over the course of about twenty minutes, as much of the raw footage and data was reviewed by John, Marlene, and the other available senior staff officers.

What had happened?

Well, it took them some hours to figure out, but I'm not going to take that much time to piece it all together for you. Here's the short version: we were trounced.

The reason we got so badly beaten really comes down to one factor, and that is the arrival in service of Mars' latest and greatest warships, the battleships (supposed 'Dreadnoughts') of the *Tharsis*-class. The same way the *Bonnies* had been devastating to the Martians in Glorious February, the three *Tharsis*-class ships had proved superior that day.

Their engagement range was longer than that of the *Bonnies*, though only by a couple of seconds. It was obviously *much* longer than that of the aged *Warlock* and *Medusa*. Added to that was the fact that the new Martian lasers were about fifty percent more powerful than the ones on the *Planetia*-class battleships — the battlewagons we were accustomed to dealing with.

These *Tharsis*-class ships were literally the Martians' answer to the *Bonaventure*-class.

The question that came from that realization, of course, was how had they been built? Years prior, we'd heard some rumblings that the Martians would try to match the *Bonnies*. The noise had come when the *Bonaventure* project was first approved, but the rumors had faded away, and after a while, we'd heard nothing at all.

Our intelligence [guesswork] had given no warning that they existed, though when we combed back over some of the [guesses] that had been made since 2231, we saw specific references to *Olympus Mons*, *Arsia Mons* and *Pavonis Mons*, as well as *Tharsis* (the name of the range those volcanoes all belong to). DCI had just assumed these were code names of some sort — not ships.

But they were ships.

When Greg and Mik had raided Mars, and destroyed battleships in builders yards, we'd assumed that we'd broken any chance of new Martian capital ship construction during the war. We hadn't seen the four ships of this class (of which one still wasn't ready for space at this point) because they'd been under construction elsewhere. I'll get into the where later on, but suffice it to say some new private shipbuilding yards beyond the Empire's purview had started hiring out their services, and the Martians had decided to take advantage.

We'll hear a lot more about this later, so I'll leave it at that for now. Suffice it to say the failure of DCI to warn us that these ships existed is not as huge a failure as it's sometimes made out to be.

Though it was still a pretty big failure.

What mattered, though, was that the Martians had superbattleships... and they'd introduced them in a very dramatic fashion.

Now Shauna had four ships left to face three *Tharsis*-class battleships, five destroyers and seven destroyer escorts.

She'd lost *eleven* ships, and killed only two in return.

I suppose this is actually proof of concept for that double-teaming theory I mentioned before. Well, partly.

What happened to the Forge Squadron was disastrous on several levels. First, the squadron had lost one of its capital ships before answer could be given. That threw everything into chaos, and the explosion took out one corvette. After that, seeing the tall odds against *Warlock*, Shauna chose to break her formations, and to try to punch through the Martian escorts to allow a torpedo run by her frigates.

The breaking of formation was a big problem, because most of the ships involved were so inexperienced. I won't pretend that, had the Jupiter Force been in the same circumstances, we would have magically beaten the *Tharsis* Squadron... I expect we'd have died too... but the inexperience on the part of some of the Forge's ships made defeat come more quickly, with fewer Martians killed in the process.

The new ships clumped together. They maneuvered just a little bit too slowly, or zigged when they should have zagged. The Martians, on the other hand, were very well led, had acted with great discipline, and had won what sports commentators often call the 'one-on-one' battles.

Because each of the Martians was just a little bit sharper in that engagement, they'd been able to tip the whole fight in their favor.

This was what we'd been doing to the Martians — up until this point in the war, we'd always had a pretty solid edge in quality and experience. But now, as our numbers increased and our core of professionals was diluted across more hulls, and as the Martians picked up more battle experience, they were getting the advantage in very select circumstances.

And so we lost.

The question was what to do next. How much time would Shauna have to prepare the defense of the Forge, and would she even attempt to stand against fifteen ships with her quartet? Was the Forge now a lost cause?

As you can see, there are plenty of pages left in this book, so obviously there's more to come.

CHAPTER FIFTEEN

LEMONADE TIME

The old expression goes that when given lemons, one must make lemonade. Defense Command had just been handed lemons laced with a neurotoxin and stuffed with hand grenades, but damned if we still weren't going to try to make lemonade.

I suppose that statement could seem too glib for this situation… but it more or less describes what had to be done. The Forge was under a devastating threat now, and we needed to figure out what possible good could come of the situation.

Yes. Very tall order.

Shauna had retired to her cabin an hour after the battle's end, and when she sat down on her bed, the world spun around her. She'd never had to cope with this sort of devastating loss — few Defense Command officers ever had. But she knew, on one level at least, that she needed to put it behind her. This is the realization any professional officer must come to in the face of a setback… and to be fair, this was more than just a casual problem.

Getting past that loss wouldn't be easy to do. Even when I'm just writing about it, I'm having a hard time putting it behind me. *Eleven* Defense Command ships lost in a completely one-sided victory for the Martians. There was no comfort to be taken, our force had nearly been annihilated. I can't think of many cases in history when a squadron from a seemingly dominant fleet was annihilated like that. Kit Craddock's defeat at Coronel in 1914 comes to mind… otherwise I'm drawing a blank.

It was a dark day for the Defense Command Navy, and a very dark day for Shauna Cass.

Now she had to try to do something about it.

The information Shauna was working with was incomplete: the Martians weren't following, but that meant she had no idea where they actually were. But the absence of a chase didn't make sense to her — why wouldn't they follow closely, chase her last four ships back to the Forge, smash them aside and take the base?

They could be coming from a different vector… perhaps they would approach the Forge from another direction… maybe they'd taken damage that she hadn't realized they'd taken and needed time to repair…

But no, there was no way she could expect them to leave the Forge alone. She had to try to figure out how to protect the base. That was her job. No matter what had just happened to her, she needed to do it — and as a professional officer, she fully understood this.

The first clear realization that came to her mind as she sat on her bed was that she couldn't run straight for the Forge. If her four ships went into orbit around the rock and waited for the fifteen Martians to fall on them, they'd all simply die.

The only advantage her squadron had left was speed. Two frigates, two corvettes…

under other circumstances that would be the makeup of a powerful raiding group. *Texas* and *Gansu* still had torpedoes as well… and what was it Marlene had done before the Battle Over Earth? She'd used fighter ordnance to create mines. To delay the Martian advance.

That was it. Shauna realized with a deep breath that she had to try to fight like her mentor — to try to be a sorceress. She had to try to slow down the Martians, because if by some miracle she could, that'd give Greg time to arrive, and with his five battleships, perhaps there'd be a chance.

But she had to delay the Martians for six days. *Six* days, before Greg arrived.

Four ships against fifteen…

She was determined to try, so she recorded orders and sent them to the Forge — along with a message to be forwarded to Venus.

DCNS *Artemis Agrotera* was pulling into orbit over the Forge just as Shauna's messages arrived. You'll remember *Artemis Agrotera* and its intrepid skipper, Captain Zail Patel, from our mission out to Jupiter. It was Zail who'd come up with the excellent idea of sending *Lion's* radiation casualties down to the hospital in Io's dome, thus saving many lives.

Now he was essentially Shauna's logistical connection to Venus. When the Forge needed specific supplies, *Artemis Agrotera* was the perfect ship to send for them, because it was fast and military. Contract civilian haulers could theoretically move the supplies more easily, but those haulers would have to operate in convoys, slow and under escort.

Fast and moderately protected by mags, *Artemis Agrotera* wasn't vulnerable to the sorts of raiders that could prey on the convoys.

Zail had just completed another run from Venus, and was this time carrying top-up supplies for small arms, medical kit, and living provisions — things that were actually difficult to come by at the Forge — and was preparing his shuttles to offload the victuals when C&C passed word of the squadron's defeat up to him.

Thinking on his feet, he immediately called down to the base and offered evacuation for non-essential personnel. Some of the Forge's personnel had families with them, and there was also a handful of civilians present, including a camera crew. If needed, Zail could take those people and any secret or sensitive materials aboard *Artemis Agrotera*.

That might sound defeatist or cowardly — how dare he not stand and fight! — but when you think about what sort of ship *Artemis* was, and what the odds were, I take it to be rather prudent. If orders came to abandon the Forge in order to save lives, he'd cram all the base's personnel into his ship and they'd run to Venus at full burn.

Contingency plans for that possibility were being put into place when Shauna's orders came in, and because he was on the line making plans with Colonel Hwangbo of Special Branch, Zail got to see them as soon as they arrived.

Shauna appeared on the screen, looking haggard… looking like hell… and she let out a sigh before beginning, "We're going to attempt to slow down their approach. Admiral Noyce, Commodore Mikaelsen and Lady Hawke are due at the Forge in six days. If we can manage to delay the Martians that long, we'll have a chance to stop them taking the base. All non-essential personnel should be loaded onto *Artemis Agrotera* when it returns, along with all sensitive materials. If we fail, Captain Patel must evacuate them to Venus. The Forge will fight to the bitter end, unless there are orders to the contrary from the First Lord. We will begin exercising communications blackouts to aid our stealth. We will report any successes or failures if possible, but vigilance will be necessary on the sensor panels. If you see the enemy coming in, you'll know that we've failed. Good luck to us all. Cass out."

Zail and Hwangbo Yang were both equally unsettled by that transmission, and neither of them were too optimistic about Shauna's chances.

With the Martians just sixteen or seventeen hours away from the Forge, it seemed very unlikely that a six-day delay was in the cards.

John and Marlene were sitting in John's office on *Bonaventure*, alternately staring at the data from the engagement, and trying to come up with ideas. Unfortunately, every idea one of them started to share died in mid-sentence, its tactical or strategic weakness all too evident.

They'd never expected Shauna's force to get shattered like that. Certainly, there'd been a chance that she'd get battered, perhaps even lose half her force... but more than two thirds? Lost to a Martian force that no one had even known existed?

The game had been shaken up, and there was so little information.

Shauna's message found them in this uncertain state.

"Does she have a chance of holding them for six days, when they're already that close?" John put the question to Marlene, as no one knew Shauna better than the sorceress.

Marlene's mouth twitched into a thin line and she shook her head slightly, "She has talent, John... but she's not ready for that. I think a day. Maybe two. I can't see six... not when they're already that close. But she'll try."

That hope wasn't a large one, but of course there were times when extraordinary things happened in war. John's confidence was still nonexistent, though. He'd picked Shauna for this job because she was Marlene's best... but the protégé was *not* the sorceress. I know that's probably painfully obvious, but it bears repeating. The Forge would have gone differently if Marlene had been there... but forgiving my coldness, I'm glad she wasn't.

John responded after a pause, "We'll let Greg know that he's heading for trouble. If she can't hold them back, we'll call him direct to Venus. I don't want him trying to assault the Forge if they capture it."

Marlene nodded, "Is it even worth trying to take back if we lose it?"

John processed that question for a moment. The loss of the Forge would be a very bad blow for morale, and it might give the Martians some momentum in the war... but the Martians no doubt were hoping to draw us into a counterattack. If we attacked a captured Forge, we'd be distracted from the Mercury assault.

We couldn't afford to get side-tracked.

That in mind, John shook his head, "I don't think it is. We have to write it off... we can't risk the resources on trying to take it back."

"I think you're correct about that," Marlene leaned back in her chair, and then a thought occurred to her, "We're only four days away."

John blinked once, then looked across his desk at Marlene, "We can't."

She stared at him for a moment, then nodded, "I know. We can't."

They sat again in silence, contemplating their options.

For once I was on the bridge when the bad news came in. Karen and I had been finding the days of this voyage refreshingly boring — not too much drama on any front, at least not any front near us. We were certainly interested in hearing what had become of the Martian force that Shauna had confronted, but we didn't have Andrea in a prisoner-shooting mood, or any wounded people.

The ship was happy.

Then Felicia Khalid started our daily check-in with Venus, and sure enough, the information package about the shocking defeat of the Forge Squadron came up on the main screen.

I think I heard a pin drop when it did.

Before the feed had arrived, there'd been plenty of joking and chatting on the bridge, but when it played there was dead silence. We watched the sensor overview of the battle, and then some of the vid footage of our ships being destroyed, and then Shauna's weary and yet determined message of continued resistance.

We watched all this, and we could barely believe it.

Jim was on the bridge with me, and after we called Karen and Andrea up, he went to the front of the bridge, studying the sensor feeds and slowly shaking his head in disbelief, "They've got longer range on their lasers than *Bonnie* does…"

I hadn't noticed the slight range advantage, but I looked closer after Jim's comment… and he was certainly right.

"My God," Shelby McLaws actually stepped down from the Helm and Navigation consoles to get a clear look, and now she began shaking her head. "Rear Admiral Cass is going to have a very tough time holding on for six days."

I was about to agree with Shelby when Andrea and Karen arrived on the bridge, so I waited and let them catch up.

Andrea's response to all this was probably the most succinct, "Christ on the cross, she's done."

"She's going to try to hold out for six days?" Karen asked, almost disbelieving. I still was having a hard time believing too.

"Reinforcements from Venus could get there sooner… about four days," Felicia Khalid offered in a tentative tone.

None of us actually had to say 'not going to happen' to that — we all knew John could never weaken Venus' defense to recover a post like the Forge. Certainly, the base was important in a tactical sense, but if the Martians had battleships with that much power available, there was no way any major population centre in the Empire was going to let go of its defensive battleships.

We didn't know how many of those behemoths the Martians possessed — could more be heading to Earth or the Belt? Well, we know now that there weren't, but hindsight is always a little more useful than what you know at the time.

Venus couldn't help the Forge — not against such odds as these. Only Greg, with a force of battlewagons that were already en route, could render assistance.

"Should we be letting Greg walk into that?" I blurted out that question very quietly, and Karen glanced at me.

"What?"

I didn't answer her immediately, and then I shook my head, "Never mind."

Wes Pellew appeared on screen four a moment later, looking suitably grim, "Have you ever seen anything like it?"

I shook my head, "I never have. I hope never to again."

Mark Gunney appeared shortly thereafter, "I never wanted to know what this felt like. I don't mind making them feel it, but I'm a hypocrite. I never wanted it for us."

"What do we do?" Wes asked after a while. "Is there anything we *can* do?"

That was the question people on *Wolf's* bridge were asking themselves, and they were all starting to look at me.

We really couldn't do much — we were three days from Venus, and Venus was four days from the Forge. But I needed to say something, for their benefit and my own, so I looked at Shelby, "Let's increase cruising speed to 198 kps, give the engines a workout. It'll get us to Venus a few hours earlier... if the Martians are playing out here, John may need us."

It was precious little, but it was all we could do.

A few moments later, the ships of the Jupiter Force and the Independent Squadron all increased to flank cruising speed, and ETA Venus dropped from seventy-one to sixty-six hours.

CHAPTER SIXTEEN
IMPROVISING

Shauna appeared on *Texas'* silent bridge some time later. Captain Tong had managed to keep the experienced ship's crew calm for the time being, but there was an undeniable tension gripping the chamber.

On Battlelink, the remaining skippers from the Forge Squadron each nodded to Shauna as she appeared before them, and she returned the greetings, then gestured Tong to join her in sight of the viewfinder.

"Our only option," she began, managing to say 'option' instead of 'chance', "is to try to delay them. I know holding them up for six days is a difficult task, but I'm confident that if anyone can manage it, it has to be us."

She wasn't confident of that — not by a long shot. And her skippers certainly weren't. But that was the sort of feeling that had to go unsaid. Uncertainty was not an option now. The Forge couldn't be abandoned, they had to try *something* to slow down these Martians.

"I want everyone to start collecting fighter ordnance into mine packages, the way Marlene did when she was slowing down the Martian Fleet before they attacked Earth. We'll give that a shot, see if we can't slow them down long enough for Greg to arrive."

The skippers each nodded in turn. I don't believe I've mentioned the COs of *Gansu* and *Hobart*: they were Captain Michael Soto and Commander Kabira Vibbard, both of them in fact regular force officers who'd been promoted to command the reservist-crewed ships.

"We'll continue retreating for the time being, but once we have those ordnance packs ready, we'll reverse our course and see if we can find the Martians," Shauna finished.

Agreements were given by way of nods, and Shauna took a step back, "Good. I need to get in touch with the Forge, I'll leave you to it. Report in when you're ready."

With that, she turned away, and headed for her cabin.

"I'm preparing everyone down here to resist landings. There's a good chance they'll just open the dome from orbit when they get here... but if they want to actually capture this place, we'll make them pay," Hwangbo Yang was explaining his defense preparations, and over realtime comms from *Artemis Agrotera*, Captain Zail Patel nodded.

"Very well. Is there anything else we have that can be of use?"

For the past hour, shuttles had been moving up and down from *Artemis Agrotera* to the Forge, carrying the storeship's haul of supplies to the Forge depots, and beginning to take up non-essential personnel. There were at least ten more hours of flying left to move all the stores and people before *Artemis Agrotera* could depart, but Zail (being an excellent skipper) had already earmarked everything that had to move... hence the 'anything else' question.

Yang shook his head in answer, "I feel bad enough taking everything you have anyway. I get the sinking feeling we're just going to end up destroying it so the Martians don't get it."

It was an unusual thing for a Special Brancher to concede, but Colonel Hwangbo was fairly certain the Forge couldn't withstand a landing assault.

With a regular complement of 1,200 personnel, only 200 of them rated SF or Special Branch, and a third of them likely departing as non-essentials with *Artemis Agrotera*, he simply couldn't believe that the base would weather a concerted Martian assault landing.

That's not to say he wouldn't put up a fight (obviously) but in Yang's estimation, if he proved successful and threw back several landing attempts, the Martians would just give up and laser the base dome from orbit. That would trap the entire base population in the single layer of underground tunnels, with limited supplies and air.

Presuming they made it down to the tunnels in the first place, and the Martians didn't just laser their way through the floor of the dome and decompress the underground complex too.

Either way, Hwangbo Yang wasn't expecting to survive the encounter.

Zail nodded at the Colonel's observation, then glanced away from the viewfinder to confirm something with one of his officers. During those few seconds, the Forge base's Sensors and Communications Officer caught Yang's attention.

"Sir, signal coming in for you from *Texas*. Marked confidential," the Lieutenant Commander offered the report, and Yang nodded, looking back up at Zail.

"Signal just arrived from Shauna, Zail. I have to go take it, I'll check in afterwards."

Captain Patel looked back to the viewfinder and nodded, "Very well, I shall speak with you soon."

Zail stepped out of frame, leaving the realtime comm up for sake of ease. Yang headed to his office.

"We're going to be holding out here for as long as we can. Chances are, by the time the Martians get to you, they'll have come through us and we'll be destroyed... if we're not, we'll make our last stand over the Forge and try to land reinforcements for you. Yang, you must hold the base if they give you the chance... if we can make it six days, we'll be set. Good luck."

Shauna's face froze on Hwangbo Yang's screen and he took a deep breath before deactivating the display. Had anyone else watched that feed (as you now can in the fleet archives) they'd never get the sense that Shauna and Yang had ever been intimate. This can be chalked up to the fact that, despite some chemistry, Shauna wasn't as close to Yang as one might expect.

When action came, her first reaction was to deal with it herself, not to share her thoughts and feelings with Yang.

Of course, in this situation, that was just as well — Yang had plenty to worry about on his own. He had officers taking stock of all the small arms on the Forge now... there were some weapons left over on the rock from *Daragh's* day, and while they weren't ideal, old-time EPKs and EPMs would still be better weapons than knives and clubs.

If they were going to arm the 600 officers and spacers who weren't part of Special

Branch or SF (but were still staying on the Forge) it'd have to be in part with those geriatric rifles.

Of course, arming them wouldn't be enough: Yang was already putting together plans, and had briefed his Special Branch Majors hours before about the need for crash courses in small-arms combat. As I'm sure isn't a surprise to you, just handing someone a weapon didn't make him or her a good soldier. Special Branchers were trained properly in tactics for a reason...

Anyway, they'd be ready. The more time Shauna was able to give them to prepare, the better. So far the Martians didn't seem to have moved, which would mean they were about sixteen hours away. The longer they stayed there, the better for everyone...

CHAPTER SEVENTEEN
DOES THIS ADD UP? SERIOUSLY, I'M BAD AT MATH. DOES IT?

Sixty-seven hours after the Jupiter Force and the Independent Squadron accelerated in their run to Venus, we pulled into dock at *Venus One*. There was fanfare, and the Lords actually asked Karen and me to come down to see them, but we had a good excuse not to go, or to do press conferences: we were still dealing with the Forge crisis.

There'd been no way (or desire) to try to keep the defeat at the Forge a complete secret. Trying to hide something like that from the media just doesn't work... as any good Public Relations professional will tell you, when you have bad news it's better to get it out there (along with your messaging) and control the spin.

So the night after the Forge Squadron was shattered, John held a press conference announcing the Martians had launched a three-battleship attack on the Forge, and that it had ambushed and destroyed the battleships of the Forge Squadron.

It didn't mention the losses to the rest of the squadron ships. John handled those questions with a look of concern (but not panic): "We know we've lost some, but we don't have a clear picture. The ships were scattered in the battle, and we've only been in contact with four of them so far."

That wasn't really a lie, it was just suggesting to the media that, in time, we'd be in contact with more of the ships in the squadron. However, when the people and the media started to wonder if there were only four survivors from Shauna's command, the Jupiter Force and the Independent Squadron arrived in port.

See what John did there? He'd made sure that just when the people of Venus were starting to worry the Martians in that area of space had trounced one of our squadrons... two of the most famous formations in the fleet arrived to allay any worries.

So Karen and I didn't do any press conferences, but we did stop for a media scrum before heading to *Venus One* C&C. You've undoubtedly seen the footage...

"We don't have time to take questions," I said loudly, managing to talk down the urgent queries from some reporters.

"We've seen all the information from the Forge, and it's a serious problem... one that we're going to deal with severely," Karen added coolly, making sure the inflection of her voice reflected the gravity of her words.

"Trust us, we're not trying to showboat when we say the Martians don't realize how bad a mistake they just made," I finished off. "We'll brief you soon."

With that, we pushed our way out and headed to C&C. Wes followed as soon as he docked half an hour later, deflecting questions with a similar mix of serious concern, anger and confidence.

So it was the evening of the third day after the destruction of most of the Forge Squadron that we all gathered in *Venus One* C&C. Greg was still three days from the Forge.

Now, if you're not already familiar with the story of the Forge, you're probably wondering what happened in those three days. Shauna's daring plan to delay the Martians with her missile-mines and torpedoes, how long had it lasted? And how had Colonel Hwangbo's resistance gone?

If you're asking those questions, then you're probably thinking to yourself that I skipped three days either because nothing happened, or as is much more plausible, everything fell apart and our meeting was about how to pick up the pieces now that the Forge was under Martian control.

To be entirely honest, that latter meeting was the one I was expecting to have. There was no way I could imagine four ships holding off that powerful a Martian formation for three days — let alone six...

And yet, we were meeting under the first scenario: nothing had happened.

This, as you'll probably agree, just didn't make sense from our perspective. There was no good reason that those new battleships shouldn't have swept in and finished the job they'd started, and that fact had us all quite worried as we got together to consider the situation.

"DCI has finally managed to sketch these three battlewagons for us."

John, Marlene, Wes, Karen and I were standing around the plot table at the center of *Venus One* C&C, and as John said that, a variety of images of the new battlewagons came up on the table's vid top.

"The *Tharsis*-class, named for the range of volcanoes on Mars. They're what became of that 'Dreadnought' project they announced when the *Bonnie* program started," he continued. "There are four built, but [best guess] says the fourth one isn't finished fitting out yet."

Karen and I had surmised as much. This, of course, is part of the problem of being the big Empire in the solar system — when we start a new class of superbattleships like the *Bonaventures*, it's basically impossible (and also unwise) to keep them from the public eye. Everyone in the solar system thus finds out the important details, and the Martians scramble to build to match.

Evidently, though, they hadn't been able to make their *Tharsis* wagons ready for action in time for the start of the war. Good news for us — if they'd had them at the Battle Over Earth, we probably would have lost.

"All we can tell about where they came from is that they *aren't* from the Mercury Squadron. Force levels at Mercury haven't changed," John finished his thought, though we were all paying only distant attention. We were looking at our enemy's new big guns instead.

I wasn't terribly impressed, "Look at this, extra engine pods... they don't have the tech to build bigger and more powerful, so they're adding more."

If you look at pictures of the *Tharsis*-class, you'll see what I was talking about: there are smaller drive pods sticking out of the engineering section on short pylons, each at a forty-five degree angle to the regular engine pod wings. This is a classic case of trying to create more capability with the same old technology. The Martians didn't have a chance of building the sort of power and drive systems that made the *Bonnies* so epically good, so to match the capability they had to put on more of the same old kit. It's like combining two old, slow computers to try to match the performance of something new and fast. It can sort of work, under certain circumstances.

"Would have been nice of Thea to give us a heads up that these actually exist," Wes said that, and coolly. It perhaps wasn't fair to Thea Fostopolos, head of Defense Command Intelligence, to expect her to know everything that was going on in the solar system...

But the existence of three... four actually... huge 'Dreadnoughts' (at some point I'm going to rant about how historically wrong that name is) would be the sort of thing she should have been able to tell us. Sorry, but that's DCI's job — I don't suggest that it's easy, but it is what they sign on to do. Some things inevitably slip through, but the existence of the *Tharsis*-class shouldn't have been one of them.

That said, they still must get much credit for the guesswork that saved us during Glorious February... and no credit for missing the Martians' plans to launch the war. Clearly, it was a hit or miss time for DCI, and after the war we'd pour a lot of effort into revamping that branch. Some things were working really well (Haley Briand had done exceptionally) but others weren't. At that moment, though, we had no option but to deal with the situation as it had been set up for us.

"So Greg's three days out... it may be realistic to think that Shauna can keep them back for that long... if they come at all," Marlene was leaning over the table and frowning. "I don't know why they aren't on top of the Forge right now, but they say you should never look a gift horse in the mouth."

"I've been keeping Greg apprised," John looked across the table at Karen, Wes and me. "He and Mik are working on the best tactics for dealing with the *Tharsises*."

I don't know if that's how you're supposed to make '*Tharsis*' a plural, but that's what John said, and it stuck.

Wes nodded, "He's not going to have an easy time... but if we can break their new ships, it should send a message to the Martians."

I started nodding in agreement with those words, but my brain was hanging a left turn, and I was no longer paying full attention to the people around me.

"If we can keep the Forge out of their hands, we should be able to stay roughly on schedule, right?" Karen asked, looking from Marlene to John and back.

Marlene was still reviewing data on the plot table, but she nodded anyway, "We're getting the last of our Imperial Army assault troops... so help us... tomorrow. After that, we have everything we need in place here."

I was staring at the plot table now, my eyes drifting from the Forge to Venus to Mercury to the icon of Greg and Mik's force and back to the Forge.

I doubt we're going to get a map again, but try to picture this. The Forge was four days ahead of Venus. Mercury, orbiting at its much faster rate, was about eighteen days behind Venus. Our plan was to wait to attack Mercury until it had caught up with and passed Venus — then we'd send forces from both the Forge and Venus to hit it.

So from their own perspective, what were the Martians accomplishing by sending their new ships against the Forge? They could theoretically menace Venus if we sent our assault against Mercury. But they had to know that the forces we had for that assault were more than double what Mercury had in terms of local defenses...

Think back to that annoying chapter full of numbers. Even if you take out the losses from the Forge Squadron, we had *ten* battleships to the five we knew were at Mercury. Why didn't the Martians just send their three new toys to reinforce the Mercury Squadron? Dividing your defensive forces in this situation didn't make a whole lot of sense...

Unless the Martians' primary objective wasn't actually to *capture* the Forge.

John, Marlene, Karen and Wes were talking while I started to ponder this.

I looked from the icon of Greg and Mik's combined force to the Forge and back.

The Martians were giving us all the time we needed to bring in reinforcements. Why? They had to know that as long as they didn't actually capture the Forge, we were going to send help to try to bail Shauna out.

They were counting on us sending backup.

Look at it from their perspective: they have three new battleships that are more than a match for any other battlewagons in the solar system, except for the *Bonnies*. What would their ideal scenario be with those ships? Well, it wouldn't be to add them to the Mercury Squadron. Tied to defending the planet and working with five older, slower battleships, the new *Tharsis*-class ships would not be able to fully take advantage of their abilities. Remember, back in Glorious February, how the *Bonnies* weren't paired with older battleships, because their abilities were different? Same idea.

So the Martians were being wise and keeping their three new ships separate, as a strike force on their own. How could that force do the most damage? Not by attacking all Defense Command's battleships at once, but by getting them piecemeal... getting two or four at a time, so that on a one-to-one basis, the *Tharsis*-class ships could deliver massive victories, as they had against the Forge Squadron.

The Martians wanted to pick us apart. They saw the Forge not as a base to be captured for their uses, but as bait for us. They knew that our first reaction would be to send support to Shauna, and to try to defeat this squadron on our flank. And when we did... *if* we did, their new monsters would fall on us. With part of our battle fleet then destroyed, we'd no longer have the advantage we needed to assault Mercury.

Theirs was a plan of divide and conquer, plain and simple.

"Those fuckers."

Yes, I said it. I actually said it myself, in public (more or less). And, because everyone around this table knew I didn't care much for swearing, they all stopped in mid-conversation and looked at me.

This, I will concede, is one occasion when I did earn my Admiral's pay. I was the first to realize what the Martians were up to, though make no mistake, if I hadn't seen it, someone else would have. I was just in the right headspace at the right moment...

"What?" Karen asked the question softly, with a concerned frown. She'd read more from the tone of my words than had the others — she knew I'd seen something.

I planted my finger on the Forge icon and let out a huff, "Look at what they have us doing."

That wasn't a really helpful remark, and realizing that fact I quickly continued: "With these new *Tharsises* out there, we can't move the *Bonnies* away from Venus. The Lords and the public would be all over us if we tried... and we're too smart to try. The *Bonnies* are the only ships that can likely hold off these new Martians one-on-one."

I looked up as I finished that first blurb, and was greeted by a few thoughtful nods.

"So given that fact, we're going to launch our assault on Mercury with which battleships?"

"Greg's," Karen was starting to read my mind, the way she could.

"And if he goes to the Forge and ends up in a firefight with those new battleships, he's going to take at least *some* damage. Odds are he'd even lose a ship or two… perhaps *Cyclops*, based on what happened to *Medusa*," Marlene started picking up the thread as well.

No offense to Mik's ship, but *Cyclops* was from the same batch of *Odysseus*-class ships that *Medusa* had come from… and *Medusa*, remember, had blown up well short of the enemy. I doubt the same fate would befall Christian Mikaelsen, but there was no question that sending a thirty-year-old battleship like his against those new Martians would be a bad thing.

Even Greg's much more modern *Empire*-class ships would be outclassed, and that was what the Martians were counting on.

"They want Greg's ships to get there, so they can shoot up our assault force," Wes said that grimly, nodding. "They're trying to divide up our offensive forces, and draw our attention away from Mercury."

That was it, that's what I saw as I looked at that map. The Martians were counting on our determination to keep the Forge out of their hands — it was the bait in their trap. If we committed forces to help Shauna defend the place, we pretty much had to give up our plans of assaulting Mercury in the near future, thus giving them time to regroup and possibly even mount a whole new counteroffensive.

So they had put us in a very tough spot indeed. How could we possibly abandon the Forge? How could we abandon Shauna?

Easy, like this.

"We have to recall Greg. Now," I said that in a flat, dark tone.

John's eyes were moving from planet icon to planet icon to base icon, and he said nothing at first in response to my recommendation. As I made it, I was overcome with a sense of stark, deathly clarity. Sort of like the moment when you realize there really is no choice, you have to pull the plug on a loved one in hospital, something I've had unfortunate experience with.

For me, at least, it's a moment when all the turmoil in my mind is silenced by a deafening understanding. It's as though my decision is in a locked room in my mind, and all those things trying to stop me from carrying it out are banging on the doors and windows, trying to get in, but they can't. And I ignore them for that moment when I make the decision.

It's only later that I start to confront them.

And if you think it's excessive to compare the decision to abandon Shauna to the decision that ends a person's life, forgive my bluntness, you're wrong. This decision was abandoning hundreds of people to death and defeat. Hundreds of *our* people. Defense Command personnel. The sort of people we'd boarded *Idaho* to find in *The Dark Cruise*, despite knowing it was a trap. The sort of people we'd gone down to Pion rock to rescue, even though it was *Pion rock*.

We weren't going to help our comrades. We were going to tell them to fight and die for a lost cause. In our business, these are the sorts of decisions you absolutely have to make, but that doesn't make them any easier.

But this was necessary. We had to win this war — the sooner it was over, the fewer people who'd die. Simple as that. If we had to sacrifice a base — mercifully, a military-only base, without a large civilian population — then that's what we had to do.

That was my assessment, and the coldness of it wasn't lost on anyone at this table, least of all John. Come to think of it, everyone at this table was a better person than me; I'm rather certain all of them, with the possible exception of Karen, were even more distraught than I was at the thought of leaving our colleagues to their fate.

We all fell silent for a long few minutes, and I turned my eyes to Marlene. Shauna Cass had been in the Venus Squadron for as long as Karen and I had been out at the Belt, and had been Marlene's protégé for a lot of that time.

Her mouth had stretched into a thin line, and the strain of the war so far seemed to pull her features tight. After a moment she nodded slowly and glanced at John, "He's right, John."

That pretty much sealed it. The sorceress isn't wrong about things like this, but more to the point, if she (of all people) recognized the need to leave Shauna and the Forge out there to be defeated, it was truly militarily sound.

John put his hands on his hips, took a deep breath, and shook his head, "Shit."

I think the devolution of our language was sign enough of our feelings about this situation.

"I'll call Greg. And I'll get the message ready for Shauna…" he continued, but I caught his eye.

"Let me send the message to Shauna," my gaze switched to Marlene. "Better that it comes from me."

Neither John nor Marlene would shirk their responsibility to tell a junior officer that they were hanging her out to dry, but it was a message I wanted to send. Some people have suggested that this was because I savored the chance to tell Shauna (who some people think was somehow my rival, even though we rarely met) that she was in a hopeless situation.

Honestly, I don't know what precisely made me want to be the bearer of this news… I think I just felt responsible for having made the recommendation in the first place, and I wanted to take responsibility for that.

"I should do it," Marlene was shaking her head.

"My job," John disagreed.

Normally, I would have backed down at this point, but again, I had a strange need to send this message to Shauna. So I suggested a compromise: "Let's each record one. I'll go first and give the bad news."

I think John and Marlene were both surprised at how insistent I was, and after a little more prodding, they agreed. It's actually not unheard of, when bad news comes in orders, for multiple officers to attach messages to it — different friends and colleagues weighing in with messages of consolation or inspiration. It was perhaps a sign of how dire this occasion was that Shauna would get three of us.

Now I just had to figure out what to say to her…

'We're abandoning you' was what first came to mind.

CHAPTER EIGHTEEN

THE SKY FALLS DOWN

Shauna hadn't slept well for three days. Her Forge Squadron was sitting between the Martians and the base, but the enemy still hadn't moved. They also didn't seem to be concerned with stopping her recon flights of Starlights — she was keeping eyes on them at all times.

That's Starlights instead of Starbursts, by the way, because she was now keeping tabs on them with planes from her ships — the Starbursts and Sunbursts that had survived from *Akagi* and *Kaga* were back at the Forge, running patrols on other vectors, making sure another Martian force didn't come in behind her.

So far, the situation was clear: the Martians were waiting.

It made Shauna nervous.

The perpetual state of vigilance — constantly being awake and wired, always ready for action — was taking its toll on her ability to strategize. She didn't yet realize that she and her base had become bait.

"Signal coming in from the Forge... forwarded up from Venus. Eyes only for you, ma'am," the report from *Texas'* Sensors and Communications Officer reached Shauna's ears, and for a brief second she didn't so much as flinch.

Then it sank in, and she nodded, coming to her feet (she'd been in her old chair), "Send it to my cabin. I need to eat something anyway."

She left the bridge and headed for her quarters, basically moving on auto-pilot. She had no jump left, or spark with which to inspire her people. She was saving her little remaining energy for the inevitable confrontation with the Martians. The moment her enemy appeared, she would become alert and capable again... in the meantime, she was roaming like a zombie.

This state of being didn't do a hell of a lot for morale, but it could have been much worse: she could have given up entirely, and become defeatist. She was acting like a zombie, but at least she was a zombie still determined to fight.

Reaching her cabin, Shauna stepped in, closed the hatch behind her, and keyed her comm screen as she tossed her tunic onto her chair. She harvested a sandwich from the kitchen and dropped onto the end of her bed, using her remote to open the eyes-only message as she did. After she provided her access code (we were carefully securing signal traffic to the Forge, out of fear of intercepts) she waited until the *Texas*Net buffering display scrolled through.

I appeared on the screen.

Shauna and I knew each other at this point in time... reasonably well. She wasn't one of our immediate Belt Squadron family, but it was like the Belt Squadron and the Venus Squadrons were different branches in the same family tree. I didn't know all the things about Shauna that I knew about, say, Wes (she may have hated soup and loved heights), but that didn't change the fact that she was one of our kin, and I was one of hers.

So think of this as a conversation between distant relatives who get along okay, and believe in the importance of family.

"Shauna, it's Ken Barron."

I started with that line, and then I paused and took a breath, looking off screen. Karen had been staying out of frame, standing next to my screen when I'd recorded this.

When my eyes darted back to the viewfinder, Shauna stared right at them.

"Mission's changed. There are messages from John and Marlene behind mine, but I wanted to tell you first because this was my idea. We're calling Greg to Venus. We're abandoning the Forge, and you."

I purposefully put it as sharply as I could… that's one thing I do when I deliver bad news that I'm responsible for — I'm blunt. When it's something like this, you can never really 'soften the blow' enough, so I don't bother trying.

"You are going to have to stay there, Shauna. You can't retreat. But there's no help coming."

Shauna, whose world had only been delicately reconstructed after the massive defeat of her squadron, now felt it vaporizing around her. She'd never expected to be abandoned. She'd been waiting for the cavalry to arrive.

"Your job now is to keep them tied up. They're using you as bait. The reason they haven't swept in to finish you off yet is because they figure we won't send some of our battleships out there if the Forge has already fallen… but they expect that as long as you hold on, we'll have to send you help. And if we did, they'd cut the reinforcements apart with those new battleships of theirs, and the Mercury assault would be off. They'd get the momentum back."

Shauna couldn't really think at this stage. Any commander knows that there's the chance of being sent to certain defeat, or death, to serve a greater strategic purpose. Knowing that doesn't necessarily make it easier when you're the one being sent.

"If the Martians realize help isn't coming… if you give up… they can redeploy that squadron to reinforce Mercury, or to attack us at Venus or somewhere else. So it is absolutely essential that you *keep them there*. Act as though you know help is coming — do everything you can to make them think we've taken the bait."

My words trailed off there, and I distinctly remember feeling surprisingly cold in that moment. I was the messenger of defeat and death in this message.

"You keep their attention. The Forge becomes the Alamo. Even if it means you all have to die, you have to keep those new ships of theirs tied up for as long as possible."

Shauna obviously had to know about the Alamo. Four hundred years later and everyone still knows about the Alamo — those Texans made a memorable statement in history.

"I'm sorry, Shauna," I said quietly after a moment. "There's nothing else for it. Do your job. I'd suggest you explain the situation to your crews. And if you're looking to hate someone for putting you in this position, I'm as good as anyone else."

I fully expected her to hate someone for this. As a commanding officer, I can tell you plainly that perhaps the greatest fear one has is receiving an order like this — an order that condemns your people to defeat and quite likely, death. And becoming bitter about it, and hating the person who gave the order, is entirely understandable.

But this is the job. We have to deal with it.

"That's all from me, Shauna. Make them feel it. And good luck."

On that note — which felt rather inadequate — the message ended, with my face frozen on the screen.

Shauna sat with her sandwich uneaten, staring at my image for a few moments. Her frame of understanding for the universe was at once gone and restored — we were abandoning her, and more importantly her *people*, but for a reason that made sense to her.

The conflicting emotions that plied through her were epic and tidal. She bore them in silence for those first moments, and then for one brief flash she let loose the anger and anguish that was billowing through her.

It was apparently a very feral scream, and it ended with her on her knees in front of her bed, flopped forward with her arms propping her up as she tried to sob, but found she had no tears. I don't know if you've ever had such a reaction, but I have. It's a strange one. It's not stereotypical anything.

It's just... painful. Part of you wants to break down and sob, part of you wants to drive your fist through something, and another part is keeping a precarious, rational control of your body. You end up doing very little — you fall to the ground, but the anger cancels out the tears, and the attempts to sob keep you from actually driving your fist through anything.

And it only lasts a few seconds. Then you try to figure out what you're supposed to be doing. Ultimately, you resign yourself to just doing your job, because it seems to be all that your brain will let you do... and it has to be done.

Take a guess as to when I learned about this reaction. I'll give you a hint: it hasn't yet been covered in these books.

Shauna gathered herself up off the floor slowly, shakily. She actually picked up her sandwich from the bed and ate it, and she became a zombie again. She blocked it all out. She hated me instantly, but in a dishonest way... that is, she hated me for having sent the message and perhaps for having made the suggestion, but she didn't really. That's complicated, I suppose. And for later as well.

For now she just stood and ate, and tried to decide what would be better: to tell her people that they had been abandoned, or to let them believe there was still hope. My recommendation that she tell them had been irrelevant. She'd decide on her own what to do.

Which option would make them better fighters? She wondered at the cold, brutal calculus of a hopeless situation, then finally opened John's and Marlene's follow-up messages.

They offered her no comfort.

After I recorded my message to Shauna, I sat silently on my bed for a few moments, and stared at the screen. Karen seated herself next to me as I did this, and after a while I glanced at her.

"There but for the grace of God goes us," I said quietly.

Karen didn't say anything at first, but then she looked at me and shook her head, "If you and Shauna switched places right now, you'd still be the one who decided this. Not her."

I frowned, and she sighed.

Maybe she was right — maybe, even it had been my own people on the line, I would have made the decision to condemn the Forge Squadron.

Circumstances didn't allow us to find out.

Chapter Nineteen
From The Trenches

Commander Bruce Arama was edgy and tired, and was determined to allow his crew to see neither fact. For the three days after the battle, he'd tried to make regular appearances everywhere aboard *Adelaide* — to make sure every man and woman saw him and his confidence each day.

It won't surprise you to hear that this confidence was entirely invented. He was about as panicked as they all wanted to be, but he was masking his fears.

Bruce was a natural-born leader, plain and simple. It's not often that you find officers in the Reserve who can be thrust into situations like this and act with all the outward calm and aplomb of experienced professionals, but there are some. That probably sounds arrogant on my part (as an egomaniacal professional officer) but I don't mean it to...

We officers who spend our careers in the fleet are trained for these situations, and we get plenty of experience commanding ships in action.

Bruce was a contractor — a damned good one — but that didn't necessarily mean he'd be a good leader in a combat situation. There's nothing that I know of in contracting that's quite the same as commanding a warship during a shooting war... I could be wrong, but I don't think so.

Anyway, what I'm trying to say here is that Bruce's excellent handling of this situation was due to his personality, and inherent skills. He was a citizen-spacer who'd proven himself very, very capable in action — a regular Arthur Currie, to draw on a very old historical allusion.

That was good news for *Adelaide*. Three days after the disastrous battle, it was probably as well-run as the venerable veteran *Texas*. Despite the odds against them, and the shock of all the destruction they'd seen, the crew of the corvette was still confident and calm.

I think any leader would give Bruce a much-deserved nod for setting that example.

The other two reservist-crewed ships — *Gansu* and *Hobart* — were not in as good condition, despite having regular officers for skippers. I think the professional officers might have been a hindrance in that case... no offense to them intended. I, for one, would have had no idea how to comfort a reservist crew in the case of such disaster — the way I'd have dealt with it with *Wolf's* crew probably wouldn't have worked for the reservists. Different styles, as I've said.

No, Bruce knew exactly what his crew needed to hear, and he made sure they heard it. *Adelaide* benefited massively.

All that good news aside, the little corvette was still in a hell of a difficult position, and Bruce was well aware of it. As he sat with his senior officers in the ship's small wardroom for a meal, they were pretty forward in questioning him about it.

"So help's going to be coming, right Bruce?"

It's not the sort of question you ever want to be asked as a commander, because if — like Bruce — you didn't know the answer, whatever you say could end up causing problems. If you say no, your people are on their own, it might have a very negative effect. At the same time, if you say help is coming and it doesn't come, it could prolong good spirits only to shatter them completely at the worst possible moment.

Theoretically, the decision of how to respond is based on the character of the crew, meaning there's no right answer. Some crews need to hear the truth, and even if the situation is grim, they'll steel themselves and push on. Others need to know there's something to fight for. So goes the argument, anyway... and it leaves a fine line for a commander. Projecting confidence is part of the job... but how much is too much, and under what circumstances? It was a decision Bruce had to make as CO, based on what he knew about his crew.

"No one's told me," he gave the honest answer — the one a 'professional' officer might not give, as we're taught never to appear uncertain before our people. "They might send the fleet out here to beat those bastards... but if they do, that pretty much puts an end to the Mercury assault."

The officer who'd asked the question was one of the junior technicians from the Sensors and Communications staff, a young man named Bill Keynes, and he frowned at the answer, "But Bruce... they wouldn't let us die out here..."

Bruce was sitting at the head of the wardroom table as an honored guest, and he shook his head, "They will if they have to."

Keynes didn't say anything else, but he started picking at his food with far less enthusiasm after Bruce delivered the reluctant assessment.

The mood at this table wasn't particularly cheery, unsurprisingly.

Francine Fuentes was the head of the mess, and thus was sitting at the opposite end of the table from Bruce. That didn't stop her from asking him the next, delicate question, "Still nothing from Cass after that transmission?"

Bruce loaded some of the food from his plate onto his fork and shook his head, "She hasn't called me yet. I bet she knows, though."

Again, not the sort of conversation we'd be likely to have at *Wolf's* mess table, in front of all the ship's senior officers. We'd tell the crew when we knew something for certain, but we wouldn't be commenting on the process of finding out (or waiting to be told) in mixed company. Not a criticism, just a difference.

The people at the table kept their eyes down as Bruce replied, none of them wanting to think too carefully about the possible meaning of the flagship's silence.

Everyone knew there had been a coded transmission marked for her eyes only, but no one knew what was in it. If there was good news, surely Shauna would have passed it on as soon as she'd seen the message that had come from Venus.

But it had been over five hours since the message had arrived, and there'd been no word from *Texas* about its contents.

Rumors were spreading like wild fire. They were all, of course, based entirely in supposition... but that didn't matter. One thing about the armed forces: rumors are almost as good as hard currency at times. I don't remark on that much when I'm talking about our veteran Belt Squadron elite, in part because we keep our people well-enough informed to reduce the rumors considerably, and in part because most of the rumors that do get around our ships tend to be personal and inconsequential.

The circumstances at the Forge made the place a perfect breeding ground for rumor, though. The stress being that high, the situation being that desperate... someone could sneeze and a rumor would start about a new secret plan.

As it was, the rumor spreading now was that help wasn't coming.

You see, rumors can be right. They often are.

Shauna was alone in her cabin, and she had been for those five silent hours. She'd talked to Hwangbo Yang about the defensive arrangements that were in place down in the Forge dome, and she'd sat staring at the scouting reports on the Martian force's location. The bastards still weren't coming in... they were still waiting...

Shauna was trying to come to terms with the fact that she and her base were now bait. The Martians were leaving her out here long enough for Greg to arrive, so that they could smash his battleships and thus keep Defense Command from being able to attack Mercury. They didn't really care about the Forge — they didn't need it. If they wanted to attack Venus, they could just cruise straight there.

So now we had to contain these new battleships — they had to be held at the Forge. That, ultimately, was Shauna's job. She had to make the Martians think that their plan was working... that Defense Command was going to divide up its battle fleet so the new Martian ships could pick it apart piecemeal.

And the only way to convince them of that was to act now as though she'd received every assurance of support from us. She had to act as if Greg was going to come in with his guns blazing — act as if she had all the confidence in the world.

But the question for her was how to do that. Not in a tactical sense, but from the perspective of morale. Should she tell her people that there was help coming, so they'd act as though it was... or should she tell them the truth, and ask them to act as if their fates weren't sealed?

I know I would have trusted my people enough to tell them. But Shauna didn't know her people as well, and she wasn't as sure.

It was a bitter question to face. And she didn't feel equipped to deal with it.

CHAPTER TWENTY
TRUST AND DEATH

"They're still sitting sixteen hours out, ma'am," Captain Calleigh Tong, *Texas'* skipper, reported as she entered the frigate's briefing room. Tong was the last of the remaining squadron skippers to arrive at this meeting, because she'd remained on her bridge to oversee the recording and transfer of a broadcast from Venus into the *Texas*Net buffers.

This, I should say, was about four hours after the end of the last chapter — nine hours since my message to Shauna, and a little over two-and-a-half days before Greg's force, had it been coming, would have arrived.

"Signal's in the root directory," Tong added as she took a seat at the table, and sorry, I should have said that seated around the table were Shauna, Bruce, Michael Soto of *Gansu* and Kabira Vibbard of *Hobart*.

Shauna nodded at her Flag Captain's words, then activated the wall screen, selected a video and hit play.

Up on the screen, before the surviving COs of the Forge Squadron, was a news feed from the network of Jessica Qing (I'm still not going to say which, I'm taking no chances of being challenged to a duel by their pros).

"We're interrupting this broadcast of the *Geraldine Coilier Show* with breaking news," the news anchor said with a certain urgency. He looked unkempt, too — the way news anchors often do when they have to cut into live programming with bad news. "It has been reported by a source in Defense Command's Venus Headquarters that the situation at the Forge base is very desperate, and that the Navy is planning a major relief effort... we have a recorded report from our correspondent, Davis Wing, to show you."

The feed switched to the veteran correspondent Davis Wing, a reporter with whom Marlene and the Venus HQ staff had a very good relationship.

"This is Davis Wing from Venus HQ. The situation here is very tense. Word has come from the famous base at the Forge that only four ships of the original squadron engaged by the Martians three days ago have survived. This confirms the rumors that have been circulating here for the last twenty-four hours. The Forge base now remains under serious threat, and is not expected to be able to hold out for very long."

The scene cut from Mister Wing to B roll of people moving in a hurry through the *Venus One* HQ corridors, and then outside to orbital space, for urgent-looking images of small craft buzzing between ships around the planet.

"One source high in Venus HQ has suggested to us that the Martians may have unleashed some sort of new battleship on the squadron, and I can only speculate that this new ship would be similar to our *Bonaventure*-class battleships. No official word has been released on this point."

Wing reappeared on the screen, "Admiral Greg Noyce and Commodore Christian Mikaelsen, of last year's raid against Mars, were bound for the Forge, but they have been called directly to Venus now. However, sources in HQ say that as soon as they arrive and resupply, a large operation will be launched. To quote my source directly, she says: 'We're assuming that the Forge will fall, but if it does, it will be recovered. No matter what it costs.' We'll keep you updated as we know more. Back to the newsroom."

The feed flipped back to the anchor, "Very serious developments at the Forge. If you're just joining us, it's been confirmed that the base squadron was reduced to just four ships by the Martian attack we reported a few days ago. The Martians may also have deployed new battleships in this attack. Information is still very intermittent, and we're working from trusted sources in Venus HQ. But it sounds like the Defense Command priority right now is very clear: the Forge will be secured, or taken back if it has fallen. We'll have more on this at the news at 1300, and again at 1700. For now, we'll send you back to *Geraldine Coilier.*"

The feed froze, and Shauna looked from the screen to her skippers, taking a deep breath.

"We need to hold out until help gets here," she said with a straight face.

That's right, she wasn't telling them what I'd said. She wasn't telling them that help really wasn't coming. That report, leaked to Davis Wing directly by Marlene, was being broadcast as loudly and frequently as it could be across the Empire, to maximize the chances that a Martian listening post would pick it up and pass it on to the *Tharsis* force menacing the Forge. It was meant to fool them into thinking that we'd do *anything* to take back the Forge — so they *had* to stay there.

And now Shauna was using it to fool her Captains and Commanders into believing that they had a chance. To be honest, I wouldn't have done this. No one from the old Belt Squadron would have.

"Did they leak that in hopes of scaring the Martians away?" Soto asked quietly.

Shauna shook her head, "As far as I know, it wasn't supposed to be leaked. But that doesn't matter. Admiral Noyce's squadron didn't ship fully loaded for action — some of the supplies in our stores were for his battleships. And they're undoubtedly going to want to review the battle records we sent before they start tangling with these new Martian ships. So we have to wait another four days or so before help comes."

That was a tall order, but Captain Soto and Commander Vibbard both smiled in a slightly relieved fashion. Their Admiral had just told them that, at the very least, there was a light at the end of the tunnel — something to fight for.

Bruce Arama didn't smile, but he nodded slowly.

"So how do we want to do this?" Vibbard asked quickly. "We remain here, wait for them to come to us… or go out there and attack. See if we can wound them with quick raids?"

"If we start raiding, they might realize we have help coming, and back off," Soto suggested quickly.

Soto and Vibbard were both solid officers, but Shauna knew that after the leaked report, there was no chance the Martians were going to back off. It was their job to draw a counterattack, and in a particularly unsubtle fashion, we'd just promised them one.

"That's exactly what we're going to do," she agreed with Soto. You see, she and her squadron now had to act as though the leaked report was true. If help was coming, it would make sense for a confident (perhaps overconfident) Defense Command squadron to start trying cute little raids.

The Martians would expect no less from us.

"Excellent, then how about we hit them with torpedoes, try to damage some of those new battleships?" Soto clapped his hands together eagerly, and Shauna paled for a second.

She knew full well that she'd lose half her ships if they tried something that ambitious. But losing half her ships would just convince the Martians that the Forge had help coming. If she was willing to throw away her ships on casual, poorly-conceived attacks, there *had* to be help coming.

"Sounds like a good idea to me. We'll proceed under attack plan one, and weigh anchor in one hour," she said with an enormous amount of false confidence, then came to her feet. "Michael, Kabira, Bruce, let's go get them."

Soto proudly saluted, then stepped away from the table and left. Vibbard repeated that sequence and followed Soto out of the room. Their ships, *Gansu* and *Hobart*, would be operating together as an attack division under 'plan one', so they'd have some talking to do on their way back to the flight deck.

Shauna expected Bruce Arama to leave as well, but instead as she glanced at him, she found his eyes were fixed on her.

"Ma'am, I'd like to speak to you in private," he didn't make those words a question or request, and she stiffened.

She'd been lying during this whole meeting, obviously, and her hope — her only hope — was that her skippers didn't see through her. Even Calleigh Tong, her Flag Captain and friend, didn't know the truth. Shauna had decided to carry the burden of this lie by herself.

She felt a chill as she received Bruce Arama's cold stare, and sensed that the Commander, the reservist contractor from Auckland, had seen through her.

"Certainly," she said in a much quieter and more sullen tone than she'd meant to use. If he knew, she had to talk to him. She had to prevent him from trying to spread a rumor that no help was coming.

"I'll be on the bridge," Tong couldn't get a read on what was happening, but she had other things to think about — namely making sure the torpedo tube was ready.

As the Flag Captain left, Commander Arama pointed at the frozen image on the screen, "The man didn't say *when* the help was coming. He said the Forge would be recovered, whatever the cost. Well is the cost us? Are they going to attack Mercury while we keep these Martians here, out of the way?"

Bruce Arama, well, that man is intuitive. Saying that takes nothing away from the other skippers in the room, I should say. But Bruce was a reservist, and every other skipper in the room was a regular officer. Regular officers are accustomed to accepting the truth in their CO's orders and explanations. Reserve officers aren't schooled quite that way.

Bruce was seeing through the careful wording we'd come up with when we'd been preparing the leak in Venus HQ — wording that loudly implied we were going straight after the Forge, but which in fact made no firm commitments.

He'd seen right through Shauna.

And now Shauna didn't know what to say in reply.

One answer, of course, would have been to order his silence on the subject. But Shauna wasn't that sort of officer.

"We all have to fight as though help's coming," she said quietly. "I can't tell anyone else. You shouldn't know. You understand, we have to force them to stay here. Keep them tied up while the assault on Mercury goes ahead."

Bruce's eyes burned into Shauna, and she felt shame. This wasn't shame that Bruce was inflicting, this was the shame that had bubbled within her since she'd decided to lie to her people. Bruce's stare just made it feel more acute.

"We're going to do this, Bruce. And you have to comply. The war effort hinges on what we do here, and it's your job. You will tell no one, you understand? Word about this cannot spread. Clear?"

Bruce had never felt so much anger, but he nodded. He understood what she was saying alright, but he had to damn her methods. I honestly don't blame him for that.

They were all about to get killed, and she wouldn't be honest with her crews about why.

He'd have to decide whether he toed that line... but for now he had to get his ship ready for a hopeless fight that was only being joined to make a deceptive point.

He left the briefing room, and standing behind him, Shauna let out a long sigh. She wondered if she'd made the right choice in lying. She didn't feel good about it, but she believed it was necessary.

That's what she told herself over and over. It was necessary.

An aside here: my editors want me to talk a bit more about what I would have done. The consensus among the editors is that lying was the wrong move — that honesty, in the end, is the best policy. I've already said that I agree with their conclusion... they want me to elaborate more as to why I do.

As I pointed out at the start of this book, I don't want to sit here and wag my finger in hindsight, but this is one point that Shauna and I certainly wouldn't have agreed on. And yes, part of that might be that I come from a squadron of professionally-crewed ships (as opposed to reservist-crewed ships), filled with people who volunteered and know the score... know that, if it comes down to it, our lives can be forfeit.

But lying, to me, is just setting everything up for a failure. The command relationship is one of mutual trust... your personnel believe you are going to do your best for them, that your respect them, and that they can believe you.

Should you always appear confident? Certainly, and this is a lie... but it's a lie about yourself. Blatantly lie to them about circumstances, even with the noble motive of giving hope in a hopeless situation, and you're betraying them.

Of course, some people will say that a lie is good for discipline and morale, and they're right... up until the lie is found out, the brighter, happier false reality is probably conducive to better working conditions.

But after it's found out...

So I don't agree with Shauna — not by half. But I'm not going to go the next step and condemn her, as many have, because whatever I say now, sitting here in comfort twenty years after the fact — I still don't know exactly what it was like for her.

It's different being there, on the ground, under the stress.

I think she was wrong, and I think I would have made a very different decision.

Circumstance, though, never demanded that I find out.

I'd like to take a moment to thank circumstance for that. I owe you one, buddy.

CHAPTER TWENTY-ONE

LIES OR NOT?

Bruce had ordered his crew to assemble in the gymnasium on *Adelaide's* rec deck as soon as he'd gotten back aboard, but now as he headed to talk to them, he found himself not sure what to say. He couldn't lie to them. He'd never be able to look them in the eye again if he did that.

He was under orders not to reveal the truth to them… but he owed them much.

It was a rough place to be in. As a skipper, your loyalty to your crew is immense. Those are your men and women — *yours*, in the possessive sense. That's not to say you own them, but they're your responsibility. When they all signed on, they agreed to follow orders from the commanding officer — from you — having faith that the CO would be qualified to lead.

This is the mutual responsibility… the symbiosis between a ship's officers and its crew.

Could Bruce lie to them? Flatly lie to them, and tell them there was hope when there really was none? It seemed like an insult to him, and he knew they would probably feel the same way.

What options did he have, then? To lie or to disobey orders?

Well, he picked the option I probably would have picked with the crew of *Wolf*, had I been in this awkward and deadly situation.

The gym had been noisy as groups of spacers chatted and tried to guess what was going to come of this meeting. No one figured it'd be anything good — there was no reason to get everyone together to tell them that help was at hand, or that they were going to be allowed to withdraw. But how bad it would be? That was the question.

As Bruce entered the gym, all the chatting and muttering died down, and Bruce wasted no time moving to a spot in front of his 143 officers and crew. Someone had kindly pulled a crate out of a nearby locker, so he stepped up onto that and held up a hand in greeting.

"I've just returned from the flagship," he called out with his deep, kiwi-accented voice. "We're going to attack the Martians, attack plan one, with torpedoes. We'll be escorting *Texas* on its run."

That drew a hush. These people weren't scared of a fight, but nor were they eager to try to get *Texas* safely into torpedo range of one of those monsters.

"The skippers of the other ships are right now probably circulating a news feed. News was leaked from Venus that Admiral Noyce's reinforcements were rerouted there, and that there'll be a big effort to come out here and either help us, or to take the Forge back if they're too late and it's already captured."

Those words, delivered in an ominous tone, started the crew looking at each other in confusion. If the other ships were getting this news feed, why wasn't Bruce showing it to them now?

"I'm under orders not to comment about the validity of that report to you. But there's a reason I'm not showing it to you. I don't lie to my crew."

There, he followed orders.

If it's possible for silence to get silenter, it did right then. This was a crew made up of people from all walks of life and education levels — middle management and tradespeople, drop-outs and valedictorians — but every single one of them immediately understood what Bruce was leaving unsaid.

"The other crews... the other skippers... I don't know how aware of the current situation they are. And Admiral Cass believes that's the way it should stay. So please don't call anyone and tell them what I haven't told you. That's between those crews and their skippers. But you're my crew."

The silence lengthened, and Bruce hopped down from the crate, "Cruising stations. We're moving out with the squadron within the hour."

His tone was uncompromising, and he turned and headed out of the gym. The men and women of *Adelaide* were left in his wake, and the chatting slowly returned.

As it turned out, the news had been bad.

Greg wasn't coming to their aid... and no one else was. They were on their own, destined to die or be captured while we went on to attack Mercury.

Of course, there were different variations with regard to the ultimate goal of their mission, and the rumors crossed each other, and rammed head on into each other. People had wildly different ideas of what the squadron's final mandate now was — to raid against the Martians... to get itself destroyed... to run and leave the base to its fate...

But while all of these questions were debated, *Adelaide's* crew did their jobs and got to cruising stations. They actually accomplished their tasks more quickly than any of the other crews in the squadron.

Ten hours later, Shauna Cass sat on the end of her bed, her head hanging while her fingers pressed her face. She was six hours from a hopeless fight with the Martians, and she fully expected half her squadron to be lost. The Martians were going to be ready for a raid, even if the report hadn't leaked to them yet.

Pushing herself to her feet, she turned and headed to her bathroom, where she splashed some cold water on her face. She then straightened up before the mirror and peered into her own eyes, trying to erase the emotion from them. She didn't want anyone to be able to look at her and realize this really was the end.

The crew had to believe there was something left to fight for. That lie — the lie of hope — would give them the extra lift that could possibly, just *possibly*, get them through the raid to come. She couldn't take that away from them. She had to be the towering statue of confidence and certainty.

That was what she'd be.

Tugging on the collar of her ship fatigues, she rolled her shoulders around slightly to loosen them up, then took a deep, solid breath. Her eyes fixed on her reflection one more time, before she turned and left the bathroom, and her quarters.

She had to be confident. She had to be certain. On the strength of the hope she was giving... on the strength of the lie she was telling... her crews might just survive this attack. They might just get through it, and even do some damage on the way.

She had to hope.

Or lie to herself, depending on how you want to phrase it.

CHAPTER TWENTY-TWO
DEBRIS

Ten hours later, *Adelaide* and *Texas* were heading back towards the Forge. Neither *Gansu* nor *Hobart* were with them. Neither *Gansu* nor *Hobart* existed anymore.

I contemplated recounting the attack, but what's the point? They went in with two separate divisions, a frigate and a corvette in each, and they got cut to pieces.

Gansu had been hit amidships by *Olympus Mons* and had blown up. *Hobart* had tried to withdraw, but had been assaulted by a pair of destroyers and was cut to pieces. Captain Tong managed to fire *Texas'* torpedo before turning her ship around and running hard, with *Adelaide* alongside, but the warhead had been shot down. Then the frigate had taken a shot to its low pod, cutting its power and its speed.

Now *Texas* and *Adelaide* were together, limping back towards the Forge with the Martians still not following them.

Shauna stood on the bridge of her ship and refused to reveal the turmoil and the agony surging through her. Her thoughts were bitter ones — give *hope*, really? Offer lies and then get people killed with them. What the hell had she been thinking?

Whatever confidence she'd had was shaken, but she had to hold things together. The crew of *Texas* still believed there was help coming — Greg Noyce would be riding to the rescue, so if they hurt the Martians at every opportunity, the battleships of the Home Fleet and the Hawke Squadron would finish the job.

Even if the crew of *Texas* died in the meantime, they'd know they were softening up an enemy that Greg would have to face.

Yes, well, that was a lie.

But it was one that Shauna needed to keep alive. She didn't want her people — even her professional spacers aboard *Texas*, all of them veterans of the Venus Squadron — to lose that one sense of purpose. The lie was all they had.

She'd take the guilt to give them hope...

Her line of thought just kept going like that. You may be sick of hearing it repeated by now... I have to admit I am... but I keep repeating it to emphasize the pit into which Shauna was descending. She was trapped by her lie, and now for the sake of her remaining people, she had to stick with it. As far as she was concerned, admitting now that it was a lie would only make things worse — her crews would lose faith in her, at the moment when they had to stand and fight.

I very nearly just wrote 'I told you so'.

So now she was in a guilt-riddled spiral. She had to shelter her crew from the truth, and it made her feel horrible to lie to them. But she was the commander, so it was her job — and hers alone — to feel that horrible guilt. She wouldn't burden her crew just to lighten her conscience.

That was the endlessly repetitive pattern of her thoughts.

But despite the mantra, and the attempts to convince herself of the correctness of her choices, she still desperately wanted to save *someone*.

As she stood on the bridge of *Texas*, looking discretely around at her bridge crew, she knew there was no way to save these brave men and women. Her ship was damaged, and it was the flagship. The flagship couldn't abandon the base, not even if she personally stayed behind. Even now, she just couldn't bring herself to do something so... 'dishonorable' is, I think, the only word.

But did they all have to die?

She felt a moment of true weakness. Then she made a decision. A decision that hard-nosed commanders, and even people like me, might say was a bad one. It served no tactical purpose... it did nothing but ease her conscience.

It's the sort of decision that many officers, myself included, might make, even though it is the bad one. I can't condemn her for it. If you can, you're perhaps a better combat officer than I am, I don't know.

On *Adelaide's* bridge, Bruce Arama was not impressed. His ship had survived the latest battle, which was undeniably a good thing, but he still had great discomfort with his commanding officer. I don't blame him for that.

"*Texas* is reestablishing Battlelink," *Adelaide's* Sensors and Communications Officer reported, and Bruce nodded, moving back to the front of his bridge.

The battle damage to the flagship had made communication intermittent — Battlelink had been cutting in and out for the whole four hours the two ships had been running back toward the Forge.

Now Shauna appeared on *Adelaide's* screen three, looking harried and marred by an unstable picture, "Commander Arama, I have new orders for you."

Bruce, at this stage, was expecting to be asked to do a suicide run, because that would undoubtedly look good to the Martians. Or perhaps, more sensibly, his ship might be tasked with close recon — it could be up to him to keep a close eye on the Martians, so that Shauna would know where they were, and when.

So as his eyes settled on Shauna's, his gaze was stern and his arms were folded.

Shauna, though, had a different order, "Get your ship to Venus, and report on the events that have taken place. Join Admiral Noyce's mission."

Bruce straightened up slightly, but he didn't unfold his arms, "Ma'am?"

"Go on, Bruce. We'll stay at the Forge and put up a good show. You won't be missed when they come," Shauna's voice revealed her exhaustion.

Everyone on the bridge stood awkwardly when those words were delivered. They weren't sure what to make of them. Wasn't it their lot to die now, as a smokescreen for the Mercury assault?

"Ma'am, we can still shadow them for you, and run escort... we're fully operational and ready to fight," Bruce's words were cold. For some reason — and he couldn't figure out exactly why — he thought right then that she didn't have confidence in him.

That she was sending him away because she didn't think *Adelaide* was fit to fight.

"Admiral Noyce will need all the information and first-hand experience he can get, so I want you to get out there and give it to him. I doubt either of our ships will survive when they finally close in, but *Adelaide* could help lead Admiral Noyce's mission. He'll need your expertise."

Her order was in keeping with the fiction. For her crew, and for the garrison on the Forge base, it would look as though Bruce and his ship — the last fully-functional ship — were being dispatched to lead the counterattack force back to the Forge, to provide them with as much up-to-date local space knowledge as possible.

In reality, she was sending *Adelaide* to the relative safety of Venus.

She needed someone to survive.

Bruce took a deep breath, and then another. He stared at Shauna on the screen, and then he looked down to his XO, and then back.

"Yes ma'am. Good luck."

It was that simple. He and his ship had been given a reprieve. They would live to fight again, while the rest of the Forge burned.

"And to you. Give my regards to Admiral Noyce. And tell Rear Admiral Barron... tell him. Tell him good luck at Mercury."

She'd wanted to tell Bruce to tell me to go to hell, but that wouldn't have fit with her fiction, nor would it have actually felt right.

Bruce saluted — something we rarely do over Battlelink, but which seemed appropriate now — and then *Texas* closed the connection.

Taking a breath, Bruce turned to *Adelaide's* Helm and Navigation Officer, "Walter, mark course for Venus and go at maximum cruising speed."

"She's letting us go," Francine Fuentes seemed as surprised as Bruce certainly was, so he caught his XO's gaze and nodded.

"Part of me says we should play hero and stay. But I'd much rather follow orders, live, and get some revenge later," his words were cool.

Fuentes paused for a moment, then looked away, "That does sound better."

Adelaide angled away from *Texas*, and then the corvette's drives fired, sending it towards Venus at high speed.

Texas labored on towards the Forge — to, appropriately enough, its own little Alamo.

CHAPTER TWENTY-THREE

GREAT NEWS (LOTS OF SARCASM)

While Bruce Arama was guiding *Adelaide* onto a vector for Venus, those of us already there were meeting to go over the latest observation reports we'd received from Mercury. I can't specifically explain how we were getting images of the ships at Mercury, but we were.

Hmm, I don't like being quite that vague. Think back to *The Jupiter Patrol*. Remember how Jim sort of got into trouble for showing Bunny our sensor suite aboard *Wolf*? Remember that it wasn't such a big deal because contemporary commercial sensor suites were just as good?

Well, do you really think Defense Command Research and Development would allow its 'best' gear to be matched by something you could buy at a civilian shipyard?

I can't elaborate any further, but suffice it to say that the corvette *Melbourne* was watching Mercury for us, from further out than just about any other ship we had could have. We were getting a preview of what was to come in our strike on Mercury... and thanks to Shauna's gambit, we had to start looking now.

Before I get into the narrative of the meeting, let me explain: had the Forge not been attacked, Greg and Mik would have arrived there in two days' time. Then we'd have spent the next couple of weeks preparing our plans for assaulting Mercury.

Now we had to turn around and launch a 'relief force' that would supposedly be headed for the Forge, but which would in fact go direct to Mercury. That meant there'd be no time to waste in planning. It had to look to the Martians like Greg's battleships were stopping at Venus only long enough to take on supplies, do a little briefing, and then set out to take the Forge.

That meant we had to lay a lot of groundwork for the Mercury assault quite hastily. The Imperial Army soldiers who were assigned to the assault forces were staying in their transports, the Special Branchers and SF who were coming with us from Venus were being put aboard combat storeships. We also had to reconfigure our intended attack force.

Under the old plan, Shauna would have brought her two battleships to Venus after the assault was launched, to cover the aristocratic colony against counterattack. Back when that plan had been made, we'd figured two battleships would have been quite enough... but now the *Tharsises* were in play. There was no way we could leave Venus without numerous battleships, and indeed, without the best battleships we had.

Only the *Bonnies* could stop the *Tharsis*-class, based on what Shauna's experience had told us. They couldn't join the assault.

That suddenly reduced our massive firepower advantage. Remember, Greg, Mik and Marlene between them had six battleships... six of ours to face as many as five of theirs, in a direct assault...

And that wasn't all, either. The *Bonnies* couldn't stay at Venus without a strong cruiser force to escort them — otherwise, they'd be vulnerable to the missiles of Martian Destroyers and DEs if the *Tharsises* came.

Which meant...

"That means us, doesn't it? We're going to miss the party?" Wes Pellew had his arms folded across his chest, and he let out a sigh.

"We'll need the Jupiter Force's corvettes to look after the storeships and the transports when we launch the assault. If the dreadnoughts come here, John will need your frigates in escort," Marlene explained quietly, not particularly happy to be giving this news.

I've discussed this before: twisted as it may seem to some people, we really do want to go into action. We don't want to be left behind while our friends and comrades get to have a crack at the enemy... we want to be there to do our share, and to help our friends. Unfortunately for Wes and his Independent Squadron, the five frigates and two corvettes under his command made for a perfect escort force for the *Bonnies* — a much better escort than the Jupiter Force's three frigates and four corvettes would have been.

He was going to miss the Mercury assault, right along with John.

At this point he nodded slowly and released another deep sigh, "Alright. Well if the *Tharsises* come, we'll be ready for them."

"Damned right you will," I patted my friend on the shoulder. I was going to miss the Independent Squadron when we hit Mercury, but it couldn't be helped.

"So, you said you had bad news..." I looked from Wes to John and Marlene, "...that was it?"

John and Marlene looked at each other, then shook their heads almost simultaneously. Marlene leaned down over the plot table that we were all standing around in *Venus One's* HQ, her fingers tapping up some new surveillance scans sent by *Melbourne*, "That was the easy part."

You never get used to hearing the other shoe drop. I glanced at Karen — she was there, along with Wes, me, John and Marlene, and she raised her eyebrows. Great. Something else fun and new from our Martian friends.

The screen in the plot table loaded up two separate display windows. One was a standard scan of Mercury, showing everything we could see the Martians had in place — five battleships, fourteen destroyers and eleven destroyer escorts, along with their orbital defenses and shore batteries.

Just for reference, that meant they had thirty ships, against the thirty-seven we were now planning to hit them with.

I'd seen sensor feeds like this before, so my eyes took a quick survey of this one to make sure nothing major looked out of place, then I turned my attention to the second half of the screen. It was a blurry vid of a couple of Martian destroyers. Again, I can't exactly explain how vid was acquired at the range from which *Melbourne* was operating, but suffice it to say it was rather more complicated than just a really, really big camera.

"Have a look at these two destroyers," John leaned forward next to Marlene, and waved his hand at the vid that was looping.

Karen, Wes and I leaned in closer, each of us wearing a frown.

"DCI briefed me this morning," John didn't sound impressed, and rightly so. "Those aren't regular destroyers."

He was right (of course), they weren't. They didn't have rear turrets — the 'tails' I so happily berate the Martians for. And their bows seemed to be built up quite considerably...

"The Mercury yards seem to have had two battleships under construction at the start of the war. When it became clear they wouldn't have time to finish either of them before we attacked, the commander of the yards stuck their bow lasers on two destroyers," the words tasted bitter to John.

I straightened up in surprise, and looked across the plot table at John, "*Monitors?*"

He nodded, "Seems like DCI hasn't been giving the Martians enough credit for their engineering creativity. And we haven't been doing any better, I suppose. But they're being innovative just when we really don't need them to be."

"That's true enough," Karen agreed with a nod, though her gaze remained fixed on the destroyers... well, call them monitors.

The 'monitor', I should say, doesn't mean 'vid screen'. During the nineteenth and twentieth centuries, monitors were small vessels carrying battleship-worthy firepower. They tended to be slow and to handle badly, but if you got close to the coast they were monitoring (hence the name, I think) they could hit you very hard. The Americans pioneered these ships in their civil war, and then the British Royal Navy took them to a new level in the twentieth century.

And now the Martians had them?

"So DCI is sure those aren't just a new class of DD?" Wes looked up at John and Marlene, and our First Lord shook his head.

"We ran those new vid scans through the comparisons database. Hull form is destroyer, but those turrets could be off a *Tharsis*."

That last word jolted all our eyes straight to John. Wouldn't that be a coup for those Martian bastards? They couldn't build enough of their new superbattleships... I still refuse to call them dreadnoughts... so instead they gave the extra range and hitting power to a couple of stumpy destroyers?

"We don't know for certain that they have that much firepower, but we have to assume they do. And that's going to complicate things," Marlene added in dry tones, her eyes drifting back down to the plot table.

"Does DCI even understand its mandate?" the question was sharp and rhetorical as it came from Wes. We were supposed to know about these sorts of developments before they even happened — and certainly before they screwed up our plans.

It wasn't terribly fair of us to be overly critical... intelligence gathering was not an easy business. It still isn't. But either way, we were in a difficult position now. Again. Yet again. Because no one at Defense Command Intelligence had been able to keep track of a few innovative Martians...

"So, do they basically have seven battleships now? Or split the difference and call it six?" Karen's question sounded exasperated, and John shrugged.

"That's what we wanted to ask you."

Great. Our planning just got even more complicated. Thanks to the Martians.

CHAPTER TWENTY-FOUR

SHORE DEFENSE

Shauna Cass had shaken her Flag Captain's hand for what she presumed was the last time before she'd entered the zero-gee chute, and now she silently pulled her way down towards the Forge base.

She couldn't command the defense of this installation from *Texas*, as much as she wanted to, because there was every chance that her frigate wouldn't survive the first ten minutes of a fight. Shauna's responsibility was ultimately to the Forge, so she had to work the defense from there.

And there was a defense. Her ruse must have gotten to the Martians, because Starbursts that had been running recon were now reporting the whole force was on its way. They knew that Defense Command had pledged to retake the Forge after it fell, so the Martians were going to make it fall. Then they'd know for certain that Defense Command's finest would come to face them.

We'd never abandon our people, obviously.

Sorry, I should stop sarcastically hitting myself over the head with that one.

Anyway, the Martians were seven hours away, so the last phase of this gambit was about to get into full swing. As Shauna came through the reorientation chamber at the bottom of the chute, she was greeted by Hwangbo Yang and two of his Special Branchers. He extended his hand and she took it distantly.

"The officers are waiting for you in the main briefing room. Most of the SF and half of the Special Branchers are stood down for another two hours, to get as much rest as they can," the Colonel explained, and Shauna nodded.

"Very good, thank you Yang."

The fact that these two had been avid lovers for all those months meant nothing now. Shauna couldn't confide in him. At least, that was the way Shauna saw it.

Their relationship was obviously somewhat opposite to Karen's and mine.

Shauna followed him and his Branchers to the briefing room, where she explained her plans and intentions to the officers who remained on the Forge. There were 800 officers and spacers down on this rock, and this would be easy on none of them.

Texas broke dock an hour before the Martian force arrived, and floated into a very low orbit just a little bit 'north' of the Forge dome. The Sunbursts, Starbursts and Starlights that remained — some 260 counting those that had been based on the rock itself — swirled up around the lone frigate in their squadron formations. None of them expected to survive.

The Forge was built as a military installation, and thus had four ground-based lasers and a dozen older mags built in bunkers around the outer perimeter of the dome, far enough away to ensure that, if they were hit, their explosions wouldn't harm the city. The crews of those weapons posts could theoretically escape into tunnels and get back to the dome, but the chances of them having time to do so if they were hit were negligible.

Importantly, those were old lasers. Being shore-based meant they did have more range than most of the lasers of the time when they were built… but the *Tharsises* could still out-reach them.

The situation was truly desperate. There was little chance that a landing of Martian Commandos and troops could be stopped… they'd have to be resisted in the dome, and then in the tunnels beneath.

And they'd have to be resisted, because proud Defense Command personnel believing help was just days away would never give up easily.

Many would die, just to convince the Martians that they weren't wasting their time here…

"Forty-five minutes out now, ma'am," Forge HQ's Sensors and Communications Officer reported in a shaky tone, and Shauna nodded.

"Very good," the standard, clipped reply was bitterly ironic. This wasn't good. Obviously.

The next forty-five minutes dragged past slowly. I suppose this could be taken either as a good thing or a bad thing… more time before having to meet one's fate could either be a plus or a minus, depending on whether you want to get something over with, or just avoid it.

For Shauna, it provided long, bitter minutes for her to think through every decision she'd made… every mistake… and to wonder how she could have changed things here. What if Holbrook had kept an eye on the Martians, instead of pulling *Akagi* and *Kaga* back? What if she hadn't charged the Martians with all guns blazing, only to lose her battlewagons in the first seconds? What if she'd told her crews that there was no hope?

You know by now how much I can torture myself with decisions. Well, up to this point in the war my decisions hadn't been nearly so *difficult* as the ones Shauna was dealing with, and she was just as good at torturing herself as I was.

What I'm trying to say is that, while her crew saw a reasonably impassive Admiral in their base HQ, she was tearing herself to pieces on the inside. She was taking the last chance she figured she'd have to attack herself.

And then the Martians came into range.

"Martians coming into range… two minutes…" *Texas'* Sensors and Communications Officer reported, and Captain Calleigh Tong nodded.

"HNO, make speed 190 and execute the bait plan," Tong ordered smoothly. She was on Battlelink with the Forge HQ C&C, so she looked up at Shauna and nodded, "We're preparing to engage, ma'am."

The Martians weren't being too cute about this: the *Tharsises* were up front, their long range guns getting ready to strip away the Forge's defenses. They wouldn't expose any of their ships to counter fire unnecessarily, so it'd be up to *Texas* to get shots on some of the smaller vessels, and to draw others into the envelope of the Forge's lasers.

With the fighters cruising out alongside it, the veteran Venus Squadron frigate started to twirl, determined to keep laser shots from gaining easy purchase on its hull. The range dropped fast, and on the bridge Tong watched and waited, wondering who the Martians would send out after her.

A frigate making a run against one of these new battleships would have to be stopped, so destroyers and destroyer escorts would have to intervene, and when they did she could turn tail and drag them back… give the Forge gunners something to shoot at.

This, I expect, is what Captain Calleigh Tong was hoping when a shot from *Arisia Mons* destroyed her ship. That, of course, was the other possible Martian response.

The Sunbursts, Starbursts and Starlights broke and attacked with desperation.

And futility.

Shauna struggled to contain the strong feelings that slammed through her when she watched her ship die, and then the pilots of the fighters started to crash into Interceptors and Martian mag fire.

"Recall the fighters. We may need them to oppose landings," she said sternly, glad that her voice didn't crack as the words came out.

The order went forth, but only a few dozen of the planes responded and turned away. The rest clawed angrily at the Martian formation, and were shot down with cool efficiency.

Then the Martian ships stopped their advance, beyond the range of the Forge's lasers. For a fleeting — bare and fleeting — second, Shauna hoped that *Texas'* sacrifice and the ferocity of the fighters might have made the Martian CO think twice… that he'd stop his attack…

But obviously that wasn't the case. He'd stopped outside the Forge's weapons range, but inside his own.

"Incoming fire!"

Three of the four laser batteries were cut from the surface of the Forge. Though dug into the rock and shielded with older battleship armor, they were no more a match for the lasers of the *Tharsis*-class than *Medusa* had been. Each battleship had targeted a single weapons bunker, meaning only one remained.

"Order the crew from the east station to make a run for their tunnels," Shauna turned to her Sensors and Communications Officer, but even as she said that, the ground beneath her feet quaked again. Her mouth thinned to a line and she shook her head, "Disregard that. All personnel prepare to repel landing parties."

Alarms started to sound throughout the Forge dome, and the Martian ships began to move forward once again.

CHAPTER TWENTY-FIVE
DAY OF DEATH

I've been trying to figure out how to describe the defense of the Forge from this point, and all I can think to do is tell the story through a bunch of short scenes. Here goes.

Lieutenant Simone Adler commanded one section in the ForgeStar Squadron, though by the time we join her, she was the only one remaining from her squadron. She'd tied in with two other planes, one Starlight and one Starburst, and now she was flying her own Starlight right at the Martian destroyer that had settled over the Forge rock.

That ship was methodically destroying the mag batteries that ringed the dome, and as soon as those were gone, the landing shuttles would be able to start raining down on the base.

"Let's have a crack at that bastard," one of the other pilots, a British woman unknown to Adler, declared over the comm, and though each of the three pilots in this improvised section knew very well that their X-9 Apocalypse missiles would do nothing to the armor of the Martian, they had to try.

The Starburst rolled out first and hit its burners. It was the weakest of the three planes, and it was probably intending to draw fire and attention from Adler and the other Starlight, who each had a marginally greater chance of doing some good.

As the Starburst drove away, Adler yanked on her stick, rolled her plane over and kicked in the burners, the other Starlight keeping with her. The destroyer was coming up fast in front of their canopies, and then they each got the red box that indicated they had a lock on the ship.

"Shoot one! Shoot two!" Adler called into her headset, and then banked to the side.

That's when she suddenly found herself surrounded by Interceptors.

A shot went through her engine before she could get out of trouble, and she ejected.

The destroyer, unharmed, finished off the mag batteries on the ground, and then the assault shuttles began to launch.

Captain Lon Negea of Special Branch had command at number three lock in the cargo building. Like the Io dome, the Forge dome had two main buildings jutting up out of it, the DC HQ building and the cargo building, the latter for moving commercial goods down to the base.

Negea had to protect one of the smaller locks in that cargo building, and for this task he had himself, three other Special Branchers, four SF and four volunteers.

Twelve people to hold the lock, which on the face of it was good… but four of those people were not trained in defense. They were engineers who had nothing else to do now, and were thus carrying mags.

"Coming in!" the alert came over Negea's headset, and he snapped his fingers and pointed at the hatch they were to watch.

The arrangements here were not particularly elaborate: a three-layer barricade had been established in the lounge that received that lock, and in order to slow the Martians, magbangs had been laid throughout the room. If the defenders were overwhelmed, or if they escaped, the Martians could be surprised by the nasty little grenades.

As the defenders prepared, they could hear the lock clunking and cycling as an assault craft nudged up to it. The color indicators over the door went from red to yellow, and then the base AI recognized that a Martian operating system was trying to interface with it. Defense Command OS XX was superior to the Martian software in every conceivable way, so it was easy enough to stop the enemy computer from overriding and taking over the lock.

But the Martians could still cut through the hatch physically, and this is what they did.

For twenty minutes, the defenders waited behind their barricades, and watched the flickering lights inside the airlock through the window in its inner door.

Sounds of fighting came into their headsets after that — at other locks, the Martians had cut through more speedily, and now yells, orders, and the occasional scream rang out over the comm as the shooting began in earnest.

"Keep a watch on our flank," Negea ordered some of the engineers. "We don't want to be flanked."

Almost as soon as he'd said it, one of his Special Branchers was knocked down by a headshot. She was dead.

Negea turned quickly and kept low, his eyes scanning the receiving lounge in a blur and discovering there was a Commando coming through one of the rear entrances. One of the engineers saw this man, turned and started spraying with his old EPK rifle. The shots went wild, and the Martian shot the engineer square in the chest. That shot didn't look fatal.

Then there was a Commando from another of the entrances. By now, the first one was down behind cover while Negea and the two remaining Special Branchers fired fast to try to contain him… the second Commando shot down two of the SF in a flash. Again, chest shots. Then that same Commando took the head off another of Negea's Branchers before pulling back into the corridor and vanishing.

One of the remaining SF grabbed Negea's shoulder, "The inner door!"

As that half-panicked warning was given, the airlock inner hatch was felled by a cutting torch, and a shower of mag fire knocked down the warning SF guard and Negea at the same time. The lock didn't hold.

Later that day, Ensign Emily Squires, a young member of the Forge's sensors staff, was clinging to her EPM rifle in pure terror. She'd never been combat trained — not beyond the basic stuff she'd muddled through at the Academy — and now she was cowering behind a barricade crewed by a Special Brancher and two bitter-seeming SF.

They were holding one of the access points to the network of tunnels that ran beneath the dome, while teams from all over tried to get here to escape below. They'd told Emily to go down there with the people who were escaping, but she was too terrified to move because of all the mag fire that was splashing around the barricade.

Things were beyond desperate. She'd taken out her headset because she couldn't handle the screams anymore. She was shivering, and she squeezed her rifle as if it could give her some comfort. She was just a sensor technician. This wasn't what she'd signed on for. She'd only come out of the Academy in 2232. This was her first post. She wasn't a trained combatant...

"Get *down* there!" the Special Brancher with this barricade, a woman whose name Emily couldn't recall, caught sight of her and barked that order.

Emily could only stare and shake her head in reply. She was numb with terror, the sort that never really leaves a person. The Brancher took a step towards Emily to haul her to her feet, but one of the SF, the only man with the team, was knocked off his feet in that same instant. The Brancher wheeled fast and caught sight of the shooter, then opened fire.

"We're losing it up here. Topside entrance four... no *Market Street*... blow the entrance in sixty seconds. Do it, redirect the rest!"

Emily heard the Special Brancher barking those words, but couldn't really comprehend their meaning just then. The soldier then looked back at the trembling sensors technician, "Get down there now, or you'll be trapped up here with us!"

But Emily couldn't move.

And it didn't help when the Special Brancher was knocked off her feet by a mag shot to the back of the head. Emily panicked as the sweaty, heavy body landed on her. The Brancher was dead, and Emily screamed. The last SF was shot down, and then there was an explosion from the entrance building they were protecting. The ground shook, and the subterranean access was cut off.

Emily writhed beneath the dead Brancher, and realized she was sobbing uncontrollably. She was trapped in hell, you see, and she'd never been one who was supposed to do this.

Three Martian troopers in their impractical red uniforms appeared above her and she panicked.

"Please, no, please..." she was pleading incoherently as the Martians trained their weapons on her exposed head.

"Check the Tree," the senior Martian ordered in a grumble, and one of his men grabbed the Special Brancher and pulled her body off Emily. As soon as the weight came away, Emily realized her hands were on the EPM that she didn't know how to use.

"Miss, please take your hands off the rifle," the senior Martian said coolly, and she nodded and pulled her hands away slowly. While one of the Martians checked to make sure that the Special Brancher was dead, the other two collected Emily's rifle and carefully pulled her to her feet.

"Miss... ma'am, I think it is. She's an Ensign. Dammit... these Defcon bastards put these little girls in uniforms," the senior Martian shook his head, then lowered his rifle, freed one hand and produced a dirty rag which he used to dry some of Emily's tears. "You're a prisoner of war, shh. It's alright. We're not going to hurt you. Hell on Earth, I have a daughter your age. You shouldn't be mixed up in this... Alright let's get her to the holding area. Report that they collapsed this entrance."

The three Martians led Emily Squires to a holding area, where she joined other

POWs. As her composure returned, she started to feel very ashamed, and very grateful, all at once.

Shauna Cass could see the entrance to the underground complex — the *last* entrance. Once it was collapsed, the Martians would have to dig their way down to get at what remained of the Forge garrison. Not that there would be more than 200 left, based on everything she was hearing over her headset.

"We have to make a run for it," Hwangbo Yang was next to her, and he said that bitterly.

Special Branchers have tactics for just about everything — they can find a way to take tactical advantage of virtually any scenario... but not this one. There were Commandos hot on their trail, and even though this was a wide open street and there could be snipers anywhere, they had no choice but to run for that entrance.

Shauna looked at Hwangbo and nodded, then glanced back at the three other Branchers who were now her escort. She'd waited in DCHQ's C&C for too long. If she'd left five minutes earlier, they would have escaped long before the Martians had moved into this area...

But she'd been stubborn, and now things didn't look good.

"We go in open order... keep a few meters between you. I'll lead, Shauna on me, then Susan, Faris and Werner. Ready... go."

No time was wasted on excess talk. The only reason Yang had actually explained that with words (instead of Charlie-esque hand gestures) was so that Shauna could follow the plan.

Once he finished speaking, Colonel Hwangbo raced out across the street, and Shauna forced herself to her feet and raced after him. The rest of the Branchers strung out behind Shauna.

She watched the first shot — she saw it in veritable slow motion — as it lunged right for Hwangbo. It was too fast for him to dodge, and it slammed into his vest and knocked him right off his feet.

"Grab him!" she barked harshly at the rest of her escort, and then she raised the MAG-90 she'd been given and sprayed the window of the nearby high rise from where the shot had come.

The Branchers didn't waste time yelling at her to get to cover, they just followed orders. Two raced forward and got hold of Hwangbo by his vest, then hauled him towards the entrance building.

Commandos appeared in the alley from which they'd emerged, and fire started to cut across the street in intense golden torrents. Realizing she was exposed, Shauna turned and chased the Branchers who were now getting Hwangbo into the building, and the last Brancher followed her.

She got hit first. And hard.

She didn't see where it came from, but she was knocked from her feet by the overload to her nervous system. Her hands dropped to break her fall, but instead the fall fractured one of her forearms.

The Special Brancher who'd been behind her crouched at her side and spun, firing back into the alley, but the sniper who'd missed Hwangbo's head didn't miss a second time. He fell across Shauna's back, and thankfully the shock was still too much for her to realize how agonizing the additional pressure of his fall was on her battered forearm, or on the burn the mag shot had left on her thigh.

Completely stunned by the impact, she just lay there, and stared at the entrance building as an explosion went off inside it.

She thought 'well they did that anyway' and then the weight was lifted off her back, and a Martian rolled her over.

Her MAG-90 was lying across her chest, but it was evident she wasn't going to use it in her stunned state. The Martians who found her kept her covered all the same, and then one of them recognized that the insignia on her uniform marked her as an Admiral. She was taken to a field hospital for treatment.

Staggering to his feet in the tunnels below, Hwangbo Yang pulled off his melted vest and swore savagely. Shauna was either dead or a prisoner. He had to do the rest of this himself.

The Forge hadn't fallen yet.

CHAPTER TWENTY-SIX

ELSEWHERE

"Say hello to some familiar faces," I said to myself, managing to smile as I did.

Wolf's main screen was showing vid feeds of the arrival of Greg Noyce's battleship squadron and the Hawke Squadron at Venus, and it was very good to see these ships again. We had lots to talk about with Greg, Mik and Lia.

Karen was standing next to me with folded arms, and she nodded in agreement with my words, "We'll be shipping out for Mercury in what, forty hours?"

"Give or take, yep," I agreed. There wouldn't be much time to linger before we launched, so we'd invariably have to go back down to *Venus One* to talk to Greg, Mik and Lia within the next couple of hours. As I've mentioned, we'd been keeping them up to speed on our plans via comm messages, but face-to-face communication was pretty important for planning like this.

Karen and I watched the ships cruise into orbit over Venus, and then begin docking with the other *Venus* stations so they could take on additional supplies. We didn't really do anything else, we just watched.

Andrea Kiley arrived on the bridge a few minutes later, "Anything new from the Forge?"

Her question was directed to Felicia Khalid, who had the watch at Sensors and Communications.

"Nothing since the alert that the attack was beginning, ma'am," Felicia answered evenly, and I glanced back over my shoulder at the Lieutenant and then at Andrea.

"I don't know if they'd be able to hold the transmitter if they got hit hard," I said quietly.

It seemed quite likely that we'd never get a final confirming message from the Forge, saying 'we've fallen'. Now that the final attack had begun, we just had to assume the base was in Martian hands. And that was all we could allow ourselves to really think about the subject — we couldn't get preoccupied with the grim fates of our comrades. There was an assault to run.

Andrea came to a stop next to Karen and me, folding her arms as she did, "Good to see the rest of the gang arriving, though. I heard we're leaving Wes behind when we ship out?"

That was a casual question, and I didn't read anything particular into it, "Yeah, he has to stay here in case the *Tharsises* come for Venus while we're out."

"Those new dreadnoughts, aye..." Andrea nodded

"Don't call them that," Karen protested, and Andrea frowned and looked past me at her.

"Er... sorry," the Irishwoman tilted her head in surprise at Karen's reaction, and I glanced at Karen too.

"I didn't think it bothered *you*," I smiled at her, and she shrugged.

"Since you explained it to me, it's started getting on my nerves."

Andrea looked from Karen to me and then to the screen, shaking her head, "I'd ask, but I don't think I'll be wanting the inevitable historical pontification from the Admiral."

Bless her, despite all that she'd been through, Andrea was recovering her sense of humor. At my expense, sure, but she was quite right: as you've probably guessed, I had a big problem with people referring to the *Tharsises* as dreadnoughts, and I was ready to tell anyone I caught calling them that exactly *why* the Martians' new battleships were not dreadnoughts, thank you very much.

Real dreadnoughts, as introduced by British First Lord Jackie Fisher in 1905, were 'all big gun' warships… before them, battleships had carried four large guns and many smaller guns. His Majesty's Ship *Dreadnought* carried ten large guns, and initially, no smaller guns. It was also faster than any battleships before it.

Basically, the dreadnoughts were loaded up with new technology that had been around for a while, but which had never been concentrated into single, powerful hulls. They changed everything to do with war at sea.

If anything in our period could be compared to the dreadnoughts, it had to be the *Bonnies* — they represented a new epoch in technology for drives, lasers… everything. All the Martians had done with the *Tharsises* was take old technology and put more of it in one hull. Sure, their lasers had longer range and more power, but the reactors behind them weren't actually more advanced, there were just more of them. Their engines weren't more powerful, they just mounted extras.

While it's true that these design choices did represent realistic solutions to new challenges, you just can't compare them to the *Bonnies*.

Bonaventure and her sisters had more advanced reactors, power systems, engines and lasers… on every level, they represented a new evolution of our military technology.

And even with that in mind, I still wouldn't call them the new dreadnoughts of our age. To earn that designation from me, a battleship needs to be able to fire eight or ten lasers at once, not the four that the *Bonnies* can shoot.

That takes nothing away from the *Bonnies*, believe you me. You know how magnificent they are, and how much we all prize them. But let's not go out of our way redefining established terms just because we want to make things sound cooler or nastier or whatever.

End of rant.

Andrea, Karen and I continued to watch as *Warspite* docked with *Venus Two* to take on supplies, and then we waited for a summons to the planning meeting that we knew was coming. We still had those new Martian monitors to worry about, and that was going to be a different kind of headache all by itself.

But let's be clear, in terms of headaches just then, the ones we had in the planning rooms in Venus didn't compare in any way to those being felt on the Forge.

CHAPTER TWENTY-SEVEN
ALAMO SCENARIO

Hwangbo Yang took charge of the defense of the tunnels, though with 203 people, the huge network of subterranean corridors couldn't all be protected. This wasn't like Io; the underground complex wasn't disused. The Forge had been an active Defense Command base since Daragh's days, and while it wasn't front line for many years, much work had been carried out there.

So the complex didn't have only one or two access points from the dome. As I should have explained during those short scenes about the fall of the dome, there were a dozen access points, and collapsing them with explosives, while a good delay tactic, wasn't nearly so decisive here as it had been on Io.

There was also a lot of digging equipment on the Forge, you see, and the Martians had brought more with them, expecting that things might develop this way. Where Charlie had been strapped for resources when he'd tangled with the Commandos during *The Sinope Affair*, the Martians had a huge squadron overhead... and we weren't going to be doing anything to distract them.

That all being the case, Hwangbo had selected a section of the tunnels with relatively limited access — only five corridors in and out — and then set up a defensive pocket. With an abundance of supplies... given some luck, they could hold out for a couple of weeks.

More than enough time for help to arrive. Because they all thought help was actually going to come.

Pacing around the perimeter of this defensive pocket, Yang nodded to the Special Branchers and SF who were on duty. More than half of the people down here were not combat trained... they were here specifically because they weren't going to survive if they stayed in the dome above.

All Hwangbo had at his disposal were thirteen Branchers (not including himself) and twenty-one SF. The rest were not trained for this, though another twenty or thirty had proved quite adept.

But it was no matter. They'd hold on, as that was their job.

"Sir," a Lieutenant appeared behind Hwangbo, and the Colonel turned.

"Friedman, the charges laid?" Yang asked the newcomer, and the young man nodded.

"Ready to go, sir. We can wait 'til they try to rush us if we want to take some of them down in the process," the Lieutenant's anger was not particularly veiled as he said that. He'd been put in charge of laying explosives in three of the five corridors leading into the pocket, so they could be collapsed and further improve the defensive situation.

If they waited for Martians to come through those corridors and *then* detonated the charges, some of the attackers would undoubtedly be killed, which might suit the young Lieutenant's desire for revenge. But it was too much of a risk.

"No, if they get to the detonators somehow, we'll be in trouble. Blow them now," Hwangbo gave his order, and the Lieutenant nodded and turned away.

"Forcing them to come this way, Colonel?" an SF spacer was sitting behind her barricade nearby, and the Colonel caught her eye and nodded.

"Want to get the first crack at them, spacer?"

She grinned, "Yes sir."

Whatever high spirits could be found would be kept up, but realistically, morale was falling fast.

Shauna Cass woke sharply, and tried to sit up in her bed. A jab of pain up through her torso convinced her that was a bad plan, but her eyes flew around and tried to get a sense of where she was. Her arm was immobilized. Her head hurt.

"Surgeon, the Admiral is awake," a foreign voice declared from behind her head, and she craned her neck with some difficulty to try to look around to see who'd spoken...

A Martian soldier, with his rifle slung.

As soon as she saw him, it all made sense. She remembered running for the entrance to the underground compound and not making it. She didn't actually remember being shot or being moved by the Martians, but it didn't take much to figure out that, if she hadn't made the entrance, she wasn't in Defense Command company any more.

"Ma'am, ma'am are you alright?" that was another, slightly more familiar voice.

She craned her neck again, and she recognized one of the Sensors and Communications staff from *Texas*. The man must have gotten off the ship before it was destroyed. Before she could even try to answer him, though, a surgeon was hovering over her.

"Try not to move, please, miss," the older man said in a paternal fashion, a traditional Martian accent wrapping his words. "You had a nasty burn, my girl. But not to worry, you'll be back to your pretty self soon enough. We'll take good care of you."

Shauna still wasn't entirely awake, so she didn't quite understand why any doctor would call her a pretty girl. That wasn't proper...

"Hey, doc, watch how you speak to the Admiral," the officer from *Texas* barked across the room, and the surgeon looked over at him.

"You DC people call yourselves men, willingly putting women in these situations. You should be ashamed of yourselves."

He said that with an almost protective tone, and by now Shauna was following enough of what was going on to take her own offense. Her hand tightened around one of his hands, "Surgeon, listen damned close. I am an Admiral in Defense Command and I want to speak to your commanding officer. Immediately."

The surgeon looked back down at her with some surprise, "Well, we'll see about that whenever he's free. But you be careful, girl, you keep on like this and the men will take you for a concubine. That's not to say we'll treat you poorly, but we won't be so polite."

Shauna wrestled herself up off the bed, "I am no damned concubine, Mister. Bring your CO to this bed. Now."

She didn't know why she wanted to speak to the Martian Admiral, but in her slightly hazy state it was just about the only thing she cared about. The surgeon tut-tutted and shook his head, "He'll be around."

He then pulled away and wandered over to one of his orderlies, "These ladies, I swear Pidge. I don't know what they do to them on Earth."

"Don't worry about him, ma'am," the *Texas* officer called to her.

"I can't see you and my ears are pounding, who's talking?" Shauna replied uneasily.

"It's Slocum, ma'am. Ensign Slocum," came the answer.

Shauna worked her brain for a moment, "Yuri, right?"

"Yes ma'am. They're treating us all well, from what I've seen. Plucked many of us out of pods from *Texas* too."

Well. At least that was something.

Shauna eased herself back down onto the medical bed. She wanted to see the Martian Admiral.

"How long do you figure before they get down here?"

Hwangbo glanced at the engineer who asked the question and then shook his head, "Couldn't tell you, spacer. They'll know that every minute they give us we'll use to dig in a little better... but they're likely regrouping and securing the dome. We probably have some breathing room."

Deep inside the defensive pocket, Hwangbo Yang was discussing the defensive situation in their little 'Alamo' with the appointed leaders of each of his twenty fire teams. Some of these were real fire teams, with SF guards or Special Branchers. Others were well-meaning groups of inexperienced but determined spacers, and others still just weren't fit for combat.

He'd seen a dozen men and women reduced to manic states so far... those individuals were all being isolated together in a rear area so they didn't spread their fear to anyone else. It was hardly the most sensitive way to deal with them, but Yang had more to worry about than the state of mind of twelve people. The other 191 officers and spacers needed to hold out.

"When they do come, it'll be through the two entrances we left open," Yang continued his explanation of the deployment, using a 'YOU ARE HERE' map someone had pulled off a wall as his visual reference.

The two corridors that were left open both led to a single large intersection — a sort of reception lounge for the section they were in. Each corridor was thus barricaded and defended separately, but when the time to fall back came, there'd be a single, central position to which they could cling.

"The trick will be defense in depth," Yang swept his hand from that 'Y' of corridors back to the room in which this briefing was taking place, the cafeteria that was at the center of the pocket. "We need to avoid getting cut off. We keep good internal lines of communication, and we keep them spread out. This is the nightmare scenario for them... fighting in tunnels... well you've seen the movies with the Pions. They're not going to want to come in here, so let's use that."

There were nods of agreement from the assembled leaders, and with that Hwangbo felt he'd said all he needed to say.

"Alright. Keep your runners ready. Listen for shouted messages. Good luck everyone."

Beneath the Forge dome, they'd set up their little Alamo.

CHAPTER TWENTY-EIGHT
THE OTHER SIDE

In deference to her rank, Shauna was moved to her own room after a few hours. The Martians had moved all the wounded Defense Command personnel into the Forge's hospital building and there were at least 100 red-uniformed troops keeping all the DC personnel in check.

Shauna, clad still in her bloody and torn uniform and with an elastocast on her forearm, had paced around to some of her wounded people and offered them sparse, reassuring words. Those words, she thought, didn't count for much, but they were all she had left to offer. The spacers and officers sometimes accepted them with artificially good spirits, and sometimes just stared at her.

She had promised them hope, now it seemed there was none, and some of these personnel didn't take kindly to the cold reality of losing. I can't say that I blame them — good spirits aren't too difficult to keep up when everything is going your way. When you've become the first sizable force to be captured by the Martians during the entire war, being down seems fair.

But now Shauna was in the protected isolation of her own room, safe from the stares of her crew, and with a window through which she could see a half-destroyed base city. The Forge had never been a delightful, bright Belt colony sort of base… but it had looked better without the occasional burning building, the scorch marks, and the red sky.

Yes, the Martians had decided to switch the sky color to red — a relatively simple software change, apparently — as a signal that they'd taken control of the dome. Sort of like running up your flag in the old days… now you just set the color of your sky to whatever feels like home to you.

It looked unnatural to Shauna. She didn't like it at all.

But then, there was very little about today, or any of the last few days, that Shauna much cared for. The level of bitterness she felt about all that had happened, along with a rampant sense of humiliation, were still only beginning to sink in. She'd have plenty of time to reflect on all of that… for now, there was a knock at her door.

"Excuse me, you're Rear Admiral Cass?"

She turned from the window, planting her good hand on her hip and deciding to look as solid as she could, despite being bloody, filthy, and shot up. At least the painkillers were keeping her from aching too much.

"That's me," she made sure her tone was cold as her eyes settled on the man who was standing in her doorway. He was poorly shaven and looked lean and gruff, like many of the Commandos and soldiers she'd seen moving through the hospital. His face had the steely look of a man who'd spent too much time killing, and knew it.

Then her eyes fell on his collar insignia, and she realized he was reasonably high-ranking, though she didn't know precisely what the various bars and crosses meant.

"You asked to see me," he stepped almost gingerly over the threshold of the doorway, and approached her slowly, his eyes taking in her sorry state. "Hasn't anyone offered you the chance to clean up?"

Shauna thought she was being patronized, "What, am I not pretty enough for you?"

The Martian stopped and tilted his head, "You look like hell."

Not sure what to make of that answer, Shauna shook her head, "I'm fine for the moment. You commanding that squadron overhead, with your new ships?"

The man was still sizing her up, "I am." He paused for a moment, examining the scowl that was dominating Shauna's face, "We've got about 1,100 of your squadron's people up there under lock and key. We'll be moving them down here as soon as we get the place secured."

If anything could have shaken Shauna's resolve right then, it was the promise that some of the people from her squadron had survived after all. The Martians had picked them up. That was good.

"Thank you for that," she said, her expression neutralizing some.

"You'd do the same for us. You have, in fact. According to what we see in your media," he replied.

"You watch our media? I thought it was all propaganda to you," Shauna's words remained sharp, and a smile twitched on the Martian's lips.

"We should watch a lot more of your media. I get to see more than some because I'm an Admiral so I have the 'know your enemy' excuse."

One of Shauna's eyebrows raised, "Well then maybe next time you'll tell your God President or whatever the hell he is *not* to start a war with us."

The Martian's smile saddened, "That's above my pay scale. I just do my job."

"Too well for my liking," Shauna couldn't resist the jab, and the Martian's smile saddened.

"Same way you and your people do it too well. It'll be better when all this is over."

Shauna caught a hint of a mournful inflection in the Martian's tone, and she met his gaze, "I can agree with that."

Smile slowly fading, the Martian nodded, then stepped closer and put out his hand, "My name's McWebsbert. Bort McWebsbert."

Quite a name on that man, I think you'll agree.

"Shauna Cass," she took his hand.

"You're... what is that, Welsh?" McWebsbert asked with genuine curiosity as they shook hands.

"Scottish," she corrected politely.

"Right, Scottish."

"You? A 'Mc' name tends to be Scottish... though the rest..."

McWebsbert shook his head, "I'm a poor Asteroid Epsilon boy. Enlisted at fourteen and rose a little higher in the ranks than most of my peers would like."

"Myself included," Shauna replied.

"I can understand that."

The two stood there, sizing each other up for another moment.

"Sorry about the surgeon, by the way. Most of our men aren't accustomed to women in... well, in the military at all," McWebsbert said after that pause. "Whenever we get women in command positions, it's usually by certain favors. Ever heard about Kitty Castillo from the Asteroid Squadron? Most of my people just assume Defense Command does it the same way."

Shauna's eyebrows went up, "That's a hell of an assumption."

McWebsbert shrugged, "Like I said, we need to watch more of your propaganda."

"So you think I got my job through whoring?" Shauna's tone was back to icy, and McWebsbert chuckled.

"No, I *know* Kitty Castillo did. If you were the same as her, we wouldn't be losing this war."

That answer threw Shauna off-balance again, and her eyes narrowed, "You call this losing?"

McWebsbert shook his head, "No, Admiral. I call this a desperate attempt to leverage new ships into a better bargaining situation when we sue for peace. If you take Mercury from us, well, we're going to have no leverage at the negotiation table."

"Pretty forthright about that, are you?" she asked sharply, and McWebsbert shook his head.

"If I said it in front of the wrong people on my own ship, I might end up being shot for sedition. Nice thing about a wrecked hospital is that no one's bugged it. Yet. So I can speak freely for a few minutes. It's refreshing."

Shauna didn't know what to make of that — or of McWebsbert in general. The man was not a stereotypical Martian, that much was obvious, but he'd also just destroyed her squadron and taken her base.

"Anyway. If you need to contact me again, just ask the surgeon. I've told him to treat you as your rank deserves, but he's an old bastard. He probably won't be looking past the obvious. You should get yourself cleaned up, though."

Shauna offered a very, very shallow single nod, "I'll consider it."

McWebsbert stared at her for another moment, then gave her a solid nod, "Good day, Admiral."

Shauna watched him leave, then let out a long breath and allowed herself to slouch after he left. The Martians had taken her base... but at least the Admiral who'd done it wasn't a complete bag of—

The explosion knocked Shauna off her feet.

CHAPTER TWENTY-NINE
ANALOGIES DON'T ALWAYS FIT

Hwangbo Yang was knocked flat by the explosion, and the massive concussion wave that shot through the corridors of the defensive pocket hit him like a ton of bricks. His eyes started to water, his nose ran, his ears rang… but he was a Special Brancher, and he was determined not to be caught lying down.

The Martians had blasted *something*, but he had no idea what.

And with them in control of the Forge C&C overhead, he couldn't risk using his comm to find out.

He and three other members of his team had been heading for the cafeteria to grab sandwiches for the rest of their unit when the explosion had thrown them. Yang could only assume it had come from behind… perhaps they'd used explosives on one of the barricades?

Well, that felt like a *lot* of explosives for one barricade, but it was about the only thing that made sense.

Staggering to his feet, Hwangbo looked down at the other three people he had with him. One, another Special Brancher, was picking himself up uneasily. The other two were communications technicians. One was unconscious and the other looked as though she'd broken her neck when she was flung from her feet.

There was no time to waste on those two, though — if the Martians were trying to break in, they had to move. All fire teams were going to be heading for the entrance barricades… that was the plan in the case of an attempted assault.

"Let's go," Hwangbo waved his Special Branch Officer into movement, and together they staggered towards the barricades.

Shauna peeled herself off the floor and winced at the pain in her broken forearm. The elastocast had kept her from doing any new damage, but dropping her body weight onto it had not been pleasant. Shaking off the pain, she turned to the window and staggered towards it, seeing a column of smoke climbing over some nearby buildings.

She had no idea what was happening.

Had Yang set a huge trap for the Martians out there? Had the Martians accidentally blown something up? What was going on?

It was at that moment that the exact nature of Shauna's situation sunk in with her. She was a prisoner of war. She couldn't demand answers about anything. Before the fall she could have pulled out her comm, or stopped a passing officer, or gone to C&C… then she'd have known what was happening.

Now, she was a prisoner… and a spectator. That reality, completely aside from the grim fact that she'd been defeated, hit her hard. She was out of this war now. She was watching from the sidelines, and that meant she couldn't make a damned bit of difference to anyone.

So what had just happened? No one was obliged to explain it to her.

She had to stand in her hospital room and look through the window for clues...

Hwangbo slowed down as he reached the fallback barricade in the reception lounge. The fire team stationed there looked nervous and disheveled but alive.

"Where'd they hit us?" Hwangbo dropped to one knee behind them, and the head of the team shook her head.

"We don't know, sir... I haven't heard from either of the teams ahead though."

Another handful of defenders arrived at the barricade over the next few minutes, but Yang sent them back.

"Defense in depth... stay within earshot. If they take this position I want you to hit them as soon as they do," he explained. That was the way this pocket had to work — they couldn't assume that any one barricade would be able to hold, but if the Martians took one, his fire teams needed to counterattack immediately to take it back.

If they all ended up in one place at one time, it would be that much easier for the Commandos and the Martian soldiers to get them.

"Do we go up there to see what's coming?" the head of the defending fire team asked after Yang sent those reinforcements away, and the Colonel took a deep breath and shook his head.

"They'll be coming. Let's not give them any easy targets."

There was no panic in the streets — at least none that Shauna could see from her vantage point. Martians were going about their business down in front of the hospital, some of them escorting wounded DC personnel into the building, other squads passing at quick marches on their way to patrols or whatever else they were up to.

No one was worried about the column of black smoke that was now collecting at the top of the dome. Someone was going to need to turn on the smoke filters, or that was going to clog up the sky for days.

Turning her back to the window and leaning on its sill, Shauna rubbed her throbbing arm with a frown. If they weren't surprised by this, then they had to have caused the explosion. Intentionally.

Which meant they were going after Yang.

They sure weren't letting any grass grow under their feet... they must have decided that every minute they waited was another Yang had to prepare...

These Martians, it seemed safe to say, knew very well what they were about. This couldn't really be considered a surprise, either — if the *Tharsises* were Mars' answer to the *Bonnies*, then it only stood to reason that they'd have the Imperium Navy's very best aboard them.

Bad news for the Forge. Bad news for Yang.

For twenty minutes, Hwangbo Yang crouched behind the barricades with the fire team assigned to protect this central entrance. There was no sign of any Martians... where were they? Had they accidentally sealed the last two entrance corridors when they'd blasted them?

"Alright… we actually do need to check this out," the Colonel said quietly as he thought that. If the tunnels were sealed… well that would change the situation yet again. He'd have to figure out new options…

If they were sealed. He had to find out.

"I can go," one of the SF guards assigned to the fire team stood up slowly, pulling her EP-5 into firing position.

"Me too," another SF stood, brandishing his old EPK.

"With me. I'm going to see this for myself," Yang nodded, then without another word he led the pair out around the barricade and down the corridor to the left.

They'd check one at a time — there was no point pulling another three people off the defense just to check both at once. Given the size of that explosion, if one barricade was gone, the other probably was too…

Moving silently, they entered the corridor, and kept to the walls. There were hatch frames to offer cover as they moved, but that blessing was mixed — if there were Commandos down here, it was a sure bet that they'd take full advantage of the cover too.

Yang kept his eye glued to the sight of his MAG-90. He swept the weapon right to left, up and down, back and forth as they moved. The two grizzled SF volunteers kept behind him, staying out of the way but paying close attention to their surroundings.

There weren't too many signs of damage up here, and Yang was starting to wonder exactly what sort of blast the Martians had used… the corridor certainly didn't seem to be collapsed…

"Sir?"

Hwangbo stopped in place and dropped to one knee, lining his MAG-90 up on the source of the voice. He found himself staring through his sight at the muzzle and sight of another MAG-90, and he lowered his weapon immediately.

It was one of the Special Branchers who'd been assigned to the barricade up here.

"Situation?" he asked sharply, and the Brancher lowered her weapon with a confused frown.

"No change here. What was that explosion? It sounded like it came from the middle of the pocket."

Yang opened his mouth to ask what she meant, then realized he'd made a grave, grave error.

He'd been knocked flat by the concussion, and had failed to figure just what direction it had come from. None of the people who'd been at the barricade had been Special Branchers… they could have had the same problem. And he'd told them that the explosion had come from this direction. Non-Special Branchers would probably defer to the judgment of a Special Brancher on something like that, even if they thought the explosion was coming from another direction.

The explosion had come from the middle of the pocket.

The Martians had blown their way through fifty meters of rock, cut a tunnel right down into the middle of the pocket…

How? He didn't know how. It didn't matter how. But he had to assume that was the situation. The Martians had breached the pocket so they would have to pull out… find somewhere else to hide down here.

"They must have blown their way into the pocket… straight through uncut rock…" Yang said those words to himself, then looked up at the Special Branch Lieutenant. "We're going to have to pull out of the pocket. You'll be lead force… we'll go for the science section. Be ready, I'll send a messenger to tell you when to go."

The Lieutenant frowned with some confusion, but nodded.

As she stood from her crouch and turned back to her barricade, Yang looked back at his two volunteers, and tried to figure out what orders to give.

He needn't have bothered — the Lieutenant he'd just been speaking too landed in a heap in front of him, shot in the throat.

Fire erupted from the fire team at the barricade, and Yang realized what was happening.

The Martians must have worked their way down through one of the collapsed entrances… found a way to dig down as he'd expected. Now they'd have Commandos blocking his escape, and they'd have troops coming down through whatever tunnel they'd just blasted.

That was all the thinking he had time for. As the two volunteers who'd come with him hurried forward to offer their fire support, Yang did the same.

Both volunteers were shot down as soon as they got close to the barricade, and another half dozen of the defenders were down by the time Yang arrived.

He didn't know what to do. And it didn't matter — a Commando took the top of his head off as soon as he rocked up to fire at the attackers.

The barricade fell almost immediately.

I don't have any viewpoint characters left through whom I can explain what had happened to this pocket, so I'm just going to have to do it myself. Sorry, I was trying to keep this whole story going through the eyes of people on the ground, but I could only manage so many interviews with survivors.

The Martians had taken over the Forge's internal security grid, and thus knew exactly where the Defense Command pocket was in the tunnels beneath the city. The system should have locked them out — Hwangbo Yang had assumed they'd have no access to it because it was shielded by OS XX security software — but when they'd stormed the HQ building, the Martians had managed to take out all the technicians and SF in the Security Centre before any of them could trip a lockdown.

Bad luck for us. Well, if I'm honest, it's a testament to the quality of the Commandos the Martians had with them. If it had been Charlie Peters or Rufus Chang, it probably wouldn't be a surprise to you or me that they managed to secure the computers before they could be locked down. But Commandos had done it at the Forge, proving that while they may not be quite up to Special Branch standards, they're still not to be trifled with.

Knowing the location of the defensive pocket, Bort had ordered a mining charge to be hurried down from *Olympus Mons*. This is an important detail: the Martians didn't mine asteroids with lasers back then — Martian civilian laser technology is even less advanced than their military lasers, so when it comes to mining, they always used special shaped charges.

That was one of the reasons their Asteroid colonies were always much less efficient than our Belt colonies were… if you need to cut 100 meters of rock, a laser can do it clean, fast, and without a concussion wave. The Martians had to blast every extension to a shaft, and that complicated mining immensely in terms of setup time and health and safety.

It *did* mean, however, that they had ready-made explosives that could be set up inside a dome… and which could easily blast through the fifty meters of rock down to the subterranean complex. Yang didn't know they had this ability, and neither did anyone else in Defense Command. Well, I'm sure some experts in comparative mining technology knew the Martians operated this way, but it wasn't something we'd have thought a whole lot about as Naval officers or in Special Branch.

Bort had figured he might need some of these charges if he stormed the Forge, and he'd been right. Go figure.

Oh, sorry, I keep referring to Bort… that's Borthias McWebsbert I'm talking about — the Martian Admiral who ran that *Tharsis* Squadron. I think it's quite obvious that he was well prepared for this mission… and that makes sense, I think. He was far and away the best Admiral the Martian Navy ever had.

In spite of the name.

I mean, I understand that Bort is a common Martian name — much more common than, say, Bart. And McWebsbert is a typical lower-class Martian mashup surname — a fact that is in itself hugely impressive. I'll explain more about that in a later book.

For now, Bort had proved himself to be a hell of an adversary. He'd turned a potential nightmare — a fight in tunnels against 200 prepared defenders — into a confused rout. Before most of Yang's fire teams knew what had happened, they'd either been knocked into comas, or killed.

The Commandos secured the underground complex with light casualties, and the Forge belonged to the Martians.

They'd paid a little more for it than we'd paid for the Io dome the year before, but I have to give them their credit: they did it as well as we could have.

Standing in her hospital room, looking out over her captured base with its now-red sky, Shauna couldn't be so understanding. Particularly not then.

The Forge had fallen.

To tie this into the title, the Forge fires had been put out.

Yeah, sorry, lame.

CHAPTER THIRTY

STAYING POSITIVE

Remember the transition between *The Hawke Mission* and *The Independent Squadron*... how there was overlap between the end of one book and the start of the next? I'm afraid I'm going to have to do that again here. I've tried to avoid it, but there seems to be no alternative.

Basically, I'm going to slice the planning we did for the Mercury assault with Greg, Mik and Lia out of the end of this book, and put it in the start of the next book. That way, anyone can pick up *The Mercury Assault* and see the whole operation, from that planning stage to the operation itself, all in one volume.

What I'm going to finish with here, then, are things that happened around Venus that tie much more into the story of the Forge than they do into the Mercury assault. These things were interspersed with the planning sessions that you'll read about at the start of the next book, but they wrap up this Forge story.

Hopefully, it won't be confusing.

Adelaide was about forty hours away from Venus when the pocket was stormed, and the ship was all quiet. Bruce had explained to his crew what Shauna had revealed to him, and his people had appreciated that honesty. The fact that *Adelaide* had been spared the fate of the rest of the Forge Squadron did help make the truth a little easier to swallow, it must be admitted.

Either way, the mood of the crew wasn't exactly chipper. People understood why we'd left the Forge to its fate, but no Defense Command crew likes turning tail, and leaving comrades behind. *Adelaide* had been a loyal part of the Forge Squadron, and everyone aboard the ship now had to assume that squadron was gone.

It wasn't easy to absorb.

Bruce himself was conflicted. He was relieved that his people were saved, but it felt wrong to run from a fight. He knew his ship wasn't the most 'professional' in the fleet... he had a corvette full of teachers, accountants, chefs, executives, middle management, and contractors. There was even a professional shark hunter in the ranks of *Adelaide's* SF. These weren't lifers, and on one level it seemed right that they shouldn't have to die for a gambit.

But they all proudly wore the black sun of Defense Command. Whatever their other lives, whatever their family situations, they were a good *crew*. And they'd given good accounts of themselves twice in very hot action against the obviously formidable *Tharsis* Squadron. Running from a fight wasn't the sort of thing Bruce Arama, or *Adelaide*, did.

These kinds of thoughts were going through Bruce's head as he sat in his cabin, forty hours out of Venus. He was slouched back in the chair next to his bed, with his feet up on the bed and a cold beer in his hand. On his screen was a message he'd received from home some weeks earlier. It was great message, with separate parts recorded by each of his three children and his wife in Auckland.

They were all looking well, and it was very fine to see the smiling faces of his daughters. Bruce was using that imagery (and a bit of help from the beer) to dull the involuntary regrets he was feeling about leaving the Forge to its fate.

He'd be dead or captured if he'd stayed at the Forge. But now he was still free and able to do his job elsewhere... and still able to call his family at home. He didn't yet chance the thought that he'd ever be home to see them again — he didn't want to offer fate any temptations to spoil his plans, as there was much fighting ahead — but at least he was free to watch this message, and to record one back.

The recording part he'd do tomorrow, though. He figured he'd probably had a beer or two too many right now to leave a good impression.

So he just watched and forced himself to enjoy his freedom. When *Adelaide* got to Venus, he figured he'd have questions to answer, and that if he answered them correctly, he might get attached to the force attacking Mercury. Or something.

Time would tell.

"Captain Patel hailing on Battlelink," Felicia Khalid called from her post behind Sensors and Communications, and I smiled as I rose from my chair at the rear of the bridge.

"Put him up on screen two," I replied with a nod, and got to the front of the bridge just as the *Wolf*Net buffering screen cleared to reveal the Indian skipper's face.

"Zail, damned glad to see you," my smile was big and genuine.

It goes without saying how happy I was that another veteran of the Jupiter patrol had gotten out of the Forge, and better yet, was now at Venus with us.

"It is very good to see you too, sir. We've heard that the Forge is presumed fallen, and a recovery will be attempted?" his smile was as genuine as mine, though his brow creased at that last part.

My own smile faded, "We're keeping it quiet, Zail... but we're not going back. We're going straight to Mercury. We're going to need you to unload the nonessentials you pulled out of the Forge, then load up with SF and assault gear. You'll be joining our dome assault squadron."

The news was rather abrupt, but Zail is a hell of a skipper. He simply nodded, "Very well. It is... not what I was expecting, but we can be prepared to leave in as little as thirty-six hours, presuming the SF and supplies are ready to be loaded aboard."

My smile returned, "They are, and you have at least forty. We're going to make sure the Forge wasn't lost for nothing, Zail. It's the best we can do."

"Indeed, I look forward to being a part of it," he nodded back. "I will begin preparations. It has been good to speak to you again, Admiral."

"Always a pleasure, Zail," I nodded once in agreement, and then the link cut.

I let out a deep breath and my head dipped a little. We had good people preparing to avenge the Forge, but would it be enough?

Time would tell.

CHAPTER THIRTY-ONE

OUT OF CHARACTER

Wes, Mik and I walked into a bar.

That isn't actually the start of a joke, that's what we did. We went into one of the bars on *Venus One's* 'strip', where spacers with money to spend tended to go to get some R&R.

This was right after one of the most important planning sessions we had for the assault on Mercury, where we'd made decisions about how to conduct our attack and deal with the monitors and so on. I'll put the actual meeting in *The Mercury Assault*, because everything that was decided will better serve that book than this one.

So, we decided to go to a bar after the meeting.

This, as the chapter title suggests, was out of character for us. Wes and I weren't particularly fond of the bar scene (to quote Wes, 'I avoid the things like the plague'), for what we both consider to be good reasons. We are, however, very unusual. Mik, as it turns out, is something of a fine beer connoisseur, and I think he was trying to share his interest with us. And after that session of planning, neither Wes nor I had had the mental fortitude to come up with a good reason not to agree to his suggestion.

So we'd decided to go to a bar to sit down and chat before we shipped out, and to distract ourselves from a variety of different problems. I think everyone probably does this sort of thing at one time or another... grudgingly agrees to go somewhere or do something that just isn't normal for them.

In the movies, such experiments inevitably lead to life-changing revelations. In reality, I find these expeditions end in awkward futility — with the 'why did we do this out-of-character thing again?' question.

But maybe that's just me. And Wes.

One of the servers came to our table as soon as we sat down, neither Wes nor I particularly impressed by the stickiness of the tabletop in front of us.

"What would you..." she then recognized us as celebrities and her eyes widened and her smile grew very large "...*gentlemen* like to drink?"

"Who's idea was this again?" I asked instantly, and Mik laughed at me.

"I'll have a pint of Vesuvian Stout," he answered the server, and she beamed.

Then she looked at me, and I felt awkward, "Orange juice for me. Thanks."

She nodded enthusiastically, "Yes *sir*."

Then she looked at Wes, and he didn't look impressed, "I'd order water... but no... no... I'll have..." He started thinking — genuinely thinking — about what to order. He looked around the bar suspiciously, sizing the place up. "Coffee. Give me coffee with four hits of sugar and four of cream."

The server nodded enthusiastically again, and then stared at us for a minute.

"Is there anyone else coming to join you, sirs... maybe Commodore McMaster?"

The way she said it, you could tell Karen was either this server's role model or her latest crush. I will not venture a guess as to which.

Anyway, I shook my head, "Afraid she's been delayed with a meeting. I can pass along your regards if you like."

I thought the server was going to nod her head right off, she was so enthusiastic, "Please do! And I'll get your drinks right away!"

She hurried off.

"Who's idea was this, again?" Wes asked quietly.

Mik laughed again, "You two seriously need to loosen up. And you should try Vesuvian Stout. I had some on Hawke One… it's a very dark beer, bitter. I think it ruined the rest of beer for me."

"That's a real tragedy," was Wes' flat answer. "This place… it's awful."

Shaking his head with a grin, Mik looked around, "It's pretty clean and nice, by most standards."

"Yeah right. Order water and they'll put vodka in it. I know their games. My coffee is probably going to be the sludge off someone's boot," Wes countered suspiciously. No, he wasn't kidding.

I nodded at Wes — and I swear I was being serious when I said this, "Take a very small sip to begin with. That's what I'm doing."

Mik laughed heartily, "You think they're going to give away free liquor without telling you? Or that they're going to mess with the drinks of people as well known as us?"

Wes and I looked at Mik with complete seriousness, and I nodded, "We had some interesting days back when we were dealing with pirates in the Belt. Once I got a dead fish in my orange juice."

"Someone replaced the water in my soup with intercooler fluid," Wes agreed.

Mik just kept laughing.

Unfortunately for Wes and I both, the stories are true. Really, could you make that stuff up? The old days in the Belt… before the war… well, those were different than the days during the war.

"This is *Venus*, they're not going to fish or poison you," Mik shook his head, and right on cue, the server returned, with a stout and slightly smarmy looking man in tow.

"I'm the manager," he informed us eagerly. "If there's anything you need, just tell me. *Anything*. It's a real big honor having you in our bar. Could we get a picture of you for our famous-people wall?"

"Sure," Mik was very easy-going about this… Wes and I less so, but we agreed.

The picture was taken, and we were left to enjoy our drinks and to catch up, as was our reason for being in the bar in the first place. Remember, the last time we'd all seen each other was when Wes, Mik and Lia had come to Belt Two just at the start of *The Canary Wars*, and there'd been no real time to catch up then. We'd found out Ian Hawke was on life support, Wes had gotten Andrea to open up a little bit about Egesta, we'd received our new assignments, and then we'd all headed our separate ways.

There were stories to tell, then, about Mik and Wes' time out in Hawke Space, and Lia's fun and games out there. That was tricky for me to listen to, because I knew about her father, and these guys didn't. I owed it to Lia not to let slip about that, so I had to be careful.

Then we wandered on to talk about Io and Sinope.

"I have to ask you about something," Mik said as we got onto that subject. "I heard a rumor."

I was almost halfway through my orange juice at this point, though Wes' coffee had grown cold as he stared suspiciously at it.

"I heard that, in the middle of the battle at Sinope, you grabbed Karen and went to the rec deck to *dance*," Mik said, sipping his beer.

I nodded simply, "Yep. When we were chasing the Martians out from Io."

"It's *true*?" Mik laid his glass down on the table with a thud. "Oh I have to give you shit about this. What the hell were you thinking? I mean, in the middle of a battle?"

I shrugged, "Well, it was weird, that's true enough. But it got the job done."

"Dancing?" Mik grinned. "Come *on*. Why dancing. That's... that's just... I have to give you shit about that."

"Well. What would you have done?" I shrugged and asked the question, sipping my orange juice.

Mik froze in place for a moment, then leaned back with a thoughtful expression forming on his face, "Now... um. Dammit. Not *that*. But that's not the point. Come on, Wes, you can't be with him on this."

Wes looked up from studying his coffee and shook his head, "Sounds like she needed it. Makes sense to me."

Mik stared at Wes in disbelief, "Seriously?"

"Didn't negatively impact combat performance, so why not?" he replied.

Mik didn't know what to say to that, so he said, "I don't know what to say to that. You Belt Squadron types are pretty special."

Wes and I exchanged a glance and shrugged, "We're unusual."

"Yes. Yes that is what you are. Wow. Maybe if you get out more you'll understand why dancing in the middle of a battle is... weird."

I nodded, "Good reason not to do this too often."

"Oh sure," Mik shook his head and drank some more of his beer. "Just don't start dancing again."

I half chuckled, and then drained my orange juice as if it would offer some consolation, "Well, you can be sure I won't be able to when we ship out. Not having Karen aboard... *that*, my friend, will be weird."

Mik's expression sobered slightly, as he realized he'd backed into one of the subjects this absurd little foray was supposedly going to keep us from reflecting on, "Yes. That will be weird."

I clunked my glass back onto the tabletop and sat preoccupied for a moment. I hadn't fought any of the battles of this war without Karen right there with me, and foolish as it may (or hopefully may *not*) sound, I was almost fearful that I couldn't do it without her. Even though for most of my career up until 2231, she hadn't been aboard *Wolf*... well, it was going to be difficult.

But it wasn't like I had a choice. I had to deal with this.

Oh, and for anyone panicking and wondering, I'm going to torture you about why Karen wasn't going to be aboard *Wolf* for as long as possible. It'll be explained at the start of *The Mercury Assault* (not just because I'm mean, but because explaining more now wouldn't work).

"Don't dwell on it too much," Wes pushed his coffee away from him. "And you'll have Andrea on the bridge... make sure you keep an eye on her, will you?"

He said that in a loaded way, indicating his thoughts about her state of mind, and about her in general. Several things bothered Wes about missing the Mercury assault, and one of them was sending Andrea out there. After she'd called him, he felt like he was obliged to be available to help her if she needed it.

But the nature of his job didn't allow him that luxury, and he'd just have to deal with that...

Now he was sitting there, preoccupied.

"Well, at least we're working together..." Mik tried to revive the brighter spirits, but that just reminded him of the incredibly dangerous job *Cyclops* was going to have to do over Mercury.

Yes, we'd be working closely with Mik's old battleship, but if our expectations were correct, *Cyclops'* fate might be sealed, as surely as *Medusa's* had been with the Forge Squadron. Mik didn't want his ship to be shot up, but there was no question that he, *Cyclops*, and his veteran crew had to take on this dangerous duty.

He sat, preoccupied in his chair.

Look at how good we were at forgetting our jobs. Even Mik was preoccupied now.

The server returned, and she could see quite clearly that we were all lost in our own thoughts. She cleared her throat and then smiled and half-curtseyed, "Sorry, I was eavesdropping. The DJ starts in ten minutes, and me and some of the other girls would be happy to dance, if you need to take your mind off something."

My God, you've never seen Flag Officers run so fast.

Although I think I heard a rumor that Mik went back...

CHAPTER THIRTY-TWO
SOMETHING TO REMEMBER FOR MUCH LATER

You hear it a lot in military-themed shows and in history: evacuate the non-essential personnel. Well, in order to get *Artemis Agrotera* ready to take on landing troops and equipment, we had to get the Forge's non-essential personnel situated on *Venus Three*. There were DC spacers and officers who could be spared — anyone who didn't work on one of the main systems... so people like cooks, counselors and so on... as well as the families of many of the people who were either dead or captured.

Dealing with these people, who have just left their friends and loved ones behind is never easy. First of all, there were thousands of them, and second, they wanted to know what we were going to do to help the Forge.

Technically, none of us actually had to do anything for these people — we were under absolutely no obligation. But the next morning, Wes, John, and I headed over to *Venus Three* to talk to as many of them as we could.

There were two motives behind this. First, we could hopefully help calm them down, and second, we could lie to their faces about our plans, and thus reinforce the impression the media was getting and loudly broadcasting — that we were going straight back to the Forge.

The way we went about doing this was fairly simple: we worked the lines. Now, I have to explain the process for accepting refugees and displaced DC personnel in order for you to picture this... and this is one time when I'm not going to apologize for boring you with exposition. No one ever seems to see or talk about these refugee lines... they're made up of people running from a fight, and thus they're not as interesting as the people doing the fighting.

When we *do* see them it's in some sort of human interest story, either as B roll explaining where someone came from (a poor refugee, coming to the Empire to make good... cue patriotic music) or as a criticism of the way DC accepts outsiders.

Well, the lines are long, fast-moving, and efficient. Every person from a ship that docks is funneled into one of two queues: DC personnel or civilians. Families can stay together, and check in as one unit. Very often, these people have nothing but the clothes they're wearing, and depending on where they were from, they may or may not have credit accounts.

The people Mark Gunney pulled from Egesta, for instance, had no accounts at Imperial banks, and thus were penniless. More about that in the last half of this chapter, sort of. The people who we brought back from Io, though, had accounts with Imperial banks, because they'd been employees of the Empire. They thus had immediate access to their accounts, as soon as they checked in.

Speaking of checking in, the process is simple: you go to the next available agent and get a DNA scan to confirm you are who you say you are. Your file is then pulled up, with information on your accounts, your military records, and so on. If you're a refugee from outside the Empire, a file is created, stating your place of origin. If you are of age and wish to stay, you can be added to the voters list and sworn in as a citizen, right then and there. The downside to that is we start taxing you as soon as you have income… the upside is you have rights protected by the Articles of Empire.

Next, you're added to the Refugee Relief List, and given a serial number. That number will get you access to your share of an Imperial fund set aside for refugee relief, and it can be used at any Imperial bank. You're then assigned temporary quarters (free for one month, and then nominal rent thereafter) where you can base yourself while you start over.

Now people constantly complain that there's not enough money in the refugee fund, or that the quarters people get for free are run down. It's true, the money we hand out is not a *lot*, but it's enough to get by. And the quarters are in fact bigger than the living accommodations for most of the crew on a frigate, so no sympathy there.

Other people complain the system gives the Empire too much access to people's lives — that privacy is a thing of ancient history, and that the 'know-everything' check-in system proves that the Empire can control everyone.

Well, sorry to contradict the conspiracy nuts out there, but there are over eleven billion people in the Empire. Defense Command is about a thousand times too small to keep track of, or so help us, *control* you all.

Not that we don't try.

KIDDING.

Anyway, this is what the people coming off *Artemis Agrotera* were standing in line for when we showed up to lie to them. They were frustrated, but as they were all Imperial citizens they knew they'd get some relief and assistance, and most had some family or friends around the Empire who could lend a hand in getting them set up. Obviously, the DC officers who'd come out would be assigned somewhere, so they had nothing to worry about.

The mood, then, wasn't one of desperation… and while there was anger, it wasn't directed at the situation these people found themselves in.

"You're going to go back there and kill those bastards, right?"

A little old lady said that to me, and I nodded very diplomatically, "Admiral Noyce is provisioning his squadron, and we're going to be loading SF onto *Artemis Agrotera* as soon as you people are squared away. The Martians won't know what hit them."

The little old lady nodded, "Good. And if they ask who it is who's hitting them, tell them it was me, Eleanor."

"I certainly will say that to them," I lied again, and she reached up and patted me on the shoulder.

"Good boy."

I stepped away from her and worked my way down the line. I didn't stop to talk with everyone… some people didn't look as if they were in any mood to chat… but I made sure to stop for anyone who seemed eager to say something or hear something.

"Will we still be able to go for Mercury?" the husband of one of the Special Branchers who'd been left behind asked me, and I nodded.

"Absolutely. We'll take care of Mercury in due time… they're not going to turn the tide of the war on us," I think I sounded rather certain, and perhaps even a bit hungry with that.

The man smiled, "Good. My Susan is dead now. You kill some of those bastards for me."

"She may be alright, and a POW," I offered that attempt at comfort, but the man shook his head.

"No sir. No she told me if they lost the base, she was going to take as many of them as she could," his voice was quaking a bit, and as he said it his young son clutched his leg.

"Ah," was my first answer. Then I managed one of my patented, stilted responses to an emotional statement, "Well, sir, we'll make certain her sacrifice wasn't in vain."

As it turned out, his wife was Susan Treacher, the Lieutenant who'd been shot in the throat when Colonel Hwangbo had gotten up to the barricade. *And* she'd survived, because the shot hadn't been on full. Susan and her husband had two more kids after the war.

Along the other lines, Wes and John were doing the same thing I was — talking to people, assuring them that we were going to have our revenge, and never once actually promising that our ships were going straight to the Forge.

The best way to lie is to actually *not* lie, just to mislead. To say things like "they won't know what hit them" instead of "we'll take back the Forge within a week".

When people don't ask too many questions, those lies work fine. And in a crowd like this one, where the people were largely ready to trust us, they worked well.

But there were other people coming off *Artemis Agrotera*, or supposedly coming off Zail's ship, who had a different attitude.

One of the darker decks on *Venus Three* is called 'the underside', largely because it's near the bottom of the station, and it's a sector that most of the wealthier station-dwellers don't bother with. If you don't have much experience with stations, think of the underside as a Belt Widow side of town… a seedy hangout for criminals and people just getting by, with no prospects. No one, not even SF, takes a whole lot of interest in it.

So when a pretty young woman, clean and fresh-faced, appeared on the deck, she might as well have had a target painted on her forehead. Carrying just a backpack, with her dirty blonde hair yanked back in a ponytail, she walked slowly from corridor to corridor, looking at the various shops along either side, and visibly trying not to get creeped out by all the leering.

She knew she was in a dangerous part of town, so to speak.

After about half an hour of pacing around, she finally found what she was seeking: an office with 'Miss Sonia Hart' written on the door. Looking around nervously again, the young woman took a step towards the door, and then keyed it open.

She didn't really know what to expect, but as she stepped into the well-lit and surprisingly clean reception area, she breathed a noticeable sigh of relief. This place seemed as professional as any office she could have expected to find in the wealthier parts of *Venus Three*… it just happened to be in the underside.

A receptionist looked up from behind his desk as the girl closed the hatch behind her,

"Can I help you, miss? Here for a homeopathic consultation?"

The girl stopped in surprise, and turned slightly red, "I... uh... I must be in the wrong place..."

The receptionist was clean-cut and professional, and he stood and slowly rounded his desk, coming up close to the girl. She made sure to continue to look nervous and awkward, though she could already tell by the way he moved that he had hand-to-hand training, and that he had a mag in a shoulder holster under his jacket.

Wait, are those the observations a fresh-faced girl in the underside is supposed to be able to make? Confused?

"Maybe you are," the man's words were warm. "But then, maybe you aren't. We offer homeopathic consultations, and we also talk about how a change in scenery can benefit a person's wellbeing. Does that interest you?"

The girl nodded eagerly, "That's what I want. I heard this was a place to come for that. If you... if you wanted to get away from it all. The Empire I mean."

Smiling, the man stood aside and gestured the girl to a chair, "Come and sit down..."

"Julie," the girl offered, smiling winningly and going to the indicated chair.

"Julie, I'll just call Miss Hart," the man passed her and went down a short hallway behind his desk, leaning in a doorway as he did so.

After a moment, a woman — presumably Miss Hart — emerged from the room, and beckoned Julie to come to her office.

Again making sure to seem both anxious and eager, Julie hurried over, nodded her thanks to the receptionist, and then entered a neatly appointed office. Miss Hart waved the girl into a chair opposite her desk, and then seated herself.

"Simon tells me you're looking for a change of scenery," Hart said as she settled herself.

Julie nodded, pausing to study the woman opposite her. Hart was young and pretty in her own right, but it seemed as though she'd been aged and worn by stress, then rejuvenated. She looked like a woman leading a new life — a second chance.

"I lost my mother and my brother at the Forge," Julie said frankly. "I'm sick of this war and this Empire."

Hart's eyebrows went up, and then her eyes darted to a screen facing her. Sensors installed in the room were scanning Julie for weapons or bugs, and none were being detected.

"Well, then our Union might interest you. It's a place we can all go for second chances... I got mine there after I was saved from Egesta. It might be just the sort of place for you," Hart offered those words with a smile. "I found a new life... love... it's a place to start over, Julie..."

"Pichot," the girl added helpfully.

Hart nodded, keying the name into her console, and bringing up Julie Pichot's file on her screen. It was extensive and well-backstopped, that file. Designed to look entirely unremarkable. After a moment's reading, Hart nodded.

"Well, Julie, I'm sorry for your loss at the Forge. Your file checks out. We'd be happy to have you join us in the Union of Solar Asteroids."

A smile spread across Julie's face, and she nodded eagerly, "Really? I'd heard stories...

I want to go."

Hart matched the warm smile, "Excellent. Our next transport leaves at the end of the week. We can put you up in quarters until then. I'm sorry, but they're located in the underside... we do have an understanding with the local gangs, though, to leave our citizens alone. And you'll qualify."

Julie breathed a very natural-seeming sigh of relief, because obviously she *couldn't possibly* take care of herself down here.

Are the hints starting to pile up?

"Thank you so much. So... is it just that simple? Or is there... paperwork?"

Sonia Hart came to her feet and smiled, "There's *always* paperwork, Julie. Several hours' worth. We have a fourteen-rock government and a full bureaucracy... all the benefits of the Empire, with only a few of the hang-ups. Paperwork being one."

With a delicate laugh, Julie stood too, "Okay."

Hart waved toward the door, "Just go across the hall, and talk to Fran. She'll get the forms together for you. But let me be the first to say welcome to the Union."

"Thank you!" Julie's tone was bright, and with that, she turned and headed out of the room, passing Simon as she did. The receptionist then stepped into Hart's office and closed the door.

"So, she's in?"

Hart's smile faded, and she nodded, "She checks out on first scan... but she feels like DCI to me. A little too average and innocent. Flag her file."

Simon frowned, "Should we be letting her in if she could be DCI?"

Sonia Hart swallowed hard at that question. It was one she'd just asked herself, and had been tempted to say no to. Perhaps Julie should have been sent away, because a spy caught in the Union, particularly on Etat Valcour, would face a death that few people deserved.

But it was necessary.

"Fifty-fifty that she is who she says she is... we need the population too much not to take that chance."

"That the President's word, or the *Governor's?*" Simon asked with narrowed eyes.

Hart was lost in thought for a second, so her answer was delayed, "Hm? They'll be the same man in a couple of years, Simon. If this plan works."

"Yeah, if," Simon didn't sound impressed, and before Sonia Hart could counter his words, he opened the door and left.

Alone, Hart lowered herself back into her chair, and remembered back to days when she'd appeared as innocent and bouncy as Julie supposedly was. Back before Egesta. She hoped one day she'd be that way again.

She was the Governor's lover. He trusted her, and he might be her ticket back to that life...

For now, though, she had other business here on *Venus Three*. Recruiting new citizens to the Union was only her cover... her lover needed eyes here, to see what the Empire was doing in its Mercury assault. That being the case, Hart turned on the news, and watched skeptically as everyone we could convince told the whole solar system that we were going to the Forge.

Sonia Hart didn't buy it, but it didn't matter if she did or didn't. She'd just watch and see, and let the Governor know.

In the other room, Julie Pichot filled out the forms for citizenship. She was leaving the Empire and going into the unexplored belt, to discover a new state, with a Governor we all knew and hated. Of course, she hadn't really come off *Artemis Agrotera*, had never in her life been to the Forge, and certainly wasn't innocent. She was no more innocent, vulnerable or naïve than Sonia Hart.

Alright, I'll stop being coy: Haley Briand, anyone? This section's been all about her.

So this meeting was the next step in something — something that, as you'll see, is going to balloon after the war. A certain new state was growing right under our noses, recruiting from the seediest parts of our own colonies, and taking new citizens with no questions asked. Sign on the dotted line and you're in... because they desperately needed the bodies to help strengthen their fledgling economy.

And one of their Governors had designs that were bad for us, and for his own government. I won't elaborate any more on that, for now.

Remember this for much, much later.

CHAPTER THIRTY-THREE

ADOPTION

Adelaide pulled into Venus orbital space eight hours before we were destined to boost for Mercury. I was in *Venus One* C&C with John, Greg and Marlene when the ship appeared on scope, and we all saw the message sent in by Commander Puruhi Arama explaining his arrival. Shauna's orders were attached to the message, just to make sure we didn't think that *Adelaide* had abandoned its squadron, and the ship was instructed to dock with *Venus One* so Bruce could report to us directly. Seven hours before we were to leave, the big commander arrived in DCHQ's C&C, and was led to our plot table by an Ensign.

He was moving stiffly, not entirely accustomed to dealing with the upper brass of the Navy. I mean, *you* know that John, Greg and Marlene are all good folks, easy to get along with and quite friendly, but because that's the way they always appeared in the press, people like Bruce couldn't really be sure if it was their real personality, or if it was just a public persona.

You know how it is — you worry that you'll meet people you see on vid and they'll turn out to be nothing like they seem? With that in mind, Bruce didn't know what to expect from us, so he erred on the side of formality.

Bringing his boot heels together with a snap, he saluted sharply, "Commander Puruhi Arama, DCNS *Adelaide*, reporting as ordered."

We'd been huddled around the table, reviewing our various jobs for the last time before we shipped out, so we hadn't actually heard Bruce come in. His announcement (along with that sharp boot click) got our attention, though, and we all looked up at the same time.

"Commander," John smiled immediately, saluting quickly and casually to allow Bruce to drop his arm. "At your ease, please."

Bruce fell into classic parade ground 'at ease' and Marlene interceded, "No, Commander… relax, please. No need for formalities."

Despite the order and the explanation, Bruce still wasn't entirely comfortable with the idea of being completely relaxed in this sort of company. As he described it later, he didn't want to risk giving the impression that his ship was somehow less professional than any other. As the skipper of the new ship — the reservist-crewed ship — standing in the presence of some famous professionals, he was understandably just a little concerned that we might think of him as a casual, incapable, Saturday-night-spacer.

I'm sure you can understand why he'd be concerned… but of course he didn't need to be.

"Well, this feels awkward," I blurted after a moment. I was the most junior Admiral in the room (the fact that I was an Admiral of any sort still struck me as *very* strange) so I decided to break the ice. As is our tradition, I stepped forward and extended my hand. "Damned good work out there, Commander. I'm glad Shauna sent you out… what your ship accomplished in both those engagements is a credit to you and your crew. We'll need you."

Bruce looked down at my hand, then took it stiffly, "Need us for the assault on Mercury, sir?"

He was pretty up front with the question, and we quite appreciated that.

"So Shauna told you," Marlene asked, stepping up behind me.

"She didn't deny it, ma'am. But the other ships and the base personnel don't know. At least they didn't when I left," he replied a bit tersely.

As I released our grip, my pleasant expression tightened, and I glanced back at Greg, Marlene and John, "Well. Dammit."

They nodded in tandem, and I looked back at Bruce, "It was my call to abandon the Forge in the first place. Not that that changes anything, Commander, your squadron is still gone. But it was for good reason."

Bruce studied me for a moment and then nodded, "You're going straight for Mercury, before they realize you're not going after the Forge?"

"That was the point of the press circus," John came out from around the plot table, nodding. "Everything we're doing is to try to sell the fact that we're about to hit the Forge with almost everything we had earmarked for Mercury."

Continuing to nod, Bruce took a deep breath, "Well, sirs, ma'am, *Adelaide* is ready for whatever task you have for us."

The way he said that made me smile, made John smile, made Greg smile and made Marlene smile too.

"That's good to hear, Commander," John said, and as he did I waved Bruce towards the plot table.

"We've got an important job for you and your reservists," I said, and at my specific mention of *reservists*, Bruce instantly figured that we were going to have him running 'important' messages or something such — that we'd give him and his non-professionals a busy-work job that would keep them out of the line of fire.

After I pointed things out to him on the plot, he realized it was nothing of the sort, and he started smiling in spite of himself.

About half an hour later, our meeting had ended, and I was leading Bruce to meet his new squadron CO.

"Sorry about the fast turnaround… you'll have first priority for resupply, so you can top up on the essentials before we boost," I was saying as we paced through the corridors of *Venus One*.

"Thank you, sir," Bruce replied, still sounding a bit cautious. "We'll need a few things."

"Good good…" I paused as my verbal cadence stalled. "Commander, I'd like to use your first name right now to try to break the rank divide and such, but I think that if I try, I'm going to completely butcher it. Even though you said it back there. Could you give it to me slowly?"

I was referring to Puruhi, his proper Maori name.

Eyebrows up in surprise, Bruce looked at me, "I go by Bruce, sir."

"Bruce! I can do that. Bruce," I probably sounded a little too enthusiastic. "Well,

Bruce, I'm glad you'll get those supplies."

We walked silently for another few steps, and then I looked at Bruce, "See what I did there? By using your first name I tried to increase our familiarity in an attempt to build comfort and rapport. How'd that work for you... feeling more relaxed?"

Bruce considered his answer for a moment, "Well... not really, sir."

My expression soured, "Oh. Well."

Commander Bruce Arama chuckled, and I smiled again.

"I really am glad someone got out of there, Bruce. We'll make sure it was worth it."

The contractor from Auckland nodded, "Yes sir, we will do that."

After the capture of the defensive pocket and the securing of the Forge dome, the hospital had taken in even more Defense Command personnel, and in a bid to do something to assuage their anger at having been defeated (even though they really hadn't had a chance, I know), Shauna had started pacing from room to room, seeing people and offering whatever comfort she could.

"When's help coming, ma'am? The Heavy Squadron going to come soon?" one dying spacer asked her.

This man had had one arm blown off by a Martian mag, and his organs were failing. They'd done their best for him —as much as she disliked the attitude of the Martian surgeon, he knew his medicine — but there was nothing more to be done.

So Shauna was holding his one remaining hand, and staring at his bloody face, and in answer to his question, she started to shake her head. What was the use of lying to a dying man?

But she stopped herself. He was about to die, and she didn't want him to believe it was in vain. Telling him the truth might ease her conscience, but how cruel would that be? Make herself feel a little better at the expense of a man who'd fought and was about to die for her.

She was trapped by her lie. Again.

"They'll be here soon. Just fitting out at Venus, and then they'll come here. And because of all the hell you put these Martians through, they'll win."

The man smiled and let out a relieved breath, "I was in *Empire* for years, ma'am. Would have loved to see it come..."

He died with a smile on his face, and Shauna gently placed his lifeless hand on his chest, then called a doctor over to confirm. She went on about her pacing, telling comforting lies — lies that were the offspring of the big one she'd started with. She didn't know what she'd do when her people realized she'd misled them. Somehow, she hadn't expected to live long enough to find out. But now, as Bort's prisoner, she would.

And how would she face her crews then?

That is where I'm going to leave Shauna Cass. I won't condemn her as some have... I do still think that, there but for the grace of God, it could have been me. But Karen was right: I do think we from the old Belt Squadron would have handled this situation differently.

Still, that's easy to say in hindsight. We were never forced to find out, and for that I'm very grateful. There were many tests yet to come for us all.

CHAPTER THIRTY-FOUR
KAREN AND ME

So my editors are frantic, slightly livid, and one has developed a very serious heart arrhythmia (which is neither funny nor actually connected to this book). They want to know what the hell is going on with Karen —why is she not shipping out with *Wolf*? How dare I wait until the next book to explain what could possibly keep her off *Wolf* as we depart for the Mercury assault?

Well, I don't know why people don't open up any number of the official history books that are out there, which explain this situation pretty well. You might assume that official histories are dull, but believe me, they get into all sorts of juicy and interesting stories about the people in them. So if you want spoilers, go to the official history.

Interestingly, movies about the Mercury assault have never figured out that Karen was *not* on *Wolf* for it. I have no explanation for this, but it's completely incorrect. Karen wasn't with us. And that, let me tell you, was grounds for much lamenting on my part.

More about that in the next book.

Yes, I'm going to make you wait. I'm cruel and horrible.

"This is… weird."

Weird was a word we were getting stuck on in the hours before we launched the Mercury mission, largely because it most accurately described our state of mind. Karen had just said it again as we walked towards the chute that would take me up to *Wolf*.

"You're telling me… how did we manage to survive whole careers without being on the same ship?" I asked right back, my question not coming out quite as clearly as it had seemed in my head.

All those years when I'd been alone on *Wolf*, and before that, alone on *Friendly*… well, we'd fought a lot of battles back then. We'd won the Battle of Deep Black and beaten Grant Merger while we were on separate ships… so I could, evidently, fight a battle on my own.

"You know, since Jupiter, Deep Black doesn't seem so *deep* anymore. Or black for that matter," Karen's tone actually revealed some nervousness, and her comment itself revealed even more anxiety.

Unflappable though she was, Karen had become quite anxious about this. And to answer my editors, I'm aware that saying she's unflappable and then saying she was anxious is sort of a contradiction.

I think writing this scene is actually putting me into the uncomfortable headspace I was in when I was walking there with Karen.

Anyway, she'd just made that comment about Deep Black, which was odd because I'd been thinking about the same battle, "What made you think of that?"

Karen glanced at me, fiddling with her ponytail as she did, "Oh, just thinking back to the last time we were apart for a big battle. That was it. And after that flight out to Jupiter, it doesn't seem that we were that far out into the black for Deep Black."

"I was thinking the same thing," I said in one of those half-exasperated tones people use when they're surprised to discover that someone was thinking the same thing they were.

Boy, my editors are going to shoot me. Sorry, I'm actually feeling nervous writing this. It's a stark reminder of how I felt when we were parting company.

"You think we actually are telepathically connected?" Karen decided to play along, asking that with the... well, I was going to say the mock enthusiasm of someone who thinks they might be telepathically connected to someone else, but being shot by one's editors twice is twice as bad as being shot by them once.

"Maybe, we could be!" I continued to play along, and Karen picked her moment to turn sane again.

"Or it could be a lame coincidence."

"Or a *sweet* coincidence," I tossed back, and she nodded shortly.

"It could be both," she suggested, and I nodded.

"It probably is both."

We were beginning to babble, which is never a good sign for us. We were like bad imitations of Lia now... albeit with a better sense of decorum.

After that, we walked in silence for a few moments. Shuffled, really. It was positively juvenile, but I think we shortened the length of our strides so that we'd take longer to get to the chute. Seriously, a Rear Admiral and a Commodore holding up the launch of an operation because they're anxious about parting company. Wait until Mik hears the rumor.

"Oh, I forgot. When Wes, Mik and I went to that bar, the server there wanted me to pass along regards to you. I sensed a crush."

Karen looked at me with mock half-interest, "Ooh, was he cute?"

"*She* seemed attractive enough."

"Ooh, racy," she purred, and I rolled my eyes.

We'd been reduced to this. Honestly. I mean, I don't even know how to try to justify this to you. Anything for a little laugh... we really were that anxious about our pending separation.

And I suppose you can understand why, having been through the gauntlet with us all the way from *The Rogue Commodore*... presuming this isn't the first Martian War book you've picked up. If it is, we just look insane. But if you've been with us all the way from that first chapter in *The Rogue Commodore*, through the politics of *The Almost Coup*, the insanity of *The Hawke Mission*, the horror of *The Independent Squadron*, the sidelining of *The Gallant Few*, the strange days of *The Jupite(e)r Patrol*, the action of *The Sinope Affair*, the viciousness of *The Dark Cruise*, and the brutality of *The Canary Wars*, then hopefully you know why.

Karen and I tended to lean on each other in this war. We kept each other upright, lucid and functional. And while we had no reason to expect that this would be the last time we were ever going to walk together, it was unnerving to think that we wouldn't be together for what promised to be the biggest planetary assault operation ever mounted.

I'd be on my own, with a hell of a mission to deal with, and she was...

"Here we are."

Ha! See what I did there? I pretended I was going to say where Karen was going, and instead cut it off with dialogue.

My editors tell me I'm going to get death threats for taunting you (including some from the editors themselves).

Would *not* be the first time.

Karen was right, of course — we were at the bottom of the chute to *Wolf*. Getting there had taken glorious ages… we'd floated like inane, bad-joking clouds through *Venus One*, but now it was over. We had to get ourselves together and go our separate ways.

"So, if all goes to plan, I'll see you again after all this is over," I said, my anxiousness driving me to state the agonizingly obvious.

"Yes. And we can send messages back and forth, of course," Karen agreed.

We stared at each other for a minute. Several minutes. I honestly don't know if there was anyone else in the docking lounge at the time. I know that sounds ridiculous or cliché, but I was paying no attention. I imagine some people would have been there, though, and noticed that we were both completely distracted. Not exactly the way you want to see your Flag Officers, particularly when much of the fleet was about to ship out.

I sighed deeply, and with the exhale any jovial energy went right out of me. Karen did the same, and to the same effect.

She reached out and put her hands on my shoulders, "Look after yourself. It'll be fine. Just… look after yourself."

I could tell she was having trouble finding the right words, which is not usually a challenge for her.

"You too," I said as her hands slid away. And then, I cupped her cheek in my left hand, "Be safe. Seriously."

Master of words, I am. Good grief.

What we couldn't say, but what we both knew, was that one of us without the other would be… *bad*. I'd faced that threat relatively recently, when Karen had been exposed to the Phosgene in *The Dark Cruise*. But she hadn't had the displeasure, until now. I'd be alone on *Wolf*… if our gallant ship died, which was a genuine fear… well.

She'd be alone.

So we were both anxious, and even though Karen was unflappable and perfect in every way, she was neither unflappable or perfect. That makes sense to me… if you have a relationship like the one Karen and I had, then you get it. We were both in rough shape about this…

And we both had jobs to do.

We decided to part company at exactly the same moment, as if we'd both been counting down from ten in our heads or something. I turned and climbed into the zero-gee chute, and Karen turned and headed out of the lounge.

It felt like taking a hit in the stomach, but this was the job.

In no way was this parting even close to being as difficult as what the Forge Squadron had been through. What every DC officer and spacer who'd been killed or wounded had been through. Or what most of those people had been through leaving their families and friends at home while they went to war.

But it was tough on us, as I hope you can understand.

By the time I got to the top of the chute, and Andrea welcomed me back aboard, I had rather determinedly shut out the cold feeling.

"Let's get ready to depart," I said to Captain Kiley.

She nodded back, "Yes indeed."

We headed to the bridge, and *Wolf* broke dock for Mercury.

AFTERWORD

So ends *The Forge Fires*, a book that became much more of a seminar on leadership than I expected when I started it. One of my editors passed me a note after reading the first draft, and I want to share it now because, as you know, I'll never pass up a chance to commend the people I served with during the war. Said she: "After reading this I've decided that if I'd been in the war, I'd have wanted to be in the old Belt Squadron. Best leaders."

She's right. As I've said, I don't intend to stomp on Shauna Cass, but I will certainly praise Flag Officers like Karen, Wes, Mik, John, Greg and Marlene. They weren't all from the old Belt Squadron, but hopefully holding their accomplishments up next to all that happened at the Forge will further demonstrate how elite they were.

One of my editors was also encouraging me to come out and say that Shauna was completely incompetent. I don't feel that this was true. I think Shauna was a regular officer (the word my editor settled on was 'unremarkable') put in a remarkable situation. If she'd gone through that war without having to fight this particular battle, she probably would have performed well enough.

But the Forge proved too much for her. Maybe it would have been too much for all of us… but then, we have some truly *remarkable* people. Make your own judgments.

Anyway, moving on: our next two books, *The Mercury Assault* and *The Fleet Clash*, will basically finish off official hostilities… though believe me, the problems don't end with them. No, things only seem to get messier after the Clash. But that's for later.

This, I've realized, is the end of the *tenth* book in the Martian War reminiscences. Ten. Can you believe that? We've been doing this for ten books already, and there's ten more to come under the Martian War brand. That's crazy. At least to me.

Ten books, and I leave you on a 'cliffhanger' with Karen. Sorry about that, but really, the explanations fall better in *The Mercury Assault*.

I'm really not sure what else to say here, except for thanks. If you've been sticking with these reminiscences since the beginning, or even if you haven't, thanks for reading. I really do appreciate it, and I'm glad that we're getting to dispel a lot of myths about the war. The success of these books is knocking the stuffing out of the worst movies, and of course now we're getting various offers for a vid series. Not sure what we'll do about that, because you know I'd be looking over the producers' shoulders every minute, making sure they didn't try to turn all of us into superheroes.

But after ten books, I really can say I enjoy sharing these stories with you. It's… well it's fun. And it lets me dig through my past, good times and bad, and make more sense out of it. It's also a forum to voice opinions — few people get this sort of chance. So, once more with feeling: thanks for sticking around for the first ten.

More to come, of course, so I'll see you in *The Mercury Assault*. Be well until then!

THE MERCURY ASSAULT

THE AUTOBIOGRAPHICAL REMINISCENCES OF ADMIRAL THE LORD KEN BARRON FOR 2233

THE MARTIAN WAR - 11

KENNETH TAM

FROM THE AUTHOR

I've been struggling with what to say about this book. As much as possible, I try to give some sort of important message with these 'From the Author' bits — to rant about something I think is significant, just because I can. But this time, between that delightful quote from Bomber Harris on the inscriptions page, and Ken Barron's rant in the Foreword, I'm at a loss.

I should say that, if you don't know who Arthur 'Bomber' Harris is, you should look him up. Quite a fascinating character. During the Second World War, he undertook the strategy of 'dehousing' the German workforce — he believed that to beat the German industrial machine, he didn't need to bomb factories, he needed to bomb the people who worked at the factories. Yeah, charming guy.

What's fascinating is that he knew precisely what he was doing, and he made no apologies for it. There's a story — I don't know if it's true — that he was once pulled over by a police officer during the War, because he'd been speeding. Said the officer, "Sir, you shouldn't drive so fast, you might kill someone."

Said Harris in reply: "My good man, do you know who I am? I murder thousands of people every night!"

The Earth Empire isn't quite so unapologetic as Air Marshall Harris — Defense Command isn't seeking to 'dehouse' anyone... though the Imperial Army might be... but nevertheless, his angry sentiment remains pertinent to the mood of many in this book. The Empire is finally getting to strike back against the Imperium with all the might in its arsenal — the Martians are reaping the whirlwind.

Good luck to them. At least they're fortunate that their opponents don't know the word 'dehousing'...

Anyway, as usual, I want to offer thanks to a number of people before we get going. Many of the characters you'll read about in this book are based on real-world friends of mine. Thanks to all of those fine people — I hope your characters do you proud!

Peter Caron, my exceedingly good friend, must be thanked for his continued insights and advice. I must also thank Wes Prewer for his brilliant handling of the images for this series, and for the Equations novels. Excellent gentlemen — I'm lucky to call them friends. I also want to mention Mikael Christensen here, for no other reason than Cyclops factors largely into this story.

Finally, and most importantly, I must thank my parents and partners in Iceberg Publishing, Jacqui and Peter. They are the best. Period.

And as ever, thanks Atlas.

– Kenneth Tam

FOREWORD

There is nothing easy about attacking a planet. Let's make that clear from the start — staging an assault on a place like Mercury is not an easy thing, and it is not a sure thing. Many history books and movies look at our attack on the Martian outer capital as if it should have been a walkover, like the Martians shouldn't have been able to put up any sort of fight at all.

Now, you know I'm always quite happy to slam the Martians. I still occasionally call them 'colonials' and 'rebels', in a truly Imperialist fashion. I think my editors have tried to remove all those references so far, but I've tried to sneak them through. I don't have much respect for the people from Mars (their colonists from the asteroids are a different matter, though).

But this was their outer capital. Mercury was important to them, and despite the insults I've thrown at them, they weren't going to be incompetent and just let us have it.

So here we go, then: the Mercury assault. To this day, there hasn't been a larger assault against a planet — never have so many ships and troops been collected into one combat force for a landing operation.

And we all believed this landing would decide the outcome of the war... or more specifically, that the fate of Mercury would dictate the outcome of the war.

It was a very big mission, and I'm probably going to hit you over the head with that fact more often than I should, because I want it to be painfully clear. We definitely weren't just going through the motions... we were fighting for our lives.

Many of us didn't win those fights. Many of us died.

Before I get on with the narrative about all this, though, just a little history about Mercury. I've been asked many times why the Martians wanted the rock in the first place — with its proximity to the sun, small size, and nasty radiation exposure, it doesn't seem like prime real estate.

Well, Mars came late to the colonizing party. Mercury was the only inner planet left, and since we've seen how well colonizing beyond the Belt goes, I think it's pretty obvious why they didn't try for Saturn.

Martian settlement on Mercury was concentrated in the northern polar region, in eight large domes that were mostly shaded from the sun by the high walls of very deep craters. This work was begun around 2160, as a response to our starting the Belt colonies. Not much of a response, though... apparently radiation levels in the early years were still so bad that life expectancy was in the fifty-year range.

Over the next five decades, the Martians thickened their radiation shielding, started a crude manufacturing economy, and seeded the planet with a reasonably strong military presence. In orbit around the planet's equator (no idea why they didn't put them over the pole), a few shipyards and orbitals were built, but they weren't the sort of stations you'd find at Venus... I think they'd have more pleasantries in common with Pion rock than with Defense Command constructions. They existed strictly to support the orbiting ships, which couldn't get too close to the surface for obvious reasons.

All these developments virtually emptied the Martian treasury, but thanks to the simple manufacturing economy that developed in the domes and the shipyards, the planet eventually started to pay for itself.

By 2188, the Martians were satisfied enough with Mercury to start seeding their Asteroid colonies, which turned into the fiscal debacle of the century. I won't get into that, but suffice it to say that Mercury's role in the Martian Imperium was primarily to add bragging rights. You know: 'you may have Venus, but we have Mercury'.

I won't do the neo-suffragists any favors by comparing the size of our planets or our economies at this point.

So, if Mercury was mainly for show, why would assaulting it do us any good? Well, we could stop the flow of razor blades to Mars, which would mean they'd lose their ability to look clean-shaven. More importantly (obviously), though, the Martians had talked Mercury up a bit too much to their own people. We weren't privy to all of Mars' propaganda, but we had a strong impression from solid [guesswork] that the people of Mars saw their outer capital as a fortress that simply could not be overcome.

If we — the evil Earth Empire — did actually take Mercury, we were hoping that the Martian people would stop supporting their absurd dictator, and that he'd fear revolution and thus sue for peace. That was our goal: destroy the Martian people's confidence in their leaders, so their leaders would cut their losses and re-dedicate themselves to suppressing their own population.

Yes, I know that probably sounds awful, but our responsibility was to the nine *billion* people of the Earth Empire, not to the 800 million people of the Martian Imperium. We'd weigh in on Martian domestic issues only after the war was over… I'm actually planning to do a little series on Op Epsilon once we get the Martian War books done.

Anyway, that hopefully sums up why we were bound for Mercury — why we thought it was an important objective, and why we didn't assume it was a sure thing.

With all that background out of the way, it's time to start.

CHAPTER ONE

CRUTCHES

For most of my career up to 2231, I'd been a ship away from Karen McMaster at all times. She and I had set parallel courses up the rank ladder, right back from our days in the Academy. We'd graduated first and second in our class, we'd both been posted to fighter groups in the Belt Squadron, we'd both taken over those groups, we'd both moved on to ship command... we'd been in lock step the whole way, defying expectations and sticking close to each other through it all.

But we had been apart. She'd had adventures without me, and I'd had adventures without her. She hadn't met Lia Hawke or the Pions... who usually don't go together in a sentence (sorry Lia!)... and I hadn't taken down the Astor family (the Belt's biggest organized crime syndicate before Grant Merger came along).

She'd taken over *Lady Grace* when I took over *Friendly*. We'd cruised together many times and fought against pirates as a tandem team. We'd landed separately in pirate-infested domes and then joined up to shoot the bastards. Then we'd both moved up to frigates at the same time — to *Wolf* and *Lion* — and continued that tradition.

We'd had all those years apart.

But then, after I got lucky at the Battle of Deep Black and happened to board Fitcher Kim's flagship while Karen boarded an underling vessel, it all changed. I got the one promotion, and for the first time we were out of lock step. Which is when you started this series. I was a Commodore (yes, a rogue one, sorry), and she became my Flag Captain.

That's when everything changed — when we started spending all our time together. It probably would have been fine if we had just gone on shooting at pirates, but no, the Martians started their bloody war, and nothing was the same.

Karen and I came to rely on each other... no, that's not enough. We had already relied on each other. Now we *needed* each other. We *survived* on each other... which I think is a grammatically incorrect phrase, but it's the only one I have.

We survived on each other. We were each others' crutches. And when we went to Egesta, and to Sinope, and to *Idaho* and Pion rock, we kept each other going. I think I've managed to make that clear so far in these books.

I go to great pains to remind you of all these truths because they rather inform this next little scene.

It was about forty-two hours before the assault force was going to boost from Venus... remember that, as happened between *The Hawke Mission* and *The Independent Squadron*, we're going to have some overlap here with *The Forge Fires*. I was sitting in my cabin, looking over reports from the skippers in the Jupiter Force, reasonably confident that we'd get through this okay.

Then Karen walked into my cabin, holding a pad, "We need to talk."

Those words always sound like such a cliché in movies, but Karen was serious. She sat on my bed as I lowered a report by Mark Gunney, and she found my eyes with hers.

There was a tightness to her expression that was unsettling, so I frowned, "Problem?"

She held up the pad, "Agenda for the meeting with Greg... to save time he's mapped out force structures for the assault. He's going to take all the corvettes out of the squadrons and turn them into an escort force for the landing ships."

I hadn't opened my mail since I'd started on the reports, so I hadn't seen this yet. Even so, it wasn't a wild concept — what Greg was doing was creating a formation of fast, maneuverable escorts who could accompany the troop carriers like *Artemis Agrotera* to their drop points over Mercury's pole.

"Makes sense..." I said slowly, trying to figure out how this was making Karen anxious. Karen was unflappable, after all.

"He says we're going to need to appoint a Flag Officer to command the escort group."

That was the sound of the shoes dropping, to butcher the colloquialism. Of course an escort group made up of corvettes from several different squadrons would need a veteran Flag Officer commanding them, because as a rule, corvettes had no one more senior than a Commander aboard.

Guess who that Flag Officer would have to be.

Greg hadn't said so in the agenda, but it didn't take much brain power to figure out who the ideal candidate was — even I could put two and two together on this one. Christian Mikaelsen was in a battleship that he'd basically designed during refit, so he wouldn't be pulled out. Lia Hawke was still learning the ropes, so she was best kept with the main force, and Greg, Marlene and I were all in critical positions.

There was one officer, and one officer only, who was in a position that could be sacrificed for the coming action. I certainly didn't need a Commodore working under me to control the Jupiter Force... and there was no better officer in the fleet for the escort command.

It had to be Karen.

And that scared both of us a hell of a lot more than it honestly should have.

We sat there for a moment... it was several moments, actually. We sat there and tried to hide our panic from each other. And I do mean panic. Trust me, I know how ridiculous that sounds... I know that, in the grand scheme of the war, this parting was a joke. It was nothing. We were both alive and healthy. We were doing our jobs. There was absolutely nothing to complain about here... we'd been hugely lucky and privileged to spend all the time we'd had together.

We both knew that, so we meant not to show our anxiety. What spoiled fools we'd be, to complain about this.

"We've really, really been spoiled for a long time now," Karen said quietly.

"Yes. Yes we have," I replied.

"No right to complain... this... this isn't anything approaching hard. Not compared to what a lot of people have been through," she added.

That was very true.

And yet, it didn't help make either of us feel better about the situation. This, you see, is why I started the chapter the way I did. We were both adults, both with successful careers on our own… but together we'd been surviving this war.

Our moods didn't brighten after this — we didn't get chipper, neither of us had a smart quip or an observation or an idea that made us feel better. We remained miserable, for lack of a better word.

But (and here we go again) we were miserable together. That made it easier.

A luxury we were soon to lose.

CHAPTER TWO

BIG REUNION

When Greg Noyce, Lia Hawke and Christian 'Mik' Mikaelsen arrived in Venus space, there was plenty of fanfare. I think I covered this back in *The Forge Fires*, so I won't get too deep into describing the hordes of pleasure craft that mobbed them as they cruised in, or the photographers who assailed them when they reached *Venus One*.

Suffice it to say they were warmly welcomed, and many questions were asked as to precisely when we'd be heading to the Forge to pay back the Martians there. I won't belabor the point that we weren't going to the Forge — obviously, we saw what happened to Shauna's base at the end of the last book.

Right now, we're going to head into the big briefing that happened upon Greg's arrival. This meeting pretty much established the course of events for the rest of this book, so it's important.

It was held in one of *Venus One's* large briefing rooms, and Karen and I were actually the first two people to arrive. Wes Pellew wouldn't be attending because he and the Independent Squadron were missing this assault, and for the same reason, John Fiora absented himself.

Anyway, Karen and I got there first because we were both more anxious than we should have been about the inevitable move Karen was going to have to make. Know how when you're nervous about something, you sometimes rush to it, and just try to get it over with? That's what we were doing.

I know, somewhat ridiculous.

We sat in silence on one side of the briefing table as we waited for more people to arrive. Marlene was the first to do that, and let me say it again:

MARLENE! MARLENE MARLENE MARLENE!

I know her first book 'back' was *The Forge Fires*, but I think she still deserves cheering. The Sorceress was coming with us on this attack, and that, as far everyone was concerned, improved our odds considerably.

"Greetings," she waved as she stepped into the room. "We the first ones?"

Karen and I nodded in tandem, and Karen added words to the reply, "Guess we're the most eager."

Marlene was wearing a slight frown, and she shrugged, "Maybe that's it. I think I'm also looking for a distraction, though. I don't like thinking about what's happening to Shauna."

Ah, indeed, I don't know if I made that clear enough last book, but since Shauna Cass was Marlene's protégé, our formidable Sorceress did have sharper feelings over the fate of the Forge. She wished the base's fate hadn't been so bleak... but that was outside our control.

Taking her seat opposite us, then, Marlene was looking for the same sort of distraction

Karen and I were — but for a much more valid reason.

It took a few more minutes for Greg and Mik to arrive. They'd been attacked by press scrums several times on the way to the briefing room (you've probably seen some footage from one of those interviews) and thus were held up.

"Goodness," Greg was shaking his head as he came in. "They're more eager than I've seen all war."

Mik nodded in agreement, "Seriously."

They both slowed as they stepped closer, and the three of us already in the room smiled and stood.

"They want payback," I offered my comment as I rounded the table, extending my hand first to Greg and then to Mik. Karen followed and did the same, while Marlene stood at her chair with her hands on her hips and wearing an evil grin.

"Well it's been a long time since we've crossed paths," she said to Greg, and he chuckled and extended his hand to her.

"Not since the Battle Over Earth," he agreed.

"Not since the two of you *saved* Earth," Karen corrected with a helpful smile as they shook hands.

Marlene laughed and shook her head, "That wasn't just us... but now I get to shake the hands of the men who raided Mars."

Greg wasn't going to accept that praise casually, "It wasn't too difficult a mission."

Modesty, you might be noticing, is something the heads of state in the Fiora Ring prize rather a lot.

"And I had the excellent support of Commodore Mikaelsen," Greg released Marlene's hand and moved aside so Mik could step forward.

"Honored to meet you, ma'am," Mik smiled broadly. "I've been reading about your missions out here for years. Between those and the stories about Lord Ryan at the Forge, I think that's why I joined the Navy."

Marlene grinned, "All that high praise, and yet you 'ma'am' me."

That was it: the banter had begun. Marlene's wit is like a razor — when she unleashes it, you better be ready.

Mik wasn't taking chances, "I err on the side of respectfulness when I first meet people. It conceals my natural insanity for a little longer."

"Well it's Marlene to you... they call you Mik, right?"

"They do."

"Well, we'll just have to—"

The door seemed to fling open (which is impossible, because it actually retracted into the wall, but it still seemed to fling open somehow) and Lady Lia Hawke erupted into the room, then planted her fists on her hips and stood in a superhero pose.

"I have saved these two from the evil hordes of the media, and now I come to join your mission!"

Well, as intros for Lia go, that's a pretty... uh... subtle one?

The five of us just stood there and stared at her for a moment, not entirely sure how to react. Karen, unsurprisingly, managed to formulate a witty counter-punch before any of the rest of us, "Really?"

Lia dipped her chin, undermining her super-hero pose as she scanned our faces, "What... too much?"

"Just a bit," I nodded. "Yeah."

"Oh," she pulled her hands from her hips and noticeably reduced her insanity level, "Sorry. But I did keep the press occupied while they made a run for it."

"We didn't exactly *run*," Mik pointed out. "But she did keep them busy."

"Team skills. We're going to need them, right?" Lia made sure to sound eager when she asked that, and we all nodded slowly.

Then, without warning, she launched herself at Marlene with arms wide for a hug, "Auntie Witch!"

Not even going to start on that term of endearment. Lia is the only human alive who could survive saying it... I take my life in my hands just repeating it. Marlene is the *Sorceress*, remember. Not a witch. Different connotation. Completely.

And she hugged Lia back while the rest of us started settling into chairs. As we did that, Karen glanced at me, and I glanced back. We both briefly wondered how Lia was holding up, given all the stress she was under — her father was dead or dying, and she was about to fight her first big fleet battle. Neither of us had any reason to doubt that she'd be up to the task when the fight started, but she was entitled to be nervous.

It'd be good for her to get some time alone with Charlie... *later*.

Meanwhile, the particulars of the meeting were much more pressing. Greg took his seat at the head of the table and Marlene sat opposite me, with Lia next to her. Mik came around the table and sat beside Karen... because it's clearly essential that you know where we were all sitting...

Sorry, I just realized that in some of these briefings, I go to some length to explain where people are sitting. Does anyone really care? I mean, if you do, I'll continue... but it just struck me as sort of pointless...

"I trust that we have all reviewed the packages on Mercury," Greg began the formal discussions, and we all replied with nods. He continued smoothly, "Good. So we know we'll combine all our battleships into a single assault force, to be escorted by the Hawke Force frigates. We will also combine all our assigned corvettes into an escort group to protect the assault ships."

Again we nodded. There really wasn't anything for us to say — we all did know this. It wasn't anything new.

"For command of those corvettes..." Greg let those words hang for just a second, and Karen was right there.

"I'll take command from *Lady Grace*, if that suits everyone."

She said it very simply — very matter-of-factly. She didn't huff, sigh, or do anything else to suggest she dreaded this job. And neither did I. Our torments, foolish as they were, belonged to us alone. They had no place at this briefing table, or anywhere else in public for that matter.

Greg smiled warmly at the words, "Thank you, Karen, that's perfect. We all appreciate the choice you're making."

I hadn't expected him to say that, and neither had Karen. He didn't elaborate, and we didn't so much as bat an eye, but it was said. And Mik and Marlene both understood what

Greg meant… they all knew this parting was significant.

"So that takes care of one problem. The other, though, is those *monitors*," Greg reached out to the desk controls in front of him and activated the briefing room's wall screen. The two monitors *Melbourne* had [detected] in Mercury orbit were displayed there.

Now, let me just backtrack to remind you what we're talking about when we say 'monitors', because we're not referring to 'computer screens'. Monitors, historically, were small ships carrying battleship-sized guns. They were unwieldy and slow, but if you got in range of their weapons, they could hurt you.

In Mercury space, two destroyers that had been under construction early in the war had been retrofitted with battleship laser pods on their bows (they had no lasers on their tails), meaning they were essentially the same sort of ships — small hulls with big guns. Our fear was that these monitors were carrying the same long-range lasers that had been mounted on the *Tharsis*-class Martian battleships… the ones Bort McWebsbert had used to destroy Shauna Cass' squadron.

If the monitors had those weapons, we were in a whole lot of trouble… and even if they were just regular Martian battleship lasers, we were still in for a mess.

Remember the situation at Mercury: they had five battleships to our six, but those two monitors could potentially give the Martians the advantage in heavy-hitters.

Our assault was in some danger.

"We need to deal with those monitors away from the action… they should be too slow to keep up with the battleships, so we can hope to isolate them. We cannot risk them getting into range of our landing forces, or even our battle line, in case they have *Tharsis* weapons aboard," Greg verbalized what we were all thinking.

Marlene nodded now, "Sounds like a special mission for a picked group of ships."

This information hadn't been in the package Greg had sent out — not in so many words, anyway — so neither Karen nor I nodded.

"It's a good job for a battleship that's been tweaked to be fast," Marlene added, looking at Mik. "With an insane man on the bridge."

Christian Mikaelsen did his very best not to look reluctant as she spoke, and he did a commendable job of controlling his expression. But I knew what was going through his mind in that second, as did we all: *Medusa*, the sister ship to his own *Cyclops*, had been destroyed by a single barrage from the *Tharsis*-class lasers. If these monitors had the same firepower, *Cyclops* might not fare well against them.

That in mind, he said the only thing an officer of his caliber says to orders like those: "We'll find a way to make it work."

"He'll need a good escort, but we can't pull too many frigates off the battle line," Greg added, without even looking at me.

Just to review our total force, we had six battleships, fifteen frigates and fifteen corvettes. Sounds like a lot, but the corvettes would all be needed to protect the transports and combat storeships carrying troops for the assault, leaving the fifteen frigates to cover six battleships. That's still a good number of frigates, but given the likelihood of huge numbers of Martian Interceptors and missiles swarming Greg and Marlene's battle line during the attack, it was only *just* enough.

In other words, we couldn't afford to get brash and peel too many frigates off the battleship-escort role to assist Mik in dealing with the monitors.

"I'll take *Wolf* and *Cheetah* for the job," was my solution.

Two frigates and an old battleship to deal with the monitors? Seems like precious little firepower as I write it now. Seemed like a lot less firepower when I said it then. But we couldn't take any more away from the main battle.

Greg nodded slowly at my words, "If you think that's enough."

I had to shrug at that, and then I glanced at Mik, "We'll make it work."

He nodded back to me, "Yes. Yes we will."

The meeting went on, but that sorts out the big stuff. Let's move on for now…

CHAPTER THREE

PATHFINDERS

Major Charlie Peters let out a long breath as he emerged from another of *Venus One's* briefing rooms. He was just being released from a long and rather intense planning session with Brigadier Peri Oktar, the senior Special Brancher in the solar system, and it had been... well, long and intense.

After collecting his thoughts for a second, Charlie turned back to the door and watched as many other Majors and a handful of Colonels departed the room behind him. Eventually Rufus Chang emerged, and upon sighting his shipmate, Charlie started off down the corridor, slowly at first so Rufus could fall into step alongside him.

"Brigadier Oktar is a no-nonsense sort of officer," Rufus observed as he matched Charlie's stride, and all the intrepid Major Peters could do was nod.

"Yes, she is."

Where our Navy planning session was moving forward with equal measures of seriousness and good-natured-but-not-too-over-the-top-humor, that Special Branch briefing had been like running a gauntlet. Peri Oktar expected a hell of a lot from her teams during this landing, and she wasn't afraid to explain that to her men and women. Clearly. Loudly. Intensely.

No one could doubt Oktar's skill, her toughness, or her general proficiency as a Brancher... but she had the bedside manner of a stampede of buffalo driving a freight train into a hurricane. In other words, she was so forceful that it took the oh-so-clever merging of three separate metaphors to convey how intense she was.

That's a lot of metaphors, I think you'll agree. Wait, are those similes? Dammit.

Anyway, as they stepped away from the briefing, *Wolf's* two Majors of Special Branch took a couple of minutes to decompress. Conveniently, this lets me do some exposition before I return to dialogue, so here goes.

There were, as I've said, eight domes in the Mercury settlement, all based in craters around the pole. Our job, as the Navy, was to get the Special Branchers, the SF, and (so help us) the Imperial Army over these domes, and to gun down any exterior defenses that might hinder their landing. That sounds easy... well, maybe it doesn't... but either way, I'll talk about what we were supposed to do later. For now, we should concern ourselves with what the landing forces had to do.

Basically, the eight domes were being divided up. Five were going to the Imperial Army, so we didn't have to worry much about how they were going to be attacked... that was up to Major General Ronald Frederick Hubert III and his 30,000 blockheads. The other three domes, including the 'Capital Dome', were left to Oktar and her 10,000 SF and Special Branch.

Now, I've thought for a while about how to explain the assault to you, and I've decided there's no way I can do justice to the landings on all eight domes. I'm not even going to try. If you want to know what happens in the general assault, there are some great books available on that subject, and at least two of the movies are acceptable.

Instead of talking about landing tactics in all the different domes, then, I'm going to focus on the job Charlie and Rufus had been given by Peri Oktar: they were to be the pathfinders for the assault on the Capital Dome.

Before any SF tried to break through the locks into that dome, it would be Charlie and Rufus and their teams who gained a foothold at an access point *somewhere* (it was up to them to choose the most tactically expedient one based on any intel they could gather prior to or during the op). Once they captured that access point, reinforcements would be funneled in behind them.

Do I even need to actually point out that missions don't get much more dangerous than this? Between their two squads, they'd have twenty-four officers to establish a perimeter... and the Capital Dome (because it was the Capital) was expected to be guarded by at least 2,500 troops. At *least*. Including Commandos, probably.

So yeah, they had been given a dangerous, dangerous job.

And just to put things in perspective, they were by no means the only teams with this sort of mission — each of the three domes being stormed by Defense Command forces would be spearheaded by pathfinders. If I remember correctly, the Imperial Army was going to do the same, but they'd be leading the way with their much-talked-about (and much-mocked) Gamma Force special soldiers.

"We got the nod for this because we survived Pion rock, didn't we?" Rufus asked the question half to himself, and half to Charlie.

Frowning, Charlie nodded, "Probably."

"I spent years marooned on Luna wishing I could get into the action. I'm getting my wish."

Rufus said that last part with neither bitter cynicism nor eagerness. He was referring, of course, to his Dave Caldecott-inflicted assignment to Luna — an exile he'd made the most of, but which he'd rather not have spent on the moon. His attitude, though, was a level one... he'd spent many years waiting for a chance to really do his job, and now he was getting it. He wasn't a fool — he wasn't excited about the prospect of getting shot up as the first man into the Mercury Capital Dome. But he wasn't bitter either. This was his job.

"I'd say," Charlie agreed, and then he shook his head. "The Martians aren't going to make this easy for us."

He knew that for certain. Remember back to *The Canary Wars*, near the end of the book, when he and I talked about the difference between Martians and Pions? Martians kill efficiently, and few officers alive knew that better than our intrepid Major Peters.

But, and again I stress this point, he didn't harbor bitterness about this mission. It was his responsibility, and quite simply, he was going to do his best with it.

The two Majors walked on for a little while, ultimately heading back towards the chute that would take them up to *Wolf*, so they could let their teams know about the assignment. As they walked, Rufus looked at Charlie.

"Casualty estimates?"

It was a simple question, and one that part of Charlie seriously didn't want to answer.

But he answered anyway, "Worst case, we all die. Best case... a third of us."

Rufus nodded, "I agree. So probably half of us."

"Probably half," Charlie concurred.

Such a cheerful prognosis.

They continued on towards *Wolf*, but after a couple of moments Rufus stopped abruptly, "Nearly forgot. I'll see you back on the ship."

Charlie frowned — he had no idea what his compatriot was thinking.

"I have to see a friend at the armory," Rufus added helpfully, and Charlie's eyebrows went up.

"Why doesn't it surprise me that you have a friend at the armory?"

Rufus shrugged, "I'm consistent. I'll see if I can get some kit to improve our odds."

Charlie nodded slowly — he'd take whatever advantage he could get just now.

Assaulting Mercury would be no simple matter.

CHAPTER FOUR
BELGRANO SCENARIO

Mik and I were sitting in an officers' lounge in *Venus One*, and thankfully the place was abandoned. It had comfortable chairs and a little self-serve canteen that was fueling our brainstorming session, and we didn't mind the chance to try to figure out our own tactical dilemmas outside the usual places — you know, offices and briefing rooms.

I was slouched back on a couch, unapologetically eating some grapes, while Mik had a sandwich he'd whipped up. We weren't saying a whole lot.

"You know what this reminds me of?" I asked after a while, and Mik looked up from his sandwich.

"The *Belgrano*?"

"Exactly."

It was incredibly helpful working with someone whose knowledge of antiquated Naval history matched or exceeded my own... but then, I suppose it doesn't help you, dear reader, if you have no idea what the *Belgrano* was. Believe me, there's no shame in it.

A couple of centuries ago, in the 1980s, the United Kingdom and Argentina went to war. The Argentineans had one ship that was a potential threat to the British squadron deployed to the area of the Falklands: the *Belgrano*. It was a fifty-year-old vessel, but one with enough armor and gun-power to still be a danger to the Royal Navy's frigates and destroyers.

The Admiralty of the time was most concerned with the *Belgrano*, so they launched a special mission: they sent one of their most modern nuclear submarines to sink the ship before it had a chance to come out to fight. Now, in the pages of Naval history, this matchup is often seen with interest — these were ships from different eras of technology, so many people who get enthusiastic about ship classes and such things can talk for hours and hours and hours about the incident.

I'm not saying *I* have. I'm just saying it's possible, is all. I mean, do you really think *I* could possibly spend hours talking about the tactical strengths of gun-armed surface combatants when set against nuclear-powered sub-surface combatants...

Sigh. Yes.

Anyway, as we sat in the officers' lounge, it seemed to both Mik and me that we had a similar mission on our hands. We were being sent out after a very specific pair of ships, our orders being to make sure they didn't get into range of our squadron.

But ours was a more complicated problem, I think, than the British faced with the *Belgrano*. Because these monitors were new, and *Cyclops* was old, and we couldn't submerge to hide from Martian sensors.

"I think the biggest problem right now is that we don't know where in the formation those two are going to be when we arrive... none of the [stuff] from *Melbourne* make[s] it look like those ships have a set orbital pattern."

"Not a regular one, no," I agreed with Mik's assessment.

"So logically, we want to figure out a way to draw them out... to separate them. But what sort of distraction could we pose that gets their attention, but doesn't bring the rest of the Mercury Squadron down on us?"

Yeah. It'd be a hell of a lot more convenient if the Martians just did what we wanted them to do, but the bastards had a habit of not being cooperative like that.

Mik finished his sandwich as he pondered the problem, and I laid down the empty fruit bowl that had held my snack. We needed to make this work...

"Well. Hm."

That was my best contribution for a while, and Mik glanced up when I said it, then chuckled and shook his head, "Yeah."

Silence rolled in again for a while, and a couple of Ensigns wandered into the lounge, only to see us sitting there and head out again. I guess we didn't look like amiable company.

"When *Shannon* needed to duel *Chesapeake*, the skipper just sent a message into the port challenging single-ship combat," Mik recalled.

That's a great story of a frigate fight from the War of 1812 — a gentlemen's duel between equally matched frigates. But that wouldn't help us either, because it seemed somehow unlikely that the Martians would answer a polite invitation to send their monitors out to fight.

I say, we live in such uncivilized times — can't even tell someone you're going to shoot them before you do it!

Er. Nevermind.

"At Leyte, the Japanese got the escort carriers on their own by drawing away the main fleet," I was grasping at straws here, completely and totally.

Mik nodded charitably, but then both of us sighed. How the hell would we convince the Martians to divide their heavy-hitters...

"Well..." I started to say something, but then I eliminated it as a possibility and stopped.

See, we were really being smart.

Eventually, I resigned myself to the simplest solution — one that seemed almost like a non-solution, and thus one that I figured had the slimmest chances of success.

"Well, if they're not completely incompetent, the Martians are going to cruise straight out to meet Greg as soon as he appears on sensors. If they tried to wait in orbit to stop us, their chances would be slim."

Mik nodded at my assertion — remember, in *every* defensive battle we'd fought since Belt Two (back in *The Rogue Commodore*), we'd done our best to keep the action away from the celestial body we were trying to defend. The Battle Over Earth was an hour out of orbit (not much, but some), the defense of Earth in *The Gallant Few* was done well away from the planet, and so on. Only in the Belt, where things are tighter, do we tend to defend a place from right above it.

And then look what can happen: back in *The Rogue Commodore*, remember how the pirates managed to land at Belt Two base despite our stiff defenses?

So, if the Martians weren't completely useless — and we figured they couldn't be

— they'd come out to meet Greg. If they let him get all the way to orbit before they tried to stop him, his troops would have an even better chance of getting to ground.

Mik was thinking all of this at the same time I was, and now he stroked his goatee, "So we're just going to count on them separating themselves by being slow?"

It was all we could come up with right then... and to be fair, it was *something*. Remember, the monitors appeared to simply be destroyers with huge guns mounted on the front. The drive power-to-mass ratio was below standard... it *had* to be. Which meant that, when the Martian battle line came out, the monitors would either stay in orbit, or lag behind.

They'd be isolated. Hopefully.

"We can keep trying to come up with smarter ways of doing it, but for now we can keep that in reserve as our fallback," I shrugged.

"And if they all stick together somehow... we'll just have to go after them in the melee. Hope it doesn't come to that," Mik sighed.

We sat quietly again for a moment, and then I grimaced and leaned forward in my seat, "I'd hoped it'd be easy to come up with a more brilliant, magic-bullet solution."

Mik frowned, "Because we have magic now?"

"I can hope whatever I like, can't I?"

Laughing, Mik shrugged, "I suppose."

We were silent again for a moment, and then the next challenge came to mind: "So we know how to get them alone. What do we do with them when we get them by themselves?"

We didn't get a chance to answer that; instead Commodore Wes Pellew turned up, and shortly thereafter we were at a bar.

As you may recall, that ended well.

CHAPTER FIVE

CORVETTE COMMODORE

Karen's return to *Lady Grace* was the cause of some fanfare. As she came up the chute from *Venus One* for the first time, she was greeted by a dozen officers and crew who had been with the ship since she'd left it years before — Ensigns who were now Lieutenants, spacers who were now Petty Officers, and so on.

There were another dozen crew members present who had never served with her before, but for whom her return was somehow even more special. Now they could tell their families and friends that they'd served with the legendary Karen McMaster in *Lady Grace*, and let me tell you, that is no meager boast to be able to make.

It goes without saying that Karen's status aboard this corvette was almost mythic. Rightly so.

That being the case, Karen's arrival was a big occasion for the crew.

The weird thing was, though, that she had come straight from our meeting with John, Marlene and Mik. She literally hadn't stopped… she'd gone directly from the briefing room to the ship, and yet somehow they knew she was coming. This is testament to the power of the rumor engines in the Defense Command Navy, I think. Some spacer must have overheard something somewhere, and then passed the word, and once a rumor started…

You get it.

Commander Elise De Winter stepped lightly through the crowd of grinning people before Karen had much chance to wonder about the welcoming committee. Stopping short of her former CO, Elise snapped a salute.

"Welcome home," she said.

Karen had to smile. There's always a connection with your first ship, I think — no matter what ships you go on to, you always feel a special bond with the first one. For me, that ship is *Friendly*; for Karen, *Lady Grace*.

Saluting back easily, Karen stepped forward to shake Elise's hand, "I'm not moved in yet… but it'll be good to be back. You and I should talk, though. You're going to be Flag Captain now."

Elise De Winter's eyebrows jumped, but she said nothing. After shaking hands with some of the crew, and absorbing some kind words from her people, Karen followed her Commander to the skipper's cabin.

"We'll clear the stateroom for your quarters, if that's alright," Elise said as she led Karen into her own berth. Because they're small, corvettes lack full accommodations for embarked Flag Officers. The newer *Noble*-class ships have 'staterooms', though, which serve as multi-purpose compartments unless they need to be kitted out as cabins for Flag Officers.

It would be more cramped than the living situation on *Wolf*, but that didn't bother Karen.

"That'll be perfect," she smiled, and then she and Elise settled down on opposite sides of the Commander's desk.

"So, when we get to Mercury, we're going to be at the head of an escort force… every corvette in the assault force will be under our command. We'll be going in with the landing forces, keeping them safe."

Karen gave that brief summary for Elise's benefit. Years before, De Winter had been Karen's very young and inexperienced XO, but over her years in command of *Lady Grace*, the Dutch skipper had been well seasoned.

Well, that makes her sound like a steak… you know what I mean. She'd gained a lot of experience. It was obvious to all of us that she'd be getting her promotion to a frigate soon enough… but for now, we needed her in *Lady Grace*, using her experience to back up Karen.

"Should be interesting," Elise remarked upon hearing the plan. "We'll have fifteen ships… three escort groups of five?"

"That's what I was thinking," Karen agreed with a nod. "We'll pick officers from each squadron to be group commanders, and then we'll try to keep our units as tight as possible. We're going to have a hard job going in there."

Elise grinned, "Hard jobs are the best kind."

It was clear to Karen that the Commander was somewhat eager about the upcoming fight, which seemed fair enough. *Lady Grace* had served through the war so far with distinction: if De Winter thought the ship was ready for more, Karen had no reason to doubt it.

But she wasn't as naturally eager as her younger counterpart, a fact she just kept to herself.

"Good. Alright, Elise, I can't talk for long now… I need to go start packing up. I just wanted to let you know what's happening," Karen stood slowly. "I'll be back in a while, and we'll figure out squadron order then."

"Looking forward to it," Elise came to her feet as well. "Thank you, ma'am!"

Karen nodded curtly, smiled brightly, and then left the cabin.

This was a homecoming, certainly.

But home felt different than it had before the start of the war…

When I knocked on Karen's door a couple of hours later, she was packing a kit bag for her move. I'd just fled from a bar, and was looking for a bit of sanity… this didn't help.

"Hey," she glanced back over her shoulder at me as I came in, and I stopped as the hatch closed behind me.

"You're… packing."

She'd looked back to her kit bag, but my brilliant observation drew a gentle frown from her, "Yes I am. Glad you noticed."

I tried to stifle a sigh, but I didn't succeed.

"You moving over tonight, or tomorrow?" I asked slowly, then moved forward to stand next to her.

She was looking down at the clothes stacked on her bed with more intensity than they deserved… because I'm observant, I realized that meant she was preoccupied with other thoughts.

"Tomorrow's soon enough," she said then, and I nodded.

"Well. That's… good."

Silence resumed, and we just stood there for a while. I know by now this is probably frustrating you… I mean, we really were having a hard time coming to grips with a paltry separation. Worse, I keep spelling that out for you, over and over… but I can't help it.

Finally, Karen turned around and lowered herself onto the end of her bed, "As awkward silences go, this one's been impressive for us."

I sat next to her, leaning over far enough for our shoulders to press into each other, "It's an awkward situation."

There was no point trying to explain it any more clearly than that — neither she nor I could accurately describe the wrenching feeling. All we both knew was that it was occupying far too much of our consciousness. That's why I keep complaining to you about it.

Eventually, she told me about her trip up to *Lady Grace* — her greetings from the crew, thanks to their mastery of the rumor mill, and her brief chat with Elise. I told her about the planning Mik and I had done, and mentioned the trip to the bar, which got her to laugh.

"No fish or intercooler fluid this time?" she grinned.

I shook my head, "Not this time, no. But Mik gave me hell for that time you and I danced out at Sinope. Remember, during the battle?"

She looked at me with a surprised smile, "Really? That rumor mill is powerful."

"It is."

She nodded and looked away again, before saying what we were both thinking, "Won't be getting away with that this time."

If you'll recall that scene in the bar from *The Forge Fires*, that same basic thought had managed to dim any hope of a good mood for me.

Now it had done the same to Karen.

"I'll owe you one, once we're done with the Martians," I said softly. It was a promise of sorts… I didn't say it with much conviction, though.

"Yeah," Karen nearly whispered that word.

There wasn't a whole lot more to say. I helped Karen finish packing, and then we both got to bed. There was still plenty to do before the fleet departed… and, obviously, even more to do once we did.

That was our last night on *Wolf* before the Mercury assault.

CHAPTER SIX

SHORT GOODBYE

The hours before our departure for Mercury were very hurried. We were moving back and forth quickly, meeting with ship skippers, checking preparations... all sorts of details had to be nailed down. For the Captains and Commanders of individual ships, victuals had to be secured, crews addressed, and so on...

Victuals. Sorry, my editor has a note on this page asking what 'victuals' are. I didn't actually make this one up: it's a terms for military supplies. I'm sure it's in the dictionary. Honest, go look. I'll wait.

There, see, bet your face is red.

Anyway, we were all hurrying back and forth, trying to get things ready for our cruise to Mercury — *and*, of course, telling anyone who'd listen that we were heading to the Forge. Don't forget that little subterfuge.

I won't bore you with too much of this stuff — most of it isn't terribly interesting anyway. I do want to include one scene, though, that was so very brief, and yet so very important in the long run.

I was coming back to the chute up to *Wolf*, having just introduced Bruce Arama (remember, the Kiwi contractor-Commander from the Forge) to his new commanding officer (Karen). *Adelaide* was joining Karen's corvette escort group, bringing its numbers up from fifteen ships to sixteen. That gave Karen an extra ship which she *could* have kept, but knowing what we were up to, she'd released one vessel to join *Wolf*, *Cheetah* and *Cyclops* in the fight with the monitors. More on that in a little while.

Anyway, I was coming back to *Wolf* after introducing Bruce to Karen, and as I got to the bottom of the chute, Charlie dropped down it.

I hadn't really had a chance to talk to Charlie at all since we'd reached Venus. I'd been in planning sessions, he'd been in planning and training sessions, and whenever he had a spare minute, he'd been with Lia, because his beloved Lady certainly did benefit from a bit of time with him, and vice-versa.

So, when he appeared carrying his kit bag and his MAG-90, I was a little surprised.

"Whoa, hey there," Charlie stepped out of the chute and then aside, letting the rest of his squad pass him as they exited it.

"Ahoy," I replied, my eyes following Ben Belete and the Special Branchers as they headed back the way I'd come. "Moving ships?"

"Moving ships," Charlie confirmed with a nod.

"Oh," I said.

"Yep," he agreed.

So much for our trademarked quasi-witty repartee.

I looked back at Charlie and frowned, "Yeah, sorry we haven't had time to... well, talk much. It's been pretty insane."

"Yes it has. It's my fault too…" Charlie shrugged, then our conversation petered out for a moment.

As if saying goodbye to Karen for this mission wasn't bad enough, my best friend and long-time partner in crime was going too.

"Moving over to *Lady Grace*," Charlie added after a moment's silence. "We'll be the pathfinders for the Capital Dome, so we may need to get in closer than the transports."

"I heard," I nodded. The dangerous nature of Charlie's mission hadn't completely sunk in for me by this stage, and it still didn't as I answered him. I knew it was a hell of a job, but as I say, the gravity of it didn't quite hit home yet.

"We're going after the monitors… *Wolf* and *Cheetah* and *Cyclops* are, I mean. And Karen just released *Friendly* to me, because we picked up *Adelaide* from the Forge."

That's what I was alluding to a little while ago — with Bruce Arama joining her escort group, Karen was able to free up Matt Baxter to join our merry little band of monitor-hunters. We'd have a fine force… hopefully enough.

"That sounds like it could be a mess," Charlie's tone was flat, and I nodded.

"Expecting it to be. Just like pathfinding into a Martian dome will be," I replied.

Seemed to both of us just then like we were heading into the most dangerous parts of this fight… I'm not sure if that's ironic, appropriate, or some other damned word that means 'strange but somehow fitting'.

"So. You be careful down there," I said lamely, feeling that this conversation had become uncomfortably stalled.

"You too… and…" Charlie started a sentence, then stopped himself. This was something he rarely did, and then to add to that, he winced.

I must have looked surprised — Charlie doesn't often start and then halt a thought, even at times like these. Reading my expression, he let out a short sigh and nodded, as if to say 'alright, I'll go ahead and say it'.

"Keep it under control," was the end of his sentence, and I frowned.

"Er. What?"

"You know. You… well. You're not going to have Karen around, and I won't be around either. Just… just keep it under control."

Ah. I knew what he meant. It was a comment that only a few people in the solar system were qualified to make, and he was one of them.

"I will," I agreed with a nod.

That seemed like enough to say, so we started to go our opposite directions, but as we began to move a new question occurred to me, and I stopped, "When you're finished with Mercury, are you going to be back with us? Or will you be looking for a promotion… and a liaison job?"

I wasn't as subtle with that question as I'd meant to be, but it was an extremely important one. Charlie stopped and his expression seemed to lock.

"I don't know yet," he said first. Then he shook his head, "I… it's possible."

"Ah."

I should have sounded more eager or helpful — should have been a good and supportive friend — but I would have been faking enthusiasm, it must be said. I would miss my friend. I'd miss his steady advice and our inane conversations… and it seemed as though, all of a sudden, we were going our separate ways. It was quite possible that we'd never see each other again, after all this time.

"Well," I recovered just a bit, "just let me know when you want to. I'll talk to John and get it sorted out."

"You don't have to trouble your—"

I held up my hand, "No trouble. You know that."

He nodded. He did know that.

"You realize, this could be it?" I asked then, rather abruptly. "I mean, off to beat the Martians, and even if we do, you could be off starting a new life, well away from my madness... do some real good out there... fix a Protectorate, bring some happiness to Lia. Our paths could be permanently parting, right here and now."

Charlie hadn't expected me to actually say that, but he'd been thinking it. He nodded once, then dropped his kit bag, "It could be. Been a hell of a run, if this is it. Been a lot of fun."

"Yes it has," I agreed immediately, and we both smiled. "Was bound to end at some point."

It might have been premature to assume it was over now... but we were both accepting that the directions were changing. This was a very, very big change, too. The end of a team... the breaking up of a band... whatever you like. This was *huge*.

And we were just bringing it up and coming to terms with it during a five-minute conversation in a boarding lounge.

"Well. If this is it, then thank you," I extended my hand to Charlie, and he took it.

"And thank you. And if it isn't, I'll see you again."

We let go after a moment, and then nodded to each other again.

"Let's go do our jobs," I said after that.

"It's what we do," Charlie agreed with a smile.

And that was it — he headed for *Lady Grace*, and I went up to *Wolf*.

Half way up the chute, it started to hit me that I was saying goodbye to a lot of close friends right then. I didn't like it one bit.

But it was inevitable.

And I had a lot less to complain about than many others did.

CHAPTER SEVEN

BOOSTING

I don't think I've paused yet to convey how startlingly awesome the fleet we assembled at Venus really was. I chose my words carefully there — it really was startling and awesome. When I was waiting with Andrea on the bridge for our departure, we had every screen displaying enhanced visual scans from orbital space — we were basically looking at pictures of the fleet, taken from fighters and others ships' cameras, and from our own.

It was startling, and it inspired awe. Beyond that, I have a hard time putting the scene into words.

Which, according to my editors, is an unacceptable cop-out.

Alright, try to picture it. We didn't just have the assault force in orbit, we had the *Bonnie* Squadron and the Independent Squadron too. That's a total of *forty-eight* ships, including the four *Bonnies,* six other battleships, twenty-one frigates and seventeen corvettes.

See, it may all just read as numbers on a page, but when you see it... it's incredible. Never in the history of Defense Command... hell, in the history of space travel... had so many warships been standing proudly together in one place. Back in the pre-war days, we'd thought it a big deal when the whole Belt Squadron turned up in one place at one time... this was on an entirely different scale.

The images that were taken by news crews and sightseers remain, to this day, some of the most spectacular pictures ever captured of our fleet. Just plain awesome. You can look up shots taken by DC Public Relations in the fleet archive, and there are countless sources of the private photos and vid. It's worth a look... impressive stuff.

And we were thinking much the same as we stood on the bridge and waited to cruise away from Venus. There wasn't too much pomp and ceremony about this — I'm sure we could have drummed some up if we'd felt inspired to, but we were all far too preoccupied with the mission.

Instead, as the launch time approached, we started pulling our skippers up on Battlelink, and warming our engines for a hard burn.

I'll join the narrative here with a few minutes to go before departure, when we had all the skippers from the Jupiter Force up on the secondary screens, and pretty images of our mighty fleet still filling screen one.

"Time to go yet? I'm really looking forward to taking back the Forge," Mark Gunney said that with a grin, and I chuckled.

"Wow, you should be an actor," my mocking bounced off him.

"I'm something better," he said. "A good liar."

Andrea Kiley was standing with me, and she half-shrugged, "That's true, he does actually *get* women."

Mark laughed, and I chuckled, though both of us were a little surprised that Andrea had come up with that barb. Either way, it was taken in good humor. I kept moving my eyes between skippers on the Battlelink screens. I wanted to get moving.

Kasia Hu, who'd taken over from Marshal Samuels on *Alberta*, looked a bit anxious, but I didn't call her on it. Matt Baxter, Katya Romanov, and Isoruku Togo all looked at their ease. And then, on the screen to *Lady Grace*, Elise De Winter was standing next to Karen.

Again, it was a very strange feeling to be seeing Karen on a screen, instead of having her right next to me. But that didn't matter. We waited quietly for another moment.

Then John Fiora broke the silence.

"Signal broadcasting from *Bonaventure*," Felicia Khalid said evenly, then pointed to one of her techs and had the feed shunted up to the main screen. A window opened there, and John appeared.

"This is First Lord Fiora to the Forge assault fleet. I just want to wish you good hunting out there. The eyes of the Empire are on you... wish I could be with you. Good hunting, God speed."

John usually isn't one for speeches, but in this case he'd made an exception specifically because it gave him a chance to say — one more time — that we were going to the Forge.

The signal closed and I clapped my hands together a little too eagerly, "Alright, folks, boost in squadron order."

"Signal from *Warspite*," Felicia interrupted then, and a new window opened on the main screen a couple of seconds later.

"Noyce to all ships: boost for the Forge, pre-established cruising order until Point Victory."

That feed closed, and I clapped my hands together one more time... then waited. Just in case there'd be any other interruptions. Waited... nope.

"Alright. We're leading, so Mark, if you please."

Mark Gunney nodded, then looked to his XO off screen, "Roger that. Erica, let's get moving. Smartly. We want to impress."

Cheetah's drives fired first, and the fleet began to uncoil into a great column, pulling away from Venus at a modest 189 kps.

For the first day of the trip, we'd hang together in our old squadrons, but once we made the turn for Mercury we'd switch around into our new groups for the assault.

We had one week until battle.

A week to keep ourselves busy...

CHAPTER EIGHT

BELGRANO MARK II

As is my habit when we have long trips to deal with, I'm going to jump around a bit for the next few chapters. Because we'd been so rushed in getting out of Venus, lots of discussion about tactics for the coming fight still needed to happen — details had to be nailed down, and so on. I obviously won't bore you with all of that, but there are some pertinent points before we get to the actual assault.

So here we go: first of all, we had to factor Matt Baxter into our battle with the monitors.

Sitting in the day cabin off *Wolf's* bridge, Andrea and I had Mik Mikaelsen, Mark Gunney and Matt Baxter on realtime comm, and were going over our options.

"I'm not sure what we can add to the gunfight," Matt was saying, referring to the absolute reality that *Friendly's* lasers simply couldn't compare to battleship-level firepower. Mark, Mik and I nodded simultaneously — it seemed unwise to let my former sloop get in the way of a gun duel...

But Andrea, *Friendly's* most recent skipper before Matt, had a notion of her own.

"Well, what if we made the most of this?"

I frowned at that suggestion, "Um, isn't that what we're doing?"

Andrea flashed a shiny smile — one that was brighter than I'd expect from her under the circumstances — and nodded, "Yes, but we can try harder. Think of it, what's our excuse for being there? If we make a line right for those monitors, they might figure we know what they are. I say we make them come to us."

Mik, Mark and Matt (alliteration!) all frowned now too.

"I'd love for them to do exactly what I want them to do," Mark said slowly.

"You think we can draw them out?" Mik began stroking his beard.

Shaking her head, Andrea looked at Mik's screen, "*Cyclops* can't. But if it looks like two frigates and a sloop are making a run on the domes, they might commit themselves."

My eyes narrowed at the thought. Mik and I had considered using the two frigates as bait for a trap, but it just seemed too fanciful — hoping that two cruisers would draw two monitors instead of two destroyers was a bit unrealistic.

But if we counted *Friendly* into the equation, would that make the Martians more inclined to commit their special ships? Perhaps it would...

"We make straight for the domes, hope seeing the three of us is just enough to draw them in?" I asked half-rhetorically, and Mark 'hmmed'.

"If it were me, I'm not sure I'd send battleship firepower to stop a little raiding force, even if it was coming straight at the domes."

A very good point, and one Mik was taking into consideration, "*Cyclops* is the real draw for them, right? The reason they'd send the monitors?"

I nodded in agreement, and we looked back at Andrea.

The Irish skipper was smiling coolly, as if she was well ahead of us, "Maybe that's the way it'd be. But if the monitors are slower, like we're all counting on, they'll *have* to send them. Because fighting us will keep them closer to the planet. They need to stay close to the planet."

She was saying things we already knew, so we all gave her the narrow-eyed 'we're following, go on' look, and she did.

"So, why don't we have *Cyclops* run dark on a separate vector? We go in loud, try to draw the monitors. If they come out, *Cyclops* can roll in behind them, get an advantage. If they don't take the bait, Mik can go bright and then they'll have to."

"But... if we don't go bright, we'll have the advantage of surprise. Maybe," Mik followed the thinking again, and Andrea nodded.

"But if they see you when you're dark, they could jump you without us there to support," Mark added cautiously. To him, this sounded a bit over-complex... and I don't blame him for his sentiment. It was bold.

Mik took a deep breath and nodded, "But might be worth the risk."

"If you're fine with it, I'm fine with it," Mark agreed after that.

"It's derring-do," Matt added.

That was one way to put it, certainly.

The final word was mine, because in the end the Rear Admiral has to make the call — even if his skippers clearly have the situation well in hand.

"Alright," I said a little tenuously. "We'll go that route — parallel courses, timed accelerations to make sure we're near each other in case mutual support is needed. And we draw them out..."

I tapered off for a moment, then scratched my jaw, "And if they don't take the bait, we'll have to go after their battle line, try to maul those monitors from behind before they can get near Greg and Marlene... or the transports."

So that was it: our solution to the *Belgrano* problem, or whatever you want to call it. Each of the elite skippers on the screen and in the room with me nodded at the plan, and then we went on with some specific detail planning — formations, signal protocol, and all manner of other particulars that you needn't trouble yourselves with.

If I'm honest, it all felt relatively good... it was nice not to be fighting Pions, or worrying about derelict ships. The last time we'd actually planned a straight gunfight had been back at Sinope. This was our job — the war we were supposed to fight.

Of course, in the end, it would probably leave more of our people dead than either the Pions or the *Idaho* trap had; doing our actual jobs tended to kill more people than the brutal sideshows. We can never forget that fact.

After the Battlelinks to the other ships in the attack group were closed, I took a deep breath and sat back, "Think we're set, Andrea?"

I'd been expecting a one-word answer — the sort that would conveniently end this scene in my usual style — but instead my Flag Captain frowned and leaned forward, planting her elbows on the desk.

"I think we'll get the job done... and I want to say, you're doing a good job."

I blinked. I was... er. What?

"I just wanted to say that," Andrea nodded earnestly. "I know it must be difficult under the circumstances… but you're settling in very well again."

Um. I realized pretty quickly that she was talking about me getting along without Karen, but for a lot of reasons it sounded odd coming from Andrea. It was clear that she was trying to make an effort… she knew I had to be uncomfortable without Karen around, and she was trying to reassure me.

Nothing that we hadn't done for her, obviously, and a very nice, supportive comment…

But in this context, it did all feel a little weird. I don't know, maybe it's because I don't take compliments well… but it was strange.

And, when I consulted Andrea about it later, I discovered that it felt odd to her too. She was consciously trying to work on 'being normal' at this point, and as we'll see, that was leading to some slightly unusual but quite well-intentioned choices.

As she said, all part of trying to re-learn how to be a normal person. Unfortunately, considering where she was coming from, that wasn't something that could be learned very easily, if at all.

But that's for later. For now, my confused reply: "Er. Glad to hear that…"

She didn't seem to notice my relative surprise, and simply nodded again. Then she stood up and we both left the day cabin.

CHAPTER NINE
SOFT SPOTS

"Is that a grenade launcher?"

Charlie asked that as he walked past Rufus Chang, and the Chinese Major nodded earnestly as he finished tightening the screws that locked the addition onto the underside of his MAG-90's barrel.

"These are coming out brand new from R&D... I had a friend get one shipped to me. I've got a couple of extras too, so we can distribute them."

Nowadays we're pretty accustomed to seeing MAG-90s with all sorts of add-ons — foregrips, underslung launchers, long sniper barrels, and so on. They're pretty popular weapons in all the action movies, and of course they're still standard issue for DCSF and Special Branch. This was the first time all those fancy modifications were being trotted out, though, so Charlie paused to have a look.

"Shoots magbangs?"

Rufus smiled in an all-too-knowing fashion, "Shoots all sorts of things."

Charlie's eyes went from the modified rifle up to Rufus' face, "I'll stick with the stock model, I think."

"Suit yourself," Rufus said happily.

Turning back towards the rifle racks on the wall (sorry, they were in the armory that Special Branch had taken over on *Lady Grace*), Charlie shook his head, "You sure you want to go into a fight with untested kit?"

Rufus practiced handling his rifle with the new addition, and answered casually, "I'll take the chance. I like the ability to throw explosives."

Charlie couldn't really argue with that. Wherever they ended up going in the Mercury Capital Dome, chances were they'd have a lot of Martians to deal with... the ability to shoot things that exploded could certainly be helpful.

But still, Charlie was going to stick with what he knew — wait to see how the new toys did in a fight.

"Looked at the options HQ sent down for us?" he asked, pulling his own rifle from its designated slot on the rack.

Rufus nodded without looking back, "None of them appear very inviting."

They were talking about the suggested breach points that Peri Oktar's staff had sent down to them — places where the pathfinders might go in and secure a foothold for the start of the general assault. There were a dozen possible sites, so I won't bore you with all of them, but I will make a point about what they all had in common: they were bad.

Sorry, that's putting it a little bluntly, so let me explain.

Oktar's staff had picked the air locks and landing bays that seemed 'easiest to secure', based on intelligence that had been gathered about the Mercury Capital Dome. I can't tell you how (go figure) but we did have some maps of the place, and so the staffers had located access points with relatively few connections to the inner dome — fewer entrances for the pathfinders to secure.

That was great in theory, but Charlie and Rufus both saw a couple of problems with those criteria. First of all, if they secured a relatively tight landing zone, and then Special Branchers started pouring through the locks, it would be easier for the Martians to block them in.

Second, if there were only a couple of entrances into the area where the pathfinding teams landed, it would be easy for the Martians to expel them... literally. I mean, think about it: there are only three or four access corridors to an area with an airlock, so what do you do? Drop the pressure doors to those sections, and then open the hatches and let Mercury's completely lethal and virtually non-existent atmosphere kill everyone inside.

"I get the sinking feeling we need to head right for a population centre," Charlie said as he began to strip his rifle. "Only way to be sure they can't decompress us."

"Or bring heavy weapons to bear. Presuming they care about their people enough not to burn them with us."

Charlie frowned at that, but said nothing. He never favored stereotyping or demonizing his adversaries, but there was a genuine concern in what Rufus said: what if the Martians really did put expelling the pathfinders ahead of the lives of their own citizens?

Well, then he'd die.

"They're going to be expecting us to try to take their base first," Charlie thought aloud. "They'll probably have troops and Commandos stacked up in the HQ buildings."

You know how a Defense Command city has a DCHQ building that juts up through the dome, providing the docking connections for ships? The Martians had the same sort of structures sticking out of their domes, though because the domes were on a planet with an atmosphere (albeit a thin one), they weren't used for docking warships, but instead for receiving smaller craft that could more nimbly handle work that close to a grav well. So essentially, they were the same as the HQ buildings on one of our Belt colony domes, just with different types of connectors on the outside.

That meant they were the last place Charlie wanted to be.

Looking up from his grenade-launching MAG-90, Rufus frowned, "Go in on the far side, then? Near those apartments?"

Sorry, we're probably not going to get a map, so let me paint the picture with words. Actually, come to think of it, picture the Io dome, which we did get a map of. The Mercury Capital Dome was similar in that it had the HQ building to the 'north', industrial buildings to the 'west', and residential areas to the 'east' and 'south'. In the middle, though, stood the government structures (instead of shopping and commercial districts).

Rufus was suggesting the teams go in on the opposite side of the dome from the HQ buildings, so on the south side.

"We'll need to secure a staging area over there... somewhere in around the apartment complex, perhaps? If we could secure the ground floors and the roofs, we might be able to make it happen."

On the south side of the dome stood three apartment buildings arranged on the points of a triangle, with a courtyard between them. Beside those buildings was a park, with an airlock behind it. If the Martians left that side lightly defended, the teams could get in, cross the park to the apartments, secure the ground floors and the roofs, and then hold from that position for long enough to allow the rest of the assault force to join them.

"We'd never be able to secure every apartment," Rufus pointed out cautiously.

That was true enough — going room to room through those tall buildings would be virtually impossible...

Which was why the Martians probably wouldn't defend them.

"We'll have surprise on our side. And snipers on the roofs. And secure positions down low," Charlie was musing as he said it. "Could be our best option."

Rufus nodded slowly, "Could be."

Ultimately, it would be the option they settled on, but there were another dozen or so that came up in the next few hours of thinking. No point wasting time on those, though. I can assure you that the one they picked was the best of the bunch, and even then, it wasn't terribly good.

Such was the job they faced as pathfinders.

CHAPTER TEN

REASSURING WORDS

The night before the fleet turned away from the Forge and headed for Mercury, I was eating supper alone in my cabin. It was a very hollow feeling, unsurprisingly... Karen wasn't there on the bed, eating with her usual wit and grace. Charlie wasn't anywhere on the ship either... no offense to Andrea, Jim Hannigan or anyone else aboard, but it just wasn't quite the same knowing those two were gone.

But I was conscious of the fact that their absence was having an effect on me, and I was actually getting frustrated about that. I'll say it over and over: this was certainly not a difficult thing to endure, not by the standards of the war. So I didn't like the fact that it was having an impact on my state of mind.

I was starting to get a bit angry with myself, in a way mildly reminiscent of how I'd been after Kate Levec had been shot in *The Jupiter Patrol*. Yeah I know, not very helpful.

During the days, I was pushing through fine. The attack had to be planned, the crews of the ships in the monitor strike force had to be prepped... lots to keep me occupied. But the evening was the worst. I've always found evening and night can have that effect on me... things that don't seem too daunting during the day get big and scary when the lights go out.

When I was younger, and still on Earth, I just assumed it was a matter of the nighttime darkness playing on my subconscious... but it still happened aboard ship, in the artificial lighting that really doesn't qualify as dark.

I was wondering about that as I ate: why I couldn't just get through an evening without more damned maudlin thinking about how different things were without my old friend Charlie around. And what it was like without Karen.

As I indulged in these questions my screen chimed with a call from the bridge: realtime message coming in. I expected it to be Karen, for obvious reasons, but as I hurriedly grabbed my remote and opened the feed, I realized it wasn't her.

Nope, it was someone else who was experiencing virtually the same inner strife I was.

I think I've effectively conveyed it so far in this series: seeing Lia Hawke when she's not masking her pain is sort of like a punch in the stomach. You know how it is... she can be so bubbly, bright and inappropriately insane, but when she drops the façade, she can wear pain on her face so vividly it hurts to see.

Sorry if that sounds a bit melodramatic, but I stand by it. She'll hate me for writing it in here, but it's true.

And, of course, she had every right to be pained just now: with her father living exclusively on a machine while she won enough publicity points in battle to be able to take over from him. Add to that the fact that the only man she'd ever really loved was preparing for a hell of a mission that could easily get him killed... well. Like I've said, my reasons for being maudlin couldn't compare with hers.

This all crossed my mind as I saw her face, and her fragile expression. I said nothing for a minute or two, which normally would have been awkward, but she knew what I was thinking. She looked away, inappropriately ashamed, and took a deep breath.

"Sorry," she said quietly.

That got me talking, and I shook my head, "Charlie's in exercises?"

She nodded slowly, and looked back at me, "Him and Chang. And I can't interrupt them... I mean, they have to be as ready as they possibly can be, so I can't interrupt him just because I'm feeling nervous. So I'm bothering you instead, because... well..."

"Because you figured I'm in the same state as you, more or less?"

She smiled tenuously, "Less or more. Is Charlie going to survive?"

It was a question she told me later she never could have put to Charlie himself, because she knew he'd have answered honestly: he'd have said 'maybe', or 'probably not'. And those weren't the sorts of things she needed to hear at that moment. She could handle them during the day, but not at night, when the gravity of everything that was coming started to gnaw at her.

"Maybe," I answered. "Probably not."

Obviously, I was not helpful.

She laughed anxiously, the way someone laughs at a joke made at a wake, and looked away again, shaking her head and exhaling shakily.

"This is ridiculous," she scolded herself.

"It's always hardest to keep composure at night. Everything seems so much worse when it's night," I offered quietly. "In the morning, you'll be able to take things in stride a bit better."

Lia closed her eyes briefly, nodded, and looked back, "Yes. Until tomorrow night?"

"Until tomorrow night," I agreed. "Then you'll remember that your dad is gone, and that Charlie could die. The same way I'll remember that Karen's off on another ship, and my best friend could get shot when he sets foot in a Martian dome."

She winced a little at the frank prognosis, and I suppose I could have regretted being so abrupt. But I didn't, and she was just as glad that I didn't sugar-coat it. I find it's always easier to cut straight to the worst case when you're talking about these things. If the worst possible fates go unsaid, it can lead to even more painful mental pictures.

"How much experience will I need for this not to happen anymore?" Lia's next question was a little bit of a surprise, not least because I thought it was clear that I — the so-called veteran — was going through the same sort of process.

I shook my head and sighed, "It never goes away. Not if you're doing your job properly. You always have to fear before the fight... personal things are harder than anything else, but no matter how many times you go into battle, you always have to worry before it starts. Key is not worrying when it happens. Get it out of your system now. Be strong when it counts."

Lia breathed sharply and nodded, "So even my dad. Even Charlie?"

I shrugged, "Probably. Charlie's always handled it a bit differently than me and you. But I think it's pretty common. It's a good thing."

A sharp laugh slipped out of Lady Hawke, "This doesn't feel good."

"Feels like total shit," I agreed, using that last word for effect. "And it'll probably get worse."

Lia laughed again, "Karen's the cheerleader, I guess?"

That got a chuckle out of me, "Yeah, I'll let you tell her she has a new job."

"I can lend her a uniform too—"

I stopped Lia with a raised hand, glad to hear a little of her humor resurfacing… however terrible it was. She smiled slightly more genuinely, perhaps feeling better too, "I don't need to hear about what you'll say to her. You just take care of yourself. And call Charlie. Honestly, I don't think a five-minute interruption is going to make any difference when he storms Mercury."

Her smile faded, and she shook her head, "But what if it does? What if that five minutes of training would have made him a split second quicker, and got him out of the way of a shot?"

A good point.

I had a better one.

"What if being distraught at not getting to talk to you caused him to lose focus with the training, or on the day? That could just as easily get him killed."

She fell silent at that suggestion, and recalling conversations I'd had with my good friend Charlie over the years, I shared a little piece of his personal wisdom.

"Times like this, one of the best things I think you could ever do is just call him to offer some support. It sounds pretty lame, but call him. It'll do you both good."

Biting down on her bottom lip, Lia nodded, then took another breath, "You've talked me into it. I'll blame you if he gets mad."

"He's on another ship. It'll be harder for him to complain," I smiled gently, and Lia mirrored the expression. She was relieved, that was obvious enough: she wanted to talk to him, and I wasn't much of a consolation prize, for completely understandable reasons.

"Talk to you later, then," she said, and with a nod of agreement from me, she disappeared.

I stared at the screen for a while after she closed the link, and sighed. I wanted to talk to Karen now, but she was busy getting her new squadron set up. Instead of calling, then, I went back to my supper, which had gotten cold.

That made it even less appealing. Dinner was now cold and lonely…

Oh God, sorry. I can't end a chapter on that line. That's just way too pathetic and melodramatic. I feel dirty.

But I did feel lonely. And that frustrated me.

The sentiment just wasn't going to pass… for many of us.

Chapter Eleven
Massive Amounts Of Exposition

There was still plenty of cruising time on the voyage out to Mercury, but I think I've covered most of what I wanted to mention. We adjusted course for Mercury once we were reasonably confident that no Martian scouts or media ships were anywhere nearby; we didn't want to tip off the Mercury defenders (or Bort McWebsbert) so we left it as late as we could afford to.

Once we made the turn, we rearranged our formations into their assault groups — remember, for secrecy's sake we had boosted in our pre-mission squadron deployments, so now we formed our new battle groups. To make things simpler later, I'm going to spell all of those out here and now, so you can see who was commanding or attached to what group of ships. If you're really not too worried about the particulars of the squadrons for the fight to come, you might want to skip ahead.

I have to apologize, though: when I listed ships bound for Venus in *The Forge Fires*, I somehow forgot to include *Lady Grace*. Seriously. If you look at page 26 [page 138 of this omnibus edition], there's no mention of Elise De Winter's ship being part of the Jupiter Force, even though I mentioned it getting out of repair dock and rejoining our formation back in *The Canary Wars*. Whoops. But we've triple-checked the following lists, so we're pretty sure they're fine.

So there, I've admitted my mistake. It wasn't the only one from that chapter... I referred to the battleship *Repulse* as the battleship *Rodney*. If you know your Naval history, that's not a completely insane mistake to make... but really, it is a pretty bad error.

Anyway, I apologize. STOP SENDING THE HATE MAIL.

Jeeze.

We begin with Greg and Marlene: they had the main strike force, including *Warspite*, *Goliath*, *Empire*, *Repulse*, and *Sorceress* — five battleships. Greg was overall mission commander, and Marlene was the official commander of this squadron. There was some overlap in terms of their lines of command, but because it was these two that didn't matter so much. Their job, obviously, would be to go toe-to-toe with the five Martian battlewagons, but hopefully not the monitors — we had to keep the monitors off their back.

Lia commanded the main escort group that was to look after Greg and Marlene. This was a powerful force of thirteen frigates: *Whirlwind*, *New York*, *Maine*, *New Hampshire*, *Utah*, *Kodiak*, *Newfoundland*, *Ontario*, *Hunan*, *Guangdong*, *Guangxi*, *Jilin*, and *Alberta*. Her job was to protect the battleships from missile and Interceptor attack, while also providing laser and torpedo support.

An aside here: one of my editors is wondering whether Lia was really ready for this kind of responsibility — thirteen ships and such a huge role — considering she wasn't terribly experienced in combat. A valid concern, honestly, but Lia had helped Mik run the

Hawke Squadron for a couple of years by this time, so she did have a good familiarity with the situation. Would someone like Wes have been more prepared for the job? Definitely. But that was why we needed him protecting the *Bonnie* Squadron. So Lia was stepping up here, and frankly, none of us doubted her.

It didn't hurt, I should add, that she had some very experienced people with her. Jake Lee was still skippering *Kodiak*, and he was undoubtedly the best frigate officer to be posted in Venus space since Daragh had retired. I haven't mentioned him much in these books, but you've probably heard his name in connection with the Forge — he's one of the people who's often suggested as a better alternative to Shauna for defending that place. Luckily, he was spared having to find out whether he could have survived Bort McWebsbert's assault. A very solid officer for Lia to rely on.

Also with the escort group was a good up-and-comer, Sela Kinder. You might remember her from *The Jupiter Patrol*, where she was skippering the communications cruiser *Semaphore*. After returning from that thankless job, she'd been granted her promised promotion and given command of *Guangxi*. Add to that skippers like Kasia Hu from our own *Alberta*, and Jim Devlin, the mischievous skipper of *Newfoundland*, and there was quite the cadre there. A lot of solid help for Lia, if she needed it.

And, of course, Marlene and Greg were going to be nearby if things seriously got out of hand... but as I'll say one more time, none of us believed Lia would be in over her head. She was cut from the same cloth as her dad, and we knew she'd prove that.

Anyway.

Karen had command of the guard force. Her fifteen corvettes were divided into three five-ship groups, each with a senior officer acting as provisional 'group Captain'. Elise De Winter was one, and her team included three Belt Squadron-veterans: *Lady Grace*, *Generous* (Isoruku Togo), and *Sackville* (Katya Romanov), along with *Trusty* (Nancy Whitehorse joined us at Jupiter) and *Adelaide* (Bruce Arama's reservist ship from the Forge).

The venerable Commander Nikhil Jones oversaw the second group: *Amherst*, *June*, *Daisy*, *Helen*, and *Nanton* (commanded by Lisa Sims... recall her from *The Gallant Few*, when she commanded *Admiral Ku* on picket duty, and was promoted immediately thereafter). The last group was headed by Commander Bernd Dozi, who'd been the XO aboard *Sorceress* at the start of the war, and had been moved over to skipper *Gallant* shortly thereafter. His group also included *Noble*, *Sydney*, *Perth* and *Canberra*.

These ships were babysitting the nine-ship troop transport force, which was led by our good friend, Captain Zail Patel. Included in this group were four Defense Command *Goddess*-class combat storeships: *Artemis Agrotera*, *Demeter Erinys*, *Athena Promachos*, and *Persephone Praxidice*. Behind them were five lumbering Imperial Army 'assault vessels', much larger and less maneuverable troop carriers, which I don't think quite do justice to their namesakes: *Fearless*, *Intrepid*, *Albion*, *Bulwark*, and *Ocean*. Between them, these ships carried 30,000 fighting men and women, their equipment, the Imperial Army's vehicles, and the landing craft for the assault.

Obviously, they needed the best protection available, which is why they had Karen looking out for them.

That all just leaves Mik, Mark, Matt, Andrea and me.

Between us, we had *Cyclops*, *Wolf*, *Cheetah* and *Friendly*, and as has already been covered, it was up to us to deal with those two monitors. Fun and joy.

So, to sum up, we were heading to Mercury with a main force of five battleships, thirteen frigates, fifteen corvettes, and nine assault transports, and a detached force (us) of one battleship, two frigates and a corvette. The Martians had five battleships, two monitors, twelve destroyers, and eleven destroyer escorts.

Dizzy yet?

Well, the good news is that's it: that's the total force for both sides. We're ready to get on with things now, so I don't see much point in waiting. I hated the long, long wait before the assault, in large part because I suffered through it alone. I do have one more piece of the story to address before we start the shooting, though…

CHAPTER TWELVE

LATE HOURS

Wolf, Cheetah, Friendly and *Cyclops* split off from the main fleet thirty-six hours before the attack, heading for our separate approach vector against Mercury. As we did that, Mik Mikaelsen took the chance to tour his veteran old battlewagon, and to talk to his crew.

You might remember some of the people on his crew from when they've been mentioned in previous books: namely his XO, Finn Yaalon (formerly Sensors and Communications Officer, since promoted) and his chief engineer, Georgina Yamagawa.

He was visiting the latter now, as he toured the engineering section of his battlewagon.

"You're going to be punching holes in my hull, aren't you?" she asked him with her usual fire.

Mik contemplated briefly pointing out that *Cyclops* wasn't hers, but he knew that would end badly so he stopped himself. Instead he laughed and stroked his goatee, "You know, I just might."

"Figures," Yamagawa said, a little disgustedly. As ever, she looked like a stereotypical ship's engineer — uniform all disheveled, hands covered in dark stains from mechanical grease. She held a rag as she stood opposite her skipper, and was presumably trying to wipe the smears away, though it looked more to Mik like she was just spreading the mess further.

"We could be shot down before we get into this, Georgina," Mik sobered a bit. "I'll need all the speed you've pretended you don't have for all these years. No faking that you're at the red line if we're not, alright?"

She scowled, "If I don't keep a bit in reserve, you'll never think I'm a magician."

Mik laughed sharply, "Maybe only Scottish engineers can be miracle workers."

Yamagawa glared a little, "No reserve, you'll get it all up front."

That drew a nod from Mik, and he took a deep breath.

"So, boss, we going to pull this off?" Yamagawa asked that question frankly, and Commodore Mikaelsen stroked his goatee again.

It took him a moment to choose his phrasing, then he gave an honest answer: "I think we'll kill the monitors. I don't know if we'll survive."

For all her prickliness, Yamagawa appreciated the frank assessment, and she nodded, "Yeah."

"But," Mik added with a shrug, "I don't want to be dead. So I think we'll try to avoid that."

"It's always about what you want, isn't it boss?"

Mik laughed, "Well, it is *my* ship, isn't it Commander Yamagawa?"

"Bullshit," she muttered, and walked away.

Cyclops was ready for a fight.

✦✦✦

Mark Gunney leaned back in his chair and lifted his glass of scotch in a toast, "Good luck for tomorrow."

Sitting across from him was Erica Martin, *Cheetah's* XO (and, as I'm sure you'll recall, *Wolf's* former Helm and Navigation Officer). She smiled and lifted her similar glass in reply, "Cheers."

They'd just finished having a final supper, and now a glass of scotch would send them off to bed. Er. Wait.

Sorry, I just realized that could be misread. They were not involved with each other — Morgan Martin and their kids would have been shocked to hear it if they had been. Moreover, Mark certainly wasn't Erica's type, in a whole lot of ways… and one thing about him that I hope has come across so far in these books: he never lets any sort of liaison get in the way of doing his job.

No, skipper and XO were having a last meal together before the big day — a last chance to talk about the plans for the coming battle, to make sure they were completely on the same page in case one of them was killed or wounded, and then to relax a bit in familiar company.

It had been a good meal, and now as they laid their empty glasses down on the table, Erica let out a breath, "Well, we'll have stories for the grandkids."

Mark smiled, "I already have stories. I don't have the kids to get me the other thing. Yet."

Erica chuckled, "I keep offering my sister. She thinks you're dreamy."

"Despite everything you tell her?" came the quick counter.

"She's not really that bright," Erica shrugged.

"You know my type," Mark grinned.

"I'm a good XO."

He chuckled, "Alright, I'll make a deal with you. If we live to the end of the war, I'll have dinner with your sister."

"You say that as if it'd be a chore."

"Well she's related to you, Erica. But I'll suspend my better judgment. As long as I don't get killed, and you don't."

Erica paused thoughtfully and frowned, "I don't know, dinner might go better for her if you were dead."

"Undoubtedly. I won't make any rigor mortis and hardness jokes, because I'm in mixed company."

Erica laughed again, and Mark sat back, satisfied that he'd managed to inject some good humor into the conversation. Tomorrow there wouldn't be time for a laugh, but he enjoyed cutting the tension while he could. These two would be ready for the assault.

Andrea was sitting in the dark, as she'd done so many times since leaving Egesta. She wasn't contemplating shooting herself (thank God), or even figuring on how to get someone else to kill her. Instead, she was focusing on two things: slowing down her breathing, and focusing her mind.

She was determined that, tomorrow, she wouldn't do anything rash — nothing that would get *Wolf* destroyed — unless it was absolutely necessary. There was no question in her mind, or mine, that our brave ship might have to die in this coming fight... but she wasn't going to ram one of the monitors the way she'd rammed *Utopia Planetia* with *Dominator* at Sinope...

Not unless she absolutely had to, anyway.

This was what she was focusing on, a goal that she could use to keep some of the regular flashbacks at bay. She had something very important to keep her mind occupied, and for this night, in the last hours before the fight, that was enough to lock her into the here and now.

She appreciated that, and it left her relatively confident in her combat judgment for the fight that was coming.

But she had no idea what her state of mind would be like after the fight was over — when she had nothing pressing to focus on. Hopefully some of the certainty would stay. Hopefully...

She meditated (more or less) on the possibilities, alone in the dark of her cabin.

Matt Baxter was sitting in his cabin alone, reading a book.

There's absolutely nothing special about this — Matt was an avid reader. But since I've mentioned the other skippers, I feel like I really should include Matt... and as is typical for him, he was all self-contained and sensible the night before the big fight.

Competent bastard.

So as I said, he was reading a book, and shaking his head at some of the absurdities. Apparently it was an old one, which speculated about a race of aliens that were in fact humanoid wolves, cats and bears. I can't remember the particulars, he only mentioned it to me in passing.

It sounds ridiculous.

By which I mean I'm sure it's actually quite good, and something people who like reading my reminiscences from this war would probably enjoy very much.

I'll bet a wolf Admiral wouldn't be as grim as I was. Well, maybe.

Sorry, that was my attempt at transitioning to the last check-in location. Yeah, with me...

I'd rewatched the message a few too many times. Or a few dozen too many.

It was foolish, but that sure didn't stop me.

"So we're all set over here," Karen said on the screen. Because we'd parted company with the main body of the assault fleet, she was well out of realtime range now.

She looked down, then up again.

"Be careful, as if saying that means anything. I'll do the same. I... well. You know. This will be done by this time tomorrow, hopefully. And then... then it'll be done. You know."

No, she wasn't making much sense. And no, I couldn't have cared any less.

She smiled her least convincing smile and the signal froze again. There wasn't much to this message, as you can see. And yet it spoke volumes.

So I watched it again and again, drawing a little more reassurance from it each time. Not much, but enough to quiet my brain for a while.

I still had to worry about tomorrow, and the fight, but this was a good distraction. Just for a little while… a longer while, because I kept watching it over and over.

Eventually, though, I had to stop.

When that moment came, I opened a new message for recording, and marked it secure for Karen.

Looking at the viewfinder in my wall, I took a deep breath, smiled, and gave my simple answer: silence. What the hell could I say? I just smiled, then let that fade. My chin sunk a bit, but I looked up again and smiled one more time.

Then I managed a tiny bit more: "Til tomorrow."

That was my message to Karen. It was the truth. That was about all I had.

Wolf and our attack group hurried towards Mercury, and the biggest planetary assault in human history.

And without further ado, I think we have to get shooting. Let's see how many of us survived…

CHAPTER THIRTEEN

LINKING IN

The biggest surprise I faced when I woke up on the morning of the attack was that I'd slept at all. I ended up with a very luxurious five hours of shut-eye that night, despite the stress and concern. I chalked it up to my subconscious taking a firm grasp of my brain and making certain I had the rest I needed to do my job.

Maybe I was just sleepy.

By the time I reached the bridge at 0520, *Wolf* and our group were about three hours out of Mercury space, meaning the main force was about two hours and fifty minutes out, on a different vector. Andrea arrived on the bridge just a few minutes before I did, Jim Hannigan and Felicia Khalid just after. Shelby McLaws, who'd had the overnight watch, resumed her post at Helm and Navigation. She'd have a long morning, but had slept late during the previous day-shift to make sure she had some energy reserves for the fight.

None of us were particularly talkative as our minds warmed up for action.

That didn't mean we were silent, just efficient with words.

"Felicia, let's bring up Battlelink with the group," was my first order as our Sensors and Communications Officer took up her post.

Nodding, she tapped the shoulder of a technician near her, and the requests for secure realtime uplinks were passed along to *Cheetah, Friendly* and *Cyclops*.

I moved to the front of the bridge and Andrea joined me, folding her arms as she did. Loading screens began to pop up on various monitors, and then faces began to appear.

Matt Baxter was first, because he'd been up half an hour before any of us, and he nodded stiffly, "Morning. We're all set."

"Excellent," I replied, in no way surprised by the report. I mean, it was Matt aboard my old ship… come on, how were they not going to be ready?

Mark Gunney appeared next, with a nod and a small grin, "All set for this very well-conceived mission to certain victory?"

"It's early for sarcasm, isn't it Mark?" Andrea raised her eyebrow and countered dryly.

"Are you implying that we're not going to win, Captain Kiley?" Mark's grin widened. Then he shook his head, "It's never too early for sarcasm."

I glanced at Andrea, then at Mark, and then shrugged without comment. Mik appeared next, making that lack of comment seem less awkward.

"Hey hey," *Cyclops'* Commodore and skipper greeted us with a nod. "We're all warming up over here. Prepared to start moving in?"

I had an answer to that: "Definitely. We'll part company in… ninety minutes. Pre-established vectors."

Everyone nodded — by now there really wasn't much creativity needed. We knew all the particulars of how we were going to get into action… the innovation and ingenuity would come when the battle actually began.

That was a few hours away, so in the meantime we'd stick to the deployment plans…
We weren't the only ones.

Captain Val Rodriguez was still Greg Noyce's Flag Captain in *Warspite*, and she nodded to her Admiral as he appeared on the battleship's bridge.

"We're getting Battlelink to squadron set up now, boss," she nodded in greeting.

"Excellent," Greg answered simply, heading to the front of his bridge.

Marlene appeared almost as soon as he reached sight of the Battlelink monitors, a wry smile on the Sorceress' face, "Morning, Greg."

"Good morning," he smiled in return. "Everything set up on schedule?"

"It is. I'm enjoying seeing all these late-sleepers up so early."

Chuckling, Greg nodded, "I suppose so, indeed."

On her bridge, Marlene chuckled as well. As she did, the skippers from her battleship squadron appeared on Battlelink — Liam Singh of *Empire*, Emma Nelson of *Repulse*, and Becky Afflighen of *Goliath*. Kyle Feldman, *Sorceress'* Flag Captain, was standing beside her.

"Morning everyone," Marlene nodded to the newly-connected Captains, and they each offered their own quick greetings in reply.

Because Greg would be commanding the overall battle, Marlene was going to be giving direct orders to the battleships during the coming fight; hence them turning up on her screens instead of Greg's on *Warspite*.

Just as this was finished setting up, then, another face appeared.

Lia Hawke wore a bright, well-practiced smile as she nodded to Marlene, "Morning Auntie Witch, Uncle Greg."

Because Lia was both a squadron commander and tasked specifically with protecting the battleships, she was Battlelinked to both Marlene on *Sorceress* and Greg on *Warspite*. As she watched both those Admirals appear on her bridge screens aboard *Whirlwind*, she put her hands on her hips and looked confident.

She didn't *try* to look confident, she simply looked confident.

With Lia, as you well know, there's no 'trying' to look anything. Her façades are perfect, and they successfully hid any suggestion that she had not slept at all the night before.

Because she certainly hadn't.

The skippers from her frigate force were appearing on *Whirlwind's* screens around the two Admirals as she greeted them — Captains like Jake Lee of *Kodiak*, Sela Kinder of *Guangxi*, and Taya Prescott of *New York*. They exchanged greetings with their Flag Officer for the day, and none would have thought that Lia had a doubt in the world.

She's very good.

While Lia was connecting in, so was Karen.

She, like me, had managed to sleep, despite all the reasons she would have had not to. Unflappable and goddess-like… you know the drill, she was completely and absolutely perfect in every respect, even the ones she clearly wasn't perfect in.

Sorry, that's not really applicable to the current chapter, but I do like to say it now and again. Never hurts to remember it.

Standing on *Lady Grace's* bridge, she nodded first to Greg Noyce as she patched into *Warspite's* network.

"Good morning," she said simply, and he answered in kind.

"Good morning, Karen."

"We're up and running," she confirmed quickly, and he nodded his reply.

Skippers from Elise De Winter's escort group started appearing on screens next — Nancy Whitehorse of *Trusty*, Isoruku Togo of *Generous*, Katya Romanov of *Sackville*, and of course, Bruce Arama aboard *Adelaide*.

Elise greeted each of them first, and then Karen said a few familiar words as well, offering warm smiles.

Next to appear were Nikhil Jones from *Amherst* and Bernd Dozi aboard *Gallant*, Karen's two other group captains. Because it was a fifteen-ship force, there was no way Karen could have every skipper on Battlelink, so those two would answer to her for their own five-ship units.

Finally, Captain Zail Patel appeared, completing the communications network.

"Good morning, Commodore McMaster," he said with a polite smile. "Our landing forces are ready to go."

"Good news," Karen smiled back.

At the same time, Zail appeared on Greg's monitors on *Warspite*, completing his Battlelink connections to the heads of his various formations. Only Mik and I, being out of realtime range, weren't on the network.

Now, I realize I've just spent a fair amount of time talking about communications, but I did it for a reason (not just to bore you, though some may argue that point).

This was the most complicated communications network ever put together for an active operation. It really forced everyone involved to strategically choose who to have on active Battlelink, and required Greg, for instance, not to have access to most of his ships' skippers.

Because Defense Command usually operates in much smaller formations, every ship can often be represented on the Battlelink screens during a fight — the way all four ships in our separate assault group were linked to each other. The benefit of this is that it makes it easy for the commander to communicate his or her intent to everyone involved.

But the size of this operation meant very clearly that Greg had to delegate — something he knew how to do, but something that would be an adjustment all the same. If he saw a problem that a corvette should deal with, he couldn't just look over to Bruce Arama and say 'go after that'. He'd have to tell Karen, and she'd have to select a ship to go and deal with it.

Now, we know that the core commanding officers here all worked well together, and as such should have no problem making those delegations happen, but I still think it's very important to point out the new layer of complexity involved.

And it is always good to remember that added complexity during a battle can lead to unfortunate consequences. Clear communication is key. Remember what happened when Shauna Cass and Jens Holbrook failed to understand each other about tracking

Bort McWebsbert's force in the last book? Yeah, we definitely couldn't afford to have that happen today.

But fortunately for us, this was a hell of a team of Flag Officers. They were confident, and so was I.

That being the case, we best move on to the first stages of the fight.

CHAPTER FOURTEEN

THE LONGEST MINUTES

I hate bluffing in a battle.

In movies, it always seems like a dynamic and effective way to get the enemy to do exactly what you want, but I think script writers often fail to realize how hard that really is. Just because you dangle a carrot (or a three-ship raiding force) in front of a pair of monitors doesn't mean they'll come running. That's one of many reactions they might have.

But we needed them to come running. If they didn't, this whole plan was bust and we'd have to scramble to join the main action, to offset their extra firepower against the battle line.

So for all appearances of calm, I spent the next two and a half hours more than a little anxious about what was to come.

As planned, *Cyclops* split off from *Cheetah*, *Wolf* and *Friendly* ninety minutes short of detection range, and cut its drives to coast towards Mercury as subtly as a battleship can ever coast. We pushed on at 180 kps, working our way a little further around so that we could approach from a different vector.

If I had a map, I could show you exactly what that meant, but once again my heinously cheap publishers won't pay to have one made. I offered to draw one for them on the back of a napkin, but that didn't go over well. So we have to work with a mental picture again...

Alright, imagine Mercury is at the center of a wheel, and we're all traveling towards it. Our courses are like spokes on that wheel. *Cyclops* had turned at a spoke and started in towards the planet, but was coasting unpowered. We kept going along the outer wheel, but at higher speed. Soon we'd turn at another spoke, and accelerate down it, so that *Cyclops* and our group would be roughly the same distance from Mercury when *Wolf*, *Cheetah* and *Friendly* were detected.

Meanwhile, Greg and the main force were going to be coming in on a spoke roughly halfway around the wheel, from a completely opposite direction.

Hope that helps.

"Coming up to our turn," Shelby McLaws warned us all that our course change was at hand, which meant we were about half an hour from detection.

I nodded, then looked up at Mark and Matt (Mik was too far out now for Battlelink), "We're riding straight in now."

"Hopefully the Martians are obliging," Matt said.

That drew a chuckle from Mark, "Isn't that the first thing they teach us at the Academy: the enemy will do exactly what you need him to do, when you need him to do it, to make your life easier?"

"I seem to remember that lecture," I managed to match humor with humor.

Andrea hadn't been paying us much heed; she moved over towards the Helm and

Navigation consoles and nodded to Shelby, "Make the turn at your discretion."

A moment later, *Wolf's* port thrusters fired to adjust overall vector, and we started accelerating in towards Mercury.

"Course change complete. We'll be on their scopes in thirty minutes," Shelby's report was as smooth as ever. We were plunging right in…

Mik sat in his chair, stroking his goatee, watching the icons of ships on *Cyclops'* main screen. The icons of our three ships turned before his eyes, and then his Sensors and Communications Officer chimed in with the official update: "They've made the turn, sir, right on schedule."

Nodding, Mik took a breath. The plan was in play now… and in about twenty minutes Greg's force was going to come barreling in from the opposite flank, making a lot of noise and drawing the main resistance from the Mercury Squadron.

And then there'd be the fight with the monitors…

Another deep breath, and Mik closed his eyes for a minute, then opened them to look at the chrono on the wall. It seemed as though the seconds were taking an awfully long time to tick past.

He wasn't impressed.

I'll attempt to paraphrase him: 'Time = FAIL when waiting for battle.' Or does he call it Captain of the 'failboat'? Can't recall. He's very proficient with some arcane idioms, and unfortunately I am not.

But the overall sentiment is absolutely right.

Tick.

A billion Mississippis.

Tock.

Greg was much less contemptuous of time as he folded his arms. He stood squared off at the front of *Warspite's* bridge, watching as the icons of all the Defense Command ships in the area hurtled towards Mercury.

Yes, *all* the ships, including ours, even though we were coming in from a different vector. My editors are bugging me to know how this was possible, because the entire point of this strategy was that we were outside of sensor range of Mercury and each other until we got much closer.

I can't tell you how. The same way I couldn't tell you how the corvette *Melbourne* had somehow made us aware of the existence of the monitors. Because I haven't mentioned *Melbourne* or its detection abilities at all in this book, and I still can't elaborate. As I said last time, do you think Defense Command Research and Development would allow commercial sensor technology to match our own?

Or maybe they had a wizard aboard.

If you look at the lists of ships involved in this fight, *Melbourne* hasn't been assigned to any squadron, but the ship was *somewhere*. And its ability to see things… its magical ability for seeing things much farther away than is possible, was somewhere too.

Have I said enough without saying too much?

So Greg was watching the icons of all our ships powering in towards Mercury with a sense of serene certainty: battle was about to be joined.

That helped the clock on his wall move at regular speed.

Apparently, though, the clocks on *Lady Grace* were suffering from the same problems as the ones on *Cyclops*. Karen never stopped looking cool and confident — you can check the fleet archives if you doubt me... but come on, it's Karen. You don't doubt me.

But time still ran slow as she stood with arms folded and watched Mercury grow larger on her screens.

Bruce Arama, our excellent reservist skipper from Auckland, made a note of that fact out loud, "So, I shouldn't ask, but is it customary for this waiting to seem ridiculously long? It did at the Forge, but I thought it'd be a little better here."

Nancy Whitehorse smiled at her Maori counterpart, "Bruce, believe me, there are worse waits to sit through."

She was referring, I believe, to the seven months she'd spent out at Jupiter, waiting for us to turn up to recapture the Io base. I think she had a point, and being a sharp fellow, Bruce agreed. Though being a reservist, his example was different.

"Right, good point. I spent nearly thirty hours with my wife when she was in labor with our second daughter. Longest wait ever."

"And you didn't even have to do the work," Katya Romanov grinned at him, and Bruce laughed.

"That's a good point too. So basically, I shouldn't complain."

Everyone laughed, and Karen smiled smoothly.

They pushed on towards Mercury.

Tick.

A trillion Mississippis.

Tock.

But the long wait was soon to be over.

Which is good, because I don't think I could drag this out any longer.

CHAPTER FIFTEEN
IN THEIR SHOES

They saw Greg first.

That hadn't been guaranteed; although Greg could see us, we couldn't see him, and there was no way to absolutely coordinate our speeds. We knew the plan was for him to appear ten minutes before us, but plans don't always work.

Here, that proved the case: they saw us only seventy seconds later. So before any of the Martians could have made a decision about how to deploy to face Greg, they were confronted by two incoming forces.

I've tried many times to put myself in the shoes of the Martian commander when we turned up. What must have been going through his mind?

First, his intelligence section had been saying for weeks that Bort McWebsbert had successfully drawn our ire — that we were going after the Forge. Seeing us appear on his doorstep with the largest formation of space-faring warships ever assembled was probably a cold bucket of water.

Second, he had tactical decisions to make — and relatively quickly. When we entered Martian sensor range, we were about two hours away from landing range (they couldn't see us any further out due to crude sensors… and, admittedly, heavy interference due to our proximity to the sun). There was no real time for him to sit around and complain to his subordinates about how he'd been had.

Action was necessary.

But what could the Martian commander do?

This is the question we'd been asking ourselves all through the planning process, obviously — what would his deployment be, and for Mik, Mark, Matt (so tempted to start saying '3M') and me, where would he send the monitors?

It was not an easy decision. I think I know what I would have done under the circumstances, though I'm possibly prejudiced by knowing what happened, and also by what I wanted him to do. Perhaps that's happened to you sometime in life: you strongly believe someone should do something, so when you try to put yourself in their shoes, you see things in such a way that makes your preference the logical answer. That could be happening to me right now, so take my assessment of what I would have done with a grain of salt.

Were it me, I would have looked at Greg's assault force and realized I needed to stop it well short of the planet. I'd have paid specific attention to the transports: if I blasted them away, there'd be no landing forces, so even if I lost the space battle, the domes might hold out long enough for a rescue.

I'd have looked at the second incoming group (3M and me) with some suspicion, wondering whether it was carrying something unexpected — a new weapon, a raiding force… anything I wasn't ready for. My confidence in my own intelligence services would be quite low, since they'd been telling me that the Forge was the target, so I'd be wary and suspicious. That being the case, I'd send some of my ships out to stop the second group.

But which ships?

Well, I'd know my monitors were slower, so they couldn't keep up with my battle line when I headed out to deal with Greg. I'd also figure that the nature of the monitors' firepower — their battleship lasers in a destroyer-sized hull — might still be a secret that Defense Command didn't know about. Though because of the failure of my own intel people, I might be suspicious that DC had gotten a better picture of what the monitors were.

Still, they were the only ships to send, under the circumstances: all my other escorts would be needed to screen for the battle line, or to attack the transports carrying the landing force. The monitors and their firepower would have undoubtedly helped a lot in a battleship duel, but they just couldn't keep up.

Monitors were a great stop-gap solution when you couldn't finish battleships... but they just weren't battleships.

So my answer would have been simple: move my main force out to meet the oncoming Defense Command assault, and send the monitors to deal with the pair of frigates and the corvette I saw coming in on another vector.

I'd be strongly suspicious that there was more to this than I could see, but that wouldn't matter. Decisions had to be made.

And they were.

The Martian commander did exactly what I would have done. I don't know if his thought process was the same as mine, but let me tell you, it was a huge relief when we watched the icons of his ships (now visible thanks to our own shipboard sensors) moving the ways we wanted them too.

I know, ridiculous to be relieved to see two mini-battleships coming your way, quite possibly to blow you out of space, but you know what I mean.

One of my editors has asked whether this Martian commander should have been punished for playing into our hands. Personally, I wouldn't think so... confronted with scenarios like this, I always recall the Marquis de Montcalm.

Here we go, a historical aside.

In the battle for Quebec in 1759, Montcalm was the defender, going up against British General James Wolfe. Quebec sits on the St. Lawrence river, and famously, Wolfe crossed that waterway and landed troops to threaten the city's flank. In response, Montcalm marched his troops out from behind the defensive walls to face the British on open ground, on the Plains of Abraham. He and Wolfe both died in the ensuing engagement, and Quebec was more or less defeated, to become a future part of Canada.

Unsurprisingly, Montcalm was bashed for centuries by historians and armchair generals, because he should have stayed behind the walls.

What I've always thought, though, is that Montcalm made the best decision he could under the circumstances. His city had been under bombardment for months from gun positions across the river. His troops were in rough shape and his city was already being rendered into dust. When Wolfe appeared on the Plains of Abraham, there was every possibility that the British were going to fortify a position, bring up artillery, and flatten

Quebec from point-blank range.

Montcalm thus decided to take a risk: he had to throw the British off the Plains of Abraham and back into the river before they could establish a defensive position.

His risk didn't work.

Nevertheless, I can understand the thought process, and I can sympathize. Sometimes I think the best military commanders are the ones who can force their opponent into having to make decisions like those — decisions with no right answer, just answers that seem a little less likely to bring defeat.

Greg and Marlene obviously qualify as two of those 'best military commanders', because this was their assault, and they had the Martians in a corner, doing exactly what we wanted them to do.

As I stood on *Wolf's* bridge and watched the icons of those two monitors coming at us, I let out a long breath.

"So, they did do exactly what we wanted them to do. How kind," Matt Baxter said dryly.

I glanced up at the screens, "Yes they did. Let's hope they're the ones who regret it."

Now we had a fight on our hands. A real hell of a fight.

CHAPTER SIXTEEN

MAIN FORCE ACTION

Greg had the main force arranged in a logical fashion: Lia and the frigates were up front, screening for the battleships and surrounding themselves with clouds of Starlights. The battleship line was obviously next, and then trailing a little ways behind was the transport force, with Karen looking after them.

For the next hour, they closed on Mercury at full speed, while the Mercury Squadron came out to meet them at their own maximum velocity. Because the monitors were slower than the battle line, these two main forces would meet before we met our two opponents. That being the case, I'm going to pay attention to the main action first, and then we'll see how the rest played out.

Folding his arms as the Martians got close to battle range, Greg looked up at his squadron commanders on *Warspite's* screens.

"Ladies and gentlemen, I wish you all good luck," he said simply.

I believe the last time he'd said that before action was at the Battle of Deep Black, which we'd won handily.

There were no immediate responses, because as he said it, Sensors and Communications Officers on the bridges of all the flagships started their final countdowns.

"Weapons range in ninety seconds."

Because battleships had longer range, Lia's escorts and Greg's battleships would both hit the engagement envelope at the same time. This was by design — Lia had put her screening forces out far enough ahead to make sure that would be the case.

Standing on the bridge of *Whirlwind*, Lady Hawke now took a deep breath and looked up at her skippers.

"Alright everyone, let's do a good job. When we get into range, I want a lot of lights. And a lot of dead Martians."

She was definitely channeling her father right there.

Shifting her eyes to Greg's screen, she retained that cool mentality, "Uncle Greg, we'll engage the escorts as soon as we have range on them, then get out of your firing tracks."

Had she been more accustomed to commanding a squadron screening force, Lia probably wouldn't have felt the need to actually say that. Still, the clarification of her orders was neither a nuisance nor unappreciated. Greg nodded on the screen.

"Excellent, thank you Lia."

On *Sorceress'* bridge, Marlene narrowed her eyes and then looked to her battleship skippers, "Lia will clear the little fish out of the way for us. We'll engage our matching battleships as we get into range. Shoot clean."

The veteran battleship skippers, all of whom had seen action during Glorious

February, nodded in agreement.

Remember, Liam Singh had been Rachel Butler's Flag Captain during that Martian attack on Earth, and Emma Nelson had been part of the Heavy Squadron. Becky Afflighen and Val Rodriguez had attacked Mars with Greg shortly thereafter… these were skippers who knew very well how to fight.

"Range in thirty seconds."

Karen waited on *Lady Grace's* bridge with her arms folded and her pulse thumping just a little. Because her corvettes were tied to the landing ships, they'd be doing everything they could to avoid the cloud of battle that was about to be created. They'd sit back and avoid contact until an opportunity presented itself to go around, and then they'd rush headlong for Mercury.

"Squadron stand by to reduce speed and adjust course," she ordered as she watched.

Twenty seconds.

Time seemed to be running regular speed again. Would this go as planned?

Fifteen seconds.

Did the Martians have something up their sleeve… a new weapon like they'd had at the Forge?

Ten seconds.

Was this hastily-organized assault force going to be able to do the job?

Five seconds.

No time left to worry about it.

Zero seconds.

Light show.

"Open fire," Lia's voice was firm, and her ships' shooting was solid.

Some of these frigates were independent Belt cruisers that had been schooled by both Lia and Mik over the years, and some were veterans of the Empire's elite squadrons. Others were reservist ships in their first-ever fight. That being the case, there was a mixed bag of hits as the thirteen frigates engaged the twelve destroyers that were screening out ahead of the red battle line.

Alberta, for instance, drove a laser shot right down the throat of the destroyer it had been tasked with engaging; the Martian vessel shuddered first, then an internal explosion shattered its power grid, and it fell off, spiraling away into the black.

Jake Lee's *Kodiak* had similar success. Direct hits were notched up by the usual suspects, too: Lia's own *Whirlwind*, Sela Kinder's *Guangxi*, and Jim Devlin's *Newfoundland*.

Two destroyers were put out of action, three others absorbed some heavy punishment, and another six took some sort of grazing hit. Not a bad first salvo at all.

As lasers recharged, Lia nodded to her skippers again, "Break by division, let's avoid as much of their counter-fire as we can. Watch for missiles."

Pulling apart in pairs, her frigates began to either raise or drop, giving the battleships free room to open fire. The Martian destroyers were going to be in range any second… here they came.

The counter-fire was not nearly the blinding onslaught that Lia had sent out, but it was still considerable. Because the frigates had separated, it was not as easy to concentrate fire against them, but the energy fire from those damned red turrets still chased some of them down.

Jilin was the first to take a hit, and once the ship was clipped it drew the fire of a second destroyer. One of its pods was quickly sliced off, and it dropped back, unable to keep up with the fight.

Things were worse for *New Hampshire*: the frigate got caught by two destroyers who were shooting as a pair, and the lasers cut right through to its reactors. Before anyone could get close to lifeboats, the ship was blown to pieces.

Lia and the frigates had taken out two destroyers: the Martians had returned the favor.

By this time, though, Lia's ships' lasers were recharged and ready to go again.

"Open fire at will. Stand by for deceleration and course adjustments," Lia gave her order, and as she did, her XO gave the command.

"Shoot!"

Whirlwind clipped the same destroyer that it had pounded before, and the Martian recognized its opponent and changed course to charge straight at the Hawke Force vessel. *Whirlwind's* division partner was *New York*, Taya Prescott's ship from the Hawke Squadron, and seeing the oncoming charge, that ship adjusted her fire to take on the attacker.

Between them, the two frigates sliced the Martian's bow pod in two, forcing it to turn away under cover of its stern lasers, and to limp back towards Mercury.

Another minor victory.

But now the range was closing, and the main event was at hand. As ever, battleships fighting each other make legions of frigates and destroyers seem entirely inconsequential.

I said it in *The Gallant Few*, and it's no less true here: when battle lines come to fight, everyone else better get the hell out of the way.

Standing on her bridge with her arms folded, Marlene was about to prove me right about this.

"Range in five seconds."

"Everyone open fire as soon as you're ready," our Sorceress said very coolly, her eyes narrow. Given the caliber of the skippers of her squadron, she didn't have to do anything more than give them clearance: these men and women were ready to deliver punishment.

Beside Marlene, Kyle Feldman turned back to his XO, "Fire when you have the range, Lijun."

A moment later, the order rang out: "Shoot!"

Battleship lasers began flying, and as ever it was a chilling and awesome sight.

CHAPTER SEVENTEEN
TITANS

Greg was watching the developments in silence, his eyes drifting from one section of *Warspite's* main screen to another as he watched his formations maneuver and engage. His mind was, as ever, assessing the tactical ramifications of every movement made, predicting the Martian actions, and coming up with counter-moves.

Beside him, Val Rodriguez was fighting her ship. *Warspite's* veteran lasers had done epic damage to the Martian war effort during the raid on their home planet, and now they were savaging the battleship opposite them. Greg didn't need to worry about how that was going — that was Val's job — so he tuned it out.

He was totally focused on the overall picture.

All of the shots from his battleships' lasers hit their counterparts, but at maximum range they hadn't done too much harm. A good first smack, but the Martians had been ready, and had spun to shrug off the fire. This wasn't going to be quite so 'easy' as Glorious February had been — as much as I don't like admitting it, our enemy had learned from their mistakes, and gone to school on our tactics.

They were more ready for this fight than any other they'd yet been a part of...

Well, except for Bort McWebsbert's attack on the Forge. But I don't classify Bort with the rest of his fleet — different calibers altogether.

Either way, the fire of five Defense Command battleships didn't kill or seriously wound any of the Martians in that first salvo. As the laser shots ended, the range continued to drop.

The Martian lasers were about to come into range, and the moment they did Greg's line would have to start shifting to avoid the worst of their fire...

And then there was the next question: would the red ships slow down? It seemed unlikely... they'd probably maintain their high acceleration in hopes of passing right through his battle line, and getting a chance to attack the transports further to the rear.

He'd have to make sure they were stopped.

"Marlene, prepare to break formation. If they try to get past us, I want each of us to latch on to one of them, and keep them from getting to the transports. Lia, prepare your frigates for melee combat support."

He said that with the same calm you'd expect of a man giving directions about how to bake a pie. Or something else equally mundane... that was the best I could think of.

Lia looked up, "Yes uncle."

Marlene's eyes remained narrowed, "We'll break line?"

"I think so," Greg nodded.

That was enough for Marlene; she passed on the orders. It was a slightly unorthodox approach — hence her question. One of the tenets of battle-line warfare was that you held your formation and reduced speed collectively to maintain the engagement. Mutual fire support, point defense, screening… all of that comes from a solid formation.

But Greg had come up in the Belt Squadron, and out there you do learn to be selective about the textbook tactics. I don't think I've emphasized that as much in recent books, but being a bit of a maverick could indeed pay off… even in combat.

For instance, Greg had won at Deep Black (against Grant Merger's Syndicate) because he'd cut all of us loose of our squadron formation, and let us hunt on our own. Now, frigates and corvettes against pirates was a different fight than battleships against battleships, but the reality here was that Greg needed to make sure nothing got past him to our transports. Not even Karen could make a line of corvettes stop a battlewagon.

So he was pulling a page from his classic playbook — one he hoped the Martians hadn't read.

"Martians entering range… now."

Val Rodriguez was all over that warning, and she looked to her Helm and Navigation Officer, "Hear that, HNO? Free and clear to maneuver."

The Lieutenant Commander replied with a smile and nod: not being locked into a battle line offered him many more options for dodging to keep *Warspite* out of trouble. Martian lasers began to sail in, but already the five battleships of Marlene's squadron were coordinating via nav computers and shifting their positions to evade.

"Shoot!" Val Rodriguez ordered almost at the same time that *Warspite* began to slide away from incoming fire.

The second burst of angry red energy erupted from the ship's pair of bow emitters, and quickly raked the counterpart it had been targeting. Still the Martian didn't slow, and cruising in close to it were a pair of destroyers.

Lia took note of those, and dispatched one of her own divisions to get the interlopers out of the way. Greg watched with a frown: the Martians were holding formation, driving straight at the space where his line had been solid a moment before. Marlene's battlewagons would simply have to fall on them, like a pack of wolves on a pride of lions.

"Isolate fire and close on your counterparts," Marlene gave that order to her skippers, virtually reading Greg's mind.

"Divisions break and escort your pre-assigned divisions. All fighter squadrons stick close for anti-missile defense. Hold torpedoes until I give the order…" Lia was, as I expected, falling effortlessly into her job.

The situation rapidly took on a different look: five battleships, each at the center of its own cloud of fighters and pair of frigates, began charging at the Martians, who were getting closer and threatening to pass.

They'd break up the Martian formation come hell or high water…

"Looks like they're going to try to blow straight through to us," Karen observed quietly from *Lady Grace's* bridge, then frowned. "Time for us to go around."

The troopships and their escort had reduced speed to a relative crawl as the fight began, ready to turn about in case things somehow went badly. But now that the Martian heavies and destroyers were about to be caught up in a big, brutal dogfight with Greg's main force, there was room to get past them.

While the titans were fighting, the enterprising corvettes and their charges could tip-toe around and get to Mercury without too much difficulty…

Just the destroyer escorts to deal with.

Karen took a breath as she looked at the icons of that cloud of little Martian ships: eleven of them to her fifteen corvettes. They were hanging back behind the battleship engagement, much as Karen's formation was, undoubtedly waiting so that they could move to intercept the landing force as it tried to tip-toe by.

"Everyone get ready for a fight," Karen said softly, looking up at the faces on *Lady Grace's* screens. "They're not going to want us to get around."

"Then they'll be disappointed," Isoruku Togo smiled in reply.

Karen said nothing to that — instead she glanced at Elise De Winter, then back up at the screens, and nodded.

"Let's go to the right. Full burn, and give the battleships a wide berth."

The invasion force began to move.

"Liam, Karen's going to take the invasion force around to the right. Be sure to block for them."

Just to repeat, *Empire's* Captain was still the elite Liam Singh, who you might recall as Rachel Butler's Flag Captain from *The Gallant Few*. Rachel was in charge of the new (provisional) Heavy Squadron that was guarding Earth, so Liam was now just another skipper in Marlene's elite squadron.

Ha, calling Liam Singh 'just another' skipper made me laugh. He was glad to have his ship back, and as Marlene gave him the head's up, he replied with a nod, "We'll see to it, ma'am."

Because *Empire* was the furthest battleship to the right of the fight, it would be the closest to the route Karen intended to take around the action. By the same token, the Martian battleship it was fighting would be nearest to the transports, and would likely be inclined to break off action with *Empire* to take a shot at them.

Liam would have to make sure it didn't get the chance.

Now, I was going to say that if you had to pick one skipper to give that job to in this context, it'd have to be Liam. But then I thought about it, and while I know this sounds like a lame cop-out, the fact is any of the skippers with Marlene would have been just as good. You can't doubt Captains like Emma Nelson, Becky Afflighen, Kyle Feldman and Val Rodriguez.

What I'm saying, I suppose, is that whatever way you slice it, the Martians were sort of fucked.

Yes, I said it. I chose my words very carefully there. I cringe a little, but it's true. Trying to get around any of these battleships would be a hell of a job — the only thing tougher would have been if John and the *Bonnies* had been present.

And just to prove my point, Liam nodded to his Helm and Navigation Officer, and *Empire* rapidly sidestepped to get between the Martian it was fighting and the course Karen was taking.

Laser shots continued to ram back and forth. The fight thickened.

CHAPTER EIGHTEEN

SCOPE OF DESTRUCTION

I need to spend a chapter, or at least part of one, outside of any one viewpoint. There's no other way I can convey the massiveness of this fight, or the chaos. The Battle of Mercury is often overlooked by historians because in a lot of ways it's overshadowed by the Fleet Clash, but it really was something different.

What made it so unique wasn't that it involved two lines of battleships fighting — we'd seen that before. No, what was different was that, frankly, the ships on both sides were very good, and because their technologies were as well matched as would ever be the case in a fight between us and the Martians, it didn't end quickly.

Glorious February was over pretty fast, if we think about it. A few very nasty volleys of energy traded, ships put out of action, and then the Martians ran.

But the five Martians we faced here were in fact veterans of the battles at Glorious February, and they'd learned from their earlier experiences. At the same time, our already-excellent skippers were even better for their experiences in that month, and our ships were superior: we'd fixed that weak point that allowed reactors to be easily overloaded. Remember, we learned that at Glorious February.

Add to the mix our desire to avenge the Forge, and the Martians' determination to protect their outer capital, and this really was a nasty brawl.

Neither side was going down as easily as the other would have liked.

The visuals themselves were epic.

Within enhanced eyesight of one another, *ten* battleships were pounding away. Greg's strategy began to tell almost immediately: as our battleships dove in from a variety of vectors, each essentially challenging one Martian counterpart to single combat, the red heavies stopped their charge at our transport fleet. Along with their destroyer escorts, they accepted the invitation for individual fights.

You can look up numerous vid records of this — every plane out there was recording the scene. Just go to the archives and check 'Battle of Mercury — Main Action'. It's epic.

Ten battleships, circling each other like prize fighters. Frigates and destroyers circling too — a pair from each side with each battleship. The stories they tell are incredible, and I wish I could give each one full coverage here, but that's not for me. Look at the official histories for that… you'll read, for instance, how Jake Lee and Cassie Pang nearly got into *boarding actions* as they circled *Sorceress*. Truly incredible.

The battleship tales do warrant more telling, though, if only to explain how the battle developed as Karen skirted it and flew into her own nasty fight. Now let's go left-to-right, so we can end with Liam Singh and then sidestep naturally over to Karen.

On the left of the line was *Sorceress*, Marlene's own elite battleship skippered by Kyle Feldman. As it ran down hard on its Martian opponent, the firing between the two got pretty intense, but Marlene's ship had the same old magic that had allowed it to hold off the Earth assault force back in *The Almost Coup*. Ducking and weaving like a frigate, the battlewagon plowed in close and held its laser fire, letting mags rain on the Martian.

"Hold for point-blank," Kyle was looking to his XO as he said that. Marlene was a little ways away from him, paying no attention — her concern was with the squadron, not with how her trusty old ship handled itself.

As the acknowledgment came to Feldman's order, he looked away, then stopped and glanced back at his XO with a wry smile, "We better not miss, alright Lijun?"

Have to give the skipper props for keeping up the humor, and targeting *Sorceress'* lasers from the operations section at the rear of the bridge, the XO grinned and nodded.

"Aye sir."

It was, of course, a valid point: *Sorceress* was going with the knife-fight strategy, pushing in through its opponent's fire, waiting until a laser shot would be the most devastating. The key to that whole plan was indeed hitting the enemy with the lasers when you got in tight. But this was Marlene's flagship — it goes without saying that they'd manage direct hits.

And they certainly did: "Shoot!"

Sorceress' bow lasers one and two erupted silently, and their red lances crossed each other at the instant they made contact with the midsection of the Martian battlewagon. The red ship shuddered under the fire, and then one laser sliced through its armor, and started gutting its innards. A moment later, the Martian jerked away and returned much less effective fire with its aft lasers, but really, that first solid hit did the job.

Kyle ended up dancing with the Martian for another eight minutes — a testament to the determination of the Martian crew — but all the Martian could really do in that time was dodge, and try to return fire. Eventually the accumulated damage made it too slow to run, and too weak to fire back. It surrendered to *Sorceress*.

Becky Afflighen hails from Wales, and she really can be a brawler in battleship fights. *Goliath's* opponent was, in fact, the Mercury Squadron's flagship, *Chryse Planitia*, under the command of Admiral Barold Dobbs. I have to give the Martian credit in this case: his ship shot very well, and when *Goliath* approached from above to engage in single combat, Becky was greeted by a spread of lasers that sawed off her ship's high drive pod.

This, I'm sure you'll agree, was a problem: *Goliath* would be slower and less maneuverable by a quarter, and there were new instabilities in its power system.

But as I say, Becky is a brawler.

While her frigate escort provided cover, she made as though she was going to turn and withdraw from the fight, and then launched both her torpedoes, under very heavy fighter escort.

The Starlights from Goliath and GoliathStar Squadrons blazed a path for those two warheads, and the Martian battleship switched all its fire to shoot them down. Energy was routed from lasers to mags (or whatever Martians call mags… EM cannons), and the point defense shooting went into overdrive.

Again, the crew of *Chryse Planitia* proved to be good gunners, and both the torpedoes went down, along with a considerable number of our planes.

But when the Martians turned their attention back to *Goliath*, which they presumed was retreating under cover of that torpedo spread, they got a face full of lasers.

With all the speed Becky had left, she drove *Goliath* straight at the Martian flagship, and before her target could re-acquire her with lasers, she was damned near in ramming distance. She didn't ram; she adjusted course to fly past the Martian at spitting distance (in olden days, they called it 'pistol shot' range), and then her port broadside lasers cut the bow right off *Chryse Planitia*.

Some counter-mag fire from the Martian chewed up *Goliath's* energy grid, forcing the mighty wagon to limp for the rest of the battle, but it was a victory.

Admiral Dobbs, who I never met or heard a thing about, died on his bridge.

Becky was out of the fight.

Val Rodriguez had *Warspite* in the middle of the battleship line, and she was doing great. Val's another excellent skipper, as I've said. She also had one advantage which Defense Command analysts have never been able to quantify.

I call it the 'Greg is awesome and you will fail if you try to fight against him' effect.

Or the 'Greg effect' for short.

Look at Greg Noyce's service record and you'll see the man has been in countless fights, big and small, over the course of his career. And somehow, in all of these messes, his ships have never been severely punished. I don't know why. Maybe it's luck, or faith, or maybe he's a super-telepathic alien who can slow the enemy down with his brain.

But whenever an adversary goes one-on-one against Greg's ship, the battle ends quickly, and in Greg's favor. It just *does*.

So Val had this working to her advantage, and it paid off. Again. *Warspite's* third laser shots on its counterpart came just as the melee began, and at first sight it looked like the Martian had twirled fast enough to shrug them off.

But then it became clear that something had been clipped. The Martian began to stagger, its firing became wild, and just as *Warspite* got into pistol shot to start trading the hammer blows that would usually be needed to decide a fight between two big guns, the red ship *blew up*.

We still don't know exactly what *Warspite* clipped — we've tried to find out, believe me, because being able to repeat that sort of victory would be very useful. Chances are, it was a fluke failure or overload that was one-in-a-million… either way, it worked.

And that, actually, was bad news, because *Warspite* was right next to the Martian when it happened.

A piece of debris rammed into the battleship's neck, causing some superficial damage, but much more importantly, one of the ship's engine pods took a sharp hit that ruptured transmission lines on the main power grid and triggered an automatic shutdown both of that pod and of two reactors.

Warspite wasn't severely damaged in the classic sense… it was sort of like it had been shot in the foot. Either way, Greg was going to have to sit further back during the rest of the fight.

+++

Of the five battleships that we sent into this fight, *Repulse* had the worst day. The Martian that Emma Nelson faced off against was tough, and may well have recognized *Repulse* from Glorious February. It sure fought as though it held a grudge.

As soon as Emma turned her sharp-shooting wagon to charge against the Martian, she caught a hard volley of laser shots that tore right through her flightdeck doors, and basically carved the bottom off the front of *Repulse's* bow pod.

That killed the ship's sensor suite, and the rest of the fight became a whole lot harder.

I don't know if you'll recall, but Emma's ship had always been renowned for its gunnery. Without sensors, that advantage was all but wiped out, and closing range became a good deal more important. As such, she ordered full ahead, and her XO started firing spreads of mags — an old trick to try to nail down a target when sensors were out.

It didn't help much, though: the Martians hit *Repulse* again, even harder. The shot drove straight down the bow laser emitters, and sent a hell of a surge back towards the ship's reactors, which promptly locked themselves off to avoid a spill.

That meant, inconveniently, *Repulse* lost power to all its forward lasers — only the stern laser was left in action. Mags could still draw power through redundant circuits, so they kept blazing away, but that's really a case of bringing a knife to a gunfight.

As *Repulse* pressed into pistol shot range, more lasers tore into its already mangled bow pod, and the bridge decompressed. The bridge crew's bags deployed out of collars and sleeves, enclosing them against the vacuum, and some among them were able to pull others into the Captain's day cabin (which didn't decompress), so most survived before the cold got them. Emma Nelson was among these survivors, though she was critically injured, and never recovered.

The ship switched to auxiliary control, which was better than nothing but a whole lot worse than having a bridge, and *Repulse* continued to fight as best it could.

Fortunately, *Warspite* was next over, and Val hobbled her ship into the picture to engage the preoccupied Martian. With excellent shooting, she carved the red ship like a roast, and it withdrew at a limp, to surrender much later that day when *Sorceress* got hold of it.

That all just leaves Liam Singh and *Empire*, blocking for Karen as she skirted this clash of titans. Getting position on the battleship he was fighting, Liam decided not to follow the pattern of his peers — he didn't try to drive right up into the enemy's face. Instead, *Empire* stood off, and its lasers did the punching.

A battleship duel at long range is something I think we're probably familiar with, and this was much the same. *Empire* shuddered and side-stepped as Martian turret-based lasers clawed at its armor, and then Liam's XO pounded back with pairs of much more powerful energy beams.

At the same time, Sela Kinder, who had *Guangxi* alongside *Empire* as escort, dropped back a ways towards Karen's formation, expecting the Martian destroyers accompanying the battleship to make a charge for the transports. One did, and in a gunfight so epic I can't do it justice under these circumstances, she cut that ship in two.

And — this is important — *Guangxi* was still fully able to fight and fly after the engagement. Good work from Sela.

And great work from Liam Singh, as you'd expect.

The Martian couldn't get around his battleship, because Liam gave no opportunity. Had the two closed and circled each other like prize fighters, the Martian might have been able to duck away at some point, and get a little distance over *Empire* — just enough to put one or two laser shots into the transport formation before being caught.

But ever wily and aware of his situation, Liam remained patient, and let steady shooting from his gunners wear the Martian down. First the ship's bow turret was jammed by one of *Empire's* laser shots, then its neck was drilled and its power disrupted, and at last it lost two drive pods.

Crippled, it surrendered half an hour later.

So ended the battleship fighting in the main force. This, I should point out, was until that point the singly most decisive battleship fight in the history of space warfare — *all* of the enemy battleships were defeated, some on site, two surrendering later in the day when it became clear that there was nowhere to run.

We fared *very* well, not least because of our excellent skippers, but if you look at the result, you'll see that only two of our heavies were completely combat-effective in the end: *Sorceress* and *Empire*. *Warspite* needed a couple of days to do the repairs on the damage to its drive pod, and then to reactivate the shut-down reactors. *Goliath* needed a new drive pod wing, and *Repulse* ended up as a write-off.

So we won, but our battleship force took some severe hits in the process.

In the meantime, the frigates fought very hard. Every time two battleships turned on each other, they released their frigates and destroyers to do a mini-version of the fight.

Realistically, these duels had no impact on the outcome of the battle, but I should say that on balance we came out ahead: seven of their destroyers survived to retreat, and eight of our frigates were left intact.

Lia, of course, distinguished herself in command… it's kind of a let down for me to tell you that, instead of showing you, but there's more yet that proves how good she is, so I'll skip this proof and emphasize the other instances of excellence in a little while.

The main forces had brawled in an epic fight. Now it was Karen's turn to ram her transports down Mercury's throat.

Ooh, the imagery…

CHAPTER NINETEEN
"I'M MORE OF A DOG PERSON"

There was no fancy trick to what came next — no special maneuver, no brilliant tactic... nothing but simple hard slogging.

Standing on *Lady Grace's* bridge with her arms folded, Karen watched as eleven destroyer escorts began to change course, moving to intercept the transport squadron. Her job now was simple: keep those attackers away from the transports that held the majority of the landing forces.

That meant a stand-up fight between the smallest warships in either fleet, and Karen was ready for the match.

"Commander Dozi, when they get into range we'll engage them. I want your group to remain with the transports. Lead them in towards Mercury, and we'll catch up," Karen glanced up at her screens as she gave those orders, and Dozi nodded.

His five ships would head straight in, then, leaving Elise De Winter's five ships and Nikhil Jones' five to deal with the eleven Martians. Karen expected that to be enough.

"Any corvettes carrying Special Branch assault groups, launch your shuttles immediately. Starlights provide escort."

That was an order for Charlie and Rufus, mainly — they were aboard *Lady Grace*, remember, expecting to be carried right to the Mercury domes on the corvette's deck. But in this situation, where the destroyer escorts had avoided getting shot up in the main battle and Karen had to go meet them, it made no sense to risk part of the landing force in a ship battle.

Two Special Branch assault shuttles rocketed off *Lady Grace's* deck a moment later, then were surrounded by the Starlights that would protect them for the duration of the hour-long flight to Mercury.

"We go straight in," Karen continued giving orders, explaining the situation a bit more explicitly than she might have if all her skippers had been Belt Squadron veterans.

"Going to be a dogfight, is it ma'am?" Bruce Arama asked evenly from his screen, and Karen simply had to nod.

"That's a good word for it, Bruce. Stay sharp, be ready for close action."

The Kiwi Commander matched her nod, then looked away to give orders to his XO, Francine Fuentes.

There wasn't much of a wait: the main action was still going on at this stage, and those destroyer escorts were paying attention. If they'd waited too long to close with Karen's force, they'd have had victorious Defense Command frigates and even battleships bearing down on their flanks. They had to move now.

I think it can be safely said that, by this point in the fight, the Martians realized they weren't going to win. I'm not sure if they ever thought they'd be able to withstand our assault, though undoubtedly Bort's success at the Forge had given them some hope.

But now there were no pretenses left: our battleships were crushing theirs, and all they could hope to do was eliminate our assault force, and thus interrupt our landing plans. Mercury's population was significant enough that we probably wouldn't be able to take the planet if our troops were dead... or at least it would take a long, long time — time enough for Bort to arrive and blast us to pieces.

That was what they had to be playing for now: a draw.

Karen wasn't about to hand it to them.

"All ships, alter course and increase to flank. Take us right at them," she said coolly. "Good luck Commander Dozi."

The escort split, two-thirds of it joining *Lady Grace* in a turn to port to face down the destroyer escorts, the rest cruising alongside Zail Patel's transports.

Whirlwind had taken a few knocks in the frigate duel, but nothing like its companion ship *New York*. Taya Prescott, the skipper of the latter vessel, had been severely wounded (and would later succumb to her injuries), and beyond that, the Defense Command cruiser had lost nearly forty percent of its power grid. It was limping, keeping close to *Warspite* which was itself hobbling along because of the damage to its drive pod.

That just left *Whirlwind* as the active fighter from that division — it still had full weapons and propulsion, just with a few unpleasant scars to show for its trouble. Three other frigates from the escort force could say roughly the same, and then four others (including *New York*) were capable of some fighting, but weren't up to heavy action.

All of that is a long way of explaining what Lia was seeing as she stood on *Whirlwind's* bridge, "I have four ships."

She said that to herself, and no one paid attention to the quiet words, though they were picked up by the microphones on the deck.

"What to do with four ships..." another question to herself, under her breath.

Her eyes drifted between icons on *Whirlwind's* main screen. Then she looked at Greg, who was standing coolly on *Warspite's* bridge, and Marlene who was calling out support orders on hers. She could ask either one of those elite leaders what to do now, but as a good squadron commander, she knew she shouldn't have to.

And frankly, as a very smart woman, very much her father's daughter in some ways, she didn't *need* to.

This was Lia Hawke. Lia who talked about zero-gee bras to make me uncomfortable. Who used sock puppets to explain diplomacy. Who many people thought was a flaky dilettante with an eye for clothes and high society, but no concept of how the world worked.

In other words, this was a woman who was more than smart enough to manipulate, outthink, or otherwise fool everyone she ever met.

She didn't need advice.

Taking two long seconds to assess the icons on her main screen, she made a decision.

"Jake, Sela, Jim, form up on *Whirlwind*. I want a tight squadron line abreast, and prepare for maximum acceleration."

Those skippers were spread across the battle line, but their ships — *Kodiak, Guangxi* and *Newfoundland* — were the other three fully-functioning ships. Now they each acknowledged quickly, ordering course alterations to bring them alongside *Whirlwind*.

As they closed, Lia explained her intent in soft, direct tones, "See the cloud of destroyer escorts that's going after Karen? Of course you do, we all can see them. That was silly. Well, whether she likes it or not, I've adopted Karen as my big sister, so I'm taking it very personally that they're trying to kill her. We're going to help her."

Lia actually made a special effort to say that like a petulant debutante… or as much like a petulant debutante as she could manage through the soundness of tactical reality.

Each of her skippers smiled at the tone, then acknowledged.

Lia turned to her Helm and Navigation Officer and smiled that classic, perfect, completely genuine-seeming smile that was her staple at court, "Let's go claw their eyes out, full speed."

One thing about having Lia commanding in action, you get some of the most unique ways of delivering orders ever recorded in military logbooks. Ever.

Four frigates leapt away from the battleship line, heading straight for the flank of the Martian destroyer escort formation.

It was clear to Karen that the fight she was driving straight into was going to be a real dogfight — no organization, only individual ship skill and guile to determine the victors. That being the case, she was quite confident that her squadron was going to gut theirs, not to put too fine a point on it.

She didn't know all Nikhil Jones' skippers, but even if it had just been the five corvettes in Elise De Winter's group, she'd have felt confident. Desperation on the Martian side could give them more oomph than they usually enjoyed, but it wouldn't change their fates…

"Ma'am, *Whirlwind* joining the Battlelink."

Karen blinked at that report, glanced at *Lady Grace's* Sensors and Communications Officer, then looked forward again to see a loading screen pop up. Lia appeared seconds later.

"Ready for the catfight, big sister?"

Somehow, Karen didn't miss a beat. Well, not *somehow*. She's Karen. That's how.

"I'm more of a dog person."

Lia grinned, then shrugged indulgently, "Whatever you want to call it. Mind if I help bitch slap some destroyer escorts?"

Bitch. Slap.

Karen nearly grinned at the incredulity, but the circumstances were more than sufficient to keep her grounded, "I… don't mind at all."

Lia's enthusiasm bubbled, "Thank you!"

They were interrupted by a report from *Lady Grace's* Sensors and Communications section, "Range in thirty seconds."

Nodding in acknowledgment, Karen glanced back at Lia, "You have the flank?"

A switch seemed to flick in Lia's mind, and her smile vanished instantly: "Four frigates, we're all running and gunning at full effectiveness. Should hit them ten seconds after you do."

Karen appreciated both the tone and the words, "Then this will be easier than I figured. Thanks for the assist."

Lia shrugged, "I'm not just an extraordinarily beautiful face."

There were comebacks, but Karen couldn't bring herself to go that far off-topic when she was twenty seconds from a gun duel. That was a skill that remained firmly in Lia's possession.

"Alright everyone, let's teach the Martians the sound of one hand clapping… or the bitch slap, as I call it," Lia started addressing her skippers, and Karen could only shake her head.

A quirky-as-hell command style that was completely inappropriate by any standards of professional decorum… but that's Lia for you.

And what happened thirty seconds later proved completely and absolutely that a bitch slap can seriously ruin your day.

The Martians hurtled in hot and angry, but their lasers, as ever, lacked the reach that ours enjoyed. Karen's corvettes thus fired first, with Karen herself giving the order: "All ships, shoot when ready."

Lady Grace and *Amherst* got the first blasts away, followed in a split second (literally) by the rest of the ten corvettes that were charging the enemy. The Martians had to shift to avoid fire, and being destroyer escorts they did have the skip in their step to manage that, though not without four laser shots connecting.

Seconds later, their own weapons came into range, and as soon as they did Karen issued the important order: "Dogfight positions. Look after yourselves and each other."

The two corvette groups scattered instantly, managing to escape the quick-targeting turrets of the DEs. The Hawke corvette *Helen* took a solid hit, and *Sackville* caught a graze, but neither was put out of action.

It was inevitably turning into a dogfight: the corvettes and destroyer escorts were picking their opponents, and as had happened with the battleships, it was going to descend into single combat.

But first, Lia was going to breeze through.

They must have seen her coming. I don't know how anyone manages *not* to see a quartet of frigates running down on them, breathing fire.

Well, they weren't actually breathing flames (which couldn't survive long in the vacuum, come to think of it), but just writing about Lia's attitude has sort of infected me with her colorful approach.

Anyway, they must have seen her coming, and yet they did nothing — the destroyer escorts continued on their course, focusing on the fight with Karen's corvettes. Perhaps they had tunnel vision, but in my experience the skippers of small ships tend to be more aware of the threats around them, since their ships are so much more vulnerable.

I sure remember being attentive on *Friendly's* bridge. But maybe I'm weird.

Either way, the Martians got a nasty intro to Lia Hawke about five seconds after they engaged Karen.

Whirlwind and *Newfoundland* teamed up, and combining their laser fire, they ripped through the hull of one Martian, forcing it to turn and run with all the speed it could muster. They didn't bother to finish it off; giving their lasers a chance to reset, they switched to mags and turned against another DE, raining golden energy on it.

At the same moment, *Kodiak* and *Guangxi* engaged yet another destroyer escort, once again combining their fire to make sure they could drive it out of the fight. This one took both frigates' lasers in the bow pod, jamming its turret and probably blowing away its bridge. It turned away and ran as well.

After that, the slaughter was almost one-sided.

On *Lady Grace's* bridge, Karen locked her jaw and refrained from giving orders that would fight the corvette. Elise De Winter was the skipper, and it would be out of place for Commodore McMaster to step in and tell her when to maneuver, or when to shoot.

It was torture, but for the right reasons.

And, while I personally could never say that Elise was as awe-inspiringly exceptional as Karen, she was still a damned excellent officer. *Lady Grace* locked onto its first opponent and went right at the Martian, laser firing and then mags raining. As I said in the beginning, it wasn't fancy or elaborate: it was a mini slogging match.

The Martian honestly didn't have a chance. And it didn't help when *Newfoundland* blasted off one of its drive pods about ten seconds later.

That quickly became the story of the engagement.

Remember back to Pion rock, when Charlie and his Branchers got into that fight in the gym? They survived going hand-to-hand with Pions because they fought in pairs, one officer keeping the Pion busy until the other had a clear shot at the bastard.

Well, these destroyer escorts had nothing on the Pions, relatively speaking. But they were getting the same treatment, and to the same effect.

Five minutes and it was over — thanks to Lia. If she'd sat on the battleship line and just watched while the corvettes and destroyer escorts clawed each other, it would have been a much nastier fight.

Instead, only *Helen* was put out of action in this scrap, to be later repaired. And, somehow appropriately, our daring corvette *Sackville* lost a drive pod again — but kept fighting. Ships called *Sackville* just don't die, it seems. The one laid down in 1940 is still sitting in Halifax harbor, open to visitors.

In return, the Martians had five destroyer escorts lost (destroyed or surrendered) and six fled, joining up with the seven destroyers that had managed to get away from Lia's frigates during the battleship fight.

They retreated in a handful of groups, none of them well organized, some of them roughly on a vector for Mercury, others just heading away from our ships.

To sum this all up neatly: we'd routed them.

It had cost us dearly, but not nearly so dearly as it cost them.

Watching them go, Karen frowned and then paused in thought. Those ships would probably reorganize and come back to cause trouble... so they'd either have to be hunted down, or the escort for the transports would need to be increased.

Or... both.

"Lia, your frigates and four of my corvettes will go after them, keep them from reorganizing," Karen reached her decision aloud. "Nikhil, rejoin Commander Dozi and get the transports in safely."

Nikhil Jones acknowledged that order, then directed his four remaining corvettes to alter course and accelerate back towards the transports.

"Patch me in to *Warspite* and *Sorceress*," Karen glanced back to the Sensors and Communications Officer.

Moments later, Marlene and Greg appeared, both looking serious but neither looking grim.

"Lia and I will start dogging them to make sure they can't reorganize. I recommend any battleship with the speed joins the transports... just in case Ken has trouble with the monitors. All damaged ships huddle up until it's over."

Notice that she basically just gave Greg's orders for him. He didn't take offense, because he knew what I did: that Karen is that good, and always a step ahead of everyone around her. Barring misfortune, she'd have his job one day.

Oh ha.

Greg simply nodded and accepted her proposed deployment, "Very good, proceed."

Marlene pitched in then, "Can *Warspite* join the transports?"

Val Rodriguez answered with a negative on a separate feed that Karen didn't have, but she presumed the answer based on Marlene's follow up.

"Alright, *Warspite* and *Goliath* converge on *Repulse*. *Empire* and *Sorceress* will join the landing forces."

That was it then: a collection of ships suffering from various levels of damage would be left behind. Marlene and two battleships would join Commander Dozi and the landing forces in their final approach to Mercury. Lia and Karen would go out and harass the wounded Martians.

Because harassing wounded enemies is a completely safe and fun way to pass the time.

So far so good, though. We still had a very strong force of active ships, and we'd neutralized or broken up all of Mercury's defenses. We couldn't have asked for it to go better...

Except for the monitors.

Oh yes, they still had to be dealt with, and that was going to be a genuinely nasty fight...

CHAPTER TWENTY
QUICK REVIEW

As is my habit, I'm going to pause here to look back over this battle, and see what we've learned. Reflecting on it all, I think I do understand one of the reasons why the Battle of Mercury is often overlooked by the history books, and particularly by the staff colleges: it was a real melee.

Back during Glorious February, when our battleships fought in line and the enemy retreated after moderate savaging, all our tactics and our theories seemed to be exercised. We saw the benefits of operating in organized lines abreast, of keeping escorts mobile, and so on.

There were no good lessons like that here. Greg had understood that the situation at Mercury was different than it had been during February of 2232: the Martians weren't going to run, and they had to be prevented from getting their lasers on a specific group of nearby ships.

As such, he'd thrown the textbooks out the airlock, Belt Squadron style. And it had worked.

But would it work again?

The short answer: not necessarily. Greg would be the first to tell you this — what he did, in terms of getting fast and loose with formations and tactical priorities, only worked because he knew that his battleship skippers and his escort groups were crewed by some of the most elite people in the Empire.

He could rely on each of his battleships to win the one-on-one fights. He could rely on Lia's frigates to mangle the Martian destroyers. He could rely on Karen to stop the Martian destroyer escorts.

If these had been different officers, with different ships and crews, his tactics could well have led to total disaster.

What if, after Marlene had broken up the battleship line, each of the Martians had proved more capable in single combat than our own ships? We'd have abandoned the advantages of mutual support, which in many respects is the great equalizer between ships of differing quality.

I suppose what I'm getting at here is that Greg took a risk, and he didn't take it blindly. He had the guts to use Belt Squadron tactics from the good old days to crush the Martians.

But if another commander fought a different caliber enemy with different ships on a different day, it could all go to hell faster than a cat can jump off a hot tin roof (and land safely on its feet, of course).

Shauna Cass comes to mind, actually. Though her circumstances were not entirely similar (since she was resoundingly outgunned), there's some truth in the parallel. Her force didn't benefit from the same experience and cohesion that Greg's did, and as such

Bort McWebsbert walked all over her.

At Mercury, the roles were reversed, and Greg did his thing.

It worked.

But again, we don't hear about it as much, despite the success. It's not one of those fights that has entered the annals of popular history, because it wasn't rife with the newest battleships and the best commanders on both sides. Ours were the best, I mean, but not knowing much about the Martian Admiral Dobbs, I don't believe he was their best.

Not that I'll insult him out of hand: he did all he could.

And, despite having lost all their battleships, the Martians still had a chance to stop our invasion force. Because there were two monitors out there which potentially had enough firepower to gun right through Commanders Bernd Dozi and Nikhil Jones, and potentially even through *Sorceress* and *Empire*…

If those monitors got to the transports, we could still lose.

So I suppose it was up to us to make sure the bastards didn't get anywhere near the assault force.

CHAPTER TWENTY-ONE
GRAF SPEE

The more I reflect on this fight, the more historical parallels I start to draw for it. I've mentioned the *Belgrano* already. Another possible comparison comes with the German raider *Graf Spee*, a pocket battleship that fought an epic battle with three British cruisers in 1939, during the Second World War.

To make a long story short, *Spee* had battleship firepower in a cruiser-sized hull, but unlike the monitors, it was fast. Its weakness was a lack of heavy armor, but its hitting power was brutal.

Three cruisers, *Exeter, Ajax* and *Achilles* — not unlike *Wolf, Cheetah* and *Friendly* — went toe-to-toe with *Graf Spee*, and ultimately forced it into a neutral port where it was scuttled to avoid being interned. It was a great victory, made all the more dramatic because, like our ships closing on the monitors, those three cruisers had theoretically been no match for a pocket battleship. Their guns weren't big enough, and their protection was hardly adequate to handle battleship attack.

That really is a very good parallel, now that I think of it.

Except we had two enemy ships to deal with.

And an ace up our sleeve.

An ace that was confusingly spelled 'M-I-K'.

"They're not turning. Looks like they're going to come straight at us," Felicia Khalid made that observation from Sensors and Communications, and I nodded in reply.

The battle between the main forces was in its last stages as we got close to the monitors, so it was entirely conceivable that the Martian ships would have turned away after seeing their battle line defeated.

But no, they'd been sent to stop what they undoubtedly thought was a landing of pathfinders against the Mercury domes. They probably thought they could easily stop two frigates and a corvette, then turn and go after the transports.

And if we hadn't known what we knew, perhaps they would have been correct.

"Range to their predicted envelope?" Andrea asked that question coolly, and Felicia checked with a technician before answering.

"If they have *Tharsis*-size lasers, it'll be seventy seconds. If it's regular battleship lasers, it'll be eighty. We'll be in range in 100 seconds."

"We'll take the one on the right," Mark Gunney sounded off from his screen, and I agreed.

"Go to it. We'll handle the one on the left. Matt, help as you see fit."

Matt Baxter nodded from *Friendly's* bridge.

"Any sign of *Cyclops?*" I turned again to Felicia, and she frowned. She was being very careful not to point any active sensors in the direction of Mik's approach, as that would have tipped off the Martians. Only passive scans were reaching out and looking for the veteran battleship…

"I have a ghost about three minutes out," Felicia reported. "Coasting at 170 kps. I think that it is *Cyclops*."

"Good… good. Keep an eye on it, Felicia. Just in case it's not him."

It seemed quite unlikely that the Martians would have a ship coasting unpowered towards a defensive fight, but it never hurt to be cautious.

Andrea moved over towards Shelby McLaws while I was talking to Felicia, and our southern belle Helm and Navigation Officer greeted her approach with a smile, "We'll be all set, Captain. They won't get a piece of us, no matter what they shoot with."

Of course they wouldn't: despite not having slept because of her night watch, Shelby McClaws was still more than ready to tangle with the Martian gunners. Andrea shrugged, "Just thought I'd ask."

Shelby nodded and turned back to her staff, who were all focused quite intensely on the consoles before them. As Helm and Navigation Officer, it was Shelby's job to coordinate all the efforts of the navigators and pilots, and to make sure they conformed with the plans aboard *Cheetah* and *Friendly*.

It was complicated and critically important… I don't know if I've ever emphasized that enough. But it was. And we were about to get solid proof of that fact.

"*Tharsis* laser range in twenty," Felicia called out, and as Andrea came back alongside me, we both braced ourselves. If they had long-range lasers and good gunners, Felicia had just given us twenty seconds to live…

Unless Shelby was better. And she was. We were confident she was.

"Ten seconds."

We didn't have to give any orders to prepare for maneuvers, obviously.

"Five seconds."

A couple of deep breaths.

"In range!"

Silence.

Standing at the front of *Cyclops*' bridge, Mik could see everything developing as he coasted towards the fight. He held his breath as we crossed into *Tharsis* range.

A second passed. Then two seconds. No shooting. He watched, his attention completely locked on the icons on the screen. If the monitors didn't have *Tharsis*-level firepower, then *Cyclops* would have a much better chance of not dying.

Six seconds.

They could just be waiting — that was always a possibility. Waiting to draw us in closer, so that we'd have a longer run to escape when they opened fire… or they might not have the biggest lasers with the longest range.

We hadn't known for sure that they *did* have that sort of firepower, we just feared they did, because that would have been the absolute worst case scenario.

Ten seconds.

Eleven.

They opened fire.

+++

As soon as Felicia Khalid warned us that we'd crossed into the regular Martian battleship firing envelope, the shooting began.

"Down twelve, rotate seventy!' Shelby ordered instantly, and with all the speed you'd expect from three Starlights peeling off into separate strafing runs, our trio of veteran cruisers shot away from each other.

The monitors had regular Martian battleship lasers, thank God.

Well, 'thank God' was the first thought. The second was 'oh damn'. Because they still had us outgunned by a mile.

"Close us right in," Andrea ordered smoothly, then turned back to Jim Hannigan, who was ready at the laser targeting controls. "Let's test their protection. Hopefully it's thin."

Jim nodded, and as Shelby turned us onto a new direct course straight for the first monitor, his sensors zeroed in.

"Range in ten," he called out, and then we all did the count in our heads.

My pulse was pounding, I'll be honest. This was perhaps the most apprehensive I'd been about a ship fight all war. We were coming in from the Martian's starboard quarter, burning ahead at 201 kps — everything that Shelby and Andy Jensen could wring from our engines for a short time.

"Shoot!"

Laser one erupted from the bow, and just as it did we started getting enhanced visuals from our external cameras. The piggish monitors were very ugly, but it seemed there was a point to that: our laser rammed home with its usual, lethal accuracy… and it fizzled off the monitor's armor without much more than a scorch mark to prove it had been there.

"Well dammit," I muttered immediately, and strangely, my heart stopped pounding. Now I didn't have to wonder if we were going to be able to carve these two beasts up: I knew we couldn't.

Instead, we'd have to help needle them to death.

"No effect from my laser," Mark Gunney announced.

"Similar results here," Matt Baxter added quickly.

Our three ships blew past the two Martians at full speed, then peeled and rolled up and down to avoid counter-fire from the aft-mounted mags on the monitors. At least they didn't have lasers on both ends… that'd be our angle.

"We'll have to stay behind them," I said quickly. "If they're smart, they'll see us doing that and go back-to-back… we keep them that way, that means they won't be able to double-team Mik when he turns up."

Matt and Mark both nodded on screen, and Andrea immediately passed instructions to Shelby: *Wolf* spun and adjusted thrust to push us back towards the monitor pair. They were, as expected, not the quickest turners… but they weren't deathly slow either.

"We'll be in their firing arc in… incoming!" Felicia was watching them closely, and as she said that Shelby barked her own quick, lady-like orders.

"Sideslip climb, right now please."

Wolf lifted up and to the side, getting away from a couple of the heavy laser shots. One did clip us, though, and that was an unpleasant sensation. The ship bucked, and Shelby gave more fast orders to jerk us away from the grazing impact. A violent maneuver combined with hard acceleration to 202 kps got us clear... and it also fooled our grav plating.

Let me be clear: Felix Wolfe grav plating is very difficult to trip up. But the combination of maneuvers Shelby just executed with the minor surge that came as the energy from a grazing laser shot pummeled our secondary energy grid was enough.

Everyone on the ship was weightless for about a tenth of a second — just long enough for anyone not sitting in a chair at a station, or standing near a rail, to get tossed a little bit out of place.

Sounds innocent enough... but when I landed it was with a thud.

When Andrea landed, it was with a sharper crack.

She was at the rear of the bridge, having gone head-first into the operations consoles. Jim was holding onto his console with an iron grip, but realizing what had happened, he looked over to see Andrea slowly trying to pick herself up, and then not being able to.

He called for medical teams to the bridge. It was just a concussion, he was pretty sure, but it warranted medical attention.

As I struggled to my feet, I realized Andrea wasn't doing the same, but had no time to worry, "Damage?"

Despite his distraction, Jim had the answer ready, "Nothing serious, though I bet we have a scar on the underside of the neck."

"I'll have a scar on my backside," I muttered as I returned to the front of the bridge, locking my grip onto the rail there and trying to ignore the ache in my tailbone. Hard landing.

"You alright?" Matt Baxter asked first, and I just nodded.

"Grav plating flicker. We got grazed..." I glanced back at Andrea, but there was no time to explain.

"Shelby, bring us right around, try to drop from on high. Let's make this less about shooting them and more about getting them to turn after us. I want them more worried about spinning than shooting when Mik comes in," I slipped into 'Captain' mode pretty seamlessly, probably a sign that it was a job I secretly missed.

Nodding quickly at my words, Shelby gave orders to that effect, and I turned back to Jim.

"Mags only for now, Jim. Let's harass the hell out of them."

Wolf's XO nodded quickly and switched the energy priorities for our weapons. As he did that medics arrived to help Andrea up into her chair.

Turning back to the screens, I looked up at Mark and Matt, "You both get that? Harassment only, mags. And let's launch Starlights. Same purpose."

All we could do for the moment was piss off the monitors. But believe me, we could do that very well — even without Lia around to help.

Oh zing.

Meanwhile, *Cyclops* was close at hand...

"They'll have us on lidar any time now," Finn Yaalon observed from *Cyclops'* Operations consoles, drawing a nod from Mik.

There was no point trying to coast silently when you were this close to a fight — it was time to wake up all his old battlewagon's systems, and to join the action.

He'd watched as we'd toyed with the relatively quick-turning monitors, so he knew a little bit more of what to expect. Now it was time to put that knowledge to good use…

"Full startup, battle stations," Mik ordered sharply. "Let's get in there."

In *Cyclops* went.

CHAPTER TWENTY-TWO

EXETER, AJAX, ACHILLES

Andrea was sitting in her chair at the back of the bridge, scowling as the medics injected her with one of their anti-concussion cocktails. Their scans said it was relatively minor, so after a few more minutes off her feet she'd be herself again.

She was pretty sure she was already herself, and she was more than a little frustrated. I think you can probably sympathize: of all the stupid things to have happen in the middle of a rather important gunfight, bumping your head just wasn't one of the ones you'd regularly worry about.

Though she had no reason to, she felt silly.

It didn't matter, though: she'd be back on her feet shortly, and in the meantime I was managing to do the job. This was the first time I'd actually skippered *Wolf* since 2231, and the first time I'd skippered my old ship in battle since Deep Black... but it was like riding a bike.

"Number two is coming around again, you see it Mark?" I looked up at Mark Gunney as the enhanced camera feed showed the second Martian monitor making another sharp turn to bring its lasers to bear.

"Got it," he nodded.

A volley of mag shots rained onto that red ship instantly, but did nothing to slow the beast down. The monitors were tough, that was becoming clear enough. Even their drive pod wings were layered with additional sheets of armor... the benefits of designing a ship you know will never go fast, I suppose.

"Slipping starboard," Mark said next, and just as *Cheetah* moved again, the monitor's lasers gave chase, coming damned close to nibbling its heels.

"Why do I get the feeling this is going to go on for a while?" Andrea asked sharply from the back of the bridge. The medics had stood aside so she started to push herself out of her chair, but a head rush convinced her to give it another minute.

"Time to *Cyclops'* arrival?" I glanced at Felicia Khalid.

Her answer was immediate: "Any second now, sir."

Less than any second, as it turned out.

As I looked back at the enhanced camera feeds, two red beams collided with the monitor we'd designated 'number one'. That gave the bastard something to think about... but the shots didn't pound right through the vessel's armor, as I was hoping they would.

Dammit.

Remember, *Cyclops* was an older battleship, and during its upgrades before being posted to the Independent Belt, Mik had done some customization, bettering its speed and protection while not completely up-gunning it. That meant its lasers were older and had a bit less punch than, say, *Empire's*... but were still easily powerful enough to break most cruiser-sized vessels without difficulty.

Unfortunately, against the armor of other battleships, they weren't as effective... and the monitors definitely benefited from that.

Now they both turned towards *Cyclops* — the Martians realized exactly who they had to fear in this fight. And they had the guns to do some harm...

Mik appeared on Battlelink as the Martians were beginning their turn, "We got our wish, I see."

"Yes, now let's just hope it doesn't kill us," I answered wryly, and Mik began to nod.

Then he was knocked right out of frame.

Surprised, I looked back at the main screen, where the enhanced pictures revealed the Martians were both shooting back. But the camera frame wasn't wide enough to show *Cyclops*, so I glanced back to Sensors and Communications, "Switch back to tac display."

The icons of regular tactical display retook the main screen, and showed *Cyclops* maneuvering as deftly as it could to clear two converging clusters of laser fire.

"Mark, Matt, back to lasers and get in close. Get your torpedoes ready too. Let's take advantage of the distraction."

Mik picked himself up off the floor of his bridge with a groan, then looked up at his main screens. Four of them had blown out, dropping shards of blunt non-shatter glass onto the deck before him.

That was one upgrade from *Cyclops'* refit that he was suddenly glad of. Standard screens from the time when *Cyclops* had been built had been prone to shattering in a manner that sent showers of sharp glass across the bridge. We'd learned our lesson about that particular type of screen, thankfully, and Mik had made a point of having new ones installed when he took command.

But that was only partially relevant to the present situation.

"Finn, lasers still up?" the Commodore asked as he found his balance, and his XO replied quickly.

"We're shooting... now!"

That was good. Mik staggered forward and looked at the situation on the main screen: the two monitors were coming right at him, and while their lasers weren't *Tharsis* level, they still hurt pretty damned bad.

"Start wiggling, let's throw them off a bit."

Cyclops began trembling, almost literally. As Daragh Ryan had discovered decades before, nothing confuses targeting software quite as badly as a wiggling ship. Algorithms are written for targeting computers that allow for tracking of a target moving in any direction, at any speed, but if a ship jolts back and forth enough, computers can start over-thinking and miss completely.

It's actually more complicated than that, but it works.

Well, sometimes.

Another laser salvo punched into *Cyclops*, and Mik swore, gripping the rails at the front of the bridge as he gritted his teeth.

Then the second monitor fired, and despite a good wiggle, *Cyclops* took the hit again. All around Mik, it seemed the bridge just exploded.

✦✦✦

"Oh shit," Mark Gunney didn't censor himself, and I couldn't blame him.

Cyclops hadn't been able to step aside in time, and a lot of lasers had pounded into its venerable old hull. It looked to us as though the ship's armor was holding, but under that modern protective skin, *Cyclops* was a generations-old warship. Its power grid was not nearly so robust, its failsafes a whole lot less sophisticated.

I'd stop here and do a rant about how the old ship should never have been in service — how Parliament shouldn't have cancelled funding for the other two ships of the *Warlock*-class (like *Sorceress*) that would have replaced *Cyclops* and *Medusa* — but now's not the time.

And Mik loved his ship, so it would also be rude.

But the age of *Cyclops*' hull and internal design was showing: its skin wasn't being penetrated yet, but inside so many things were overloading or falling apart that I strongly doubted Mik would be able to stay in action.

So Mark summarized it quite nicely: oh shit.

"Torpedoes against number one, right now," I ordered quickly. "Contact Adrienne, have Wolfstar escort them in."

There was no delay; the torpedoes lanced out from both *Wolf* and *Cheetah*, and made a rush towards monitor number one. We were close, so as Adrienne Thompson's fighters from Wolfstar Squadron moved in to escort, they knew they didn't have long to run.

The monitor saw the attack coming and began to turn, its laser fire fell off and its turret EM cannons started blazing away, throwing up a field of energy flak that was meant to shoot the warheads down.

While its colleague was occupied with our torpedo attack, the other monitor dipped below and charged right at *Cyclops*.

"Matt, harass that bastard, buy Mik some time," I said quickly, and Matt Baxter answered by ordering *Friendly* to chase the red vessel.

One torpedo was shot down.

"Move us in close for another laser shot, see if we can get number one's attention," I looked first to Shelby, then to Jim as I said that. It was starting to become clear in my mind: we had to split these two up, or together they could pound *Cyclops* to bits.

The second torpedo blew up short of its target, and I contained a curse. Now monitor number one began to turn, its lasers coming around to bear on *Wolf*.

At least we'd done our job... it wasn't looking at *Cyclops*...

"Shoot!" Jim called from the back of the bridge, and our laser gave the Martian a little heat before Shelby turned us to run out of its line of fire.

Mark positioned *Cheetah* off the monitor's stern and drilled it with his laser three. That did it: the red ship wasn't paying attention to *Cyclops*, at least for now.

We were two predatory animals, trying to keep a buffalo distracted so it wouldn't trample us...

Mik's face was wet and warm, which he was pretty sure meant covered in blood. He wasn't squeamish, though, so he wiped his eyes with the sleeve of his ship fatigues, and got to his feet.

It would have been easier if there'd been some light.

"Report?" he tried that query halfheartedly, and then sure enough, Finn Yaalon answered him.

"I have a piece of metal in my knee, sir. There aren't any lights on either."

Mik followed the sound of the voice and started shuffling, running into a couple of people on the way. After a moment, someone got to the arms box and pulled out the flashlights. The bridge was eerily lit, and Mik could see that half his crew was down.

Someone quickly checked him, too, and he was indeed covered in blood. The good news was at the same time the bad news: it wasn't his blood... the bad part (from Mik's perspective) being that that meant one of his crew was almost certainly dead.

"We have no power up here, sir..." one of the Lieutenants from Mik's bridge crew made the obvious observation, and Mik nodded.

But he knew his ship — he could feel the vibration through its deck. The engines were still running. The ship was still alive. The control systems and their relays had probably just been overloaded.

So it was time to be creative.

"Finn, get to aux weapons control. I'll head to engineering. We'll fight the ship over the comm," Mik said as he started for the bridge hatch, but Finn held him up.

"Sorry sir, internal comms are down."

Mik stopped, managed not to say 'figures', and then stroked his goatee. That proved to be an uncomfortable experience, as like the rest of his face, his beard was drenched in blood.

"Somebody get me a bucket of water and a towel," he ordered quickly. Was that all he could control right now — cleaning off the blood?

His ship was alive, but it had literally been deprived of its command and control network... Finn could direct energy weapons fire from aux control, Mik could direct course and speed from engineering...

But how would they coordinate?

"Handheld comms, get a bunch out of the arms locker," Mik decided quickly again, then started for the door once more.

"Sir, they'll be jammed by static from the wrecked grid."

Coming to a stop, Mik turned back to Finn Yaalon, "Are you fucking kidding? Sorry. Finn, let's just figure out a solution!"

The XO nodded, "I have an idea, sir."

"Good. Let's get this ship fighting..." he turned back to the hatch, just as a rating stepped through with a bucket of water. "Ah, splash me in the face with that, quickly."

The spacer nodded nervously, then tossed the bucket of water over her Commodore before anyone behind him had a chance to get clear. The water blasted a lot of the blood off his face, and then she handed him a blue towel that he used to wipe away most of the rest. Draping that around his shoulders, he led the way off his bridge.

Matt Baxter was clinging to the heels of monitor number two as it gave chase to *Cyclops*, and he got the feeling that *Friendly* was irritating its adversary.

The space around my old corvette was being positively filled with mag fire from the Martian pig.

"Keep at it, Matt," I encouraged from *Wolf's* bridge, and just as I did, Jim called out again.

"Shoot!"

Wolf's laser two had the honors this time, and the shot went straight into the drive pod of monitor one.

And did *nothing*.

"Those can't be interplanetary pods," Mark Gunney grunted on his screen. "They're taking too much punishment."

In case you've never noticed, the drive pods that traditionally carry ships between planets tend to be more vulnerable than the simpler, much less complex short-range engines that are used for orbital operations, or movement to and from moons. And the simpler something is, the harder it can be to break.

"Keep pounding it," I looked up at *Cheetah's* skipper.

Mark nodded, "I love to give a good pounding."

Andrea, by this time, was on her feet next to me, scowling and keeping one hand on the top of her head as she waited for the large bump to inevitably appear.

"Drop us to port, Shelby, he's coming again," she ordered sharply, and Shelby obeyed.

Wolf drove in closer to monitor one, sweeping to the left to get ahead of its counter-turn. Jim was lining up another laser shot, and *Cheetah* was firing.

"Try a mag storm," I suggested as I watched the icons. "Maybe we can saturate its shielding and fry the pod."

It was hugely unlikely that such a thing would succeed, but why not give it a try under the circumstances? The big brute was absorbing everything else.

"Come on, Mik..." I muttered then. We needed *Cyclops'* big guns to make this work.

Or there was a good chance we'd all die.

Georgina Yamagawa stopped to stare at Mik for a minute as he appeared on *Cyclops'* engineering deck with a dirty towel around his shoulders and a few drying streaks of blood on his cheeks.

"You look like shit, boss. Don't know if you should be allowed on this deck looking like that."

Somehow, she managed to sound relieved, even as she said that, but Mik ignored her tone, "I'm taking command from here. You have any sensor readings on the aux nav panels?"

"Lidar only. We've got one monitor behind us, and *Friendly*... we assume it's *Friendly*... is keeping it occupied. I've got us running away until we get internal comms back up."

Since the engine room literally sat between the four wings that carried *Cyclops'* engines, it made for a good secondary steering position when the command and control grid was down. In the end, the orders sent to change course on the bridge ended up being executed by the computers down here anyway, so now they'd just cut out the middle man...

The only problem with that was that none of the other systems a ship needed in order to fight were directly connected to the engine room. That's why ships need bridges — singular places from whence all the different essential combat functions can be controlled.

Whoa, I just used 'whence' in a sentence.

But now, Finn Yaalon's suggestion meant that there was a way for the other crucial system to report in.

"Why is my hatch open? We're in a battle!" Georgina started to pass Mik when she noticed there was a person standing in the hatch to the engineering bay, but he grabbed her.

"That's internal comms for now. Until your people can get the power to the main internal grid switched off so it stops spitting the static that jams our handhelds."

Yamagawa frowned, "Wait... what?"

Mik shook his head and looked back to the door, "Report laser status."

"Report laser status," the spacer there repeated, and then both Mik and Yamagawa could hear another spacer out in the corridor repeat the words, and then another.

"Human chain. Finn's idea. I like it — very old school," Mik looked back at his engineer. "But I'd rather have handhelds, so clear the air, would you? And send me your aux navigator."

Nodding and managing to contain her surprise, Georgina Yamagawa hurried off to assign personnel to deactivate the scrambled comm grid. A Chief Petty Officer appeared near Mik a moment later, "Your navigator, sir."

Mik recognized the man, "Good, thank you, Jonah."

As he said that, the man at the door called out the reply that had come up the human chain from Finn Yaalon, "All forward lasers non-responsive, sir. Aft laser online. All mags responding."

Mik cursed softly, then called back, "Reducing speed. Shoot at monitor as soon as in range."

The order started to work its way back down the human chain: up one deck, and down two more corridors to Finn Yaalon in aux weapons.

"Slow us down, give our aft laser a good shot," Mik nodded to the Petty Officer.

"Aye aye," he answered immediately, and headed for the controls.

This was a hell of a way to fight a ship, but Mik would take anything he could get.

Absently, he dried his blood-sticky beard with his towel, and waited.

CHAPTER TWENTY-THREE

NEVER EASY

"He's not quick enough to hit us, we're not strong enough to break him," Mark Gunney was thinking aloud. "Problem is, we're more likely to make a mistake and get hit than he's likely to throw off all his armor and say 'hit me.'"

It was a very accurate assessment of our situation, and it described our problem quite well. We were in a spot of bother...

"*Cyclops* opening fire on number two!"

My eyes darted back to the main screen just as the line that indicated a laser shot crossed from the battleship's icon to the monitor.

"Solid hit... they must have flaked armor on that one, I see some debris," Felicia Khalid was leaning over the shoulder of one of her spacers, reading off the news.

"That's the style. Mik's still in this..." I nodded a bit eagerly, then looked back at Mark.

"Let's keep concentrating on that pod. It has to break eventually."

"That's what they said about my determination to die miserable and alone," he quipped back, then started handing off orders to his crew.

We continued to circle monitor number one faster than it could turn.

"Direct hit!"

As that announcement came through the door into the engineering bay, the crew there cheered, but Mik had other things on his mind, "Keep spinning, don't let them get a lock."

That order to the Petty Officer running the navigation panel drew another 'Aye aye', and with that done Mik turned back to the door, "Maintain fire."

It was feeling almost absurd to him to have to give orders this way — you get spoiled by just being able to look at the guy you need to talk to and say what you need to say, be that in person on the bridge or via Battlelink. But there was none of that now.

"Any idea how much damage we did?" Mik looked back to the Petty Officer, and he nodded.

"Lidar shows flaking. Must have stripped some of their armor."

That was something, then...

"Sounds like another shot!" someone nearer the reactor rooms called out, and sure enough, the sound of energy running through buffers filled the compartment. Finn Yaalon was shooting again.

"Track that for me," Mik moved over closer to the lidar screen at the navigation controls, and the Petty Officer leaned a little to his right to allow an unobstructed view.

More debris: the laser had cut into something unprotected...

"That looks like he's turning to shoot, sir," the Petty Officer pointed quickly at a shift in lidar profile, and Mik had to agree.

Reading intent from a lidar panel was not easy, and frankly was something we rarely had to do anymore in the era of modern sensors, but he could still manage it.

"Climb and turn," Mik put a hand on the Petty Officer's shoulder, and the man did exactly that, manipulating the rudimentary helm mechanisms on the panel to push *Cyclops'* thrust in the appropriate direction.

"Switch to mags, maximum fire," Mik called back to the door. He would have loved to be able to talk this through personally with Finn, but that wouldn't be feasible by human chain. They needed to keep hitting this monitor, but always presenting *Cyclops'* rear to the enemy wouldn't be the safest way.

The mags would have to rain too…

"Incoming now, sir," the Petty Officer remained quite calm as he saw the distortions that indicated inbound laser fire. "Not going to be able to avoid all of it."

"Brace!" Mik warned loudly.

Then his ship was jarred, and the top third of its bow pod was ripped off.

"Hard hit on *Cyclops!*" Felicia called our attention to the shot, and my eyes darted back the main screen. Mik had torn into the bow pod of monitor number two, and was starting to rain mags into its guts. It needed to go down soon… but it was shooting back…

"That carved a piece right off *Cyclops'* bow pod. I'm closing in," Matt Baxter narrated for us, as *Friendly* was obviously nearer the ship it had been harassing.

Andrea and Mark remained focused, giving orders to keep *Wolf* and *Cheetah* in the fight against monitor number one. I watched as Matt Baxter dove in on that other monitor, and with laser number one of my trusty old corvette, did something unexpected.

A laser shot from *Friendly* found the chink in the monitor's armor, and drilled down deep, decompressing sections and probably clipping the vessel's power grid. *Cyclops* had at last stripped away the battleship armor, so now even a corvette could cause pain.

"Emergency starboard, he foxed us!"

I barely heard Shelby's warning before *Wolf* began a rapid change in direction. Not willing to drop onto my backside again, I clung to the rails.

"*Friendly's* engaging again, sir," the Petty Officer was keeping the weight off his right leg, because that last jar had sent him knee-first into the side of the console, with a sickening crack. Good chance he'd need reconstructive on that one…

Mik appreciated the man's dedication, though, and answered with a nod, "Good. Turn us back towards the bastard. We'll rain mags on him, Chief."

"Yes sir… incoming again!"

Friendly was pushing attacks home, but monitor number two was not allowing itself to be distracted… or perhaps it had tunnel vision. Either way, it realized that it was more important to take *Cyclops* out of action than to swat a corvette. Without *Cyclops*, we probably wouldn't be able to break the armor of the other monitor, at least until reinforcements arrived…

Something towards the rear of the engineering compartment burst. It didn't explode with flame and fire, just simply *burst*. Chunks of it killed two nearby engineering techs, and Mik distinctly heard another piece as it ripped past his left ear and embedded itself in the wall.

He ducked a little, then started to cough as a putrid smoke began to pour into the engineering chamber.

"Dammit," he muttered. "Rebreathers, Chief?"

The Petty Officer pointed Mik to one of the nearby lockers, where techs were already hurrying to collect the full-face masks that would allow them to work in a situation like this. Hurrying over, Mik grabbed two, pulling one on immediately and bringing the other back for the Petty Officer.

"Engaging mags!"

That call came from the door, and Mik waved in reply. Wearing a mask was going to make this already crude system even cruder…

Then his comm chirped.

"Aux control to engineering, read me now?"

Mik's comm was on his belt, so he pulled it out and lifted his mask, then coughed again as he held the unit up, "Here, Finn. We're filling with smoke, I need a headset. You're engaging mags?"

"Yes, get me closer boss. He's got a hole in his armor, I can pour mag fire right down it, but you have to keep me on an angle."

That was good news, "Got it. I'll patch in the man on the wheel, so we can all talk directly."

Hurrying to a nearby console, Mik grabbed two headsets, put one to his ear and pulled on his mask. He returned with the other and handed it to the Petty Officer, "Put it on, you'll get direct maneuvering instructions from aux weapons."

"Aye aye," the man coughed as he put on the headset and replaced his mask.

Turning for the engineering hatch, Mik waved to the spacer there, "Comms are back, close that hatch and get to action stations!"

The human chain had done its job for now.

As the hatch shut, Georgina Yamagawa arrived next to him, "That last hit took out coolant to two of our reactors. We auto shut down, all non-essentials are offline now. That's why the comms are back — we killed the power to all internal C&C systems."

Mik frowned, "Did we have to get them to do that for us?"

Yamagawa shrugged, "The controls were fused, I didn't think blowing them out into space and killing fourteen people was the way to correct the problem. The Martians disagreed."

That, I think, was an inappropriate way to reply to one's skipper, but Mik didn't react. He sympathized — Georgina had lost fourteen people in that shot — but they were his people too, and he knew it wasn't time for bitterness.

"All the power you've got we'll need. This isn't over," was his reply.

Yamagawa moved off, and Mik headed back to the navigational controls just in time to see the distortion of mag fire appear on the lidar screen.

On *Friendly's* bridge, Matt Baxter watched as a battleship-worth salvo of mag shots started to rain down on monitor number one, all of it zeroing in roughly on the rupture in its armor.

"Laser that breach again. Let's give the mag fire more room," he said sharply.

Friendly's laser lanced out.

Mik normalized his breathing thanks to the mask, though the thick smoke was really filling the compartment now, to the point where it was starting to obscure the screen. After a couple of moments, someone managed to route power to an atmospheric pump, though, so it started to get better.

When the screen was clearly visible again, it showed the Martian dead in space.

Then Finn's voice came into Mik's ear, "I think we fried it!"

Watching the still shape on the lidar for a moment, Mik continued to breathe normally. After a moment of stillness, he nodded, "Good. Let's get after the other one. Ken doesn't have our firepower."

There's a testament to Mik's commitment to getting the job done. His ship was literally coming apart, and he was still determined to get into the fight.

The Petty Officer running navigation keyed up *Cyclops'* acceleration, and the maimed battleship limped our way.

CHAPTER TWENTY-FOUR
INSANE SOLUTIONS

"Cyclops is turning to rejoin us," Felicia Khalid made the announcement as she saw it on her panels, and I noted the same turn on the main screen. Mik would be back in range in about five minutes, at his current rate of approach.

That would help, but he only had one laser online, meaning he'd need a good stern shot to be able to hit the monitor. And since this monitor had just undoubtedly watched him destroy its sibling, that wouldn't be easy.

Cyclops was limping too slowly to evade much more punishment... somehow, we had to keep that Martian busy long enough for Mik's battleship to limp up, turn around, and fire.

"So how do we keep this fucker from atomizing Mik before he gets a shot off?" Mark Gunney was following quite directly, and I looked up at him.

Very good question. Torpedoes had been expended, lasers and mags weren't cracking the main armor, and none of the usual soft spots seemed all that soft. It was getting down to the stage where ramming was the next logical progression of tactics, but I definitely didn't want to have to go that route.

We just needed to keep this beastly red ship from turning fast enough to pin Mik...

A very stupid idea drifted into my head around then.

Incredibly stupid. I mean, this is a level of stupid that is so stupid people at the Academy get confused and start calling it 'brilliantly-innovative combat thinking'. But trust me, it was stupid. Daragh Ryan in his heyday stupid. *That* stupid.

I looked at Andrea, then bobbed my head to indicate both she and I should go back to speak to Jim.

We talked about a very, very stupid idea.

And then we started executing it.

"I think one of the frigates just launched a shuttle," the Petty Officer on the navigation consoles said with a frown, and Mik hurried over to the panel.

There was a small icon on the lidar — a new small craft entering the fray, and being surrounded by Starlights as soon as it turned away from its mothership. It looked as though there was a distortion of some sort following it, but the resolution on the lidar image was just too poor.

Presumably we were up to something that would be helpful — at least, that's what Mik hoped. He was even more aware of the difficulty of his situation than I was... asking himself how the hell he was going to get his ship into range of that relatively undamaged beast and get a shot off without being obliterated.

"Hopefully they're going to lend us a hand. We close to range?" Mik put the specific questions of what we were doing out of his mind with that inquiry, and the Petty Officer nodded.

In his ear, then, Finn Yaalon pitched in, "We should skirt range… make a starboard turn as soon as we get close, and then back in."

Mik nodded, then looked at the Petty Officer, "You get that?"

"Yes sir."

Patting the man on his shoulder, Mik turned back to the engineering compartment. The chamber was almost cleared of the smoke now, but everyone still had their masks on, so Mik didn't remove his. It was annoying, because he couldn't stroke his goatee.

"We're about forty seconds out," the Petty Officer reported, and Mik nodded.

"Get ready," he said.

Watching the shuttle we launched dodge and weave was a hell of a thing. The pilot, Lieutenant Sasha Ryan (no relation to Daragh, though that would have been ironically appropriate), was one of Shelby McLaws' best, and she was proving that she had a knack for making ships dance.

Adrienne's F-194s were putting on a clinic too: as the shuttle closed in on the monitor, the Martian mags started tracking it. We fired our mags at the Martians to give them something to think about, but it was mainly Adrienne who kept them distracted with Wolfstar Squadron. After all, Starlights with weapons aboard were actually far more dangerous than a regular old shuttle, right?

Well, yes actually. Mostly.

"That's great, Sasha. Get around that drive wing…"

Andrea had a headset up to her ear, and she was passing on encouragement to the pilot.

"It's handling a bit badly, ma'am, but I've got it," the voice came back over the bridge speakers.

She did have it… but time was running down.

"Will she have it in time? Or should we tell Mik to slow down?" Mark Gunney asked the sensible question from his screen, but Matt Baxter pitched in with an equally sensible answer.

"No way to tell him. There's nothing left of *Cyclops*' comm gear."

"Shit."

Mik was coming straight on, and if this didn't work there'd be trouble.

"Shelby," I glanced over at our southern belle, "get set."

"Aye sir," she said with a smile.

She was most certainly ready. Lieutenant Ryan just needed to finish the job…

"Executing the turn, sir."

Mik nodded, then was surprised to find his weight shifting as *Cyclops* banked away from the monitor — usually grav plating made certain that no one felt the sharp changes in momentum that came with maneuvering in combat.

But like most other things on his ship, the grav plating was starting to suffer.

This needed to be over soon…

"Getting a lidar lock on the bastard," Finn Yaalon's voice returned to Mik's ear.

"Good. Shoot as soon as you can. And Finn, if we get cut up by their return fire, I want this to be clear: we do anything we can to finish this bastard off. Even if it's a ram. It doesn't walk away from this fight."

Mik obviously wasn't playing games.

"Yes sir," his XO replied.

Live or die, they were going to kill the monitor.

"Reversing into range now, sir," the Petty Officer reported.

Mik folded his arms and took a deep breath. This could quite realistically be his last minute alive.

"Crossing over the line now, sir... reversing thrusters... opening the hatch. Kyla's EVAing now..."

As ever, listening to live reports of something incredibly dangerous happening had my heart rate up. Kyla Delancie, one of our mag techs (no idea how she got this gig today) was doing a spacewalk in the middle of a rather nasty gunfight.

"She's on it. The coupling... the coupling is on! I'm reeling her in and bugging the hell out!"

The shuttle ripped away from the fight, Starlights closing in behind it to provide rear cover as a cable pulled Kyla Delancie back into its aft compartment.

"That's it, do we go?" Andrea looked quickly at me, and I narrowed my eyes.

"Wait one," was my answer.

My gaze fixed onto the icons on the main screen. The monitor was turning to face *Cyclops*, completely ignoring our mag fire and *Cheetah's* lasers. Mik was backing in at full speed... they'd probably fire at exactly the same moment, based on the Martian's rate of turn.

But if we went too soon, we could throw off *Cyclops'* targeting solution, and we needed the first shot from the maimed battleship to count. We had to cut this very fine... as always seems the case with needlessly (or, in this case, needfully) stupid plans.

"Shelby, get ready..."

I watched the icons. I waited until it felt like the right moment.

The Martian had nearly completed its turn. Laser range was about to be reached.

"Now, Shelby. Full burn."

I didn't yell, I said that quite quietly — even though, in the movies, the consensus seems to be that barking it out loudly would have been more dramatic. But I didn't yell, and neither did Shelby.

Patting one of her pilots on the shoulder, she repeated part of my order, "Full burn, on the 146."

Wolf turned hard to port and accelerated to 202 kps, heading away from *Cyclops*.

The slack on the tow cable was taken up almost instantly.

Oh yes, we'd roped the bastard.

Sasha Ryan had carried a standard tow cable out to the Martian, and since they hadn't been polite enough to offer us one of their towing points, she'd flown it right around their high drive wing. Then Kyla had EVA'd to secure the cable to itself, making it a lasso.

Like I said, completely bloody idiotic plan.

Which is probably why the Martians never saw it coming.

The monitor didn't get to finish its turn because our acceleration countered its slower momentum. In the last moment, when its lasers should have come to bear against *Cyclops*, it was yanked out of position, but not far enough so that Finn Yaalon could miss.

Mik's aft laser cut out viciously, and pounded right into the Martian's bow pod. It was a long, sustained hit, and some of the armor started to flake away.

"We'll keep dragging the bastard around, Mark. You exploit any breaches."

Mark didn't even answer me, he simply ordered *Cheetah* onto the attack.

Shelby wore a brilliant smile as she started giving orders behind her bank of consoles. She watched the orientation of the Martian and then gave course alterations to make sure the big ship's lasers couldn't bear on either *Cheetah* or *Cyclops*.

At one point, the monitor wisened up and tried to turn right at us, but she was too quick, and we got around behind the Martian without difficulty.

Cyclops fired again, and then again, and finally once more. And then the breach was made — not a huge one, but enough. As Mik's battleship hobbled closer to assist with mag fire, *Cheetah* poured laser shots into the hole until the monitor finally shut down.

A quiet sort of end to a loud sort of fight.

We released our tow cable, and all of us on every ship took very, very deep breaths.

Then someone on *Wolf's* bridge let out a cheer, which is not something we often do, but a lot of people joined in with clapping and handshakes.

Andrea was smiling — genuinely smiling — when I shook her hand, and then I went over to Shelby to pat her on the back and congratulate her pilots.

We had won this very brutal little fight, and the frigates and corvette involved hadn't suffered much at all.

That was good.

The situation for Mik's ship, however, wasn't good. Not at all.

"We done now?" Georgina Yamagawa appeared next to her Commodore as he let out a sigh of relief.

Mik glanced at her and nodded, "They're both finished. Start damage-control work."

"Ship's probably not salvageable," she countered immediately, a little bitterly.

At first, Mik didn't know how to react to those words. Then, he decided that he didn't quite like what he was hearing, "We've still got some power, propulsion and weapons. Shore them up enough so we can keep maneuvering."

Yamagawa nodded slowly, then turned away.

Mik didn't like hearing anyone pronounce his ship dead — he'd poured a lot of heart into this ship. He'd shepherded *Cyclops* through its refit, refined its systems and its crews out in the Independent Belt, and fought this whole war in it.

He wasn't willing to give up so casually.

But a little voice in the back of his head was saying that Yamagawa was right, because honestly, she was. It would have been cheaper and more logical to build a whole new battleship than to rebuild *Cyclops*. The old veteran was going to be paid off for scrap after the war.

And yet, as Mik said to me later, if you had to pick any way for a glorious old battlewagon to meet its end, it had to be this way. You couldn't ask for better.

Well, the Martians could, seeing as *Cyclops* clobbered them.

But Mik couldn't.

Our risky job was done. But, of course, there was much more risk to come on this day.

Before I push on, I just want to make a quick note about the insane lasso tactic we used in this fight. Unsurprisingly, it has never entered the Academy playbooks, because realistically, when the hell is anyone ever going to be in a position to do it again? Against a proper warship — a battleship or a destroyer — the plan would have failed, because the target would have been too quick, or too powerful.

But it did work against the monitor, because its engines weren't as powerful as ours, and because its secondary armament (mags and smaller lasers in the Martian case) was thin. A battleship, for instance, would have been able to saturate our shuttle with mags, and the plan wouldn't have worked.

Why am I going to such pains to explain this? Well, two reasons. First, movie writers have gotten it into their heads that this tactic is the best new thing ever, so all their fictional skippers are doing it.

Trust me when I say we've looked into repeating it, and it won't work. Just trust me.

Second, while the dangers of doing this to a monitor were less than they would have been when attempting it against a proper warship, it was still batshit insane totally massively fucking dangerous.

Yes, I swore again. That's how dangerous it was.

That's why both Lieutenant Sasha Ryan and Leading Spacer Kyla Delancie were nominated for the Black Sun, and both received them personally from the next Emperor. Ahem. More on that later, but I wanted to mention now that those two did something very special. It's fine to be the one with the crazy idea, but making it actually happen is something else entirely.

I'm not sure if I'll get a chance to cover this fact in later books, so let me also say now that both of those ladies were quickly to be promoted. Their services that day had helped kill a very nasty opponent, and had helped save the remainder of *Cyclops'* crew.

A good day's work from two of *Wolf's* elite spacers.

As I've said before, ours was an incredible team of men and women.

Alright, my editors are telling me to stop gushing. So I will.

Wolf's crew is awesome.

And so was *Cheetah's* crew, and *Friendly's* crew, and of course, so was *Cyclops'* crew.

The monitors were finished.

CHAPTER TWENTY-FIVE
RESPITE?

The day's fighting was not over — far, far from it — but I think we deserve a brief break before we start shooting at more people. Unfortunately, there aren't too many places to go to find that respite just now. Karen and Lia were off harassing Martian escapees, Greg was still overseeing the battle from *Warspite*, Marlene had taken over the escort of the assault ships, and Mik, Matt, Mark, Andrea and I were beginning search and rescue operations to evacuate survivors from the two monitors.

Nothing there that I'd really call respite from the destruction.

In fact, the only people who were enjoying some quiet at this time were those yet to begin their battle: Charlie Peters, Rufus Chang, and the thousands of men and women of the assault forces.

And let's be honest, they weren't all just lazing about, having a quiet morning.

Charlie's assault shuttle was tucked under the shadow of *Sorceress'* starboard drive wing, burning its engines at full to maintain the 194 kps speed that allowed it to stay in formation. Rufus' shuttle was next over, and a wing of Starlights surrounded them both, offering protection in case Martian Interceptors popped out of nowhere.

They had a relatively long flight down to their target dome — another half hour or so from this point.

Sitting back in his seat, Charlie was checking his MAG-90 again. There wasn't anything wrong with it, the weapons drill just passed the time, and practice helped keep the motions instinctive. Beside him was Captain Ben Belete, someone you'll probably remember from the squad. Next down was the medic Terry Schroeder, another familiar officer, and then a number of new faces who'd joined to replenish losses after Pion rock.

Across from them sat Gina Bertram, who had been with us at Io, and a number of her officers who'd come through that fight as their own team before more recently being blended into Charlie's.

Chet Srisai, the veteran pilot of this assault shuttle (and the Brancher who'd helped a great deal when Kate Levec had been shot at Io) was at the controls.

There was no idle chit-chat, no particularly good humor. That's not to say there was any bad humor either — no one was complaining about the mission, or making defeatist remarks. It was just as you might expect from a shuttle full of Special Branchers heading into yet another meat grinder: everything was quiet.

Nothing else to say, no way to change what was coming. The job simply had to be done, and these people, some of whom had fought the whole war together, others who'd come through many nasty fights on the same battlefield, were going to work together to do their part.

I suppose you could complain that me reinforcing these realities is starting to verge on the needlessly cliché, but I want to keep doing it, because it's what we continue to do when we're in the midst of the situations. It's not difficult to have a moment of lucidity, and to ask yourself what in the merry hell you're doing storming a Martian dome, or battling a monitor, or all the rest of it.

Well, the reason is simple: it's the job.

Not everyone in the uniform agrees with the whys or the hows, but the simple reality is that they signed on — were not conscripted — and agreed to do these things. There was no point complaining about that when the going got tough… complaining would be more likely to get you killed than help your situation.

I don't believe anyone on Charlie's shuttle was complaining. They never would. To be in the company of an elite team like Charlie's, you needed to actually believe in the job… and by that I don't necessarily mean you think your government is always correct, or that you can do no wrong.

No, to be on that shuttle, you had to have the absolute, certain knowledge that you were the best at a certain sort of duty, and that because of your talent and training, the responsibility rested on your shoulders to do your part. To do the job that others just weren't cut out to do. To spare their lives.

Sounds a bit like martyrdom, I suppose… but another reality was that, in order to be on that shuttle, you had to be awfully difficult to turn into a martyr.

Though as Charlie pointed out at the end of *The Canary Wars*, the Martians are quite capable of turning anyone into a martyr.

And as he sat in his seat and cycled the power cell of his MAG-90, he knew it was quite possible that he'd be one of their first victims. Or perhaps more generously, one of their first twenty-four victims.

This pathfinding squad, along with Rufus', might not make it through the airlock.

But on they went, silent and certain. You ever want to talk about what courage looks like, you go ahead and start with that.

If you find that assertion too cliché, I invite you to sit in Charlie's chair on that landing craft and keep your composure. Hopefully everyone can agree that it's not an easy thing to do.

Anyway. This chapter of respite from the shooting is fast turning into my pontification about the quality of our fighting women and men, which is a subject I could easily spend a whole book on. That being the case, I'm going to move on to the assault itself.

Let's find out just how many of our elite Special Branchers end up as martyrs in the first hour of the Mercury invasion…

CHAPTER TWENTY-SIX

DOOR KNOCK

Marlene had taken over control of the assault forces, and as she paced back and forth at the front of *Sorceress'* bridge, she was deciding how best to approach the situation. Of course there were plans in place for the landings — she wasn't going to undermine those — but no one had built a contingency that included her leading the landing forces in with two battleships at their head.

Sorry, let me try to clarify that: the strike force was intact and very well escorted — better escorted than we'd dared hope, because it had two battleships with it, *Sorceress* and *Empire*. And because we'd handled the monitors, those wagons had no credible threats against them.

The shore-based defenses which would have required deft handling by the corvettes could now simply be bashed aside by battleship laser fire. Any attacks on transports or the landing shuttles would be driven back much more easily. These were advantages the Martians had to be conscious of, and Marlene was trying to decide how best she could leverage that.

Turning to her Sensors and Communications Officer, she frowned, "Hail their Capital Dome."

Nodding, the Lieutenant Commander sent the signal. There was no response.

That wasn't particularly, surprising — Marlene doubted she'd have answered either — so she paused again, then shook her head. Seemed like they were going to be stubborn.

But planting seeds of doubt never hurt.

"Alright, give me wide broadcast on a channel we know they can hear," she said again to the Lieutenant Commander.

A signal was established, and Marlene looked up into the viewfinder at the head of *Sorceress'* bridge, "This is Vice Admiral Marlene Stoll of the Defense Command fleet. As you've no doubt observed, we've defeated your defensive squadron, and we're preparing a landing that will overwhelm your domes in the coming hours. We are willing to do what is necessary to take Mercury's domes, but we have no desire to inflict unneeded casualties, particularly upon civilians. We're thus making the offer for you to surrender. At any time during this landing, you can surrender, and you will be treated as we would treat our own. Do not fight us out of misguided bitterness. Stoll out."

It was a complete and total long-shot, and Marlene knew it.

"Liam, take four corvettes and silence the stations and the yards. We'll handle the ground defenses," she ordered quietly. *Empire's* Captain nodded in reply, and then detached his ship and four escorts to knock out Mercury's very rudimentary orbital presence, most of it around the planet's equator.

Marlene led the rest straight in against the domes, situated at the pole. As the strike force got near, the Martians replied to her suggestion: lasers and mag bolts started flying off the surface with all the fury they could muster.

Charlie's assault shuttle remained tucked close under *Sorceress'* wing as the battlewagon rode in shooting. Interceptors started rising from Mercury's domes as the Defense Command force approached, so all but two of the escorting Starlights raced away to engage them. It was down to Chet Srisai's flying and some luck now — if things went poorly, Charlie and his warriors wouldn't even get to ground.

Rufus' shuttle tucked in close with Charlie's, and then both were joined by a shuttle that Kyle Feldman had kindly volunteered from *Sorceress*. Originally, the third shuttle was supposed to come from *Lady Grace*, but that plan had gone out the window when Karen departed, so Charlie had made a quick call and secured what he needed elsewhere.

You'll see what that means later.

For now, Charlie moved up into the cockpit of his own shuttle and strapped into the seat next to Chet. This was unusual for our intrepid Major, but to be quite frank, he wanted to see the fight that was going on outside the window.

Two battleships and ten corvettes sweeping down on a planet, firing torrents of energy at Martian installations that were firing back… this was the only time in human history that an actual planet had been invaded from space, and he had no intention of saying he'd missed the sight of it for no good reason.

What a sight it was.

There's plenty of footage of this in the archives, and that in itself is quite breathtaking. I can only imagine what it looked like for Charlie as he sat in that chair. There were Starlights weaving back and forth in front of the shuttle, tangling with Interceptors that were outnumbered but determined. Corvettes were descending towards the planet at high speed, skimming Mercury's almost-not-there atmosphere as they started unleashing mag and laser fire at stationary ground targets.

And every minute or so, a new pair of vicious battleship lasers drilled down into the rock, taking out some of the shore batteries that were trying to stop the onslaught.

The Martians really didn't have a hope. While Mercury was indeed a planetary colony, it had a lot more in common with somewhere like Belt Two than it did with Venus, Mars or Earth. There just weren't enough people or enough infrastructure to put together a layered, powerful defensive system.

"Atmosphere in one minute," Chet's words brought Charlie back from being just a spectator. I was going to say 'back to reality', but come on, it's Charlie. He's always at least a little bit grounded in reality.

The shuttle was plunging through a dogfight now, its escorts blazing a clear path through waves of Interceptors. It was indeed close to landing time.

Keying his comm, Charlie turned and looked out the window at the other shuttles in company — Rufus' and the one from *Sorceress*, "Major Peters to *Sorceress* shuttle. Begin your run."

"Affirmative, Major. Good luck!"

"And to you," Charlie replied with a nod he knew the pilot of that craft couldn't see, then watched as it peeled off.

"Make us invisible, Chet," Charlie looked back at his trusty, long-time pilot. Chet had flown the shuttle for us when Charlie and I had been back on *Friendly*, so we knew damned well that he was a good pilot.

Now, as he pointed his ship right at Mercury and punched up the throttle, he'd need that skill. Rufus' shuttle followed closely, and in seconds they'd shed their fighter escort and were accelerating right into Mercury's very thin atmosphere at a speed unsafe for just about anyone to attempt.

They looked, in fact, like they'd taken hits from Interceptors and were crashing into the planet, destined to leave big craters on impact.

Charlie leaned forward and flipped the screen in front of him to a sensor display, and then centered it on the icon of *Sorceress'* shuttle. Kyle Feldman had found a volunteer pilot for that craft — someone willing to go in for a very, very dangerous job. By the look of the scans, the volunteer was a good flyer, though… someone who had a good chance of coming back from this.

The Starlights, having been briefed during the approach, stuck with that shuttle, as if it was the last of the charges they could protect. Together they dropped into the atmosphere in a very controlled fashion, heading straight for the Capital Dome at full speed.

"We'll be pulling up in fifteen seconds, everyone hold on," Chet Srisai warned, and Charlie shifted back in his seat and tightened the straps.

His eyes remained fixed on the icons of the assault force. He didn't allow himself to get distracted when the Imperial Army assault boats started launching from their troop transports, or when other Special Branch and regular DCSF shuttles began launching from *Artemis Agrotera* and the other *Goddess*-class combat storeships.

All he could focus on (and all we will focus on for now) was what was happening with the Capital Dome.

The assault shuttle roared as Chet reoriented it, using all the small craft's thrust to keep it from driving into Mercury's surface. He leveled out just above the unpleasant-looking landscape, and as Rufus' shuttle came up alongside, the pair accelerated towards the pole at 100 kps, keeping low enough to avoid most sensors… hopefully.

Ahead, the shuttle from *Sorceress* headed for the docking runways of the government dome. I'm actually struggling with what to call these 'runways'… they were sort of lips that jutted out next to the docking bays in the Martian HQ building — places where small craft could put their feet down while they waited for entry into the bay, if there was a delay in the doors' opening.

The *Sorceress* shuttle touched down on one of these, and then edged over to one of the locks that Peri Oktar's staff had recommended for the landing. Starlights circled close by, strafing any mag turrets that they could find and making sure no Interceptors came close. This, as far as anyone watching from the inside was concerned, had to be the first wave of attackers, heading right for the most important target in the dome.

That's what Charlie was counting on, anyway…

"Hope they take the bait, eh boss?" Chet Srisai asked the question without looking away from the ground and sky ahead of him, and Charlie answered with a nod.

"Hope so," he agreed.

They'd find out whether their ruse had succeeded very soon: the pair of shuttles reached the pole, and dropped into the high-sided canyons that shielded the domes from some of the sun's radiation at this close range. Before any Martians could get a good look, the pair was skimming the smoother surface of the crater floor, heading for the airlock they'd chosen on the civilian side of Capital Dome.

"It's all smooth now, boss," Chet said. "Better get back there."

Charlie nodded and unbuckled, then got to his feet and headed back into the main compartment. In a moment, he and his officers would be the first Defense Command personnel to set foot inside a Mercury dome. *Ever.*

CHAPTER TWENTY-SEVEN

TOEHOLD

Getting through the airlock was, thankfully, not difficult. It could have been — there could have been welds, or booby traps, or even just a tougher software lock on the emergency hatch that Charlie and Rufus had chosen… but there were none of those things. Small favors, as they say.

When Charlie's shuttle extended its chute to the lock, and Rufus' shuttle extended its chute to the rear access hatch on Charlie's shuttle (the one, remember, that I'd docked my Starlight with back at Io), there were no complications. Both small craft were landed silently on the lip outside the lock, both seemed to be unnoticed in the general din of the attack.

"Ready," Gina Bertram was working the docking chute controls for the two squads, doing a job that before might have gone to officers like Raza Weiss or, of course, Carly Henderson. But Raza was getting his arm reconstructed, and Carly was dead. Now, Gina was doing a good job.

Charlie nodded to her as Rufus entered the back of the shuttle's cabin through the chute from his own ship. He nodded to Charlie as he appeared, and with a nod back, our intrepid Major took a breath.

"Go."

There were, of course, no pep talks or hesitations. There was no time for any of that. The decoy landing by the shuttle from *Sorceress* wasn't going to convince anyone for much longer, presuming it had helped at all. Just had to go.

Gina popped the hatch and led the way into the emergency airlock beyond, her MAG-90 up and at the ready. The rest of the squad followed at open intervals, about two meters between each, to minimize the number who'd be caught in the lock at one time if something went wrong.

"Clear," Gina called as she reached the inner hatch and applied a crack pad to the lock.

"Jarammer up," the officer right behind her announced as he came to a stop. I don't know if you recall, but a jarammer can interrupt the detonation signals of many types of trigger devices, so Charlie's squad was keeping one active in case someone was trying to blow them up.

Of course, there were plenty of ways to blow a charge that the jarammer couldn't stop…

None of them dwelled on that as they filed into the lock and waited for the inner hatch to open. It did feel like an interminably long time as Gina worked the keys, using the Defense Command OS XX software in her handheld to strong-arm the Martian operating system.

It didn't take long for the inner hatch to pop.

As it opened slowly, Gina let go of the code breaker, leaving it attached to the panel, and raised her rifle again. Once the door retracted, she stepped into the Mercury dome — I believe the first Defense Command officer to enter any of the Mercury domes that day.

She was greeted by silence.

There were no yells, or sounds of energy fire, or *anything*. The Martian dome was in the midst of what appeared to be a normal red-sky day, with occasional horns going like old-time air raid sirens, presumably telling people that an attack was imminent or occurring, and to stay in their homes or shelters.

No defenders.

This lock proved to be a good choice: it was exposed in as much as it wasn't contained within a building, but the park before it was full of what can best be described as strange landscaping features that obscured it from easy view of the street about 400 meters away. Gina hurried up to a red-leaved hedge and dropped to one knee for cover, then the rest of Charlie's squad followed smoothly.

As he entered the dome, Charlie found the air tasted a little odd, but he ignored that as he swept right, towards the triangle of apartment buildings. He stayed low and found a thick bush to get behind, then leaned up a little and looked through the scope of his rifle for any sign of defenders in this area.

Rufus was beside him by the time he crouched down again, and made hand gestures indicating that he'd seen a squad of fifteen Martian troopers in the courtyard between the apartments. Defenders who didn't look like they were expecting company from this direction.

All things being equal, that wasn't too bad a discovery — they could handle fifteen regular Martians with relative ease, so long as that was all there was here. For the moment.

The plan still stood, then: one squad would secure the rooftops of those three apartment buildings, set up sniping positions, and then cover the entrance they'd just come through for further landings. The other would stay low and dissuade any Martians from trying to come through on foot.

That in mind, Rufus made hand gestures that amounted to 'I'll go low, you go high'.

Charlie nodded.

That was it, the plan was in place.

Using more tactical hand gestures, both Majors got their officers on the move.

Captain Zail Patel was emptying his shipload of Special Branchers and SF, and as he watched that process from the bridge of *Artemis Agrotera*, he was joined by Brigadier Peri Oktar, who looked on with stern anticipation.

"Signal from Major Peters' pathfinders. They've entered their dome and are securing the entry. No resistance so far. They recommend immediate landing of all forces."

As that note was read by *Artemis Agrotera's* Sensors and Communications Officer, Oktar grunted, "Good. Order LCV006 down there immediately. Order all group one ships to begin landing now."

Those orders sent a flood of small craft towards the domes, the first of them —

LCV006 (Landing Control Vessel 006) — to be pulling up to the lock in about eight minutes. By the time it arrived, Charlie and Rufus would need to be pretty well situated, because the bigger, more heavily-armed dropship would certainly be noticed when it replaced the two assault shuttles at the lock.

I should explain the LCV. It had been designed specifically for this sort of job. It could hook up to a lock, send its complement of about fifty shooters through that lock, and then have a dozen other shuttles dock with it. Basically, once it connected to a lock, it was designed to be a temporary base of operations… a sort of toehold on the outside of a dome, within which assault waves could be marshalled from other shuttles.

It would thus replace Rufus' and Charlie's shuttles, and other small craft could dock with it and send their Branchers through it into the dome…

Presuming the way into the dome was secured by Charlie's and Rufus' squads.

Without any sort of darkness to aid them, the Special Branchers of both Charlie's and Rufus' squads could only be so stealthy. That being the case, they focused on speed, crossing the hundred-meter distance to the perimeter of the apartment complex in quick runs.

Because securing the ground level was going to be Rufus' job, he moved up first. His officers hurried to the base of the nearest apartment building in an open-order line, and then waited there for Charlie's squad to work their way around to the other side of that building.

As they both got closer, it looked increasingly like the position was not actually configured as a defensive point — it wasn't a place where these Martians would fort up when an attack came through. Instead it looked like a rallying point for reserve forces… a place away from the expected epicenter of the fight (the HQ buildings) which would allow regrouping and organization.

Well, it goes without saying that it wouldn't fulfill either purpose for our red-clad adversaries.

Charlie led his squad as they lined up against the wall of the apartment, and then he quickly glanced around the corner to get a clearer look. The courtyard between the buildings appeared to be both a garden and a parking strip for hovercars, of which there were four military ones on the ground. Fifteen troopers in the open, possibly more in the vehicles or in the buildings…

Tapping his comm once to release a single, unnoticeable burst of static to Rufus, Charlie took a deep breath. They'd have to shoot down all of those troopers fast.

Using his hand gestures, he lined his squad up to go around the corner. He told them not to engage until they were seen, so that they could have as many rifles ready to open fire as possible when the shooting started. Rufus told his people the same.

When the Chinese Major was ready, he tapped his comm to reply to Charlie with a static burst.

All set, no time to waste.

Charlie tapped his comm twice more — two 'squawks' of static — and then turned the corner.

The rest of his squad hurried out, coming around that corner in a line that swung like a door, all of their MAG-90s up and leveled. On the other side of the building, Rufus' shooters did the very same.

For a second, they went unnoticed — they were approaching from 'behind', from the wrong direction as far as the troops collected here were concerned.

Then one Martian saw a line of black-clad Special Branchers. Charlie watched this man's eyes go wide, and then at a range of thirty meters he shot the man in the neck. His shot was the signal, and twenty-four MAG-90s sounded off at the same time.

Of the fifteen Martians in sight, twelve instantly dropped, and the last three didn't get a chance to respond before they were mowed down too.

You only get results that resounding when it's Special Branch doing the shooting, believe me.

Both squads hurried forward, covering their angles as they entered the courtyard area. Two Martians were found in vehicles, both getting on the comms to their HQ building. Neither Charlie nor Rufus knew if they managed to get through to the base commanders before they were knocked out, but it didn't matter — speed was of the essence, either way.

Rufus found Charlie quickly, "We can use the hovers to get you up to the roof quickly. And we can use them to redeploy ourselves as needed."

"Roger, you're transport," Charlie agreed.

Confirming with a nod, Rufus directed three of his officers to become temporary drivers, while Charlie split his squad into three four-person teams, one under him, one with Ben Belete and one with Gina Bertram. Each team took a shoulder laser in case vehicles came hunting them, and then they were up and on their way to the roofs.

Below, Rufus' nine remaining officers broke into teams of three and checked the lobbies of the apartment buildings. Security guards were stunned before they realized what was happening, and then security panels in each of the structures were hacked, allowing decompression lockdowns to be triggered. In each of the three buildings, pressure doors sealed on every floor, trapping the occupants within… so long as they didn't have weapons with them that could blast through sealed hatches.

If there were troops in these towers, then they could shoot their way out and threaten Charlie's and Rufus' positions… but there was no time to worry about that. The pathfinders hopefully wouldn't be staying here long enough for that to become an issue.

With the lockdowns complete, Rufus moved his nine officers towards the dome-side of the triangle, and positioned them on the ground so they could make the most of their firepower.

When the cars finished depositing Charlie's teams on the roofs and dropped back down, Rufus waved them to land and park close to the defensive line, in case it became necessary to make a quick run somewhere.

The situation was thus as good as Rufus or Charlie could have hoped.

That, it has to be said, was a very good thing. Because not seconds after Charlie's teams had picked positions on the roofs with the best cover, the dome-wide invasion alarms started blaring.

Across the wide city, at the tall HQ buildings, vehicles quite clearly began to stir, and both Majors knew full well that those hovers were coming their way.

"Get set," Charlie warned his team.

They were set.

But the next part was going to be hell.

Five minutes of hell.

CHAPTER TWENTY-EIGHT

FIVE MINUTES IN HELL

LVC006 entered the atmosphere and burned hard for the Capital Dome, and a dozen shuttles chased it, each carrying a payload of Branchers. Between them, they could put about 200 officers into the Mercury dome — a force of operators that would hopefully be able to tie up the in-dome defenses for some time, while more locks were secured and reinforcements summoned in.

But LVC006 was now four minutes from docking, meaning the first reinforcements were realistically at least five minutes away.

And in that five minutes, the Martians were going to do whatever they could to secure their breached lock.

Now, I've been asked why we didn't just send LVC006 first, to land and send through a huge force in the first go.

Well, if the lock had been a trap, or defended, that would have tied down a larger number of officers and resources, which would have delayed the assault. And, had a big ship like an LVC come down, it would have had a lot tougher time going unnoticed as it docked, meaning its landing would have probably been contested. And no matter how many troops you have in an LVC, they still have to get through the airlock alive.

That would have been tough without the element of surprise.

What actually happened, believe it or not, was going to be easier.

Easier like it's easier to cut off your own foot than it is to perform surgery on your own intestines.

Er. Sorry, what a macabre analogy…

"Three hovers in the first wave," Rufus said into his comm, remarking on the vehicles that were now floating their way from the HQ buildings. The comm frequency was encrypted so it was unlikely the Martians could hear it, but even if they could have, it was necessary to pass the observation up to Charlie on the rooftops.

"See them. Me, Ben, Gina, left to right. Shoot."

Wasting no time, because he never does when it matters, Charlie had just ordered the shoot-down of the trio of troop-carrying trucks.

Next to Charlie, the officer with the shoulder laser raised it and looked down the sight. The weapon was a Special Branch model, with more than enough range to reach across the dome to the trucks.

She fired.

The first truck was hit solidly — an excellent shot, worthy of Charlie's squad — and it staggered before making a half-controlled descent down behind the government buildings. The second truck was hit by Ben Belete's gunner on the next roof over, and it exploded outright. A sorry fate for the troops inside. The third truck was clipped and dipped low, smoke billowing out from under its hood.

Not a bad start.

Then the sniper fire began.

Mag shots crossed the rooftops of the three apartment buildings almost simultaneously, forcing Charlie and his squad down.

"Ben, look for the shooter," he called. "Rufus, snipers have us down. Call the shots."

Down below, Rufus acknowledged with a quick sound just before opening up on a squad of Martians who hurried up the street outside the apartment complex. Five of the red-clad troops fell before their comrades backed into the alley, and then more troops came from further to the left, firing over Rufus' head to provide cover for their fellows.

The Chinese Major wasted no time: he loaded a magbang into his new underslung grenade launcher and fired it in their direction. A handful fell, and the rest scattered.

But this was just a drop in the bucket: as the shooting began, Martians started coming from all sides. Dozens of them.

Turning fast, Rufus started what could best be described as a shooting drill — it was like one of their training scenarios, where targets kept popping up (spawning, as they say), and the officer had to shoot them down.

Rufus' shooting was beyond exemplary.

Movies often tone down the number of headshots Special Branchers make in scenarios like this, because most average viewers believe it unrealistic for a shooter to be able to do that much damage on his own — they think it's just movie excess.

But it isn't.

Special Branchers are our elite for a reason, and when the attackers are coming out into the open in a panicked rush, it makes hitting them easier.

That was the key for this first minute — there wasn't much organization. The Martian Generals in HQ had called out that there were Defense Command troops at the apartments, and a lot of junior officers who'd been held in reserve had taken it upon themselves to respond.

Commandos would be coming soon — that was almost a certainty.

A grenade sailed up over the street, arching straight for Rufus' position.

You'll never believe this, but it's true: the officer next to the Major looked up, took aim, and shot it out of the air.

It had been an underhand toss, and it had hung up there, which made it easier... but yes, a Brancher shot a grenade out of the air. They can do that. They do do that.

And it helped just a little.

They sprayed fire in all directions.

"Sniper spotted," Ben Belete's voice came over the comm, and as soon as he said it the shoulder laser from his roof let off a shot. Charlie didn't see where the beam went, but the mag fire racing over his head stopped immediately.

"Street suppression," was what Charlie said next, and he rolled up onto one knee, then leaned over the rooftop wall that had just been sheltering him.

There had to be at least sixty Martians in the street below, so he just started picking and shooting.

Two of the other officers with him did the same: lean over, choose a running Martian, aim, fire. Repeat.

On Ben's rooftop, the shooters mirrored the action, while on the third roof, which was the furthest back from the street, Gina Bertram's shooters engaged a squad of Martians that was trying to flank around the far side.

"Going to ground behind that truck, see it?" Ben called out his observation on the comm. Charlie paid no attention, knowing what was coming next.

A shoulder laser shot blew the landed hovercar right off the ground, and scattered the men who'd been hiding behind it in all directions.

Several dozen Martian troopers were down in the street by now, and with that explosion, the rest started to back away. The defenders had been overenthusiastic, but they weren't entirely without sense — while they couldn't have ascertained the number of invaders they were facing, they knew there was very heavy and very accurate fire coming both from ground level and the rooftops, and trying to charge in against that was never going to work.

That was the end of the first minute — a very long minute, I think you'll agree.

The next one would be worse.

"Tanks! Tanks on the right!"

Rufus' eyes jerked up and he looked to the right, but he couldn't see any tanks, obscured as they were by the high buildings.

"Tom, shoulder laser and truck: go technical!"

Without acknowledging, one of his Lieutenants hefted a shoulder laser and hurried away from the firing line. He skidded to a stop next to one of the hovertrucks they'd commandeered, and in a second the vehicle was in the air, with the Lieutenant and his shoulder laser in the back seat.

Charlie watched the truck rise past his roof just as he sighted the section of four tanks floating down the right side of the dome towards him. These weren't heavy tanks in the Imperial Army sense of design — they didn't need to be robust enough to operate in a real outdoors scenario, the way blockhead tanks did on Earth. No, these were more like armored hovercars with mid-sized mags on top... but that was still enough to clear both squads of Special Branchers out of this dome.

They were sweeping down to the right, towards Ben and Gina's side of the triangle. That meant those two would have to deal with them.

"My team suppress ground, Ben and Gina take them out," Charlie gave his orders, and as soon as he said it the first shoulder laser blazed from Gina's rooftop.

It clipped the lead tank, but proving its resilience, the bastard staggered but kept coming.

Ben's gunner hit the same one, and it dropped back in formation, but didn't fall away.

"Keep pounding," Gina said sharply into her comm.

Charlie couldn't focus on that, though: more troopers were below, trying to use the distraction to get closer to Rufus' line. A lot of them, too, and they were managing to get across the street...

Rufus shot down two Martians just short of his line, and then a third one leapt in screaming some sort of battle cry. Our Major cut this trooper's throat with his Japanese-style tanto, then went back to shooting.

The next firing position wasn't so lucky: a whole Martian squad managed to get on top of it (the survivors of a platoon that had made the rush). Rufus watched out of the corner of his eye as his trio of officers fought eleven Martian marines in a brutal, close-quarters fight.

His officers, remember, had survived Pion rock — that is the greatest testament to their close quarters combat skills. But the Pions didn't have mags. One Lieutenant took a shot in her vest and had to stagger back for a second. In that time, one of the Martians shot her face off.

The Captain who'd been commanding the post had turned to help her, but was shot in the back of the head, the back of the vest, and the back of the knee simultaneously. Only the last of the team managed to leap away to escape, and as the Martians came on again, they got caught in a crossfire from the drivers of the two hover vehicles that were still on the ground, and the pair of shooters in the final rifle position.

"Down two. We're not going to hold static for long," Rufus reported into his comm.

On the rooftop, Charlie nodded in understanding: he was still firing down into the quickly-moving teams of Martian marines, but they were getting organized and making it harder for him to get easy shots.

Then a burst of mag fire sprayed the roof, and hit the officer next to him in the vest. It wasn't a kill shot, except that it stunned her momentarily. She fell off the roof — plunged to her death.

The Special Branch teams were down to twenty-one.

Off to the right, the shoulder lasers were still hammering the oncoming tanks, but those vehicles had gotten into range: three of them fired on Gina's roof simultaneously.

The Special Branchers scattered very quickly, getting further back on the structure and going low. Because there were still civilians in the building, the tanks were shooting carefully — they had to scrape the roof, but not hit the levels below. That gave Gina's team room to duck. A little bit of room.

Ben's laser gunner got a bead on the lead tank as this fire was being exchanged, and shot again. This time, the shot grazed the hoverpad, and the tank dropped like a stone, regaining gravity control just enough at the bottom of its fall to cushion the impact. The crew still probably died.

As soon as that shot was made, though, Ben waved his team to scatter, and sure enough, the heavy tank mags blazed away again, this time chasing his team instead of Gina's. Using that distraction to their advantage, Gina got her people back out of cover and fired again, the laser shot glancing off the armor of one of the Martian vehicles.

That did it: the three remaining tanks divided their fire, but kept it constant, aiming to keep heads down on the two roofs that were challenging them. Importantly, the third tank became preoccupied with those same two roofs, and didn't shoot at the third — the roof Charlie was on.

A mistake, that. Understandable in the heat of battle… but still quite a mistake.

Charlie and his remaining shooters were able to continue leaning over the edge of their roof to fire down into the oncoming marines. That was slowing the progress of the ground assault, and giving Rufus a little breathing space — at least a dozen seconds worth — to decide how to proceed.

Rufus knew he needed to pull back: being overrun was bad tactics, and the Martians were proving determined enough to do just that.

"Rolling retreat to the rear end. Let them have the courtyard, we'll cut them down in here. Trucks first, park back there, establish first perimeter."

I don't know if that makes sense to you, as it didn't make sense to me until I followed what happened next. Basically, Rufus' first line had been facing the street, using the various concrete walls and plant furniture as cover. Now he was going to pull his squad back from that line, through the courtyard between the buildings. His officers would take up positions on the far side of the open space, so that when the Martians charged into the courtyard, they would be gunned down in what can best be described as a killing field.

The two hover vehicles would withdraw first, and their drivers would hop out and offer cover fire for the rest of their squad as it retreated.

That was the plan, then: two drivers to cover the fallback move by six of Rufus' officers who remained at the front.

It all happened very quickly — getting into minute three here.

The two vehicles moved, landed, and the drivers got out and under cover. They called to Rufus that they were in position and then the Branchers started to leapfrog backwards.

It went three and three: three covered while three pulled back.

Knowing what was happening, Charlie and his two remaining shooters laid down as much interdiction fire as they could from the roof.

One Special Brancher went down on the pullback — but only one. He was left in the middle of the courtyard while the rest made it to cover, and keeping with the over-enthusiasm they'd demonstrated so far, the first two squads of Martians came rushing in, disorganized and making no use of cover.

Two thirds of them were shot down instantly, the rest diving for cover in scattered positions while Rufus' shooters kept their heads down.

Because Gina's team had been forced to the back of their roof by tank fire, two of her shooters had a good look straight down on those Martians who'd taken cover in the courtyard, and after some quick shooting, none were left active.

Gina would have directed that fire, but she was with her laser gunner, trying to line up another shot against the armor, despite the continued mag fire that was countering her efforts to get in position. She was leading the gunner, running between bits of cover on the roof. They found a concrete half-wall that offered a good vantage point, so they dove behind it. Then, with as little delay as possible, they both rose up halfway behind the wall, and took aim at the nearest tank.

The tank shot first.

The mag shot burned off everything that was exposed. That's the least gruesome way to describe how they died.

Down to nineteen.

Charlie realized he and his last two shooters were now surrounded: their building was flanked on all sides by Martian troops, some of whom would undoubtedly be coming up to get the Special Branchers on the roof.

But there was no question of getting lifted off the roof: any hover vehicle that tried to reach them would be blown out of the sky.

It was up to Rufus to keep the Martians as distracted as possible on ground level.

"Maximum fire support into the courtyard," Charlie ordered with that in mind.

Ben acknowledged: he and his laser gunner would keep on the tanks, but for now his other two shooters, the two survivors from Gina's team, and Charlie and one of his shooters would rain mag fire into the courtyard, to support Rufus' ground position.

Charlie's laser gunner separated herself from him and his other shooter, and turned on the tanks as well.

But the Martians were getting wise, and their marines had stopped running headlong into the killing field that was the courtyard. They'd be working their way around the outside of the apartment complex, trying to flank Rufus... and they'd be trying to get to the rooftops, or even just to higher-storey windows inside the buildings, to get better angles on his officers.

And soon they'd have tanks right above to help.

This was minute four.

Ben Belete and his laser gunner crept up from behind cover, and their shot punched the hoverpad of one of the tanks. It swerved and dropped, then began to regain control... but not before it went sideways into a building. The crew probably survived, but it was out of action.

The other two tanks were set to drill Ben and his gunner.

Fortunately, the hovertruck that Rufus had dispatched had reached a good firing position.

Because of the relative confusion of this fight, the Martians didn't entirely realize that the red, military-built vehicle floating into formation near their tanks was in fact being flown by a Brancher. It only became clear when the door flew open and a shoulder-laser shot punched the pad of the next tank in line, causing it to roll over and crash straight into the ground below.

Realizing the subterfuge, the last tank of the quartet turned on the truck. No way that vehicle would survive a tank shot, but the two Branchers inside would be damned if they let the last Martian escape to menace the apartments.

The tank gun and the shoulder laser fired at essentially the same moment. Both vehicles plunged to the ground in flames.

Seventeen Branchers left.

Ben turned back to the courtyard, and then waved his gunner to join him at the edge of the roof, to put some laser fire down on the Martian marines.

Behind him in the distance, eight new tanks lifted off from their depot: the Martians had probably been holding them back, fearing this was just a feint. But whether it was a decoy or not, they had to respond with enough force to contain it.

Marines managed to get around Rufus' flank relatively quickly. His position was essentially on the back corner of one of the rearmost apartments, so Martians coming around the outside (the direction the tanks had been approaching from) made first contact.

One of Rufus' drivers had been covering that direction, and he shot three of them before a blast caught him in the vest... and then two more caught him in the vest. Already melted, the panels in that body protection shattered, sending molten shards of alloy through him like a rain of daggers.

Rufus himself redeployed as he realized the threat, and shot three more Martian troopers. Another of his officers joined him, and together they drove back the attack from that direction.

But then another attack came from the opposite side — the side that was between his squad and the airlock they'd come in through. Three of his officers turned to drive that attack back, one of them almost instantly being shot through the head in the crossfire.

Down to fifteen Branchers. And the Martians were coming from all sides to get Rufus' team.

He started shoveling grenades into his underbarrel launcher, and letting them fly.

As the explosions started to sound from the various types of grenades Rufus had to shoot, the two survivors of Gina's team hurried to another corner of the roof, where they knew a platoon of Martians was rallying for the attack. Leaning over the side, these two officers dropped grenades, and chased them with intense mag fire.

The attack was literally a straight-down one, and as the Martians scattered for cover, they left nine of their comrades behind on the ground.

Little moves like that bought seconds, or tens of seconds, all of which were important.

One of Ben's shooters got caught in the neck by a lucky return of fire, and went head-first off the roof. The Captain could not afford to pay much attention to that, and simply continued shooting at the Martians below.

But then his laser gunner tapped him on the shoulder, "Eight tanks coming!"

"Eight tanks coming!" Ben repeated so Charlie and Rufus would hear.

He then turned and joined his gunner as they looked for positions to begin opening fire.

Charlie looked back out towards the right of the dome, and saw the tanks approaching. He then swung around and looked down into the courtyard, and saw the Martians moving in tactical columns along the sides of the buildings. He shot five more of their troopers as he watched them deploy.

Then he got a feeling there was other trouble.

"Stairs!"

It was a well-timed warning: his laser gunner dropped her shoulder weapon and managed to get her MAG-90 up in time to shoot the first Martian who threw open the door to the internal stairway.

Martians were coming up to throw Charlie's team off the roof.

"They're on our roof. Be careful," Charlie called.

"Got them here, boss," his gunner assured as she shot two more troopers short of exiting the stairway. She was joined by the other shooter just in time to stop a rush. For the moment, stopping incursions onto the roof from the stairway was relatively simple... but the Martians would learn quickly, and try alternate routes.

Charlie kept shooting down into the courtyard, but he switched his mind to automatic — he targeted and shot on instinct. He needed to think.

He was down to fourteen people, from twenty-four. They'd killed dozens... probably over a hundred Martians by now. But they were going to be overwhelmed any moment.

Had they held on long enough?

He didn't know. Charlie wasn't completely superhuman: he'd lost track of time. There wasn't a clock conveniently placed on the roof for him — nothing that would constantly remind him of how much time he had until reinforcements arrived.

Hopefully it was soon. Because if it wasn't, the Martians would secure this area and the assault would fail.

After five minutes in hell, that would be a terrible turn of events.

But sometimes, the cavalry does show up, right when you need it to.

CHAPTER TWENTY-NINE

HANDOFF

When forty-eight Special Branchers come hurrying out of an airlock in open order, shooting with the lethal precision we know Special Branchers possess, and using cover to its maximum effect, that pretty much ends a fight, doesn't it?

Especially when, behind that first forty-eight, another 144 are coming?

Ha. No.

Not even close.

The Martians on the ground near the lock didn't know what hit them, though. They were focused on dealing with Rufus and Charlie, and they were by no means ready for the lethal influx of attackers on the flank. As such, the Branchers from LVC006 gunned them down by the dozen. We don't know exactly how many Martians went down — all we do know is that, in this area of the government dome, the bodies of more than 450 of their troopers were later cleared by medics.

How many of those were shot by the pathfinders and how many were taken down by the influx of reinforcements is anyone's guess, but it does go to show just how devastating our elite operators are. That's why we lead with them — that's why regular SF come later.

But by no means was this fight over. The ground around Rufus got cleared pretty quickly, but there were still Martians in the three apartments, climbing to the roofs to get at Charlie's squad, and there were still eight tanks hovering, angry and determined.

And there was no question now that the main landing was coming from this direction, so the Martians were mobilizing their last eighteen tanks, and over 3,500 marines and Commandos, to evict Special Branch from the dome.

That would take time, and frankly, I'm not going to try to explain how all of it happened. Right now, the question we have to consider is simple: how many of Charlie's people would die before the newly arrived reinforcements could get between him and the eight tanks that were already on the way.

Because, despite what the movies and the games often suggest, the arrival of the reinforcements does not automatically make the holding force invulnerable. Far from it. Charlie's teams in particular were on rooftops, very exposed to the tanks and with no easy way out.

And, because they were Charlie's Special Branchers, they were picking a fight with the eight tanks. I mean, they had nowhere else to go, so why not be productive while they sat and waited for relief?

Ben Belete's gunner sent a laser shot right into the front of the lead tank, and cracked its armor plate. That vehicle backed up in formation, so one of its fellows with intact armor could lead the way. Charlie's gunner fired next, and managed a glancing hit on another tank, but nothing to really put it down.

The tanks were still out just a little too far for their mags to return accurate fire, so they waited, not wanting to chance hitting the apartments with a wild shot.

Charlie paid little direct attention. He knew where the Martians were, but his MAG-90 wasn't going to do anything to them, even when set on full. Instead he focused on trashing the nervous systems of Martian troopers below, who were now starting to hastily redeploy and withdraw under the threat of fresh Branchers from the lock.

On the ground below, the assaults against Rufus' position began to melt away. He looked around, saw black-clad Branchers hustling out of the lock, and actually allowed himself to breathe a sigh of relief. Then he waved a couple of his officers to the hovertrucks, "Let's get Charlie's team."

Without delay, Rufus and two drivers got to the remaining commandeered vehicles and fired them up.

"Keep the buildings between us and the tanks. Up and down like an elevator," Rufus ordered quickly, then let Charlie know he was coming up. "Side elevators, hop onto the roof."

Again with the short and choppy combat communications, but Charlie was completely on the same page as Rufus; it was all either of them needed.

Staying low, the vehicles hovered to the bases of the first two apartments and then climbed up vertically, until they were almost level with the rooftops. Charlie's team had access to one, and they unceremoniously jumped onto the roof of the vehicle. The remains of Gina's team repeated the process on the other.

Both cars went straight down again, with the Branchers on the roof holding on tight, while shooters on the ground made sure no Martians tried to bring the cars down more hastily than intended.

When they were two meters from the ground, both cars stopped and allowed their passengers to hop off. Charlie waved to the driver of his vehicle, then used hand gestures to order his laser gunner to get in. This car might be able to get a shot or two against one of the oncoming tanks, while the other one, which Rufus was in, collected Ben Belete's team.

Both cars floated off, and Charlie looked around him.

He was literally surrounded by red-clad bodies. Martians carpeted the courtyard, some of them groaning, others dead, some in comas. It had certainly been a killing field.

And there was no time to dwell on that; with the last shooter from his team in tow, he found a good position and laid down additional suppressing fire to help cover the arrival of the newcomers.

Ben Belete hopped onto Rufus' car just as the mag shots from the approaching tanks started blazing over the roof. The car began to drop immediately, and the veteran Captain nearly lost his grip and slid off the vehicle, but his gunner got a hold of him.

Once they descended to the ground, Rufus hopped out and Ben's team jumped off. Looking them over, Rufus nodded to the gunner, "In the car?"

She frowned, then shook her head, "I'm better from ground level."

"Go to it."

Dialogue that fired as rapidly as Branchers' MAG-90s. The gunner and Ben's other shooter hurried off around the side of the building they'd just come down from, getting set to take more laser shots at the tanks from ground level.

Overhead, the hovercar with Charlie's gunner got into position and opened fire on the tanks, only to be slammed by two mag shots. The driver was clever, though, and with the last of his hoverpad's energy he swung the vehicle behind one of the apartments, and then stabilized its descent into a crash-landing, instead of a crash.

Both Branchers crawled out of the wreck, and stayed on their feet.

True to her word, Ben's gunner brought down one of the tanks a moment later, and then hurried back to join her Captain and Rufus behind the building.

There was no point waiting there: together they all hurried towards the rest of their respective squads, and towards the reinforcements that were continuing to pour through the lock.

Charlie repositioned so he had a direct line of sight to the lock.

"One tank down, one damaged. Seven coming total."

As that came into his ear, he nodded. There were fewer Martians to shoot at now, so he was keeping low and easing off on his fire as he assessed the situation. Those tanks would be over this park area in a moment, and that could be trouble for the assault forces—

"Major Peters or Major Chang, you there?"

That was a new voice in Charlie's ear. He tapped his comm, "Peters here."

"Ronald here, commanding LVC006 assault company. Situation?"

"Martians running on foot, seven tanks will be over the park in thirty seconds."

"Roger."

That was Lieutenant Colonel Garth Ronald, who was commanding the Branchers coming out of LVC006. He'd just stepped out of the lock with his Command and Control team (I believe the jargon for that is C2), and was looking for the clearest available picture of the immediate situation. Charlie had just given it to him, with more of that rapid-fire dialogue that clearly suited the occasion.

Charlie could see Colonel Ronald from his vantage point. He didn't know the tall, lanky man, but he had to assume there was a reason he'd been put in command of the first LVC to reach the Mercury Capital Dome.

Turned out he was right: Garth Ronald had a good head for dome invasions.

As Charlie watched, the Colonel called in a gunskiff from the LVC. Defense Command never bothered with tanks — they were virtually useless in assault operations, and it was a strongly-held doctrinal belief that high-mobility, high-firepower units were more effective. The simplicity of that assertion was going to be rethought after the war, when this assault was reflected upon, but that's not relevant right now.

What matters is that SF and Special Branch did keep a force of 'skiffs' for this sort of mission. We never saw them in day-to-day operations, because they'd been developed explicitly for assaults like this one... so I suppose it makes sense that they used one under the current circumstances.

If you've never seen a picture or vid of one, a skiff is basically... well... it's about half the width of a hovercar, with high armored sides and a heavy weapon at the front. It's designed to be quick, and to be able to fit into alleys and other cramped spaces. It's also small enough to come through a personnel lock, instead of needing to go through a cargo lock like most vehicles.

This particular skiff was a two seater — one officer piloting from the rear, one gunner in the front, and it mounted a double-barrel laser cannon that had about four times the hitting power of a shoulder laser.

As it appeared out of the lock, the vehicle pulled up next to the Colonel for instructions, then it turned towards the apartments and glided at about five meters altitude, clearly keeping the buildings between it and the tanks.

Charlie watched it come, then tapped his comm, "Rufus, skiff coming. Support fire."

Rufus still had two shoulder lasers from his own squad, and both Charlie's gunner and Ben Belete's were with him too — that was four shoulder lasers that could support the skiff when it went up against the tanks.

A second skiff popped through the lock as Charlie gave that order, and it hurried after its comrade. They were, on the face of it, quite outgunned… but that's never stopped Branchers, as probably doesn't surprise you.

Repositioning to the corner of the building, Charlie looked up and to the right, where the seven tanks were rolling in. They weren't firing yet, because the Branchers weren't clustered anywhere to give them a big target. Hopefully the Martians didn't realize how much firepower was waiting for them.

The skiffs started to climb: they'd pop up over the tops of the apartments and open fire. Seeing this, Charlie tapped his comm, "They're up."

Rufus didn't respond, but his four gunners hurried out from behind cover — all of them very well spread out — and cut loose with the shoulder lasers.

One tank took a nasty hit and plummeted, and one more side-slipped and banged into one of its fellows. They all started to nose down to send mag fire into the clusters of Special Branchers who'd done the shooting.

Right on time, then, the skiffs popped up, lasers blazing.

Two tanks immediately went nose-first into the ground, and one more started spewing smoke, and swung away. The last three began reorienting, and the first of them got a solid mag shot off, which nastily batted one of the skiffs aside.

It managed to spiral to a non-lethal landing, but its gunner had been burned away. Only the pilot survived.

The second skiff pounded the shooting tank, and it went down. Before the last duo of tanks could return fire, the skiff dipped behind the apartment again. Seeing the confusion, Rufus ordered the gunners to shoot at the tanks, and though neither was brought down by shoulder lasers, they both withdrew in confusion.

A little more time bought.

In turning back the tanks, Rufus and the skiffs had eliminated the immediate threat to the toehold here. The Martians were now forced to regroup and reorganize — it would take them at least five minutes to get deployed again. Maybe ten minutes.

And that was enough time for the Special Branchers to set up a rough perimeter.

For his part, Charlie hurried back towards the lock, moving low and keeping his rifle up in case there was a quick counterattack somewhere. He found Colonel Ronald behind the first line of hedges Gina had used for cover when they'd breached the lock, and he nodded as he knelt beside the assault company commander.

"Charlie Peters," he introduced himself.

"Garth Ronald," the Lieutenant Colonel extended a hand. Charlie took the hand, though it seemed a little odd to do so under the circumstances.

"Good foothold," the commander continued after a second.

"For now," our intrepid Major agreed.

Ronald was about to agree when a voice came into his ear, "Where? Okay, secure both, I'll call up." Ignoring Charlie by necessity, the Colonel tapped his comm to patch in to *Artemis Agrotera*, and Peri Oktar. "Ronald, LVC006. Firm footing. Have two locks in industrial sector…" one member of his C2 team put a map pad in front of him as he spoke, "…numbers 010 and 011. Secured. Request SF support for stabilization."

Charlie couldn't hear the response from Peri Oktar's side of the line, but I can tell you that she immediately dispatched LVC026 and LVC034 to those two locks — two more emergency airlocks that had just been located and secured by Ronald's Branchers as they hurried into the dome.

Because Charlie and Rufus had drawn so many Martian defensive units off station, there were gaps in the line now, and the Branchers were exploiting them. The industrial sector and its many warehouses were to the 'west' (left) of the apartments, and two of Ronald's teams had headed right for them, and secured the airlocks there. Now reinforcements could enter those locks as well as the one Charlie and Rufus had come through.

This was how the whole assault would work: a new force would come in, secure additional locks, and more reinforcements would arrive. They, in turn, would secure even more locks, and even more reinforcements would arrive. Eventually, the balance would tip completely against the Martians: they'd have no way to contain the invaders, and would undoubtedly be scattered and confused by the many incursions…

But the risk wasn't over. If the Martians did manage to stop reinforcements arriving, they could turn the tide. It was still a bitter fight… just one that was leaning increasingly in Defense Command's favor.

So now there was another five minutes of hell coming, as LVC026 and LVC034 hurried down with their loads of SF guards, skiffs, and other equipment.

However, Rufus and Charlie had done their part.

"Alright," Garth Ronald turned back to Charlie, "losses?"

"Ten down at last check."

A nod was Ronald's first answer, then he bobbed his head back towards the lock, "Break time for you. Collect both your squads and take five to rearm and reequip. Then you're my reserve."

Charlie wasn't going to complain about that — five minutes off in this sort of situation was a veritable vacation. And then their squads would be in reserve… meaning they'd see a ton of action, but not two tons like everyone else.

At least until the Martians counterattacked… then they'd see two tons or more.

Because there was no real place to get a rest when you were invading a dome. Just places and times to stop for a second and catch your breath.

That's what Charlie, Rufus, and their squads had earned. At a dear enough cost, I should say.

Charlie called his officers, and together they hustled back into the belly of LVC006, where they replenished their energy cells and grenades, and took a minute to see who was left and who was dead.

Then they went back out to fight.

CHAPTER THIRTY

SUMMARY

I could spend 200 pages talking about the rest of that invasion. In many ways, it was textbook: we took locks all around the perimeter of the Capital Dome, and eventually overwhelmed the defenders. Over 800 Martians died, and 1,104 were wounded. Sixty-one civilians died as well, which was very unfortunate, but almost unavoidable.

Not that it being unavoidable makes it any less horrific.

We ended up putting 4,100 Special Branchers and SF into that dome; 562 were killed, and just about 1,000 wounded. The reason our losses as the attacker were less than the losses of the defenders in this case is usually put down to the fact that a huge number of Special Branchers were part of the landing. When the regular SF started arriving, our losses climbed greatly — they just aren't trained the same way Branchers are, as we know.

The happiest news from our perspective: neither Charlie nor Rufus lost anyone else that day. That *whole* day. In fact, they didn't lose another officer before the civilian government surrendered. Though, as you probably know, the fighting didn't stop with that declaration of surrender, which came during the night.

More on that next book, of course. But just to sum up, the fighting in the Capital Dome went our way, and did so relatively quickly.

The other domes that were invaded by DC forces had similar outcomes. I know it probably sounds like I'm being self-congratulatory here, but it's true. We put roughly 3,000 Special Branch and SF into each of the other two domes we'd been assigned, and in both cases our losses were in the 450 dead, 900 wounded range. In return, the Martians suffered roughly 800 dead and 1,000 wounded, the spread again coming from the superiority of Special Branchers.

The Imperial Army had five domes to take, if you'll recall, and 30,000 men (yes, men) with whom to make that happen.

Now, you can say I'm being a Defense Command elitist, or a prejudiced fool, or just a plain old asshole, but the blockheads did a real dastardly job.

The numbers bear this out: each of their domes took 6,000 of their troopers, of whom roughly 1,000 never came home, and 2,000 were wounded.

That's nearly 5,000 *dead*, and 10,000 wounded, from their own forces. Half of all their combatants. The Martians didn't have particularly large numbers of troops in any of these domes — roughly 2,500 to 3,000 in each — but because the Army's Gamma Force Commandos failed to do the job Charlie's pathfinders did, things went much worse.

Imagine what would have happened to Colonel Ronald if all those troops and tanks that Charlie and Rufus had held up had simply been in place, ready to shoot his assault forces as soon as they came through the lock?

Imperial Army-level casualties would have happened.

Charlie isn't nearly as critical of the blockheads as I am in this case — he sees what he and Rufus experienced as being a near-run thing… they could have had bad luck and been driven back as well… but I don't buy it. The Gammas, the Army's supposed elite, were up against the same sorts of Martians, just fewer of them. And they failed.

And then General Ronald Hubert Frederick III had ordered his commanders to simply overwhelm the defenses at the airlocks they breached. Walls of blockheads sent into the teeth of the enemy, until finally the enemy was overwhelmed and a toehold gained.

As I say, Charlie cautions me about criticizing the Imperial Army for suffering this, and perhaps he's right… but it seems to me that, for all their vaunted expertise, they didn't do so well.

What really gets me, though… what's probably really at the core of my disdain right now… is how the blockheads reacted when they got into the dome, having suffered such massive casualties.

Furious at their own losses, and refusing to blame themselves for not handling the situation adeptly, they unleashed hell on their five domes — five domes that were largely residential and commercial.

In the Capital Dome, sixty-one civilians died. Numbers were similar in our other two domes. The average for the blockhead domes was over 300, with the worst dome seeing 916 civilians killed.

We didn't actually get these numbers until the following year, for reasons that you might already know. They reported numbers much more in line with our own during these days of the attack, and when the Martians screamed bloody murder we just assumed they were trying to cause trouble.

Because surely, for all our bitterness and prejudice against them, the blockheads couldn't so callously target and destroy civilian groups in the street. They'd never treat unarmed persons that way.

That, I believe, is what they call black humor. And the last time I remember mentioning black humor in these books was back in *The Independent Squadron*, when Charlie's team — many of whom were now dead — had been going around in a hover truck with 'Your Floral Specialists' emblazoned on the hood.

Ironic that the last mention of black humor was on Egesta… the place where the blockheads who assaulted Mercury had done their training. The Martians really didn't know how lucky they were — the blockheads here had been well behaved by comparison.

But that's more for next year's books than it is for now.

To finish this sum-up, we took Mercury, and by the next morning every dome had officially surrendered… meaning the next stage of fighting would be far more complicated and messy. We'll deal with that in *The Fleet Clash*.

For now, we just had a lot of pieces to pick up, and a lot of deep, relieved breaths to take.

The Mercury assault was over. And we'd won.

Now let's tidy up the loose ends…

CHAPTER THIRTY-ONE

GOT AWAY

"We're not going to catch them, are we?"

It was nearing 2330 hours... the middle of the night... and Lia Hawke didn't look the slightest bit tired. Courtesans never look tired. They always look perfectly awake and lively, and when they retire to their cabins they have throbbing headaches to show for it.

Or so Lia tells me.

Karen didn't bother to put on a brave face — she was weary from a full day of action, and knew there was no shame in that fact. Of course, being that she's made of goddess stuff, she didn't look half bad at all.

Who am I kidding, forget 'half': she didn't look at all bad. But then you know I'm hugely biased about these matters.

Anyway, this scene (and this chapter) occur the night of the surrender, but not before it. Lia had just observed that the last Martian destroyers and destroyer escorts they'd been chasing weren't going to slow down... and she was right.

Remember, Karen and Lia had been sent to chase the retreating destroyers and destroyer escorts after the main force action, their mission being to dog those ships and make sure they didn't double back to Mercury to interfere with the landings.

Now that the landings were well underway, though, there was no reason for those ships to stick around. Five destroyers and six destroyer escorts (all that remained of the survivors after a couple of close encounters with Lia and Karen's force) were running full speed away from Mercury, and it didn't take a genius to figure out where they were heading. Even I could have managed it, so it goes without saying that both Lia and Karen knew it.

They were running to the Forge, to tell Bort McWebsbert that he'd been fooled and that his battle group was the only Martian force left this side of Earth. In fact, one of them might have already sent off a message to the Forge to warn him.

Because those surviving Martians were running so quickly, it seemed highly unlikely that Karen or Lia would catch them. It was clear they weren't going to endanger the landings, so that meant the ladies' job was pretty much at an end.

"Let's turn back for Mercury," Karen decided aloud, and Lia nodded.

"I think so," Lia said almost casually.

She completely concealed her desire to get to the planet. But as she told me later, those hours of eventless chasing had given her plenty of time to start worrying again. There'd been no updates from Mercury beyond the most general 'we're doing well'.

The fate of a certain pathfinder was of huge interest to Lady Hawke, and she wasn't going to be hours away when she learned of it.

Led by *Lady Grace* and *Whirlwind*, the frigates and corvettes of the chase force turned back to Mercury. They let the survivors of the Mercury Squadron flee to the Forge. We'd see them again. In fact, *Melbourne* would be seeing them very soon... and they wouldn't be seeing *Melbourne*. But again, I can't elaborate on that.

For now, Karen and Lia turned towards Mercury.

Towing *Cyclops* to Mercury was quite an operation, and it wasn't until around the same time that Lia and Karen were turning away from their pursuit that the haggard battleship was safely adrift in a loose orbit around the planet.

Mik was finally getting off the ship.

I waited for him in the observation lounge next to landing bay two, feeling more than a little fatigued myself. After finishing off the monitors, we'd had quite a lot of searching and rescuing to do — hundreds of Martian survivors were taken, and were at this moment being delivered to *Athena Promachos* where they'd be interned for the time being. After that it had been a matter of rigging up our well-used tow cables to *Cyclops*, and along with *Friendly*, pulling the veteran to safety. Mark Gunney had kept *Cheetah* free from towing, to serve as our escort.

But soon we'd be able to steal a few hours' sleep, and figure out the next steps. The wreckage of the day's carnage would all be collected in one place — over Mercury — and after that we could take stock.

Mik's shuttle came into the bay smoothly as I thought about that. I watched as it landed and the doors shut, and once the compartment repressurized I headed out there to greet him. The shuttle's ramp dropped, and first off were a bunch of haggard-looking spacers who clearly needed a shower and a cot. One of the Lieutenants on deck took charge of them while I waited.

The hundreds of wounded from *Cyclops* were already on *Persephone Praxidice*, which was serving as our medical ship now that it had unloaded its SF. Too bad that ship hadn't been named *Persephone Sotiera*... sorry, classicist joke. If you've ever wondered, the second part of the names on those *Goddess*-class combat storeships is an epithet — what the ancient Greeks used to classify the characteristic of the God they were referring to.

Persephone, for instance, was the Goddess of the underworld, after a kidnapping incident that saw her taken by Hades. An incident, I feel completely inappropriately compelled to point out, that would not have happened had Charlie Peters or any of our superb Special Branchers been there to intervene. Oh yes, I am quite randomly asserting that the men and women who just stormed the Capital Dome on Mercury could in fact stop a lusty Greek God from kidnapping a girl.

Go ahead and prove me wrong.

Sorry. Anyway. In *Persephone Praxidice's* case, the epithet meant 'exacter of justice'. Had the ship been *Persephone Sotiera*, it would have been 'the savior', which would have been more appropriate for a hospital ship... though let's be honest, assigning hospital duties to a ship named after the Goddess of the underworld feels like stacking the deck against the wounded.

They might have done better on *Artemis Agrotera* (Artemis the huntress), *Demeter Erinys* (Demeter the furious), or *Athena Promachos* (Athena who battles from the front lines).

Or. Hm. Not. All of them sound pretty mean, actually.

And really, this is all quite irrelevant. Sorry, little things like this distract me, as you well know by now.

Mik was coming down the ramp. Let's get back to the narrative and talk to him.

"Long day," I made that rather obvious remark as Mik saw me.

"Yes," he agreed, managing a tired smile. "Yes it was."

Stopping at the bottom of the ramp, he extended his hand and I took it.

"You did an excellent job," I said firmly. "How's your ship?"

Mik laughed the way you do when you damned well better laugh, because if you don't you might as well fall over and die. Not to put too fine a point on it.

"Some of it's still there. Honestly, I don't know if they're going to salvage it... probably be cheaper just to build a new one."

I nodded slowly, then bobbed my head towards the lounge, "Come on. We're taking sixty of your crew aboard here until *Demeter Erinys* is set to receive you in some comfort. It'll be a bit crowded, but we'll make do."

"Figured," Mik nodded. "Thanks."

"Not a problem. We couldn't let you sleep over there... who knows what's left of your radiation shielding. This close to the sun..."

"Yeah," Mik agreed solemnly. He was determined to keep his spirits up, but he was both exhausted and saddened. His ship was dead or dying, and with it many of his crew.

For a skipper of his caliber and character, that was one of the worst possible fates. But of course he had nothing to be ashamed of, and he'd be well rewarded for his fine work this day.

Well, 'rewarded' is one word for it. I'll explain that later. In the meantime, we headed off to grab some food before I directed him to sleeping quarters. It had indeed been a long day.

"Five minutes," Charlie announced as the word came through his comm.

There were a few groans of relief at that. It was dark in the dome, as the Martians were still clinging to their HQ buildings. If we'd been able to, we'd have turned on the daylight to make clearing buildings a little easier and safer.

Rufus sat down next to Charlie. They were actually in the lobby of the Mercury Government House, where the Governor had been during the day, before he'd retreated to the HQ building. There'd been a sniper on the roof of this building, taking shots at SF as they exited a nearby airlock, so Rufus and Charlie had been sent in to clear the place.

Job done with one dead Martian and no one lost from their teams, they'd earned a five-minute respite from Colonel Ronald.

That, for them, was enough to completely recharge and get ready to go out again.

Alright, that's an exaggeration, but still, it was a good break. And they were going to keep going all night. Like the other couple of hundred Special Branch in the dome, they'd be doing sweeps and dealing with improvised attacks until morning.

And then tomorrow, Charlie figured they'd be on to the tunnels, where Commandos and hard core resistors would have almost certainly fled.

That would be deadly, as I think we've drummed into you over and over by now.

But Charlie sighed and put all of that out of his head. Five minutes of peace and quiet.

"You sent a message up to let her know you're fine?"

Rufus' question caught Charlie by surprise, and immediately he frowned. It took him a whole second to shift mental gears and figure out what his counterpart was talking about. He wasn't used to having Lia so close to a fight... if she'd been this close to his battles over the whole course of their relationship, she'd probably have ulcers.

It was a good point, then.

Tapping his comm, Charlie connected to *Artemis Agrotera's* signal grid. When a technician acknowledged him, he inquired, "*Whirlwind* in realtime range?"

He just went ahead and assumed that the ship still existed, because he'd watched it come through the main force action. It seemed hugely unlikely that anything would have happened to it after that, and he was right.

"No sir, just reversed course and is coming in. Want to record a message?"

Charlie paused. He hated the thought of recording a message to Lia saying he was fine, and then have her open it, feel relieved, and then find out that just after he'd recorded it someone had shot off the top of his head. He couldn't do that to her.

"No... is *Wolf* in realtime range?"

He hadn't actually asked about us yet — the outcome of the fight with the monitors had not been clear when he'd landed (I know it may not have read that way, but that's because I was trying to keep things more organized than chronological). Still, he assumed that we'd survived, because he knew *Wolf's* crew, backed by Mik, Matt and Mark, could get it done, even with me tagging along.

"Yes sir, should I patch you through?"

"Yes please."

I'd just gotten back to my cabin after meeting with Mik when my screen chimed, indicating the realtime signal. I activated it instantly, and heard the thump of an audio feed kicking in. Since it was Charlie's headset comm, there was no picture, but that helped me figure out who it was.

"How'd it go down there?" I asked without checking to see if I was right. Because I was.

"Messy, but it worked. We lost ten, but we'll have the dome soon."

"Ten... Glad it's almost finished," I sat down on the end of my bed and began pulling off my boots. "*Cyclops* is a writeoff, but we got the monitors. Mik did a hell of a job. So did Mark and Matt and Andrea. And Karen and Lia chased the last of the Martians away... they're on their way back here now. Lia will probably be looking for news."

"Thought so," Charlie replied. "I don't want to record a message saying 'I'm fine' in case something happens. Call her for me?"

I looked up at that. The fight was over for me, so my perspective on things had already begun to shift away from that somber acceptance of possible death. Charlie was still in a fight, though, and he made a good point. At least I thought it was a good point.

"I'll call her as soon as she's in range. Try not to die, will you? I'm terrible at breaking bad news to people."

It was a lame attempt at morbid humor, which probably will make events in next book seem somehow more unpleasant. Charlie charitably laughed once, very shortly, "That's not the only reason I'll try not to."

"Good point."

We were silent for a moment after that, and then Charlie closed things off, "We're moving out again. Talk to you later."

"See to it you do," I concurred.

The feed cut, and I sat on the end of my bed wondering if that would be the last conversation I ever had with my friend Charlie Peters. That sort of grim thinking seemed inevitable on a day like this, more than any other day that had gone before it.

But we had won. That was something.

CHAPTER THIRTY-TWO
SETTING UP THE CLASH

John Fiora and Wes Pellew were in *Venus One's* C&C, looking over the reports that we'd sent back from Mercury the next morning.

"Went as well as we could have hoped," Wes observed quietly as the information rolled. He was still more than a little disappointed that he'd had to miss the action — that his Independent Squadron had been assigned to remain on the defensive at Venus. But he knew, based on watching these reports, that action was still going to be coming his way.

Nodding slowly, John folded his arms, "The Martians won't be happy. And the *Tharsis* Squadron is probably going to be coming out and looking for a fight."

Still sitting at the Forge, the *Tharsis* Squadron under Bort McWebsbert included three battleships, five destroyers and seven destroyer escorts… and based on things *Melbourne* may or may not have been watching, the five destroyers and six destroyer escorts that Karen and Lia had chased away were going to join them.

A force of twenty-six ships, three of them the mighty *Tharsis* battleships, would be looking for blood.

The question that John and Wes had to consider was where those ships would head. By the time the escapees from the Mercury Squadron reached the Forge, the orbits would have changed… that is to say, Mercury and Venus would both be roughly equidistant from the base — both in the same general direction, too.

So the Martians could cruise out of the Forge in the general direction of both, and then catch us off guard by turning one way or the other at the last minute.

If they went after Mercury, the battered assault force wouldn't be in particularly good shape if the *Tharsis* battlewagons and their long range lasers appeared… if they went after Venus, Wes' Independent Squadron would be at a huge disadvantage, outnumbered more than two-to-one as it tried to escort the *Bonnie* Squadron.

The Defense Command fleet was divided in the face of an enemy who was concentrating. Which, as far as John and Wes were concerned, meant one thing.

"So, we go out there and meet them in open space?" Wes asked the question first, and John looked up at him.

"I think so."

That was all they could do: summon some of the active ships from Mercury and rendezvous with them in the space between those two planets and the Forge. Then they'd have to try to run into the *Tharsis* Squadron well short of either planet — catch them on the move.

I probably don't need to say (again) that trying to catch an enemy in the middle of the black is never an easy proposition — space is big and it's empty, so it's more than possible that you could cruise right past the force you've been sent to intercept.

But there was a trump card in our pocket: *Melbourne's* shipboard wizard (let's call him Joe) was probably watching something of use... something cryptic and sufficiently non-descriptive to not get me in trouble, but which would be hugely helpful to John in making this interception.

"We'll need to call in more escorts from Mercury," Wes observed quietly, folding his arms. "They'll have quite an advantage otherwise."

John nodded, "Yes. And we'll need to put a couple of battleships here as well. Or bring them out with us, to offset their advantage in escorts... we'll have to see. But we need to regroup our forces. Or they could still win."

Indeed, from Bort's perspective this could have been an ideal setup — we had divided our fleets while he was taking in reinforcements from Mercury... if he attacked either of the planets we were holding now, he'd have a superior force.

He couldn't know (as you can't) that we might possibly have had a way to keep an eye on his movements, that would allow us to concentrate and intercept him short of his target. But even if he had known, this was still probably the best opportunity he'd have to tip the balance of the war.

Because if Mercury remained in our hands, there was very little chance of Mars winning. And I know how choked up about that he'd be.

Ahem.

"Alright, let's pick a rendezvous point and get a message ready. We should be out there as quick as we can."

Wes nodded, and together those two started work on the plan that would lead to the Fleet Clash.

Greg had expected the message to come, so it was no surprise: he had to move most of his ships out of Mercury space and send them to rendezvous with the *Bonnies*. And he wouldn't get to attend, because he needed to oversee the occupation of Mercury. That fact left him a little disappointed — he certainly would have liked to be a part of the last battle of the war (and he was convinced that fight would be the last), but his duty required he remain where he was.

Sitting in his office on *Warspite*, though, he had to consider who to send. The escorts were relatively easy: he had fifteen corvettes, for instance, and he needed perhaps five to run patrols in this area. He'd send Karen with ten corvettes.

Frigates weren't too tough either: he'd keep five for his operations, some of them perhaps the damaged survivors of the main force action, and then send the rest out with me and Lia.

But what about the battleships? Neither *Warspite* nor *Goliath* would be in any position to move, as both were suffering from drive problems of one sort or another... that was fine, though, because they could remain on station at Mercury as defensive battlewagons. *Repulse* and *Cyclops* were both virtually out of action, so they would stay as well.

The case for *Sorceress* and *Empire* had to be made, though: both ships could fly out, but reducing the Mercury defenses to two active-but-wounded battleships would be a risk...

A risk Greg was willing to take.

So *Sorceress* and *Empire* would cruise out as well, though John would still have to decide where they should go — back to Venus, to appease the Lords there (who wouldn't like watching their mighty battleship protection fly away to fight the *Tharsis* Squadron), or out to join the battle. A choice to be made a little later, anyway.

For the time being, Greg had made his decisions. He leaned forward in his chair and tapped some controls on his desk, raising the bridge, "Contact *Sorceress*, please. I'd like realtime with Admiral Stoll."

Word filtered down to us about an hour later. I was in my cabin, reading through some after-action reports when a realtime call came in from Mark Gunney. I opened the message and he popped up on my wall screen.

"I just heard. We're going back out to get the bastards who took the Forge?"

I nodded, "Us, *Kodiak*, *Guangxi* and *Whirlwind* will be the frigate group. Karen will bring ten corvettes, and Marlene and Liam will either be coming with us or going to Venus to hold there."

Mark nodded slowly, "Sounds like a party."

"That's one word for it. How's *Cheetah*?"

Mark tipped his head with a little swagger, "We'll bring beer and chips."

I managed to smile at that, "I'll let John know. We're departing in a couple of hours, so be ready."

"Always am," Mark nodded, then the link cut.

I paused for a moment after he vanished, and thought through what was coming next. At least four *Bonnies*, ten frigates and twelve corvettes would be going out into the black to stop a Martian force of three *Tharsises*, ten destroyers and thirteen destroyer escorts. If Marlene and Liam didn't get sent to Venus to appease the Lords, that would tack on two more… though I won't be coy: the Lords got their protection. Because as tactically useless as separating out two battleships was, it was politically expedient.

But that was the setup for the Fleet Clash: twenty-six ships per side, and a hell of a fight ahead.

And Karen still wasn't going to be aboard *Wolf*…

I tried to ignore that fact and go back to my reading.

The attempt pretty much failed…

CHAPTER THIRTY-THREE

WARTIME GOODBYE

I don't think I've ever included a scene with Lia and Charlie that I wasn't personally there to witness, but I think I'd be murdered by my editors and possibly by you if I didn't give a little more information on what they were doing just before *Whirlwind* joined the battle group headed out to rendezvous with John.

Now, I should say that I've been roundly supported by the individuals featured in this chapter — they're alright with me including this. That's my polite, roundabout way of saying Charlie won't kill me. Probably.

Well, if I'm honest, he has a romantic side to him. Seriously. He could kill you with the condensation on the side of a glass of water (yes, in fact, it is getting harder to come up with random things that he could kill you with), but he's a bit of a romantic too. Believes in love and all that stuff that I obviously deny any belief in.

Okay, *now* he'll kill me.

Anyway, as you can probably tell, this chapter will involve Lia and Charlie connecting. This wasn't an easy thing to set up, largely because Charlie and Rufus were two of Colonel Ronald's go-to people when it came to dealing with problems in the Capital Dome. Their success as pathfinders had been a curse — it was decided they could be depended on to handle the most unforgiving of situations.

That meant not many chances for a break, and very few opportunities to get on the comm to a ship in orbit when there was no pressing tactical business that required it.

Finally, though, Charlie had a break. This was about three hours before our departure, so it was cutting it close. Word had filtered down to him that a large part of the orbiting force was going to pull out, and he was determined to say something to Lia before we all left.

Probably a good thing he made that decision.

Lia hadn't slept a wink. Despite her fatigue from the previous day, she couldn't switch off her mind. She reflected on the day's events, she wondered what was coming next for her ship and squadron, and she feared for Charlie.

At any given moment, any one of those concerns could be foremost on her mind, and it was wearing on her.

But then her screen chimed. She was tossing and turning in bed on *Whirlwind*, so that alert ping was a welcome interruption — even if it just turned out to be fleet business. Hell, if it turned out to be a battle alert because the Martians were returning, it'd still be better than being caught in that middle-of-the-night purgatory that comes when you can't make yourself sleep. I hate that. You probably do too.

Of course, it wasn't *just* a little respite: Charlie had gotten aboard LVC006 and found a room with a comm screen, and he was on the line.

As she sat up in bed, Lia fumbled with her remote, activated the signal, and opened the message. She was then rendered speechless.

You know by now that Lia being speechless must be a sign of something significant.

Her expression, which had been a bit strained, seemed to melt instantly. Relief took over, and a little bit of happiness, and a larger sum of worry… but relief.

"Hi there," Charlie said awkwardly. For his part, he looked just as relieved — so much so that everyone could have noticed it, not just me. He wasn't maintaining his usual Special Branch façade… he rarely did when it was just him and Lia.

"Hiiii…" she replied, letting the word drag and then following it with a very deep breath.

That threatened to be the sum total of their conversation, as for the next moment they just collected their thoughts and feelings while they stared at each other. Both were so emotionally drained that this wasn't easy.

"I'm doing alright," Charlie finally said, anticipating some of Lia's worry. "We're in a lot of close fights… nasty ones… but so far I'm okay."

Lia's expression was quickly overcome by worry, "So you're still fighting?"

Charlie nodded slowly, "Yeah. The really complicated operations start now."

"Dangerous?"

Because he's a fundamentally honest fellow, Charlie nodded, "Pretty dangerous."

Lia looked away and rubbed her neck, "You could lie about that. I wouldn't mind."

"You know me better than that," he shrugged.

She looked back at him and sighed, "Yes I do."

"Things go well for you? I heard from Ken that you were out there with Karen."

Lia nodded, "They went well. Lost some ships. Lost some people. But… it worked out. And now we're going to hit the force that took the Forge."

"I heard that," it was Charlie's turn to look worried. "Ken's going with you?"

Nodding again, Lia stared at Charlie, "Yep."

She didn't really want to say much more on that subject. Just then, she wanted all this fighting to be done, because it was getting to be too much, even for her. Not that she'd ever let anyone else see that fact.

But that was what made it so difficult: there was one person she absolutely and totally trusted — who she could be completely honest with — and there was a reasonable chance that he'd be killed, or she'd be killed, in the coming weeks.

Gee, that's something into which I think I have some insight.

It wasn't easy for her — especially her, because of the rest of her circumstances. And it was, again, the middle of the night, so the fear and doubt was at its worst.

She didn't want to talk. She wanted Charlie to jump out of the screen so she could hold onto him. Yes, I expect that sounds incredibly sappy, but you know what, it's what she wanted. And I'm sure Charlie wouldn't have been opposed to it.

But that wasn't allowed. They had jobs to do, and as I've been repeating a lot recently, there were others who were in far worse positions than these two. And both of them knew it.

"Please… um. Look after yourself," Lia decided that the conversation needed to move to an end, because it wasn't helping either of them.

Or at least she didn't *think* it was helping.

Charlie disagreed, "Is that really the last thing you want to say to me, in case I die?"

"NO," her eyes jumped to his with the protest. "Don't talk like that."

"You know you'll survive just fine if I don't," Charlie countered quietly. "It would be hard, but you'd survive it. So you have to promise me you'll be careful. Do your job... but be careful."

Lia shook her head, "I wouldn't survive..."

Her protest wasn't accepted, "Yes, you would. I don't want you to have to. I'm going to do my damndest to make sure you don't have to find out. But you need to stay safe, alright? If you don't, I'll probably just stay in this job until it kills me. One way or another."

Unconvinced but unwilling to argue, Lia let her chin sink, and she nodded once, "Let's just both not die, so this doesn't become an issue. It's upsetting me talking about it. Okay?"

Charlie winced a little and looked down.

"Okay," he agreed gently. Then he looked up again, "I'm glad I called, though. Because talking to you is a good thing. Hearing from you actually makes it a little easier."

Lia smiled sadly, "I'm sure."

Charlie repeated the sentiment, "It does."

He wasn't lying. It was a comfort in the midst of a really nasty operation — a taste of the sort of happiness that was so easily forgotten when you attacked an enemy's outer capital. That he could talk to Lia now really gave him a boost.

"Well, knowing you're still alright helps. So stay that way," she countered. "And when I'm back, and you're off that planet, then we'll... we'll hang out more."

Charlie wasn't sure whether that was just a half-jumbled hope, or a plan for the future. But he had a very distinct moment of clarity when she said it. His answer reflected that certainty: "Deal."

She frowned a little, "Deal?"

He nodded, "Once this is done. Then... well. We'll talk then."

Lia bit her bottom lip, not entirely sure what commitment he'd just given. But she didn't get a chance to find out.

"Listen, sorry, I need to get back out there. Stay safe on your mission. I will see you when you're back."

"Okay... yes," Lia nodded. "I... um. Goodbye. Love you."

"Love you too," he smiled, and the link died.

As he told me a little later, hearing Lia say she loved him actually did put a skip in Charlie's step. He felt like an idiot for having such a clichéd reaction, but in his words, 'Seriously, I was lucky there was no crossfire nearby. I'd probably have waded right in, feeling ten feet tall. And gotten blown in half. Which would have been the opposite feeling that I wanted.'

Lia was buoyed by the words too, though they certainly didn't help her sleep. She flopped back in her bed and took a deep, shaky breath, then closed her eyes. The stresses were piling up on her — her dad's death, hiding that death, her first combat commands, and the threat to Charlie... all at once.

And you know what, despite it all she was still proving that she could command a formation of warships with as much aplomb as Ian Hawke ever had... or more. As I'd always figured, she belonged in the Fiora Ring's pantheon of strong fleet officers.

That's a remarkable Lady. Charlie was a lucky man. I was lucky that she figured herself my little sister.

I was reading pads when the screen chimed. I looked at the clock as I hit the remote to open the message, wondering if it was already time to talk to Karen—

Nope it was Charlie.

We stared at each other for a second, then he asked, "Lia's going with you tomorrow?"

I nodded.

"Watch her back for me?"

"You don't even have to ask."

Charlie nodded, "Thanks."

"Watch yourself down there."

He nodded again, and the message ended.

And yes, I again wondered if that was the last time I'd ever speak to Charlie. I was full of such morbid fears during this mission, it seems.

But I couldn't decide his fate — time would tell.

For now it was back to paperwork. We'd be cruising soon.

CHAPTER THIRTY-FOUR

STILL ON OUR OWN

"Lia did great today."

Endorsements don't get much clearer than that one, and I smiled as Karen said it. I was sitting on the end of my bed, and Karen was sitting on the end of hers. It was as close to dinner together as we were going to get.

"I knew she'd have the knack for it."

Karen smiled a little impishly, "She did order her ships to 'bitch slap' the enemy."

My eyebrow went up, "Oh… really."

"Really," Karen nodded. "It got the job done."

"We all have our quirks."

It was true, we certainly did. Karen looked down for a moment after I said that, and began playing with her ponytail as it sat on her left shoulder. I watched, completely unashamedly staring and wishing I didn't have to see it in 2D. What a magical world it would be if we could have three-dimensional live projections for communications. But that was the stuff of some crazy future. Maybe the one Matt Baxter had been reading about in that book with the wolves, cats and bears.

Ha, yeah. Right.

But two dimensions were better than none, and I just took a deep breath and watched. That fact didn't escape Karen's notice.

"Are you watching me?"

"Like a creepy guy hiding in the bushes."

She laughed brightly and looked up, "I thought you looked familiar."

I shrugged, "Sorry about trampling the flowers."

She chuckled again, "Well, I shouldn't have planted them outside the bedroom window."

"It's true."

The humor tapered off after that, and we just sat and sighed. Neither of us wanted to be grim in this conversation — we'd both come through a hard day's fighting and were intact. With that behind us, we were finding something of the rhythm we'd once had when she'd been on *Lion* and I'd been on *Wolf* — before this series started.

Back when not being in the same room with Karen for weeks hadn't been a problem for me. Or for her, if I'm honest.

"It's not the same as before, is it?"

Karen's question made me blink — as usual, she was inside my musings, predicting my thoughts.

"It isn't," I agreed.

It wasn't the same as before. That was clear to both of us. Now we were enjoying this moment because it was all we'd get, and we both knew we were lucky to have it. Before the war, this moment in itself would have been special enough. I don't know if that makes sense… I hope it does.

But when you get used to having someone close, and then they're gone, that's tricky…

Sorry, I probably don't need to explain this to you yet *again*. I suppose the fact that I keep trying to re-explain (and perhaps justify) it indicates that I feel a bit uncomfortable with it, and with my inability (then and now) to get over it. But it's true… so I suppose I shouldn't be uncomfortable.

"How do you think Charlie and Lia survive, being apart so much?" Karen's next question was one I didn't see coming, and I leaned back and frowned.

"I… well. Charlie's a different sort of guy, I suppose. And Lia's obviously unique. They just… they do what they have to do, I guess. When you find what they have, you don't let go of it. Whatever the circumstances."

Karen's smile returned, and she shrugged, "I wouldn't know anything about that."

I laughed, "Obviously not. Me neither, clearly."

"And keeping a deep romance like that out of the public eye, no idea what that's like either," Karen's lips twitched a little with those words.

I laughed again, "Is this a secure channel? If someone's eavesdropping, what will they think?"

Karen chuckled once more, then exhaled and let the humor fade, "Sometimes… to hell with what they think. You know?"

I did know.

"Doesn't change what we think," I said.

That was so very true.

"So, tomorrow we boost… and if we win the battle that's coming, that could be it," Karen changed subjects.

"It certainly could. If we can break the *Tharsises*."

"We can. We will," Karen's tone became more somber, and more firm. "Whether we live through it, though. Well."

There was no being coy about that subject with Karen — she knew the gravity of the situation just as well as I did. We hated it, but we were more ready to face what was coming now than we had been, say, during *The Dark Cruise*. At least if one of us fell in battle against the Martians, it'd be on the job, and in an important fight near the end of the war.

Small consolation. The sort of consolation you draw sitting alone on the end of the bed, while you talk over the comm with the person who should be sitting with you.

"What happens if one of us dies? What would I turn into without you?"

That was another surprising question from Karen. She was starting to remember the times we'd been apart before we'd even known each other — her younger years full of anger, pain, and recklessness. The days before the Academy, and Defense Command.

It wasn't a subject we needed to get into — talking about how we'd changed each others' lives, blah blah blah…

So I frowned, "If we go down this route, we're both going to start trying to out-compliment each other. It'd be pointless."

She paused, frowned, and nodded again, "We really have to be careful what we talk about these days."

"No kidding."

We fell silent after that, each of us looking away from the screen. What else was there to say? What would be productive… what would feel right under these circumstances?

Nothing was coming to mind.

Finally, I glanced back at Karen, "So. Hm. This is productive. Should we just wind down this call and get back to our duty-bound states of repression and denial?"

Looking up from the end of her ponytail, Karen wore one of the rarest expressions I'd seen from her to that point… the genuinely uncertain one. Her brow wrinkled as she frowned, and she shook her head.

"No, not yet. I miss you enough as it is… so let's just sit and pretend like we're in the same room."

Could not have said it better myself. And who could argue with that?

Call me sappy or stupid or a hack or whatever the hell you can think of, but I wasn't budging from the end of that bed. And Karen wasn't budging either.

And that, in the midst of everything else, was a good feeling.

We'd take it while we could get it, and then fly off to fight Bort McWebsbert and the elite of the Martian Navy after it was done.

To invoke Winston Churchill: the Mercury assault was over, and the Fleet Clash was about to begin.

AFTERWORD

So ends the story of our assault on Mercury. Looking back, many do think it was a sure thing, and that the battles in space somehow don't rank among the most epic in history. But they do. And a lot of good women and men died in them.

Of course, it goes without saying that the battles on the ground were equally important, and even more brutal. The only planetary invasion in human history had gone as well for us as it possibly could, but that wasn't setting the bar very high. At least Charlie, Rufus, and some of our veterans from the squad had survived. For now.

But across the board, the losses were heavy, from ships like *Cyclops* to people like Gina Bertram. The job got done, as I keep saying, but it was at some heavy cost.

What was to come, the Fleet Clash, is a battle that has been saddled with a lot more significance than I think it deserves. That isn't to say it's unimportant, just that it isn't fantastically more important than what I just covered.

But that's an argument I'll make next book. In *The Fleet Clash* we'll learn more about the fates of many people who were near and dear to me. Belt Squadron veterans… old friends… new friends… people yet to be friends… all sorts of people.

We'll lose Charlie. Once and for all.

So there's plenty ahead as we wrap up 2233, and I for one won't be sad to see this year of books go. There weren't really many upswings during those twelve months… though let's be honest, 2234 isn't going to be a joy-fest either. Let alone 2235…

Sorry, I'm getting way ahead of myself. For now, let's call it a book. I'll see you next time to talk about the colossal final battle.

Until then, keep well!

THE
FLEET
CLASH

THE AUTOBIOGRAPHICAL REMINISCENCES OF
ADMIRAL THE LORD KEN BARRON FOR 2233

THE MARTIAN WAR - 12

KENNETH TAM

FROM THE AUTHOR

We come to the end of hostilities — to a time that some would suggest is the bitterest to lose friends. One thing that I'd never thought of before reading personal histories about the Second World War was the notion that dying on the last day of a war would have to be a pretty damned horrible thing. So close to making it through… then robbed of survival at the very end.

That's not to say, of course, that dying any time during a war is good. I feel like an idiot for even implying such a thing. But getting close to the end, and then being killed…

As that observation might imply, we're about to lose people, in the last battle of the Martian War. A climactic final fight between ships will rob many of their lives, and will reveal once again some of Ken Barron's flaws. Consider those a preview of things to come, both in 2234 and much more potently in 2235. I don't think admitting that gives too much away… many people have predicted what's to come, in part or whole, so I'll just add more fuel to the speculative fire.

This book will close the chapter on some old friendships, and start new ones. It will preface political power struggles, and end wars. It'll be quite a ride, and as of now, I think it may well be my favorite book in this series.

Though I know books to come will usurp it, because there's a lot ahead.

Anyway, enough self-serving prattle: I have people who deserve a great deal of thanks.

Once again, there are numerous characters in these pages who are based on real-life friends of mine. I thank those friends for their indulgence, and hope that their characters do them proud!

Peter Caron, my very good friend, was again instrumental to this book, providing advice and perspective on all that takes place. Of course, Wes Prewer must be thanked to, for another brilliant cover image, and his continued help in fleshing out this universe, both visually and through story.

Finally, as ever, I must thank the most important people: my Iceberg partners and parents, Jacqui and Peter. You guys are the bestest. Not just the best, the best*est*.

Yes, I know, it's getting lame. But I'm going to keep thanking you. Deal with it.

Atlas, old friend, thank you.

– Kenneth Tam

Foreword

Welcome to *The Fleet Clash*.

This is a book about an event that's been subject to a lot of myth-building, a lot of popular history, and a lot of movies that really haven't gotten it right. That's not to say that everyone has gotten it wrong… but if I'm honest, most have.

If you ask the average person on the street what the Fleet Clash is, they'll probably tell you it's the biggest space battle in history.

Nope.

They might say it was the most important space battle in history.

Nope.

They might say it was the most decisive space battle in history.

Not really.

It was big, and important, and decisive… but I've always felt that it got swept up by the media, and turned into the crowning achievement of the war — the climax to a long story of battle and suffering. I can understand why this happened. The media, and popular historians, and even some professional historians sometimes need to see things in the context of metanarratives — the big story, that makes every event flow together as part of an epic, huge plot.

As I've said before, those metanarratives often exclude seemingly unimportant events (like our visit to Pion rock in *The Canary Wars*), and they often attach a hell of a lot more importance to certain actions than they really warrant.

An example of this — and I'll get in trouble for saying this — is the Canadian fixation on the battle of Vimy Ridge. This was a battle to take a ridge on the western front during the First World War, and it is to this day known amongst Canadians as a moment of national triumph, when the Canadian Corps fought together as a single force for the first time, and took an objective none of Canada's allies had been able to take.

All true.

Details that aren't mentioned: the Canadians were involved in this action explicitly to support the main battle, which was being fought by British on the Scarpe below. No question, it was essential that the Canadians took that ridge, because it protected the British flanks, but in the end our great national triumph was a supporting action.

Granted, it was the only part of the operation that was a success, but why was this moment — as opposed to earlier victories or later ones — considered such an outstanding event in Canadian history?

Well, it made for a good story, and fit into the metanarrative pretty well. It was the first time the Canadian Corps had fought as one, so that made it unique, but if you look at things in pure military terms, later fights were more exclusively Canadian, and much more successful for us. But they're largely forgotten, because they don't make for quite as convenient popular memories.

Vimy checked off all the boxes: a win for Canada, operating on its own, where others had failed to go, in an easily-summarized action that could be packaged and retold to great effect by the propaganda machine of the day.

I'll say it one more time, in a futile attempt to prevent people calling me a traitor to my home country: Vimy was a solid win. But it was blown out of proportion by fond recollections, and in reality, was actually no greater than many other hard-fought victories won by those same men in that same war. It certainly wasn't as significant to the outcome of the war as some of the Canadians' later fights.

So, with a setup like that, you've probably figured out where I'm going with this book. The Fleet Clash was an important battle, and it was ultimately the last one of the war. But I firmly believe that many other battles fought over the years had more to do with us winning the war.

My apologies to the many producers and historians who've made their way by suggesting otherwise, but the Clash wasn't the be-all, end-all.

I suppose I'm a bit bitter about this, and I'll tell you why.

According to popular history and the movies, every woman and man who died in the Clash was a hero of the Empire, while all the people who fought and died to take Mercury were just folks doing their duty. All those poor saps invading the Martian outer capital were just fighting a battle to *set up* the Fleet Clash.

That's bullshit.

Mercury wasn't assaulted just so we could set up a Fleet Clash. That's garbage.

If anything, the Fleet Clash happened so that we could preserve the gains we'd made at Mercury. There's no question that Mercury was the vastly more important objective, and it frustrates me that it gets sidelined as a 'setup operation' by people who don't know better, but who *should* know better.

A lot more people died taking Mercury than in the Fleet Clash — Special Branchers, Security Forces, and so help me, even blockheads. Suggesting they did all that just so we could draw Bort McWebsbert into an open-space duel of battleships is crap.

We fought Bort so that those men and women wouldn't have died for nothing.

And that's why I'm bitter.

Sorry. Hopefully I don't have to vent so much during the book now that I've gotten it out of the way off the top. And hopefully I haven't alienated you and compelled you to declare me a blood enemy of your family, for a feud unto death. Alright, so that might be a slight overreaction. But you know how I am…

Anyway, chances are I'll spin off into some complaining as we go along, but less than I would have otherwise. For now, that's enough of me jumping up and down on my soapbox. Let's get started.

CHAPTER ONE

A STRANGE START

I'm going to start this book in a way I've never started a book before. If you're not sitting down, please sit down now. I'll wait.

Alright, ready?

Here we go.

Vice Admiral Borthias McWebsbert was just leaving the hospital in the Forge dome when his communicator (the Martians don't call them comms) pinged on his hip. Drawing the device from its holster on his belt, he came to a stop in the street.

Some of his troopers were passing by, and they nodded to him, so he waved back as the communicator's channel opened.

"McWebsbert."

"Sir, we have a communication from a ship claiming to be part of the Mercury Squadron. It's claiming the Defcoms just hit Mercury in force."

Bort froze in place as he heard that, and then something made him turn and look back at the hospital. Shauna Cass was standing in the window of one of the rooms, staring at him. It was apparently a creepy moment.

He turned away again, frowning, "You validate that ship's identity, Hawk?"

"We're doing that, sir. But it would explain why the bastards haven't gotten here yet."

"Yes it would," Bort grunted.

Again he paused, and then he sighed, "Alright, I'm coming up. Get confirmation. And get the ships ready for departure. We may have to go to Mercury."

"Yes, Admiral."

The call ended, and Bort McWebsbert let out a second sigh, then looked up at the red sky of the Forge dome.

There'd always been a chance that we'd out-fox him when he took the Forge. He'd been sure to warn the Grand Admiral Staff of that possibility when he'd suggested the operation, and they'd been only too happy to tell him that he'd be cashiered and probably shot if it did.

So it sounded like the bastards would finally get him. They had wanted an excuse to evict him from their ranks for a long, long time, and now that Ben Conflans was dead, he didn't have any friends left to protect him.

The jumped-up Admiral from the humble mining family would finally be put in his place.

But not before he did his job. He'd have to take the *Tharsises* out and see if he could do something about our occupation of Mercury. He had the best crews and the best ships in the Imperium — ships and crews he genuinely believed were a match for the best in Defense Command.

That might be enough to make a difference… or in the end, he and his best might just get swept away by Lord John Fiora and his elite Navy.

There was only one way to find out.

Bort headed for *Olympus Mons*.

"They went to Mercury after all? All those people, sir..."

Bort held up a hand to stop his Post Captain's verbal musing. Art O'Thomson skippered *Olympus Mons*, and had been with Bort McWebsbert for many years. He was one of the few fleet officers who Bort was certain he could trust, and as such had been given command of the flagship.

Now, the Post Captain wore a scowl. He didn't share Bort's certainty that a lot of the propaganda about Defense Command was inaccurate.

"What about the women, sir?" Art asked somberly, ignoring the raised hand. "The civilian women, I mean. You know what they say... they put their own women in uniforms. God only knows what they'll do when they capture ours."

Bort winced and shook his head, "Don't worry about that, Art."

Despite all their years together, O'Thomson still didn't understand how his Admiral could be so tolerant of the Defcoms. He trusted Bort implicitly, but this was one of those subjects they'd just never seen eye-to-eye on.

"Sir... not thinking about it isn't going to change what happens to those women."

Frowning, Bort sat back in his chair. They were in his cabin, by the way, reviewing the message that had come in from the Mercury Squadron ship.

"Art, *thinking* about it isn't going to change what happens to them either. Right now we just have to think about the job. Agreed?"

O'Thomson fell silent, then nodded, "True enough, sir. About the job."

He didn't stop thinking about the women, though — Bort could see that clearly enough in the man's eyes. O'Thomson had a wife and four daughters back on Asteroid Kappa, and every time anyone suggested that Defense Command might attack the Asteroid colonies, the Post Captain virtually frothed at the mouth.

Bort didn't have family. There was Casey, back on Asteroid Epsilon, but the only relationship he had with her was such a clichéd 'we never both seem to be in the right place at the right time to be with each other' scenario that he refused to speak of it to most people. He missed her like hell, though.

But anyway, he could understand why Art O'Thomson would be sensitive to the many publicly-issued vids that indicated Defense Command would gladly rape every woman they captured, and that they'd torture men taken in combat.

A hedonistic culture of excess, that's what the Earth Empire was. Mixed-gender crews fornicating on duty, murdering indiscriminately, and leaving the economically less fortunate to fend for themselves.

Man, we really are bastards.

And Art didn't want us... ahem, sorry, changing perspective when I shouldn't be... Art didn't want Defense Command to inflict its horror on any women who lived under the relative safety of the Red Banner.

Even if the Banner did tend to stifle (suffocate) their freedoms. A small price to pay for safety from the many monstrous people of this solar system — namely us.

Bort rubbed his jaw while some of this was pondered. Unlike a proper, upper-class Admiral, McWebsbert hadn't shaven in a couple of days, and he'd probably go a couple more before he bothered.

"So are we ready to sail, Art?" he finally pressed his Post Captain out of musing, and O'Thomson glanced up again.

"Sorry sir. Yes. I spoke to Post Captain Wallazevedo and Post Captain Fredhopanov twenty minutes ago, and they're warming the engines. All our escorts have been put on ten-minute sailing notice."

Nodding, Bort leaned forward in his seat, "Alright. When the Mercury survivors make their next scheduled communications stop, send them the rendezvous point. We'll sail in two hours."

"Yes sir," Art O'Thomson came to his feet, saluted (with his palm down, in Martian style), and left Bort's cabin.

Bort sat in silence after his skipper left, and then turned back to his desk. He knew damned well that, if Defense Command had gone for Mercury, they were going to be ready for him to charge in after them.

The *Bonaventures* would be hunting him. Defense Command ships might even be trailing the survivors from Mercury to their rendezvous, so they could locate him. But he'd need the additional ships from Mercury if he was going to have a hope of matching a concentrated Defense Command squadron... so he'd link up with the Mercury ships, and shortly thereafter he'd probably be in a gunfight.

Who would it be? He gripped his forehead as he wondered about that. Martian intel was not terribly good to him, but he'd always been a watcher of our news feeds — one of the few Martians allowed to do so, because it helped him 'know his enemy'.

It'd probably be John Fiora. He'd commanded the *Bonaventures* to great effect during the failed February 2232 attacks on Earth. But Fiora wouldn't be alone. Probably Wes Pellew on the escort — an officer whose efforts in the free belt had stymied many of Bort's less capable colleagues.

And Bort knew that, if he was really unlucky, there'd be two other officers with John. The two who had been able to beat Ben Conflans in that ridiculous mission out to Sinope.

If it was Fiora, Pellew, McMaster and Barron, Bort would have a problem winning the gunfight.

But he still had to try. That was his duty.

He might not survive it... but at least then he'd never have to see the smug bastards on the Grand Admiral Staff again. Might almost be worth it...

Sighing at the prospect, Bort tried to switch off his thoughts.

Two hours later, his squadron sailed, and left the Forge behind.

CHAPTER TWO
HOLY! DID YOU READ THE LAST CHAPTER?

That's crazy! Officially, that previous chapter is the first time I've *ever* presumed to do a scene from the Martian point of view. It felt weird, I won't lie. But I think it made for a different start than we're used to, and of course it'll be significant later.

The reason I took that approach is so we could look at what Bort knew. I think the movie and popular history crowds could learn quite a lot from this.

We often assume the Martians were simply dumb and duped into fighting the Fleet Clash — that our assault on Mercury was a setup for it, and that they didn't think 'sailing' (weird, that's what they call it) to support their outer capital would be dangerous at all.

Clearly, they were much smarter than that. At least Bort was.

But it was a situation with no real alternative. Because of poor leadership and decision-making in the early phases of the war, the Martians had a limited number of options available to them by the start of 2233. Taking the Forge was a clever play, but it was by no means sure to deliver victory.

Now, cruising to try to break the occupation of Mercury was a mission that Bort and his people knew probably wasn't going to meet with success... but they had to try. And if, as they expected, John, Wes, Karen, and I ended up in their way, they'd just have to fight and see how it went. They had no illusions about the risks involved and knew defeat was a very real possibility.

At the same time, they were well-trained men, and they were aboard the best ships the Martian Navy had ever put into space. That being the case, they did *believe* they could win. They knew it wouldn't be easy — by now everyone on both sides was aware of the epic superiority of the *Bonnies*, even if only by hearsay and rumor. But they believed in themselves, they trusted their ships, and they were devoted to their CO.

That's why they came out to fight us.

Unfortunately for them, Bort was pretty much entirely right about who they were going to face... except he didn't know about Lia. As Earth Empire all-star teams go, this was another excellent one.

Though we'd left Greg, Marlene and Mik out of the lineup for this fight, we'd added John Fiora and Wes Pellew. Talk about depth on the bench. I mean, come on, the deck was bloody stacked in our favor. Not that we were taking victory for granted... the opposite, really. But we had a very strong force, and people who knew how to use it.

And now, for a convenient segue.

It was the formidableness (shut up, it's a word) of our soon-to-be-merged battle group that was distracting me from paperwork as I sat in my cabin. My productivity was low due to the musing, and as we start this scene, my screen chimed to add to the distractions.

Checking the clock, I saw it wasn't yet time to chat with Karen — *Lady Grace* and *Wolf* were near enough to each other in our cruising formation to allow the occasional realtime chat, but we were trying to be disciplined about those. Too much time on the comms would be distracting and mildly torturous. So we strictly rationed ourselves to only two hours a day...

Anyway, it probably wasn't Karen.

Grabbing the remote from the floor beside my chair, I opened the line, and Lia Hawke appeared.

For some reason I hadn't really thought it could be her, which is foolish — she'd been calling me daily, just as Karen had, though for completely different reasons.

"Hey big brother," she smiled halfheartedly and waved at me.

"I am so not related to you by blood that it isn't even funny," I replied straight-faced, and she adopted a look of shock.

"You're mean."

"Oh, so maybe we are related."

Lia's eyebrows went up, "Well, someone had their wheat-based cereal for breakfast this morning."

I frowned, recognizing the obscure joke, and then realizing there was probably a little more than Lia's humor to it. I was being a bit tetchy.

"Hm. Sorry."

Lia shrugged, "No... I shouldn't really keep bugging you."

That was a little bit of a guilt trip. Lia knew it and I knew it. She might as well have stuck out her bottom lip and crinkled her brow.

So that's exactly what she did.

I groaned and let my head flop back against the chair's headrest, "I said I was sorry. I'm not going to rhyme off all the reasons it's better for you to be calling me than anyone else."

Lia tilted her head, thought about my answer, and then erased her pouting expression, "Well, as long as you acknowledge there are reasons..."

"He's probably still fine, Lia. You know how good he is."

I switched subjects abruptly there, because I knew why she was calling — why she always called — and my answer to the question hadn't changed. While we were in transit to the rendezvous with the *Bonnie* Squadron and the Independent Squadron, there was no communication with Mercury.

For all either of us knew, Charlie Peters was dead.

And that possibility was having a profound influence on Lia.

Now, I want to be very clear about *how* it was affecting her: she wasn't roaming around *Whirlwind* (her flagship) a blubbering basket case. She wasn't making bad decisions. She wasn't incapacitated by worry. I point all of this out because I fear the neo-suffragists will think I'm saying Lia was no good unless her man was around.

Hardly. You should know better, you neo-suffragists!

But in private, in those moments during a cruise when her duties for the day were done, she was worried. And that's no sign of weakness. Well, if it is, then people like Karen and I must be pretty damned fragile.

Lia and Charlie were lovers trying desperately not to become star-crossed. And they were simultaneously managing to be exceedingly good at their jobs, and not to let anyone down. So if Lia wanted to let herself be a basket case in private, that was entirely her right.

And let's be honest, she wasn't even a basket case then. Just anxious, and worried.

My preemption of her question now made her sigh, and she reached up to rub her eyes, "This should get easier every day, shouldn't it?"

I frowned, "Why would it?"

Looking up over her hand, she shrugged, "Well, I *should* get accustomed to it. Especially with my history with Charlie... I mean, this is just stupid."

This was slightly new territory for our conversations since leaving Mercury, so I shook my head and maintained my frown, "The separation isn't really the same now. Similar, but not the same."

Lia lowered her hand and raised her eyebrow... then said nothing.

I stared silently at her, wondering if she was contemplating my words or waiting for me to continue. She stared back.

Finally, she bobbled her head and threw her hands up in front of her, "Well are you just going to leave me hanging, or do I get a dose of brotherly wisdom?"

I snorted a laugh and leaned forward, "Since you asked... you know this better than I do, Lia. Your dad is gone. And you're going to go back to Hawke One and all those responsibilities you've been able to avoid so far are going to get you. Life is going to get very serious very fast."

The truth was sharp, and Lia's expression saddened involuntarily — one of the few times. Usually it was well controlled, but now her eyes darkened, and her mouth stilled. She nodded slowly.

"You've always loved Charlie. But now you really need him... and you can have him, since your dad won't be getting in the way... which, of course, means there's a good chance that a fickle universe would choose this moment to steal him from you. That's why it's more worrisome now than ever before. And I don't think you're going to get used to it."

Lia let out a long breath, then anxiously rubbed the back of her neck, "I sound like such a... a... I don't even know. Damsel? Or flake?"

"Sure, that's exactly what you sound like. Heiress to the Protectorate and now a combat officer in the Fiora Ring. You're absolutely a flake," I let loose with the sarcasm, and that sparked a disapproving look.

"Come on, go easy on me. I'm fragile."

"You totally are," a small smile crept onto my face, and she scowled.

"Here goes mister wheat-based-cereal breakfast again."

I shrugged, "Sorry. I'm fragile too, and lashing out to hide it."

"Figures," she muttered. Then she frowned, and looked up, "Karen's been sounding different lately. Is it the same thing? I mean, I expect you to be pathetic when she's not around. But her too?"

My smile grew, and I shrugged, "You'd have to ask her. Just don't jam up her comm, we're due for two hours of staring at each other in a little while. And I won't have my little sister spoil that."

Lia instantly smiled, and then she shrugged girlishly, "I wouldn't dream of it, bro. Same time tomorrow? I love the pep talks."

"Yeah, sure. I hate paperwork marginally more than I hate pep talks."

She beamed brightly (for effect), and then agreed, "It's on. See you tomorrow!"

"Joy," I replied, and then Lia vanished.

As the screen blanked, I stretched and closed my eyes. I really had given a pep talk. A mushy relationship pep talk. Sort of.

But I didn't know what I'd say to her if Charlie died. I didn't even know what I'd say to myself if he died. I hoped to high heaven that he was alright.

So… was he?

CHAPTER THREE

INSURGENTS

For centuries, surrender has basically meant nothing. They might as well change the meaning of the word in the dictionary, because honestly, no one seems to understand that when you surrender, you STOP TRYING TO KILL THE OTHER SIDE.

The Martians didn't get this memo... and to be fair, neither did our people on the Forge after they were captured. Not that Bort gave them much chance to resist...

Anyway, Mercury was rapidly becoming a clear case of surrender meaning relatively little. I suppose that's not fair: the civilians had surrendered, and were living under martial law. The government had surrendered, as had the military high command, but 130 Commandos had decided they were smarter than their Generals... and this time, an estimated 200 regular troopers were with them.

That probably doesn't sound like a lot of resistors, but remember how tough it could have been on Io when just that handful of Commandos failed to lay down their weapons? Well, multiply that problem by a bunch, because not only were there more resistors on Mercury, they were being silently aided and abetted by members of the civilian population.

And because the population was present, we couldn't simply knock down entire cities to get the bastards.

That made the job of maintaining order rather difficult.

Now, as had been the case during the assault, Defense Command was responsible for three of the Mercury domes, while the blockheads had the rest. The blockheads did a fair bit of collateral damage when they crushed resistors, while Special Branch went far out of its way to be as precise as possible.

But it wasn't easy. It was downright exhausting.

The population was essentially hostile, being kept in check only by the presence of soldiers or SF on their street corners. They had hoped that their freedom fighters would somehow find a way to throw out our occupation force... or to keep us busy long enough for Bort to come and save them all.

And many of them believed that, as soon as the last of the resistance stopped, the rape gangs would start working their way through the domes.

Yeah, they really thought very highly of us.

All of these circumstances made living and fighting in the domes very difficult for our people — and particularly for the Branchers, who were the ones always sent out to run dangerous patrols, or clear mysterious packages that could explode... those fun sorts of jobs.

Returning from one of these missions, then, was *Wolf's* Special Branch squad. Ten now remained — four fewer than had survived the invasion that you read about in *The Mercury Assault*. Two of those missing were wounded, two were dead. Of two squads that had once numbered a total of twenty-four officers, fewer than half remained.

And two of those remaining were Majors, and they were essentially sharing command.

"I need to find some more grenades," Rufus Chang was first through the door of one of the safe houses Special Branch maintained in the Capital Dome.

"The SF barracks might have some," Ben Belete followed the Major in, and was already stripping off his rifle and vest. "I'm starving. Anyone want anything?"

He headed for the kitchen before there was any chance of answer.

Next through the door was medic Terry Schroeder, who was sporting a hell of a black eye after getting into a tiff with some Martian industrial workers earlier in the day. Both those Martians had been allowed to walk away... well, hobble away. But one had managed to hit Terry with a shovel before he adjusted both of their backs for them.

Special Branch medics may not be licensed chiropractors, but let me tell you...

The rest of the squad filed into the safe house, and began collapsing onto chairs and couches that had been rounded up in the dwelling's living room. Groans of relief echoed through the building, because this was the first time in nearly forty-eight hours that any of these people had been able to relax.

Relatively relax, anyway.

This safe house was on a street that was owned by SF — standing roadblocks, regular over-flights by skiffs and hovercars... it was secure enough that you could sit down and even take off your tac vests for a little while.

That was a great relief.

Of course, Charlie Peters was the last person through the door. And no, not because I was trying to build suspense about his fate, but because he and Rufus had started being first man/last man on their operations. That way a lucky bomb was less likely to get both of them.

Not that it would really matter if they both got blown up — Ben Belete could easily take over. Hell, all the Branchers on this team had been around the block plenty of times, even before they'd gotten to Mercury. They were all probably better qualified to command an outfit like this one than, say, anybody in the Imperial Army would *ever* be.

I may be a little biased, but I'm still right about that.

Anyway, Charlie was last in, and he closed the door behind him, because he wasn't raised on a raft. And also because it was a heavy door, and it would absorb plenty of concussion and shrapnel if someone tried to blow them up.

"Do I hear *Wolf* shooters?" a familiar voice came from the stairwell, and Charlie turned just in time to see Marcus Atallah descend to the ground floor.

Marcus, I hope you recall, was *Cheetah's* Special Branch Major. I don't think we've seen him since Io, but he'd obviously been a part of this assault too.

Now there was a great big bandage around his head, securing a pad to his left eye.

"How'd that happen?" Charlie asked with a frown, letting his MAG-90 dangle from its harness as he approached his long-time colleague from the Belt Squadron.

Shrugging, Marcus patted the eye, "Hear that pop last night in the warehouse district? Wasn't a big one, but I only closed the scope eye."

"Ouch," Charlie winced.

What Marcus was referring to was something Special Branchers were trained in, but which I never knew about: if there's an explosion nearby, they close the eye they use for aiming through a MAG-90's sight, but leave their other eye open so they can see what's going on around them. Problem is, that eye is then open and exposed to whatever the explosion kicks up. That can mean temporary blindness from a flash. It can also mean tiny bits of debris that might normally be stopped by the eyelid can get through to the eyeball and do some harm.

"Could be a lot worse. It was just some bad luck that I caught the flash. They applied that pasty healer stuff… apparently I'll be alright in a couple of weeks."

"Meantime they're keeping you down here," Rufus approached the pair of Majors, and Marcus grinned.

"I still have my scope eye. Squad's just running without me for a couple of days until I can get down to a patch."

Charlie chuckled a little grimly and patted Marcus on the shoulder, "Well I'm glad you're still around."

"Me too," Rufus agreed. "Got any grenades?"

The Majors laughed, but Marcus actually *did* have grenades, so those two went off to collect them. Charlie headed for the kitchen, opening his vest as he did. He was pretty hungry and thirsty, so he'd get something to eat. A lot to eat, really.

And then he'd be ready to go again.

Because Charlie is mildly superhuman, see — able to go into elite combat on very little sleep, so long as he's fed. Or even if he isn't fed.

Ben Belete was frying simulated bacon on the Martian stove. It was starting to smell good, so Charlie grinned at his Captain, "Save me some."

"I suppose," Ben shot back.

They didn't get to say anything else: there was a loud explosion.

Both men froze, looking out the barred kitchen window to see if there was any smoke in that direction.

Nothing wafted up.

Then Charlie's comm chirped, and he tapped his headset, "Peters."

Lieutenant Colonel Garth Ronald was still Charlie's direct superior, "Charlie, sorry about this, but you're on the job again."

Charlie was half-tempted to ask if there wasn't anyone else who could do this… but he'd come to know Ronald well enough. If the Colonel was calling, there was good reason. The Branchers were spread thin in this dome right now, and incidents were still happening with such frequency that rotations out to quieter domes literally couldn't happen.

Hopefully things would slow down soon.

Meantime, there was more work to do.

"Roger, tell me where."

While Ben Belete turned the fryer up on maximum to finish the simbacon quickly, Charlie listened to his next mission. As Ben wrapped up the bacon to take along, Charlie headed out into the living room and told the exhausted squad where they were going next.

There were groans, and there was a good measure of swearing, but the officers got to their feet and headed back out the door a couple of moments later.

Mercury had surrendered… now someone needed to hit its population over the head with a dictionary until they understood what that meant.

CHAPTER FOUR

SOME OF THE BEST

Commodore Wes Pellew hadn't been at Mercury, and frankly, that was our bad luck. Just to remind you of what's gone on over the last eleven books, Wes used to skipper *Cheetah* as part of the Belt Squadron, and then after 2231 he'd been promoted to Commodore and given the unenviable task of rehabilitating the reputation of the Independent Squadron. He'd done that, shedding the ghosts of Sean Cook, and replacing them with a track record of beating any enemies the Squadron was sent after.

Having even one or two of his ships with us in that battle against the monitors might have made a big difference. With their special abilities, installed during construction to enhance pirate-hunting ability, his frigates were in many respects even handier in a gunfight than ships of the *Predator*-class.

And much, much more importantly, Wes is a top-notch ship-handler, and an equally adept squadron commander.

Also, Wes likes soup. And hates heights.

Everyone who knows anything about Wes knows that.

Ahem.

Anyway, Wes was commanding the escort for John's *Bonnie* Squadron. That meant he'd be linking up with Lia, Karen and I when our two forces merged, and between the four of us, we'd be charged with keeping Bort's destroyers and destroyer escorts away from our four mighty battleships.

"So they broke up command by class?"

Wes blinked and looked up at that observation. Roslyn Young, his Flag Captain, was frowning at the pads in front of her. They were meeting in her day cabin, off the flank of *Nova Scotia's* bridge, and it was the first time she'd had a chance to look at our order of battle coming out of Mercury.

"For the assault, yep. It may not stay that way when we link up, but we'll have four Flag Officers and twenty-two ships... so who knows how we'll divide them up," he let his voice trail off in thought.

There was no question in his mind about who would command his own squadron — namely, it would be him. That wasn't because he didn't like us, it was a simple matter of practicality — the ships of the Independent Squadron had been fighting as a team since 2232, and it wouldn't make sense to shake up their formation now.

So perhaps, he thought, the old Belt Squadron/Jupiter Force might be put together, and then a third force of ships out of the Hawke Protectorate. That wouldn't be his decision, but he speculated it might be the way things went, since he knew me well.

He knew, for instance, that I hate soup and am ambivalent about heights.

"Well, it'll be quite a force we have to hit them with," Rozy Young observed, and Wes looked up at her again.

"True enough," he agreed. "I'm pretty confident we can deal with their escorts. But the key will be what John can do against the *Tharsises*. If we win and he loses…"

Rozy nodded, "Ramming speed?"

Wes winced at the suggestion. He'd gone through phases in his life where the preservation of his own survival hadn't really mattered to him, but this wasn't one of those periods. He'd rather not have to ram *Nova Scotia* — or any other ship — headlong into a Martian battlewagon.

But if it was necessary, he'd do it.

Time would tell.

"Let's hope it doesn't come to that," he said quietly. "But check with engineering to make sure our jump drives are ready for it."

Rozy nodded, "I will."

She went back to reading pads about the Mercury action, and Wes pretended to read one too. But he was stuck thinking about how the escorts would be divided up… and about who was coming.

After a long spell working in the Hawke Protectorate during the last half of 2232, Wes knew many of the skippers who'd been based in the Independent Belt. Names like Nikhil Jones and Lisa Sims — corvette commanders from *Amherst* and *Nanton* — were very familiar. He obviously also knew Lia, though he'd never fought alongside her.

Other skippers were known to him by reputation… people like Jake Lee from *Kodiak*, and Sela Kinder from *Guangxi*.

And, obviously, he'd fought alongside all the old Belt Squadron veterans for years against the pirates. He knew me, Karen, Mark Gunney, Matt Baxter, Isoruku Togo, Elise De Winter, and Andrea Kiley.

He wondered how Andrea was doing, too. He was the only one she had really talked to about what she saw on Egesta. Now she was coming back from a big battle at Mercury… how would she be?

That question distracted him more than he expected it to.

But Roslyn Young wasn't paying attention, so it didn't matter. Eventually he shook himself out of his musings and went back to reading. He'd see us all soon enough.

John Fiora was spending a lot of time on *Bonaventure's* bridge… and really, who could blame him? Let me reinforce a point here: *Bonnie* and all her sisters are fundamentally, unquestionably, totally and absolutely awesome.

Epically so.

And though I've been mentioning them offhand for a number of books now — casually mentioning them as if they're just four more ships in the fleet — let's remember that they remain the most universally beloved ships in the service.

So, with that reminder in place, John was spending a lot of time on *Bonnie's* bridge. The place was about as big as Admiralty House C&C, it was always bright and featuring some action, and frankly, being there was better for our venerable First Lord than sitting alone in a cabin would have been.

He knew damned well that this was going to be a tough battle, and that it was theoretically possible that the super-duper-epic-wondrous-awesomely-good *Bonnies* were at a technical disadvantage to the *Tharsis*-class… but pacing around that bridge gave him confidence, plain and simple.

Occasionally he'd stop to chat with some of the officers and techs on the deck. Most were the same men and women who'd followed John into battle during Glorious February — people like Jorge Allende, the Sensors and Communications Officer.

And, of course, Captain of the Fleet Lennox Williams was still running the ship with a steady, masterful hand.

It was Lennox who came up alongside John when the First Lord stepped up onto the stage before the main screens.

"Anything you want to see?" the Trinidadian skipper asked, pointing to those many massive bridge screens. John paused, then shrugged.

"Nothing I haven't seen a dozen times already, Len. I'll let you know if something comes to mind though."

Smiling easily, Lennox nodded, "Don't think watching them a thirteenth time could make us more lucky?"

John laughed, "I didn't realize we were that desperate."

"I don't know if there's a way to be too lucky. Unless you're in a room full of beautiful women… escorting your mother."

"Somehow I doubt that'd stop you," John countered wryly.

Lennox shrugged, "You know me. No matter how complicated it gets, I always do my duty."

Chuckling again, John looked back at the screens, "I'll keep that in mind next time I see your girlfriend. Or your wife, for that matter."

"You wound me, skipper," Lennox laughed, then left the stage.

John leaned back against the rail at the back of the stage and folded his arms. Patience was a virtue, and some days, he wished he was just a little bit more virtuous…

CHAPTER FIVE
PICK TEAMS

"So, do we draw lots to see who gets the first pick?"

I blinked, "What?"

Lia was grinning in her window on my screen, and from her own window, Karen smiled the way a big sister smiles when she's amused by her younger sibling's antics.

"I think we're a bit more mature than that," Karen said brightly. "You might not be, but we are."

"Ouch," Lia pouted before smiling again. "Well I suppose."

We were doing a realtime conference to address the concern Wes had been considering last chapter — specifically, the breakdown for our squadrons.

"I'm thinking three groups," I said, glancing at a pad which listed all our ships.

Here we go, this is who we had with us: the frigates *Wolf, Cheetah, Whirlwind, Kodiak, Guangxi*, and the corvettes *Lady Grace, Friendly, Trusty, Generous, Amherst, Nanton, June, Daisy, Perth*, and *Adelaide*. That's five frigates and ten corvettes total.

We'd be linking up with the four battleships, *Bonaventure, Terra Nova, Hibernia*, and *Bonavista*, as well as the Independent Squadron, which consisted of the frigates *Nova Scotia, British Columbia, Nunavut, Yukon*, and *Prince Edward Island*, as well as the corvettes *Corner Brook* and *Port Aux Basques*. Five more frigates and two corvettes, bringing our totals overall to four battleships, ten frigates and twelve corvettes.

For our purposes in this meeting, we were only picking from the first paragraph there — John was obviously going to command the *Bonnies*, and Wes was keeping his ships.

So the question was how we'd divide ours.

"I don't know if we have enough to justify three groups," Karen said thoughtfully. "I'd say two groups, and either divide them by class or by prior affiliation."

Karen, as ever, made a very good point.

"Yeah, you can command the escort overall, right Rear Admiral?" Lia said that mischievously, though I don't really know how there could be mischief in that plain statement.

She did have a point: I was the only other Admiral (aside from John) who was going to be present for the Fleet Clash (Fifth Lord Lynn Bokai, who'd officially commanded the *Bonnie* Squadron during *The Gallant Few*, was now overseeing Earth orbital defenses for Daragh). That being the case, it would make sense for me to oversee the whole escort group, and its component squadrons.

That put Karen and Lia in command of the two squadrons we'd draw from the ships with us... and as Mercury had proved, that was a very good leadership combo. If the burger joint I can't mention for trademark reasons had a combo that good, I'd eat there more often.

Er. Sorry. So lame on so many levels. Comparing Karen and Lia to burgers... just no.

"So how should we do the break, then... by class or by experience?" I asked, then looked up at the two ladies on screen.

Lia bobbled her head side to side and frowned thoughtfully. There were good arguments for either division. See, generally when you assemble a squadron, you want to put ships together that have experience with each other. Remember the effectiveness of the Jupiter Force and the Belt Squadron because the ships were used to each other? That's what you wanted to maintain, particularly when going into a big fight.

But all of the ships with us had some experience with each other, just from different times and contexts. Many of the ships hailed from the Hawke Force, and had been with Mik, Wes and Lia for long months in 2232, while most of the others were from the Belt Squadron and Jupiter Force, and thus had been fighting together for ages.

That said, during the Mercury assault they'd worked together in squadrons defined by ship class... the corvettes from the Hawke Squadron and the Jupiter Force had worked together, as had the frigates.

So, divide them based on the more recent battle experience, or based on the months of cruising and occasional combat prior to that?

After the fact, I've asked many different officers how they'd have handled this, and the choices have been pretty divided — there's no right answer.

That in mind, I went with my gut.

"Well. I think... hm. Let's go by old affiliations. Let's put the Hawke Force and the Jupiter Force back together," I said.

Karen and Lia looked at each other and shrugged... but because it was realtime comm and we were all looking at roughly the same viewfinders, they could just as easily have been looking at me and shrugging.

"Works for me. I'll have lots of pretty blue ships," Lia smiled brightly. She had a point there: *Whirlwind, June* and *Daisy* were all ships from Hawke Command. It probably wasn't a bad idea to put them together.

"So... let's see. I'll take *Wolf, Cheetah, Lady Grace, Friendly, Generous, Trusty...* and *Adelaide*," Karen looked down to read ship names off her pad. She could probably have named them from memory, but she was being thorough.

Lia checked her own list and read off the rest, "So I get *Whirlwind, Kodiak, Guangxi, Amherst, Nanton, Perth, June* and *Daisy*."

"Seven for Karen, eight for Lia," I did the math in my head (well, counted them on my fingers).

"Exactly," Lia nodded. "Great. So, I'll call the appropriate skippers and tell them they're stuck with me now. I'm sure they'll scream."

"I can't imagine Nikhil Jones screaming at anything, ever," Karen frowned a little, and Lia laughed.

"I'll record it for you."

Karen chuckled, "I'll look forward to that."

I said nothing. With the business taken care of, I'll admit I was getting a little distracted... the two most important women in my life (excepting my mother, obviously) were on my screen, and just to make that a little sweeter, we were all getting ready to go fight a big battle together.

I'm sure that sounds delightfully insane, but there was something fundamentally brilliant about it. I've never envied those people whose loved ones are at home while they go out in space to make war... I feel for the lonely fighters, and I empathize with the worrying loved ones.

But, while Karen being on another ship was still having a certain effect on me, it was starting to sink in that this was going to be a story we could all tell our respective grandkids... about how we all went off together and fought in the last battle of the war.

And about how we all hopefully came back.

Seeing both Lia and Karen on screen helped drive that revelation home. And because it was still mid-afternoon, not late at night when my anxieties about being a ship away from Karen were at their worst, I was enjoying the feeling.

"Is he staring at us?" Lia had obviously noticed my lack of attention to her mindless blather.

"He probably is."

"Well I hope it's you he's staring at," Lia frowned. "I can never tell on the realtime comms. But it's probably you. You're so pretty, big sis."

Karen's eyebrows went up, "Well. Um. Thanks. You're much prettier though."

I don't know if Karen had ever uttered a more awkward sentence in her life. The uncomfortable way she said it got me chuckling, and Lia latched onto that without mercy.

"Seems Ken has an opinion. So, Ken, which one of us is prettier?"

A bright smile leapt onto Karen's face with the question — she was beginning to enjoy being Lia's wingman far too much for my good.

Of course, I had a clever solution: a useless historical (actually, classical) tangent, "There's a cautionary tale from ancient Greece..."

"Oh here we go," Lia rolled her eyes, though Karen kept smiling.

"Once upon a time, a few goddesses... Hera, Athena and Aphrodite I think... they had a beauty contest, judged by a mortal named Paris. Ended badly."

Lia released an exasperated sigh — the sort of sigh you release when you're letting someone get to the punchline of a bad joke — and then indulged me, "How badly?"

"Trojan War."

She frowned, "Really?"

"In a roundabout way, yep."

"Goddesses were total bitches," Lia shook her head.

"Hey, don't talk about Karen's people like that."

Oh listen to me, mister bloody smooth.

Karen turned a little red, which was awesome, and Lia howled, "Aha, so you've decided. Well, I'm starting a war as soon as we're done with this one!"

I laughed, "You can't see my feet, so I'll tell you I am indeed quaking in my boots."

Lia nodded over-earnestly, "Damned right you are."

We were clearly being very mature and focused in our preparation for this fight. It'd pay off, I assure you.

Chapter Six

Big Happy Space Reunion

Seeing the *Bonnies* never gets old. As far as I'm concerned, it doesn't matter how many times you've seen them before: they always strike awe. They're massive, and elegant, and superior to anything else Defense Command has ever put in space.

It was doubly rewarding to see them at a rendezvous point knowing that you were going to cruise into battle alongside them. We escorts were going to be the sideshow in the battle to come, and ours would be a dangerous job considering the amount of firepower that was going to be lobbed from one side to another... but it still felt like a privilege to be going.

We all had the feeling that it'd be important for us to one day be able to say, 'yeah, I cruised into battle beside *Bonaventure*.'

"That's impressive," Karen was up on Battlelink as we approached the rendezvous, and standing on the bridge, I smiled up at her.

"It really is."

Andrea Kiley had settled into place beside me, and now she nodded severely, "The Martians are going to learn what *real* superbattleships are."

Slightly surprised by the level of gritty determination in her tone, I glanced at her, but decided not to comment. To my own discredit, I hadn't spent a great deal of time trying to interpret Andrea's actions and words since Karen had left... I hadn't been concerning myself as much with her wellbeing.

Perhaps that was appropriate — Andrea was obviously an adult, and an exceptional skipper. She didn't need someone following her around, raising an eyebrow every time she said something that, before Egesta, would have been out of character for her.

Or maybe she should have had the attention. Either way, she wasn't really getting it, for better or worse.

She tells me she thinks it was for better, so I'll defer to that.

Anyway, as she gave that pledge, Lia appeared on another Battlelink screen, a bright smile on her face, "Well well well, looks like poppa John beat us here."

"Signal coming from *Nova Scotia*... another from *Bonaventure*," Felicia Khalid cut in before I could answer Lia, and Andrea made the acknowledgement.

"Put them up."

*Wolf*Net loading screens popped up on two of the bridge's blank monitors, and after a moment both appeared.

"Welcome to the middle of nowhere," Wes spoke first with a grin. "Ken, Karen, Lia, Andrea... good to see you all!"

"And you," I answered with a smile and nod. "You too, John."

"Didn't forget about me, did you?" the First Lord asked wryly, and I chuckled.

Karen had the answer first, "Don't think that's even possible, actually."

John shrugged, "Oh I don't know about that. And how's Lia doing today? We saw the reports from Mercury. Greg was very impressed, young lady."

"Thanks pop," Lia batted her eyelashes and tried to look aw-shucks-ish. It was amusing, and John laughed.

"You're very welcome..." he paused, and then we simultaneously got the sense that there wasn't really time for more niceties.

John said something at this point that I can't repeat word for word. The gist of it was simple: he was giving us Bort's current position, which he knew because it had been relayed to him from the corvette *Melbourne*, and the magical wizard embarked on that ship. And I can't be any more specific than that.

"They must have gotten moving quickly," Karen frowned at the news. In order for Bort's ships to be where they were — nearly halfway from the Forge to Mercury — they'd have to have left days before we really expected them to.

I should have already pointed this out (can't recall, maybe I did?), but Mercury and Venus were in roughly parallel orbits at this point, so they were essentially equidistant from the Forge. Now, Mercury orbited much faster, so soon the Martian outer capital would be closer to the Forge than Venus was... but for right now, they were both the same distance away.

That meant we couldn't be absolutely certain of which one the *Tharsis* Squadron was bound for.

"We're thinking it's Mercury?" I asked, matching Karen's frown, and John nodded.

"That's our best guess. Their course could work for either, but if it were me, that'd be my route to Mercury."

"And," Wes added quickly, "if there's ever been a Martian who we can liken to our elite First Lord, it's the guy who took the Forge."

Karen, Lia and I all nodded with sounds of agreement — mmhmms.

"So, we have to turn right around and cruise for an intercept, right? No time to waste, get them while we know where they are?" Lia was sounding a bit eager to get on the road, and the enthusiasm revived some smiles.

"As a matter of fact, yes we do," was John's answer. "We've worked out the coordinates... we'll intercept in twenty-two hours. And they shouldn't see us coming."

"Hopefully," I agreed with a nod. "Let's get started then. We can figure out battle order on the way."

"Agreed," John concurred, and then we all took a break from the conversation to give orders to our respective commands.

Over the next five minutes, the Jupiter Force, the Hawke Force, and the Independent Squadron oriented themselves around the *Bonnie* Squadron in a roughly triangular formation, with Wes' ships and their specially-tuned sensors (great for pirate hunting) taking point.

As soon as we got ourselves properly arranged, our drives fired and we started off for the intercept coordinates.

We doubted Bort McWebsbert would have any idea we were coming.

+++

"Some of them look pretty shot up, sir," Post Captain Art O'Thomson folded his arms as he stood at the central databank on *Olympus Mons'* bridge.

Bort was walking behind his trusted skipper when that remark was made, and he paused and looked up at some of the pictures being displayed on the bridge monitors.

O'Thomson was right: at least half of these ships were showing very visible signs of damage. But he'd take what he could get.

"Communications Chief, I want to talk to their senior officer," Bort ordered, and after a moment one of the bridge's main screens began loading up a livecom (realtime) feed.

It took a minute or so, and because it would be untoward to do so in this sort of scene, I won't comment on the relative speeds of Defense Command OS XX and MarsCorps' Vantage Combat Operating System.

Ours was faster, more stable, and much superior. Also much cooler.

Sorry, that just came out.

After the delay, a fully zipped-up Captain appeared. Evidently, none of the Commodores at Mercury had been able to escape, and only battleships carried Post Captains, so a Captain was the best these survivors could show him.

By the stern, haughty look on the man's face, Bort could already tell this was one of the hereditary officers — one whose father had served, and whose father's father had served. One who assumed that good Naval skills came from breeding.

He wouldn't like being subordinate to Bort, or to Colm Haysrandov, the Commodore commanding Bort's escort ships.

But that was too damned bad for this Captain.

"*Meridiani Planum* reporting, sir. I am Captain Jason Winchester Nudle."

No. Kidding.

I guess because Martians have so many crazy made-up names, they don't get phased by guys called 'noodle'. Not that there's anything wrong with that name, if you happen to own it yourself… but in this case, it seems a little much to me.

But that was what he was called.

"Captain Nudle. You'll be joining my battle group in our attempt to relieve Mercury."

"You are Vice Admiral McWebsbert?" the Captain managed to spit that question out with as much contempt as he was allowed, considering he was speaking to a superior officer (if not a superior specimen of humanity, in his view).

"Bort McWebsbert, yes," Bort replied disinterestedly. "You'll be joining Commodore Haysrandov's escort squadron. Get in touch with him on *Promethei Planum.*"

"Sir," Nudle sounded like he was going to protest, so Bort took a deep breath and scowled. Owing to his non-haughty upbringing (and his failure to shave in accordance with Imperium Navy grooming standards) he tended to have the look of a bruiser when he scowled. Looked like he could beat you stupid, which would have left a man like Nudle, who was already an idiot, seriously lacking in brain power.

Still, the haughty bastard protested, "My ships are a coherent and excellent force. We will be of much better use to you in battle if we remain in my hands, because I am an experienced and generational Naval officer."

This was one rich son of a bitch.

Ooh, rhyme.

I'll get to the mangling of that sentence in a minute. First, let's talk about what a prick — oh yes, prick — this noodle was. Typical of his class. Not all Martian officers 'of breeding' were this bad, but many still were. Think of people like Kitty Castillo, from all the way back in *The Rogue Commodore*. There was a strange, self-righteous attitude amongst those who came from Navy families... Kitty, for instance, being the only child of Marvin Castillo, had been required to go into the Navy to maintain her family tradition. But after her father died, she'd traded her way up the rank ladder... 'traded' being my polite word for what some might call 'whoring'.

But no one could ever tell her that she wasn't the best of the best, because she came from a line of Naval officers dating back a century.

Family reunions must have been real festivals of hereditary underachievement...

Sorry, that was harsh. But accurate.

As I was saying, though, not all were like this. Benjamin Conflans — who'd been killed during *The Sinope Affair* when Andrea had rammed *Dominator* into his flagship — had been a real professional.

But honestly, it seems to me like there weren't that many good ones. A pale percentage, especially when compared to the general professionalism of Defense Command.

Anyway, this fellow was trying to tell Bort that because he came from a professional family, he should be promoted to Commodore and given command of the ships that had joined him in fleeing Mercury.

And he was making that demand with a very precarious grasp of assigning the correct plurals and pronouns... I mean, if 'we remain in my hands'?

Bort wasn't impressed, "Is that what you think, Captain Nudle?"

"Of course, I wouldn't trouble to say it otherwise."

Looking away for a moment, Bort reined in some of his frustration — a skill he'd refined over the years, because a lower class Asteroid boy didn't fare well in the social circles of Imperium Naval officers.

After that pause, he looked back at the screen, and at haughty, dense, useless Captain noodle, "Captain Nudle, you just fled from Mercury. Left our outer capital to be taken by Defense Command. I will happily bring you up on charges and shoot you, if you like. Or you can redeem yourself by loyally serving under Commodore Haysrandov's command. Choose right now."

Aghast, the noodle opened his mouth. To be so treated by an un-bred officer... unthinkable!

"My family will see you—"

"Shut up about your family. They're not skippering that destroyer. Do what I say, or there'll be charges. We can sort out the indignity with your family when we get home. Presuming your incompetence doesn't get us all killed... and right now, I'm thinking there's a good chance it will. Now get off my screen."

Nudle turned red (appropriate for his allegiance) and started vibrating with rage, but Bort's no-nonsense threat hadn't been missed.

The bastard disappeared from the screen.

A little surge of triumph passed through the men on *Olympus Mons*' bridge — all of the crew up there were either from Bort's social strata, or were like Ben Conflans... they all appreciated seeing a shit like that being handed his orders, and kicked in the pants.

Of course, the Captain hadn't been bluffing — after a slight like that, Bort might certainly have problems when they got back to Mars, but he wasn't convinced he was going to get through this next fight, let alone back to Mars, or home.

One problem at a time.

For now, his force linked up with the Mercury survivors, and resumed its course.

We'd be seeing them within a day.

Aside here. I really want to highlight the differences in culture between the Defense Command Navy and the Martian Imperium Navy... specifically, see how hostile they are towards each other?

I don't mean that as a criticism of Bort, but as a realistic observation. Not everyone gets along in Defense Command, obviously, but it's part of our professional culture to do our best to interact smoothly with each other. Doesn't always work, but usually it at least makes working relationships survivable.

There was no similar tradition of cooperation within the Imperial Navy. You think John's rivalry with Dave Caldecott was bad? At least in that one, no murders took place. Dave got exiled as an enemy of the Empire, but that was entirely because of what he'd done to tie up communications during the almost coup.

Mostly, if we hated each other, we at least agreed that our first duty was to the Empire.

The late George Parks-Dawes comes to mind on that front. Remember him from *The Almost Coup* — one of Caldecott's staunch loyalists, who'd been killed with most of the Light Squadron at the Battle Over Earth? For all the other politics going on, he was still determined enough to do his job... to suspend the grudge when it counted.

Some Martians had that same perspective (ironically, these were usually the ones with no close ties to Mars itself), but these professional family types were just disgusting. It was all family politics to them... like the garbage that would go on in Ian Hawke's court.

Always focused on their personal status and advancement... small wonder we had such a solid track record against these people. Sometimes we faced their best, but often we were going gun-to-gun with their family divas.

And people who spend more time worshiping the familial coat of arms, and telling each other how great they are, really are at a disadvantage to those of us who focus on doing our jobs properly.

But it was bad luck for us that the Martians' very best Admiral — the one who believed completely in fulfilling his oath and doing his duty for Mars — was commanding the best ships they'd ever had.

That was a problem.

And in less than a day, we would discover how much of a problem.

CHAPTER SEVEN
BUSY DAY

"Sniper?"

Major Carrie Walsh nodded and let out a frustrated sigh, "A good one, too. I think he must be a Commando."

Charlie scratched his brow and sighed. It was another long day in the trenches for his squad, now down to nine people. One fatality the day prior, just before they'd gotten into a safe house for two hours of rest (finally).

Right now, he and Rufus had been called in to assist Major Carrie Walsh, who you might recall from *The Almost Coup* and *The Gallant Few*. She and her squad had been part of the Admiralty protective detail, so they'd bailed Greg and John out of the courtroom when Caldecott had started the coup, and later had escorted John to find Daragh in Ireland.

Remember how they got stuck in Daragh's minefield, but it wasn't really a minefield? Yeah, good times.

Five of the members of that squad were now dead, two of them blown up by a mine. I suppose that might be bitterly ironic. I just call it bitter.

So, down to seven members, they'd been going into a neighborhood to sweep it for Commandos when a sniper had started taking shots at them.

And because the sniper was in the second floor window of a house that probably still had people in it, they couldn't just call in a skiff to level the place.

Instead, they'd called Charlie.

Now crouching next to Carrie behind some cover, Charlie considered his options. Best bet was to work around and try to get access to that house from behind, though if the sniper was clever, the place would be rife with booby traps.

Still, nothing else to do.

"Keep his attention, we'll get behind him," Charlie sounded a little more exasperated than he meant to, but Carrie nodded.

"Thanks."

He nodded, then crouch-walked back to the alley where his squad was staying out of sight.

"Sniper, house at the end of the street. We need to get around behind him."

Rufus nodded from the opposite end of the squad line, "Right. Back this way and left turn."

Leading the way, the Major with mismatched eyes charted a course down the alley, and then left into another one which ran behind the block of oppressive, mass-housing dwellings that fronted the street where Carrie was pinned down.

The squad was relatively rested after the recent couple of hours of downtime, so they were noticeably fresher as they checked their angles and crept along smoothly.

Another mag shot sounded from the street Carrie was on, but there was no comm call noting a casualty. That probably meant Major Walsh and her shooters were now purposefully drawing the sniper's attention. Hopefully, he wasn't terribly good, and he'd be so tunnel-visioned on his scope that he wouldn't notice a Brancher creeping into the room behind him.

At the front of the line, Rufus held up his fist, stopping the column. He leaned away from the wall they'd been moving along, looked carefully at the building he was beside, then did hand gestures saying 'this one'.

Four officers were put on the perimeter, to make sure the alley stayed secure for as long as they were here. Ben Belete commanded them.

Charlie and Rufus edged up to the back door of the dwelling; it was slightly ajar, which made pushing it open awfully tempting. Instead, though, Charlie snapped his fingers and got Terry Schroeder to start up the jarammer. Hopefully that would keep anyone from detonating the house from afar... now they would just have to disable any trip sensors, or even trip wires.

Rufus was on that: he pulled a fresh kit of bomb bugs out of his vest and carefully emptied them on the door ledge. The tiny robots, not unlike the spiders that intubate patients, or the tracking bugs that we used on Pion rock, began creeping into the house, and scanning for explosives and sensors.

Pulling out a hand control, Rufus frowned and watched the bugs' search results.

"This door is rigged, antipersonnel," he whispered just loud enough for Charlie to hear.

It took a few minutes for the quick bugs to cover the dwelling's ground floor, and then for two of them to start up the stairs.

"All ground floor doors and windows trapped. Two adults and two kids in the kitchen, look like they've been bound," Rufus reported as the results came in. Then he and Charlie waited patiently, letting the bugs reach the second floor.

"One mine at the top of the stairs... that's it. They put the shooter in the front-right room, set back from the window."

Charlie nodded. Traps set up and civilians — volunteers or more likely hostages — in position so that there'd be innocent deaths if Defense Command went off blockhead style. And the sniper wasn't a complete amateur: he was set up back from the window, where he was a much harder target for shooters from the outside.

"Alright, get the bugs to suicide the triggers on the doors and stairs," Charlie whispered after reflection.

Rufus nodded and keyed in the commands. The clever little bugs began roaming again, locating the trigger sensors for the various doorway traps. As soon as they clung to one, they sacrificed themselves, emitting hefty EM bursts that fried — or usually fried — the trip controls.

The team would still have to be careful going in, but chances were good that nothing would explode.

Well, chances were *decent*.

It took two more minutes for that process to finish, and then because it was his turn, Rufus was first through the door. Terry Schroeder and two more shooters followed, and

Charlie came last.

Hand-gestured orders immediately sent Terry and one of the other officers to the kitchen to release the hostages, and then Rufus led the way to the stairs.

Because the home was a Martian concrete dwelling, the stairs didn't creak as Rufus' boots hit them… one of the surprising perks of these abysmal places to live. He crept up, with the next shooter behind him, and Charlie last again.

It was slow going, and as soon as the anti-personnel bomb at the top of the stairs came into view, Rufus stopped. The fact that it hadn't taken off his head as soon as he set eyes on it was a good sign… but the Major wasn't terribly interested in trying to tip-toe around it.

He had another idea.

Quietly and quickly, he drew a frag grenade out of his vest, and slid it into his MAG-90's special underbarrel launcher — the one, remember, he got from a friend in R&D. Charlie winced, but said nothing. It was undoubtedly a risk, firing something explosive in a house that was wired to blow, but it would save them going upstairs to deal with that sniper.

The doorway was only partially visible from Rufus' position, but he was getting pretty handy with the launcher.

He brought his MAG-90 to his shoulder, lined up the shot, and fired the grenade.

There was a nasty explosion in the room, far enough away that it didn't have much impact on the three Branchers on the stairs. Then there was a scream, and a second explosion that shook the house.

Shook it in a way that Charlie recognized.

"Oh shit," was all he needed to say before he led the Special Branchers out of the building at a dead run.

Yep, the building was collapsing.

It was Rufus' turn to bring up the rear, so he was last to hustle out the back door and sprint away from the collapsing home. He slowed from his dash further up the alley, where the rest of the squad had withdrawn. Standing with the Branchers were a Martian couple and their two sons.

"Sorry about that," Rufus panted as he noticed their presence. "The sniper had your house rigged to blow… maybe a dead man's switch. He didn't want you to survive, no matter what we did."

The Martian husband gently put an arm across his wife's front, and guided her to step back behind him. Rufus frowned and glanced at Charlie, who frowned back. They still weren't used to the different social order here — women had to be protected by the men, remember. Martian society 101.

With his wife safely away from these terribly savage Special Branchers, the man put one hand on each of his boys' shoulders, "We appreciate your letting us escape. But I will not stand for any exactation of rewards."

I'm not sure if we think 'exactation' is a word, but he sure did.

Rufus looked properly confused, as did Charlie.

Then it dawned on them both: the Martian thought they'd pulled out his family because they wanted to rape his wife.

Honestly.

Sigh.

Propaganda, I tell ya, is a powerful thing.

It didn't help that the three women left in this squad were not right in front of the Martian fellow — he was looking at four Special Branch men, each of them pretty sweaty, a bit bloody, and not really looking their parade best.

Charlie wiped his brow with the back of his hand, then stepped in closer to the Martian, "There's nothing to be exacted, sir. We're sorry about the house. You need to visit the Operations Post for this district... it's over at the football pitch on Third Street. Talk to Major Atallah. Tell him Charlie sent you, and that we accidentally flattened your house. You'll be set up with temporary accommodations, and once we're secure here you'll be compensated for your property losses. In Martian currency."

The man frowned at Charlie, clearly confused.

"Seriously," Rufus reinforced the promise. "If you like, we can escort you over there."

The man's eyes darted back and forth from Charlie to Rufus, and his expression slowly went from confusion to very cautious gratitude, "Well, thank you."

"Our pleasure," Charlie nodded, patted him on the shoulder, and then did a few hand gestures that got the squad moving.

Just another little operation for Charlie, Rufus and their squad.

Nothing dramatic, none of their officers lost. The best kind of mission they could have on Mercury.

I bet you were worried that Charlie was going to get blown up, or otherwise die.

Nope.

Not yet.

Chapter Eight
A Reminder Of Things To Remember

Twenty-two hours to intercept seemed like an eternity while we cruised. Realistically, it was less than a day — not much time at all — but as you know well by now, the clock gets slower when you're cruising towards a fight.

But, fortunately for us, there was business to discuss, so we were trading realtime comm calls the whole way.

I, for instance, was on with John for an hour or so. Most of the time we were talking about plans for the battle... as expected, I'd be overseeing the escort squadrons while he focused on defeating the *Tharsises*. My mission was simply to keep as many of the Martian escorts as possible from getting into missile range of the *Bonnies*.

We got all that sorted out in the first forty-five minutes of discussion, and then we changed gears when John asked something unexpected.

"Have you heard anything new about the Emperor?"

Frowning, I shook my head, "Haven't been tuning much into the news lately. Is he complaining again?"

John shook his head, "Daragh's watching him for me... last I heard he was calling Mercury a great victory for the Imperial Army."

"Of course he is," I grumbled, then leaned back in my chair (I was in my cabin, sorry). "Think he's going to try to leverage it against us after hostilities are finished?"

"Of course he is," John grimaced. "Since we got that warning from Haley Briand, I've been waiting for something. I don't know exactly what it's going to be, yet, but this is part of it."

You'll hopefully remember Haley Briand's warnings to Daragh Ryan and Mel Samuels back in *The Gallant Few* — her suggestion that the Emperor was going to come after John and the Fiora Ring again, as revenge for his loss to us in *The Almost Coup*. We hadn't forgotten, and we had some cards to play against his Excellency, the bastard.

But it was going to be a nasty fight when it happened, and we needed to be ready to jump all over him as soon as he started his trouble.

"If we win this coming battle, and secure Mercury, I think the Martians are going to sue for peace," John went on thoughtfully. "I'd bet a month's salary he's going to try to take over the negotiations personally... he needs to do something he can spin as a victory for himself. And when his approval ratings are at their highest, he can come after us."

I frowned at that suggestion, "Well then we're going to need to be ready to get in the way of his glory grab. Negotiations should be the Prime Minister's job, or Foreign Affairs, or at least the Foreign Minister."

"True," John nodded. "But I bet dear Luther Gregory is going to have plans to keep us out of his way... dammit, I dislike this mess. I shouldn't be worrying about it right now."

I shrugged, "True, probably not. But it's still important to keep in mind."

"Yes it is," John agreed, then took a deep breath. "When I retire, I'm not going to miss this crap."

Chuckling, I shook my head, "Hope you're not in any rush to get away from it. We're going to need you around here for a while."

John laughed and shrugged, but before the good humor could continue, another question occurred to me.

"About Haley Briand... any word about her lately?"

I hadn't been privy to briefings from Thea Fostopolos on the whereabouts of the star agent who'd gone missing after delivering the cryptic warnings, seeing as I'd been out with the Jupiter Force in action or in transit while they were happening.

Unfortunately, the briefings really hadn't added much to the obvious: she'd disappeared.

"Not much," John said. "She got a tip and apparently went out to check a new government forming in the unexplored belt... Solar Asteroid Union, I think it was called. We haven't heard a damned thing since."

We didn't know, for instance, that she'd been on *Venus One* during *The Forge Fires*.

"Hope she's safe out there... she did a hell of a job, I've heard."

She'd stormed the Government Palace with John and Greg, so he needed no prompting to agree, "Best agent I've ever met."

I smiled, "Haven't met Mel Samuels, then?"

John frowned and shook his head, "Sounds familiar."

"She was Mel Fox back then... she's the agent who got close to Grant Merger for us... became one of his skippers, and I think Grant was carrying a torch for her. But she scorned him," I smiled when I said that, because as you know, Grant and I did not like each other then. "She led us to Deep Black. Then when Marshal picked up her escape pod after the battle, they had a whirlwind romance and got married."

John laughed as I finished the brief story, "You Belt Squadron types always have the swashbuckling stories with the unlikely romances. I love it!"

I joined in the laughter — it was true. And though John was the patriarch of the Fiora Ring, he'd never actually served with the Belt Squadron... our eccentric, maverick methods were similar to his, but they had their own frontier flavor.

I missed that eccentricity... maybe it would come back soon, once we finished off the Martians in the battle ahead.

Time would tell.

Wes Pellew was just settling in to do some paperwork when his screen chimed. He'd already talked to me, John, Karen and Lia, so he wasn't sure who'd be calling. We were a good eighteen hours from the fight, though... time enough for lots of talking yet. Picking up his remote, he opened the window, and Andrea Kiley appeared.

That was a surprise — a rather pleasant one, but a surprise.

Dropping the pad he'd been reading back onto the pile beside his chair, Wes smiled, "Hello Andrea."

A quick scan of the Irish skipper's features gave no suggestion that she was in any particular distress — both previous times she'd called him out of the blue, he'd gotten the distinct impression she'd just had nightmares, or flashbacks, or whatever they were called.

"Hello Wes," she returned his greeting, her expression neutral... actually almost verging on serious.

"How are things?" his returning question was open-ended. He didn't want to pressure her into talking.

She frowned a little, and then took a deep breath, "So far they're alright. Pretty well, actually. I just wanted to call to let you know that I don't think I'll need to be calling anymore. I appreciate that I could, and that you haven't been pressuring me. So I wanted to just let you know that, I think I'm doing well enough that I won't need to any more."

That surprised Wes, but he managed to not show it.

"Of course," he said. "Though... you can still call to catch up. As friends do."

She nodded, "Yes, I can do that. I'm sure I will. Just. Well, I didn't want you to think that I didn't appreciate you receiving the other kind of call from me. I just won't be needing to make those kinds of calls anymore."

Wes read through the various layers of certainty and uncertainty in Andrea's tone, and decided it was unlikely that her assertion was correct. He guessed that she was feeling better lately — undoubtedly because she was back in action — and that was helping keep her flashbacks at bay. Though it had been different for him after Sara's death, he distinctly remembered that his greatest difficulty had been during downtime.

So Andrea was probably feeling a bit better, and because of that she was making promises to herself — promises like 'I'll never let anyone else see that I'm vulnerable about this again'. That meant no more calls to Wes.

But if she got through the battle ahead of them, and things calmed down again, Wes had to guess that the pain would start coming back in the lull.

Hopefully she'd change her mind and call him when it did.

He contemplated very briefly saying that to her — saying that if she changed her mind, he'd still be happy to talk to her, or more importantly, to listen. But he decided not to. He didn't want it to seem like he was doubting her.

"Understood," he said instead. "I'll look forward to our regular catching-up chats, then."

"Me too. But right now I have to go," Andrea replied a little more quickly than she meant to.

"Okay. If I don't talk to you again before the fight, good luck."

"You too."

She killed the link.

Frowning, Wes wondered if Andrea had been embarrassed at the end of the conversation. She was clearly keeping it together quite well, but she wasn't yet comfortable with her state of mind.

Only time could let such wounds heal. Time, peace and quiet.

Andrea wouldn't have any of those things for a while, so in the meantime she was doing what she needed to do... she was keeping it together.

That was Wes' assessment, as the completely untrained counselor whose only experience was in a different sort of trauma.

Funnily enough, he was right about all of it.

Andrea herself has since confirmed his interpretations.

He understood the Irish skipper very well, and that was to their mutual benefit.

CHAPTER NINE

DIFFERENT PERSPECTIVE

You're probably used to (or sick of) hearing me talk about how we get ready for a battle. Well, seeing as the Fleet Clash is the last fleet battle of the series, how about I change it up this time? How about we see what it was like for our evil adversary, Bort?

The circumstances weren't quite the same for him, obviously — he was mentally preparing himself for a fight, but the one he expected was at Mercury, not fifteen hours away from him in open space. Still, it was the same mental process... the same time warp that made seconds tick by slowly.

On this particular day, he'd spent several hours doing pads (their way of saying 'doing paperwork') for squadron business. All sorts of things came to him for approval, but today's labor had been his least favorite: disciplinary authorizations. The Martians had some interesting notions about how to keep crews in order, and on unhappy ships, it often meant corporal punishment.

Most of the ships in his original squadron had been relatively happy — only occasional pockets of troublemakers who needed lashes or a beating to put them back in their place. But the new ships that had joined from Mercury seemed rife with problems, despite their completely and unquestionably elite professional family leadership.

Ha.

Bort understood that ships running from a defeat like the one at Mercury had to have very low morale, but some of the charges he was seeing on his pads were ridiculous. It frustrated him to know that these people were going to be his backup when they reached Mercury...

But, of course, he had no choice but to keep them. He'd make the most of it... and probably catch hell from the family connections of people like Nudle back on Mars.

That thought crossed his mind, and he swore at himself and dropped the pad he'd been working on to his desk.

There was so much bullshit crowding his job. I mean, we all have our share of inane distractions, but in Defense Command those distractions tend not to get in the way of actually *fighting the enemy*. Even Luther Gregory III was smart enough to hold off on his power-play politics until we won the war.

Many Martians just didn't seem to understand that, during a conflict they were *losing*, focusing on the job at hand might have been a valuable exercise.

Actually, Bort figured that because they were losing, a number of the professional bastards were lining themselves up politically to make sure they wouldn't be blamed for the defeat. Even though clearly they were more responsible for it than anyone else.

Taking a deep breath, he tried to put them out of his mind.

It was tough, though, so he decided to pull out the big guns. He turned to his desk screen and punched up a video file he kept handy for moments like this.

A window opened, and a youngish woman appeared. This was a vid of Casey Flynnboldak, who I mentioned earlier. She'd sent it to him almost two years prior, when Bort had been overseeing the construction of the *Tharsises* with Ben Conflans at Etat Concord, and he'd kept it all this time.

Casey danced professionally in a famous Martian troupe called 'Light', and this recording was of her repeating a routine she'd done on stage the night they'd met. Then a Post Captain, Bort had been attending a show on Asteroid Beta when he'd spotted her. He'd never been mesmerized like that before in his life, so after the show he used his rank to talk his way backstage. Then he'd managed to walk in on her naked. Not kidding.

Now, in the Earth Empire, this story would be pretty amusing, but you have to understand it in the Martian context.

According to the usual niceties of the colonials' society, fleet officers should not become interested in any women who work for a living. As a Captain, you should be married to a woman with no career, who sits at home and wrings her hands, waiting for you to return. So Bort's interest was, in itself, wrong.

Officers of his rank also were never supposed to trick their way backstage to actually meet anyone. Captains were above such foolish pursuits… but since Bort had no breeding to teach him better, he decided to actually take the initiative, and get backstage.

And the walking in on her naked part? I think they shoot people for stuff like that… or maybe I'm exaggerating.

Either way, Bort's courtship of Casey was incredibly unusual, and it was one of the few things in his life that he enjoyed. It wasn't going very smoothly for either of them, because she was still dancing professionally, and he was still fighting a war professionally, but they were trying.

And that helped keep him sane.

So he sat back at his desk and watched Casey Flynnboldak dance like an angel, and he forgot about flogging crewmen and fighting battles alongside incompetent fools for just a little while. He looked forward to a time when the war was over, and presuming he lived through it, he could go back to the Asteroid colonies and convince Casey to marry him.

He'd even be happy to marry her if she kept her job, because honestly, he didn't care whether his wife stayed at home and worried about him, or toured with a dance troupe. He just wanted *her*.

A sentiment I think we can all understand.

But the first requirement of that plan — that he survive the war — was going to be a tough one. And he didn't even realize how tough it would be, or how soon it could become a problem.

Because we were on our way to destroy evil Bort and his monstrous squadron of bad people.

Sorry, that's a little over the top. But we were, indeed, fifteen hours from intercepting his ships, and fighting the final battle.

Would he live?

Would any of us?

Well, I obviously did. I'm not writing this as zombie Ken Barron. Or am I?

Sorry, lame, moving on.

CHAPTER TEN

ANOTHER DANGEROUS MISSION

"I heard Carrie Walsh got hit."

Charlie was checking his MAG-90 when Rufus said that, and he looked up with a frown, "When?"

"This morning. Shot in the throat. Last I heard she was on her way up to *Persephone Praxidice* in critical condition."

That was bad news. Charlie hadn't known Carrie particularly well, but she had a very good reputation from working with Admiralty House and people like John Fiora.

And she was a Special Brancher, one of the family. It was bad news that she'd been hit... another sign of the dangers of operating on Mercury.

I suppose by this point in the series I've railed enough about how bad fighting in built-up areas can be. Danger around every corner, civilians to watch out for... well, Mercury was exactly that.

But so far, at least, the population in general was remaining outwardly quiet. A widespread uprising would have been a serious problem, but the fact that Defense Command was proving far more genial than any of the civilians had expected was a help.

Hell, Martian propaganda had set the bar so low for our conduct that even the blockheads in the other domes were making a generally positive impression. That's how poorly the Martians thought of us... as if we needed any reminders.

But anyway, it was still dangerous. Commandos and regular Martian troopers were resisting, along with some hardline civilians. And the fact that the resistance was continuing this long after the official surrender was a sign to everyone from Charlie right up to Brigadier Peri Oktar: insurgency was going to be an ongoing problem.

Perhaps if we kept impressing the ordinary men and women of the Mercury population with our good behavior, we could beat this thing... if the hardliners had a tough time drawing more fighters into their ranks, then Special Branch could theoretically kill all the troublemakers.

Eventually.

But it would be slow and dangerous.

Since last we've seen them (not all that long ago), Charlie and Rufus had lost two more officers, one wounded by a sniper, the other beaten over the head with a frying pan. Not kidding about the last one: she'd been scoping out an apartment for overwatch in another counter-sniper op when the tenant turned up and thought she was a looter.

It's sort of funny, but really not. She had a fractured skull and was out of the war, though the tenant learned a lesson too: he wasn't murdered for his trouble. He wasn't even roughed up. He became more cooperative after that.

Anyway, that meant just seven shooters remained, including Charlie and Rufus.

It was actually getting to the stage where Charlie was genuinely wondering when his time would come, and whether any of the officers he and Rufus had led into the Mercury Capital Dome would leave alive and uninjured.

Grim sort of question, and unsurprisingly, it wasn't one Charlie was letting himself dwell on.

"Okay," he said finally, closing his MAG-90's cell chamber and setting it to medium power. "Tunnel entrance down the block?"

Rufus nodded, "The one next to the liquor store. If you're thirsty."

Charlie grinned, "No, I don't think that'd be wise."

I obviously should explain: they were getting set to sweep a tunnel network that ran under the commercial district. These were tunnels similar to the ones at Io, and the ones at the Forge… you know, the ones I always say will be hell to clear if the enemy gets a chance to fortify them?

Yep. Just their luck.

The squad had been patrolling in this area when Colonel Ronald received a tip that some Commandos were going to be down in these tunnels, preparing to launch an attack. Such a tip was a perfect setup for a trap, obviously, but if there were indeed insurgents to be found, it was worth the risk to get those bastards.

Better to fight them underground, where chances of hurting civilian bystanders were nil, than to have a shootout in town. Going down there was more dangerous for the Special Branchers, but it was the job.

And you know how they are about shutting up and getting on with the job.

Rufus and Charlie took a couple of moments to brief the rest of the squad, which still included Ben Belete and Terry Schroeder, and then they set off down the street towards the tunnel entrance building.

The area was reasonably clear, but it was by no means secure, so they moved tactically, MAG-90s sweeping the storefronts and rooftops around them.

It was creepy, honestly. The Martian stores had a very surreal quality about them — bookstores with displays telling people what books the state thought they should read… clothing stores with clearly marked sections for 'State Sponsored Wear' and 'Individualist Styles'…

I'm too embarrassed to tell you what their 'Physical Intimacy Shop' storefront looked like. It caused some open-mouthed stares as Charlie's squad passed by, and Ben Belete had to ask the most obvious question: "How the hell can the state regulate *that*?"

We'd had very few windows into Martian planetary culture up to this point. We got the broad strokes — the status of women, and so on — but the details of how their government's oversight played out in day-to-day life was a revelation. I'm sure there were reports on some of the quirks of the relationship buried in the DCI archive somewhere, but they weren't made public, or even available to us during the invasion, because if the Martians realized we had ways of knowing what their day-to-day lives were like, it might have tipped them off about some of the [guesswork] that was occasionally saving us from getting blindsided during the war.

Yeah, I can't explain.

Anyway, it seemed quite clear that the Martian government, which had been created to free the people of Mars from the supposed tyranny of the Earth Empire, believed it was duty-bound to regulate Martian day-to-day life, at least on its core planets. The asteroids were at arms length, but Mercury and Mars were under their boot… or, no, that's not it. The police didn't kick down your bedroom door if the wrong person was on top, but propaganda would tell you constantly that if you were doing it wrong, you were a hedonist Empire-type who secretly fantasized about molestation, rape and murder.

I'm not kidding, this is right out of some of the literature that was confiscated at the time.

It's so over the top I have a hard time believing it worked… but then, based on the reactions our people were getting in that dome, the Martians were convinced of some damned unlikely things about us.

Genuinely frightening. But then the Martians aren't history's only example of this… and there are too many examples of propaganda leading to blind, often ridiculous obedience for me to repeat them all here. I'm sure you know some.

So, citizen of the Empire, be glad you live in a place where the sanctity of your individual rights is considered to be as important as the safety of the state. The government doesn't recommend clothing, tell you what to read, or… er… other stuff about who you spend time with.

Enough said.

Sorry, that was a long tangent. But it was appropriate, because that's the sort of thing Charlie and Rufus and their officers were seeing as they approached the underground access point.

"I think it's more shopping below here," Rufus said quietly as they came to a stop outside the tunnel entrance.

"Jarammer up," Terry Schroeder reported as he switched the device on.

"Bomb bugs," Charlie ordered smoothly.

This was all pretty old hat to them by now — and when I say that, I don't mean they were getting careless because they'd been doing it too much. They were used to taking their time and being cautious.

The bomb bugs went into the access stairway and started sweeping. Two anti-personnel mines were found on the way down, and each was zapped. At the bottom of the stairway there was an open food court, probably with state-recommended burgers. Eat the one with the wrong kind of cheese and it means you secretly want to eat puppies.

You monster.

Sorry, that's inappropriate.

"Clear down to the food court," Rufus reported, then edged into the stairway. He took a few steps down, covering the descent with his MAG-90, and then looked up at Charlie with a nod.

The bots had been right: no bombs here.

Charlie took one step down into the stairway, then remembered himself — he had to go last this time. Turning back, he looked to his squad. They were lined up in a tactical column, crouching in front of the liquor store window, and keeping their eyes up.

They had to go first, and deploying them would be a challenge in itself. What was the best way to sweep a food court? Each kitchen would have to be checked separately, and there could be more traps in any of them.

It was going to be a chore.

He started doing hand gestures.

And then the liquor store exploded.

Simply *exploded*.

With Charlie and everyone right in front of it.

It was a huge blast — not the typical improvised bomb they'd seen a lot of, but enough of an explosion to shatter the building.

For a long time I struggled with how to describe it to you… to describe it with enough reality to be fitting of the blast that got my friend Charlie. So, speaking with experts, I've tried to reconstruct what happened to him… what he must have seen. It's still not enough, but maybe it helps make it understandable.

This is probably how it went:

A flash from inside the store.

Right eye — scope eye — snapped shut.

Other eye went white, then nothing.

Air was ripped right out of his lungs.

Vicious tearing sensation.

Nose began to bleed.

Eardrums ruptured and bled.

Pressure wave hit him like a sledgehammer.

Reflected off the wall, hit him again.

Powerful enough to liquefy soft tissue.

Debris reached him next.

And heat.

Blades of glass from the window.

Pieces of bottles covered in flaming liquor.

Fractions of microseconds before they hit him.

Somehow he got his arm up.

Protected his face with his forearm.

Glass went through the combat mesh in his sleeve and embedded in his arm.

More slammed into his vest.

Protection of the central panels saved his organs from shrapnel.

Blast wind threw him like he'd been hit by a truck.

Protective panels couldn't stop that.

Feet were lifted off the ground.

Back hit the inside wall of the stairway.

Dropped down, onto the stairs.

Tumbled down towards the food court.

Head first into the support post for one of the rails.

Jerked to a stop.

Sound of the explosion caught up to him.

+++

Rufus stared down at Charlie's limp body. His ears were ringing and he knew he had to be bleeding from various openings — the pressure wave had raced down the stairs, but the blast wind with the debris hadn't been able to follow because of the concrete wall.

Charlie was down there, thrown twenty meters down the staircase, and Rufus had no idea if he could have survived.

He tapped his comm, knowing that he couldn't hear an acknowledgment on the other side of the line if it was given, "Rufus Chang, *Wolf* SB1-2. Explosion at my location. On surface. Six casualties. Request medical support. Reinforcements."

Rufus, for the first time in his life, didn't know what to do next — check Charlie, or see if any of the squad that had been next to the liquor store was alive.

He decided to check the latter, because his subordinates were his first responsibility and because it was a little quicker — a few steps up onto the street.

When he reached there, he found the ground was littered with body parts.

All had to be dead.

He didn't know that Ben Belete had actually survived, through the sort of luck that convinces people there is a God. He lost both legs, but he survived. That's one of the reasons I've been able to bring him into so much of the storytelling so far this series. He tracked me down after he read *The Independent Squadron* and offered to help fill in some blanks.

But from Rufus' viewpoint, Ben was out of sight (under rubble). He wouldn't be dug out until the backup teams arrived.

Everyone else was dead and in pieces.

And Charlie?

Rufus didn't know.

He went to find out.

CHAPTER ELEVEN
FIND EACH OTHER

What would Lia say if she knew about that?

Well, she didn't so it doesn't really matter, I suppose.

What she did know is what we all knew: the battle was fast approaching.

"We're about forty minutes from intercept," Felicia Khalid looked up with that info, and I nodded.

Having *Melbourne* out here somewhere took a lot of the drama out of finding Bort, and I really wasn't going to complain. Even having one detail taken care of — like where to find the enemy — was a good thing. It meant the Martians wouldn't get the drop on us, which considering the *Tharsises'* firepower, was good news.

But we'd still have to fight them in the end. There was nothing *Melbourne* or its wizard (sorry, I'm loving that mental picture) could do to change that.

"Bring up Battlelink," was my next order, and with a nod, Felicia started getting her staff to send out the necessary signals.

Faces began appearing. Because Karen was squadron commander, she was going to connect directly to all the skippers from our group, while I was going to have Lia, Wes, Karen, and John up on *Wolf's* screens. It didn't take long for each of them to appear.

"Latest from *Melbourne* puts them on course," John told us as soon as he appeared.

I nodded, "Alright. Then we stick with the plan?"

John nodded, "No reason to change it now."

He was right about that. And the plan itself was quite simple: the escorts would move in first to draw off the Martian screen, and then John and the *Bonnies* would face off against the *Tharsises* in a rather climactic firefight.

Simple, flexible, hopefully effective.

"All screening forces forward," I switched my gaze to Karen, Lia and Wes, and each of them nodded quickly before passing orders on to their ships.

For the next few minutes, we got into formation and continued our acceleration towards the intercept point. Soon enough, we'd see Bort for the first time.

Like us, Bort didn't spend all of his time on the bridge, but even though there was no reason for him to think that this particular time of this particular day was going to require attention, he'd decided to pull a shift on *Olympus Mons'* bridge that afternoon.

He sat in his chair (in general, Martians rely on their command chairs a lot more than we do, so theirs are the central focuses of their bridges), working on some pads about repair authorizations. Sitting in the chair beside him was Post Captain Art O'Thomson, who was similarly working on his pads.

At one point, the Captain stopped and leaned in closer to his long-time commander, "Sir, question."

2233 · REAP THE WHIRLWIND

Bort blinked and looked at his old friend, "What's on your mind?"

O'Thomson narrowed his eyes thoughtfully, "Well, sir... I got a letter in the last comm package from home. My eldest daughter is to be married as soon as the war is over. She wanted to know if you'd be willing to attend."

That wasn't anything Bort had expected to hear, but he smiled, "Trina's getting married? Of course I'll make it."

These two had been in ships together for nearly twenty years, and Bort had been with Art when he'd gotten news that his first child had been born. She had to be nineteen now, and evidently she'd found someone who made her happy.

"Did you give your permission?" Bort asked after a moment's thought, and Art winced a little more.

"I didn't. But I approve of the man. He's one of the Governor's staff, a good man. I've met him a few times during visits back."

"Ah," Bort nodded in answer.

It was customary in Martian culture for a father to be asked for permission before a daughter could be married, but as I've said, the asteroids really were at arms length from the culture of home. They had a frontier feel not unlike the Belt colonies, though they were incredibly destitute.

It's significant, I think, that many of the senior officers in the *Tharsis* Squadron hailed from the Asteroid colonies, starting with Bort himself. They were the rejects of Martian military culture, granted their position because they were simply too good at their jobs to be relegated to their 'proper station'. And that made them our biggest headache.

To put it mildly.

"Why'd you wait til now to ask?" Bort frowned with that question, realizing the last comm package from home had reached *Olympus Mons* days prior.

Art O'Thomson smiled wryly, "Don't know, sir. Just got a feeling I better ask now."

Strange sort of feeling to have.

Some might call it a premonition.

"Sir..." a concerned voice sounded from *Olympus Mons'* Scanning Section. "Sir, I'm reading signatures at long range."

Time was up.

"There are the bastards..." Andrea muttered as she folded her arms and squared off next to me.

The Martians appeared on our screens in a large, well-organized cloud, three superbattleships in the middle of a flock of escorts. They were on course for Mercury, and we were closing on them from an oblique angle — if you take a letter 'A', we were coming up the right leg, they were coming up the left, and we were going to converge at the point.

"No surprises in numbers. I like having eyes everywhere," Wes remarked softly from his screen, then folded his arms and ordered his ships to prepare for action.

"General quarters everyone," Lia added from her own screen. She didn't sound one little bit nervous, because her façade remained impenetrable. But she was anxious, and that was fair enough. It'd pass soon.

"Jupiter Force to action stations," Karen said it last, so smoothly and graciously.

I smiled at her — it really wasn't a time for smiling, but I did anyway.

Andrea gave the orders that moved *Wolf* from standby readiness to full action stations, but really that was just a formality at this stage. The crew was ready.

"Lasers and mags crewed and energized. All compartments report ready for action," Jim Hannigan started reading off the usual reports from his operations consoles.

"Sensors tuned for battle, communications tied to secure frequencies. Aux systems on standby," Felicia Khalid reported for her section.

"Engineering reports all reactors battened down, full speed available. Aux nav systems on standby. Helm ready for battle maneuvers," Shelby McLaws added after that.

Wolf had been fighting battles for many years now. I had skippered the trusty frigate through some, Karen through others, and Andrea through others still.

And there were no frigates better for the job, in my biased view.

Today would be another big challenge for us.

"Give me a count to weapons range, *Tharsis* and otherwise," I glanced over at Felicia, and she replied with a nod.

"Understood… range is now… five minutes. Closing."

"Is there any point to turning away?" Art O'Thomson asked that question very quietly, so only Bort could hear it.

But both of them knew the answer — there really was no point. Chances were the *Tharsis* Squadron wasn't any faster than ours… perhaps it was slower. No, it was better to stand and fight, and if things went well, then they'd remove the *Bonaventures* from our arsenal, and truly give Mars a victory worth talking about.

If anyone in the red fleet could pull that off, it'd be Bort McWebsbert.

"General quarters sounded and confirmed throughout the fleet, sir," the Comm Chief reported at that point, and Bort nodded.

"Thank you, Chief. Give me intership comm."

There was a brief pause, and then a distinctive whistle sounded on every ship in Bort's battle group. The Admiral came to his feet and cleared his throat,"This is Bort McWebsbert. Looks like Defense Command has found us, and they have the *Bonaventures* with them. Our counting shows even numbers, us and them… they have one more battleship, we have one more destroyer escort. We're going to have to fight. A victory here will rock our enemy, put them on the defensive. We'll be able to relieve Mercury. We'll take the Empire's best ships from them. We're the only ships in our Navy who can do this, but we'll all need to give our very best to make it happen. Good luck, fight hard."

He gestured for the link to be cut, and then he moved over to the central information pillar, and watched the screens on the rotating column.

We were right on his heels.

John took a deep breath and looked at Captain Lennox Williams. Then he looked up at our faces on screen — he had me, Karen, Lia, Wes, as well as the skippers of *Terra Nova*, *Hibernia* and *Bonavista*.

"Alright, ladies and gentlemen. Goes without saying that this is important. Let's win it cleanly."

My answer was simple: "Good luck, John."

That sentiment was repeated by everyone else.

Standing on *Wolf's* bridge, I then turned my attention to my three squadron commanders. The two most important women in my life (excepting, again, my mother), and one of my very best friends. Who liked soup and hated heights.

"Everyone look after yourselves."

They each nodded and smiled.

"You too," Karen said.

A moment later, the Martians turned straight at us, so we turned straight at them.

CHAPTER TWELVE

FACE EACH OTHER

Escorts lead the way. We do a job they call 'screening', which I think I've explained before... basically, it boils down to making sure that no one interferes in the clash of the titans. The last thing epic battleships need to worry about during a fight with other epic battleships is the appearance of a destroyer spitting missiles.

We were there to stop that, and as you well know by now, the fights between the escorts can be as vicious as they can be inconsequential.

A little trivia: Shamus Czarnecki was the last commander of escorts for the *Bonnies*, and his squadron, if you recall *The Gallant Few*, had been gutted for its trouble.

It was going to be a tough fight.

"They're leading out with their screen... damn, I was hoping we'd get a chance to flank them," Wes was offering his observations, which I certainly didn't mind.

"Range in fifty seconds," Felicia offered the countdown, and I watched in silence.

Their escort force seemed to be moving in two halves, each roughly equal in strength, with a very small gap between them — a gap too small for us to exploit.

"Launch all fighters," I ordered. There was no point holding them back.

What would be the best way to deal with the Martians...?

"Lia, go left, Karen, go right. Wes, up the middle. If one side proves tougher..."

"I'll turn and flank them," he agreed.

It was very easy to lead these people, because frankly, they barely needed leading. Just coordination.

"Forty seconds," Felicia was keeping the count now, and we all watched the icons moving on the screen.

Karen started handing out targeting priorities, followed quickly by Wes and Lia. We'd go one-on-one for the first exchanges — no doubling up, just straight ahead shooting.

"Thirty seconds."

"The *Tharsises* might try to sweep some of you out of the way," John warned quietly. "Be ready for that."

He didn't really need to offer the warning — the possibility of being swatted by the mighty battleships couldn't be lost on any of us — but his concern was paternal and appreciated as such.

"Twenty seconds."

I glanced at Andrea, and she nodded and looked back at Jim Hannigan, "Open fire as soon as we're in range."

He replied, "Will do."

"Ten seconds."

The air on the bridge went silent. You could virtually count seconds by heartbeats in those last ten seconds — they seemed both so long and so short.

"Coming into range…" Felicia began evenly.

"We have a solution on our target," Jim overlapped her.

"…now," Felicia finished.

"Shoot."

Wolf's laser number one was the first beam to fire during the entirety of the Fleet Clash, though I hardly need to tell you that it wasn't the last. Space filled with silent red light, our lasers ramming into the Martians in those few seconds before their own weapons came into range.

I counted those seconds in silence, watching as the data from our first shots came back. Jim's laser solution had been true: we'd drilled a destroyer pretty nastily. All of Karen's ships made some sort of hits, and all of Wes' did too. Only a couple of Lia's ships were off the mark, and that's nothing to be critical of.

But we didn't stop any of the Martians — it wasn't that easy, they weren't going to be that helpful.

"They're in range… now."

"Evasive," Andrea's order followed Felicia's report, and I looked up at the screens.

"Keep formation as long as you can, then pile on."

Karen, Lia and Wes each nodded at my order, and then my eyes darted back to the main screen. Our three lines of ships started to fluctuate as individual vessels maneuvered, but basic formation held together enough that mutual fire support was still possible.

We kept charging straight at our Martian counterparts.

But I wasn't watching that. I should have been, but I wasn't.

The *Tharsises* hadn't opened up on us. They were waiting to engage the *Bonnies*. And their first shots could determine the fate of this battle. Arguably even the fate of the war.

Bort knew the significance his battleships' first shots were going to have. He could have opened up on the escorts, but he decided to wait — to save his ships' might for the symbolic beginning of the battleship fight.

Sitting in his chair (I can't imaging commanding a battle from a chair, but he managed), he took a deep breath.

The Scanning Officer was reading off the range in whatever units the Martians used: "Eight thousand… 7,500… 7,000… 6,500… 6,000…"

Art O'Thomson was sitting next to Bort, gripping the arms of his chair. If our bridge on *Wolf* was tense, then I don't know what word even applies to *Olympus Mons'* bridge. Everyone on deck knew this was the fight for which their ship had been built — the enemy they'd always been meant to face.

A supposed 'dreadnought' against a proper superbattleship.

"Prepare to open fire," Art gave the order.

"Laser batteries at the ready, sir," the Gunnery Officer replied immediately.

Bort steepled his fingers, and waited for the range to hit '5,000'.

John put his hands on his hips. He stood on the stage at the front of *Bonaventure's* bridge, waiting for his battleships to cross that line into the potential dead zone — where the *Tharsises* could fire and the *Bonnies* could not.

"They have us in range… now!" Jorge Allende reported.

"All hands brace," Lennox Williams called from the center of the bridge.

They wouldn't alter course. They wouldn't do anything that would slow them down — they had to get within their own laser range before they could afford to start maneuvering.

Which meant the *Bonnies* would have to accept laser fire that had literally blown up other battleships.

John stood his ground and waited for the Martians to dish it out.

"They're not altering course! Lock solution and fire!"

Bort took a deep breath as Art O'Thomson gave those orders, and then turned his eyes to one of the screens tracking the exchange of fire.

Olympus Mons, *Pavonis Mons*, and *Arsia Mons*, each named for a volcanic mountain in the Tharsis range on Mars, opened fire.

I remember watching this from *Wolf*'s bridge. For all the frigate and corvette skippers I talked to later, this was the absolute defining moment of the fight. Everything hung on what happened when those lasers lanced between us and rammed into our mighty *Bonnies*.

I've been trying to figure out the best way to describe the effect. I think this is it:

John felt *Bonaventure* shift under his feet, as though it was a hovercar taking a corner with the dampeners turned down.

And that was it.

Sixteen lasers raked our beloved ships, and you better believe they scorched her armor. But you don't smack a lady like *Bonnie* or her sisters and get away with your life.

No sir, you pick a fight with those four ladies and you're going to need something special on your side.

Because there's never been a warship like any of them in the history of the human race.

Sitting on his bridge, Bort tightened his jaw when he came to that realization.

All at once, the reality of what was going to happen next became clear: his ships, the best warships the Martians had ever put into space, weren't going to have the stuff. Of course you can say the first shots don't make the whole battle, but for so many reasons he just *knew* it was all going to go badly after *Bonaventure* walked right through *Olympus Mons*' lasers.

Those were war-winning lasers.

Or so the Martians had hoped.

"Hit them again, guns!" Art O'Thomson wasn't about to stop shooting, and the lasers lanced out sharply.

But the mighty beams just slid off *Bonnie*'s armor, and then Lennox Williams started to twirl his ship to scatter the targeting solutions just a little.

Bort looked at a clock and ran the numbers in his head. The seconds dragged out, but not enough.

Bonaventure came into range.

♦♦♦

"Shoot."

John took a breath as he heard *Bonnie's* XO give that order, and then space *really* turned red. Four lasers, more powerful than any other beams in human history, came from each of the four *Bonnies*. Space itself seemed to rupture with the power.

Hibernia and *Bonavista* had teamed their fire on what proved to be *Arsia Mons*. The ship's armor was strong, but three of its four extra, smaller drive pods were sheared off immediately.

It's to the credit of the Martian Navy, and to the builders of these ships, that the fire from those two *Bonnies* didn't simply obliterate *Arsia Mons* in the first go.

Terra Nova had *Pavonis Mons*, and instantly took off two of its supplementary drive pods.

Bonaventure set her sights on *Olympus Mons*, and didn't fool around: four mighty lasers converged on Bort's bow pod, and blasted away almost all of his ship's mighty bow armor in the first blow.

Olympus Mons' bridge filled with smoke as relays were fried by the heat of the shots, and several conduits blew out around the deck.

Bort coughed and got to his feet, moving forward to the monitor column. He knew the battle was lost immediately, but that didn't mean he'd give up. His ships might not survive, but he'd still accomplish something if he managed to do harm to the *Bonnies* — enough harm that they couldn't cruise straight to Mars after finishing him off.

"All *Mons* continue fire, aim to disable!" he grunted his order, and as his ship bucked, he kept his feet through sheer experience and determination.

The fight was on.

CHAPTER THIRTEEN

THE CLASH

While the battleships were slogging, we escorts were really starting to get into the thick of it. But in the interests of trying to keep the chaos for you as the reader to a minimum, I'm going to stick with the battleships until the end of their clash, then go back in time a little ways and explain what was happening to us while they were doing the heavy lifting.

That in mind, it's back to *Bonnie*.

John felt his flagship shift again, but not too dramatically. The armor that R&D had spent nearly a decade developing — which was a couple of generations newer than what had been on *Medusa* when it had been blown up — was handling the onslaught very well.

"Passing the escort line now, sir," Jorge Allende narrated the images John was seeing on screen, and our First Lord nodded.

"Straight at them," he ordered. "Let's get in close."

Bonnie fired again as he said that, and the lasers flew true.

Bort struggled to a railing near the central information column and held on as *Olympus Mons* jerked out from under his feet. He turned to the gunnery officer, "Anything getting through?"

The Lieutenant looked up at him with wide eyes, shaking his head.

Gritting his teeth, Bort went through his options.

The new lasers — the war-winners, according to their designers — were no match for the new *Bonaventures*.

But over time, they could wear John's squadron down... if they hadn't been outnumbered, perhaps they could have even beaten them. For now, they just had to keep swinging...

"Missiles — start hitting them with everything," Bort ordered sharply, and the gunner nodded.

Olympus Mons bucked again as the armor on the starboard side of its bow pod absorbed massive punishment.

Missiles were launched in reply.

"Missile separation... incoming."

Lennox Williams hopped up onto the stage next to John and checked out the icons of incoming missiles on one of the screens. Starlights were turning on the warheads now, but the Martian battleship *Bonnie* was squaring off against had fired fifteen. That would be a tall order for the pilots to shoot down as Martian Interceptors kept them preoccupied.

"Switch to mag batteries," Lennox gave the word with that revelation. "Warn all

Starlights to clear the fire zone."

The signals went out, and *Bonnie's* XO switched energy priorities from full lasers to full mags. What resulted was a hurricane-driven rainstorm of golden energy.

You'll genuinely never see anything else like it in your life.

Starlights peeled away from the missiles as eighty quick-firing mag batteries opened up, and Interceptors that hadn't been attentive were wiped from space, along with the fifteen missiles.

But the switch from lasers to mags had bought *Olympus Mons* precious seconds, and now the Martian flagship had turned to starboard and was presenting its relatively unharmed port side to *Bonnie*, with the range closing down to nothing.

Because of stupid Martian design principles, only a fraction of the ship's lasers could be brought to bear at that approach angle, but being so much closer, those lasers would have much more tell.

"Hold on!" Lennox Williams grabbed the rail behind him, as did John, and then a sledgehammer hit *Bonaventure*.

Martian lasers dug into armor up and down the top of the ship's neck, cutting into dozens of the mag batteries that were positioned on the tops of her dorsal fins. The deck under John's feet vibrated with the impact, and a relay at the rear of the bridge blew out from the overload.

"Full broadside!" Lennox roared back to his XO, who was already finishing the targeting solution.

A moment later, he barked the order: "Shoot!"

Because *Bonaventure* was well-designed, she had four lasers available for broadside fire, and now all of them spoke in anger.

At close range, the four powerful red beams carved into *Olympus Mons*.

Just before *Bonnie's* reply got to him, Bort was checking on the success of his ship's passing shot, "What did we do to them?"

After a brief delay, the Gunner's Mate looked at his Admiral, "Cut through dorsal armor, sir… must have damaged some EM cannon and some of their power grid…"

Then *Bonnie's* lasers rammed home.

The bridge had been smoky and scorched, with some control systems collapsing.

Now the entire front wall seemed to explode.

Bort was carried off his feet, landing hard on the deck behind a console as a cloud of shrapnel showered the bridge. He was stunned by the landing, and was sure some of his ribs bruised on impact. But he didn't have time to worry about that.

He struggled to his feet, wincing in pain, and looked to see who was left.

Both the Gunner and the Gunner's Mate were standing, so he called to them, "Keep firing as we pass. Try to disable them!"

He then turned to the steering section, and saw no one left alive.

"Call the aux steering position, tell them to hold course…" he barked, and someone left from the comm side did just that.

Then he turned his eyes towards the Captain's chair.

Art O'Thomson was sitting there, looking down at his chest. Blood was coming out of his mouth with every breath.

"Shit," Bort hurried to his friend's side, then looked back at the survivors in the comms section, "Med staff to the bridge, the Captain's wounded."

Art looked up at him with wide eyes as he said that, so Bort put a hand on his shoulder, "Hang on, Art."

Somehow, the Admiral doubted his long-time friend would have the ability to do that.

"Moderate damage to our high mag batteries," *Bonnie's* XO gave that update.

It was obviously a far cry from the damage her opponent was suffering — the bridge around John remained bright and smoke free.

"Turn us to port as the bastard passes, HNO," Lennox looked down to his Helm and Navigation Officer, who nodded.

"Aye sir."

"As soon as the broadside is presented again, hit them," Lennox said that to his XO, who nodded in turn.

Bonaventure was turning as *Olympus Mons* passed going in the opposite direction, so our mighty fighting lady would present her port lasers again at the stern of Bort's flagship. Now, because of Martian design, Bort would be able to engage with a dozen lasers when that happened, but Lennox had the feeling his opponent was in trouble.

Now was not the time to back off.

John turned his attention to the main screen — to the icons of our ships engaging the destroyers and destroyer escorts, and to the other three *Bonnies*.

I'll save talking about how many we'd lost for the moment: the story with *Terra Nova, Hibernia* and *Bonavista* was worthy of note.

Those three battleships had tried to split up *Pavonis Mons* and *Arsia Mons*, but the Martians had hung together, and seemingly realizing that neither of them was going to survive, they'd decided to choose one of the *Bonnies* to take with them into oblivion.

By chance, the *Bonnie* they had selected was *Hibernia*, and they were hitting the superbattleship with masses of lasers, thirty-two beams at a time.

Hibernia's bridge, I'll tell you, was full of smoke, and her Captain, Abdul Ji, had a piece of console sticking out of his thigh, but the ship didn't just roll over and die. Much of its armor held, though its dorsal mags suffered, and its power grid was tested.

Mainly, though, the damage was not to critical systems — the ship was simply being pounded, its armor buckling but surviving, its lasers and mags cutting back intermittently.

I think it's safe to say that, if she'd been on her own, *Hibernia* would have been destroyed in that fight.

But she wasn't alone, obviously.

Her sisters *Terra Nova* and *Bonavista* each chose one of the two *Mons*, and while the red ships did everything they could to pound *Hibernia* out of existence, those *Bonnies* started to cut them to pieces.

It didn't take too long…

"Incoming again," Jorge Allende warned *Bonnie's* bridge, and the mighty ship shuddered as more lasers pounded into its armor.

"Laser five took a direct hit... offline!" the XO barked. That was unfortunate — it cut *Bonaventure's* port broadside strength down by a quarter.

But there were still three lasers left bearing on *Olympus Mons'* stern.

"Shoot!" the XO called next.

Those three lasers lanced out, and didn't miss.

Medics were just seeing to Art O'Thomson when *Olympus Mons* took that hit.

The main lights went out and the secondary lights came up, and then an alarm sounded.

Bort looked up at the ceiling as he heard the peculiar klaxon — a klaxon he had never expected to hear in this ship. *Olympus Mons* was too powerful, too robust.

"That broadside cut right through the stern pod... sir, the reactors were hit. We're looking at a huge radiation spill, possible overload!"

Eyes widened, Bort turned to the engineering officer who made that report, "How bad a spill?"

The man looked down at his console and began shaking his head, "Category... nine, sir. The engineering section was automatically sealed."

A stillness overcame Bort McWebsbert — a second-long pause to recognize the destruction of humanity that was taking place around him. Everyone in the engineering section would soon be dead — 150 men were going to fall to massive exposure, or an explosion if the reactors went critical.

And then the radiation would breach the shielding and irradiate the whole crew. Unless the reactors blew and killed everyone first.

Olympus Mons could fight and fly at about two-thirds efficiency until that happened. They could still take shots at *Bonaventure*.

But that would be certain death for Bort's entire crew, and he strongly doubted any of his shots were going to seriously limit *Bonaventure's* ability to go into another fight after this one.

That was the decision in front of Bort McWebsbert — the Martians' most hardened spacer. Would he abandon ship and save his crew, or fight on out of spite, and get them all killed on the off chance that he could do some damage?

Take a guess what he decided.

John's attention was on *Terra Nova* and *Bonavista* now, and he watched as those two ships protected their sister with angry lasers.

Arsia Mons was the first to lose power, and then as escape pods began bursting away from the hull, the ship started to explode.

Frowning, John looked up at the skippers from the other *Bonnies*, "That one just explode?"

Tasha Tate from *Terra Nova* nodded, "Must have scuttled, sir. We didn't hit it that hard."

Her assessment was quite correct: the Martians weren't going to let us get our hands on the *Tharsises*, out of pride, and out of a desire to keep their latest technological advancements secret.

Even though those advancements weren't superior to ours... or technically even *theirs*.

Both *Terra Nova* and *Bonavista* then closed on *Pavonis Mons*, which was doggedly hammering *Hibernia*.

That didn't last.

Eight lasers crossed the *Tharsis'* neck, four from either side, and damned near cut the ship in two. Its central power core was severed, and the ship fell dark.

Then the same routine repeated itself: the escape pods launched and the scuttling charges took the ship apart.

That just left one, and Lennox Williams was turning *Bonaventure* to chase the staggering *Olympus Mons*.

But as *Bonnie's* bow lasers turned to bear on the last Martian 'dreadnought', its escape pods started to fly.

It was almost anti-climactic for John. He let out a breath as he watched the Martian flagship burst into debris.

None of the *Bonnies* destroyed — some chopped up, to be sure, but they'd met the Martians' secret weapons and proved more than a match for them.

That was a good feeling, but it didn't quite sink in immediately. After a few minutes of trading lasers, the main clash was over.

But that wasn't the end of the battle.

Looking up at the screens, John redirected the attention of his skippers, "Alright, prepare to launch SAR teams. But first we need to clear out the rest of the escorts. Support Ken's squadrons."

We were still fighting our counterparts, and the help the *Bonnies* could provide with their epic firepower would be hugely welcomed.

It'd save a few lives.

Many were already dead.

CHAPTER FOURTEEN

THE ESCORTS

While the battleships were having their rumble, we were in knife fights with some of the best Martian escorts we'd ever seen. Bort's hand-picked destroyer and destroyer escort officers were the Martian equivalent of the Belt Squadron, and though they only made up half the forces we faced, that was enough to give us hell.

When the battleship lasers started flying, we had no choice but to break formation to stay clear. Squadron ships remained near each other, but we couldn't keep our lines because we needed the ability to completely change course if we got stuck in the crossfire.

So it came down to a melee similar to the one at Mercury... while our Starlights were dogfighting with their Interceptors, our ships were dogfighting with their ships.

There was no particular sequence to events. In fact, it was chaos.

"We're sticking with you," Mark Gunney appeared on one of our Battlelink screens as the divisions broke up, and *Cheetah* paired off with *Wolf*.

I didn't acknowledge because he wasn't talking to me — he was telling Andrea that she had a partner in crime.

Two destroyers seemed to have marked us, so I let Andrea and Mark deal with them while I kept an eye on the entire situation.

"Lia, there's a bunch of them coming right at you," I pointed out.

She nodded back to me, "On it, don't you worry!"

I switched my gaze back to the main screen, my eyes tracking different icons as they split apart. A destroyer and two destroyer escorts were going after Karen's division — *Lady Grace* and *Friendly*.

They were outgunned.

"Karen, you see them?" I asked instantly.

"I do," she nodded.

But seeing them wasn't in itself enough.

"Is that one of the destroyers from Mercury? It looks familiar."

Karen frowned at Elise De Winter's quiet question. They were watching the trio of Martians approach on enhanced camera visuals, but Karen certainly wouldn't have thought to try to identify the individual ships coming in.

"How could you tell?"

Elise pointed towards the bow of the Martian, "The scorching on the bow there, I remember it from one we were chasing."

With a shrug, Karen nodded, "Probably is then. Grudge match."

"Well that's delightful. We'll deal with him this time. Right and left?" Matt Baxter interrupted from the Battlelink screen and Elise looked up with a nod. "As usual."

Lady Grace and *Friendly* were going into battle together. The history of these two ships was such a partnership — one always being there for the other.

And now, outgunned as they were in this little corner of the massive dogfight, they'd need to be as good a team as ever.

There was no squadron command left for Karen to give now — like me, she was more resigned to coordinating ships than to fighting them. It was a real waste in some respects, but this was Elise's job.

"Open fire at will," *Lady Grace's* newer skipper ordered, then looked to her Helm and Navigation Officer. "Spin to port."

Almost simultaneously, both *Lady Grace* and *Friendly* parted company, shooting and spinning to dodge opposition fire.

Wes Pellew folded his arms as he stood before the screens at the front of *Nova Scotia's* bridge. Because his ships had been going up the middle, they were now scattering more completely than either of the other squadrons, which left him relatively little to do.

Nova Scotia shuddered as he stood there, and Roslyn Young looked back to her XO, "Target that destroyer."

"Aye," the XO replied immediately, and *Nova Scotia's* number one laser prepared to fire.

Teamed with *British Columbia*, *Nova Scotia* was facing two destroyers and a destroyer escort, and that was a fight Wes was confident his elite ships would win.

"Let's surprise them," he said as he watched the approach. While he didn't have ship command here, he was still squadron commander — he could coordinate this little engagement. "Prepare for a jump acceleration to the flank. We'll catch them on the turn."

It was a plan that took advantage of the special pirate-hunting abilities of Wes' ships — in this case, their ability to accelerate faster than any other warships of their size.

Roslyn Young passed on the orders to her Helm and Navigation Officer, and *British Columbia's* skipper did the same.

The courses were planned, and just as the Martians began to open fire, Wes gave the word, "Now."

Nova Scotia and *British Columbia* hurtled off on a vector to starboard, making a velocity that I don't think I can reveal because it's classified. Suffice it to say they moved a whole lot faster than the Martians expected them to. Nearing the apogee of their run, the frigates then spun without changing momentum, presenting their bow lasers as they passed.

"Shoot!" *Nova Scotia's* XO called, and the frigate cut loose with its laser one.

One destroyer caught the shots from both *Nova Scotia* and *British Columbia*. The beams sliced into its drive section, and nearly trimmed off its high drive pod. It spun away, venting atmosphere. The other destroyer and its destroyer escort turned to face Wes' ships, but the Independent Squadron veterans had already changed vectors.

This is what anyone who faced Wes Pellew got: frigates that could move and shoot with such precision and speed you'd swear they were from Ami Cairn's 141st Flying Squadron.

Er. I have no idea what I just said.

Nova Scotia and *British Columbia* set about tying their opponents in knots. Elsewhere, other frigates and corvettes fought hard.

+++

Whirlwind was fighting with *June* and *Daisy* alongside — all of them Hawke Command ships. It was a great moment of pride for the spacers of the Protectorate: they were able to join a hugely important battle, and to fight through it as a blue-hulled team.

The other ships from Lia's squadron had paired off and were looking after themselves, so she was enjoying this chance at small-unit command.

It was no mean test: she was up against some of Bort McWebsbert's best. While Karen and Wes were dealing with Mercury survivors, these destroyers were fighting craftily, keen on salvaging some wins from this clash.

"Watch the one on the left, he's going to jump," Lia was paying close attention to the three destroyer escorts and the destroyer that were coming straight at her, and as *June* turned its laser against the target Lia had selected, her intuition proved correct: the Martian tried to accelerate.

The shot from *June* dissuaded it, burning a scar into some of its armor, but it was by no means out of the fight.

Whirlwind was shooting rapidly at the same time, its laser one drilling the Martian destroyer while the Martian shot back, raking the Hawke ship's bow pod.

This ship, I should point out, was *Promethei Planum* — the flagship of Commodore Colm Haysrandov. In other words, it was probably the best destroyer Bort had, and arguably was one of the best destroyers in the Imperium Navy.

Lia had her work cut out for her.

Daisy took a hard hit to its bow pod, and as it staggered, two destroyer escorts pressed in close to the blue corvette. Watching this, Lia turned to her skipper, "Get us in their way. *June*, keep that other destroyer escort busy."

There was no time for bitch slaps or other fun orders in this context. It was turning into what I've previously called a squadron knife fight. The Hawke ships were going to look after each other.

"Shoot!" *Whirlwind's* XO called, and this time it was the starboard laser that lanced out, punching a hole in the drive pod wing of one of the DEs. The ship's acceleration dropped off as its drive pod threatened to tear itself away. As that red ship pulled up, *Daisy* shot at its partner.

"Switch to mags, gun that damaged one," Lia looked back to her XO.

He began to nod. And then *Whirlwind* bucked under her feet.

Promethei Planum was still bearing down, and Lia's face went cold. She was going to have to deal with that opponent, and hope *Daisy* could deal with the two destroyer escorts in the meantime.

"Alright then, turn us back towards that bastard," she said sharply.

"We're going right," Mark Gunney said from his screen on *Wolf's* bridge.

"Left for us," Andrea matched the statement, and I simply nodded, arms folded. These two skippers didn't need me getting underfoot, trying to coordinate them. Right back to when Andrea had skippered *Friendly* and Mark had *Honesty*, they'd been a fighting team.

Remember, it was these two who had found Egesta together, back during *The Hawke Mission*. They knew how to operate in tandem.

Unfortunately for all of us, we were up against two more of Bort's destroyers. Doubly unfortunate: both of these had ended up in his squadron after they'd returned from… wait for it… Sinope. Remember back to *The Sinope Affair*, those destroyers at the end that chose to turn away instead of engaging us? Yep, these were survivors of Benjamin Conflans' squadron, which Bort had gladly brought into his command.

And you better believe they recognized *Wolf* and *Cheetah*.

"Opening fire… now. Shoot!" Jim Hannigan was calling the shots from behind his operations consoles, and as usual, his laser gunnery was second to none.

Wolf's laser one plowed into the destroyer on the left, and as it did, Shelby McLaws turned us fast and climbed, kicking velocity to over 200 kps to get clear of counter-fire.

The Martian absorbed the punishment and staggered, but then turned after us with its lasers blazing. It shot better than I think any other Martian destroyer I'd ever seen, and caught us on the underside of the bow pod.

Wolf jerked, but Shelby again demonstrated her excellence, calling in a quick twirl that got us free of the shot before it could do more than burn some of our armor.

"Close us in," Andrea looked to Shelby, then glanced back over her shoulder at Jim. "Mags this time."

Jim nodded and started the necessary targeting calculations. I kept my eyes fixed on the icons of our ships, and on some enhanced visual feeds that Felicia was feeding up to the screen.

Then I saw something I hadn't really expected to see — the first of the unexpected things I'd see in the next few minutes.

It was a very long few minutes, I can tell you.

"Belay mags!" I almost shouted that order. "Shelby turn us back, over the top. We need to support *Cheetah*…"

Mark frowned at me on screen. Andrea looked at me in surprise. It wasn't my job to override the orders of *Wolf's* Captain, but I'd seen something she hadn't and in that moment of shock I forgot myself.

Shelby and Jim both listened, though.

Good thing they did.

On *Cheetah's* bridge, Mark had been standing with arms folded as he watched his frigate approach the Martian destroyer he'd been targeting. The ship didn't look to be flinching at all — it was coming on straight and level, and as *Cheetah's* XO controlling the lasers from the operations consoles, Erica Martin was all set to fire into it.

What had I seen? I can't even describe it, but *something* in my head triggered. A hint of something… some notion that the Martian was beginning an early turn. I've reviewed the logs and I haven't found anything objective that indicates it was going to happen, but I had a very strong feeling at that moment.

Take it for whatever it's worth.

And the Martian did turn — sharp and fast. It accelerated and twirled with the sort of skill you'd expect from a Belt Squadron ship, and as such Erica Martin's first laser shot almost missed it entirely.

It replied with mags, raining EM shot down on *Cheetah* while Mark Gunney frowned, "Clever bastard."

"Missiles in the mag fire!" his Sensors and Communications Officer called out quickly, and that got Mark's blood pumping harder.

"Starlights get in there. Helm, spin us away. Mag counter-fire!"

The Martian had closed the distance to *Cheetah* so that the missiles would have the shortest possible flight time, and was still chasing them with its mag fire. Starlights turned away from duels with Interceptors and tried to get in there after the warheads, but that covering mag fire was too intense, and there wasn't enough time.

As *Cheetah* backed off and spun fast, its own mags went after the missiles, but the pair came in with the sort of damned luck these things sometimes can have.

They both hit the bow pod, one right after the other.

"Jesus wept," Andrea Kiley was unable to say more than that for a second, and then she turned back to Jim. "Catch that bastard in the stern!"

Jim was ahead of her, "Shoot!"

We'd turned in time to get onto *Cheetah's* assailant before it could deliver the coup de grace with lasers. Our red beam raced down on its stern and sliced hard into its tail, and thanks to Jim's excellent shooting the bastard wasn't able to squirm out from under our beam for nearly ten seconds.

In other words, we got a chance to burn deep.

The destroyer turned away, but Andrea wasn't going to let it go.

We chased: *Cheetah* reeled.

Mark Gunney had never seen a bridge decompress around him. It wasn't a common thing to have happen — the bridge of a ship is buried deep in the bow pod to afford it maximum protection from that sort of thing.

Oh, completely inappropriate aside: those who think the comms/observation tower on the top of the pod is actually the bridge are incorrect... otherwise we'd probably all be dead. Several times over.

The last time I can think of a bridge taking this much damage (without the ship being destroyed) was back in *The Almost Coup*, when *Ark Royal* was carved up like a roast, and George Parks-Dawes was killed.

Well, the two missiles hitting in the same area, one after the other, had blown away a little over a quarter of *Cheetah's* pod. The bridge ceiling and the deck above it were ruptured. A breach four meters long and about half a meter wide appeared, and sucked the atmosphere right out of the compartment.

It all seemed to happen so slowly.

The microfilament bags deployed to save the bridge crew from the effects of vacuum — remember, those bags in the seams of collars and cuffs that explode out and surround exposed skin in airtight bags, buying people time? I think I explained them in *The Hawke Mission*... if you live in the Belt, or Venus... well, anywhere other than Earth, you know about them.

Mark's deployed fine, and as he realized what was happening, he turned towards the operations consoles.

There's a popular and incorrect notion that there's an endless amount of suction when a compartment decompresses. Obviously, as air rushes out it sucks objects and people with it… but when a compartment is sealed, as the bridge was, there's not that much air to rush out, and thus no lasting suction.

Open the hatch to the corridor beyond (presuming it hadn't decompressed too) and that would get you a new rush of air, and additional suction. But once the atmosphere was gone the first time, it was just a vacuum in there.

Very, very cold.

The grav plating — trusty Felix Wolfe manufacture — kept working, so Mark was able to walk back towards the operations consoles.

Along with the CO_2 scrubbers in his collar, his emergency heaters had kicked in, but all they could do was keep his body from dipping below minus thirty degrees Celsius… and they could only manage that for five minutes before the chemicals causing the warming reaction (woven into the interfacing of his uniform clothing) were used up.

It was the same story for everyone on the bridge.

They had to get out, which was a job for the XO.

Erica Martin wasn't at her post, though.

Frowning, Mark looked around. But she wasn't there.

She wasn't anywhere.

We never found her remains.

Our assumption is that she was one of the few unlucky ones from the bridge to be sucked through that fissure before the air was expended.

Erica Martin, my old comrade, was gone.

Mark didn't have time to dwell on that fact. He moved to the operations controls himself, and began cycling the atmosphere outside the bridge hatch — turning the corridor beyond the door into a makeshift airlock. It hadn't ruptured, just buckled, so if they could empty it of atmosphere, get out there, then repressurize, they'd be relatively safe.

But Mark's extremities were already numbing. The heating filaments were not going to last long, so he needed to work fast — before frostbite set in.

The systems were sluggish, which didn't help. Some of the relays had probably been fused. He worked fast, drawing on command computer skills he hadn't used in years to employ work-arounds to control the atmospheric system. It took long seconds, and he realized as he stood there and worked that his legs were genuinely beginning to freeze.

Ice crystals were appearing within his cells… a sort of damage he'd never experienced… hoped never to experience. He could lose his legs if this went on too long.

He had to get the door open, for his sake and more importantly for the sake of his bridge…

The pressure settings worked. The hatch opened.

He tried to hurry after his people as they started going through, but his legs dragged, and he ended up falling through the hatch. Someone else closed it behind him, repressurized the corridor and activated full heaters to flash-restore minimum living temperature.

Cheetah spiraled away from the fight, and medics arrived to carry most of the bridge crew to med bay.

Erica Martin, the young Ensign who had flown me to my first command, and who'd been my Helm and Navigation Officer both on *Friendly* and on *Wolf*, was gone.

CHAPTER FIFTEEN

LOSSES

Lia didn't see the damage to *Cheetah* because her attentions were fixated on *Promethei Planum*. The Martian destroyer with its elite skipper was running down hard on *Whirlwind*, and Lia had no interest in losing this gunfight.

"Over to port," she ordered directly, and then turned to her frigate's XO. "Stick with lasers."

The answer to that was a nod, and Lia turned back to the front screens on *Whirlwind's* bridge just in time to see her ship's laser one firing on the main monitor. Those enhanced visuals reached as far as *Promethei*, and she could make out the impact of the beam.

A little more damage done.

"Close us in," she ordered next. "Watch for missiles, stand by our torpedo."

Ahead, the Martian began twirling and climbing, and Lia frowned at the maneuver. Clearly this adversary knew how to handle his ship — she wasn't going to assume he was as dense as some of her opponents at Mercury had proven to be.

"That might be a move to get into close missile range... switch to mags!" Lia was thinking out loud, and she watched as her ship's forward-firing mag batteries began showering the destroyer with golden energy.

That would suppress any missile launches — if the Martians let loose their warheads and one of them happened to be detonated too early, it could damage their vessel.

The Martian figured this out, and turned back towards *Whirlwind*. There was a laser shot coming — Lia just knew it.

"Stand by to sidestep," she warned, and then as the beams came she waved her hand. "Go now."

Whirlwind's Helm and Navigation Officer was swift, and the frigate took only a glancing blow from the laser salvo.

"Back to lasers, hit him," Lia gave her XO that command.

Laser one fired again, its angry red beam settling on the Martian's bow pod for just long enough to cut into its turret base. It jammed in place.

"Gotcha," Lia smiled. Without the ability to spin its lasers, the Martian's effectiveness was down — it'd have a harder time tracking Lia's movements. Turning back to Helm and Navigation, she decided to take full advantage, "Start a spiral, since they can't track us. Let's get in close."

That order got *Whirlwind* moving in such a way that the destroyer, now having to actually turn ship to point its bow-mounted guns, couldn't easily hit it.

"Back to mags," Lia continued. "Don't let any missiles at us."

See, as I think I spent some time telling you last book, Lia was a total natural at this — she had all her father's instincts, and none of his less endearing qualities.

My little sister knew how to kill the enemy.

And Bort's escort squadron knew how to look after its own.

"Missile from astern!"

Lia's eyes went wide, and she looked to the sensor display on one of the screens. It had been fired by the destroyer escort they'd wounded. *Daisy* was keeping the other one busy, but this one was riding up *Whirlwind's* tailpipe.

"Reprioritize mag fire!" she turned back to *Whirlwind's* XO, and he did.

The maneuvering became more violent, and Lia grabbed the rails at the front of her bridge to stay on her feet.

Then the worst happened: in a maneuver to side-step the missile, *Whirlwind's* Helm and Navigation Officer inadvertently put the ship into the path of *Promethei Planum* again.

A solid laser shot burned into the Hawke frigate's bow pod, and that was chased by two missiles.

"Spin us away!" Lia's voice was tightening as she realized she was in a vice. If any of those missiles hit…

The one from the destroyer escort was caught by a mag shot. Two more to go.

Whirlwind writhed away from the lasers of its opponent, and Starlights swooped in now, realizing there was a serious problem facing their base ship. Lia's mags went to work again.

One more missile shot down. Lia's grip on the railing got white-knuckle tight.

The other missile was shot down.

She closed her eyes for just a second, and let out a sigh of relief.

Then she heard the strangest sound she'd ever heard in her life — like an explosion, or metal tearing. Air burst.

She released her grip on the railing, straightened up, and opened her eyes.

The wall of screens in front of her was dark… no, that wasn't right… the screens had all blown out, and the bridge had gone dark. Emergency lighting popped on, and she took a couple of unsteady steps back towards the center of the bridge.

There were people down at Sensors and Communications, and Helm and Navigation, and behind her at operations. Some people were rushing to help other people. She had no idea why.

"Where are my screens?" she asked, and then realized her chin was wet.

She wiped away the water with the back of her hand and turned to look for the XO.

"Did we take a hit? I didn't think I felt anything. Can we get these up again?"

She was getting a bit light-headed, probably from all the stress.

The XO wasn't answering, which made no sense to her.

"Come on, people, we're in a battle… answer me."

Lia's Helm and Navigation Officer stepped down from his bank of consoles and approached her, a funny look on his face.

"Staring at something, Josh?" she asked with a frown.

So light-headed.

And why was she wet? Did somebody turn on fire suppression?

No, that didn't make sense, ships used atmospheric suppression, not water. She wasn't home on Hawke One.

She looked down, and discovered what she thought was water was actually blood

— so much that it was seeping right through her uniform.

Her mouth was full of it, actually. She didn't know why she hadn't tasted it before.

But who's blood was it? She didn't feel anything.

"M'lady... m'lady come sit down," her Helm and Navigation Officer said gently. Then he turned and bellowed, "Medics, now!"

Someone interrupted with something that mattered but didn't matter: "Main power back online."

Lia blinked a few times. She had blood running into her eyes, so she wiped her brow with the back of her other hand. It was frustrating, all the blood. Whose was it?

She turned away from the Helm and Navigation Officer, back towards the brightened wall of screens.

They'd all shattered.

Lia's chest started to hurt. She frowned.

She couldn't see anything.

She tried to take a step forward, but that didn't work.

"Dammit," she muttered to herself.

Then she started to fall.

The Helm and Navigation Officer caught her, and as soon as his grip got around her waist, the initial shock started to pass. Her mind numbed with pain, and as her officer fell to one knee, trying to lay her down gently, her jaw hung slack, and she tried not to wail.

She had been peppered with shards of combat glass from the screens at the front of *Whirlwind's* bridge. I think I mentioned it last book... remember Mik's screens on *Cyclops* had shattered into soft fragments, because he'd upgraded from the old-style glass that tended to shower the bridge in sharp daggers? Ian Hawke never made that conversion for his ships. He'd been the First Lord who had overseen the adoption of the old stuff, and though he knew it could shatter like this, he always said he thought it produced a *crisper picture*.

The bastard.

Now his choice had sent forty-one individual pieces of glass into, and sometimes *through*, his daughter's body.

And I know all of this because, while the screens had blown out due to a power surge when *Promethei Planum's* lasers had crossed *Whirlwind* again, the camera that picked up the Battlelink feed had stayed on.

Fluke thing, that.

You could have heard a goddamned pin do a bloody fucking tap dance on *Wolf's* bridge.

In the same minute, I watched *Cheetah* get gutted, and Lia Hawke collapse to the floor, covered in her own blood.

For a second, I had no way to respond. Then I did the only thing I could think to do: my eyes darted to Karen.

"Can you get over to her? We need to protect *Cheetah*..."

Karen nodded.

And then the minute got worse.

The feed from *Lady Grace* winked out.

CHAPTER SIXTEEN

BAD TO WORSE

Everything seemed to stop, all around me.

All stopped. And then started up again, in slow motion.

It was almost like that moment Kate Levec had been shot at Io: my conscious grasp on reason was gone.

I looked down and to my left at Andrea Kiley, and something on my face made her eyes widen.

She said one thing to me: "It's all yours."

I don't know if I understood right then what she was saying, but I took her up on her offer. The rest of this I don't properly remember. I'll tell you when I started feeling things again. I'm going mostly by the bridge recordings now. And me reconstructing what I must have been thinking.

"Felicia, all skippers in range on the link now," my voice was sharp but controlled, and then I moved over to Shelby. "Get us on this bastard's broadside."

I was referring to the destroyer that was still trying to engage *Wolf*. Remember, we'd shot up the one that had damaged *Cheetah*, but there'd been two. If we left this one now, Mark was done for.

"Jim, keep hitting him, everything you have," I turned back toward the operations consoles and he nodded.

Andrea simply stood aside and waited.

Moving back to the front of the screens I looked up at Wes — the only Flag Officer I had left, "Can you get to Lia or to Karen?"

Wes, bless him, knew immediately that the message was for him, and he nodded, "Going right now for Lia. I'll get that bastard off her."

That was all I needed to hear. I didn't acknowledge.

"Shoot!" Jim called from the back of the bridge.

I think everyone here sounded sharper… angrier now. Mark was one of us. Lia was one of us. Karen was one of us.

It all became very personal, very quickly.

The destroyer we'd been fighting turned in sharply and tried for a laser shot of its own, and my face twisted with cold anger, "Shelby, turn in on him. Head to head. Right now."

Of course Shelby could make that happen: a sharp maneuver, and just as the Martian lasers reached us they found we were bow-to-bow, and closing straight at each other.

"Jim," I called, and saying his name was order enough.

"Shoot!" he commanded, and laser one raked that son of a bitch.

"Torpedo, we'll do it point-blank," I announced icily. It was dangerous, but imagine how much I didn't care.

"I'll be ready to move us, not to worry, sir," even saying something as seemingly friendly as that, Shelby sounded mean.

We ran straight at that Martian, and he came right at us. This was one of the ships from Io and Sinope. He wasn't going to blink. He probably still had two missiles aboard, and he was probably thinking the same damned thing we were: get close, fire warheads, pull away.

Mags started raining back and forth, and *Wolf* shuddered, but the ship was too angry to be dissuaded.

"Launching torpedo... now," Jim called.

"Peeling away," Shelby added.

"Missiles coming out, I'm tracking them," Jim continued.

I didn't hold my breath. I didn't so much as doubt.

This was my ship, these were my people. They weren't going to be defeated by some son of a bitch Martian. Not now.

We were all angry.

Mags continued to fill space, and Starlights and Interceptors swapped dogfighting for missile and torpedo strafing.

Adrienne Thompson and Wolfstar Squadron were out there. And they were better than anything those damned Martians had. Even Bort's pilots.

The two missiles went down.

Our torpedo went in.

The destroyer exploded.

"Find me *Lady Grace*, Felicia. Shelby, get me there."

Nova Scotia was hurrying towards *Whirlwind*, but there was a lot of fighting to get through. This all was still within the confines of the battleship fight, believe it or not. The Martians were soon to start scuttling their *Tharsises*, but all of this happened in the time before that began.

Like I said earlier, it was a big, chaotic, mess of a dogfight.

And *Nova Scotia* wasn't having much luck getting to *Whirlwind* because of it. But *Promethei Planum* wasn't stopping its attack.

Other frigates, like *Kodiak* and *Guangxi*, were tied up in their own duels. Remember, we'd started this fight with even numbers — there weren't too many extra ships to go around.

So it was Nikhil Jones in *Amherst* and Lisa Sims in *Nanton* who got on scene first. Their two older *Canada*-class corvettes were in tough against the crafty Martian, but they kept him distracted.

Watching this on his main screen, Wes folded his arms and forced himself to control his anger — something he did much better than me.

"Range?" he asked, his tone quite level.

"Almost there," Rozy Young was next to him, her voice as soothing as it could be.

Nanton hit *Promethei Planum* with a laser shot, and then *Amherst* got in close and pounded the destroyer with some mags... only to be rewarded with a laser shot to one of its drive pods.

It staggered aside, and *Promethei* turned on it. *Nanton* got in the way of a more serious shot, though, and hit the Martian with another laser. These two together didn't have the firepower they needed to win, but they were keeping themselves alive...

Wes decided he wasn't going to let them be killed for their trouble.

"We're in jump range... now," the Sensors and Communications Officer reported.

Roslyn Young looked at Wes, then past him as she gave the order, "Pounce."

Again that massive acceleration made itself apparent: *Nova Scotia* went from far away to right on *Promethei Planum's* back bumper, so to speak.

And unlike the determined corvettes, this frigate *did* have the firepower.

Commodore Colm Haysrandov was clearly a good cruiser officer. I have to respect him. Based on Bort's assessment of him, I'd probably have liked him personally, too. But if, in the middle of a battle, you attempt to kill one of ours... and especially if you succeed... you're going to suffer from the anger of our guns.

"Shoot," Wes gave the order himself.

Laser one drilled straight into the Martian's stern, before he even realized there was something behind him. At the same time that *Bonnie* was cutting into the engineering section of *Olympus Mons*, Wes' laser was reaching *Promethei's* reactors, and cooking them off.

The destroyer went dark and tumbled away, shedding escape pods as it did.

Commodore Colm Haysrandov died with his ship.

Wes turned *Nova Scotia* around to find out if Lia had died with hers.

Matt Baxter held onto the railings at the front of *Friendly's* bridge for all he was worth, and my trusty old corvette dodged another sledgehammer hit from the Martian destroyers that were ganging up on him.

Three of them now — all of them Mercury survivors who evidently knew they'd die quickly if they picked fights with ships their own size. Because of the relative chaos of the battle, there were no frigates nearby to help Matt, so he was doing the only thing he could: fighting three ships with one.

Three bigger ships with one smaller one.

"Any sign of life on *Lady Grace?*" he demanded.

That was why he couldn't run: two of the destroyers had hit *Lady Grace's* drive section with concentrated laser fire, and from what he could tell from the outside looking in, all the corvette's reactors had either shut down... or gone wild. In the former case, the ship was heavily damaged without power. In the latter, it was heavily damaged, without power, and irradiated.

He wasn't about to leave his fighting partner, its crew, and Karen to be used as target practice.

"Shoot!" his XO called from her station again, and *Friendly's* laser three clawed at one of the destroyers.

As it turned out, that destroyer belonged to a certain piece of garbage, Jason Winchester Nudle — it was *Meridiani Planum*.

It turned, again too slow, and tried to swat *Friendly*.

That surely did not work.

And then a laser drilled into it from below.

Matt blinked, and as he did a *Friendly*Net loading display popped up on his screen six.

A second later, a face he hadn't expected turned up.

"Watch that one, Walter, I think we might have ticked it off!"

Bruce Arama was in almost the same pose as Matt Baxter, holding onto the front rails of *Adelaide's* bridge with all his considerable strength.

Our damned fine reservist, who'd been added very quietly to Karen's lineup in her revised Jupiter Force for this fight, was proving yet again that he and his crew were something special.

"Shoot!" Francine Fuentes, his XO, called from the back of the bridge, and again *Adelaide's* laser burned *Meridiani Planum*.

Looking up to see Matt Baxter's surprised expression, our elite Kiwi Commander managed a smile, "Here to assist, sir."

"Well bloody done, Bruce!" Matt replied instantly.

A second after that, Walter Borjigin linked *Adelaide's* nav plots with *Friendly's*, and the two ships partnered as smoothly as if they'd been doing it forever.

The three Martian destroyers were in trouble now. They kept trying to turn back on *Lady Grace*, to finish off the limp and stricken corvette, but they'd get a laser in the chops every time.

And when they turned to chase these two elite, fast-flying frigates, they couldn't manage it.

I don't need to remind you how elite *Friendly's* crew was. They'd helped keep a monitor from finishing off *Cyclops* at Mercury, and now they were doing the same sort of job again. This was their profession.

But let me just say this one more time: Bruce Arama was a general contractor from Auckland. Francine Fuentes — who was not missing a single laser shot — taught preschool. Walter Borjigin was a tax accountant.

And they were fighting this battle like it was their full-time job.

You better believe these are spectacular individuals.

They saved *Lady Grace* for a little longer.

And then we showed up.

The first destroyer didn't see us coming. And Jim made them pay for that.

Meridiani Planum was nearly cut in half by his laser shot, no mean feat at all considering we were racing down at 200 kps and the Martian was moving.

As their lead ship took that hit, the other destroyers realized they had more trouble coming than they expected. One turned up to face us, the other continued to keep *Friendly* and *Adelaide* busy.

I start to remember feeling so cold around this point. I was just… I can't even describe it. Not without sounding like a complete cliché. Honestly, I would have throttled any Martian I saw right then. Or shot them, cut them.

You know how Karen praised me at the end of *The Canary Wars* for keeping it together? I wasn't keeping it together just now.

Andrea had realized that immediately. She recognized it all too well. And she understood it to the point that she'd done the unthinkable: she'd essentially let me take over as Captain for this fight.

My job was to coordinate, not to command a single ship.

But at this moment, the bridge of *Wolf* was mine again, and I was so damned mad.

They were going to die. And if Karen had gone before them, as I feared she had, then I did not give a shit what that would cost.

Out of control, you understand. I'd lost the even keel that I'd been keeping.

And now the Martians suffered for it.

"How close do you feel comfortable getting, Shelby?" I sounded positively hungry.

Shelby, though a southern belle lady of the highest caliber, wasn't much more controlled, "Right up to them, sir. As close as I know you want to be."

I turned back to Jim, and his expression was level. He and I had been together as long as I'd commanded ships. I don't say that often enough, but he was an original, and he knew exactly how damned angry I was.

He was angry too.

"Just get me close," he said sharply.

They were his lasers, his mags. I trusted that he'd kill with them.

"You heard him," I nodded to Shelby, and *Wolf* plunged towards the Martian destroyer coming to meet us. It was a collision course, plain and simple, with both ships moving at well over 190 kps.

But Shelby was in full control. As the Martian panicked and started to weave away, strafing us with mags at point-blank range, she put us right above it on a matching course. We were so close we could pick out the destroyer's airlocks with the naked eye.

Mag bolts from the destroyer's turrets seared our armor for a second, but then we rolled and laser two came to bear.

"Shoot," Jim's word was low and cold.

Our beam hit the Martian's drive section right where the four drive pod wings meet. And it burned deep, and deeper, and it punched right through the reactor room, melting the power plant, and then burned out the other side.

The Martian ship darkened, stopped firing, and coasted away.

We could have done more — we'd all have loved to cut that ship into small pieces right then — but we needed to get the pressure off *Adelaide* and *Friendly*... and obviously, we had to get teams over to *Lady Grace*.

"Turn us at the other one," I looked back to Shelby, and she nodded.

It came up on screen in enhanced visuals, with both corvettes keeping their distance and prodding it with lasers as it turned and shot back.

"I have the solution," Jim informed us all.

And then, before he could say another word, the bastard blew up.

A pair of giant red lasers had cut right through it: *Bonaventure* was coming to the rescue.

+++

In the next minute, the whole battle changed. Our tough bloody fights were ended with almost mechanical disinterest by *Bonnie, Terra Nova* and *Bonavista*. Destroyers that were so brutal for us to deal with as frigates burned like paper under the firepower of the superbattleships.

Wolf, Adelaide and *Friendly* coasted towards *Lady Grace*, and I didn't say a damned thing as I left the bridge and headed for the hanger bay. I was going over with the SAR teams. No one was fool enough to try to stop me.

CHAPTER SEVENTEEN
UNPROFESSIONAL

I stepped out of the lock into *Lady Grace* and found the corridors visible only through emergency lighting. There were people moving in the corridor — some of them technicians hurrying from relay panel to relay panel trying to restore power, some of them medics looking for the injured, and some of them officers and spacers from other SAR teams who had come aboard ahead of us.

Behind me, a team of engineers led by Andy Jenson started emerging from their shuttle, and with a few waves from their leader they started to work.

"We'll get power back for you," Andy said quickly as he passed me. "Good luck."

Like Jim Hannigan and Erica Martin, Andy had been with me since we'd been on *Friendly*. He understood very well how I had to be taking this.

Alicia Morgan and her medical staff were coming in through another lock, so I stepped out into the corridor to see if I could see where they were arriving. Instead I spotted Matt Baxter coming out of an intersection down the hall.

He sighted me immediately, "I figured you were coming personally. Been to the bridge yet?"

I shook my head, "You?"

"No. Let's go then."

This was a personal affront to him. As you'll probably recall, Matt was very protective both of me and Karen, and of his fellow ships. This had been a fair fight — that was the only reason he was holding his temper in check.

But he was not pleased.

He led the way now as we moved through the familiar decks of *Lady Grace*. The same class and vintage as *Friendly*, we could navigate the ship in the dark if we had to... and in some areas where emergency lighting had blown, we did have to.

The bridge was our destination, for obvious reasons.

I had no idea what had happened to Karen. None of us did. There'd been no communications. The destroyers that had bracketed *Lady Grace* had wiped out its power grid instantly.

At least the reactors hadn't spilled. Engineers from *Adelaide* — part of the first Search and Rescue team to get aboard — had confirmed that. *Lady Grace's* reactors were shut down without incident, and most of the reactor and engineering staffs were actually alive.

But there had been a huge number of secondary explosions through the ship. There was no telling how many were dead.

Hurrying through the darkness, I was too focused on the fate of one person to think on the rest of this. How could I not be?

When we turned the corner into the corridor that accessed the bridge, Matt was ahead of me.

We both saw the medical team crouching over someone in the corridor at the same time. A few of *Adelaide's* technicians were standing between us and them, blocking part of the view.

"Report," Matt called as we approached quickly.

I didn't intend on waiting to be told.

"It's the CO, sir. Bridge was empty, they tried to get her out of there but she's died," one of the spacers replied.

I was already starting to pass Matt when his hand locked down on my shoulder.

"Wait. Don't get in their way," he said sharply. He was clearly the one calling the shots here — it didn't matter what our ranks were. It was Matt. Who stopped Karen and me from doing stupid stuff.

But if he was calling, I wasn't listening: I pulled away from his grasp and hurried down the corridor, until I got a better angle. Doctor Krista Lapolo was leaning over a woman's body, hammering it with defib pulses, trying to get the heart going again. Another med tech was crouched next to her.

I couldn't see the woman's face. Did I really want to?

The thoughts that went through my head, in that one second… what would it all mean without Karen?

Matt got in front of me, two hands on my chest, "Let them save her."

He was being optimistic there. He knew it, but he hoped it'd stop me.

I held my ground for a moment, and then I looked closer at what I could see.

I looked that body up and down, even as Doctor Lapolo worked on her.

The rush of relief I got, in that one second. The incredible rush of relief.

I turned away. She had to be somewhere else…

Matt didn't understand, "Wait, come back. Come on, dammit."

"That's not her, Matt. That's Elise," I said sharply. Elise De Winter was the CO, Karen wasn't, though I'd automatically thought of her.

Looking back at the body, with people in the way of her face, Matt frowned, "How can you…"

"You think anyone knows her body better than I do, Matt? She must be… Aux Control. Aux control!"

I literally started running. Matt remained in the hall, staring down the corridor after me until I turned at an intersection and was gone.

The *Adelaide* techs were staring too, but as I vanished they looked at Matt.

"You never say a bad word about him, you two understand that?" my former security chief was as protective as ever.

They both nodded solemnly, and Matt turned back to the fallen Captain De Winter.

Doctor Lapolo stood up, shaking her head, and as her med tech did the same, Matt saw I was right. Elise's build had been very similar to Karen's, but I knew the difference.

Karen was alive. I was going to find her.

Elise De Winter, one of our Belt Squadron veterans, was not.

"Is that her shuttle?"

Wes Pellew entered the observation lounge for *Nova Scotia's* flight bay two just as the doors were starting to close behind a blue shuttle. The medical team waiting in the lounge seemed a strong indication that Lia was coming in, but he asked to be sure.

His chief surgeon nodded, "Yes sir."

Whirlwind's power was too unstable for anyone to operate on Lia in their med bay, and *Nova Scotia* was the closest ship.

Hopefully the doctors aboard Wes' frigate could help her, but there were no guarantees. Just the process of moving her from one ship to another might have been enough to kill her.

As the space doors shut and the bay repressurized, the medical team hurled the hatch open and hurried to the landing shuttle. It set down gently, its pilot all too aware of the importance of its cargo. Then, as the ramp dropped, a team of Hawke Command medics carried a stretcher down.

As soon as it was on level ground, a hover field was activated, and then as Wes stepped out into the bay, the teams hurried past him.

He got one look at Lia, and he's never forgotten what he saw.

When it came down to describing her, he actually had to say 'Swiss cheese'. It's a dismally absurd description — it almost feels cruel and tacky — but Wes couldn't think of a clearer way to say it.

There were so many obvious wounds. A lot of blood. They were pumping her full of plasma, and trying to stabilize her, but Wes had been around enough death in his time with the Navy. He didn't think she was going to survive.

He grasped his jaw with his left hand and let out a long, deep sigh.

Lia didn't deserve to die like this.

He wondered how Charlie would deal with it. Because we didn't know about Charlie.

After a few moments, Wes left the flight bay. He'd come down to see her arrive, but now he couldn't bear to go down to medical to watch the surgeons try to keep her alive.

Instead, he went back to the bridge, and waited for word.

Mark Gunney couldn't sit up in bed.

What he could feel felt reasonably alright, but it was what he couldn't feel that worried him. No arms below the elbow, no legs below the hip.

"Well fuck," he said in a typically brusque tone, and *Cheetah's* passing surgeon stopped.

"Problem, sir?"

Mark looked up, "Was too slow getting us out of there."

The Defense Command uniforms with their microfilament bags did the job in keeping him and the crew who weren't sucked into space alive — if not for the bags and the heaters, death would have been instantaneous.

But as the heaters wore out right at the end, Mark had been exposed to the cold of the vacuum, and that had frozen his arms and legs right through. Extreme frostbite, to borrow the civilian term. He was under high-efficiency warming blankets to thaw his nerves right now, and they'd hit him with a painkiller to keep the agony away when the thaw kicked in… but there was a good chance the damage to his limbs would be severe.

"Well, sir, you're alive. Can't complain about that, can you?"

Mark still felt nothing in his limbs, but he winced a little, "I'll find a way."

She said nothing, just moved on.

Lying back, Mark waited for the pain of the thaw to start... and he hoped like hell it did. There'd be a lot of damage to fix... potentially a lot of cell and nerve regeneration. He was out of the war.

But at least the war would soon be over...

That reminded him of a promise he'd made to Erica, at their last dinner before Mercury. In *The Mercury Assault*.

Dammit all.

He'd have to be the one to tell Morgan and their kids. He'd have to get himself better enough to do that job. He owed at least that much to Erica.

Really, he decided, he owed her a lot more.

The Auxiliary Control room was empty when I got there. I was convinced that Karen was alive. I had to be convinced. The reality of things would get far too sharp if she wasn't.

What was I with her dead, exactly?

What had I become in the last moments of that battle, when I was taking command of *Wolf* and fighting mean and not nearly as disciplined as I should have been?

I didn't want to think about that. I stepped into the darkened Aux Control room instead, and looked for any sign of life.

Nothing. No one here.

She had to be somewhere.

She had to be alive somewhere.

Then a hand slipped around me from behind, and a familiar scent crept into the air.

The feeling I had right then, in that moment. The relief was unlike anything I'd felt before. Because there was no doubt this was Karen. Who else could it be.

"Elise died."

She sounded uncommonly weak, and I wondered if she was wounded, but as I turned around and we got arms around each other, I realized it was just pain. Not unlike what I was feeling. Completely unbecoming of officers of our level and our caliber. But we were both so relieved to see each other.

"They just fell on us," she said quietly as our chins found each others' shoulders, and we pressed together. "Nothing we could do. Lost main power. I came here to try to fight the ship but there was nothing. I was... pretty sure we'd be dead."

I swallowed when she said that.

"It looked bad. I... overreacted. We did some damage to the bastards who were after you."

She squeezed me a little bit tighter, and I returned the favor.

So many mixed emotions on so many different levels, but all of them being overshadowed by immense relief.

"It was Matt and Bruce Arama who kept them busy," I said next. "We came in as fast as we could, but those two did the business."

"Bruce?" Karen asked, letting the surprise out openly.

That's no offense to Bruce, I don't think anyway. It's just proof of how exceptional he and his crew were. They fought like Belt Squadron professionals in the last battle of the Martian War.

Contractors, teachers and accountants had saved Karen's life.

Real heroes of the Empire.

"Lia," Karen breathed that name, and we pulled apart enough to come face to face.

I must have looked like I was at a wake, because Karen bit her lip and her eyes twitched against some stabs.

"We don't know," is what I said, and Karen let out a long breath.

"They saved the nastiest fight for the very end," she whispered.

I nodded, and then our foreheads fell together, and then our noses, and so on.

Matt Baxter turned up at the door several minutes later, but he backed out quietly, and then stood guard. By his estimation, we were allowed to have a quiet moment. He was going to make sure we weren't interrupted.

It was completely and totally unprofessional. Indefensible. My job was on *Wolf*, helping organize SAR operations. Karen could come back with me. We had work to do. We should save all of this for later.

But imagine how much I didn't care.

And if Bruce doesn't mind me invoking his name here, I had very recent, very real proof that being good at this business didn't always mean being a 'professional'.

I still had Karen.

For a little while longer, at least.

CHAPTER EIGHTEEN

FRAGMENTS

Karen's return to *Wolf's* bridge was a real homecoming. Jim stepped away from his station as she came through the door, and she smiled and nodded as she shook his outstretched hand. Andrea came back too, and shook her hand, and squeezed her shoulder.

"Glad you're alright... I was sorry to hear about Elise."

"She did a hell of a job," Karen replied softly.

I was two steps behind, and it was probably obvious to everyone that I was far less tense than I'd been when I'd left.

As Jim returned to his station and Karen, Andrea and I moved forward to our old spots at the front of the bridge, Felicia had news for us: "Message came in from *Nova Scotia* a few minutes ago, Lady Hawke is in surgery. They're not optimistic."

I stiffened when I heard that, and turned to her, "Any news you get... let me know immediately."

She nodded, "Aye sir."

"We should start search and rescue for other pods. There aren't that many ships left out there to do the job," Andrea suggested after a moment.

I frowned, then realized I didn't actually know how the battle had turned out — aside from the fact that we'd won.

Turning my eyes to the main screen, I got a dismal picture.

Seven Martian ships had escaped: three destroyers and four destroyer escorts.

But the rest were destroyed or surrendered.

It was, after all, a decisive win.

But we'd paid dearly.

Obviously, there are the losses we know about: *Cheetah, Lady Grace* and *Whirlwind* each suffering from severe damage. *Kodiak* had been disabled, though with light casualties. Of Wes' frigates, *Nunavut* and *Prince Edward Island* had paid dearly, the latter being destroyed outright. *British Columbia* had lost two drive pods, but was otherwise intact.

In the corvettes, Nancy Whitehorse had managed to get herself and her crew off *Trusty* before it exploded. Isoruku Togo had lost a drive pod off *Generous*, and Nikhil Jones had managed to keep *Amherst* basically operational despite a huge hit to its drive section. *June* and *Daisy* were both heavily damaged, as were *Perth* and *Port Aux Basques*.

I suppose it might be easier to say what we actually had left in full fighting condition: four frigates, *Wolf, Nova Scotia, Yukon,* and *Guangxi,* along with four corvettes, *Friendly, Adelaide, Nanton* and *Corner Brook.*

From a force of ten frigates and twelve corvettes, we were down to four and four effective. The Martians almost managed to get away with as many as we did.

But, of course, that doesn't count the *Bonnies,* of which even *Hibernia* could theoretically continue to fight, if needed. The damage to her armor was severe, and several of her main systems were working on backups… but she was a hell of a tough ship.

I suppose I should do an after action on this. But what can I say?

We managed to win, because in the end, the ships the Martians had built to counter our superbattleships weren't up to the job. Bort and his people — for whom I'd very recently had a vicious rage that somehow passed when I saw Karen alive and well — were good. No question of that.

But the *Tharsises* just weren't powerful enough to stop the *Bonnies*. Nothing ever was. It'll be a long time before anything is.

I said it back in *The Forge Fires* when we saw them first: the *Tharsises* were a case of using more of the same old technology to make something better. The *Bonnies* were filled with technology that was simply decades ahead of what the Martians (or their builders) had to offer.

Some people dismiss ships like *Olympus Mons* out of hand for that reason, but that's a mistake. Remember, those three *Tharsises* stood up in a slogging match to four *Bonnies* — they didn't go down in single hits, and in fact, they scuttled themselves before the *Bonnies* could destroy them.

It would thus be too much to say the ships were no good: they were.

They just weren't good enough.

Things like that always fill me with a tragic fascination. So many people, from designers to engineers to dock workers poured blood, sweat and tears into building those Martian monsters. So many good men crewed them. Yes, I'm saying good men, because they're Bort's people.

All of them believed in the power of their ships — believed that they were war-winners, and that they could really make a difference, and stop our supposed tyranny.

And yet for all that effort, and for all that faith, their hopes came to a shattering halt when they ran head-first into our best ships.

Ships that our designers, engineers and yardworkers had poured blood, sweat and tears into. Ships that were crewed by men and women who believed they were war-winners.

One side had to be wrong. In this case, it was the Martians, and that's really no surprise to me… they were at a disadvantage to our industry and our experience.

But they believed they could win. Their belief was now floating in a debris field all around us, but they'd believed.

There but for the grace of God… it could have been us.

But now, it wouldn't be us. Because we all knew it then: the war had to end.

So our immediate task was to save as many from space as possible. Starlights and shuttles were out sweeping for life pods, and all the ships with enough control over their thrust to assist had to do so.

Because even the Martians deserved saving after this fight. Whether they hated us or not… whether I'd wanted to kill every one of them or not… they deserved to survive to see the peace.

That all in mind, Andrea turned to Shelby, "Coordinate our search grid and get us moving. All Starlights to run a sweep pattern on the usual vectors."

Wolf moved to find those left alive.

Karen and I stood shoulder to shoulder and watched in silence.

CHAPTER NINETEEN

THINE ENEMY

Not a lot of people think what I'm about to describe actually happened, but it did. I know it comes off as a convenient movie plot point, but life does have some of those unlikely moments, and this was one of them. Frankly, I'm glad it happened the way it did, for reasons you're probably aware of.

Our first hour of SAR operations was the busiest, and we pulled in pods from all manner of ships. Most were from our side, as we worked an area near where *Trusty* had been lost, but eventually we moved on, into a zone filled with Martian pods.

Security Forces were thin aboard *Wolf*, most having gone with Omar Cunningham to fight on Mercury, so we had to get volunteers with EP-5s (the return of those damned rifles, because all our MAG-90s were down on Mercury) to guard the prisoners as they came aboard. There was, of course, a finite number we could take safely, and they were going into two of our cargo bays, which had been locked down for the purpose.

For some reason (and I really don't have a good, rational reason), I decided to go down to bay one to supervise. Andrea didn't need me on the bridge, and Karen had headed to her cabin to clean up after the ordeal aboard *Lady Grace*.

So I went down to bay one, I suppose because I wanted to actually look some of these Martians in the eye.

Maybe it was my subconscious guilt at having killed so many of them today. Or my subconscious frustration at having killed too few.

Or maybe I was bored and it just seemed a good idea at the time.

However you slice it, I ended up there.

Chief Eugene Sengooba was the senior SF left aboard. You might remember him from *The Jupiter Patrol* and *The Dark Cruise*... he was a real fixture in *Wolf's* SF section, so I'm sure I've mentioned him a fair bit.

Now he waited with me and a dozen guards and volunteers in the viewing lounge as shuttles towed in three large Martian escape pods.

Behind us, the hatch opened, and Alicia Morgan, our excellent doctor, stepped in, a medical team with her.

"I just cleared the last injuries from the med bay... just in time?"

I nodded to her, "Martians. You'll have to treat the minor wounds with the rest of the prisoners in the cargo bays."

Alicia nodded, "Understood."

It was a routine she'd been through many times — there was no reason for me to explain it to her again, but talking passed the time. She didn't take offense.

The shuttle that had towed the pods in laid them down on the deck, then swooped back out to collect more. The bay doors started to close, and Eugene and his guards got ready. Once the bay repressurized, we opened the hatch and headed out. On the deck, hands in EVA suits removed their helmets, some taking mags from the deck arms locker just in case.

One Chief simply hefted his number twelve wrench, ready to knock out some teeth if there was a scrap.

As we got clear, the hatches on all three pods opened simultaneously. They were on a timer, actually — as soon as a pressurized, breathable atmosphere was surrounding them and they were firmly landed, the doors were set to open automatically. Not sure if that's clever or not, but it's the way the Martians did it.

Then out they came: dirty, sweaty, sullen.

They looked around at the flight bay as if it was made of gold. It was probably brighter and bigger than any bay they could have had on a destroyer... and it probably felt very, very alien to them.

"Drop any weapons!" Eugene bellowed, and then along with his SF and volunteers, he started moving between the survivors, checking that they were unarmed. In his wake, Alicia's medical people went into action.

All the Martians looked so beaten, they just stood sullen as our people checked them. There was no anger or defiance left... they seemed resigned to their fates.

Which was just as well: they had nothing to worry about as prisoners of war.

No comments about Andrea, please. She was well past that now.

I didn't see any senior officers, which sort of surprised me. You could always spot the Martian senior officers because their uniforms were damned near Teutonic. The high, starched collars, the overbearing attitudes... well, you know.

None seemed to have come out of these pods. Perhaps they'd all nobly gone down with their ships, or some other damned thing.

Then I saw one.

He was bleeding, and limp, being carried over the shoulder of a big spacer as he came down the side of the pod. The carrying man looked around the bay, saw his people, saw our people, and then saw Alicia.

Curious, I headed for the officer and the man carrying him, and neared them just as they approached Alicia, "This is Post Captain Art O'Thomson of the Imperium Battleship *Olympus Mons*. He's got shrapnel wounds in the chest. We tried to stabilize him but he's going to need surgery or he's done."

Alicia frowned at the analysis but couldn't supplement it with her own scans until the big man put the Captain down. She waved over a gurney and then helped ease the Post Captain onto it.

As her scanner checked his condition, I looked at the man. He had the right uniform, but by no means did he seem overbearing... though that could have been because he was unconscious.

"His daughter's getting married soon. He should be there to see it," the spacer who'd carried him said quietly.

I found myself nodding, and then I looked at Alicia.

"Tough, but they stabilized him pretty well. I'll get to work immediately," she said that and set off all at once, leaving a team of medics behind to mend broken bones and the like.

I sighed and turned back to the Martians… and was startled to find them clustering around me. Eugene was suddenly at my shoulder, and his guards had their weapons ready.

"We'll need all of you to come down to a triage area. Please don't resist, you will not be harmed in any way. You are our prisoners of war. And despite what you might have heard, we will treat you well."

The Martians stared at Eugene, then stared at me. None of them moved, and I exchanged a glance with the African SF Chief. Beyond the cluster, flightdeck hands with weapons started to form a ring, just in case. We expected the worst.

"It's alright, guys. All of you, listen. You did a hell of a job today. No matter what anyone else tells you, I'm proud of you. We lost this fight. I told you I thought we could win it, and I thought we could. But we lost to the best Defense Command has. There's no shame in that. Hold your heads high. I'm proud to be with you. That'll never change. So listen to what they say. I believe they're going to treat us right. Officers and non-commissioned alike."

That all came from the spacer who'd carried the Captain in. For the first time, I actually paid attention to this guy (though you probably figured out who he was immediately). There were a bunch of tarnished clusters on his collar, but he was wearing a regular-enough seeming ship fatigues uniform.

No tunic.

Still, there was no mistaking the sound of an officer speaking to his crew.

"Atten-*hut!*" someone in the Martian crowd barked in their overzealous but genuine manner.

All their boots came down as one. Shoulders back, chests out, salutes up.

"Go on," the man next to me said, a sad smile on his face. "I'll be down soon. I need to speak to this officer first."

I stood in silence next to the Martian officer as Eugene led his men away. I nodded to the Chief when he looked questioningly at the officer (who was obviously Bort, so I'm going to stop calling him 'the officer') — I didn't expect this man to cause trouble.

And there were deck hands with wrenches around if he did.

As the prisoners left, then, Bort looked at me, "You're not going to make a liar out of me, right? You'll treat them well?"

I nodded, then looked at him with a frown, "You're an officer."

He nodded, "So are you. I recognize you, actually. Ken Barron, right?"

That caught me by surprise, and I nodded, "You have me at a disadvantage."

Bort smiled sadly, "You had me at a disadvantage when it really counted."

Very, very true.

"Bort McWebsbert. Vice Admiral. I commanded that fleet you tore up."

It's a testament to how preoccupied I was that his name didn't sound strange when I heard it. But that's irrelevant. I needed to say something to this man. He'd commanded the fleet against us, he was clearly a different sort of Martian… what could I say?

"You're a real bastard, you know."

I said it with no anger, just resignation… fatigue. Bort blinked, and looked at me, then back in the direction his men had gone.

"Yes, I am most certainly that."

His agreement spoke volumes about him. I knew instantly I couldn't hate him. His next words confirmed that truth.

"You're a bastard too."

In that moment, I thought the same sorts of things he'd thought when I put the comment to him: all the deaths I'd been responsible for today, and over the course of the war.

"I'm definitely one."

My friendship with Bort McWebsbert — one of the more unlikely friends I could ever have — started there, with that common understanding. It's been said of enemies in many wars, but sometimes you do have more in common with the person fighting to kill you than you do with anyone else.

In this case, we both knew what it was to lose people, and to cause others to lose them.

Bort's people had killed some of my friends, and maimed others. And I'd hated them for it. But irrationally, that didn't matter at this moment. Because I'd done the same to him, and the fighting was all over, and here we stood, survivors who could agree that better men and women than us were dead. And that we were bastards for getting them killed.

But we didn't say all that then. Not even close.

"You should get cleaned up and see to your crew. I'm sure we'll speak later," was my next line.

Bort agreed, "Yes, I should."

At that point I realized there was no one else to take him out of the bay, so I led the way. We said nothing.

After we left, the deck crew tossed the three Martian lifepods out into space to make room for others. More lives to save.

CHAPTER TWENTY

AFTERMATH

Karen and I took a call from John in my cabin a couple of hours later, and Wes patched in from his cabin on *Nova Scotia*.

"We shouldn't try the Forge yet," John was saying. "Back to Venus and secure Mercury first. Hopefully the Martians are going to see the light and surrender now, but if they don't... well."

He didn't need to finish that sentence: if the Martians didn't surrender, *Hibernia* would get patched up in Venus' yards and then the *Bonnie* Squadron and whatever escort we could pull together would be going on a trip to the red planet. The temptation existed to send ships immediately to the Forge, to try to reclaim that base, but there were undoubtedly Martian troops on the ground there, and we'd left all our ground combat personnel on Mercury. Shauna Cass would have to wait a while longer for rescue.

So it was back to Venus. Sounds simple enough... but really, not at all.

Wes looked away from the screen as his internal comm sounded. The realtime feed automatically muted so there wouldn't be signal overlap. Then he listened with a frown while John, Karen and I watched him.

I had the distinct feeling he was getting news about Lia.

Turns out my feeling was right.

As his feed unmuted, he looked back at us, "Surgeon's report on Lia is grim. She's alive on a machine right now... they say if they can get her to a real hospital her chances improve."

What Wes was saying there was that, if they could get Lia to Venus as soon as possible, she might live — so *Nova Scotia* needed to leave immediately to make the two-day trek. But most of the ships here at the battle site weren't ready to cruise... we couldn't all go.

That complicated things. Though we were pretty sure we'd defeated the Martian mobile forces in this area of space, it still seemed like a bad idea to casually scatter our forces. If we were going to divide, it had to be done thoughtfully.

"Two convoys, perhaps?" Karen suggested quietly, and that idea drew a nod from me.

"Makes sense," I said.

John frowned. It was his decision, and it wasn't an easy one. What about the *Bonnies* — would they stay out here until the second convoy left, or return with Wes?

Plenty of options to consider, so he paused a moment, then began to nod slowly.

"Alright, I like the sound of that. But the first convoy will be strictly medical. Take in the most seriously wounded and some of the prisoners. You said you have the Martian Admiral aboard?" John addressed that last question to me and I nodded.

"McWebs... something. Lower class name."

"Really? Didn't think they got to be Admirals," John shook his head, but then pushed himself past that relatively irrelevant observation. "Well, get him back to Venus. So you and Wes go, and I'll see to things here."

"Two ships?" Wes asked.

That was a good point: remember, seven Martian ships had escaped. If a pair of frigates ran across them it could be trouble for us.

John tipped his head to the side, "Good point. Alright, Captain Ji tells me *Hibernia's* drives are working fine... he can make the cruise back at 195 kps. So escort him. And take a couple of corvettes with you. I'll hold the rest here while we finish patching up, and then we'll follow as a slow convoy."

That made sense — a reasonably strong first convoy, moving fast, and getting the most damaged battleship home for repairs... along with the most damaged people...

And then once the rest of the damaged ships were shored up and made ready for the cruise, they could all limp home together, under the mighty protection of *Bonnie, Terra Nova* and *Bonavista*.

"I'll send word out for all critically injured patients to be moved to *Nova Scotia* or *Wolf*," Wes began to nod. "What corvettes should we bring?"

I glanced at Karen, then back at the screen, "*Friendly* and *Adelaide* would be my choices."

My faith in those two little ships was at an all-time high just now. Because (just to remind you) Karen was alive and sitting in front of this screen with me.

Wes didn't disagree, "Works for me. Let's get to it then. Depart in an hour?"

"Sounds good. We'll call in as we're leaving, John."

Our elite First Lord nodded, "Right, talk to you then."

He vanished from my cabin screen, and Wes remained just a moment longer, offering a nod, "I'll let you know if anything changes with Lia."

"Thanks," was my only answer to that. I couldn't say any more for now. I didn't want to dwell on that too much.

Wes vanished, and I took a long, deep breath. Was doing a lot of that, lately... not just breathing, I mean. I do a lot of that all the time. Most people do. But noticeably sighing and huffing. I suppose it's something I do in stressful times.

"There's been no word from Mercury?" Karen asked quietly, and I glanced at her.

"No... you worried?"

She had a thousand-meter stare, her eyes hitched onto the bulkhead ahead of her. At first she said nothing, then she sighed (yeah, her too).

"I have a feeling."

Honestly, I didn't want to hear that.

But if Karen said it, then I had to trust it... because you trust the feelings of goddesses.

Grabbing the remote from the bed, I keyed the ship intercom and got the bridge.

"Felicia here, sir."

"Felicia, could you try to get a signal off to Mercury, see if we can get casualty updates? And let Andrea know we're boosting for Venus in an hour, along with *Nova Scotia, Adelaide, Friendly* and *Hibernia*."

"Yes sir, I'll let you know if we can get anything from Mercury."

She cut the link, and I dropped the remote.

"You think the universe would do that to us?" Karen asked softly. "Charlie *and* Lia, all at once?"

It was one of the rare times I'd heard Karen sound quite so… exhausted. I nearly called it 'defeated', but obviously she wasn't defeated. She'd won, and lived. But it had been a long day and her humanity was obviously stinging for all the losses. Mine was too, but as a much more selfish brute, I was better consoled by her presence.

"I don't know if the universe does anything to us," I replied, a bit too analytically. "I just hope to God Lia pulls through. And Charlie's fine. Though I have no idea what I'll say to him if Lia dies."

Funny, I wouldn't have to face that problem.

And frankly, I don't want to talk about what it was like when Felicia called in her next report — the casualty report from Mercury.

Wes was grabbing a quick meal in his cabin before he headed to the bridge for our departure. He was just settling down with a bowl of soup when his screen flashed, so he gingerly grabbed the remote, checked to see that it was a realtime message from *Wolf*, and activated the feed.

He was looking down at his soup when the feed switched on, "News, Ken?"

Then his eyes darted up, and he discovered it was Andrea.

"Oh, Andrea. Hello…" he lowered his soup bowl carefully. "Glad to see you alright."

"You too," she agreed.

She was sitting in her day cabin, based on the angle of the picture.

And she said… nothing.

She looked like she wanted to say a few things, but she didn't actually say anything.

Wes frowned a little as the silence dragged on, and then he smiled a bit wryly, "Just calling to *not* talk?"

Andrea blinked, and her eyes seemed to jump to his (even on the realtime screen).

His smile grew, "Like we said last time. No need to talk anymore, right? So we can just call to… *not* talk. Right?"

Andrea opened her mouth to say something, but then Wes' screen flashed again — another signal from *Wolf*.

"Er. Can you hang on just a minute, Andrea. Ken's calling."

She nodded, and then I appeared.

I had no idea that Andrea was on the other line, not that it mattered. When Wes saw my expression, he knew something was up.

He turned and leaned over the side of his chair, laying his soup bowl on a tray on the bed. It was never a good idea to get bad news with hot soup hovering over one's lap.

"News?" he asked.

I rubbed my forehead, as if that'd help, and nodded.

"Casualty reports in from Mercury."

Wes blinked. He thought for a few seconds, then asked the question: "Do we tell Lia?"

I let go of my forehead, "I don't often say this, but she might be too fragile. Literally."

Wes swallowed, "Maybe."

He sighed.

"Maybe."

CHAPTER TWENTY-ONE

PAROLE

An hour later we boosted, and there wasn't much fanfare in that. We just got cruising, tucked in around *Hibernia* with *Adelaide* and *Friendly* guarding *Wolf* and *Nova Scotia*.

As we did this, our passengers were getting situated.

In deference to his rank, we'd given Bort McWebsbert a rather small cabin down near the cargo decks. It wasn't much of a room, but it was better than a cot in the cargo bay. He cleaned up there, sent his uniform to wash, pulled on the clothes we provided (black pants and white shirt out of stores, with some Admiral's bars quickly appended to the collar so our people would realize he was an officer) and then asked his guard to be taken to see his crew.

The SF was happy to oblige, so Bort went down to the cargo bays where his men were being held. Many of them had been coaxed out of their filthy (and sometimes mildly radioactive) uniforms too, and were dressed as he was. Others were making the transition. I bring up this point because our rooms full of prisoners were not rooms full of red.

For some reason I find that significant.

He wasn't ostentatious; he started moving among his men, talking to them individually and in small groups, finding out how they'd been treated and how they were feeling. He reassured many of them that they didn't need to worry... that Admiral Barron would respect the Ceres Accord, and that there was no shame in being defeated by a superior force.

Several people asked about Post Captain O'Thomson, and he didn't have an answer for them. He promised to find out — he wanted to know too. He didn't want Trina O'Thomson back on Asteroid Kappa to be weeping on her wedding day.

After he'd talked to everyone who wanted to talk, he turned to Eugene Sengooba, and asked to see me.

The veteran Chief passed on that request, and it reached Karen and me just as we were finishing supper.

"You want to meet a Martian Admiral?" I asked as we cleared our trays in the kitchen.

She glanced at me, "You said he called you a bastard?"

I nodded.

"And called himself one too?"

I nodded again.

"Sure, I'll meet him."

We finished clearing up and headed down to the cargo bays.

Karen drew some strange looks when she stepped into the cargo bay beside me. Of course, this was to be expected — recall that delightful discussion she'd had with a

Martian Ensign back during *The Dark Cruise*, and what Bort had told Shauna Cass about how women were perceived in his Navy.

But there were no jeers: Bort's crew was well-behaved.

They did stare at Karen, though. Both of us, but Karen in particular.

Part of that is obviously down to the fact that it's incredibly difficult not to stare at her. She might have been tired, just had her other former ship crippled and seen some of her fellow officers killed… but there was still an unflappable quality about her that commanded attention.

Some were probably looking at me a bit too, recognizing me from the landing bay or having heard about the same. I was one of the evil Admirals who'd done some harm to the Martian Navy over the past couple of years.

They were well within their rights to stare.

Anyway, as we stepped in, Eugene Sengooba and his guards stayed close enough to us to offer some protection in case trouble started, but again, none of us had the feeling it would. Probably a good thing, since we didn't have Charlie… Rufus, I suppose… to bail us out.

Bort approached easily, some of his men clustering behind him to make sure he had his own protection with him, even if they weren't armed.

"Vice Admiral Bort McWebsbert, Commodore Karen McMaster," I introduced Karen to Bort rather formally, stepping aside so they could shake hands.

Bort smiled politely, "McMaster. I would have suggested our families might have similar origins, but my family name evolved on Asteroid Epsilon."

Karen didn't catch his meaning at first, then their common 'Mc' struck her and she matched his polite smile, "Yes of course. Nevertheless, Admiral, we do hold a profession in common."

She was being almost painfully cordial, not just for Bort but to maintain the proper appearances before all the Martian spacers. Any frank comments like the ones he and I had exchanged in the bay would probably not do well with an audience.

"Is there any news about Post Captain O'Thomson?" Bort queried next, and Karen glanced at me.

"We've been tied up speaking with the First Lord, so I don't have any reports for you. If you'd like, we can head up to the med bay now, and see for ourselves…" I paused and studied Bort for a second before deciding whether to say the next thing. Whatever I saw convinced me to continue, "As I understand it, there's a custom in your Navy… you offer parole to captured officers?"

I'd heard bits and pieces of that during and after Io and Sinope, and I knew what the historical precedent was. Parole (in Napoleonic times, for instance) was the idea that as a fellow gentleman, a captured officer could be permitted to move around freely (not be imprisoned in a jail) provided he did not attempt to escape.

The Martians still did believe in that, theoretically, though during the war they hadn't been wed to it.

All the same, I was inclined to extend the opportunity to Bort, for reasons that weren't terribly clear. I suppose I just got the sense he deserved it.

"We do offer parole," Bort replied slowly, clearly not sure what we were getting at. He decided to give a little more, to sound us out. "We offered it to Shauna Cass, though she didn't accept."

Shauna's mention got both Karen and me to perk up a little more. Obviously, there was plenty for us to talk about with this fellow.

"Well, we're extending the offer to you, Admiral," I made it plain, and Bort sized up both of us.

As you can probably tell, we were all trying to get reads on each other. Made for a slightly awkward conversation.

"I'll accept," he answered eventually.

"Very good. Let's go check on your Captain," I turned and gestured towards the door, and then Bort looked back to his men, said a few things to them, and joined Karen and me in exiting the bay.

Once we stepped out of the compartment and the hatch closed, the mood changed.

"Thanks for this," Bort said more plainly.

I nodded, "Sure."

Karen glanced at the SF guard who'd been on Bort's door, and who'd followed him to the bay and out again, "You can stand down for now."

The SF looked from Bort to us and then acknowledged, "Yes ma'am."

He turned and left the area.

"No guards?" Bort glanced at me.

"That's what parole means, isn't it?"

He shrugged, "It does."

"Then no guards," I concluded. "It's this way, come on."

I led, and Karen brought up the rear, largely so we could keep our guest bracketed. As I keep saying, we didn't expect trouble, but he was a Martian Admiral... and an a-typically large and strong one at that. Better safe than sorry.

We arrived at the med bay after a few moments and entered quickly. The compartment was reasonably busy, though I got the sense we'd come after the storm — that it had been much busier there an hour or two prior.

Alicia was going from bed to bed, checking the patients she was keeping for observation and care during our cruise. Four critical cases had come aboard from other ships before our departure, so she was keeping a particular eye on them. Since she hadn't done the initial surgeries on them, she couldn't be as sure of their status.

Post Captain O'Thomson was on one of the beds to the left, so we moved over his way, and I waved to Alicia. After finishing her checks on one of the others, she joined us.

"Alicia, this is Admiral McWebsbert," Karen introduced them.

Bort nodded to her, and then looked at O'Thomson, who was unconscious, "Doctor, how is he?"

Alicia took a quick look at the panel next to his bed, "Critical but stable. We had a lot of internal bleeding to stop, and we pumped quite a lot of plasma into him... I'd give him an even chance, at best."

The lack of overwhelmingly good news kept Bort's expression tight, but he did appreciate it nonetheless, "Understood. Thank you for your efforts on behalf of an enemy combatant."

A little surprised at that remark, Alicia looked at Karen and then at me, "Er. Certainly."

She wasn't accustomed to getting thanks quite like that — there usually weren't Martians around to offer them. But it seemed just then that Bort appreciated the fact that his friend, critical though his condition was, lay on the same sort of medical bed as our own wounded, clearly receiving the same quality of care.

Without saying anything further, Alicia went back to tending her other patients, and I looked at Bort, "We should probably go somewhere and chat for a while, don't you think?"

"Yes, I'll be most interested to have a conversation with you, Admiral," Karen added, just in case he thought that was a suggestion.

"Be my pleasure," he answered.

We went off to talk.

CHAPTER TWENTY-TWO

FRAGILE

Wes Pellew had never been Lia Hawke's closest friend. They'd gotten along very well when working together, but recall that their first meeting actually took place within the books of this series, back in *The Dark Cruise*. Knowing that, Wes felt somehow unequal to looking after her during the cruise to Venus. It would have been better if Karen and I had been seeing to her, while he was dealing with Bort… but it didn't turn out that way.

Lia's condition was critical and we couldn't move her just because it'd be a little easier on us.

Of course, Wes being Wes, he didn't let his own concerns stop him doing his job. He might have been convinced that Karen and I were better suited for the role, but he was all Lia really had in terms of a friend, so he wasn't going to let her down.

That in mind, he spent quite a few hours that first day in *Nova Scotia's* med bay, sitting next to Lia's bed while he did paperwork. The doctors had said she might slip in and out of consciousness, so having a familiar face around could help if she did wake up.

We join them during one of these conscious periods.

Wes heard Lia shifting on her bed and looked up over his pad. Sure enough, her eyes were opening. One of them had suffered a ruptured vessel or something to that effect, rendering its white part blood red.

That was the least of her problems, though… I suppose I should describe just how bad her condition was.

Most of her head was bandaged up, as was her neck. Then up and down her body, literally from head to toe, there were a variety of wrapped bandages, seal patches, braces and any other things the surgeons had available to close wounds.

Her body was literally riddled with holes. She was on so many painkillers that she couldn't feel much at all — her lips and tongue were slightly numb, which made speech of any sort a very difficult proposition.

But her brain was intact, which was almost miraculous.

That said, she was in shock, and she was so laden with drugs that even our supposedly side effect-free medicines were likely messing with her state of mind.

"Where 'm I?" she gurgled.

Wes put his pad down on the tray next to his chair and stood up, "Lia, it's Wes."

Her eyes jumped to him, and then she blinked repeatedly until his face came roughly into focus.

"Wes?" she managed to say.

He nodded, then reminded her of things he figured she wouldn't have remembered since he'd told her last time, "You're aboard *Nova Scotia*, we're taking you back to Venus for further treatment."

She stared at him as he said that, and then remained silent for a few moments. He could see her thinking — or trying to think. Her groggy brain and her seemingly lifeless body were wrestling for her focus, but through sheer force of will she was managing to keep a hold of Wes' words.

"Ken? Karen?"

The damage to her diaphragm and to her left lung made speaking quite difficult, but she continued to pull it off with great determination.

"Both fine, they're on *Wolf*. You'd be there too, but we picked you up first. The doctors don't want to move you until we get to Venus."

Lia stared at Wes again, processing the words. He waited patiently.

Wes will be the first to tell you that he's not the best at this sort of thing. This isn't his specialty any more than it's mine. When it comes to figuring out what to say to someone who's hurting, we always tend to come off too analytical, too wooden. I guess it's just a function of the job... or our personalities. Who knows.

But for the moment he knew his explanations were probably letting his side down a bit. He wasn't saying anything soothing or comforting, and he figured that if he tried, it'd come off as so forced and phoney that Lia would either see right through it, or worry that he was lying for her benefit and assume the worst.

Even in her heavily-injured and medicated state, he expected she'd be more than a match for his rudimentary deception skills... well, that's putting it too harshly. But his reassuring-despite-genuinely-dire-circumstances skills just weren't a match for Lia's court-bred people-reading abilities.

I mean, what could he say? If it were me on my deathbed, he'd probably say what I'd say to him: 'Good chance you're not going to survive here. Can I do anything?'

But he could say that to me because he'd know we both tended to be more analytical. What could he say to someone with a healthy concept of what giving comfort actually meant?

Probably not much, without causing offense.

So he did what I'd have done, and remained taciturn. He didn't lie or promise everything would be alright, he just waited for Lia's mind to decipher his words.

As the moments passed and she did that, her eyes reached his again, "Charlie?"

Wes stiffened. The exact question that passed through his mind was 'why the hell did she have to ask?'

He contemplated his answer. He contemplated it knowing very well that Lia was, as I said, fragile. Not in the sense that macro-chauvinists would usually claim when calling a woman fragile, but in the way where a spike in her blood pressure might literally kill her.

So Wes quickly considered his options for answering the question. He could promise that Charlie was alright, but then later when she realized he was lying her blood pressure spike would be massive.

And she'd probably hate him for life. Rightly so.

He could tell her the truth, but that might kill her immediately.

Funny, back in *The Forge Fires* I railed about the importance of telling the truth to your people, but under these circumstances it just wouldn't have been right to. Goes to show how important context is to decision making.

"We haven't heard from Mercury yet," Wes lied blatantly.

He sold the line pretty well — he focused on saying it with the same cadence he would have had he meant it. He concentrated on keeping his expression as neutral as it would have been had he meant it. All in all, a solidly-performed lie.

Unfortunately, Lia saw right through him. Bleary-eyed and drugged, she was still her father's daughter, and a master courtesan. She had spent decades learning how to identify a lie when it was told by people who were much better liars than Wes. Seeing as Wes didn't lie at all, and thus had no practice, he really didn't have a chance.

That was bad for him, and worse for Lia. Her monitor beeped, and the panel next to her bed revealed how fast her heart rate began to climb.

"Dead?" her voice raised painfully.

"No, wait, no…" Wes staggered with that attempted reply, and she started to struggle on her bed.

"Lying!" she gurgled and tried to sob. "Not… both of us…"

Her monitor started flashing, and *Nova Scotia's* medical team hurried over. Wes took a step back to let them work, and watched as they injected a sedative into her bloodstream. She went limp.

Wes just had to stand there, jaw open and arms held a little away from his sides… you know the way you look after you've just pulled your arms off something you weren't suppose to touch. Like that.

He looked at Lia and felt a pang of sadness.

The doctor turned to him as he stared, "Sir, we have to make sure she doesn't panic like that."

Nodding slowly, Wes let out a sigh, "I know… I tried. But I'm no good at lying to her."

Looking back at Lia, the doctor frowned, "Well then we're going to have to keep her asleep until you have genuinely good news for her."

That might be a problem, Wes decided, because if they kept her asleep until he could promise her that Charlie was…

Yeah.

"Can you put her in a medical coma?" he asked quietly.

"Sir?" the doctor looked back at him. "Well, yes… but… is it necessary?"

Wes took a deep breath, "Well I doubt she's going to forget that I was lying to her. Next time she wakes up it'll only be worse. So better that we keep her sedated."

It was not a suggestion that he made lightly, and the doctor realized that.

"I… yes. Alright. I'll see to it."

Wes held up his hand, "As long as it doesn't put her in any greater danger."

"No, it'll be fine, sir. It's just usually you want to be able to talk to the wounded people. Not the opposite."

Wes' mouth thinned to a line, and he looked down, "Usually there's something left to comfort them with."

The doctor opened her mouth to say something, then decided against it. She went on about the business of putting Lia into a medically-induced coma, and Wes took his paperwork back to his cabin, where he collapsed into his chair with a weary sigh.

Venus was thirty-six hours away, and then Lia would have closer friends with her.

As long as she survived the trip.

CHAPTER TWENTY-THREE

MY ENEMY

Bort, Karen and I tried to have productive conversations several times during the first thirty-six hours of our cruise to Venus, but that didn't work out as well as we might have liked. We ended up with occasional bursts of actual conversation, scattered amongst long stretches of uncomfortable positioning.

We were learning how to interact... and it wasn't easy. We were enemies, and that's something that's not easily overcome, no matter how positive a vibe you get when interacting.

We did eventually manage to get a bit of a flow going during one of these conversations. Though it wasn't because the subject was cheerful.

"So you took out Ben Conflans," Bort was sitting back in a chair in the briefing room, and Karen and I were sitting across the table from him.

We'd just finished explaining that we'd been at Io, a mission he evidently knew about.

"Admiral Conflans? He went down with his ship," was my cautious answer.

"Never got to meet him?" Bort asked, and Karen and I both shook our heads.

"Met some of his spacers," she added. "They didn't think much of me. But they spoke highly of him... and he looked after his prisoners very well."

Bort smiled sadly and nodded generously, "Yeah, that's Ben. Friend of mine... he was actually supervising the *Tharsis* project until he got assigned that mission. He always had an instinct for technical matters, so they sent him to raid your R&D. Left me in charge."

It's an incredibly awkward feeling when someone sitting across from you speaks in a warm, nostalgic way about someone you went out of your way to kill.

What makes it even stranger is when you feel no guilt at all, despite hearing that the man on the other end of the laser had been human afterall. It had been our job to stop him. It was a shame he was killed. But we'd lost *Honesty* in that fight, Kate Levec had been shot, and *Lion* had been cooked with radiation. Kris Jacobs was still undergoing very, very painful gene therapy to undo the damage.

So I didn't feel guilty, even though it was quite obvious that Ben Conflans' death had been sharply felt by Bort.

And, to switch to his perspective, he didn't expect us to feel bad. It was very surreal, this. I can't think of a better way to put it... we were here talking to someone who had successfully defeated more Defense Command ships than anyone else in his fleet, and we were sharing with each other information about the people we'd killed.

Without a whit of anger.

There wasn't even tension. Just awkwardness.

Though there was one unpleasant issue that came to mind, "What about... you ever hear anything about *Idaho*?"

Bort had been looking at the table as he reflected on Ben Conflans. When I mentioned

Idaho, his gaze jumped up and shifted from me to Karen and back.

"That wasn't Ben."

Karen raised an eyebrow and looked at me, then looked back at him. For understandable reasons, this subject was… *close* to her. She's the one who'd been exposed to the Phosgene on that ship. She was the one who still… well. Who bore the scars, and carried the anger at being tricked, and made weak.

Karen hated to be weak.

Now, though, she maintained the atmosphere that had been set for our conversation with Bort: calm.

"You know about the incident, then?"

Bort's eye twitched slightly, and he nodded, "I told you I watch your news feeds when I can. To get to know my enemy. I saw the one by the man who died."

"Jocko Kent," I said that name with dry reverence.

Nodding again, Bort's eyes turned back to the table, "And I was sorry to hear about it. I can tell you, though, that wasn't Ben Conflans. His honor would never allow that sort of bollocks."

He said that with a grave certainty, and I glanced at Karen. He sounded genuine, and I had no reason to think he was lying, but we didn't have a better suspect at the time.

Then he drummed his fingers on the table, and looked up again, "There are Captains in our Navy who would try something like that. I can't imagine any of them being out that far. But we have some real… unpleasant officers. As you've no doubt seen."

Between the fate of *Idaho* and the destruction of Simon Kishko's *North Carolina* over Pion rock, I certainly couldn't disagree.

Karen leaned back in her chair, "I'm sure both our fleets have their share."

Bort looked at her, "You hung yours at the start of the war."

I was genuinely surprised at how much Bort seemed to know, though it bears noting that the facts he had were all the ones we'd broadcasted through the media, loud and clear. That said, it's an important lesson in keeping intel secure. If, for instance, we'd been undisciplined in our lies about going to the Forge before Mercury, the Martians almost certainly would have found out, and redeployed.

There's an old saying from World War Two: loose lips sink ships. It means the enemy is listening, so be careful what intel you give up casually.

Bort's the reason why we had to be careful. He was smart, and he listened. The worst sort of adversary to have.

Anyway, the bad ones we'd hung were, of course, Sean Cook and his Captains from the old Independent Squadron, and Bort had a point: they were some of the very worst to ever disgrace our fleet.

There were other poor officers. Some we met out at Jupiter, others I simply haven't talked about. I'm sure some of you think I'm covering them up, but frankly, I don't care. I'm not dedicating any more page time to those bastards than I have to — not when so many good men and women deserve recognition for doing things right.

Anyway, sorry for the tangent.

"Maybe once the war is officially over, we can find out more about who staged the *Idaho* incident," I suggested.

Bort answered with a rather severe nod, "I'd certainly like to know."

That was definitely a sentiment I could agree with.

We sat silently for a moment after that, and then Karen leaned forward, her eyes narrowing as she studied her adversary.

"I'm going to be honest," she said, "you're nothing like what I... we... would have expected."

Bort snorted a laugh, "Guess I'll take that as a compliment."

"You should."

I joined in then, following Karen's line of thought, "A lower class spacer from an Asteroid makes Admiral? We didn't think that sort of thing happened on Mars... well, not that we really knew. Just doesn't seem to fit your Navy's character."

Chuckling bitterly, Bort nodded, "I don't look like Garvey, or Kitty Castillo, who I take it you still have prisoner?"

My eyebrows went up — it had been a long time since I'd thought of my former counterpart from the Martian Asteroid Squadron.

"So you remember her," Bort noticed my reaction. "I got here by being good at what I do. Good enough at it that they couldn't ignore me."

"That's what we've seen. Officers... like Kitty, for instance. Well," Karen shook her head slightly in recollection.

"I'd been put up for that job — Asteroid Squadron CO. I didn't get it. They actually tried to drum me out instead, but Ben took me in on the *Tharsis* project. And here we sit."

That made me think of some things. What if Bort had been the Martian we faced at the Battle of Belt Two, right back in the beginning? The whole engagement could have gone a whole lot differently... we could have lost.

Because where Kitty Castillo had been no match for us, Bort could have been. Against the old Belt Squadron, that would have been tough... but I'm sure it would have been a much nastier fight, at the very least.

And if he'd won, and we'd been unable to warn Earth or protect the Belt colonies... well.

"No offense, but I prefer meeting you here and now. Back then, I don't think we'd have had this chance to talk after the dust settled," I said quietly.

Bort looked at me, and I could see he'd been thinking similar things. Sometimes wars come down to the right people being in the right place at the right time. At the beginning, it came down to Karen's landing gear not working properly one morning... and that led us to uncovering the plot to start the war.

Little things like that made all the difference.

Bort being in charge of the Asteroid Squadron most definitely could have altered the course of history.

But he hadn't been, which was probably a good thing for everyone involved. We all came to that realization as we sat around the table. It was one of the realizations that, over time, helped us get to know each other better, and to find a framework for friendship.

Because, I suppose, we were the right people together at the right time for that to be possible.

To all of our benefit, in the end.

CHAPTER TWENTY-FOUR

OUTSIDE OUR HULLS

While we were focused on the people close to us, the Empire was celebrating, and the Imperium was preparing for the very worst.

First to our enemies. I can only speak in generalities about them at this stage, but that should be enough to get the point across. Once they realized their outer capital and their most powerful battleships were gone, their Admirals Staff (or whatever the hell they call their Admiralty) met in a panic.

As I understand it, two members of that staff were executed shortly thereafter, and their families disgraced (possibly executed too, that's been tough to confirm). Then the President-for-Life, Barnaby Godwin, started cracking down on his people with some very harsh curfews and communications restrictions.

He was worried that there'd be a revolution, and I think he was on to something. You could certainly draw parallels between the Clash and Tsushima… but that's for a later book, obviously.

Despite what the movies suggest, our comm didn't ring the next day with Godwin begging for peace — it was not a decision he came to overnight. The Fleet Clash wasn't actually *that* decisive. The Martian Navy still had plenty of battleships — *Ascraeus Mons*, the last of the *Tharsis*-class would probably be online soon, and the Martian home fleet still included five of the heavies.

So he had forces to work with.

Just not enough.

Factoring in the actual losses from Mercury, we still had four *Bonnies*, four *Hokkaido*-class, four *Empire*-class, and one *Warlock*-class. Even *Ark Royal* — the supercarrier that looked a lot like *Bonaventure* but boasted only *Empire*-class firepower — was coming back online. So it was roughly three-to-one in our favor in capital ships.

What I'm getting at is that peace seemed highly, highly likely to us under those circumstances, but the Martians didn't just throw their hands up and yell 'done'. They considered their options, searched for any possible way to salvage the situation… and then threw their hands up and yelled 'done'.

While we waited for them to come to their senses, though, we had our own little problems to deal with. And as I think John and I prefaced earlier, politics were chief among those concerns.

"The Emperor is reportedly assembling his personal travel guard, and packing," Thea Fostopolos, the head of Defense Command Intelligence, was sitting in the office of our favorite mad Irish lord.

Daragh Ryan was slumped back in his chair, and the mention of Luther Gregory III brought a sour look to his face, "Is that a fact? Planning a vacation, is he?"

Thea nodded, "Word is he wants to be ready to head to Mars aboard *Ark Royal*. He wants to oversee the peace process."

"There isn't a fuckin' peace process, yet," Daragh said sharply. "It takes the bastard so long to pack that he has to start months in advance?"

"Seems so."

Daragh groaned and let his head fall back against the headrest of his chair. Point of interest: he'd managed to get rid of Dave Caldecott's old back-breaking chair before the end of 2232, so sitting at his desk no longer robbed him of feeling below his waist. Probably a good thing.

"So I need to tell the PM he's going to have a silk stocking full of shit looking over his shoulder while he's putting the screws to the President-for-Life?" was the Second Lord's question. Thea frowned, not recognizing the insult, so Daragh helped her, "Talleyrand was a silk stocking full of shit, according to Napoleon Bonaparte."

That still didn't help her in the slightest, but Daragh wasn't about to educate her on the political maneuvering of a Frenchman who'd been dead for 400 years. And you know what, I'm not going to either.

"I can brief the Prime Minister if you'd prefer," Thea offered softly, but Daragh shook his head.

"No, better that I do it. I'll get something booked for tomorrow. What else do you have for me now?"

Thea had a pile of pads which she now started shuffling through, "First close images of the *Tharsis* wreckage tells us they definitely weren't built by the Martians. That new Asteroid Union was probably the builder."

Daragh frowned, "The new kids have the tech to build ships that powerful?"

"Our people think it's more likely they had cheap labor pools… made it more economical and faster to build them to Martian spec," Thea said evenly, and Daragh narrowed his eyes and shook his head.

We already know what he thought of most shipbuilders (his dealings with them often involved his shotgun, remember). The thought that some jumped-up Union of Solar Asteroids might have the gall to build battleships for the Imperium didn't sit well with him.

It seemed equally ridiculous to him that the Imperium — with all its supposed might and its probable lack of true concerns for its citizens — didn't have the yard capacity and the skilled labor pool to build its own superbattleships.

So as a result, these Solar Asteroid people were getting their noses into our war.

"Anything from your agents about these Unionists?" Daragh's question was sharp, and Thea shook her head.

"Haley hasn't reported anything at all. As soon as any of our people get out there, we don't hear from them. Either they're getting caught or they're in a situation so covert they can't risk comms."

"Christ wept," the Second Lord leaned forward in his chair. "Well when the peace comes we might send a squadron to knock on their door and ask who the fuck they thought they were toying with when they built ships for our enemies."

Daragh's lack of sympathy for the Asteroid Union was acute — the argument that, as a neutral third party, they would have built ships for us if we'd asked, didn't work. He'd taken the loss of the Forge a little personally, since it was his old stomping ground, and as far as he was concerned, anyone working with the Martians in any way had earned our ire.

All that will be important later, but for now it was on to other matters.

"There's one other thing," Thea switched pads again, then took a breath and looked across the table. "We've lost Dave Caldecott."

Daragh had been slightly lost in a quiet rage — thinking about what he'd say to those Union bastards if he got a chance. Thea's words brought him back: "Excuse me?"

The head of Defense Command Intelligence paled slightly. Remember, after the number of things DCI had missed during this war, her stock was at an all-time low. It wasn't necessarily fair to her or her organization, given some of the news they'd brought us, but it was true.

And the stock sunk a little more right then.

"The Coalition intel team on him got chewed up by some professionals, and when the dust settled he was gone," she said quietly.

Remember, Dave Caldecott had been exiled to the Coalition of Unaligned Asteroids, which was friendly towards the Empire. As a favor to us, Coalition agents had been keeping a watch on Dave, making sure he didn't get up to any mischief. He was a declared Enemy of the Empire, after all — we had to know where he was.

And if he ever set foot in Imperial territory again, it was the duty of every Imperial citizen to do him harm.

But now he'd slipped away from our Coalition colleagues… or more precisely, a professional team of operators had broken him out.

Just what Daragh wanted to hear.

"Keep all the ears open for that piece of shit," Daragh grunted. "I don't expect he's stupid enough to come back here… but if he does… watch for him."

"We will," Thea agreed, and Daragh sighed.

Sitting in her office in the underside of *Venus Three*, a supposed homeopathic specialist called Sonia Hart knew a lot more about Dave Caldecott than we did… and she wasn't worried. Instead, she was finishing a report to send to the Governor of Etat Valcour, summarizing all the information she'd been able to gather about the Mercury assault and the Fleet Clash.

Her last line read 'the Martians must surrender soon'.

The Governor wouldn't be terribly pleased.

His plan had allowed for the Imperium to win or lose… but it would have gone so much better had they won. A stronger Empire had greater potential to be a problem for him.

But Sonia knew he had plans for every contingency. He'd started laying seeds during the war — intricate little threads that he could pull later, which could unravel the Empire. And even if that failed, he could use the strength of the Empire to his political advantage…

It was impossible not to be impressed by the Governor's designs. He clearly was as smart and deadly as his reputation suggested.

And there was something compelling about him. She'd found that impossible to deny. People had always said he was very much like Ken Barron — cut from the same cloth as Karen and Ken... she could see that. She'd shared his bed often enough during their whirlwind courtship... she knew more about him than many.

Soon, too, she'd be called back to see him. When the war ended, the political intrigue would undoubtedly start, and after that the threads would be pulled... and the Governor would become President of the Union of Solar Asteroids.

He'd finally seize the status he'd always believed he deserved.

Sonia looked forward to seeing that. She'd be right there next to him, ready if someone tried to take it from him.

And considering who he was, she had to assume someone would try.

He was probably the most famous enemy the Empire had ever had. And if Ken Barron found out about him... if *I* found out about him, there'd be hell to pay.

I'd just have to go through Miss Sonia Hart.

To get at this bastard.

You know who he is.

CHAPTER TWENTY-FIVE

CULTURE SHOCK

Bort McWebsbert was on parole, and that meant he had the run of *Wolf*. Yes, I know, that's a risky and slightly unprecedented way to treat an enemy Admiral, but particularly after our conversations with him, neither Karen nor I were concerned.

And I suppose it bears mentioning that Eugene Sengooba was personally keeping an eye on him, either via internal surveillance or in-person tracking, even though that proved unnecessary.

Bort had a tough time sleeping the night before our arrival at Venus. He'd spent most of the evening with his crew, who all seemed strangely gratified to see him receiving special treatment — it seemed that, to them and their culture, making sure their Admiral was treated with due respect was a point of pride. Now, though, all those men were sleeping, and Bort wasn't about to trouble them. Instead, he wanted to satisfy his own curiosity — he wanted to see what a Defense Command ship was *really* like.

It was culture shock in the extreme.

Word had been passed through the crew that the POW wearing black and white and Admiral's bars had been given parole out of courtesy, but that he wasn't to be allowed to mess with anything. That meant people who passed Bort in the corridors eyed him carefully while still offering polite (if somewhat forced) smiles.

They also didn't salute as he passed.

At first Bort thought that might be because he was an enemy officer, but as he saw more people go by, and some officers pass some non-commissioned persons, he realized that no one was saluting.

That was one difference.

Another, probably more obvious one was that more than half the people he passed were women. Bort didn't really share the prejudices of many in the Imperium, but it was still a fair and honest shock for him to see so many females going about their business, operating without difficulty alongside male compatriots.

As he passed through the corridors, and nodded to these women, he found the air about them to be different, too... to be similar, in fact, to the air which had drawn him to Casey, back in the asteroids. She was confident, strong, and capable — qualities not usually displayed by the women of the Imperium. That's not to say the women there weren't as good, just that they so often hid their qualities, because that was the proper way... Casey had never done that, and it appealed to him.

Evidently, Defense Command (or at least our Belt Squadron elites) expected such quality in all of its officers, men and women alike.

It was a real eye-opener.

Taking his time, Bort made his way around to parts of the ship he'd looked up on the internal map, but hadn't yet seen. He avoided the weapons sections for reasons that weren't entirely clear to him — somehow he didn't want to see our mags or lasers from the inside. Instead he visited our engineering section, where he found Andy Jenson doing a late night's work rewiring some monitoring systems.

Our veteran chief engineer was quite polite, and gave him the very basic tour of the engine spaces. Bort was truly impressed by all of this: our safety equipment, our powerful reactors, and just the general sophistication of our engineering compartment seemed a generation ahead of Martian technology — even the systems aboard *Olympus Mons*.

It became very clear to him that one of our key advantages during the war had been our superior energy systems.

From there, Bort moved through the neck and stopped at the bridge.

He obviously expected to be unwelcome there — the nerve center of our ship was not necessarily a place we wanted an enemy Admiral… but he had parole.

Jim Hannigan had the watch that night, and as the hatch opened he looked back to see a slightly tenuous-seeming Admiral McWebsbert poke his head through.

Bort looked around uncertainly, "Sorry."

"No, sir, come in," Jim shook his head and then beckoned with one hand.

Uneasily, Bort took a step onto a very foreign command deck.

His hands linked firmly behind his back, he took a few steps from the hatch, moving between the last few Helm and Navigation consoles and the left-most operations consoles, then stopping as he emerged into the open central 'courtyard' of the bridge — the open space where Karen, Andrea and I usually stand and command.

This reminds me, actually: I can't remember if I've ever fully painted the bridge for you… oh boy, if I haven't, I'm sorry. If you think of the bridge as a square, the front wall is consumed by the screens, and the 'stage' in front of them. Along the right wall is the Sensors and Communications section, along the left is the Helm and Navigation section, and along the back wall is the Operations section. Back left corner is the doorway in and out, back right corner is the door to the Captain's day cabin, and the arms locker.

Bort was now standing near Jim Hannigan, right at the center of the open space between all these consoles. He turned around slowly, looking at the very sensible, ergonomic array of consoles, then up at the high ceiling, and then around to the front wall, where our screens were mostly showing *Wolf*Net graphics.

He'd seen brief clips of bridges in our news feeds, and he'd seen Battlelink simulated on a couple of movies about pirate fighting… but standing in the midst of *Wolf's* bridge right then, he really *got* it.

I know this will sound self-congratulatory, but we do deserve congratulations. Our engineers had built the most effective bridges in the solar system, making the process of going into battle so much easier than what Bort had ever enjoyed, even aboard *Olympus Mons*.

Instead of having to lurk around a rotating pillar of screens on a dark bridge with narrow aisles constantly interrupted by steps and low beams, we had a very open, very bright space to work in. We didn't have to yell at each other. As commanders, we were surrounded by the information we needed.

And here again, our personnel seemed relaxed, confident and obviously competent.

It was as he stood on this bridge and really soaked in the relaxed, professional atmosphere our people projected, that Bort decided the Martians probably could not have beaten us. I take issue with this: I think they could have, but for the grace of some luck on our side… but what Bort said to me later is worth mentioning.

After the war, I once said to him that luck sided with us more times than it sided with him, and he said that the reason it did was because we did all these little things — these things we take for granted — that helped push luck our way. Our ships were practical, bright, and frankly undramatic in terms of lighting. It was easy to move around. There were women aboard. These points all seem a little absurd, on the face of it, but they lead to a point we often overlook: more often than not, Defense Command makes its ships good places to work.

Remember the point from ages back about the advantage of having a happy ship — about having people in a positive state of mind, and how that contributes to success? Well, environmental factors play a role.

Bort could vouch for the Martian failure to appreciate this. His ships had always been cramped, dark and uncomfortable. And maybe that cost his crews a little tiny bit of their efficiency. It didn't make good crews bad, but maybe it made good crews a little less fresh when it came time to fight.

I don't know if Bort is right about this, but I can understand the point. We were generations ahead of the Martians in terms of making ships friendly to crews. And really, given what we were soon to learn about the relationship between the Martian upper and lower classes, that shouldn't be a surprise.

After leaving the bridge, Bort was rather beside himself. Jim had suggested he go down to the officers' club on the rec deck for a night cap, so he followed that advice. The last time we visited the officers' club in this series, I'm pretty sure it was in *The Gallant Few*, when we interrupted a flagging date between Jim Hannigan and Adrienne Thomson.

Well, oddly, Adrienne was in there again, and having a good deal more fun, though this time it was with Shelby McLaws. It was quite empty aside from those two — they were staying up late, being their usual troublemaking selves. Incorrigible officers, always up to no good…

Or, wait, they're the opposite of that. And even if they weren't, they were entitled to get themselves into trouble. They were the damned best, after all.

Anyway. They were at a table near the door when Bort stepped in, and they were both witness to the dropping of his jaw. There was a full bar-restaurant on *Wolf*… well, actually there were two, but the non-commissioned club wasn't really the place for a Martian Admiral.

This place was just unthinkable. Warships didn't have this.

Seeing the rather stunned look on Bort's face, Shelby put down her glass, shot a quick 'oh dear' glance at Adrienne, and then stood, "Sir, can we be of any help?"

Bort blinked, then his eyes jumped to Shelby.

"I'm Lieutenant Shelby McLaws, Helm and Navigation Officer. If there's anything you need…"

"No. Thanks. Don't let me interrupt… your… conversation."

Like I said, Bort was suffering from some culture shock.

Shelby looked back down at Adrienne, who raised an eyebrow and then stood, nodding to Bort, "Lieutenant Commander Adrienne Thomson, Commander Flight Group. We could order you a drink, sir, if you like."

Apparently, realizing that Adrienne was a combat pilot pushed Bort over the edge. Women simply did *not* fly Interceptors.

"I'll take something strong, then," Bort accepted with a nod. "Thank you."

Adrienne smiled, then waved to the Ensign working the bar, "A pint of Black Sun."

The Ensign nodded, then emerged from around the bar with the beer, which he handed to Bort with a polite bob of the head, "Here you go, sir."

Bort took it, and then he drank it. All of it, in one go.

Remember, Bort's not your typical Martian officer.

Apparently it didn't taste too bad, though it offered him some consolation in not tasting better than his favorite brew from home. If, on top of everything else, our beer had been better, that would have been too much.

Both Shelby and Adrienne watched as Bort finished his drink, and then took the empty glass up to the bar. As he lingered there for a refill, the pair sat down and got back to their chatting. Bort finished off another pint and then pushed the glass away. He turned around at the bar, looking over the officers' club with continued disbelief.

He watched Adrienne and Shelby laughing and chatting in such a relaxed manner, realizing that they had to be two of the ship's senior officers. Relaxed, clearly professional… had they been so at ease through the whole war?

He stopped himself. The two pints of Imperial beer, combined with the overwhelming things he'd seen and the late hour, were making him wonder too much. Realizing that he'd probably had enough, he pushed off from the bar and headed for the door, pausing as he passed Shelby and Adrienne again.

"Thank you for your help, ladies," he said, making a point to try and sound like he was addressing officers, not Martian ladies. "Um. Enjoy your… evening."

With that, he left.

Adrienne and Shelby watched him go, then looked each other with confused frowns. Bort got back to his cabin a few minutes later and tried to get some sleep.

CHAPTER TWENTY-SIX

AND NOW FOR POLITICIANS

Generally speaking, Daragh Ryan hates politicians. If you happen to be a politician, there's a very good chance that Daragh hates you. Sorry about that. It's nothing personal, he's just pretty sure you're evil.

Ironic, I suppose, but there it is.

Now, I introduce this chapter that way because we're going to be dealing with two politicos who, all things being equal, Daragh didn't hate.

I know — unusual to say the least!

So here we go… Daragh was waiting in the reception lounge in the Prime Minister's Office, arms folded as he paced around and looked at the portraits hanging on the walls. A lot of people get confused about the PMO: the term doesn't just refer to the office the Prime Minister works in, but an office complex across the way from the main Parliament buildings (but still on the hill). The PM's staff works in the building, and he hosts state guests and meetings there.

And, of course, he has an actual office there too.

Daragh was waiting in the lounge outside that office for Prime Minister Douglas Pope to return after Question Period. Our mad Second Lord was again to be the bearer of bad news… something he didn't really like, but then, Daragh's never had a problem doing jobs he didn't particularly like.

Oh ha. See what I did there?

Anyway, it actually wasn't the PM who arrived first for the meeting: another politico walked into the waiting room carrying a briefcase and wearing a coat, which he quickly shed and tossed on a nearby couch.

Upon seeing Daragh, the man groaned, "Oh great, the Irish are here."

This, of course, was the Empire's rather colorful Foreign Minister, Craig Bernard Macdonald.

Daragh didn't miss a beat in the exchange, "Oh Christ, the Scots have arrived."

"Bet your ass I have," Macdonald grunted, then closed with his Irish opposition. "Don't pretend you're actually happy to see me, you'll hurt yourself."

Daragh glared at Macdonald for a moment, and then with about as much insanity as you'd expect, he grinned, "Aw fuck off, Scottish."

"You first, Irish," Macdonald grinned back, then whacked him on the shoulder. "Come on in, PM said we should go through."

Turning to the office, Macdonald tapped his personal combination into the keypad beside the door, then held the door open so Daragh could lead the way. They settled themselves in a couple of large armchairs just inside.

I should pause here, because it bears pointing out that a Foreign Minister having this sort of access to a Prime Minister's office is a bit unusual, seeing as they're both politicians.

In politics, there tends to be a distance, even between close allies… they don't *actually* trust each other completely.

But the relationship between Pope and Macdonald was different. While Olivia Bennington was Deputy Prime Minister, Macdonald was in fact Pope's most trusted friend on Capital Island. I don't know the specifics of why, but I do know both men were genuinely good individuals, and that seemed to be a basis for their friendship.

Still, it was tricky. Bennington was Deputy Prime Minister because she was the head of one faction of the Empire Party — the faction that Pope's people had defeated during the last leadership race. Now she was being kept close out of necessity, but really it was Pope and Macdonald who held the power.

Good thing for us, I must say. The Empire would need people like Pope and Macdonald in charge during the coming year… but I shouldn't get ahead of myself.

"So, you fall off the wagon yet?" Daragh shot the question at Macdonald with a grin, and the Foreign Minister groaned.

"I'll be sixteen years sober next month," he fired back.

Daragh chuckled, "As long as you don't count the gin as liquor."

Macdonald laughed, "Well who does?"

They were about to go a few good-natured rounds, as they were more than capable of doing, but the door opened again, and Douglas Pope strode in with his usual, Prime Ministerial gait.

As the door shut behind him, he headed straight to his desk to lay down his briefcase, and then he turned to the circle of chairs in which Daragh and Macdonald were sitting.

"Don't let me interrupt your banter," the Prime Minister said as he approached, and I suppose significantly, neither Daragh nor Macdonald stood to acknowledge his arrival.

Instead, Pope rounded a chair opposite them and then collapsed into it with a very un-Prime Ministerial huff. The façade was down for a little while, so Doug Pope could relax.

"I wouldn't call it banter," Macdonald replied as Pope sat. "That implies he's giving as good as he's getting. He's not."

Daragh 'oohed', "Yeah, you're just bloody lucky they took my shotgun at the door."

"That I can agree with," Macdonald conceded.

Pope smiled a bit sardonically — he was recovering from Question Period and the media scrum, which by this time in the war had started taking more out of him than it used to. Time in politics aged a person pretty quickly, so while Pope appeared his usual, dynamic self in public, he tended to need a few minutes to decompress before he got on with regular business behind closed doors.

Neither Daragh nor Macdonald had a mind to rush the Prime Minister, so they went back to inane point-counterpoint fighting for a few minutes, neither of them winning.

Eventually, they trailed off, and Pope took a deep breath and looked at Daragh, "So, you must have bad news."

"Do I bring any other kind?"

"You just showing up is bad news enough," Macdonald observed, and Daragh snorted another laugh.

"That's true," he nodded. "Well, no word from DCI about peace yet. But we do know the Emperor is probably going to butt in on the negotiations himself. Probably as a first step towards trying to take all of us down."

Macdonald sighed and looked across at Pope. The Prime Minister was pressing his right temple with two fingers, and he took a deep breath, "To be expected. Your intel on him is still safe?"

Daragh nodded. I suppose it tells you something that Daragh and John had trusted the Prime Minister enough to let him know Haley Briand had given them something on the Emperor — even though they hadn't told him what it was.

"He tries, and we can let it out. It'll be damning... though we'll need more than just that, I expect," Daragh shifted in his seat, "Other wee piece of news: DCI lost Dave Caldecott."

Pope blinked, and his eyes widened.

Macdonald looked at Daragh in disbelief, then did a double take and managed a sort of laugh, "I'm sorry, what?"

Daragh winced, "Lost him. Some sort of professional team extracted him. Took out some Coalition observation operatives to do it, too. So someone wanted him loose."

"Somebody with enough resources to break a surveillance team," Macdonald looked back at Pope. "That's just great."

The Prime Minister sighed, "I take it we've heightened our alert for him?"

The Second Lord nodded, "He shows up on our grid, he'll be finished. But we don't know if he's going to. Either way, I think we need to be careful... man could end up anywhere. Could even be the Emperor who got him out. So we should be prepared."

Daragh's warning was answered by a moment of thoughtful silence, and then Douglas Pope looked at both men, "I get the feeling that the end of this war is just going to be the beginning of the real mess. We need to be careful, and look out for each other."

Exchanging glances, Daragh and Macdonald nodded.

There were many troubles ahead. The good news was that the Admiralty and the PMO were going to be on the same side for them.

The bad news was that the Emperor, and possibly a faction of Defense Command, were going to be against us.

CHAPTER TWENTY-SEVEN
DANGEROUS MOVES

There was plenty of fanfare when *Hibernia* returned to Venus local space, and unfortunately, that ship didn't draw all the attention. *Wolf* and particularly *Nova Scotia* needed to dock with *Venus One* as quickly as possible, so we could transfer our wounded to the superior medical facilities on the orbital...

But the shuttles were swarming. Some were media craft, most were privately owned, and they were all in the way.

It's very rare that you hear Wes Pellew swearing, but by the time he got through that cloud of spectators looking for snaps for the scrapbooks, he was doing it with some regularity. That was a simple matter of frustration — he knew that Lia was in dire need of a better hospital, and after coming all this way with her clinging to life, the thought of there being a crucial delay because some yacht owner wanted to say 'I saw them come back'... well, it tested his patience.

And no, I'm not going to give in-depth descriptions of anything he said. He was entitled to be aggravated, and his words don't bear repeating.

By the time he turned his bridge over to Rozy Young, he was feeling some relief. He headed down to the medical bay to witness Lia's transfer through the zero-gee chute and down to the station.

Now, this actually does deserve some explanation. You hear it a lot in stories of various types — 'sorry, it's too dangerous to move her'. Is it just a convenient plot device?

Sometimes, yes. But in a case like Lia's, no.

Moving a wounded person through zero-gee can be a serious problem. These days, intravenous fluids are pumped instead of allowed to drip via gravity, but there are all sorts of things that can go wrong if organs suddenly become weightless. What, for instance, happens to blood clots?

Wounds that are supposedly closed can be opened instantly, or clots can be pressured into the bloodstream, leading to death. I mean, think of it like this: a room with a table full of knives, each in its own slot but none of them actually pinned down. What happens if gravity fails? All those knives can start floating around as they like.

It's one of the disadvantages we face, having evolved on a planet where gravity was constant.

So yes, moving Lia was a big deal, but there was no other option — she needed far better medical care than a frigate's med bay could provide. Of course, by this time we did have grav-gurneys specifically designed to make these transitions safer, but something could always go wrong. One in 500 critical patients transferred through zero-gee chutes do still die as a result... but the risks from harsher gee environments to be experienced during transfer to and flight aboard small craft is even greater.

Sorry, all of this is to say that Lia was in the most danger she'd been since she'd been successfully brought aboard *Nova Scotia*, and Wes was going to be right there for her.

He described the moment to me later as one of 'profound helplessness'. As his ship's surgeon led the way to the docking lock, Wes trailed behind, watching Lia lie almost lifelessly in her medically-induced coma. He kept up a steely, unfeeling expression, and stayed nearby.

When they arrived at the lock, he stood back and let his very experienced medical technicians check her gurney's grav field, then ease their way into the chute. He waited by the lock and listened for any sounds of distress, then followed when they were far enough down.

The whole float down to *Venus One* seemed slower than usual… and it was. There's no fast movements when you have a critical patient in zero-gee. You take no chances.

But the pace was steady, and eventually the medical team made it to the reorientation chamber at the bottom of the lock, where the fun really began. If you've never been in one of these chambers (if you've never left your hometown on any sort of space flight), remember, they're basically like walking down the inside of a letter 'L'… with constant gravity on both 'insides' of the letter. That corner at the bottom is tricky enough when you're a nimble, experienced spacer. Getting a gurney across it without too much disruption of grav is pretty damned difficult.

But again, Wes' crew knew their jobs very well. They got Lia down carefully, and then they exited into the reception lounge on *Venus One*, where some pretty impressive doctors met them and led them to intensive care.

Wes followed, and as he emerged he saw me, Karen and Andrea already in the lounge. It had taken us less time to come down from *Wolf*, because we hadn't been following a critical patient. Normally we would have greeted each other properly, but for obvious reasons we were all more worried about following the doctors.

Nods were swapped, and then Karen and I led the way. Ahead of us, and ahead of the medical party, a team of SF were clearing any bystanders who'd come to watch. We were going in through DC locks, but there were still some people around who would have rubbernecked if they had the chance.

And Lia really didn't need any interruptions.

Karen and I were right behind the doctors, while Andrea and Wes trailed further back. It was as they walked that Andrea glanced at Wes, and took note of his expression.

"How are you today, Wes?"

The question seemed somehow absurd when Wes heard it, and he glanced at our Irish skipper with a frown, "Better off than Lia. But not feeling too great."

Andrea's reaction to that was yet another surprise coming from her: she reached out and clasped the back of Wes' arm as she walked beside him, then gave a reassuring squeeze. Well, I suppose that shouldn't be a surprise, as such… but then the last time Andrea deliberately reached out and touched someone, it had been a knee to Charlie's groin.

"When you accept there was nothing you could do…" she started to say, and then she looked at him.

By now, he was looking at her, a surprised half-frown on his face.

Of course Wes knew he couldn't have done anything for Lia, and in this area he had very credible experience. He'd come to realize there was nothing he could have done to save his wife, so by comparison, this was honestly much easier to cope with. With no offense to Lia, she didn't matter to him nearly as much as Sara had, so while he was frustrated, he wasn't in anything like the pain he'd suffered during those dark days.

Andrea had realized that as soon as she'd started talking, and she felt a fool for bringing it up. To use her words, her 'relative pain scale was broken'… she was having a tough time detecting different levels of discomfort in others, depending on the circumstances. When I lost my head because Karen was in trouble, she'd assumed that I was very, very upset. And she was right.

But now, she was sensing discomfort, and reading a bit too much into it.

That was, as far as Wes was concerned, not a problem at all. What interested him — and what shook the frown off his face — was what Andrea's question said about her own state of mind.

Hm. I think that's a typical case of me making something sound terribly analytical. Let me try again: Wes was surprised Andrea was worried about *him*, and then he wondered if she was projecting her own mental state onto him.

He and Andrea matched stares for a moment, and actually slowed down to a stop, letting our convoy with Lia get well ahead. Andrea looked uncomfortable, as if she'd been caught knowing something that she shouldn't.

Wes considered a clever, sideways remark, but then decided to be direct: "Andrea… do you really not want to talk about… that sort of thing, anymore?"

She immediately looked away. From her perspective, she was still trying to get past the problems she was having, all on her own. But as Wes had predicted, not having actual battles to focus on was making it more difficult to maintain perspective than she'd previously hoped.

This was very much a matter of personal pride for her. She didn't want to have to talk to someone — even a trusted friend like Wes — about these things. It seemed entirely ridiculous to her that she couldn't keep it all under wraps by herself. That was her duty as a Captain, one she'd failed at once already.

It's not a healthy state of mind, but I understand it. You might too.

And she did need to shake it. Wes was extending a hand… well, actually, she'd extended the hand — she was still holding onto his arm.

Realizing that, she let go, and nodded up the hall after us, "We're getting left behind."

Wes was still looking at her, and his frown returned, and deepened, "No shame in it. It's just talking."

Andrea nodded again, this time in answer to his question, "I know. I'll… see. Come on."

There wasn't much room to argue with that: she set off up the hall, and Wes followed.

I suppose you could say there were many people in various stages of 'unhealthy' in that corridor just then. Sorry if that sounds melodramatic, but it's true.

And if you're finding Andrea's aloofness frustrating, then you're not the only one. Setting aside me, Wes and Karen, she was finding it difficult as well. It would have been great if she could have just had a violin-backed moment of catharsis, probably with tears and hugs, and then been okay again.

Unfortunately, it didn't work like that. She still closed her eyes and saw a little boy staring at her, until the airlock closed behind him and he was sucked into deep space.

Over and over and over. Like being there.

I love violins, and I don't mind hugs, but they don't fix that.

So she walked on, and Wes did too. Eventually, they'd have to try again. And again…

For now, though, Karen and I were paying them no attention. We were worried about Lia, because as much as Wes and Andrea are dear friends, she was the closest thing I had to a little sister.

And she was even worse off.

Chapter Twenty-Eight
Medical Coma

Venus One's Defense Command Hospital was ready to receive. As we followed Lia's gurney in, we found the ER lined with beds, and the large open triage bays filled with even more. There weren't too many staff around just yet — they were all off duty now, getting the last scraps of rest they could before *Persephone Praxidice* arrived with the first load of wounded from Mercury. The place had a very eerie feel to it.

I distantly noticed that fact, but mostly I was focused on Lia.

She looked very bad.

Comas in movies tend to be very stylish things, but in reality they're the opposite. Between the immense number of bandages covering Lia and the ashen look that was exaggerated by the zero-gee transfer, she looked more like a corpse than a living person.

Seeing that doesn't do your state of mind any good, believe me.

Karen and I followed in silence, and when we finally reached the room Lia had been assigned, we stood back as the doctors carefully moved her off her gurney and onto her new bed. The room, at least, was private... for the moment. If enough wounded came in, the second bed in there would have to be occupied — it didn't matter who Lia was, medical priorities demanded that every space be filled.

But for now it was quiet.

"Can we wake her?" I asked a little too hopefully as the doctors finished conferring with each other about her current condition.

Both *Nova Scotia's* surgeon and one of *Venus One's* very best physicians, Doctor Heinrich Fields, looked at me. His answer was pre-empted by a voice from the door: "Better be ready with a very good lie."

We hadn't seen Wes and Andrea slip into the room behind us — we hadn't even been paying enough attention to notice they'd been trailing behind. His words now earned him a frown from me, "Really?"

Wes nodded, "You can probably convince her better than I could... but if you can't, she should stay in that coma."

My mouth seemed to go dry, and I looked at Karen. She took a deep breath, then shook her head slowly, "She's too good at reading through lies."

"The truth could literally kill her," Wes added.

In that moment, it seemed so absurd to me — how could hiding from reality help anyone? But this was a very unusual case. Normally Lia was fully fit to handle whatever bad news came her way, be it about her dad or Charlie... but now she was literally in pieces. So going to pieces over bad news was probably a bit more than a foregone conclusion.

But keeping her in a coma... that seemed wrong.

"I..." I started, then stopped. It would have been a very, very bitter fate to have Lia die in that comatose state, never able to speak to her friends again.

Karen looked at me and read my thoughts with that seemingly telepathic ability of hers. She frowned, and then she looked at the doctors, "Let him have a chance to calm her down. Lia deserves to be awake… especially if she never recovers."

The doctors exchanged glances, then nodded. We spent the next couple of moments arranging what amounted to a careful piece of theater: Lia's bed was cordoned off from the rest of the room with a curtain, and after the wake-up drugs were directed into her intravenous, the doctors were going to step out so it would just be me and her.

I doubted she'd want an audience.

Of course, the doctors would be just a step away, able to come through the curtain and hit the switch to put her back into a coma at a second's notice, if that was necessary to keep her from hurting herself.

After all that was arranged, we got things started. The doctor flipped the appropriate switch, the chemical cocktail flowed, and Lia started to regain consciousness.

I held one of her hands as she woke up, then leaned over her with what I hope looked like a concerned frown. I was going to do my best to be my most convincing.

Her eyes started to open slowly, and then she blinked repeatedly to clear her vision as the light began to pour in.

"Wha…" she started to look back and forth in confusion. The coma hadn't given her any peace.

She finally locked onto my face, but it actually took her a couple of minutes to recognize me. Her vision was too blurry and her head was swimming, but eventually things cleared and she squeezed my hand.

"Hey, kiddo," I said, instantly realizing I was trying too hard to sound familial. Even doped up like this, I had to assume she could read a lie.

"Okay?" she croaked.

I didn't know who she was asking about, so I started with the true answers: "Karen and I are fine. Wes too, they're just outside the curtain…"

I trailed off, and reading what I could of her expression, it was clear she wasn't going to conveniently forget to ask about Charlie. Wouldn't that have been helpful?

"Charlie…" I had to pause, and then focus on absolutely everything I said very carefully. "There was a blast on Mercury, Lia. But he was… lightly injured… which means… he's on *Persephone Praxidice*, and they'll be here in less than a day. And then he'll come visit you."

Oh man.

I figured the odds were about one in a million that she'd buy it, but apparently I underestimated the level of trust she had in me.

"Truth?" her eyes were locked onto mine.

Obviously it wasn't the truth.

But right now, it would be better for her if it was. So I nodded, and squeezed her hand, "Yes."

As lies go… well, I don't put it up there with lying to your people about their chances of living through a fight, but I think it was relatively bad. I thought Lia would hold it against me, once she was up and around again.

I'd deal with it later.

Lia, for now, seemed to relax — she'd directed a lot of her very limited supply of energy into trying to get answers, and having heard what she needed to hear, she could release some tension. We chatted briefly about her condition, and her chances of recovery — which were honestly much better now that she was safely in *Venus One's* DC hospital — and then the doctors came back in.

I slipped out from behind the curtain to find that Andrea and Wes had gone for drinks in the cafeteria (which they enjoyed in utter and somewhat uncomfortable silence). Karen took the same hand Lia had been holding, and the difference in their grips actually struck me. Karen was so warm and smooth and alive. Lia was virtually the opposite.

"Good work," Karen whispered to me, and then we stepped out of the room and moved down the hall, out of any possible earshot of our wounded Lady.

"She bought it," I said that, though obviously Karen didn't need me to tell her. I think I just needed to say it. I sort of felt dirty, ridiculous as that probably sounds.

Remember on Egesta, when I became best buddies with the Guild checkpoint leader at the drop of a hat? I felt sort of like that, because while my lie was innocent-seeming in some respects... well.

Karen, fortunately, wasn't going to allow too much of that sort of thinking, "It was necessary."

I nodded. Of course it was.

But there was a pretty serious question to ask... so I did: "But what happens when *Persephone Praxidice* shows up, and this place fills with wounded, and Charlie doesn't walk through her door?"

Karen didn't have an answer for that. We'd start coming up with options — with ways to give bad news, or other possible solutions, if circumstances allowed... but it could simply end up very, very badly.

And if it did, Lia quite possibly would never forgive me.

But hopefully she would recover.

That was the more important thing.

CHAPTER TWENTY-NINE
ENEMY EYES

The first thing Bort McWebsbert noticed when he stepped out of the chute into *Venus One's* receiving lounge was the height of the deckheads. Martian stations apparently tended to be very cramped, many of them having been built generations prior and to smaller scales, so seeing the very wide and tall corridors of the *Venus* orbital was, in fact, something of a revelation.

Scale aside, the relative poshness of the reception lounge earned his notice as well — it was carpeted, and instead of exposed and unfinished metal pipes gratings, and conduits, it was paneled very crisply.

Now, this wasn't a particularly fancy lounge — pretty run of the mill for us — but compared to the relatively impoverished Martian standard, it was positively decadent.

As the POWs from *Olympus Mons* emerged from the chute behind their Admiral, they were even more startled by the sight. In their culture, stations were backwaters — you were always better off either in a dome, where there was room to build and grow, or in a ship, which was built more recently and thus more spacious.

Many wide eyes greeted the SF guards who approached to take the column of prisoners under escort to *Venus One's* large DC brig. There was no resistance.

Eugene Sengooba had come down with the prisoners, and now he moved over to stand beside Bort. As the guards moved in that direction, Eugene caught their attention, then explained to them Bort's situation — the parole I'd granted him. That parole didn't give him the run of *Venus One*, but I'd suggested he be allowed to see Marlene. She did have the power to grant that sort of latitude, and I figured she also might want to come face to face with the guy who'd so handily defeated Shauna Cass.

Might make her feel a bit better about the fate of her protégé if she got to see how capable Bort clearly was.

With approval from Venus SF, Eugene led Bort through the corridors of the DC section of *Venus One*, towards the C&C and Marlene's offices. There weren't too many stares as he went — the white-and-black clothes we'd given him and the POWs did serve to disguise their identities from casual viewers. If the prisoners had come aboard in their reds, it probably wouldn't have been such a subtle greeting.

I'd commed Marlene to let her know she was probably going to have a visitor, so when Eugene led Bort into her outer office, the duty officer was expecting them, "Good day, sir. Vice Admiral Stoll is ready for you."

Eugene stood aside, and Bort wordlessly followed the Lieutenant down a short corridor to an office with an open door. Knocking on the doorframe, the Lieutenant stuck his head in, "The Martian Admiral, ma'am."

Marlene was sitting at her desk, working on a few pads. I hadn't filled her in on what Bort was like — I figured it was better for him to make his own impression on that front

— so she was being quite cool.

Dropping her pad, she laced her fingers and laid her hands on the desk in front of her, "Thank you, Roman. Close the door please."

As Bort stepped through, the Lieutenant shut the door behind him. He stood there for a moment, studying Marlene, and she studied him in turn.

She didn't stand — that was a sign of respect that she genuinely doubted a Martian Admiral would warrant, and to be honest, she was ready to be quite unpleasant with the man who'd taken the Forge. Shauna Cass had been under her wing for many years. The loss still stung.

Bort, however, defied expectations, "Admiral Cass would have sent her respects, but neither she nor I expected that I'd have this conversation with you."

Marlene's expression didn't change, but the introduction surprised her a bit.

"She's alright. Put up a hell of a fight," Bort went on, slowly. "And it seems her sacrifice paid off. Has my government surrendered yet?"

"You expect them to surrender?" Marlene countered, and Bort smiled sadly.

"Not as quickly as they should," he said. "They're good at hanging on to delusions."

Again, the frank assessment of his own government helped Bort break the ice.

Marlene wasn't about to soften easily, though — remember, Sorceresses can have sharp edges to their personalities. She gestured for him to take a seat opposite her, and continued to study him as he sat.

"Ken said he gave you parole. I assumed it was because you whined until he got fed up and granted it to you. Though that didn't make sense, because he's more the type to lock up whiners. Or shoot them."

Bort laughed once, "Something else we have in common."

Marlene leaned back in her chair, frowning at her Martian counterpart. She was beginning to think he wasn't quite like the other red Admirals she'd encountered...

"Let me save you some time, Admiral Stoll. I'm a lower class Asteroid boy who's not too well liked by the Grand Admiral Staff. I got my job because I'm too good at what I do to be ignored. And like most of us Asteroid folk, I'm smart enough to suspect the propaganda Mars likes to spew. So Admiral Barron and I got along pretty well on the flight here. And Admiral Cass and I had an understanding. Though I'm pretty sure she'll never forgive me for killing her people and taking her base."

Marlene definitely hadn't expected that. She shifted in her seat, "You want Shauna to forgive you?"

Bort's expression remained impassive, "If it were me, I don't think I ever would."

"With some reason," Marlene countered.

Bort simply nodded.

She wasn't sure about this fellow. Obviously, I had to see something redeeming about him if I'd given him parole, but going from enemy to friend isn't something that happens in one meeting. I certainly wouldn't have considered Bort a 'friend' at this point. So it was baby steps along the way.

Marlene decided she'd follow my judgment, and learn more about Admiral Bort McWebsbert as circumstances allowed.

"I don't really have time for a chat right now, Admiral. But in deference to Ken's decision, I'm going to give you parole to move freely around the Defense Command sections of this orbital. That doesn't extend to the civilian areas outside, only the military section. We couldn't protect you from angry citizens if you went out there anyway. You'll be given quarters near your men. You'll be monitored at all times. We expect good behavior."

Bort nodded, "You have my word."

"Fine," Marlene nodded, then immediately picked up a pad.

Taking that as a signal to leave, Bort got to his feet and turned for the door. He was about to key it open when Marlene remembered something she'd seen on a pad not long before, "Admiral, you have a Captain called... what is it... O'Thomlin?"

"O'Thomson," he turned back to face her again.

Shuffling pads, Marlene found the one with the information on Bort's old friend.

Frowning, she scrolled up and down and then looked up at him, "I got a report about him not long ago. I'm sorry to say he succumbed to his injuries during the zero-gee transfer."

Told you transfers were dangerous. Dammit.

Bort's impassive expression faded into a much sadder one. His eyes fell to the carpet of Marlene's office and he shook his head slowly, before clutching his jaw with his left hand.

A lot of thoughts went through his head — memories he and Art O'Thomson had shared over years of service together. *To draw parallels, this was similar to me losing someone like Charlie or Karen. People who'd been with me for so long... gee, wonder what that feels like.*

Bort knew. He closed his eyes, and said nothing.

"I hope you know we did everything we could for him," Marlene lowered the pad to her desk, her tone still a little cold. *Later she'd express regrets about that — she always felt she was a little too chilly the first time she dealt with Bort. He never held it against her.*

Now he simply nodded, "I saw he was well looked after on *Wolf*. And I don't doubt you tried."

He sounded grim, but not unconvinced. *As a professional in our line of work, he just understood that sometimes the doctors can't make the miracles happen. People do die, as Elise De Winter had already discovered, and more were yet to find out.*

Marlene watched Bort as he stood in silence for another few seconds, then he opened his eyes and shook his head, "When the war is officially over, I'll need to get a message through to his family. His daughter's going to be married soon, he was supposed to be there."

"Bitter business," Marlene said quietly, shaking her head. "As soon as channels are available, I'll make sure you have access to one. For now, your government's not allowing us any access to their comm grid, obviously."

"Of course they're not," Bort said, a little exasperated. Then he turned and slapped the door frame with an open hand, "Because if they let you send humanitarian messages through, we might lose the war."

No questioning the bitterness in those words. They were the last of the conversation; Bort opened the door and left Marlene's office without even a formal farewell. She didn't mind.

After sparing a few seconds to reflect on how Bort McWebsbert defied expectations, Marlene sighed and got back to work. The war would be over soon.

CHAPTER THIRTY

PEACE AT LAST

Later that same day, the Martian government contacted us through their embassy on Ceres (the same asteroid from the accord) and called for an immediate cessation of hostilities.

No surrender was offered, because that would have been embarrassing, but they offered an immediate ceasefire. They also had a few conditions to go with that request: a freeze on all warship movement on both sides, an admission by the Empire that we started the war, and an exchange of prisoners. Interestingly, they also demanded we turn seven of our officers over to their custody — officers who reportedly committed war crimes against Martians during the conflict.

But none of the seven officers they listed actually ever existed. My guess is they were invented people, created by the Martian propaganda machine as effigies that could be used to blame the Empire for all the evil that happened in war. But the Martian people probably believed these men (all men) were genuine monsters, and thus the Martian government had to be seen to at least be making an attempt to bring them to justice.

Fortunately, officers like 'Post Captain Killer Stryker' and 'Commander Lance Dye' didn't really exist. Honestly, the propaganda…

Anyway, our Foreign Office laughed their asses off at the demands, and sent back their own terms: a ceasefire would be accepted, but Defense Command ships would be fully mobile. All of the other conditions were taken as a poor attempt at humor by the Martian government. We weren't giving an inch.

And we absolutely didn't have to. Their subsequent request for an unconditional ceasefire was received by Douglas Pope and Emperor Luther Gregory III at 0441 Earth Standard Time, on 28 November 2233. It was accepted, and by the end of business that day, Parliament had ratified it.

There were literally celebrations in the street. All across the Empire, people went a little bit nuts. There was some drinking and some looting, as is prone to happen during that sort of celebration, but I won't get into any of it.

I'll take this chance, instead, to visit some friends and see their particular reactions.

Marshal Samuels had just gotten to sleep in his house on Belt Two. Because of different time zones, it was obviously night there when the news arrived. The comm beeped on his bedside, which always woke him instantly, but his wife Mel (the DCI station chief and gymnastics coach) beat him to the key.

"What?" he asked, sitting up in bed.

The answer came back in an excited outburst: "Sir, word from Earth: peace!"

Marshal heard the word, but it didn't register. He looked at Mel, and she looked at him, and it still didn't register.

Then it sort of did.

"Alert all Defense Command bases to prepare for operations in support of the civil power. We may have looting to deal with," Marshal ordered, swinging his legs over the side of his bed, then getting to his feet.

"Sir?" the Lieutenant on the comm was confused. Wasn't this the greatest news ever?

Mel was out of bed and grabbing her comm next. She called into the DCI station, "We just got word. I want reports on any troublemakers who could try to use the chaos as a chance to execute attacks."

Marshal pulled on his uniform tunic, then went over to the bedside comm, "I'll be up in a minute. Call Commander Kellerman to oversee base security."

He then killed the comm.

Marshal and Mel Samuels went to work. That's how they celebrated the arrival of peace. Talk about dedicated to their jobs!

It took most of the following day for it really to sink in for them — that the war really was over. It wasn't license to relax, because there was so much left to do, but when it finally did click they had a celebratory supper.

And then went back to work.

Mark Gunney had been transferred to *Bonaventure* for treatment of his extreme frostbite. As he put it, though, if he had frostbite, then he'd been bitten by something rather large — possibly a shark, or a prehistoric water creature that survived undiscovered for millions of years in the ocean depths.

Both legs and both arms were out of action. Parts of them were alive, but other parts had been murdered by buildups of ice crystals within their cells. It was going to take close to a year for surgery and gene therapy to regenerate the damage, and he honestly wasn't looking forward to the wait.

The doctor who brought him word of the end of the war had just taken over his case, and he'd be lying if he suggested he didn't find her very attractive. Double torture for him, then.

"Peace," she said with a smile as she came to his bedside and started checking the vitals on screen.

"Shit," was his reply, so she frowned at him.

"I thought you'd be pleased?"

He shook his head, "You must know my reputation. There's fun to be had during tonight's celebrations, and I'll be stuck here with no working appendages."

Yes, he was testing her.

She didn't let him down.

Checking the monitor, she narrowed her eyes, "According to my scans, you do have one working appendage."

Sigh. Yes. She said it.

He grinned, "But no stabilizers."

"That would mean more work for me, wouldn't it?"

Oh man.

"You'd be well compensated."

"Well, spacer, one of the perks you get as a DC officer is free medical service."

Not. Kidding.

Anyway, I'd say Mark had his hands full, but they'd been rendered useless by ice crystal damage, so… well… no, there is absolutely no way I can finish this scene without getting into trouble.

Though most comm lines were jammed almost as soon as the news of peace arrived, Bruce Arama had gotten his hands on a code that let him send signals through the secured Admiralty net. This code was only available to Flag Officers, so there's no way to know how he got it.

I mean, I gave it to him, but other than that who's to know how he got access to it.

With the much-appreciated ability to send messages through the din, he sat down on the end of his bed aboard *Adelaide* and recorded a message to his wife and daughters. They wouldn't yet have had confirmation that he survived the Fleet Clash — there was no communication from officers to families that soon after a battle, because we didn't want to chance giving up too much information on our casualties to Martian listeners.

But now, it didn't matter. And Bruce, to whom Karen and I owed a whole damned lot, and who frankly deserved some recognition for his outstanding service, got to call home. Lines were jammed across the Empire, but not for him — or for *Adelaide's* crew, because that code made its way around.

Those survivors of the Forge, Mercury and the Clash got to send warm wishes to their families.

Aboard *Wolf*, there was a lot of celebrating too. Jim Hannigan and Bunny Philips curled up in front of a fire (a vid of a crackling fire that Jim played on the wallscreen in his quarters) and enjoyed a bottle of champagne.

Felicia Khalid wrote a letter to her family.

Alicia Morgan and Andy Jensen went to a movie being screened on the rec deck.

Shelby McLaws and Adrienne Thomson went for a swim.

Andrea Kiley sat in her cabin in the darkness.

It was a momentous day.

But Karen and I barely paid any attention to it.

Because *Persephone Praxidice* had docked with *Venus One*, and the hospital was filling. Pretty soon there'd be no keeping the truth from Lia, so we had to find out exactly what the situation was, and then try to minimize any damage.

The war that had done so much to change both Karen and me was over.

And we weren't really paying attention.

CHAPTER THIRTY-ONE

CUE VIOLINS

Tragic romances suck.

I mean, some of the movies are good and compelling and emotional blah blah blah.

Reality: they suck.

When people you care about love each other, and then all this shit (yes shit!) happens, it sucks.

It's bad.

It's awful.

So whatever the movies tell you about how tragically romantic and moving a wounded warrior is, or a wounded heiress is, or whatever... it's all crap.

It is by no means easy. How do you deliver bad news to someone who is in critical condition, and near death?

Well, there was no more getting around it now.

Karen and I went down to the *Venus One* hospital together, and as we entered the emergency reception area and passed the triage bays, it really was a completely different place. There were wounded women and men on every bed, and the medical staff was moving around in blurry streaks, giving drugs, stabilizing a few patients who had indeed gone critical or blue during the zero-gee transfers, and basically squaring away 2,700 injured personnel.

We were briefly taken aback by the scale of the chaos, but eventually we moved through it, remembering the way to the corridor where Lia's room was located.

Before coming here, we'd managed to contact Rufus Chang, who had come aboard *Persephone Praxidice* even though he wasn't seriously wounded. Being the last man left on his feet (or with feet, as Ben Belete joked later) from *Wolf's* Special Branch teams, he'd been given a pass on the rest of the Mercury operations.

He'd be meeting us outside the room, because even though he didn't know Lia at all, he'd been Charlie's partner through the assault, right up to the end. That would hopefully make things a bit easier on everyone.

True to form, the Major with the mismatched eyes was waiting outside the door when we arrived. He straightened up when he saw us, and then we shook hands with him as we got close enough.

"Great to see you, Rufus," I said earnestly, and he shook his head.

"I wish there could be more of us."

Karen and I nodded, and then we went over the plans again. We had to do this right. It might seem ridiculous, but we couldn't just blurt it out — we had to do everything possible to ease Lia into the news. Or she'd be back in a coma, and that would be very unfortunate.

It took a few moments to sort out all the details, right down to who would stand where, and who had the mirror. After all that was sorted out, we went in.

I was going in behind the curtain alone — now that the hospital was packed with wounded, the curtain was an extra shroud of privacy that Lia dearly deserved. I entered reluctantly, but kept my discipline.

She was awake now, and her eyes jumped to me as soon as I walked in. I had a speech all ready to go for her, but dammit, she read my expression.

I don't know how it was even possible for her to grow more pale than she already was, but she did. Her blood pressure and heart rate started climbing too, though in her eyes I could see her making a conscious effort not to jump to conclusions.

"Hi," I said lamely, then edged up to the side of her bed and took her hand.

"Hey," she replied.

I nodded. There was nothing to nod at, but I nodded.

She closed her eyes, "You lied before."

This time I didn't nod, even though I did have something to nod at.

"I wanted to believe you."

I still didn't manage to nod.

"Charlie's not lightly injured."

She didn't want to say 'Charlie's dead'.

None of us wanted to say that.

"He's not lightly injured," I repeated.

She turned her eyes away. She didn't really want to hear what I had to say next.

"After the way you reacted aboard *Nova Scotia*, we didn't want to just blurt it out. Didn't think it'd be good for your health."

She said nothing.

"Rufus," I called, and the Major stepped in.

"I don't think you've met, but you know of Rufus Chang, Charlie's counterpart."

Lia nodded as much as she could with her head largely immobilized.

Rufus moved up the other side of the bed, staying near the curtain, "Pleased to meet you, m'Lady. I'm sorry about the circumstances."

She was locking her jaw now, feeling like she was in a nightmare she couldn't escape.

"The blast, m'Lady, killed everyone left in our combined squad, except for Captain Ben Belete."

She closed her eyes.

"Charlie suffered severe internal injuries, and was put into a medical coma. The prognosis was not good."

She bit her lip and waited for the news.

"The doctors still don't know if he'll ever wake up."

She closed her eyes tighter.

Rufus' last words took a few seconds to register.

And then her eyes opened, and you better believe her blood pressure spiked, "He's alive?"

Rufus nodded, and drew back the curtain that was behind him. Karen was standing there, holding up a mirror.

Lia couldn't turn her head, but thanks to that mirror she could turn her eyes enough to see that, lying in the next bed over, and even more bandaged up than she was, was a comatose Charlie Peters.

"Oh God," she just about wailed, I think it's fair to say — but she wailed it with joy, not distress.

She'd convinced herself Charlie was dead and gone. But he was still breathing. Some of the time under his own power.

Some say if it had been anyone other than Charlie Peters, he'd be dead. And not because Charlie was innately tougher than every other human being, but because people knew Charlie's reputation, and there were people like Greg Noyce and Zail Patel in orbit over Mercury after the blast.

These people, who knew Charlie and knew what he meant to people like Lia, Karen and myself, refused to just let him go. There was a very good chance that he would never wake up... but they hadn't given up hope, and neither would we.

Because the real world is often much less forgiving than the movies. But sometimes — just sometimes — the real world out-impossibles the fictional world. If anyone could wake up after that blast, it had to be Charlie.

Dammit, it had to be my friend Charlie.

We hoped.

So we'd held off on the news for as long as we could, because we didn't want Lia worrying about whether or not Charlie would survive the cruise from Mercury, or the zero-gee transfer, or the move onto his new hospital bed. Now she knew, and she could actually see him, and listen to the chimes from his monitor panel.

She would have wanted to be next to his bed for this, no matter what condition she was in, and now she was.

It was as much as we could do to take the edge off for her.

So now they'd live together, or die together, or one of them would be witness to the death of the other.

Like I said, tragic romances are crap. Bastards.

"I think I hate you," Lia looked at me after a moment, but it was only a fleeting look before her eyes turned back to the mirror, and Charlie.

I shrugged, "That would be entirely fair."

For all the work Lia does on façades — and despite her ability to keep them up in some form, even when mostly immobilized in a hospital bed — she couldn't fool the monitors. Her heart rate and her blood pressure started to decline as she continued to stare at the mirror. She was putting things together in her head. We hadn't taken anything away from her by not telling her about Charlie's condition — it wasn't as though she could have seen him any sooner.

All we'd done was save her worrying about him until she was right next to him.

And being right next to him was as much as she could have asked for if she was healthy under the same circumstances. Actually, this was better.

"I don't hate you," she said quietly, and whacked me lamely in the leg with her hand. "And now they can't throw me out when visiting hours are over."

Dammit, Lia is awesome. And don't you forget it.

That was as much good humor as she could muster just now, which was more than fair enough. Eventually Karen wheeled a cart over and propped the mirror on it so she could move, and we left Lia in silence half an hour later. There was nothing more any of us could do — we'd just have to wait and see whether Charlie Peters could survive.

CHAPTER THIRTY-TWO

POSITIONING

Emperor Luther Gregory III was making a public address to the entire Empire.

That, of course, was his right — one of the powers he still retained, despite the erosion of privilege the throne had been suffering from for forty years. I don't know if I've explained this particularly clearly in these books, but the reason Luther Gregory was so determined to go after the Prime Minister — and by extension, Defense Command — was because decades of political evolution had been rendering him increasingly irrelevant.

Remember, Defense Command was such a huge (arguably cumbersome) operation because it gave Parliament a single, unified force with which to battle the Emperor's power. He couldn't use his army to overpower local police or government garrisons because all those police and garrisons were, in fact, part of Defense Command.

To attack a Detective Inspector in Canada was to attack a Special Brancher on Belt Two, or a frigate at Venus. Having that sort of backup made police immune to intimidation from the Imperial Army.

Predictably, a man with Luther Gregory's ego disliked this situation. He was the Emperor, after all. He wanted to command the Empire with as much personal might as Luther Gordon the Great, our first Emperor from the twenty-first century.

What Luther *Gregory* failed to appreciate, though, was that having a similar name didn't make him at all like the man who created our Empire. Luther Gordon the Great united a divided world that had nearly been shattered by terrorism and war. He snatched the Earth Empire from the jaws of destruction. Some think that, had he not come to power, the Omega plague would have been released, and the human race might have been eliminated... except maybe for some survivors shot off into deep space on a desperate mission.

If you ever want to be depressed, go to the pre-Imperial archives and look up the planning documents for the Genesis mission... especially the false 'bible' the United Nations created when they decided the surviving colonists would need a new religion to keep them united. Classy stuff. I can't imagine how the mission could have succeeded, let alone brought about anything good...

Anyway, sorry, I digress. Luther Gordon had managed to save our planet through a mix of good political instincts and personal force. He brought governments together, inspired people, and mobilized big business for the greater good. His support for the Felix Wolfe Corporation led to us developing grav-control technology, which really made space travel possible.

His shoes are kind of tough to fill.

And certainly, they could not be filled by Luther Gregory III, who could only claim to be a snappy dresser, and a decent public speaker.

These were the kind of bitter thoughts that were running through Daragh Ryan's head as he viewed the Emperor's address from his office in Admiralty House. He was alone, watching the bastard speak, and that was just as well.

"Fucking stupid fucking arrogant fucking bastard..." he was grumbling.

Yep, literally every second word out of Daragh's mouth was—

"Fuck you fucking fucker..."

Daragh was talking over parts of the speech, but I should repeat the salient points, for no other reason than to set up the massive problems the Emperor was creating for 2234, and to decrease the amount of colorful language in this chapter.

"Now Defense Command has accomplished its aims, and the Imperial Army has cowed resistance on Mercury, the Martian enemy has been forced to succumb," he said. Notice how the Imperial Army did all the work in winning the war, according to him? "With peace in the offing, I see it as my duty as your Emperor, and the head of state for this great Empire, to go to Mars, and to personally lead the peace discussions."

Of course he did. Refer to Daragh's remarks above for my feeling about what that made him.

"I am, of course, very specially skilled in these matters. The interaction of our Empire with outside forces is not simply a legislative concern, but one that draws upon the very soul of our collective identity."

WHO DOES HE THINK HE'S KIDDING?

Sorry. First, in no way was he 'skilled' for this. Second, what exactly *is* the 'soul of our collective identity'?

"With the help of the Prime Minister and his people, I will extend the branches of peace to our lost Martian children. They will come to see that we are a benevolent relation, and all the bitterness that has come before will be washed away. A new, bright and peaceful future will await the solar system. This is my mission as your Emperor, one for which I was truly chosen."

I honestly have a hard time believing anyone who says they didn't roll their eyes at this bucket of shit. I'm sorry, you know I don't usually swear, but COME ON.

Charlie and Lia were sharing a room on their respective deathbeds because *Venus One* was choked with Defense Command wounded — people who had served Parliament and the Empire, not Luther Gregory III.

But he had the gall to go on vid to the entire Empire and proclaim that he was the anointed one, set to fulfill his destiny as our great leader?

What's scary to me is that a solid twenty to thirty percent of people seemed to approve of him. That's not a majority, obviously, but it was enough of an approval rating for him to believe he had a strong mandate from the people. Don't ask me how he worked that out — clearly mathematics was one of those skills that really qualified him to be the epic savior of our solar system.

But realistically, he did have billions of people on his side, or at least saying 'yeah, okay'.

"I look forward to this great endeavor, and to making this solar system a more wonderful place for our mighty and unprecedented Empire. As your Emperor, it is my right, privilege and joy to speak for all of you. I have heard your voices, and through me the Martian President will hear them too. I bid you all anon!"

Okay, just in case you're wondering, 'I bid you all anon', when translated into non-pretentious-asshole-speak, means 'I bid you all tomorrow'. That used to be the way people talked, a few CENTURIES ago.

Fortunately, it was the end of his broadcast.

Daragh nearly — nearly — blasted out his office wallscreen with his shotgun. Honestly. The only thing that stopped him was a secure call from the PMO, that showed up on the screen before he could load his gun.

Douglas Pope and Craig Macdonald appeared, both looking suitably disgusted.

"Wait now, I wasn't finished basking in the afterglow of how awesome that silk stocking full of shit thinks he is," Daragh protested their appearance, and at least that got a laugh from the two politicos. You really had to laugh.

The fact that Luther Gregory III was our Emperor was less and less tolerable. But there was nothing we could do — we had a peace treaty to negotiate and sign. We couldn't even think about asking the House of Lords to recall the Emperor... that was a whole constitutional problem that I'll explain in a later book.

For now, we had to be focused.

After Daragh cooled his hot head (just a little), Pope got on to business.

"We're going to have to go out there too. Can you recall a strong force of ships for a convoy to Mars, probably in late December?"

Daragh nodded to the PM, "I can. I know shitbrain is going to take *Ark Royal*, so I'll find a good skipper to put aboard that ship too. Someone who can keep tabs on the fucker."

"Do you really need to keep up with the profanity?" Pope asked with a gentle frown.

"Fuck yes," Daragh said. "I'm Irish."

For some reason (perhaps the amount of Irish in my own family), that makes me laugh. I guess all my Irish swearing genes were suppressed by my Chinese politeness genes. Wait, is that stereotyping my multicultural ancestors? I can just hear Lord Tam mounting another staunch defense of Chinese rights in the face of supposed bigotry.

Anyway.

"I'll ask John to come in with some elite ships. We'll get you there safely, Prime Minister. And then it'll be up to you to keep that asshole from destroying this victory."

Pope's eyebrows raised, and he sighed, "I look forward to that."

That was sarcasm. He obviously didn't.

But this was the challenge he, and we, would have to deal with in 2234. This Emperor and his designs on us would have to be stopped... even if that meant a coup that wasn't 'almost'. His reckoning was coming.

And after that, so was mine.

And Karen's.

But that's still to come. How about we shift gears here, and get away from the self-absorbed and completely useless supposed leader of the Empire, and get back to the supposedly (but not really) self-absorbed and entirely capable actual leader of the Hawke Protectorate.

Because who wouldn't prefer Lia Hawke to Luther Gregory III?

If you don't, then as the Martians say: it means you secretly want to eat puppies.

CHAPTER THIRTY-THREE

YOU KNEW IT WAS COMING

One of my editors is pretty livid with me, for a reason that I personally think is both slightly nonsensical and completely hilarious.

This editor, who I'll refer to as 'F', has been working on this series with me for two years. Last year, when we held that big gala thing to celebrate some award or something, I introduced him to two of my dearest friends in the world: Charlie Peters and Lia Hawke.

Keep that in mind.

Now, as he read this draft, he got very mad. He still edits manuscripts with pen and paper (sorry, trees), so his anger was reflected in much red ink in many margins. And all of it was to this effect: 'Stop holding us hostage — tell whether Charlie lived or died'.

At first, I thought he was trying to take the perspective of a reader who's never watched vid news. Because it's pretty hard to do that and *not* see news about either Lord Peters or Lady Hawke and their excellent governing practices in the Hawke Protectorate.

But apparently, he really somehow failed to remember meeting Charlie and Lia in person. And he actually didn't put 'Lord Peters' from the news and 'Charlie Peters' from the books together in his head.

This baffles me. Either he's sort of joking about not realizing, or he really didn't pay attention. Or maybe he hit his head.

But that last one isn't funny, because when people hit their head so hard they forget things, it's serious business requiring gene therapy on the brain.

Anyway, let me apologize to you if somehow you were being held in suspense about Charlie's actual fate. I thought that the number of times I've mentioned talking to him in the here and now (at the time of writing) would have made it pretty clear that he's alive and well.

I was just excluding him in an attempt to replicate the uncertainty we all felt, and specifically, that Lia suffered during those long days.

And, I suppose, if you're reading this years and years from now, and couldn't turn on the news and see Lord Charles Peters on the vid, you might have wondered if he actually did die.

But obviously, he didn't.

Come on, it's Charlie. Even when immobilized in bed, he could still kill you with water vapor. Seriously. He could make that stuff explode. Somehow.

He's always a big hit at birthday parties.

Now, there's no question that Charlie was in extremely rough shape. The worst thing — the near-fatal thing — was the brain swelling. It had been pretty intense, to the point where they'd drilled some holes in his skull to relieve pressure. I know, ick. Brain swelling is a very tricky thing to treat — most of our drugs are only moderately effective, because when you're playing in the brain you always have to be exceedingly careful.

Gene therapy can rebuild pathways that are destroyed, but often it can't restore lost memories or personality. Kris Jacobs battled with this, after her radiation dose.

But the swelling started to come down on its own with time. Because I'm secretly a bit of a romantic, I think it was some cosmic thing that involved Lia being in the next bed over.

Yeah, go ahead and groan. I still think the two of them being together in the same room actually helped. Karma, the power of love, luck… call it anything. I think his chances of dying decreased when he got into that particular hospital bed.

Even if it was only because he was too stubborn and thoughtful to die with Lia watching. He'd never inflict that on her.

Once the brain swelling started to subside, the other injuries weren't actually that horrific. One of his lungs and one of his kidneys had been rendered to mush, but his tac vest had saved him from a fair amount of upper body harm. Being thrown down that flight of stairs had also given him extra cover against the blast wind.

Some joints and tendons were screwed up, and numerous bones were either fractured or shattered, but those sorts of injuries were pretty easy to fix, all things being equal.

Growing a replacement bone is generally pretty straightforward these days. It's the injuries where you have to repair damage to dead or partially-dead tissue that take the longest, because you can't just cut out the old and install the new. Again, ask Kris after her recovery from the rad poisoning. Or ask Mark Gunney how arduous it was, trying to breathe new life into shredded cells that needed to heal enough to replace themselves.

This is all to say that, once Charlie was on the mend, we were all pretty confident he was going to make a full recovery. He'd have a hell of a lot of scars to show for the war, but as prices to pay go, that was a fair one.

He was alive.

Most of his people weren't.

When he woke up in his hospital bed, that was the first thought he had, too.

Well, not quite: first he thought the stairs he'd landed on were surprisingly squishy. He didn't realize he was in a hospital. He just remembered the flash — and that's all he'd ever remember of the explosion itself.

Waking up, then, he expected to be injured, and he expected to see pieces of his team lying all around him.

He knew no one could have walked away from that… pardoning the black humor in relation to Ben Belete's lack of legs.

But as Charlie blinked a few times, his keen Special Brancher senses became fully aware of his new reality. It felt like a hospital. Not an infirmary or med bay, but a proper hospital. He could feel the unpleasantly numbing effects of various drugs, which suggested he was severely injured. There wasn't much sound of commotion outside, either, which meant he probably wasn't at any sort of a frontline hospital.

Pulling all that together in his head, Charlie determined that he must have been virtually killed by that blast, and transferred all the way back to Venus for treatment.

See, he's a sharp cookie, even when slightly maimed. Er. More than slightly.

What the hell is good about a 'sharp cookie', by the way?

Soon Charlie discovered he was in a neck brace, so there would be no head turning. That was a minor frustration, but being a Special Brancher with special skills, he could still move his eyes without turning his head. Wish I had that ability... oh wait.

Jeeze, listen to me. Even as I write this, I'm starting to channel the completely immature glee I felt when I got the message that he was awake. But more on that in a while.

Charlie spotted a mirror on a stand next to his bed, and he did his best to frown at it. Why would they put a mirror on a cart, and why would they put it in an inconvenient spot between the two beds in the room?

Focusing on the reflection, he found he was looking at a very bandaged individual — so bandaged that her pale face was barely visible.

He literally didn't recognize the face at first — Lia was so pale and so bandaged that some of the normal cues to her appearance were muted, and more importantly, he had absolutely no reason to think that she'd be heavily bandaged and sharing his hospital room.

I mean, how likely would it be for them both to be grievously injured like this and...

"Sweet merciful crap... Lia?"

Charlie's first words after waking up. I think he wouldn't have minded having them back — to say something more dashing.

Lia blinked, and her eyes leapt to the mirror, where they caught his.

Holy God, what a moment.

I'm assured by both of them that time stopped. Just simply stopped. Because both of them were thinking similar things: thank God it's him/her... oh hell, what really happened to him/her?

Lia had expected that she'd start bawling as soon as Charlie woke up — she'd convinced herself that she'd finally be overcome by emotion, and that violins would be piped in over the intercom and she'd cry and cry.

Instead, she was completely surprised, so she answered unremarkably: "Um. Hi."

Then she actually felt a little embarrassed, which I find monumentally funny, in a strange way. She was embarrassed that she'd been shot up during a big Naval battle?

"You're not just bandaged up to be moral support for me, are you?" Charlie's question was a little bit hopeful, and a lot absurd.

Our Lady Hawke contemplated saying 'yes' and then trying to sell the joke, but instead she sighed and tried to shake her head. That didn't work because of the various wraps, but Charlie got the message.

"What the hell happened? I told Ken to watch your back..." he didn't sound angry, just confused. He also discovered that he was short of breath due to being down a lung, so he had to control his breathing and not get too worked up.

"He did, but they got a lucky shot and I got... well... lots of glass shrapnel. But they got me out and here, and now the doctors are pretty convinced I won't die."

Charlie opened his mouth to say something, and then didn't know what to say, and then figured something else out. Something I don't think I would have expected him to say, and which I don't know if he expected to say himself: "Well, you're too pretty to die."

Lia smiled, "Aw, really? Even all bandaged up?"

"Well. That's not my favorite look on you. I'd prefer you weren't, you know, covered in bloody bandages."

"Oh so you get blown up and that turns you into a fashion critic?"

Charlie would have shrugged, but there were too many things braced, "I must have hit my head."

"Your brain was very swollen. They had to drill holes in your head," she confirmed.

"Well that explains it. But you are still pretty."

Lia smiled even more brightly — no easy feat, given her state.

They stared at each other in the mirror for a moment more, then he said what was really on his mind, "I'm really, really happy to see you."

"Me too," she beamed. "Love you."

"You too."

A profound sense of relief settled in after that. They didn't stop staring at each other... why would they? Together in a Venusian hospital room, both bandaged virtually from head to toe, both going to live.

Why the hell would they not look at each other?

Lia's emotions didn't hit a low ebb, either. She expected them too, but the elation at Charlie being awake seemed to melt all the angst away. I'm sure it would have been more movie-like if she wept and such, but she didn't feel like it.

In fact, it wasn't too long before she'd gone the opposite direction: "So, how long before you think we'll be able to start comparing sexy scars?"

Charlie didn't skip a beat, "What's to compare? Yours will be sexy, mine will be manly."

"Don't pull out semantics when I'm trying to proposition you!" she protested in reply.

If he could have, he would have turned his head, and so would she. Instead, they grinned at each other via the mirror, and then they started laughing at the complete and utter absurdity of that statement, for so many reasons.

These two were back together. And you know what, they weren't going to really be apart ever again.

So there.

CHAPTER THIRTY-FOUR

KAREN WAS DANCING

Of course Karen was dancing.

The war was over, Charlie was alive, and all things being equal, it was a good day. It had been a while since her last 'boogie', though, so she lost track of time as the music went on. When she didn't turn up for supper, I guessed what was going on and headed next door to confirm my suspicions.

I was entirely correct.

I knocked and got no answer, so I opened the hatch and stepped in. The music was up pretty loud, and she was entirely lost in it.

Or she simply didn't care to stop when I stepped in.

Her back was to me, and the music this time was different than her usual fare — her body was rolling to this stuff more slowly, more rhythmically than usual. It appeared, at least to one who claims to have no rhythm for dancing, to be a much smoother, more relaxing way of contorting her body.

I'm sure she must have heard me come in, but she didn't turn around. Her hips kept swinging, and she seemed to be reaching up towards the ceiling with no particular purpose as she twisted and counter-twisted.

Ha, I'm making this sound like a frigate doing maneuvers.

Just picture… well. Nevermind. Picture what you like, I know what I was seeing.

And I was in a damned gleeful mood. I'd just come from the hospital where I'd seen Charlie and Lia, and watched for a few minutes with unabashed joy as they taunted each other. They were both trapped in really torturous conditions but they were keeping each others' spirits up.

That was simply great to see. After all the pressure and the worry and stress… that was very good to see.

Combine that complete elation at their improving situation with the fact that the war was over, and you'll get something that approaches a loose explanation for what I did next.

Like I say, I'm pretty sure Karen heard me come in, so when I appeared right behind her, she wasn't surprised.

No, I didn't start dancing. Pfft.

Well, maybe I shifted my weight from foot to foot a little, but I promise it was out of time with the music.

Well, mostly out of time.

Partially.

Alright, so maybe it *was* in time with the music, but honestly, no. Come on. I don't dance. You know that.

My right hand ended up around Karen's waist, which evidently was an invitation for her to lean back, shoulders against chest, while she continued to sway and twist with the beat. So that sort of guided my motion a bit, because as her shoulders moved my body had to move with them. Otherwise she could have fallen over.

So I wasn't dancing, just helping make sure she didn't fall over. Which I think we can all agree was a noble pursuit.

Clearly not dancing, though.

Don't start any rumors that it was dancing, because Mik will give me hell for them.

Though, if you're going to catch hell for something, it should really, absolutely be this.

After a moment, Karen turned her head so that her nose was nearly pressed into my cheek. Her eyes were closed, but her smile was so relaxed. It was as though, for just a few moments (or hours, however long we could manage without dinner), the weight of the job was off her shoulders.

Karen loved to dance. She loved the feeling in her muscles when she could just let them move. It made her feel strong. Perhaps that sounds strange, but that's what it gave her. Confidence in her own strength, without requiring any violence of action to prove it.

She could be strong and smooth.

So this was her celebration. This, to her, was a way of saying that after all the shooting was said and done (we thought), she was still here, and still strong, and she didn't have to worry about shooting ships, or people, or driving spikes through heads.

This is a very strange analogy, but it was like a dog who finally got out from behind his fence after years of having to stay in there, relentlessly patrolling. Now he could run and play.

Now Karen felt like she really could let herself dance again. Sure, she'd done it now and then during the war, but that wasn't the same. This felt different to her.

I could use this opportunity to start fore-shadowing for all the trouble that was yet to come, because there was plenty. I could talk about the Emperor. I could talk about Egesta. I could talk about the Governor of Etat Valcour.

I could point out that this was one of the last times I'd get to dance with Karen before... well.

But I'm not going to. Because in deference to the peace that she was feeling, I'm just going to say that it really was brilliant. The expression on her face said it all: the war was truly over. And whatever else we had to deal with, at least it wasn't going to be a war.

I could dance to that.

I don't think we said a word to each other for hours. We really didn't need to. I'm sure we ate some dinner at some point, but I hope to always carry the very vivid memories I have about that carefree evening. It was a pocket of peace in the midst of a whole lot of madness.

We danced together, and all around us, *Wolf* prepared for the next stages: the chaos after the war.

There was plenty left to do.

We'd worry about it tomorrow.

CHAPTER THIRTY-FIVE

END OF AN ERA

I always end these books on the last chapter with Karen and me, but I started this book oddly (with Bort) and now I think I'm going to finish it oddly too.

The day before *Wolf* pulled out of Venus space, I went to visit Charlie. Lia was out for some minor surgery when I arrived — nothing serious, just cleaning up some wounds ahead of stem cell grafts and such things — so Charlie was on his own. Meaning no offense to Lia, that was probably just as well.

This was around two weeks after the end of the war, and Charlie had been making progress. He could now turn his head, and sort of sit up. Slightly. He was still mostly immobilized, but all things being equal he was recovering quickly.

Anyway. I came by to visit him because we were heading to Earth to start putting together the convoy that would take the Emperor and the Prime Minister to Mars for negotiations (by the way, next book I'll explain how stupid it was to go there instead of bringing them to us). When I arrived, he was leaning slightly up in bed, reading a magazine pad that one of the nurses had left for him.

Even though half his head was wrapped, he still heard me coming from a mile away, so without looking up he started talking, "Have you seen this? *Scientific Imperial* has an interview with Forrest Douglas about us rescuing him at Io..."

I hadn't seen it, so as I paced over to the side of his medical bed, I frowned, "News to me."

Charlie sort-of-nodded (as best he could), then held the magazine up and turned it towards me, scrolling the page so I could see one of the featured vids: Major Peters and Forrest Douglas chatting in the lobby of Io's DCHQ building. It was probably one of the vids Jocko had recorded while he'd been down there.

Now, if you'll recall, Forrest Douglas was the smartest man in the Empire, and he looked the part, thanks to his gray frizzy afro. Charlie had been delighted to meet him, and had chatted with the man as much as he could before getting on to the business of destroying the Io dome.

Leaning to look more closely at the magazine screen, I read the caption beneath the vid, "Douglas enjoyed his discussions with Major Charlie Peters, of Belt Squadron fame, on the subjects of artificial intelligence. He thinks the Major could have a career in the field, should he choose to leave the service."

Charlie sort-of-nodded again, "That's what I read."

"Nice of him to say," I straightened up with a smile. "Career change time?"

That question was probably a lot more loaded than it sounded, and Charlie knew it. Lowering the magazine, he sort-of-nodded again, "I think so."

Of course it was. Leaving aside the fact that he was in pieces right now — a fact that good doctors would correct, mostly, over the coming months — the war was over, and his squad was dead. All of them, except Ben Belete, were gone.

We both drifted to that line of thought at the same time, and the kind words of the Empire's smartest man fell from our minds.

"I'm going to start recording messages to their families as soon as I can sit upright," Charlie said.

I sighed, then nodded. Taking a couple of steps backward, I sat on the side of Lia's empty bed, then folded my arms.

"All of them. Except Ben."

Charlie stared ahead for a moment, then nodded, "All of them."

I hope I've done enough in these books so far to convey how significant that revelation really was. Even after two weeks, it was still just sinking in. For years, the officers from Charlie's squad had been the ones who we turned to in the most dangerous moments, and who kept us alive. There'd been turnover during that time, of course, but 'Charlie's team' had always existed.

Now, only Charlie did. And that was profoundly sad.

Worse for him, too, because he wasn't with them. Survivor's guilt is a bit of a cliché these days, I think. It's casually thrown around in movies, to make the audience love the hero a little more when she or he alone walks out of the fire, scarred but living.

In reality, it just damned well hurts. Charlie knew he'd be a fool to curse his luck at being alive — and to sharing a room, at long last, with the woman he'd been apart from for all these years. But knowing that all his people — *his* people — were gone... well. It was good that he loved Lia as much as he did. Sappy as it sounds, that was one thing he could use to reconcile himself with the guilt. He had something brilliant to look forward to, and a chance to make a real difference. His squad had helped give him that chance, keeping him alive through many dangerous days, and he wouldn't let that effort be for naught.

But they weren't the only losses, and Charlie knew that: "I heard about Elise. And about Erica."

Elise De Winter, as a member of the Belt Squadron family, was a sharp loss... but Erica Martin had been with us back aboard *Friendly*, in the old days. That one hit us both.

"Mark's down with severe frostbite," I replied slowly. "So I'm sending a message to Morgan and the kids. I'm also going to ask Marshal to go and see them."

Erica's family — including her two beautiful young daughters — was on Belt Two. Eventually, we'd all make our way there to see them, but for now it would just be messages.

"I remember that wedding," Charlie said quietly, and I nodded. Erica and Morgan had finally tied the knot shortly after we'd moved from *Friendly* to *Wolf*.

These were just some of the people who were gone.

For a long few minutes, neither Charlie nor I said anything... we just thought about them, and everyone else who had been lost. And about those people who were still with us. Because remember, the good news was that many of the wounded — people like Kris Jacobs — were recovering, and they'd be back.

But when you boiled it all down, if you took the Belt Squadron that fought at the Battle of Belt Two, there was precious little of it left. For one reason or another, the old team had broken up.

And right here, that was going to happen again.

"So. You going to make an honest woman out of my little sister?" I asked that question with as much humor as I could manage, and Charlie chuckled briefly.

"She's your sister now, is she?"

"Something like that. Don't break her heart, or I'll challenge you to a duel, and you'll have to kill me."

Charlie winced slightly, "A duel? Really? Who actually duels anymore?"

Obviously this was before these books came out, and I started having to fight lots of people who felt their honor was besmirched. Though that's tapered off, lately — word must have gotten around that I'm a good shot.

"Stop evading. You and Lia, happily ever after, right? There is good news to end this war on?"

Charlie would have shrugged, but with his various wraps, he couldn't even manage to 'almost' do that.

"We figure we can pretend we fell swooningly in love while we shared the room. So we can keep our pasts to ourselves," he said.

And that worked... right up until *The Hawke Mission*, when I blew it for them. I'm so evil.

"That works," I said. "And then... when you're fixed. You'll be with her. Off to Hawke, to help her run the place?"

Charlie sort-of-nodded again, "We'll see how that works out when the time comes. But I'll be with her."

"Rightly so."

I meant that when I said it. Sure, we were breaking up the central partnership of the old team... while Karen had been on *Lady Grace* and *Lion*, it had been Charlie and me on *Friendly* and *Wolf*. And though obviously Karen and I had history that long predated me and Charlie... well. I'm trying to explain this too much, aren't I? You know.

"End of an era," Charlie said simply, and I nodded.

"But the right way to end it. You're going to go run a government... which can only mean great things for the people of Hawke. And I'm going to stay on the job, next to Karen. Which can only mean great things for me."

Charlie laughed, then added, "And for her."

"Not so sure about that," I countered, and we chuckled again.

After a moment's silence, I stood up and approached the side of the bed again. Charlie extended his usable hand and I took it, "Alright then. We'll obviously keep in contact."

"Indeed," he agreed.

"You take care of Lia," I went on, sounding a little protective of my 'kid sister' (though I obviously didn't need to be). "And... have *fun*."

"You too," he smiled. "And don't let Karen go."

I tipped my head, with a cat-ate-the-canary smile, "Don't think you need to worry about that. I don't ever plan to."

Really, I shouldn't have said that. I shouldn't have tempted fate. But I did. And Charlie's advice stayed with me for a long, long time. For now, though, we'd said our bit. I left the hospital, and Charlie went back to his magazine, reading how Forrest Douglas felt about Defense Command, intelligent machines, and Special Branch Majors.

A few hours later, *Wolf* departed Venus with a mixed squadron, bound for Earth. I suppose it's not too overdramatic to say we were at last leaving the war behind... but the fighting certainly wasn't over.

Now we had a much more clever enemy to deal with. He wore white and fancied himself the absolute ruler of the Empire. And after him, a jumped-up 'Governor' from the Union of Solar Asteroids.

Charlie would be back to help us with them, as would many familiar faces, but for now the war was done, we were heading home, and that was a good feeling.

Let's close 2233 on that bright note.

AFTERWORD

Well, that finishes the Martian War. If you're thinking you can at last stop subjecting yourself to my prattling… that you have all the closure you need… well, you may be right. Depends on if you want to know what the Emperor's up to, or what happens to us after that. I leave the decision to you. When we start up in 2234, it's going to be political backstabbing, Martian intrigue, unexpected combat, a visit to Egesta, and of course, the final battle with Luther Gregory III.

Then there's 2235, or as I sometimes like to call it, 'hell'.

Anyway, *The Mars Convention* is next. It'll deal with our arrival at Mars, and the disastrous diplomacy that follows. Now, you know I'm prejudiced, but I'm going to say right now that virtually all the blame for that debacle falls on the shoulders of the Emperor, and his ambitions.

For a preview that doesn't spoil the actual story (though these events are relatively well-known), look up the aftermath of the Russo-Japanese War of 1905. If you ever needed proof that the Martian Imperium had more problems than its military, 2234 will prove it.

For now, that's all I'll say. Take care of yourselves, and I'll see you next time!

THE
EQUATIONS NOVELS

The Earthers evolved after humans were driven from the Earth by an intelligent bio-weapon dubbed 'Omega'. They are faster, stronger, smarter, wiser, *better* than humans, and they are the only hope for the survivors of the human race as an interstellar war between two great alien powers absorbs the galaxy. But all is not as it seems, and the humans and the Earthers face challenges that overshadow the wars of alien empires and threaten to destroy their civilizations...

The Equations Novels by Kenneth Tam

Book One: THE HUMAN EQUATION (Oct 2003)

Book Two: THE ALIEN EQUATION (May 2004)

Book Three: THE RENEGADE EQUATION (Dec 2004)

Book Four: THE EARTHER EQUATION (July 2005)

Book Five: THE GENESIS EQUATION (July 2006)

Book Six: THE VENGEANCE EQUATION (July 2007)

Book Seven: THE NEMESIS EQUATION (July 2008)

Book Eight: THE DESTINY EQUATION (July 2009)

The Equations Novels are complete, but there are spinoff series and new stories in the Earther universe still to come!

For more information, please visit
www.earther.net

ABOUT THE AUTHOR

Born in 1984 in St. John's, Newfoundland, Kenneth Tam holds both a Bachelor's and Master's degree in history from Wilfrid Laurier University in Waterloo, Canada. His MA thesis examined the creation and operation of the Caribou Hut, a hostel for Allied servicemen in St. John's during the Second World War.

In 2006, Kenneth received a prestigious Canada Graduate Scholarship from the Social Sciences and Humanities Council of Canada. He was also awarded a Balsillie Fellowship at the Centre for International Governance Innovation during 2006-07. In that capacity, he worked for Mr. Paul Heinbecker, Canada's former ambassador and permanent representative to the United Nations. He presently serves as a Communications Consultant for Kitchener–Waterloo's federal Member of Parliament, Peter Braid.

Since releasing his first novel in 2003, Tam has promoted his books across Canada, speaking with junior and high school students, delivering writing workshops, and doing book signings at bookstores and Iceberg-organized events. He frequently appears as a guest author at science fiction events across the country.

Kenneth is a partner in Iceberg Publishing, the company he and his family started in 2002. He has authored many of the company's existing titles, and is also responsible for graphic design, including the company logo, website, banners, advertisements, and other marketing materials. He acts as a primary contact with printers and suppliers, and is also key in new author development and recruitment.

He remains very lazy about writing his author bios. When they told him to make this one longer, he mostly copied and pasted it together from the Iceberg website, www.icebergpublishing.com.